NOT OF WAR ONLY

"*NOT OF WAR ONLY* is historical novel writing AT ITS VERY BEST." —*Albuquerque Journal*

"EXCELLENT...MEMORABLE...*NOT OF WAR ONLY* richly merits the praise it has gained from such authorities as Tony Hillerman, New Mexico's most successful novelist. SOME HISTORICAL NOVELS BREATHE NEW LIFE INTO HISTORY. *NOT OF WAR ONLY* IS SUCH A NOVEL." —*Amarillo Sunday News-Globe*

"REWARDING...UNIQUE...COLORFUL...THIS SUCCESS-FUL NOVEL IS SURE TO PLEASE MANY AUDIENCES..." —*Library Journal*

"*NOT OF WAR ONLY* IS BREATHTAKING, THE BEST NOVEL ABOUT THE MEXICAN REVOLUTION I HAVE EVER READ." — Dale L. Walker, columnist, *Rocky Mountain News*

MORE PRAISE FOR *NOT OF WAR ONLY*

"Norman Zollinger is a modern master of historical fiction. *Not of War Only* shows him at the peak of his powers."
—Win Blevins, author of *Give My Heart to the Hawks*

"Readers of newspapers might want to keep Norman Zollinger's latest novel close by while scanning the morning's headlines. It is not often that art and life dovetail to produce such high drama. ZOLLINGER'S FICTIONAL CHARACTERS MAY NOT HAVE BUILT A NATION, BUT NO READER WOULD BE BLAMED FOR THINKING THEY DID. *Not of War Only* is historical novel writing at its very best."

—*Albuquerque Journal*

"Zollinger paints bright pictures of Villa, Zapata and other Mexican generals as they jockey for position amid governmental chaos. His historical explanations render the complex politics comprehensible without trivializing the power struggles, and the shifting rivalry and friendship between Lane and Martinez proves engaging ..."

—*Publishers Weekly*

"THE FINEST NOVEL EVER WRITTEN ABOUT THE MEXICAN REVOLUTION."
—Kathleen O'Neal Gear and W. Michael Gear, authors of *People of the Sea*

NOT OF
WAR ONLY

Norman Zollinger

A TOM DOHERTY ASSOCIATES BOOK
NEW YORK

NOT OF WAR ONLY

Cover art by Jeffrey Terreson

A Forge Book
Published by Tom Doherty Associates, Inc.
175 Fifth Avenue
New York, N.Y. 10010

Forge® is a registered trademark of Tom Doherty Associates, Inc.

ISBN: 0-812-53013-6
Library of Congress Catalog Number: 94-2336

First edition: May 1994
First mass market edition: May 1995

Printed in the United States of America

0 9 8 7 6 5 4 3 2 1

For Ginna—*mi amor último*

"Not of war only nor of death I sing
but of the sadder stillness
the heart's pause before it fills again
and beats more deeply than before."

—Narciso Trujillo

". . . who makes revolution ploughs the sea."

—Simón Bolívar
The Liberator

PART 1

LOS PEREGRINOS

1

¿Un milagro? Quizá.

The tall man tracking Jorge María Martínez would have caught him by nightfall if an epic sandstorm hadn't roared up from deep in the valley of the Rio Grande, pulling a curtain of unexpected charity across the trail they both had ridden for three grueling days.

Jorge had only seen the tall man twice after he began his run from Black Springs, but he had been conscious of him every second of the long ride, conscious of him closing in with that earnest single-mindedness Jorge had known during the years he was growing up in those two completely different towns which masqueraded as the one they both called home.

He had gotten his first distant look at him just after they broke through the *malpaís* south of Three Rivers, and his second when he watered at Antelope Wells this morning. The gap between them had narrowed from six or seven miles to three. The tall man was no longer on the spotted horse he had ridden the first day out. Somewhere on the journey he had gotten a fresh mount, a heavily muscled black that looked ready and able to pound hard down every inch of the lower Jornada's road through hell. Jorge's own pitiful *caballo* was faltering, and he couldn't turn off the trail to trade for another as the Chupadera County sheriff had.

What would he do when the sheriff caught up with him? If he only had a gun. *Sí,* if he had a gun he could slip from the saddle and flog his exhausted pony down some yucca-lined bend in the high desert trail, lie in wait, kill the tall man, and take the black for himself. He would get but one chance. The sheriff of Chupadera County was good at his job.

But Jorge didn't have a gun, and his knife—the knife he had buried in the chest of the blond anglo in the cantina three days ago—would scarcely be a match for the other man's rifle.

Besides—could Jorge María Martínez, son of honorable Andreas and gentle, God-fearing Ismelda, kill that way, even when running for his life? An ambush in the noonday heat would still be a cold, cowardly murder, not at all like the affair back in the cantina, which for all its stupidity at least took *cojones*.

No! He was a killer now, but he wasn't an assassin or a murderer—not yet, at least. He would stay in the saddle, and the knife would stay in the top of his boot until the sheriff caught up with him and took him in.

He first saw the sandstorm when it was still miles away, a broad, lumpy, saffron-colored *rebozo* rolling up from the low desert stretches near the Rio. Just before it reached him, he left the saddle, soaked his bandana with almost the last of the water in his canteen, and tied it across his mouth. As the storm struck with all its fury, he stripped off his jacket, wrapped it around the horse's head, and led the terrified animal stumbling and blind through the dark yellow wind until he found an arroyo deep enough for them to huddle in.

He lifted and bent the pony's foreleg and got it to lie down and flung his slender body across its heaving flanks, while above the lip of the gully the wind sounded like the late night Southern Pacific freight when it raced through the town he would probably never see again, and he knew he wouldn't even hear his pursuer if by bad luck he entered the arroyo now. Then he breathed as deeply as the storm and the pony's manic restlessness would let him.

No one, not even a man as determined as the sheriff, would try to move a foot against this battering wind. He was safe as long as it blew, and probably for a good while afterward.

Torrents of grit and sand turned his hands raw and stung him even through his shirt, and once a fist-sized rock rolled into the arroyo, missing his head by only a hair before it settled in the bottom. From time to time the wind slacked off, long enough once to tempt him to get back on the pony and set out again, but then it punished him even more wickedly than before.

It was two hours before the sandstorm at last sucked in its hot, heavy breath to where he could rouse the pony with any hope of going on, but within minutes the trailing edge of the saffron robe was clearing the baked, high sections of the Jornada he had crossed earlier in the day, and when he was up in the saddle again he could see behind him for nearly a dozen miles.

No black horse and rider appeared in all that barren grassland.

Somewhere south of Warm Springs he left the upland plains for good and headed down toward the Rio. The pony needed rest and water. So did he.

He laid up in the last heat of the day where the river made a sweeping bend around a small floodplain with a thick stand of cottonwoods and patches of good grass. He let his animal have its fill of the brown water at the river's edge, drank passionately himself, first from his canteen and then from his cupped hands, amazed to find they didn't shake nearly as much as he feared they might. The water had turned dark and bitter in the wake of the storm, but he topped off his canteen, knowing it might be the only water of any kind he would find for another day. He dug the last of the grain from the gunnysack tied to his saddle, and got the feed bag on the pony's muzzle, wondering if the sheriff knew about this bosque, and deciding no, he didn't. If he did he would have already shown himself on the empty approaches to it. Even the lawman and the powerful black, for all their strength and purpose, would need water by this time, too. They must be miles away now, holed up at another bosque or water hole, waiting out the storm as Jorge had.

Sí. He was safe for the moment. He could even spend a few minutes reading the book that had been the last thing he put in his saddlebag before he rode away from the Cantina

Florida. He had time. The words of Molinas would anger him as they always did, but keep him from the clutches of despair. Then he would have to saddle up again and ride on through the night, even if his mount collapsed beneath him and he had to make the rest of the way on feet that could know exquisite torture before another day dawned. The man on the black horse wouldn't rest long, no matter where he was now, or how much doubt he had as to what Jorge's next move would be.

There were two questions to ask himself now that it seemed he had given the sheriff the slip for the rest of this long day at least.

Should he try to cross into Mexico the moment he reached the border, and if he did, where? At El Paso behind the Franklins rising on the southeastern horizon? Or at one of the smaller border towns to the east or west?

There was a fair argument against El Paso. Now that the lawman had lost him for a while, and with the odds so long against him picking up tracks after the storm, he could pretty well figure on the sheriff heading directly for El Paso to wait for him there. He would have all of the Texas city's big police department turned out to look for him an hour after he arrived, if he hadn't already telephoned ahead or sent a wire, and every bridge and ford across the Rio within the city limits, and for miles upstream and down, could already be under guard.

El Paso would be dangerous, *sí*, but on second thought it wouldn't be much better anywhere else.

At Anapra or Columbus, or any of the other tiny border crossing points, he would stick out like a red chili *ristra* on a gloomy day; the sheriff of Chupadera County would by this time surely have alerted every lawman's office from Laredo to Douglas, as well as the big one in El Paso. In the three days since the knifing they could even have printed wanted notices, nailed them to every telephone pole, and pinned them up in every saloon, town hall, post office, and bank along the border.

But he *could* lose himself for a while in the El Paso *barrio*, where a fugitive Mexican from a little-known tank town back up the line could, for a few weeks, anyway, merge with all the Mexicans who lived there, stay in hiding more or less until the police tired of the hunt. Then he could cross the river when they were no longer looking for him with such intensity. To pick him out in the overcrowded Chihuahuita *barrio* would be difficult, perhaps impossible, for searchers who didn't know him as the sheriff did. Didn't the gringos always say that all "greasers" looked alike?

Of course, bypassing both El Paso and the border villages and crossing straight into the Chihuahuan desert itself would be the quickest and easiest way into Mexico—if the Revolution hadn't been raging in nearly every square mile of Mexico's northern states. As a lone, unknown foreigner, he could be gunned down by the very people he wished to fight with, even before he could tell them.

Sí. El Paso was the answer—not a good one, but the best under the circumstances; perhaps the only one.

2

"Corey Lane!" The fat man behind the desk stuck his hand out. "Good to see you, *amigo*—but Jesus! You sure look all wore out."

"Got caught in a sandstorm out on the Jornada, Jim Bob." When Corey told the Doña Ana County sheriff what he had been doing out there, it would bring a condescending smile to Jim Bob Stearns's moon face. Although a dogged, hardworking peace officer, Jim Bob would never be caught in a million years tracking a fugitive across the desert. Fighting crime was purely an administrative matter for him, and chasing possible killers a chore for deputies, not one for the principal law enforcement officer of a New Mexico county. In fairness, Stearns wasn't the only sheriff in the state who felt that way. Corey Lane of Chupadera County was the maverick.

"May I use your telephone to call my office, Jim Bob? I've been gone three days, and I should check in. Chupadera County will reimburse you. I'll pay you myself if they don't."

"Sure, Corey. Hey ... you been out on the Jornada for three days? What on earth for? You *like* misery?"

"Been chasing a kid wanted for a stabbing back in Black Springs. Lost him in the storm."

"Oh, yeah. I read your wanted bulletin when it came in on the wire. His name's Martínez, right? Homicide?"

"It wasn't—three days ago—but it might be now. That's why I want to call Black Springs. The victim was in bad shape when I left, and I've been completely out of touch."

"The bulletin didn't say who got stabbed. Anybody I know?"

"Jamie MacAndrews from the D Cross A."

"Kin to Douglas MacAndrews?"

"His son."

"In college here at Las Cruces a few years back?"

"Yes."

"Sure—I know him. Hell of a football player, but kind of a crybaby for a big, strong dude. I had to run him in once after a nasty scrap he had with a frat brother half his size over a girl in the Home Ec school. The brother was beat to a pulp, needed doctoring. MacAndrews was scared shitless when I put him in a cell overnight, but when the D Cross A's Mex foreman came down with bail money to get him out, he turned cocky as hell."

"That sounds like Jamie."

"Bet my badge the stabbing was *his* fault—and about a girl again. That's one leopard won't never change his spots." Stearns was shrewd.

"You're probably dead-on right. The girl was Jorge Martínez's sister. She almost died aborting a baby. Her brother thinks the child was young MacAndrews's, and people in Mex Town say he was mad enough to kill Jamie."

"You know the man you're hunting, Corey?"

"Not really. Oh, in a way I do know everybody in town, of

course. Black Springs is still just a wide spot in the road compared to Las Cruces."

"Well, make yourself right at home." Jim Bob lumbered to his feet. "Use my desk when you make your call. I'll clear out so's you'll have it a little more private-like. Will you need help looking for your man?"

"No thanks, Jim Bob. It's my job. I wouldn't want any of your men getting hurt because I let him get away. He's probably out of your jurisdiction by now, anyway."

"You figure Texas?"

"That's my guess. I'll have to get extradition papers if he holes up in El Paso, which seems as likely as anyplace right now."

"Well, you're lucky in one way, Corey. He probably ain't about to jump the border, what with all the ruckus and killings going on down there now."

"Strangely enough, that's my biggest fear. Jorge Martínez is kind of a radical about Mexican politics from what his friends and neighbors tell me, and getting in on the Revolution might seem a lot more attractive to him than coming back to what he figures could be a date with the gallows."

"We can't win them all, Corey." Stearns didn't sound as if he believed it. Jim Bob Stearns probably felt he did win them all. It was one of the things that made him an effective lawman. "A radical? Maybe you ought to kind of herd him into Mexico then, and save Chupadera County the expense of feeding him until they stretch his neck. Practical *hombres* them Villistas. Don't cotton to radicals no more than white men do. I'll scoot now, Corey. I'll see if I can rustle you up some grub, and if there's anything else you need, holler."

Stearns's office could have been Corey's own, except for the telephone on the wall in back of the sheriff's swivel chair. Corey and his deputy, Ben González, had to walk upstairs to the county clerk's desk to use the one instrument Chupadera County felt it could afford. No complaint. More often than not it was the only on-the-job exercise he and Ben got in an entire day.

He dreaded making his call. If Jamie MacAndrews had died while Corey and Jorge were playing their deadly game of hide-and-seek, he would have to accept Jim Bob's offer. He might have to make a street-by-street search of Las Cruces, and get started on a thorough combing of the rest of Doña Ana County, no matter how his instincts were calling to him that Jorge wouldn't linger here, or even in nearby, heavily Mexican Mesilla. He almost hoped the boy had headed for the more immense *barrio* of Chihuahuita in El Paso, with its warren of adobe-lined *calles* and, dusty, unnamed *avenidas*. As much as he dreaded making the call, he dreaded accepting Jim Bob's offer of help even more. Stearns, who took few chances in enforcing the law, would insist on a posse to support his deputies. Corey hated posses. They posed dangers he didn't want to consider even in the abstract. According to Jorge's sister, Concepción—the girl MacAndrews had apparently compromised—her brother had ridden from Black Springs without a gun, but the youngster could have gotten one by now. If he made one panicky move to draw on the itchy, overeager amateurs who made up most posses, he was dead. The boy should pay for his crime, but death was a heavy penalty for something no witness had yet described as cold-blooded murder.

He went to the telephone and lifted the receiver.

"Las Cruces Central," the operator said.

"Hello, Central. This is Sheriff Corey Lane of Chupadera County. Could you put me through to my office in Black Springs?"

"Yes, Sheriff Lane. I'll ring when I have them on the line."

He hung up and cranked the handle at the side of the wooden box.

No, even if he ultimately had to take Jim Bob's help, he didn't want it. He much preferred going it alone, with all its risks, just as he had done the past few days. The past few days? Going it alone had been his abiding habit for most of his life, and certainly for the last dozen years. He had been lucky during that time, serving as sheriff of one of the three or four most thinly populated counties in the state, lucky that he had been *allowed* to go it alone, by apathetic voters who didn't care much what he did as long as he didn't do it to them and county commissioners who often cared even less. He was luckier still that the burdens of office hadn't ever grown to where he couldn't devote long, contented hours to the hobby that was so much more than hobby: his writing, and the studies which went with it. When his term as sheriff ended in another month, he could spend all his time on it, and fend off some of the boredom that had plagued him more and more the last few years. Even with his weighty manuscript *Republican Beginnings from Sonora to Morelos* at last done and published to his satisfaction, if no one else's (witness the lack of reviews or sales), there was still a lode of intellectual ore to be mined and smelted into books and articles. A new project such as the study of General Felipe Ángeles now engaging him would give his spirts the lift they might need when his time as sheriff was behind him. He had met the general on his pilgrimage to Chapultepec before the Revolution, and although there had been no opportunity to get to really know him, he had learned enough about the brilliant man who had become Villa's strategist to make him want to learn a good deal more.

But he couldn't complain. If in the past he had to interrupt what he felt to be his real life's work from time to time to impound a ballot box at an election, settle a quarrel between two stockmen over water rights or fence lines, or to pacify a violent drunk, it was a tiny price to pay. He had paid it, for the most part, without even muttering.

Not so with the price he might have to pay in the matter of Jorge Martínez.

He went to the window of Jim Bob's office and looked out across the cottonwood-ringed plaza. The black horse nodded at the hitchrail in front of the county building. It was the only animal there. Stearns and his men must do most of their law enforcement from automobiles now. Corey and Ben had one at their disposal sometimes, too, but they still did most of their work from the backs of long-outdated horses.

"You seem to know the man you're hunting," Jim Bob had said.

Corey hadn't, of course, exactly lied to him, but he hadn't come totally clean, either. He had shown the Doña Ana County sheriff the bland face of the professional lawman. He hadn't once in Stearns's office, for instance, referred to the man he was sworn to take into custody by anything but his full name, but until he entered Jim Bob's office he had never even thought of Jorge as anything else *but* Jorge. And before he had uttered the word to Jim Bob, he had certainly never thought of Andreas Martínez's mercurial son as a "radical."

Jorge had first nosed into Corey's ken nine years ago, when he was still a student in the Black Springs high school, one of only three boys there with Spanish surnames—small back then, wiry, but almost delicate in appearance. Ellen Stafford of the *Chupadera County News* had dragooned Corey into judging an elocution contest the paper was sponsoring. The contest differed a little from the few others he had seen throughout the county, where "Horatio at the Bridge," the Gettysburg Address, Marc Antony's eulogy, and Washington's Farewell were the standard fare; Ellen, dauntless lady, had required each of the contestants to write their own piece for delivery from the stage of the auditorium.

After the first few predictable, embarrassingly halting renderings, a slim lad he didn't at first recognize—it might have been the brand-new suit he wore—stepped to the lectern and began to speak—in Spanish. Something like a gasp issued from the audience, something felt rather than heard. Corey had smiled at the impudence of the speaker just as he identified him as Jorge Martínez, son of the owner of the Cantina Florida across the tracks. The smile carried more than a little rue. There would, he was sure, have been voiced objections, or at the very least indignant exits, except that something in the speaker's young eyes, as black as the lava rock of the *malpais*, and in a startling way as hard, seemed to keep his listeners fastened to their seats. "Spellbound" hadn't seemed at all excessive to describe the manner of the Black Springs merchants, teachers, and parents in attendance—and the few

Mexican farmers from the Rio Concho who were seated way at the back with Jorge's family.

He was so pleasantly surprised at hearing the Spanish in this unlikely setting that he failed to take in the full meaning of the boy's words at first, but at last the message began to seep through.

It was a bitter polemic attacking the anglo society of Chupadera County in general, and that of Black Springs in particular, couched in intense but graceful phrases almost Castilian compared to the regular Ojos Negros patois. Young Jorge Martínez had style, even if most of his listeners failed to notice it through eyes veiled by prejudice and ears stopped by ignorance.

From the stunned expressions on most of the faces near him it was likely none of his audience understood much, if any, of what young Martínez was saying. The workaday Spanish the anglos present used to some extent just to deal with their neighbors at all couldn't see them through this lofty use of the language of Cervantes.

With the speech in the unfamiliar language it would be days before Jorge's listeners realized they had been attacked. By that time none of them would care. *"Just another jumped-up Mexican brat who ain't quite learned his place yet."*

Jorge reached what appeared to be the end of his presentation and made a small half-bow mostly hidden by the lectern. There was a light scattering of painfully polite applause from the people seated around Corey, and a ripple with perhaps a bit more enthusiasm from the half dozen farmers at the back, certainly not enough from either group to raise an eyebrow. When Jorge returned to his place in the row of contestants he would be forgotten even as he took his seat, unless . . .

. . . unless Corey judged him to be the winner, as something devilish in him was suddenly urging him to do.

But Jorge didn't return to his seat.

After a short pause, he began again—this time in English. The Spanish had been but the faint flicker of distant lightning; the English words and phrases were the heavy crashes of close-in thunder. It was a storm of words, imprecations really, words like "oppression," "injustice," and—particularly delicious to Corey—"intellectual, economic, and political serfdom."

He had his winner, the winner he couldn't pick on the scant evidence of the speech in Spanish. But that his "winner" had provoked a storm to equal that of his impassioned words became instantly apparent. There was a good deal of shouting, a few chairs were overturned. Hattie Spletter, the town librarian, abandoned her customary decorous "shh . . ." for a well-modulated, ladylike cry of alarm. Blessedly there were no injuries. Still, it was scary for a moment. And these were the *genteel* inhabitants of Black Springs, not the ruffians.

It hadn't been funny at the time, but in Jim Bob Stearns's office he smiled at the memory. Poor Ellen Stafford. The newslady had been beside herself: too courageous and honest to back off from objections which no longer went unvoiced, too sensitive not to be hurt at the way in which her contest became a shambles when Jorge finished for the second time; in the end she decided that no prize would be awarded. Of course the decision satisfied no one, least of all Corey.

After he had shepherded a defiant but surely frightened Jorge out the back door and sent him hurrying toward Mex Town, he took Ellen to a late supper at the Sacramento House and pretended not to see her tears, even when she reached across the table, plucked the handkerchief from his breast pocket, and wiped her eyes. Perhaps it was a good thing he and Ellen were no longer seeing each other at the time. He had never been proof against a woman's tears. Of course, fair-haired, fair-minded Ellen would never have stooped to take advantage of him or any man that way.

There had been a time, two years before the contest, when it seemed Corey and Ellen might make a go of it together.

They were regulars at dinner at the Sacramento House, and for the few parties that constituted the social life of Chupadera County, and there had been a brief period of something approaching intimacy, culminating in a weekend in

Santa Fe at an opening of what was then only the *Territorial* Legislature in the last days before statehood, a session Corey testified before, not as a small-town sheriff, but as an expert of some minor standing on Mexican-American affairs. They shared a suite in La Posada with every intention that the door between their rooms would remain securely locked. It didn't. That part of their relationship seemed, for that one brief episode, to bode well for the future. Surely much worse things could have happened to Corey Lane than if he had married Ellen.

But the famous spark he had heard always accompanied an enormous passion never evidenced itself. Not in Corey, at any rate. He couldn't speak for her. In the end it was Ellen who called it quits.

"It will never work, Corey," she said one night across the candles at the Sacramento dining room's corner table. "Lucy Bishop is still there."

The mention of the Apache woman, lost to him but still alive at the time—and dead seven long years now—shocked him speechless for a second. He truly had felt until then that while he never had forgotten Lucy, never would, she had faded deep enough into the recesses of memory to stay hidden until deliberately recalled. "Lucy's gone, Ellen," he said at last.

"No, she's not. It's something every woman who knows you will have to come to terms with, whether they know they're doing it or not. I can't. Probably because I knew Lucy—loved her only slightly less than you did."

"If you're right, it presents a bleak outlook."

She laughed. Ellen was always quick to laughter, but there was something bittersweet in her laugh now. "For Pete's sake, don't despair! You'll find someone, someday. I'll give you some free advice, though. Don't tell her about Lucy."

They were friends now, he and Ellen, good friends, but only friends. Santa Fe was never repeated. They buried themselves in their respective workaday worlds.

At Ellen's prompting, Corey was sure, her boss, Tom Hendry, editor and publisher of the *News*, had set a pretty good editorial about the Jorge Martínez incident in a front-page box:

> While falling victim to the passion and exuberance of youth, the orator last Saturday night uttered some home truths. Is the dominant element in our small society too obtuse to profit from them? Why not, if such is indeed the lamentable case? It has profited in so many other ways from the labors of the Jorge Martínezes of our town and county. Contrary to some of the remarks passed at the time and reported to this writer, the young man in question is every flamboyant inch an American. He has a right to be heard, indeed would have that right in this free country even if he weren't an American. Let's not forget that.

It was only a nine-day wonder, but now it bothered Corey that it might be remembered to Jorge's disadvantage by a jury of his "peers," when and if Corey caught him and took him back to Black Springs to be put on trial, possibly for murder.

It might also be remembered that although he hadn't graduated, Jorge had gone to college here in Las Cruces—ironically at the same time Jamie MacAndrews was playing football for the Aggies—and that he had compiled a brilliant record as a scholar, with a gift for language, his own and English, too, that was the talk of at least *some* academic circles in the southern counties of what had been back then the Territory of New Mexico. A Chupadera jury would get reminders from the prosecutor that Jorge had been notable as at least an intellectual troublemaker, a sometime contributor of "inflammatory" articles to a small Spanish magazine published in El Paso. Corey had wondered at the time how Jorge could return to Black Springs after such a promising beginning to be just a bartender for his father.

After a wait that seemed interminable, the Las Cruces central switchboard finally got him through to Black Springs.

Ben González came on the line. "Sheriff's office. Deputy González speaking." Good feeling that Ben was running things in Black Springs when he wasn't there. Ben should be the next sheriff when Corey's present term ran out and he turned to full-time writing, but recalling the fuss about Jorge's speech made him wonder now if such a thing was possible for a "greaser," even in this second—and supposedly more enlightened—decade of the century.

"Corey, Ben."

"You've got Jorge?" Over the telephone the fact that Ben had none of the Mex accent so usual in Black Springs—Jorge's speech, despite his astonishing skill with words, was thick with it in his second tongue—was even more pronounced. Ben's more customary western-states drawl must have come about from his early days up in Colorado, that and having had an anglo mother.

"No, he's still at large."

"Well, you can relax, *amigo*. The MacAndrews kid pulled through. It was touch-and-go for a day or two, but Doc Colvin says he's going to be okay. And get this. Jamie's old man is seeing to it that all the charges against Jorge will be dropped. He's off the hook unless the D.A. wants him to answer for it. That ain't likely, is it?"

"Don't think so. Kincaid is a pretty reasonable district attorney, and the fact that Douglas MacAndrews won't make a fuss probably will satisfy him. Sure is good news." Yes. It was as if a noose had been removed from around *his* neck. "Of course, it means I'll have to hit the trail again, to tell Jorge before he does something else as silly as stabbing Jamie."

Yes, he had to move fast. Thinking he was still wanted, and, for all Corey knew, believing himself a killer, Jorge could be on the verge of something truly desperate. He would need another horse for the getaway he would still think he had to make, and would probably feel there was only one way to get one—and the food he needed. Doña Ana County and Jim Bob wouldn't cast a kindly eye on him if he took to stealing. There was always the specter of him ducking into Mexico as well, and an innocent such as Jorge might not last a week in the turmoil below the border.

"Jim Bob Stearns has offered help, Ben, and I might have to take him up on it. Hold the fort for me, please. Don't know exactly how long I'll be, of course."

"Sure would like to, Corey, and I know what telling Jorge must mean to you, but I think you better head back to Black Springs, *pronto*."

"Why? What's up?"

"You got a mighty important-looking letter on your desk."

"A letter? Where from?"

"Washington, D.C. It was hand-delivered by a courier who came down from Albuquerque the day you rode out of here. It's from the Office of the Secretary of State of the United States of America. No kidding."

"What does it say?"

"Haven't opened it."

"Why not?" Odd. Ben knew Corey kept no secrets from him. "Open it now, Ben."

"Can't. Says on it that it's for your eyes only."

That was odd, too. Backwater lawmen just didn't get that kind of correspondence. Made no difference, though, with what faced him. "It will just have to keep. I've got to find Jorge before he gets himself in more trouble."

"I think maybe you'd better forget him for the time being."

"Why?"

"There's been a call from Washington, too. Day before yesterday. About the letter."

"A call? Who from?"

"Some dude in the State Department named Henry Richardson. Says he's an undersecretary or something like that, and that he knew you in Cuba during the war."

Henry Richardson? He had all but forgotten the man he served under in Havana thirteen years ago, after combat. Henry an undersecretary of state? Not surprising. He had been headed for the top even then.

"What exactly did he say?"

"Wanted to know if you'd gotten the letter yet and if you'd read it. He says it's about something of national importance. He actually said 'pressing national importance'—with a hell of an emphasis on 'pressing.' When I told him you weren't here, he said to track you down. Of course I didn't know how to do that, and he seemed pretty damned upset when I told him so. He went on to say I'm to tell you he's coming in by train on Monday, regardless."

"Day after tomorrow?"

"That's what he said."

"Damn it! That means I can't reach him by telephone. Look, Ben, I've simply got to get to Jorge."

There was a pause at the other end of the line. At last Ben came on again. "I don't suppose I got any business telling you what to do, Corey, but I sure feel you better get back here quick. This Richardson is an impressive *hombre*. I don't think he's kidding one bit about this being important."

Ben wasn't all that easily impressed.

"All right. I'll head right back."

He found Jim Bob in a saloon a block from the courthouse, where he had ordered a sandwich and a jug of coffee for Corey. Corey told him about the charges against Jorge being dropped. The sheriff grunted as he finished off a schooner of beer.

"We'll look for him, Corey, but I ain't about to bust my ass since he ain't wanted anymore."

"No posse, Jim Bob. Just find him and tell him."

"Okay, no posse. Not unless he misbehaves here in my backyard."

"I don't want him hurt. He's a good kid."

"Good kid? He stuck a knife in an anglo."

"The charges have been dropped. He's not a criminal."

"You can count on me." The Doña Ana County sheriff grinned then. "But maybe you should bear in mind that he *ain't* a kid. And even though he ain't technically a killer yet, it sure sounds to me like he just might want to be one. I reckon he *ought* to hightail it for Mexico. Get it out of his system down where they pay for killing. Good kid, shit!"

3

He awoke in the crooked alley that lurched away from Calle Rinconada deep in the El Paso *barrio.*

After he cracked his eyes at the sun's first weak peep and stepped to the wall of the nearest adobe to relieve himself, he found someone had robbed him of every last cent of the money his father and Concepción had pressed on him when he left Black Springs. *¡Mierda!* He had thought it as safe as if it were in God's pocket when he reached the alley at two or three this morning, whenever it was. Now his pants pockets, front and back, were turned inside out. He had put the larger bills he carried into the pocket of his one extra shirt, wadded it up, stuffed the shirt inside his jacket, and rolled the jacket up to use as a pillow. It was still lying on the poncho he had wrapped around him. He raced back to it without even buttoning up. The jacket was as empty as the alley he could just barely see now. Even the shirt was gone. The thief had stripped the knife from his boot top, too.

After a sick moment that brought him close to tears he told himself, *No llores, estúpido.* He couldn't let himself cry. Anger flooded him, but anger wouldn't help much, either. He should look on the bright side, dim as it was. He had, after all, been blessed with far more luck than he deserved. His exhaustion from the long walk after the pony died had probably saved his life. He had slept the sleep of the dead. If he had lifted one eyelid while his phantom robber was stealing his few belongings, his ripped throat would probably have poured every last drop of his blood into the caliche.

Of lesser importance, but still something he should be thankful for: the silent predator with the sure hands and the nerve of a *torero* hadn't found or hadn't wanted the Molinas book. He probably couldn't read.

But even calming himself and sending murmured thanks

to *los cielos* didn't alter the fact that he was, as one of the Cantina Florida's gringo patrons, the surly, apelike telegrapher Gibbon, was so fond of saying, "hungry enough to eat the ass out of a skunk." He hadn't eaten since he bolted down the last of the food in the saddlebag he left beside the pony's carcass, and when he reached the *barrio*—dark and empty as a graveyard at three in the morning—he had chosen sleep over a search for a meal. Now he had to get food. If he didn't, hunger and fatigue would soon pull him to the gutters.

There was something he hadn't been aware of when he went to sleep. An army of other bums before him (*sí*, he was a bum now as well as a killer) had pissed against the adobe wall as he had, and the stench rising on the damp air of first light was bringing his empty stomach close to mutiny.

He had to leave this alley and its stink and its gray, nightmare shadows before the sun cleared the tops of the *barrio*'s adobes. And he had to be careful. Whoever had visited him during the night might be close at hand, just beyond the corner, the stolen knife in hand, not convinced he had taken everything worth taking. There might be any number of other armed *ladrones* roaming the streets now, too.

On one side of the alley, where it opened into Calle Rinconada, sheets of newsprint and faded hoardings hid the raw adobe wall, and across the narrow way advertisements for three different kinds of beer were peeling around a giant poster plastered over the mud and straw. In spite of the gnawing in his belly the poster stopped him in his tracks.

"¡ATENCIÓN GRINGO!"
For GOLD & GLORY
Go South of the Border and
RIDE
with PANCHO VILLA
el Liberador of Mexico
WEEKLY PAYMENTS IN GOLD TO
DYNAMITERS * MACHINE GUNNERS
Enlistments taken in Ciudad Juárez, Mexico

January 1914
¡VIVA VILLA! ¡VIVA LA REVOLUCIÓN!

After a flush of excitement made him forget his hunger for a second, he sobered. Gold and glory? Shouldn't the glory be enough? Odd that the plea would be addressed to "gringos" this deep in the Little Chihuahua *barrio*, but when he nosed cautiously out of the alley he saw that the dingy street he hadn't really seen at three in the morning was lined with just the kind of cantinas and saloons the gringos liked, and with wine and liquor shops stretching for a block or more in either direction. Two doors down the *calle* and across from him, a gilt-on-black sign over a green lacquered door read, "El Paraíso—40 Lindas Mujeres 40—Ten Cents a Dance." The street here must be a playground for exactly those gringos General Villa wanted: the hardcase soldiers of fortune and professional delinquents not above rubbing shoulders with "greasers," desperate men not entirely welcome in the brighter, if only marginally cleaner and quieter, avenues of pleasure in uptown, modern, strictly "American" El Paso.

He ducked back into the alley and read the poster again. *Sí.* For the needs of an army fighting Victoriano Huerta and the well-armed, well-trained killer regiments of his illegitimate government, gold would be the lure. Glory was only a *salsa picante* for the kind of mercenary the general had to have. The *campesinos* of Chihuahua and Nuevo León weren't machine gunners or dynamiters. Few of them had read Molinas, either.

All the same, it hurt a little.

It hurt, too, that the old Calle Rinconada *barrio*—remembered with affection, and sometimes longing, in the nine years since he had been in El Paso last, when his grandfather died and he made the trip down here from Black Springs with his mother and Concepción for *el abuelo*'s funeral—had fallen to such a state. He had come here almost without thinking in the lonely dark this morning. In 1905 it had been a wonderland, a magic, friendly place of small shops, artisans and craftsmen, gentle, soft-spoken people, of pigs wandering the mud street, fat cows, and flocks of chickens in every fenced-in yard—a place that truly lived by "love thy neighbor." Now, from this first look at it, the *barrio* had become a slum every bit as depressing as the ones in Chicago and New York he read about in the magazines Ignacio Ortiz passed along to him—a latrine, a *sucio tocador*, where night prowlers stole from lone travelers even as they slept. He hoped Ismelda Martínez never had to visit her girlhood home again. He would avoid it himself for whatever short time he was forced to stay here. Not hard to do this morning. There was no tiny, brown grandmother here any longer to slip him *bizcochitos* and candy over Ismelda's tongue-in-cheek objections.

What he wouldn't give now for one of *la abuela*'s biscuits, or a steaming plate of the *albóndigas* she took such pride in. *Sí.* Food.

As he stepped into the sunlight in the *calle* he heard a faint throbbing sound from down the street on the left, opposite the dance hall. He wasn't alone now. It came from an automobile idling in front of a gaping door fifty feet away. The vehicle was an open-topped touring car, a shiny black Pope-Toledo like the one J.J. McIntyre, the Socorro banker, drove. Jorge's schoolmate Juan Serna said the car cost nearly four thousand dollars—almost as much money as the Cantina Florida in Black Springs took in all year. In its glistening arrogance this one looked even more out of place in the squalor of Calle Rinconada than Señor McIntyre's did back in Mex Town.

An ox of a man dressed in a business suit much too tight for him leaned against the hood of the touring car. He was alternately looking into the open doorway in front of him and paring his fingernails with a silver penknife.

Jorge's heart skipped a little before he decided there was no way this *hombre gigante* could be his nighttime sneak thief. He looked far too prosperous. Prosperous? *Sí.* Perhaps he could get this stranger to stake him to a meal. Then again, probably not. The man had a hard, wide, flat face under a gray felt fedora, a face Jorge somehow knew wasn't given to smiling. But with his stomach in agonizing knots under his belt it was worth a try.

He swallowed the remaining lump of pride in his throat and walked toward the man, who obviously hadn't seen him yet, wondering if he should speak to him in English or in Spanish. A closer look revealed blond hair under the hat and skin the blotchy pink of so many gringos. Still, this deep in Chihuahuita, it was probably best to speak to him in Spanish first.

"*¿Cómo estás, señor?*" Did the pleading he heard come from *him*? He winced. "*¿Por favor, me puede?*"

He could almost feel the street shake under him when the man jumped away from the car, landed on the rock-hard caliche with a thump like that of a jackhammer, and turned to face him.

"What the fuck are you doing here, *muchacho*?" The man took a heavy step toward him.

The menace staggered him, but he found a small part of his voice again.

"I thought perhaps, *señor,* that if you could spare—"

"Never goddamn mind what you thought. *¡Vamos!* Clear out. Get the hell over to the other side of this here *calle, pronto,* or I'll rip off your *cojones*!"

Then he noticed out of the corner of his eye that the open door framed a woman. She apparently had been there all along. Weak as he was, did he have to take this with a *woman* looking on? No! He doubled his fists and braced himself. Then he saw the bulge under the left armpit of the big man's coat. He was beaten and he knew it. The man reached inside the coat and took one more step.

"No, Jimson. *¡Por favor, no!*" It was the woman. "The general would not be happy if you called attention to him."

The man stopped in his tracks. He dropped his hand to his side. "All right, Carmen. But this kid had better move along. Is the old coot about ready now?"

"*Sí.* Ramírez will have him out here in a second."

The gringo took one step back.

Jorge turned to the woman.

At any other time he might have laughed. A brocade dressing gown encased a heavy-breasted body like a hard shell. Some dried white ointment covered a fat face from chin to forehead, but not so completely that patches of brown skin didn't show through. He had been wrong about the man—Jimson, was it?—but the woman was every bit as Mexican as he was, despite the brassy gold hair wrapped around tiny, ringlet curlers. Her accents gave her away, too. This outlandish, comic apparition had saved him from a nasty beating, and by rights, regardless of the injury to his feeble pride, he should thank her.

"*Señora.*" He managed a small bow. To do or say more would be too great a surrender.

"You'd better listen to him, *niño,*" the woman said. "*Es un hombre muy peligroso.*"

He started across the *calle.* On the far side he looked back. The woman had stepped into the street to let someone behind her come through the door.

A man as big as Jimson, wearing an apron, and about whom there could be no doubt that *he* at least was as Latino as Jorge and the woman, was half carrying another, much smaller man, out of the darkness behind her. The second man, also a Mexican by the look of him, was dressed, or rather half-dressed, in a khaki uniform with a splash of colored ribbons above the right breast pocket of an unbuttoned tunic. He looked sixty or sixty-five, faintly oriental, black hair plastered to his skull, with a gray mustache stained brown at the edges curling down over his upper lip. The man helping him carried the military cap that went with the uniform in his free hand. The man in the uniform looked ill, close to his final breath, but the years in the cantina told Jorge he was only drunk. More than tobacco smoke and coffee had passed under the mustache. This must be the general the woman had mentioned.

Jimson shot one more threatening glance at Jorge, then helped the big Mexican pour the general into the idling automobile. The older man in khaki collapsed into the rear seat. The big gringo walked to the driver's side, got in, and in a moment the black touring car bounced away past the dance hall and the alley. Jorge watched until it was lost from sight on its way out of Calle Rinconada.

He turned and began to walk away. There must be someplace open in the long street where he could beg a handout.

"*¡Niño!*"

When he stopped and turned, he found the woman was alone in the open doorway. The Mexican in the apron must have gone back inside the building. The woman beckoned to him with both arms. "Come here, *por favor*."

Above the door he now noticed a small sign that read "Casa Estrellita," and beside it an electric light in a globe fixture. The light was off, but the sun streaming through the globe had turned it a brilliant red. A rooster crowed from somewhere behind the building. He crossed the *calle*. Close to her again he found the woman every bit as grotesque as she had looked at first. The bloated cheeks under the bone-white salve made her look poisoned or—he shuddered—poisonous. She smiled suddenly, showing a mouthful of teeth by turns black and gold, the gold a match for the violent yellow hair beneath the curlers.

"You said you were hungry, *amigo*. Come in and I will have one of the girls fix you *almuerzo*."

He pulled himself together as best he could after his belly groaned again. "I am not a begger, *señora*." A small lie. He had been ready enough to beg from the gringo Jimson or some shopkeeper who opened early, hadn't he? "But I will work for food."

"It is '*señorita*,' *amigo*, not '*señora*.'" She gave him the same half-rotted, half-dazzling smile she had given him a second earlier. "Work? *¡Magnífico!* But what work can you do for Casa Estrellita? What is your *profesión*?"

Well, what was his profession? Killer? Beggar? Bum? "I tend bar, *señora* . . . I am sorry—*señorita*."

She laughed, throwing her head back and revealing a neck wrinkled like the skin of a lizard. She laughed until she cried, the tears streaking down through the ointment. "You tend bar, *niño*?" The laughter stopped. "It is *providencia*, *verdad*. A bartender is the one thing I need. Can you take care of drinkers like the *hombre* in uniform you just saw?"

By ten o'clock that morning, fed and washed, and a little stronger, Jorge María Martínez had become an employee of the second largest brothel in the Chihuahuita *barrio*.

He didn't see the general again for almost two full weeks.

4

▲▲▲▲▲

"You must never, never have anything to do with the *muchachitas* who work here, *niño*," Carmen Padilla told him his first day on the job. "Some of my girls might try with you. You are a handsome *hombre*, and young, and they tire sometimes of the *viejos* they take care of, but their services are reserved for Casa Estrellita's clients, *solamente*. Remember that I will be watching—and so will Ramírez, my majordomo. Besides, there is something better in store for you."

Although he said nothing, he was outraged that she would think for a second that Jorge Martínez, son of Andreas, would go with *putas*.

The outrage dissolved in bitterness when he remembered that he had in a way, by the simple fact of taking the job, become a whore himself.

But he wouldn't be one long. As soon as he saved some *dinero*—and when he felt it safe to try crossing into Juárez—he would be gone. Three or four weeks should do it. He could hide from Corey Lane here in the *barrio* until then.

"We must do something, too, about your clothes," Carmen said. "You look like an *hombre* on the run." ¡*Dios*! Had she guessed? Probably. He supposed harboring a fugitive made little difference to her, not with the business she was in.

Ramírez, who she said was Casa Estrellita's *mayordomo*, and who turned out to be a quiet, friendly old brute, gentler than he first appeared, showed him to a cell-like back room. Ramírez pulled a uniform with a short, brass-buttoned jacket from a dilapidated armoir. Jorge almost smiled. His father had chided him since he was fifteen about his love for fancy clothes.

His first night at work presented him with demands for a bewildering variety of drinks he had never been asked to make by the patrons of his father's bar—even the gringos. Carmen asked him if he could read, and when he told her yes—piqued a little that she might think he couldn't—had Ramírez bring out a dog-eared bartender's guide for him to study. Ramírez sampled Jorge's first Sazeracs, sloe gin fizzes, and six or seven other drinks he hadn't even heard of, and pronounced them fit before he fixed them for the amused regulars of Casa Estrellita.

Ramírez revealed an almost encyclopedic knowledge of the myriad of drinks in the guide, and Jorge wondered why Carmen hadn't installed the old man in this more elevated position instead of *him*. It surely would have been a promotion, for although she called him a *mayordomo*, Pedro Ramírez was in fact merely waiter, janitor, and handyman, doing all those onerous tasks around the house that could have easily been done by any of a hundred men in the *barrio*. Why, then, had she hired Jorge? Never mind. It was better, in his present need, not to look a gift *caballo* in the mouth.

Pedro helped him at the bar in the evenings, where the customers, never identified by surnames, but who Ramírez catalogued for him by their preference for girls or liquor, proved as exotic as the drinks he made. He tried not to look as awed and wide-eyed as he felt. On his first three shifts he served a Texas congressman, two bankers, a junketing Italian tenor, and a slim, tight-lipped, splendidly dressed gambler Ramírez whispered had killed seven men below the border.

Below the border. He left the house each day for a few minutes stolen from his free time to walk to the alley and gaze at General Villa's poster.

Carmen had been right when she made that warning about the girls. The entire house, Ramírez, Carmen, and the nine regular, full-time prostitutes—there were others Pedro said worked in the house on weekends—took all their meals as a *familia* by the madam's fiat, and his second night at the table one of them, the tiny, impish Yaqui Indian, Isabel, wasted no time in making a try for him.

"If you have no woman, *amigo* Jorge," Isabel said, "and if it is not a busy night, perhaps you would like to become *friends* with me." No, he wasn't fooling himself. There was no mistaking what she meant.

"I saw him first, Isabel." This came from the spectacular blond gringa named Belle. Isabel made a face, and the table erupted into a chorus of salacious giggles.

"*¡Basta!*" Carmen exploded. "That is enough! You both have work to do tonight." The table shuddered into silence. That her girls lived in mortal terror of the brothel keeper was all too obvious.

He didn't look at anything but his plate for the rest of the meal. He knew he would have to guard himself as long as he remained at Casa Estrellita. It wouldn't do to get himself thrown out of this unlikely haven by breaking Carmen's rules before he was ready to cross the Rio into Juárez with money in his pocket—and with no one after him.

He discovered that the paste that had covered Carmen's balloon face the first morning, and which she must have applied every night, was some kind of bleaching agent. It wasn't working. The cosmetic acid or whatever it was left her skin white enough above the high collars of the long-sleeved dresses she seemed to favor, but it couldn't eat away the brown in the folds of her neck, at the hairline, and around the eyes. Even had it done the job well, it failed miserably with her hands, which gave the game away whenever she stroked her wrinkled cheeks or patted her metallic-yellow hair.

If she was a tyrant with the other inmates, her tyranny didn't extend to him. It became plain by his third day that he was Carmen's pet. She merely smiled her indulgence when he did something wrong, as when he served a margarita instead of the whiskey sour one of the patrons ordered. Even poor Pedro Ramírez, with whom he had quickly come to be the beneficiary of seemingly genuine affection, would have been the victim of a titanic, hellish fury had the big old man made the error.

Why had he become so special? *¿Quién sabe?* Perhaps it was only because he was something new.

He did his job, kept his mouth closed around the girls, and—it seemed wisest—held his talk with the patrons to a minimum, while trying hard not to speculate about what went on in the warren of rooms at the back, when the whores led their clients away.

But of course he watched and listened. And during his first Thursday stint at the bar he made a discovery that sickened him.

All nine of the girls were occupied, and none of the part-time neighborhood whores were on the premises. The bar lounge was empty. He took advantage of the lull to go to the backhouse.

The way outside led him through that section of the ancient adobe building where the girls worked. Some extraordinary moans and groans issued from two or three of the rooms he passed, and he was mildly shocked at the strange excitement they provoked.

In the hall in front of him light splashed across the frayed carpet, where the door to the last room was ajar. When a shadow flickered across the carpet, he realized this room, too, was being put to the sordid uses of Casa Estrellita, and he knew it would be difficult for him not to look into it as he passed on his way to the backyard and the outhouse.

When he reached the doorway, he couldn't help himself.

An older patron of the house named Clifford, gray-haired, and with a gross, fleshy, pink body, leaned fully unclothed against a chest in the room, turned sideways to the door. A boy—he couldn't have been a day past twelve—also naked, with dark hair and mammoth black eyes, kneeled in front of him. As Jorge watched, the boy took the man's penis in his mouth.

He didn't sleep that night. Of course he had heard that disgusting things like this happened in the world, but not in the world he had known. There had never been a hint of such depravity in Mex Town, and never so much as a whisper that it went on across the tracks, even among the most corrupt, and for Black Springs worldly, gringos.

He felt himself sullied, as if he had been smeared with excrement, and he scrubbed his skin brutally in his bath next morning. Then, knowing full well the risk he might be taking, he found Ramírez and told the majordomo what he had seen.

"Do not upset yourself, *amigo*." The old man reached to him to pat him on the shoulder. Jorge shrank form his hand. "It is the way with some strange *hombres*. It has nothing to do with you. Casa Estrellita offers many services. Carmen does not talk about it, and the *muchachos* are never put on show. It is all done by arrangement. The boys come in the back way. The general you saw your first morning here is one of the special customers who likes that kind of thing. He wants them a little older than is the boy Chico you saw, but he does prefer other men to girls. For your own good, forget you saw it. And do not worry. I, Ramírez, will forget. Carmen would go *loco* if she knew one of our 'guests' had been watched. Except by someone who pays to watch. There are some who only like that, too."

He spent more time than usual in front of the recruiting poster that afternoon, and reread the first fifty pages of the Molinas book before the dinner hour.

Tuesday morning of his second week Carmen asked if he knew how to drive. *"Bueno,"* she said when he nodded. "Ramírez has never learned. I want you to take the Metz and run some errands for me—uptown."

His heart almost stopped. Uptown? Surely the police were still looking for him. The only thing he could hope for was that they wouldn't be looking for him in a motorcar.

It was a golden April day presaging the even brighter ones to come in May, and he felt more at ease as he nosed the Metz Special out of Calle Rinconada into Wyoming Street. He kept a light hand on the throttle. It would be disastrous to be stopped by the police because of his driving, and then be recognized as the fugitive killer Martínez, wanted in two states. He had a bad attack of nerves when he saw a policeman taking an apple from a vendor's cart at the side of the street, but by the time he reached the center of town he had himself under control again. He picked up an order of linen supplies Carmen had placed with the C.C. Shelton store on South Oregon. The woman clerk scarcely looked at him. He was just another greaser hired hand to her. From Shelton's he walked to the Carl grocery on San Antonio for another pickup on Carmen's list, only to find the fancy canned goods marked for Casa Estrellita far too heavy a burden to carry any distance. On the way back to South Oregon to get the Metz, he passed the post office and remembered that Carmen had wanted him to get a supply of postage stamps.

As he stood in line he tried hard not to look directly at the postal clerk behind the grilled window, and he pulled his hat down a little more and turned his head when he reached him and mumbled what he wanted. An alleged killer would have been the last thing on the mind of the woman at Shelton's, but this clerk in the black leather bow tie came to work every day where the faces of men like Jorge were on display. He probably looked them over frequently. Some of them surely offered rewards for information. But, as the case had been with the young woman, the clerk hardly glanced at him. When he stepped away from the window he scanned the lobby.

Sure enough, a whole rogues' gallery of wanted posters covered a sidewall.

Did he dare look at them? An anglo woman had taken his place in front of the clerk, and there was no one else in the lobby now.

He forced himself not to hurry toward the wall, and he didn't get so close as to be seen looking too intently at it.

To his vast relief, but mild disappointment as well, none of the faces that stared out at him was his.

After he picked up the order at Carl's, emboldened by not finding himself on the post office wall, he took almost an hour to drive the streets of the city, a fairly easygoing *turista*, *sí*.

El Paso was without a doubt a wonder of the world, perhaps not one of the famous "seven," but fabulous enough. Four years ago William Howard Taft and white-haired old tyrant Porfirio Díaz had held their famous *dos presidentes* meetings here, first on one and then the other side of the International Bridge. The grand pronouncements of the two aging heads of state that day had been a sham, clever stratagems to produce more profit for the gringos, more pomp for the Porfirianos, and more poverty for almost every Mexican.

Now that he had seen this city, the town of Black Springs one hundred and seventy-five miles back up the Southern Pacific tracks was less than *nada*. Still, his heart longed for it. *¡Basta, muchacho!* He would soon be a revolutionary fighter, not a homesick calf.

He drove back to Casa Estrellita sobered, and not without a twinge of shame. In spite of his not appearing among the other wanted men, he still didn't feel quite secure enough to make the try for Juárez. The crossing points would still be watched. There was the matter of his finances, too. Except for some pocket money, Carmen hadn't paid him yet.

What a different picture Chihuahuita presented from that of the modern city he had just left behind. This district of El Paso was a *barrio* every bit as much as his own corner of Black Springs was, but it was so much bigger it had its own peculiar power, its own soul. The seedy, honky-tonk look of Calle Rinconada notwithstanding, a spaciousness of spirit belied the huddled adobe houses, stores, and stables covering every inch of caliche from the *calle* to the Rio. Already he had learned that a man could go days without seeing a gringo, particularly a Corey Lane, days more without hearing a word of English.

He should take comfort from the fact that he could stay hidden here until he got his money and his chance.

Two nights after Jorge's excursion to uptown El Paso, the general came back to Casa Estrellita. Carmen was busy with the account books in her office when he arrived. The few patrons in the lounge hardly glanced at the general, but it was clear he was a regular here of a very special kind.

The gringo Jimson came with him, and so did another man in an officer's uniform, a Mexican like the general, but much younger and clearly subordinate to him. Jimson looked at Jorge, but it was the assessing look of the professional bodyguard he was, not one of recognition. Obviously he didn't remember his meeting with Jorge in the street outside the *casa*. He sat apart from the general and drank beer, and not much of that. The girls must have accepted that he was only here on business. None of them approached him as they did the lower-ranking officer, a sallow, nervous type given to stroking and pinching those who climbed aboard his lap in relays. The girls didn't come too close to the general, either. They must have known all about his preferences. The two Mexicans drank cognac, with the general swallowed by the oversized wing chair in the corner of the lounge, reading the *El Paso Times* Ramírez brought him. He only looked up when he fished a *cigarro* from his breast pocket and motioned Pedro to him and had him hold a match to it. Drunk as he had been that first morning, he had looked harmless, even pathetic. Now his oriental features lent him an air of cruelty and power.

An hour passed. The young officer—Belle had called him "Colonel"—disappeared at about half past nine, led by the hand into the rear of the *casa* by the well-padded girl from Hidalgo County, Flora Medina. Jimson looked every new arrival over with a practiced eye. The general was still deep in his newspaper. Jorge began to think that for this evening at least, he wasn't set on indulging the unholy sexual tastes Pedro said he had. He only smoked and drank. But *Dios*, how he drank! Ramírez ferried an ocean of cognac to the table at the general's elbow.

It was almost eleven when Jorge came to the realization that the little man with the cruel, yellow, Mongol look hadn't uttered a single word since he and his two companions made their first appearance in the lounge. From time to time Jimson would leave his seat and walk across the room to him and whisper in his ear. There was no sign that he heard the body-guard. He was now sinking into the same drunken state as when Jimson and Ramírez bundled him into the Pope-Toledo.

At eleven on the dot, Carmen entered the smoky lounge.

"Epifanio!" It was a cry of pleasure, feigned or not Jorge couldn't tell, but with alarm in it, too. The general turned his bleary eyes toward the madam. "It was unforgivable of me to keep you waiting, but no one told me you were here." She turned to Pedro Ramírez, who was serving another patron. "What is wrong with you, Ramírez? You will hear about this, *estúpido.*" She wobbled to where the general sat. "It will take me a few minutes to make arrangements, *mi amor.* In the meantime, let us have a drink together, but not out here." She crossed to the bar. "Jorge, give me a bottle of the cognac the general drinks and a pair of glasses, *por favor.*" She winked at him coquettishly. Over her shoulder he saw the general, who had risen on a pair of unsteady short legs, look-ing at him. His eyes were glazed, but it seemed an exquisitely searching look nonetheless.

They left the lounge, as bizarre a couple as Jorge had ever seen. Just as they passed Jorge on the way out, Carmen whis-pered to the general, and her words, although low, reached as far as the bar.

"I am sorry, Epifanio—tonight it must be Chico. There is no time to get one of the others for you."

It was that second "Epifanio" that did it.

Jorge knew this general now!

This was the hated butcher Epifanio Guzmán, who had been second-in-command to Victoriano Huerta the usurper. This monster had commanded the death squad that blotted out the lives of President Francisco Madero and his hapless vice-president, Pino Suárez, in the most heinous crime of the Revolution. Even the backwater *Chupadera County News* had reported the atrocity in grisly detail. Old Huerta kept Guzmán north of the border these days partly to buy weapons for the Federalista army, partly because the little toad was a living reminder to all of Mexico of Huerta's own role in the death of Madero. U.S. Government men in El Paso, according to the *News*, were keeping a sharp eye on Guzmán, had even had him under arrest for a while, twice, first at Fort Bliss and then at Presidio, but had shown a strange reluctance to deport him. He lived in luxury at the Hotel del Norte, according to the paper.

Huerta, in Mexico, would pay with his own guilty blood when Pancho Villa and the *insurrectos* under Carranza and Obregón eventually triumphed, but who would ever make this reptile Guzmán pay if the Americans never sent him back?

Jorge didn't sleep much that night, either.

In the next two days his visits to the poster in the alley took on something of what he had felt in childhood when he went to church on Sundays at tiny San José, the adobe church where the Martínezes had worshipped for so many generations. He had been only a sporadic communicant since the age of fifteen, to Ismelda's dismay, but he still considered himself a faithful Catholic.

He should reaffirm his faith at least by making confession now, but to venture too far from Casa Estrellita too frequently would be to invite discovery, and the church Ramírez and three of the girls attended was on the edge of uptown El Paso. No, he decided, he would set himself straight with God and the Church once he was safely across the border. Safely across the border? Strange thought. If things went according to his half-formed plan there would be even less safety there than here. He had conveniently forgotten that it was a war he was going to. It wouldn't be an end to troubles, but rather the beginning of troubles still distant and phantasmagoric.

But he couldn't now afford to consider what he would face when he crossed the river.

Still, it was difficult not to consider it; as devoted as Calle Rinconada and Casa Estrellita were to lower pursuits, he heard enough opinion on the street and in the house about the great events occurring in Mexico. The name of Pancho Villa was uttered frequently by the patrons and the girls, two of whom, Chita from San Antonio and the Kansas City redhead

Ruth Ann, claimed to have slept with the general, claims met by hoots of derision from the others, and detonating anger from Carmen.

"Impossible!" she screamed. "He only goes to bed with *mujeres* he marries, not that there haven't been enough of *them*."

The daring, perpetually attacking, seemingly invincible Villa was a hero to everyone in Chihuahuita, even Carmen. The adulation of the notorious revolutionary seemed so universal Jorge wondered if he wasn't a hero even to Guzmán. It wasn't an entirely *loco* notion, given the worship of Mexicans here in the *barrio* and as distant as the jungles of Yucatán for a strongman, whatever his politics, provenance, or morality. Guzmán could hate or fear Villa and still admire him.

"I saw Pancho," Flora from Hidalgo County said one slow evening in the lounge when Carmen, as usual, was locked in her office doing the books. "And fat-ass Carmen can't say I didn't."

"We all saw him, you silly slut," Belle said. Two of the other girls joined Belle in assent. Belle went on, "She *is* telling the truth for once, Jorge."

"When was this?" Jorge asked.

"When he captured Ciudad Juárez a year ago. Get the pictures for Jorge, Isabel."

The Yaqui skipped across the room to the battered desk behind the armchair where Guzmán did his marathon drinking, opened a drawer, and returned to the bar with a stack of snapshots.

When the photos were spread on the bar in front of Jorge the girls bent over them and the story spilled out. It wasn't the same sober recounting of the battle he had read in the *Chupadera County News*.

The management and the staff of Casa Estrellita were pictured on the flat roof of the whorehouse—bejeweled, caparisoned, and parasoled—as they watched the fighting across the river and the executions afterward.

"It was a *función magnífico*, Jorge," Isabel bleated. "We all wore our best clothes and perfume. We had music. Three *mariachi* bands. They must have played 'Adelita' and 'La Cucaracha' for three straight hours. We danced when Carmen let us."

There were shots of hawkers peddling fruit ices and enchiladas down in the beaten dust of Calle Rinconada, and others of the smoke rising from the battle across the river. For all that the girls agreed they had actually seen Villa, there were none of the Tiger of the North, but Jorge made out tiny horsemen riding against a barricade, Dorados maybe. Bodies littered the far bank of the river, and on the near bank half of El Paso, it seemed, had turned out to gawk. In one view, Carmen herself surveyed matters through a pair of porcelain-barreled opera glasses, and in one other remarkable photo an anglo in the frock coat of a banker stared across the mud fences of Chihuahuita, looking out over the soupy Rio while a street urchin picked his pocket.

"We didn't work at all that day," Belle said. "The *barrio* streetwalkers picked up a lot of easy money."

"It was a *fiesta*, Jorge," Flora said.

Chita broke in. "Some *fiesta*! After the battle Pancho's *hombre* Fierro sent more than a hundred Federalistas to the wall."

Excited as he had been first at the pictures and then at the only firsthand report on Pancho Villa he had ever heard, none of it was the kind of thing Jorge María Martínez was particularly pleased to learn. It turned the tragic, portentous matters of life and death, the nobility of the struggle for *la libertad*, into an afternoon's painted entertainment, a show, a comedy.

Then he retrieved the knife stolen from him that night in the alley.

To help Ramírez, suffering from a chronic case of sciatica, he had gone to the fruit store two blocks from the house to buy produce for a Saturday luncheon Carmen was giving for some unidentified wealthy gringos. The little shop, redolent of mangoes, pears, plums, and tomatoes, was crowded, and as he waited for the owner-clerk to free herself to take care of

him, he spotted the boy prostitute Chico sitting on an up-
turned barrel behind hanging clumps of bananas and a display
of chili *ristras*.

At first all he saw were the two huge dark eyes the boy
turned on him. The eyes suddenly filled with fear. Chico had
been cutting into the tough skin of a cantaloupe, and he now
tried to hide the knife he was using behind his back, but he
wasn't quick enough for Jorge not to see it was *his*, the
weapon he had used on Jamie MacAndrews.

Rage almost melted him. His immediate thought was to
rush the boy and choke a confession—and his money—out of
him. Then the rage drained away. He had come within a step
of ruining everything he had suffered for at Casa Estrellita.
To force the issue now could stir up the hornet's nest that
served Carmen for a brain. Chico had more value to the
madam than did a man who merely tended bar. The stolen
money was probably long gone now, anyway, and when payday came he should get at least as much as this little piece of
mierda had taken from him.

The boy made a sudden, skittering move toward the door
of the shop, but Jorge stepped in front of him.

"*Por favor*, Chico," he said. He was pleased at how low
and calm he kept his voice, calm, *sí*, but lethal, too. It shot
something electric through him. "I believe that is my
cuchillo. May I have it, please?"

Chico handed him the knife without a word. His dark eyes
paled.

None of the customers in the store seemed to notice the exchange.

He washed the knife and stuck it in the drawer of the chest
in his room. Then he took it out again and tucked it under his
pillow. Perhaps the sensible thing to do would be to get rid
of it. The knife, after all, was partly to blame for the predicament he was in. But *was* it the knife when all was said and
done? In his fury in Black Springs he would have used a broken bottle, a bung starter, or his bare hands, to the same
deadly effect.

Even with it safely under his pillow the knife seemed visible. The thought of it haunted him. It was still dancing before his eyes that night when Epifanio Guzmán and the ever-watchful Jimson, together with two other junior officers this time, came again to Casa Estrellita. Carmen greeted the general with the same effusiveness as before, but with a considerably easier air about her. Perhaps her contentment sprang from the fact that whatever arrangement she had made for Guzmán's pleasure tonight would be more to his slimy taste.

But the "arrangement" would have to wait. There was for the general some very serious drinking to be accomplished first. The glasses of cognac Ramírez ferried to him from Jorge's bar went to Guzmán's bloodless lips with the regular beat of the pendulum of the carriage clock on the white-washed wall of the lounge. It was the sick, obsessive, mindless drinking Jorge had seen in a few, very few, of Andreas Martínez's *campesino* patrons over the years. Most working-men couldn't afford to drink as the general did. He wondered how this *borracho* could have been such an efficient brute while indulging such appetites, and how he could have commanded troops in the battles that put Huerta in power two years earlier.

Then the knife, Epifanio Guzmán, and the desires of Jorge María Martínez all came together.

He would bury the knife in the heart of this *sucio puerco* of a general or, even more fittingly, cut the throat through which that river of cognac flowed!

His *destierro*, his fate, must have led him to Casa Estrellita. Certainly fate had led him to the knife again.

But a big question remained: how could he reach his target?

All the glory that would cover him, all the deep personal satisfaction this act of public vengeance would bring, would go glimmering if he botched it. Jimson and the general's entourage, which might even now be growing by the week, were the paramount problem. He had to find a way to get Guzmán alone. He pondered it for an entire day with no result. The girls by now liked him, he was sure of that, and it might have been possible to enlist the aid of one of them had the little yellow turd been normal. But he wasn't, and that was that. Could he track Guzmán to whatever room he and his "arrangement" used? Not a much better scheme, but perhaps the only one.

Another day of puzzling over it brought no solution.

Then Carmen Padilla on a fine Thursday morning handed him Epifano Guzmán on a plate, and at the same time settled the question of why Jorge Martínez had become a favorite of hers, as well as making clear what she had meant that first day when she said, "Besides, there is something better in store for you."

She came to his room, where he was washing up for breakfast.

"You like it here at Casa Estrellita, Jorge?" she said.

"*Sí,* Carmen."

"And you wish to stay, *no*?"

"*Sí.*" He had better be careful, keep his face a mask. This gross creature was not stupid.

"Of course you would like to earn more *dinero*, is that not so?"

"It is only natural, Carmen."

"*¡Bueno!* I adore an ambitious *hombre*. You know that Epifanio, the general, is a very special *frecuentador de nuestra casa*, don't you?"

"Yes."

"And that we always try to give him what he wants."

"*Sí,* Carmen."

"Well, then, *caro* ..." She winked the same coquettish wink she had the night she steered Guzmán to the boy Chico. "The general has decided he wants *you.*"

He kept his face blank. "He wants me? I do not understand, Carmen."

"Oh, but you do." She winked again. "He wants you to be his lover."

5

By Thursday night doubts and misgivings attacked him. Through the long dark hours they camped around his hard bed in threatening legions. *¡Dios!* He had been so sure.

Elated as he had been at what Carmen had given him, and as ecstatic as he was at the celestial justice of the appetites of Epifanio Guzmán bringing about his twenty-times-earned execution, the thought of Carmen possibly telling even the filthy amoeba who swam in this sewer that Jorge Martínez would go with a man brought him close to nausea. No matter that it was the linchpin of his plan, he felt soiled, scabrously unclean, encased in *mierda* even as his intended victim was.

He found, too, that the perceived meaning of what he planned to do had made a complete turnaround in his mind.

He had persuaded himself at first that the killing of Guzmán would be an act of nobility when compared to what had happened back in Black Springs. The stabbing of Jamie MacAndrews had been driven by red rage. He had castigated himself for it ever since. But, no matter how he might regret it now, it had been an act of honor. Given Jorge's temperament and his victim's arrogant dismissal of what Concepción had suffered and would forever suffer, it was still right. The death of Guzmán, on the other hand, would be a calculated thing. As thoroughly despicable as the man was, as much as he deserved to be a feast for worms and maggots, he was still a man, a human being in the eyes of the law. Shouldn't he have his day in court?

Sí. But only if there *were* a court. There wasn't one. Even when Victoriano Huerta fell from power, his henchman Guzmán would be safe here in the United States, out of reach of the people he had wronged. Washington might eventually lock him away for years as an embarrassing nuisance, but no *norteamericano* judge would ever pass the sentence of death his crimes shrieked to *los cielos* for. If Jorge Martínez shrank now from becoming the instrument of retribution, who would step forward to take his place? Visible as this archcriminal was, no one had yet stepped forward in the year and a half since he killed Madero. Perhaps no one had ever had the chance. Jorge Martínez had it. It might be the only chance *anyone* would ever get.

By the time sleep took him it was settled again.

It must be done.

If his course wasn't exactly set in stone, it was etched deeply in his fast-hardening resolve.

He still had to work out the mechanics of his plan. In essence they were simple. Friday after lunch Carmen called him to her office and told him to be ready for his time with Guzmán Sunday night. "When he comes to my office to have a drink with me, Ramírez will take the bar. You go to the last room down the hall and wait." It was the room where he had seen Chico and the gray-haired gringo Clifford. He swallowed down the sick revulsion the memory brought.

Then his mood brightened. The door to the backyard was but a step away from the room where he would meet with Guzmán. Once his knife had found its mark he could be out of the house in the flicker of an eye, over the adobe wall of the yard, and gone—across the river into Juárez.

Saturday would be payday at Case Estrellita, his first. He would have money in his pocket, and time in the afternoon to buy the spangled *charro* jacket he had seen at Mercado Gómez a block away on Avenida Cuerva. No one else would think so, but the jacket was important. When he boarded the streetcar for the ride across the Rio into Juárez he couldn't wear the Casa Estrellita uniform he tended bar in, or the old clothes he had worn when he rode from Black Springs. The new jacket would make him look less like a wanted man. He could hide it in the room before he began the regular evening shift.

"Be ready, *amigo*," Carmen said. "Undressed and ready. He will want to look at your body first."

¡Mierda! Well, he shouldn't have expected there wouldn't be a hitch. He would have to do as she said, but he would cut the looking short, then put his clothes back on after he used the knife. He would lose precious seconds. *Easy*, amigo. It altered nothing. It only meant that he had to be doubly sure he struck so swiftly there could be no outcry from his victim. A deathly silent "moment of truth." *Sí.*

Carmen went on. "You have never been with another man, have you?"

Unable to manage a real reply, he shook his head.

"It is not as hard as it might seem," she said next. "You might even enjoy yourself. *¿Quién sabe?* The other *muchachos* tell me Epifanio is not actually hard to please." She cackled. "They say he is often not hard at all. Maybe you will be lucky. If you don't like it, keep thinking about the money."

He almost asked her then for his pay. It would mean one less time he would have to talk to her or look at her between now and Sunday night. No. He must keep everything as close as he could to what passed for normal until then.

When he left her he found Ramírez and begged a whetstone from him to sharpen the knives he used at the bar. "I could hardly slice the limes last night." He asked if he could keep the whetstone Pedro brought him until suppertime, and took it to his room. He prayed Carmen would never discover that poor Ramírez had become his unknowing accomplice.

When someone discovered Guzmán's body, Pedro would probably suffer as much at the hands and tongue of Carmen as if he had done the deed himself. He would miss the simple old *hombre*. None of the others in this evil house would remain in memory a second. Perhaps the Yaqui, Isabel. After her one squelched attempt to share his bed, they had become almost friends.

At bedtime he put the finishing touches on his knife. The blade was a mirror in the lamplight. He held it closer to the lamp and looked at his reflected eyes. Fear looked back at him. But there was something else looking at him, too. *¡Dios!* He was ready.

* * *

Impatience such as he had never known before attacked him so strongly Saturday morning he had to force himself to the breakfast table.

He had to take a grip on himself, calm down, look innocent. Carmen peered at him quizzically through her white ointment mask as they ate breakfast, but wasn't that to be expected? If he was to be paid extra for his services to the general, surely she had much more money riding on his performance. All she wanted now was reassurance. Somehow he managed to smile at her. The mask almost cracked when she smiled back.

"Jorge, *mi amigo,*" she said. "You look tired. You must keep yourself in good health. Be strong." Again that gruesome wink. "Why don't you take a nice walk after breakfast? Then drink some red wine. It is good for the blood."

"I will get plenty of exercise putting out the empty beer barrels for the brewer's *hombre*, Carmen," he said.

Only another thirty-five or forty hours. He could stand her that long, couldn't he? *Sí.* But not one second longer.

It was true about the beer barrels. There were half a dozen empties in the storeroom next to the areaway between Casa Estrellita and the boot and shoe repair shop across the narrow space. They were heavy and cumbersome, and ordinarily the teamster who drove the brewer's wagon helped him carry them out after he and Jorge rolled a full one to the lounge. The driver had been rushed on his deliveries of the past two weeks, and the empties had mounted up. This time Jorge would put them in the areaway by himself. He certainly had enough excess energy, most of it nervous energy, to do it. The work might relax him. The wine wasn't an altogether bad idea, either. But not wine from the *casa*'s cellar. He wanted nothing more from this foul place except his money—and his chance at the general. If Pablo's wineshop on the other side of the *calle* was open, he would put a bottle on the cuff. The grouchy Sonoran would trust him this morning. He might not have at any other time, but he knew when Carmen paid her people.

"Don't strain yourself, *mi amor*," Carmen said as he left the table.

"Jesus!" Belle hooted. "He's *mi amor* now!"

When Jorge rolled the first barrel out he glanced across the *calle*. *Sí*, Pablo had opened up his shop, and there was a customer standing in the window, a tall man who could be nothing but a gringo from the way he held himself. The gringos who came to the *barrio* on a Saturday began their weekend drinking early.

He returned to the storeroom for the second empty. When he had wrestled it to the areaway he upended it and looked across to the wineshop again.

The gringo was still in the window. There was something familiar about him.

He looked at him more carefully—and stared straight into the gray eyes of Corey Lane.

6

At the sight of Jorge Martínez, Corey breathed a sigh of thanks. Sitting in the wineshop this morning might not be a total waste of time, after all. General Epifanio Guzmán hadn't come to the house across the street as Agent Jake Cobb said he might, but the discovery of Jorge was an unexpected gift. Tough Jake Cobb would think it a small catch.

Cobb thought Corey himself a small catch.

"I've told Henry Richardson I don't like working with amateurs," he said at their first meeting here in El Paso after Henry entrained for his return to Washington. "Have you ever done undercover work, Sheriff Lane?"

"I know I'll need help. How do I start?"

"I want you to keep an eye on a Mex general named Guzmán. He stays at the Del Norte with a pack of Huerta's exiled rats. If you miss him there, there's a place in the *barrio* he visits regular as clockwork once a week—a whorehouse. You know what to be on the lookout for, don't you?"

"Gunrunning. Private American financial backing for Huerta. Mexican nationals from across the Rio. Europeans—the British and the Germans."

"Yeah. See if you can meet with Guzmán. If you find him at the whorehouse you might even have to act like you just want to get laid. Don't waste a lot of time, though. If he doesn't show up at Carmen's Friday night or by ten Saturday morning, he'll come for sure on Sunday." The U.S. State Department man apparently expected a battalion of agents, arms and munitions magnates, the gunrunners who worked for them, politicians, and soldiers of all ranks and of unmistakable Mexican origin to be paying court to Guzmán this weekend, either at the Hotel del Norte, which Cobb himself was now watching, or here at Carmen Padilla's. "Bank records show the little bastard got a mammoth wad of money, probably from Huerta, just this week. Once you're in Little Chihuahua you'll be on your own. After this business you can take a week or two off." Cobb dismissed him then with an offhand wave.

Now Corey ordered another glass of the Monterrey red. The waiter had hovered near him for the last five minutes, clearing his throat from time to time. Smart as Cobb seemed to be, and as good as his advice probably was, there was no way Corey was going to pose as a client in the house across the *calle*. He had seen enough of the distasteful little general with the one glimpse of him he had gotten with Cobb in the lobby of the hotel. There had been no chance to get to him then, surrounded as he was by men in Mexican uniforms. That was two days ago. His only chance now was to beard the general here at Casa Estrellita.

He smiled. New England Puritan Henry Richardson would take to his bed to think that discussions of affairs of state, even pitifully minor ones such as the one he might have with Victoriano Huerta's dog-robber of a general, might be conducted in a second-rate Little Chihuahua whorehouse.

This was now all beside the point. Despite Cobb's confi-

dent predictions, no one from below the border had contacted
the general yesterday or today. It bore out the opinion Corey
had expressed to Cobb at their last meeting in the Wyoming
Street office. Recent political cannonading by the Carranza
forces was blowing even more holes in Huerta's ship of
state—already rudderless and listing since Villa had beaten
his army so soundly in the second battle of Torreón—and the
last rats were deserting. The time was nearly at hand for
Corey to move on to Mexico City and the real task Henry
Richardson had set for him. Things in the capital would happen at the speed of light once the three armies of Obregón,
Villa, and Carranza converged and ran headlong into Zapata's
hordes now streaming northward from Morelos. Huerta
would be in a vise.

If Washington and Henry Richardson ever truly needed
him, it would be when those armies met. The only soul who
needed him now was the boy who had hauled the huge barrels into the areaway. Finding him had been an astounding
piece of luck. Some part of his conscience still insisted he
had deserted Jorge in Las Cruces.

The last three weeks had been almost pure futility. Still, the
low-key watching and waiting here in El Paso had been good
training for the bigger game he would have to play below the
border. Guzmán's lieutenants had seemed completely taken in
by his yarn that he was just an unknown historian on the
prowl for something to write about. It had cost a small fortune buying wine and beer for Guzmán's hangers-on, loosen-
ing further the tongues of his already talkative junior officers
with their senior thirsts. Thank God the giant Jimson wasn't
a problem in that regard. If *he* had been a drinker, filling his
big belly might have scuttled the U.S. Treasury. Through
Cobb, Henry had already complained mildly about his expense account.

Henry's fancy description of him as a "Special Foreign
Service Officer" to the contrary, he wasn't, hadn't been, since
he reached El Paso last week, more than a mediocre spy. It
was suspiciously like a game for little boys. But he guessed
that getting his cover firmly in the minds of Guzmán and his

staff *was* important. Carranza's and Villa's people should buy his story, too, when he reached them. Cobb was sure a few of *them* were already watching him, so he had better not get smug and careless; a historian wasn't supposed to loaf about in wineshops in Spanish-speaking *barrios* looking like a two-bit spy.

Things were going well at the moment. In addition to his retrieval of Jorge, there would be time now to take that promised leave of a couple of weeks, bring Jorge back to Chupadera County, and mend at least temporarily the fabric of his personal life Henry Richardson had ripped so casually nearly a month ago.

The searching instant scrutiny the boy gave him—not his actual appearance—told him who he was. He had turned and ducked back in the side door a great deal faster than he had come out of it. It was exactly the sort of behavior a fugitive would show.

Thank God Corey would have time for him. What he now owed Henry Richardson could be deferred for the moment.

His thoughts about a historian looking like a spy came to mind again. Henry had said at the outset, when he came to Black Springs to recruit him a month ago, that he *wouldn't* be a spy. But hadn't Henry immediately backtracked on the denial?

What a strange thing that conversation had turned out to be.

"The President of the United States wants *me*?" Corey had at first laughed outright at Richardson's proposal. "Did he send you out here from Washington to get my vote? The election's still two years from now. Surely you're joking, Henry!"

"I'm *not* joking." Henry Richardson's lean body stiffened. "I would never joke about a thing like this."

"Sorry. I suppose you wouldn't." The man sitting across the desk from him hadn't been famous for levity when they fought together in Cuba, fifteen years before, nor when they had both served in the occupying force in Havana. Of course, Corey had never looked on Harvard men as a particularly comic lot; apparently the climbers of the State Department's steep and slippery upper slopes didn't try to be funny, either. Henry Richardson had been shaped by both institutions.

"All right, Henry. I'll take you seriously. But how could the President even know about a small-time peace officer like me—and why would he want me?"

"I didn't say he knew about you—yet. As for wanting you, *I* want you. That means Secretary Bryan wants you. And if the Secretary wants you, the President will, too."

"To go to El Paso and then Mexico as a Special Foreign Service Officer?"

"That's what we have in mind. You must know Mexico well."

"Sure, but to go there on behalf of the United States sounds too important for a country boy like me."

"You know what's going on below the border, don't you, Corey?"

"Oh, I've *watched* the Revolution a little, sure, but my vision from here in the sticks is pretty myopic."

"So is that of almost everyone else in this country, including the seers of the Fourth Estate. We certainly don't expect *second* sight. Still, we feel you have the critical insights about Mexico that we sorely need."

"Insights? There must be a thousand other Americans with better insights than I have."

"There probably are, but I don't have time to look for them."

"Thanks, Henry," Corey said. "You never did let anyone's ego get out of hand. Level with me. Why do *you* want me? You and I haven't even talked in more than a dozen years. What made you even think of me?"

"That book you did two years ago, the one on the origins of the Revolution, *Republican* something-or-other I think it was called. I read it."

"You what? How on earth did you come across it?"

"I hold the Mexican desk at State. Anything serious the Library of Congress catalogues that so much as mentions Mexico is automatically sent to me. Most of it is worthless. When your book appeared in my reading file, I almost passed it up, but then I saw your name as author. The historical stuff didn't particularly interest me, but your analysis of the political situation in Chihuahua and the capital when you were down there did. I was impressed. When this new project came up a couple of weeks ago, I dug out the journal I kept in Havana in '97. The observations I made back then in Cuba reminded me of what a faculty you had for working with the difficult people in the Cuban government in those days, and of your grasp of Latin American politics even then. You can't have lost your talent altogether."

"For Pete's sake, Henry! What I did in Cuba was day-to-day administrative stuff. You were the brains of our section. Hell, even the county commissioners here don't seek my advice, never mind the President of the United States. All I've handled in the past dozen years has been the town drunk and an occasional brawl at an election rally. I'm no diplomat."

"My sources here tell me quite another story."

Sources here? Who in Chupadera County could be a "source" for Henry Richardson?

The Washington man went on, "You've been in this office a dozen years, and you've stopped at least two small wars among your three different constituencies."

"They weren't wars, and wouldn't have been, with or without me. Tempers got a little hot a couple of times, that's all."

"You're too modest, Corey. Now, will you accept this appointment from your President?"

"You want an answer this minute?"

"I want it by the time the Western Union office closes." The firm, set lips curved into the closest approximation of a smile Corey had seen on Henry's sandy face since he had stepped down from the Pullman on the noon train, looking as tailored and unruffled as the man in the Arrow shirt advertisements in *Harper's*.

Richardson pulled a watch from his vest pocket. "That's an hour and forty-three minutes. I'll need ten minutes of that to encode my signal to the Secretary—if you agree. You've got an hour and a half, say. Take all of it before you say yes."

"Not until you tell me what saying yes means. I want chapter and verse before I even consider it."

"Sorry. But I must have a 'yes' before I go into the details."

Corey shook his head. "Not good enough, Henry. I want to know what I'd be getting into."

"I suppose that's fair. All right. I'll tell you everything my instructions *allow* me to tell you . . ." He stopped when Ben González entered the office, and didn't speak as he watched the deputy place a sheaf of reports on the corner of Corey's desk. Ben seemed to shrivel a little under Richardson's gaze.

"Sorry, Corey," Henry said after Ben left. "I don't like to upset your people, but I'm not comfortable talking here. Does the bar in that hotel you've put me up in serve a passable Bordeaux?"

"The Sacramento House? I doubt it—but I think we might get a decent glass of Mexican wine at the Florida, across the tracks."

"Then that will have to do." Henry rose. His posture was still the parade-ground ramrod he had maintained all the way up San Juan Hill under blistering Spanish fire, and in the office they shared in postwar Havana. "As I tell you what I can, please keep in mind that to a good citizen a call from his President is a call to duty."

"Let's find out what passes for Bordeaux at the Florida, then," Corey said. "Why do I suddenly feel I need a drink myself?"

"I've no idea. I must confess I never have *needed* one."

Corey didn't doubt that for a second.

At the Cantina Florida, Concepción Martínez, the daughter of the owner, showed them to a table in an alcove well away from the bar. Beautiful young woman, even with what she had been through recently. She gave Corey a questioning look as he and Henry seated themselves.

He never saw Concepción without the sight striking him,

almost physically, how much she looked like Lucy Bishop. This was hardly the time to think about that.

"You know, don't you," he said to Henry as they settled into the table, "that I'll be sheriff here for another two months?"

"Yes, but you have nearly half a year of accumulated leave coming—you've kept your nose to the grindstone like a Calvinist—and that deputy who seemed so uneasy with me in your office is fully qualified to fill in for you. Your own reports indicate that."

"I have other obligations."

"As a single man with no discernible commitments beyond an occasional dinner with that lady at the newspaper, Ellen Stafford, you have *no* obligations I'm aware of. You don't even figure in your mother's ranching operation." Henry had certainly done his homework. Ellen was probably one of the "sources" he had spoken of. Yes, *Chupadera County News* owner Jim McPherson had sent her to Washington on a story a year ago. A State Department story. The diplomat swirled his wine around the bottom of the glass, passed it under his nose, inhaled deeply, and lifted it to his prim lips for a careful sip. "It's not a robust pressing. Look, Corey, we're only asking you to make periodic visits down there. It wouldn't be as if you were stationed in Mexico on a 'permanent party' basis."

"All right, Henry—give me the rest of the drill."

Richardson didn't play with his drink now. He tossed the rest of it off firmly and finally. Corey's recollection of the man's temperate habits in Havana told him he wouldn't order another. Richardson fixed his eyes on Corey over the rim of the empty wineglass.

"You say you've followed recent events in Mexico . . . and the Wilson administration's reaction to them? This Revolution is four years old now, and no closer to a conclusion than it was when Díaz was overthrown. In my opinion we should have jumped in when Victoriano Huerta had Madero murdered and usurped the presidency. Now Huerta in turn is in deep trouble with the Chihuahuans and the Coahuilans closing in on him, and with Zapata opposing him in the south. Our feeling in Washington is that if Huerta falls there will be a real chance of things stabilizing in a way not entirely unacceptable to us, that the mantle of Francisco Madero could fall quite naturally on the shoulders of Venustiano Carranza. But lately we have been, frankly, amazed at the strength General Villa is showing. The President doesn't really care which of the two of them comes out on top—as a matter of fact he seems sometimes to lean toward Villa, even though the general is by all odds the more radical of the two—but he wants one of them to emerge as the clear-cut victor. What has us concerned is that with Villa and Carranza contending for power and possibly weakening each other, there's a strong chance that even after his defeat Huerta might sneak back to Mexico City and stage still another coup. That would be intolerable. We want to pick Carranza or Villa or one of the others soon—and give him complete American backing. We need good counsel from someone on the scene, someone to get into all the important different camps."

"I can't understand why the President is even considering Villa for a second. The press has pictured him as more of a brigand than a serious politician."

"Do you agree with that?"

"No, Henry. He is a far more sophisticated leader than the world thinks, even if he is somewhat limited in scope."

"You're an admirer, then?"

"I admire his ability to surround himself with truly capable men. Felipe Ángeles, for instance."

"Who?"

It was discouraging that a bright man like Henry, privy as he was to the deepest intelligence reports, wouldn't know the subject of the book Corey was working on. What would it take to make the exalted thinkers in Washington realize they were overlooking the best of all choices in Felipe Ángeles? Lamentably, Henry didn't look as if he even expected an answer to his "Who?"

"I suppose Woodrow Wilson's view of Villa is a bit puzzling at first," Henry said next. "Partly it's because the President feels that in the long run Carranza, the 'First Chief,' as he calls himself—while not a Victoriano Huerta—may prove to be more inimicable to American interests than Pancho would. He's not exactly an adherent of democracy in the U.S. sense." He paused. "There's something else. It isn't secret or even sensitive in the way the other matters I'll discuss with you are, but I'll perjure myself rather than confess I ever said it. As enraged as Woodrow Wilson sometimes gets with Villa, that 'natural animal'—as the President is fond of calling him—holds a strange fascination for him. Thug though Pancho well may be, the President's tolerant view of him seems to be shared by millions of Mexicans. A million others, including the men under him, adore him. In Wilson's case it's rather like the way some highborn women can be attracted to stablehands and stevedores. And Villa for all his faults does admire the United States."

"Who are the 'other' people Washington is watching?"

"Obregón, two or three shots left over from Francisco Madero's regime, Maytorena in Sonora, the Vásquez Gómez brothers . . ."

"Zapata?"

"No."

"Why not? He's the unquestioned power in the south."

"I know. But there's something self-destructively messianic about him. He has intense loyalty from the peasants in Morelos; in the rest of the country we feel his influence is a mile wide, but only an inch deep. We don't think he will survive ultimately.

"Why does the President feel we have to do anything, Henry? I thought he was committed to self-determination right down the line. I know he tends to preach to our neighbors down there, but I didn't think it would ever amount to more than just that."

Richardson looked uneasy—for him. "A great many influential people in Boston, New York, and Philadelphia— including our old boss T.R.—are after the President to go pell-mell into Mexico and enforce a *pax Americana*. Some are even talking annexation. The President feels that intervening in a military or strongly political way would be catering to extremely narrow interests. He doesn't want some mother's boy from Ohio getting killed to guarantee a bank loan or guard Rockefeller's oil rigs or the Guggenheim silver mines. What he wants in Mexico above all else is that stability I just spoke of."

"And he's thinking of a preemptive move."

"I didn't say that, Corey."

Corey felt then that Henry was holding something important back that he *could* tell, and was choosing not to tell it for his own reasons.

"If stability is all we want, why not cast a more kindly eye on Huerta? For all his faults, he could provide it. He did until just recently. Of course it has been the stability of a prison camp." That should get a rise out of Henry.

"Corey! Victoriano Huerta is the last person we want running Mexico. The President may have become a bit more pragmatic, but he's not a hypocrite." Then Henry turned suddenly and uncharacteristically sheepish. "Of course, we would like to know what he's up to. We need a man to assess Huerta's strength on the border, discover how he's getting munitions out of the United States, and some other things, and we need that man fast."

"As in the next hour and half?"

Henry had regained his composure. He pulled out his watch again. "As in the next hour and sixteen minutes."

"My first strong feeling is to decline, Henry." Not quite true, but he did have massive doubts.

"There's something else I'd like you to consider before you do, and this is the sensitive matter I spoke of. It's something quite apart from what we've talked about so far ..." Henry looked around, as if assessing the chances of being overheard. There wasn't another soul in the cantina except for Andreas and Concepción, and they weren't watching, and certainly couldn't hear from where they stood. "We now have almost completely persuasive evidence that German agents are swarming over Mexico. We know they've been cozying up to Huerta, and now we think Carranza is listening to them, too. This thing at Veracruz doesn't help matters. The President will certainly hold his ground on *that*."

"He will? When it comes right down to it, don't you feel that's pretty arrogant? After all, Huerta's government and the port authority did release those sailors. No physical harm was done them. Carranza, too, was sharply critical of us, and supported Huerta for once. We were probably wrong and, damn it, you know it, Henry."

"I certainly agree, but the President has American pride to deal with. When Huerta locked up that landing party, the press in the East fulminated outrageously. It was 'Remember the *Maine*' all over again. I will admit, though, the Germans may trade on it and embarrass us in Mexico. They may even be contacting Villa, too, although he has stood firmly with us so far. In any event, we must know what the Kaiser's men want from Mexico, and what exactly they are promising to get it. You know what this could mean, don't you?"

"Sure. If war should break out in Europe we would be vulnerable on our southern border. War's not likely, though, or is it? Surely the cooler heads in Berlin and Paris have some idea of what a great war would do to the world."

Henry shrugged. "I wouldn't place any sizable wager on cooler heads prevailing."

Something had been ticking inside Corey's head since the walk over from the office. It was the word "duty" Henry had planted there. Was it too late to defuse the time bomb it was wired to?

"I want you to tell me the truth, Henry, and without any more nonsense about my becoming a Special Foreign Service Officer. I'd be a *spy* in Mexico, wouldn't I?"

Richardson recoiled. "I despise that word, Corey." He fell silent for perhaps five seconds. "I won't lie. Yes—part of the time you would be a spy."

"And subject to the penalties spies must face if I were caught?"

"I suppose that's true—*in extremis*. But we're not asking you to steal the plans to Chapultepec, or assassinate a cabinet Minister, and we're not at war with Mexico. The worst you could expect if you were caught would be that Carranza or whoever winds up in charge might expel you from his dismal country. With the last-resort credentials we would arm you with, international law should protect you against physical harm. A man like Carranza would never lock you up or shoot you."

"Nice to know. But that's Carranza. What about Huerta, if he survives? And Villa? Regardless of his supposed affection for us, I'm not aware Pancho has made a fetish of abiding by the law—not even the ones he makes himself. From what I've heard, he's shot his own men because he didn't like their table manners."

"Come now, Corey. That's stretching things a bit."

"It could be my neck that gets stretched. What exactly did you mean when you said 'last-resort credentials'? Why wouldn't I be presenting my *bona fides* and securing diplomatic immunity immediately?"

"We think you should arrive in Mexico City as something other than an official U.S. agent."

What little Henry was telling him was probably the truth, but as for the whole truth, Corey would have to whittle it out of him, sliver by tiny sliver. Henry was still holding something back.

"Not an official agent? Well, then. If I do agree, what do you suggest my pose should be?"

"We call it a 'cover,' not a pose. I thought I would leave that up to you in order that you might be comfortable with it. I've found that best in the past. I have one little idea, though. That book. I would say you have strong claims as a social scientist."

"You're confusing a couple of different disciplines. If I'm anything other than a lame duck sheriff, I'm just a would-be historian."

Henry seemed to think that over. "That would work just as well for getting reports back to us. We wouldn't want direct contact, but as a writer you'd have to keep in touch with a publisher or two here at home, wouldn't you? Better yet, three publishers. It would avoid a noticeable pattern."

Corey broke into laughter for the second time. "Even the *giants* in the field don't have *three* publishers, Henry. I'm luckier than most in having found that one. I've never cracked the big ones in New York."

"We can *get* the three for you, I assure you—or ten. But perhaps you're right. One will do. It should be in New York or Boston, though. In order to give you credibility it would be wise for us to see to it that you do get published by one of the 'big ones,' as you call them."

Small wonder Henry had risen so high in Washington. He knew which button to push, and his finger was firm when he pushed it.

This could mean not only the study of Felipe Ángeles that Corey was working on but the hopes which had risen in him for Pancho Villa's great lieutenant as he learned more about Ángeles's quietly distinguished career. Should he mention the general again in the context of the 'strongman' State was fishing for? There was little chance he could articulate the excitement suddenly bubbling in his head. It might sound as if he were presuming to *make* history, not just write it.

Henry continued, "There of course would be a windfall in it for you."

"Windfall?"

"Someday you may want to write the history of all this. Wouldn't it be particularly rewarding to write it with the authority that would accrue to you from having lived through it on the inside?"

"Damn your eyes, Henry Richardson. And to think I was actually glad to see you when you stepped off that train this noon."

Henry pulled out his watch again. "One hour now, Corey. By the way, I said the President didn't know about you yet. That was when we began to talk. His habits are fairly predictable on some things. He does his reading at the same time every day, and he should be reading your book this very minute. He'll know you when he finishes it. As you will recall, he's a historian, too."

Corey signaled to Concepción for another drink. The questions were still in her dark eyes. He turned back to Richardson.

"All right, Henry. I surrender. If the President still wants me after he's read my stuff, I'll say yes."

Henry Richardson actually smiled. "With that said, Corey, I'm going back to my room at the Sacramento to get the confidential briefing file you'll have to read before you leave for El Paso and Mexico. I'll meet you at the telegraph office. Fifteen minutes, Corey."

"You're *that* sure of the President's reaction?"

"Yes, I am." He stood up.

"And you're that sure of me, too?"

"Yes. I was sure of you before I left Washington. Goodbye, then, for the moment."

When Henry left, Concepción brought Corey's second drink. She still hadn't regained the weight she had lost during the "illness" before the fight between her brother and young MacAndrews. Andreas, at the bar, looked almost as bad. The elder Martínez had fought with him in Cuba, and Corey never forgot that he owed him his life, although modest Andreas would never call the debt, in this existence or the next. He had cleaned a Spanish sniper out of a tree Corey was headed for. There was little he wouldn't do for this decent man. One of the worst things about chasing Jorge down the Jornada was the constant recollection that he was Andreas Martínez's son.

As the girl placed his drink in front of him, he said, "Any word from your *hermano*, Concepción?"

"Nothing, Sheriff Lane. I have a letter ready to send Jorge the moment we hear from him."

"Then he probably doesn't even know the law isn't looking for him any longer, that all the charges against him have been dropped?"

"No. I should never have let him run away. I know that now."

"Don't be too hard on yourself."

"How is Jamie, Sheriff Lane?"

So there was still something left of that, after all. Concepción Martínez not only looked like her but clearly loved as Lucy Bishop loved. He shouldn't be surprised. "Doing well, last I heard. We can all be grateful. He was lucky. Another inch to the left and Jorge's knife would have . . ." He stopped. The pain his words were causing was all too obvious. "Don't worry. We'll get Jorge back."

"Muchas gracias, señor."

When Corey met Henry at the Western Union office in the Black Springs depot at 4:55 to send Henry's coded signal to Secretary of State William Jennings Bryan, they found one from the Secretary waiting there for Henry.

After the man from Washington had retired with it to a depot bench, fished a tiny black book from his inside coat pocket, and made some notes on a telegram blank, he called Corey to him. It was hard to believe that Henry Richardson's superbly sober face could suddenly look even more so.

"We've gone ashore and occupied Veracruz, Corey. There's been a fair amount of killing, but the Stars and Stripes are flying over the port. I won't pretend that this doesn't make your job more dangerous and difficult, but with time running out for Huerta, we mustn't lose any advantage his deposition might afford us. Can you leave for El Paso with me in the morning?"

Suddenly Corey's saying yes to his old friend was underlined. He wanted this assignment very much.

The one question here in Calle Rinconada was: should he walk across the way and collect young Martínez now—or come back for him tomorrow? Jorge, perhaps not knowing he was no longer wanted, might panic and run again now that he had seen a Chupadera lawman. Corey would have to spit the news out fast. Martínez was mercurial, swift as a sidewinder, and impulsive to boot. Witness the attack on young MacAndrews.

He hadn't appeared in the areaway again. Corey had better get him now.

Wait. He was forgetting something. Talking with Jorge might very well ruin his cover story with Guzmán's people if any of them were already in the house, and news like that would fly southward faster than by telegraph.

He would pick the young man up tomorrow, but only after Guzmán came and went. Whatever kept Jorge here this long would surely hold him here another day.

Then Corey would be able to keep his promise to Jorge's sister.

This mission for Henry Richardson—not even properly begun—had already brought him one small comfort.

He hoped it wouldn't be the last.

PART 2

THE
DOGS
OF
TORREÓN

7

Misión de Guadalupe—Ciudad Juárez, México—May 1914

She wanted to stay a little longer here in the wonderful old mission church, where the haze from the candles softened everything in sight and their flames chased shadows up the walls and lit the giant *vigas* that roofed the nave, making that fantastic dance of light and dark she still loved—but she had to get to the *mercado* and back to Avenida de Los Árboles to fix Papá's supper.

The church was nearly empty. Not another soul approached the altar after she knelt there, and the nave itself was bare of worshippers. A legless beggar sprawled just inside the wide front doors, and an old woman who had been praying to the Virgin when she entered the church was now walking through them, ignoring the tin cup he held out.

Papá didn't know she was here today, but she would have to tell him about the visit before they ate. She wouldn't try to hide it from him; even if she did, he would smell the wax and incense on her hair and clothes and know exactly where she had been. He wouldn't say a word, but it would trouble him that she still felt this old need for confessional and prayer. He no longer felt such need himself, and sometimes even denied he ever had. He wouldn't be happy about hers, but he would understand it.

It was pleasant to be alone in the musty, silent place. She seemed to need this time more every year. This year her saint's day was particularly special—it was her seventeenth birthday, too.

And it was five years to the day since Mamá died.

She finished her prayer, the same short prayer for Mamá's soul that was the only prayer she ever said, crossed herself, got to her feet, smoothed her full skirt, and pulled the *rebozo* close about her head and shoulders. She untied the handkerchief that held the money for the food and *cerveza* she had to buy for Papá's supper, and pulled out two centavos to drop in the beggar's probably still-empty cup.

If she didn't hurry now, she would be late getting to the market. Papá turned fierce when his supper wasn't ready on time, only mock fierce, though. Bad-tempered old bear that he could be when crossed or out of sorts, he had never struck her once in all her seventeen years. A few other people hadn't been so lucky.

She started for the doors at the front of the church, but hadn't taken five steps when a young man carrying a *ranchero* jacket in one hand and a huge book in the other came out of the far confessional, dropped to his knees across the dark nave from her, letting the book and jacket fall to the hard floor beside him. His eyes were closed, and his lips began to move in prayer.

She stopped short. It wasn't often young men came to church this time of day.

In the dim light it was hard to see his face, but a candle flame suddenly burned down through a thicker section of its wick and a splash of light spilled from the dark shadows behind the altar, reaching his features and touching them with flame for an instant, too.

Except for the moving lips, he was motionless, head bowed, his chin with the silky, clearly brand-new beard tucked down on his chest. He hadn't looked at her when he knelt under the serene plaster gaze of the Virgin, and she wondered what there possibly could be about him that made her stop and look at him. It must have been that sudden flare of the altar candle.

His eyes were still closed, but he could open them any second and catch her staring at him. She had better look away. And she had better leave—now. She had things to do, places to go.

She couldn't move, couldn't stop looking.

¡Dios! She had never looked at a man quite this way before, nor for anything like as long.

There was at least one reason why. Despite his immobility, there was something about the way he held himself that spoke of great exhaustion and agitation, as if he were just ending a long, hard journey, or beginning one—or both.

He was slender, not terribly tall, but even fixed in prayer, there was something almost frighteningly compelling about his straight, firm shoulders, the arch of his back even as he knelt, the strong supple neck. She wished she could hear his voice, but she didn't dare move closer.

Was he poor? He hadn't placed a candle at the feet of the Virgin or any of the saints, and *los hermanos* here at Guadalupe asked less for candles than they did at almost any church since Santa María del Oro six years ago. There were certainly too many poor here in Juárez; two of every three of the women she met at the market or at the Division's Los Árboles office—looking for men to feed and protect them, and maybe, just maybe, to give them something they could feel was love—were truly destitute, certainly more of them ground down to nothing by poverty than she remembered back in Santa María. If this young man was poor, he wasn't poor in the same way they were poor. He didn't have the haunted look she knew too well.

He was probably a workman of some kind, out of a job at the moment and only temporarily without a peso, his pockets empty, as were those of so many men these days with the Revolution now at its very worst—the sort of man Papá was always looking for and seldom managing to find: young, strong, and perhaps desperate enough to do Papá's work.

No, a closer look told her he wasn't an *obrero*, not a common laborer, at any rate. The hands clasped in prayer in front of him weren't the horny, scarred hands of a digger, a carpenter, a drover, or a porter. He looked like he actually might read the book beside him. Contrary to what she had just thought, it was hard to imagine a man who read books as one of Papá's people.

He wasn't very old, not much older than she was herself. And no, he *wasn't* poor; poor men didn't have smooth hands and carry books to church, and his clothing—a sort of uniform, but not an army uniform, and at odds with the rough woolen jacket—was new and stylish, except that his dark blue, striped trousers looked wet, soaked to above those knees pressed down on the hard floor, and with mud beginning to cake at the wide cuffs *norteamericanos* along the border seemed to favor.

He had come from across the big river, *sí,* and not too long ago, probably had waded it within the hour, slogging through the Rio's soupy brown water because he lacked the money for the El Paso–Juárez trolley car. She had seen enough men like these since she and Papá came up to Juárez from Torreón last week.

Norteamericano, sí, but not a gringo.

His hair was as black as hers and his skin as brown. Like her, he was Latino, but not *mestizo*; his nose straighter and more prominent than the blunt ones of most of her countrymen, the ones back home or the ones she had known in the four years she and Papá had traveled with the army.

So again, why this interest? Just turning seventeen couldn't have made the difference. She had been old enough for men for a long time now without looking so keenly at any man. Half the *soldaderas* who followed their men on the railroads and through the war camps and battlefields were younger than she was, and hundreds had already given birth to a child, often more than one. She had never once let herself get involved with a man. It hadn't, of course, been due only to her own unguided choice. When she was only half past thirteen, Papá, blushing, hinted broadly at what men would want from her.

"You have become . . . *Dios,* how to say it? . . . *interesting* to these *hombres, querida.* Remember always—no matter how sweet their talk or how *magnífico* their promises, they are after one thing only. You have time enough for men, all the time in the world. You are too good for any man we have seen so far."

Too young to think so grandly of herself back then, she nodded, agreed tacitly that he was right. Actually, she hadn't needed his warning to know the folly, worse, the danger she could face if she let men get too close to her. She remembered Mamá all too well. With the army, all through Durango, Coahuila, and now Chihuahua, she had heard and seen things women with husbands and families back in Santa María never heard or saw all their lives, and wouldn't believe if they had, although her still-longed-for village may have changed since Mamá died, when Papá took her to the mountains.

The intrusive, filthy sameness of the spoken and unspoken demands of the soldiers and civilians she and Papá had been thrown in with these past four years, the hard, grasping hands, had certainly made her wary enough of men, alert as a sparrow to the subtlest of their advances as well as the crudest. She had learned to fend off even the boldest and most persistent, puncturing their ballooning egos with a tongue as sharp as an awl, and she had built a reputation in the brigade as the worst kind of spitfire, a hellion better left alone. Sometimes—she was only a *little* ashamed to admit—it was fun. One deflated corporal had called her a *bruja del infierno*, and she had taken perverse pride in his look of utter defeat. And if she didn't get rid of them herself, Papá did. Papá knew how to handle the few too brutal and gutter *macho* to shrink from her scalding tongue. He never said a word when such a man approached her, but a look or a threatening gesture warned the man off more times than not, and if some slavering animal persisted, he disappeared for days or weeks—even the few officers among them who Papá should have feared and yielded to—and when she saw such a man again he treated her like a stranger. She never asked Papá what he said or did to dissuade these few.

Sí, Papá was right. There would be time enough for men when the Revolution ended. She needed no man to feed her, to protect her, and be a comrade. Papá was all she needed for such things now, wasn't he? He would be all she needed for a long, long time. And if sometimes in the dark of night in her bedroll in camp, or on the long marches when the army was fleeing an enemy or seeking one, her mind and her *corazón* craved a different kind of love from Papá's, her body, while vaguely stirring from time to time with desire she couldn't have described, hadn't yet.

But now, as she had told herself moments earlier, she had places to go and things to do. She couldn't daydream here forever. Papá might be looking for her even now.

Still, there was something about this young man that held her almost as if he had taken her by the hand ...

Suddenly she knew what it was. The book. It set him apart from almost all the others she had known, back home or in the army. It didn't matter, either, what book it was. Books had fueled her dreams since she learned to read in Santa María's mission school ten long, lost years ago, back when Doña Luisa lent her books from the *hacienda*'s library. No one else on either side of her *familia* had ever leaned to read, not Papá, Mamá, or any of her cousins. In the army she could count on the fingers of one hand the men she knew who could read—or write. Most of those who could were officers, far too old for her, and, except for Trini, living in a different and sometimes *indifferent* world from the one she and Papá knew. A young man who read would surely be more like her, wouldn't he, even if he came from another land?

Perhaps—it wasn't too much to hope for—he would even have dreams that matched her own. They could talk, at least. Papá wasn't big on talk.

But all this speculation was monumental silliness. When she and Papá went south to Torreón tomorrow to rejoin the Division, she would never see this young man—or his book—again. Just as well. Papá and she had a lot of work to do.

She clutched the *rebozo* even more tightly about her. She *must* leave now.

A little sigh escaped her as she walked past the kneeling figure and headed to where the church's open doors framed a broad shaft of sunlight. As she passed she fought back a small, throbbing impulse to bend toward the book and read the gold lettering on its spine.

Outside, she lingered a moment on the wide stone steps, reluctant to walk away from the dream which had flickered so briefly—but so brightly, too.

She shrugged, and set off for the market plaza.

When she was a dozen steps down the cobbled street a voice came from behind her. *"¡Señorita! Un momento, por favor."*

It was the young man from the church. He had donned the *ranchero* jacket. The book was tucked under his arm and held tightly to his side. She swallowed the beginnings of a gasp.

"¿Sí, señor?" Her mind whirled. She nearly gave way to dizziness.

"I wish to ask you something."

"¿Qué es?" She forced herself to meet his eyes. They looked faintly glazed, the slight glassy look barely masking a deeper one of anxiety and trouble, overlaid with sudden high excitement. His mouth worked soundlessly for the time it took her heart to beat just once. He was going to have great difficulty getting his next words out. Bad sign. Even the worst of them sometimes had this kind of trouble at the start.

Dios, por favor—do not let him be like all the others. Probably a vain hope. It all too often began just like this: feigned shyness at the start, next the suggestive leer, then the inevitable try for conquest and deceit. Well, she would be ready for him. She would send him on his way and forget all about him by suppertime.

"Could you tell me, please, *señorita*, where a man could go to join the army of General Francisco Villa?"

Now *she* was the one who couldn't find her voice, but at last she got it out. "Half a kilometer straight down this *avenida, señor,* at the corner of Los Árboles and El Portal."

He mumbled *"Gracias"* and moved swiftly past her.

She watched him until he was lost in a knot of other walkers.

It was a small reward, but at least he wasn't like the others. Then her heart dropped. He hadn't looked at her, hadn't really seen her. It was almost worse than if he had grabbed for her.

A small nagging pain started somewhere under her breastbone, near her heart.

Maybe Papá was right about something else. Going to church today was perhaps not the best idea she had ever had.

8

"*¡Tosco!*" Sergeant Paco Durán bellowed. Jorge froze. Durán went on, softly now, but with even more genuine threat. "You have wrecked an expensive weapon, Martínez. In the field against the Federalistas I would shoot you—*nombre de Dios,* I would. *¡Marrón!*"

There wasn't a great deal Jorge Martínez could say in his own defense even had he dared. He had, after all, dropped the machine gun in the Coahuilan desert rocks because he *was* careless and clumsy—*tosco,* as Durán said—and the ugly tear in the gun's water jacket gaped at him like one of *el sargento*'s accusing sneers. The sun became more merciless as he looked down at the damaged gun. There were sneers from the other recruits, too. They came with painful regularity now. When they began training together six weeks ago they had winced at the sergeant's bullying outbursts as much as he had, but now he was alone in Paco's Purgatory. He wondered if he would ever get *anything* right. Something had gone wrong between Durán and him almost from the first, but this thing with the machine gun was the worst disaster yet. His face burned. It was doubly humiliating when he recalled how affable this big angry bull of a man had been in the recruiting office on Avenida de los Árboles back in Juárez, how pleased when Jorge signed the enlistment papers, how persuasive when he said that before the sun rose twice Jorge would be a superb *soldado de caballería.* Something had indeed gone wrong.

Perhaps it happened at that first inspection after the truck ride through the desert from Ciudad Juárez to the tent city south of Torreón, when the sergeant inspected their kits and pulled the Molinas book—*Los grandes problemas nacionales*—from Jorge's pack. From the gingerly way he held it and turned it in his ham-sized hands, and his look of suspicion as he did so, it was clear he couldn't read. To Durán's credit, he didn't try to disguise his deficiency.

"What is the name of this, Capitán Cucaracha?" he said. Jorge told him, half expecting admiration or at worst jealousy. Neither showed on the massive features behind the heavy beard. "Tell me what it is about." Jorge explained how the book had been the Bible of the struggle against Porfirio Díaz. Beyond an animal grunt there was no flicker of seeming interest. "I will keep this for you. You won't have time to read for the next month or two."

Durán, who apparently had only been in Juárez as a temporary recruiter for Regiment Bracomonte, was a regular, a dynamiter and cannoneer, a veteran of the regiment and of Brigade Ignacio Zaragoza—General Eugenio Aguirre Benavides commanding—the unit that had opened fire first in the second battle of Torreón. The brigade had slashed the rail line to Monterrey northeast of the city on the Río Nazas, keeping the Huerta forces there from coming to its relief. Then Pancho Villa and his master gunner, General Felipe Ángeles, had reduced the Federalista stronghold under José Refugio Velásco to rubble. Paco Durán had been prominent in that first lightning interdiction and in the week-long siege that followed. He had never once mentioned it himself, but every one of the recruits with the exception of Jorge seemed to know the sergeant's exploits in great detail. "Three wounds," someone said. Jorge looked in vain for evidence, but couldn't find it. He noticed, though, that Durán never removed his shirt in the middle of the day as the other drillmasters did. "He blew two trains in the first six hours," another *cucaracha* added.

Jorge Martínez had done very little, no *nada*, that seemed to please the giant sergeant-of-recruits. It brought even more shame when he remembered how he had been prepared to like the man from Durango, *sí*, to learn from him and fight for and with him as a *soldado de caballos*, even—was it so wild a dream?—as one of the famed Dorados of Pancho Villa.

Dorado? *Soldado a caballo? Mierda.* In the six weeks since El Paso and Juárez he hadn't even been near a horse, never mind on the back of one. Not quite true. After the cavalry-in-training rode out on maneuvers each day, he had shoveled enough horseshit from the brigade's stables to make a mountain the size of Cuchillo Peak back home. At this rate, and with this kind of training, he could never become a Dorado.

When he complained to Durán, the sergeant maintained a contemptuous silence for almost a minute before he said, "This, I think, is the limit of your *capacidad*, Capitán Cucaracha. *Muchachito*."

Words like these, and Durán's glares at him, reduced him to such a state that he wanted to scream at him, "I am not a child or a moron, Sergeant. I am a man, one to be feared. I am wanted! I have killed." He never said any of it. The stabbing death of an unarmed gringo in a barroom in a distant New Mexico town wouldn't have impressed Paco. Killing Epifanio Guzmán would have.

But he hadn't killed Guzmán. He hadn't even made the attempt.

He had fled Casa Estrellita less than five minutes after he had seen Corey Lane, running like a madman the three blocks to the Rio with his jacket and the Molinas book clutched hard against a heaving side, the knife in his boot top once more. He had waded the hundred yards of foot-deep water in the river as beaten as he had ever been, almost penniless, feeling hunger mount in his belly after the meager breakfast of that heartbreaking morning. He hadn't even looked behind him to see if Lane was following. And he hadn't stopped at the riverbank to see if any guards were posted to prevent his crossing. Jorge María Martínez reached Mexico as blind to the world and as low in spirit as he had ever been.

Now, at the end of each grinding day of drill and forced labor under the blood-red Coahuilan sun, he swore that one night soon he would bury his knife, the knife he hadn't used to slit the throat of Epifanio Guzmán, somewhere deep in the huge body of Paco Durán—*if* he could find a weak spot in that tough, bulging, saddle-leather hide for the blade to enter. But when the ragged squad Durán kept him in (long after he had promoted the other recruits who had signed up with Jorge back in Juárez into a regular cavalry troop) was dismissed at day's end, he found he had no strength left to do more than eat, find his bedroll, and collapse.

Strangely, though, by each following morning the bitterness and the killing anger had dissipated, and he knew in those dawn moments that the knife would stay securely where it was. He faced the new day—and *el sargento*—almost eagerly. He wondered about that. Was there something of the masochist in his nature?

He wondered, too, about the obviously pejorative first word of the epithet "Capitán Cucaracha" Durán reserved for him. Why the "Capitán"? The other recruits were cockroaches to Durán, too, but without benefit of rank. Pride kept him from asking the harried new men in Paco's charge if they had any idea what Durán meant by it. He finally decided it was only to put him on the same lowly level as the other insects in the squad, but with the "Capitán" making doubly sure the rest of them knew he was the biggest and stupidest *cucaracha* of them all.

Sí, the thing with the machine gun was possibly the lowest point of his brief career with Brigade Ignacio Zaragoza.

Durán stared balefully down at the fractured weapon in the sand and then lifted a gaze as belligerent as that of a Miura bull to Jorge's face. "Since you have earned no pay yet, Capitán Cucaracha, I will take its price out of your miserable hide if it can't be fixed."

Life with Paco Durán, Jorge knew to a sinking certainty at that moment, could only grow more difficult.

But as the next few days went by, a subtle change began to take place in the sergeant's "training" of him.

Durán didn't give him nearly as much physical work to do, and what he did demand wasn't quite as onerous. The manure detail at the stables all but disappeared from Jorge's daily regimen, as did his tours to duty as *el jardinero*, the "landscape gardener" who cleaned the company street and dug the new latrines.

He received his first pay. It was just as pitifully small as he had feared, but to his surprise his paybook didn't mention any deduction for repairs to—or a replacement for—the wrecked machine gun. He was positive it was an oversight, but he didn't mention it to any of his comrades—and certainly not to Sargento Paco Durán.

Durán required his presence on the firing range with the 7.5mm carbine a good deal more often and for longer sessions than in the past. Jorge reveled in the target work, even when the repeated volleys and blazing sun made the barrel of the short rifle agonizing to the touch. It was something he seemed to have a natural ability for, and once Durán even grunted something suspiciously like approval after a run of rapid-fire high scores with twenty-three of twenty-five rounds well within the red.

The map-reading drills went even better, although he reflected that the sergeant might have rated him higher than he deserved because he couldn't read at all himself. Jorge recognized his own mistakes all too well. He was still having trouble making the adjustment from inches, feet, yards, and miles to centimeters, meters, and kilometers. Changing the thermometer readings to Celsius from Fahrenheit during Durán's short course in explosives gave him no end of trouble, too.

Then, on a morning hot enough on either scale to make the devil himself whimper in surrender, Durán put him on a horse.

The animal was one of the skinniest, most ridiculous-looking beasts he had ever seen, with a head an insane-asylum inmate might have designed, a swayed back, and with hooves that were not only too large but over which the hairs of the fetlocks hung down like matted buckskin fringes. Strangely, it was at least a willing, easy goer—to a point. The silly animal apparently couldn't defecate while on the move. No amount of coaxing, cursing, spurring, or use of the quirt Jorge found looped around the saddle horn could get it under way until it had done its business.

For a moment he thought he and Durán were going to ride together. He had seen the sergeant mounted only once before, but he had gotten a fair idea of just how good he was despite the fact that not many horses were big enough to carry him easily, and his heart beat a little faster at the prospect of being schooled in *military* equitation by this veteran, even on the sorry Rosinante he was riding. A fair horseman himself, he was ready to imagine how much better Durán could make him.

But a lesson wasn't to be this morning. Durán reached down into his saddlebag and drew out a worn, flat leather case he handed Jorge. "Take this, Capitán Cucaracha. Find a major named Trinidad Álvarez and give it to him."

"*Sí, sargento,*" Jorge said. "And just where is this Major Álvarez?"

"How should I know, *señor bufón*? It is *your* mission. Find him!" With that he wheeled his horse around and in the wink of an eye was at a full gallop, and in two winks out of sight where the company street ducked behind a row of tents.

So—he was, as he had been by everything Paco Durán did or said, still being tested. *Entonces,* he would face it without complaint. It couldn't be much of a test, anyway, if this major was in the División del Norte.

He had heard "Álvarez" before somewhere and had some cloudy recollection that the officer was straight up the ladder of command from Durán, but he couldn't recall ever hearing the name put to any of the rankers at *la tropa*'s headquarters tent on the few occasions Durán had taken his *cucarachas* anywhere near it. Still, that was logically the place to begin the search. Runty Sabine Sánchez, one of the batch of recruits who came down from Juárez with him, was now assigned there as some kind of clerk. Sánchez, almost a dwarf, wasn't very bright, but *mierda*, he had been promoted when Jorge hadn't.

The tiny, twisted Sánchez was alone in the tent where the *tropa*'s guidon hung limp on a staff jutting from the ridgepole.

"Álvarez?" Sánchez shrugged his shoulders. "There is no officer by that name in this *tropa*, Jorge. *¿Quién sabe?* Maybe you should try regiment—or brigade. *Un momento.* There is a kind of roster somewhere here, *amigo.* If I can find it."

He began rummaging through the drawer of a field desk sagging on a bent leg. At last his hands came out with a folder that had seen better days. He handed it to Jorge with an apologetic look that told Jorge that he was, as was the case with Durán, hopelessly illiterate. For an instant Jorge seethed. A clerk who couldn't read?—while *he* was held back and kept from taking his place as a true *soldado*? *Mierda, mierda,* and again *mierda!*

He almost ripped the folder from Sabine's hands. Inside it sheets of paper were covered with names, ranks, and the numbers of individuals and units.

Adolante . . . Aguirre . . . Altemirano . . . Álvarez! *Sí*, there were four Álvarezes, but only one named Trinidad, a captain. Paco Durán's Álvarez must have been promoted since this list was made. Another thing: there was no *tropa* or *compañía* number after the "Capitán Trinidad Álvarez," no name of a regiment such as Los Bracomontes nor of a brigade like Jorge's own Ignacio Zaragoza—just the single word "Dorado."

That sent his blood racing. Trinidad Álvarez was a major of Dorados! It was hard enough to be a mere private in Pancho Villa's personal striking force, but to be a high-ranking officer? A major? The man Paco Durán had sent him to find must be an *hombre muy importante, muy guerrero.*

"Where are the Dorados bivouacked now, Sabine, *por favor?*"

Sánchez spread his hands. "I don't know, Jorge. Not south of the river here. I think if I were you I would look for them near the headquarters of the Division."

It made sense. If the Dorados were anywhere at all inside

the ten-square-mile encampment strung along both sides of the rail lines to San Pedro de las Colonias and Paredón, they would be at the heart of things with General Villa. The last Jorge had heard, the general had settled in at the foot of La Pila on the other side of the Río Nazas. With only the railroad bridge across the Nazas still intact, but rattling with freight and ordnance day and night, he would have to ford the river, now running full to the top of its banks with the last of the late spring runoff.

God *damn* Paco Durán!

Well, at least that brute of a sergeant hadn't said *when* he had to deliver the case to Major Álvarez. It was nearly eleven now. He couldn't cross the Nazas and be anywhere near La Pila for perhaps another hour. He would have to cadge food somewhere on this side of the river, from some other horse *tropa*'s noon mess on the way to the riverbank, or from the cooking fire of a friendly *soldadera*, if he could find one whose man wouldn't raise a stink. Near the encampment center across the river it might not be easy, perhaps not even possible. Without any real experience to base it on, he nonetheless had the sure instinct that the closer to power one ventured, the more difficult the people encountered would turn out to be, with even the lowliest camp followers ungenerous and mean.

Crossing the *río* wasn't as hard as he expected, until he neared the far side. The horse, tractable and foolishly gentle to that point, suddenly broke for the bank, splashing through a knot of women doing a wash. Screams erupted as the women scattered, some of them gathering naked brown children into their arms.

Curses hot enough to singe his new short beard and mustache followed him up the slope from the water, and one of the women proved accurate enough with a gob of mud to catch him full at the back of his neck. Actually, with the solid-brass rays of the sun playing a bastinado on him, hammering him deep into the saddle, the cool mud felt good. He let the horse run a few more paces until he was sure he was out of range of any more such missiles, reined up, turned back to the women, swept his sombrero from his head, and made a little bow.

Two of them applauded. One other laughed, then raised and shook her skirt back and forth across the tops of her legs like a dancer, movements obviously practiced many times. No wonder. Her legs were marvelous, and she knew it. They were like his sister Concepción's, but even longer. Her right hand was black with mud. Without a doubt she was the one who had pelted him.

"*Por favor,*" he said. "Can one of you *lindas mujeres* tell me where the Dorado camp can be found today?"

A chorus of shouted words mixed with hoots and jeers answered him. Then it subsided and the girl with the good legs and the muddy right hand took over.

"What do you want with Los Dorados, *muchachito*?"

Muchachito again! It sounded exactly like Durán. The blistering sun had never burned his skin half so much as the word now seared his insides.

"That is for me to know, *señorita*."

"Dorados would chew you up and spit you out."

There was a ringing challenge in her voice he decided to ignore. He turned the horse back toward the center of the camp and urged it forward at a walk.

The animal started readily enough, but after a few feet it stopped dead in its tracks. The damned old bag of bones had to shit again. He felt like a fool.

"You will not tell me what you want with the Dorados, *amigo*?" It was the girl again, standing beside him. She was watching the horse and smiling broadly. Then she turned her face up to him with her mud-caked hand shading her eyes against the sun. "I know all the Dorados. They are all friends of mine." *Dios,* she was extraordinarily pretty, pretty enough to make him forget his embarrassment, probably beautiful in a light softer than this harsh, unflattering sun and with other clothes—although the clinging, flimsy gray blouse and full red skirt did look good. Close up like this she was also younger than he had thought when she first spoke to him. Fifteen?

Sixteen maybe, surely not more than seventeen. Then he was struck by the idea that he had seen this girl somewhere before, but where? No answer came.

In Black Springs she would have been far too young for him. Here? Perhaps not. Isabel at Carmen's in Chihuahuita had been no older, and she had more or less invited him to bed with her, but he could no more have slept with poor, used-up Isabel than he could have gone with Carmen.

He knew that if this long-legged creature, who at that moment reached up and grasped the bridle of the big horse and held its lantern head steady, invited him, he wouldn't be proof against the invitation for a second.

Wait. Such speculation might be the stupidest thinking he had done; and he had done some. What was it Paco Durán had told him and the other recruits about women? Oh, yes—sooner or later they would all want *soldaderas*, women to travel with them and share their bedroll, to cook and mend, even clean a rifle or a pistol, and above all to care for them if they were sick or wounded. "What else you do with them is up to you. One important thing to remember, though. Do not try to take one of the women already in the camp. They belong to someone else. You are asking for a knife between the ribs if you even look at them. Find a free woman in one of the towns we reach when we move again. Until then keep your cocks in your *pantalones*."

He wondered where the man who owned this girl might be, if perhaps the knife was already on its way.

He looked down at the girl, and again came the thought that he had seen her before today. "You know *all* the Dorados, *señorita*?" The girl nodded. "Do you know a Major Trinidad Álvarez?"

"El mayor Álvarez? *¡Sí!"* Her face, bright enough under the black hair to begin with, became suddenly even more luminous. "You are looking for Trini Álvarez?" *Dios,* maybe the major he was seeking was this girl's man.

"Are you his *soldadera*?"

Brightness of an entirely different sort lit her face now, the vivid flare of anger. "I am *no* one's *soldadera*! Not that of Trini Álvarez or any other *guerrero*. Trini is just an *amigo*."

"If you are not a *soldadera*, who looks after you?"

"I look after myself." A shade too much defiance perhaps? "And *amigos* like Trini Álvarez look after me, too, if I let them." *Sí*, he could bet there were many would-be *"amigos"* only too glad to look after her.

"Can you take me to your *amigo* Álvarez?"

"Sí, soldado . . ." Impish, but at least the *soldado* was an improvement on the *muchachito*. Then she went on, "For a cigarette."

He laughed and fished in his pockets. "I have no cigarettes, *señorita*. Will a *cigarro* do?"

"All right, José. A *cigarro*, then."

"Match?"

She shook her head. "I will save the *cigarro* for someone else."

"Show me the way."

"Swing me up behind you. I do not walk."

He put his left arm down. She grasped it with two slim hands and then almost floated up to the broad back of the horse just behind the cantle of his saddle. Her two brown arms slipped around his waist, and then she leaned forward, her soft chest close against his back. Too young for him? It didn't seem so now.

"Straight ahead. Along the railroad tracks that come out of the yard," she said. "Cross the tracks when you reach the flat-car that carries El Niño."

"El Niño?"

"The big cannon. You don't know El Niño?"

"No."

"That's right. You weren't with us when we took Torreón."

Us? We? "No, I'm new." How did she know he hadn't fought in the battle? A guess, most likely.

"In the fighting for this town, El Niño almost blew off the top of La Pila, that hill up ahead. What is your outfit?"

"I have not been assigned yet. I think I will be with Regiment Bracomonte, Brigade Ignacio Zaragoza."

"Then you are still a recruit? A *cucaracha*?"

"I suppose so." It was a terrible admission to have to make right now. His face burned and he wanted to dig at the still-infant beard that was suddenly itching as if it were home to a full *tropa* of *cucarachas*.

"You joined the División del Norte at Ciudad Juárez, then."

"*Sí.*" Again, how did she know? Another lucky guess?

"You are an *americano*? A *Mexican* gringo?" Before he could answer she began to laugh. At any other time and under any other circumstances it would have been a wonderful thing to hear, but he knew the laugh was at his expense. With the laughter shaking her, her chest heaved against his back. Perhaps he could take it for a while.

At last the laughter subsided. Her arms left his waist and her hands came to rest on his shoulders as she apparently leaned back from him.

"*Conque . . .*" she said. "Then you are the famous *Captain* Cockroach. *¿Sí?*"

He turned in the saddle so swiftly he feared for a moment he would knock her to the ground.

"How did you know that?" he said, his voice the dry rattle of a diamondback.

"Because my father is Sargento Paco Durán!"

9

Major Trinidad Álvarez rubbed his eyes with a hard fist while his other hand held back the netting at the opening of the tent. Deep in *siesta* as the major must have been, it hadn't taken him fifteen seconds to answer the girl's call, and when he pulled the fist from his eye he was wide awake, fully alert, black eyes now keen and piercing. Jorge had the certain feeling Major Álvarez could have reacted to any emergency with the same paralyzing swiftness and without thinking. *Sí.* He must be *muy guerrero, verdad, muy Dorado*. Four or five years older perhaps than Jorge, he was built as powerfully as Paco Durán, if not on the same awesome scale.

He was dressed in the familiar khaki of the Northern Division, but he wore no insignia, no shoulder pips or epaulettes, and nothing at all on his collar, which was unbuttoned and sagged open and limp with sweat.

When he saw the major's full, glossy *bandido* mustache, Jorge put his hand to his mouth in an effort to cover his own scraggly, half-grown one, if only for a futile second. He realized then that he hadn't saluted, and he shot his hand to his sombrero hard enough to knock it cockeyed. *Dios,* what a bad beginning he was making with this Dorado officer, particularly after arriving on the comic cart horse Paco had inflicted on him.

The major's eyes had been solely on the girl until then, but now he looked at Jorge and returned the salute with a light brush of his forehead. It wasn't a contemptuous gesture; it wasn't offhand, either, just easy, comfortable. His eyes were steady on Jorge's face the whole time, as if to say, "I see you there, *amigo*. I am not going to ignore you." The eyes moved away from Jorge and back to the girl now, but with a subtle, unspoken promise to return. Had there been a trace of a smile, too? *Sí.* Why not? Jorge's salute must have been high comedy to this professional. Jorge was lucky his awkwardness had only been greeted with a smile. Some other more rigid officer might have handed him his head. He almost wished Álvarez had. That would be the way of a Dorado, wouldn't it?

"*Qué tal,* Juanita?" Álvarez said to the girl. "And how is your father?" There was something like sadness in the smile he gave her. Why would a Dorado look sad?

"It goes well with Papá, Trini." It was hard for Jorge to think of Paco Durán as anyone's "Papá," but at least he knew her name now.

"His wounds are healed, then?" The voice matched the smile.

"Healed well enough for Papá, Trini," Juanita Durán said.

"But you know how he is. I have to be hard with him to slow him down. As long as he can lift a carbine or set a charge of dynamite, he *thinks* he's healed."

Álvarez laughed. A laugh, yes, but again that sadness. "Perhaps in his case it's the same thing, Juanita." He turned to Jorge again. "Speaking of Juanita's father, I believe you have messages from Sargento Durán for me, *compadre*."

Jorge, intent on listening to Álvarez talk to the girl—and just a little bit put out that this slim young girl was hinting that she could run his sergeant, father or not—was taken by surprise. He jumped, almost skittered the way a cockroach does when a light flashes suddenly in a dark room. *Sí*, a cockroach. If only the girl hadn't been there to see it, but she had. He felt his face redden. But why should he worry about her or what she thought? If she said anything to her father, so be it. It was Álvarez's reaction alone which should concern him now.

"Yes ... sir," Jorge said. It was mortifyingly close to a stammer.

He turned, reached into the saddlebag on the horse, and dug out the leather case. How had Álvarez known he come to him from Paco Durán? Clearly the major had expected him—and the leather case he brought. But how? Because the girl had come along? No. Álvarez hadn't looked as if he had expected her at all, and even if he had, he couldn't have known Jorge would meet her at the river. Perhaps in his ignorance Jorge had now become part of some kind of messenger service. Was that all they would ever let him do in this army?

Álvarez took the case from him with a soft *"Gracias,"* opened the flap, and started to pull out a sheaf of papers. He stopped. "Forgive me, *por favor, amigo*. I must be alone when I read this. It might take as much as half an hour." It sounded almost too apologetic, with nothing of the arrogance Jorge might have expected, even wanted, from a great Dorado. "I do wish you to report back when I have finished, *soldado*. Part of what I must read bears on your permanent assignment." Álvarez turned back to the girl. "Will you look after our young friend here while I do my studying, Juanita? Perhaps you will want to spend a few minutes with your Captain Espinosa. It might be good for the captain to have a look at this *guerrero*, too." It was too good to be true—this splendid officer calling him a *guerrero*.

"*Sí*, Trini. That is a really good idea, even if he is not yet a real *soldado*." What was going on here? This girl, this *child*, was presuming to pass judgment on the comments of a Dorado cavalry officer, and by extension was passing judgment on him as well. Was her sergeant father that important to the major that he would ignore what by rights should be treated as impudence? Something else. Álvarez had said "*your* Captain Espinosa." Was this Juanita, despite her angry denial, a *soldadera*, after all? That shouldn't bother him. As he had just told himself, she was not his concern, daughter of his sergeant though she was. He wanted to tell Álvarez he could look after himself, and that he had already eaten, but the Dorado major had already dropped the mosquito netting and was back inside the tent.

"Are you hungry?" Juanita said now.

"No. I ate before I crossed the river."

She laughed. "*You* didn't cross the river. Your funny-looking *caballo* did. You just went along for the ride."

¡Mierda! His face burned and his wispy beard itched even worse than earlier. *Dios*, what was wrong with him? He had gotten pitifully thin-skinned lately. Well, this girl's father hadn't helped matters much in that respect—nor had the girl herself. She had seemed to be spoiling for a fight from that first moment at the river's edge. It couldn't have all come from his horse having splashed her. Maybe anyone in the Division of the North named Durán would always be bad news for him.

"*Vamos*," she said now. "*I* have not eaten. Let's see if we can find something."

"I said I wasn't hungry."

"If I were you I would eat—hungry or not. Good habit for a *soldado* to get into. *Norteños* sometimes don't know where the next meal is coming from."

Now she was trying to tell him how to be a soldier—as her father had for all these impossible last six weeks. "I think maybe I should wait here—the major wants me to report back . . . and there's this Captain Espinosa of yours I should see." Should he ask if Captain Espinosa was a Dorado like Álvarez? No. No questions. Questions always made a real man seem weak and ineffectual.

"If Trini says half an hour, it will *be* half an hour. I will find the captain for you. Come on, *muchachito*."

Muchachito again—*Aiyee!!!* He put his foot to the stirrup.

"We're only going two hundred meters." She pointed back toward the railroad yards they had crossed on the way to the Dorado bivouac, but a little farther to the north than the way they had come. He started to tie the horse to a hitchrail in the company street in front of Álvarez's tent. "Don't be *loco*," she said. "If you leave it here two minutes someone will steal it. How would you face my father then? Lead it, *soldado a caballo*." Again the mocking laugh.

Two hundred meters she had said—a bit more than six hundred feet. He looked up and down the crowded tracks. Where would there be a Captain Espinosa in that tangle of cars and equipment, field guns, ammunition boxes, and endless stacks of crates, who could possibly have anything to do with him? His heart sank. Was he to be reassigned from the regiment to railroad work? And would the assignment be permanent? Was that what Álvarez really meant for him? Would he do his fighting by laying track, while better men and—even more humiliating—*worse* ones were using rifles and grenades against the enemies of the Revolution?

The girl had started walking toward the tower and the signal bridge that crossed the tracks between them and the hill she had called La Pila, but the tower was a good deal more than a hundred meters away and couldn't be their destination. Where, then, was she taking him?

She turned toward a spur of rails leading off from the main yard, where a boxcar had been positioned some distance apart from the other rolling stock. On its rust-brown side a huge white cross all but obliterated the legend "Ferrovía Central de

México." As a brand-new recruit on the truck ride down from Juárez he had passed a number of railroad cars just like it pulled off on sidings. Like them, this one was one of the Northern Division's mobile hospitals.

When they rounded the end of the car he discovered it had a twin parked on a track parallel to the spur. Sheets of olive-drab canvas stretched between the two cars, and tall poles propped them up into a tent not too different from that of the one-ring, fly-infested circus that had come to Black Springs the summer he was twelve.

There were enough flies in this tent, too, but this was no circus.

Cots were jammed together with hardly room enough to walk between them, and each of the cots held a man, or, as he discovered when they drew nearer, part of a man. No, they weren't *all* amputees. The staggering effect of his first look only made it seem so. He heard someone choke. It was a second before he realized the sound had come from his own throat. Had the girl heard it, too?

"This is *nada*," she said. "Right after the battle there were wounded from here all the way to the foot of La Pila. Most of them are in Ciudad Juárez now. The ones who lived, that is."

"I . . . thought we *won* here at Torreón." He felt colossally stupid, as stupid as Paco Durán said he was.

"We did. There were many more Huertistas lying here that day than there were of our *guerreros*—many, many more. We took care of most of their wounded, too. I was a nurse for three days. Now you can tie your *caballo*. Here no one will need it. These *pobrecitos* aren't going anywhere."

She pointed to a hitchrail, and when he had tethered the animal she turned, beckoned to him to follow her, and led him toward the closest of the two boxcars.

As they made their way through the ranks of cots it occurred to him that it was strangely silent under this canvas "big top," with none of the moans and groans he might have expected. But then few things had gone quite as he had expected since he crossed the border a jump ahead of Corey Lane six weeks ago.

The odor of pus and piss and fetid breath was overpowering. The eyes that followed him and the girl were hollow, as if a great hot thirst consumed them in spite of the water jugs he saw beside every cot.

Again he wondered exactly what he and the girl were doing here. Was this Captain Espinosa one of these casualties? Was his assignment going to be here in the hospital or somewhere else in the Division's medical section? Well, at that it would be a whole lot better, certainly more honorable, to be a litter bearer, perhaps under fire, than it would be to pound spikes into railroad ties and shovel ballast as he had shoveled horseshit for Durán. Just as long as he wasn't a nurse, as the girl said she had been. By God, he would *not* fight this war with a bedpan, no matter how many Sargento Paco Duranes they fed him to.

Juanita had reached the ramp leading up to the open door of the boxcar on the left. When he reached her, he found that the smell of the wounded men wasn't nearly so overpowering here, but only because of the mingled, quarreling odors of disinfectants and *Dios* knew how many different kinds of medication pouring out of the door. It must be an oven inside the boxcar.

A woman in a uniform deeply darkened by perspiration appeared at the top of the ramp. On the collar of her shirt was the Maltese cross emblem of the medical corps of División del Norte. She was shielding her eyes against the sun behind them, but even with her face partly covered, and with her squinting as hard as she was, he saw she was handsome— perhaps thirty years of age; it was hard to tell. Full-figured, she made Juanita a *latilla* by comparison. A pair of sharp eyes took Jorge in and then swung to the girl. A broad smile deepened the squint.

"Juanita!" she called down. "*¿Cómo estás?*"

"*Hola,* Margarita."

"What brings you here? Why aren't you taking *siesta, muchachita?*"

It brought some small satisfaction to hear the girl addressed in the embarrassing diminutive, but not much. He couldn't be too satisfied about anything, with all the human wreckage on the cots behind him still burning the retina of his mind's eye. Still, for some reason, he found himself liking this *mujer* in the sweat-stained khakis. It felt good. He hadn't found many people or things to like in recent days.

"Trini wanted you to meet this *soldado*, Margarita." Juanita turned to Jorge. "You had better make that *mentecato* salute again, *amigo*. This is Captain Espinosa. She is the head nurse for Regiment Bracomonte. Someday you may need her. She is another *Mexican* gringo like you. I worked for Margarita after the battle." She turned back to the captain-nurse. "This is Jorge Martínez, Margarita. Trini wants you to meet him. He comes from Nuevo México. Papá is training him."

"New Mexico? Where from exactly in New Mexico, Jorge? I did hear 'Jorge,' didn't I?" Captain Espinosa said in English. "I know your state almost as well as home. I worked for a while in the hospital in Roswell." Her accent, in the tongue that suddenly seemed awkward after six weeks of little but Spanish, sounded faintly familiar, but it wasn't the Rio dialect he had heard—and for the most part spoken—all his life.

"Black Springs, Chupadera County . . . *capitán*."

She smiled even more broadly than when she had greeted Juanita, with her head now cocked to one side and a teasing, playful look suddenly on her face. "*Sí*, if I remember them correctly, a Chupadera County man named Martínez *would* have trouble calling a woman 'captain.' I had forgotten what the men of the Ojos Negros can be like. You don't have to 'captain' me, Jorge. 'Margarita' will do just fine, or 'Margaret.' Maybe you won't have the trouble with 'Margaret' Juanita does. You don't have to talk English, either. Are you hungry? I haven't had my own lunch yet, and I'm starving."

It came to him now: her way of speaking. It must have been the fact that she was a medical person that enabled him to make the connection. In English she talked very much like Mrs. Bannister, the widowed nurse or whatever she was in

Dr. Colvin's office, the one who was always looking at Ignacio even if the self-effacing *vaquero* never noticed. The young widow, who was the doctor's sister, too, came from somewhere in the east. New York, he thought. Yes, she sounded like Sally Bannister. But what was a New York woman doing with Pancho Villa's army here in the high southern deserts of Coahuila and Durango? And how did she know as much about the men of the Ojos Negros as that teasing smile claimed she did? *No, no questions,* amigo.

"*Are* you hungry, Jorge?" the captain said again.

"No. *No, gracias, mi cap . . .*" He must not slip about the way he addressed her, either, not after what she had said. She had sounded as if she had truly meant it when she said he could ignore her rank. "I have eaten well."

"I haven't, Margarita," the girl said. So, she understood English, too.

The captain-nurse laughed. "I've *never* heard you admit to having eaten, Juanita. How do you stay so slim? One extra bite of *queso* for me and it's here forever." She patted her hips. "All right. I'll send an orderly for something. Will you at least take a *cerveza* with us, Jorge? It will probably not be cold, but it will certainly be . . ."

She broke off as if someone had struck her in the mouth. She was staring over Jorge's shoulder into the area of cots and stretchers. He had just begun to wonder if he dared turn and follow the stricken look when she lunged forward, burst between him and the girl, spinning them about with the force of her rush. "No . . . no . . . no!" she screamed, while Jorge searched for the cause of her alarm.

In the center of the outdoor ward a squad of men carrying rifles had stopped by one of the cots. Two of the riflemen were digging their hands into the armpits of the man in the cot and were dragging him from it just as Margarita Espinosa reached them. The wounded man, hardly more than a boy, no older than Juanita certainly, was making a feeble effort to break their grasp. It was not contest. The riflemen were burly, the boy was slight—and he only had one leg.

The captain-nurse flew at the two riflemen holding the boy,

her nails clawing at the cheek of one of them, drawing a bright spurt of blood. For a second the man lost his grip, but the one-legged boy only sagged, unable to break free. Other riflemen closed around Margarita, prying her loose from the one she had attacked and holding her away from the other and the boy.

One man in the group carried no rifle. He had a holster with an automatic pistol strapped to his waist. Now this one, obviously some kind of officer, stepped toward those battling with Margarita.

"Control yourself, Captain. This is not an *escuela de crianza*, a nursery. This man is a traitor. I have a *decreto de prisión* from Colonel Fierro himself." Fierro! Jorge knew that name! Fierro, the man called "Villa's Butcher." The man who had executed hundreds of traitors for the general, and, according to malicious gossip Jorge wasn't yet prepared to think about, some who were only *called* traitors because they opposed Pancho Villa.

"A traitor?" Margarita said, her voice thin with anguish. "How can he be a traitor? Tell me. Tell me how!"

"He ran from his post in the battle."

"Don't be *loco*! How could he possibly have run? Look at him, for God's sake! And he's not a man, not really. He's a boy, a child."

"He is a *soldado*, Captain. He received the wound that took his leg only when he started running. There are witnesses."

"Did he have a trial? A court-martial?"

"Colonel Fierro was his court-martial, Captain. That is proper and correct."

"No. That's insanity." Margarita had calmed herself some, but her shoulders quivered for another few seconds. Now she seemed to exercise a slight, precarious control over them, too. "Major," she said, "I will not release this child. He is in my care and he will stay here until I say he can go. If he was guilty of something, hasn't he been punished quite enough?"

"That is not for me to say, Captain. I only know you may *not* keep him. General Villa is waiting with his guests."

"Guests? You mean this horror has now become some kind of social event? *My God!* We've turned into even worse animals than I feared."

But with that last despairing eruption, all the fight went out of Captain Margarita Espinosa.

The major marched his squad away, the two powerful riflemen dragging their prisoner between them, his one leg trailing in the dust, as useless to him now as the stump which seemed to have begun to bleed again through its dressings.

Margarita dropped to her knees at the side of the cot the boy had occupied. She put her head down on it and her back heaved. In a bit, though, she straightened herself, only to bend over again, reach under the cot, and pull out a pair of crutches. "Well, we needed these, anyway." Her voice was biting acid. She stuck the tip ends of the crutches hard into the earth beside the cot and pulled herself to her feet almost hand over hand. Then sobs broke the silence.

Juanita moved toward her.

Jorge hung back. There was nothing he could do.

Juanita was at Margarita Espinosa's side. She had her hands on the nurse's shoulders.

It wasn't quiet in that valley of damaged men now; a low muttering was rising in rounded waves, the sound not breaking apart into individual words or phrases, but swelling gently as he had heard the surf do once on a beach in California when he and Concepción had been sent to visit the cousins. A fat cop had chased them from the water. "White man's country, *chiquito*," the cop had said. "Greasers ain't allowed here. Get your little brown asses back to wherever it is they keep Messkins." He had only been eleven then, but he had boiled over the top as fiercely as he ever had again, even when he stuck the knife in Jamie. Eight-year-old Concepción had saved him from a beating or worse that day when she burst into tears and begged him to take her home. Funny thing. "Home" at that moment had been the basement apartment in the big house of the cousins' rich employers, living space the likes of which the cop himself probably couldn't even dream about.

"Let's go see Trini," Juanita said. Margarita hadn't spoken yet, and now she only nodded. She seemed dry-eyed again.

At the tent Álvarez came through the mosquito net as quickly as he had before. He took one look at Margarita and gathered her in his arms.

"*¿Qué pasa, querida?*"

"It's happened again, Trini. Fierro's work, of course. Will it never stop? It was Porfirio this time. They say he was a traitor. If Porfirio is a traitor, who then isn't? He begged the doctors not to take his leg so he could *fight* again. My girls and I stayed up five nights saving him. What's the use?" She began to sob again.

With her mouth against the major's shoulder the words, for all their anguished intensity, had come out muffled, and it had been all Jorge could do to make them out. Álvarez was stroking her back, looking out over the company street apparently oblivious to the stares they were getting from a group of soldiers lounging in front of another tent across the way. He paid no attention to Juanita or Jorge, either. From the way he held her, a blind man could have seen that Margarita Espinosa was his woman, a *soldadera* of quite a different kind and on a different level.

The sobs stopped. Margarita broke away from Álvarez. "Forgive me, Trini. I should be able to take this sort of thing better now. I know how this embarrasses you. You'll have to send me back to the Bronx if I can't do better." She turned and looked at Jorge and Juanita. "I'm sorry. I never did do anything about the food I promised you. Maybe Trini can . . ."

"Of course," Álvarez said. He turned his head and called, "Esteban!" It wasn't loud, but pitched so it carried across the street to where the small group of soldiers in Dorado uniforms were idling. One of them detached himself from the others and hurried across.

"*¿Sí, señor mayor?*"

"We need food for the captain and these *amigos*, Stebbi— and camp stools."

"It is done, *señor mayor.*" Esteban hurried off. Álvarez turned back to the other three.

"I am sorry about what happened, *amigos.* There might be even more of this. With El Primer Jefe and his people here in Torreón, it would not do for General Villa to show weakness."

"Carranza is here?" Margarita's voice was tight.

"*Sí.* He came in this morning with González. Obregón from Sonora is here, too."

"You were at their meetings today?" Álvarez nodded and Margarita hurried on. "We will go on the offensive again?"

"Yes. That is another reason why this thing happened to Porfirio now. The Division will march in two days' time, and no more men can be spared to guard prisoners than the ones who have already gone back up to Ciudad Juárez. *La guerra.* It is always this way. The general must get agreement from the Coahuila people for the attack General Ángeles wants us to make."

"Then it will be Zacatecas, Trini?"

"That has not been decided yet. It will be made known at tomorrow's meeting. Zacatecas? *¿Quién sabe?* But there will be an attack somewhere, that much is certain. Felipe is pushing hard for Zacatecas."

"And no one was going to tell the doctors and nurses so we could get ready for it?"

"I'm telling you now, Margarita."

"But you aren't *supposed* to tell me, are you, Trini?"

"No."

"And what about these two?" She gestured toward Juanita and Jorge. "If Fierro finds out they heard you, he will have *them* shot—and me—right after he sends *you* to the nearest wall." She shuddered. "The idiotic games you stupid men play!"

"I won't argue that with you now, Margarita. All I can say *por el momento* is that I am truly sorry." He shrugged an end to this particular exchange. Then he turned to Jorge. "In Paco's file on you it says you can read and write with skill, *soldado.* This is true?"

"*Sí, señor mayor,* I think so," Jorge said.

"And that you are familiar with *Los grandes problemas nacionales?*"

"*Sí, señor mayor.* There are many. I know some of them, but of course I do not know much of what has occurred in Mexico since I've been in training." Was it too much big-sounding talk at this point?

Álvarez smiled. "I did not mean the problems themselves, *amigo,* although I am pleased to find you think you know them. I meant the book. Molinas."

The book! How could he have missed what the major was really saying? Of course he hadn't read it or thought about it since Paco Durán had taken it from him on that first day. So—Durán had passed along the word about the book in the very briefcase Jorge had carried across camp.

The major went on. "Perhaps you and I are the only two men in the brigade who have read it. Pity. I have the copy Paco took from you. Step inside my tent, *amigo.*" He turned to Juanita and Margarita. "You will forgive us, *señoritas, por favor?* This won't take long, and Esteban should be back in just a moment. Eat without us if we are not finished." He turned and stepped his way through the flap. Jorge hesitated. He should move quickly. The major had just given him an order—but he didn't want to push. Álvarez was holding the flap for him. He went on through. Why in *el nombre de Dios* would the sergeant give his book to this Dorado? Perhaps, despite what seemed encouragement from this exalted major, ordinary soldiers like Jorge Martínez weren't supposed to own pernicious things like books. *Nada,* it seemed, went right for him in this army.

10

▲▲▲▲▲

"*Buena fortuna,* Capitán Cucaracha," Juanita Durán whispered as she watched Jorge Martínez follow Major Trinidad

Álvarez into his tent. He hadn't heard her. ¡Bueno! She hadn't meant him to.

She should take this time Trini granted to try to console Margarita. Even though the *yanqui* woman was a captain, she hadn't been with the Division as long as Juanita had, and she couldn't yet put things such as the one-legged boy out of her mind. Bad as it was, she would have to learn. The nurse was still sobbing softly even though the major had gathered her in his arms and tried to comfort her himself. It would turn even worse if they heard the sounds of the firing squad, and unless a train roared by, they would. It could come any minute now.

Verdad, this was serious agony for Margarita, and Juanita knew she should help, but she couldn't pull her eyes from the flap of the tent after it closed on Jorge Martínez and Trini. She wanted to see the North American's face the very moment he emerged, no matter how long it took.

During the last six weeks, since Papá's return to duty here at Torreón, she had caught glimpses of the young man who had prayed so rigidly in the Misión de Guadalupe, seen him from afar a dozen times in the past six weeks, when Papá kept her, as he always did, a sanitary distance from the new men on the training grounds, out of the way of any *cucaracha* who, as he said, "might get ideas," and the meeting today at the bank of the Nazas brought her first close look at this particular *cucaracha* since coming south to Torreón.

She hadn't told Papá about going to church back in Juárez or about her encounter with the recruit from north of the border, after all. Perhaps it was just *because* she had met this young man that she avoided mentioning the trip to the mission. *Sí,* there were still a *few* things she and Papá didn't talk about. With his terrible hot prejudices and those keen *peón* instincts, he might decide she was more at risk with this particular *cucaracha* than with any of the other recruits or veterans.

It could be true, of course. But this Jorge Martínez certainly hadn't behaved the way men did with women they had designs on. Even today. From the way he acted toward her when they met at the Nazas he didn't even *remember* her. It hurt a little, until she considered again what a troubled man he must have been at the church, and still was, after training with her father.

But it was this small hurt that made her turn so shrewish at the riverbank and even worse riding behind him to Trini's and during the time they spent with Margarita. One would have thought him one of the apes she usually saved such behavior for. *Sí*, she had indeed been a *bruja del infierno* with her scorching tongue. Even Margarita must have noticed.

She had to admit she liked what she had seen of him so far, even if she had gone to such pains not to let him know. It was more than just his good looks and the appealing way he held himself erect on the back of that comic horse her father must have forced on him in some last, mildly sadistic display of power. Even a raw recruit wouldn't have chosen such a sagging bag of bones himself. And the way he tried to ride it—as if it were the charger of some reborn *conquistador*. More than any of these, she had been jolted into a visceral awareness of him by the astonishing open smile he flashed when he bowed to her and the other women on the riverbank. There had been no such smile in Juárez, nor in any of the occasional distant glimpses of him here in Torreón. The electric feeling it brought her pleased and frightened her at once.

Was it only a *chance* meeting at the river? Mamá, were she still alive, wouldn't have thought so. Florencia Durán attributed everything that happened in life to some force that didn't remotely allow for chance. *Destierro* was everything. Papá was a little that way, too, but *his* belief in fate was nothing at all like Mamá's. Hers had been shaped by a passionate devotion to God and the Church; Paco Durán had abandoned the Church a month after Mamá died so horribly—if he hadn't abandoned God as well. It was one of the two things he and his daughter didn't talk about. The other was Mamá's death itself.

For a week now, Papá had talked of little else but this young man and his upcoming talk with Trini. She had wanted to say something every time he mentioned his name. No matter how the meeting inside the tent came out, she would have to let Papá know about this afternoon, of course. She wouldn't tell him of the smile that had taken her breath away.

Sí, the smile.

Small wonder she hadn't seen it before today. There could have been little enough for this recruit of Papá's to smile *about.*

Oh, how he must have suffered under Paco Durán's tyranny. So, of course, had all the other recruits in the new detachment—Papá played no favorites among his *cucarachas*—but from her sergeant father's talk at night at the cooking fire in front of their tent, she knew he had singled this Jorge Martínez out for treatment of an especially brutal sort. Only this morning had he told her why. She had seen him this way twice before with a new man he planned to pass along to Trini, a former lawyer from Sonora and an odd little man who had been a Nuevo León postal worker. Unlike them, Martínez had never complained or whimpered, according to Papá. And he hadn't quit. Not that quitting was a genuine option in the División del Norte. The two others tried to quit the División, but Paco Durán stopped them in their tracks, reassigning the lawyer to one of Calzado's track-laying companies, sending the funny little ex-mailman into a labor battalion. Papá was very hard on quitters. The fact remained that Jorge Martínez hadn't even *tried* to quit.

"Whatever else I think about him, Paco will grant that he is *muy hombre, mi hija,*" Papá said this morning when he told her what was in store for Martínez today. For a new *soldado* to be *muy hombre* was of more than passing significance in the sight of Sargento Durán of Brigade Ignacio Zaragoza. "But I, of course, will not have the final say about him."

Yes, the fact that her father was softening toward him would mean nothing if Jorge (was she already thinking of him as Jorge?) failed with Major Trinidad Álvarez today.

She knew some at least of what was going on inside the tent right now, but she would have given almost anything to actually be there the moment the young man said yes or no. More than what he finally said to Trini, the way he said it would tell her things about him she wanted desperately to know.

But why was she *desperate* to know such things? Why such interest in just another *cucaracha*?

Interest? *Tell the truth, Juanita Durán. This new, strange feeling is more than interest.*

It was perhaps another thing she couldn't discuss with her father. To Paco Durán she was still a child, a little girl. If she talked with him about Jorge he would be bound to get it wrong. She felt in her heart that Jorge Martínez had about him none of those things her father feared.

Besides, it was perhaps time Juanita Durán decided something about her life without asking her father first. She trembled. The biggest reason she had always felt so sure of herself in dealing with men was that Papá was always there to rescue her. Could she really take charge of her life herself?

She had learned new and different things about men when she worked for Margarita in the hospital. As much as she thought she had come to know men in her time with the army, she discovered new things when she cared for the poor maimed creatures who wound up on the cots between the two railroad cars. She had learned a lot of the secrets those men harbored; few of them could read or write, and she had written letters for them, more than a few touching on intimacies she had never until then thought too much about, growing up as she had in a devout home in her tiny village. She had known about them, of course, what Santa María girl didn't? Everyone in the village knew what almost any other villager was up to day or night, and there had been times when she wondered what it might be like to be loved that way. She had dreamed about it, *sí*, but only in the vaguest way.

Perhaps she could let Margarita into her thoughts. The captain-nurse had treated her like a grown woman almost from their first meeting, even before Juanita worked with her in the nightmare days in the hospital after the battle here.

Jorge (*sí*, she *was* already thinking of him as Jorge) looked as if he might be very good at the things men did with women the *soldaderas* joked about when they met on the riverbank or at the market *carreta* stalls, the things which were hinted at or spoken of with sometimes embarrassing frankness in the letters she had written for the wounded. *Dios* knew she had *seen* men and women doing things together; it was hard to hide even the most furtive act in an army on the move. But it was still much too early to consider herself that way, even with the young man now in the tent with Trini.

As for Juanita herself, Papá would flay her with his rough tongue if he suspected she was thinking about such things at all. It wasn't that she was too young. Mamá had been no older when she married Papá, and he had told her wistfully on more than one occasion how much he wanted grandchildren someday—"before this Revolution kills me." But when she teased him about it once and told him she could see to it pretty quickly, he had bellowed like a bull. "Do not let your thoughts run that way yet, *mi hija*! This struggle will go on for years. There is the matter of marriage, *también*." For a man who had turned his mammoth back on the Church so firmly and, he swore, finally, he was a strong believer in family and marriage; he still didn't believe in the first without the second.

But it was a different world from the one they had known in Santa María. Even Papá must know that now. Did any man and woman in the army even bother to get married anymore?

It must be a different world, too, for Jorge Martínez, coming as he did from that comfortable, peaceful, gigantic, and, to a girl from a mountain village or to any other Mexican, often worrisome country north of the great river.

Unlike Margarita Espinosa, who with her blond hair and hazel eyes looked as *norteamericana* as many of the wealthy *gringas* who passed through Juanita and Paco's village on their way to visit nearby Hacienda del Sol—her heart stopped for half a second at the thought of the *hacienda* and Mamá's last time there—Jorge outwardly was as Mexican as anyone in the *familia Durán*. But coming from the United States did make a lot of difference. Why was he here?

The reason lay somewhere behind those sad, troubled eyes. Had he left a woman back there somewhere?

She would rather not think about *that*.

Yes, she liked what she had seen of Jorge Martínez so far.

In spite of his attempts on the ride from the river and to Margarita's hospital to appear as tough and *macho* as the other men in the regiment and the brigade—the grinning animals who reached for her and would have found her if Paco Durán hadn't bulked so formidably in their path—this *cucaracha* couldn't hide a certain . . . not softness . . . but a certain manly ease and *cortesía*, made even more attractive because he seemed unaware of it. A young man like Jorge could become *muy caballero*. Or was that just a dream of *hers*?

In some ways—even if she wasn't and could never be *muy hombre*, as Paco said Jorge was, and even if she wasn't a fighting soldier or true *soldadera*—Juanita Durán was tougher than Jorge Martínez had yet learned to be. Soldier or not, there was a gentleness about him even Paco Durán's training couldn't beat away.

Had something about *shared* dreams occurred to her back at the church? The thought of Jorge becoming more to her than just one of Papá's long-suffering, thoroughly cowed recruits wasn't a dream. It was instinct. Seventeen was old enough for instincts about things such as this.

That's why she had thrown the mud from the bank of the Nazas earlier today, knowing even as she hurled it that if she were wrong about the young *soldado* on the silly horse and he turned out like all the others, she might well feel the quirt he carried sear her cheek. She hadn't been wrong. Jorge Martínez passed the first test Juanita Durán gave him without even knowing he was being tested.

She wondered if he was passing the test inside Trini's tent as well.

"You are very much taken with this *yanqui*, aren't you, *cara*?" Margarita said. She had stopped crying. *Bueno*.

What had her face given away? She couldn't talk about this yet. No. Not even to Margarita. Someday perhaps, but not now.

"To me he is *nada, mi amiga.* Less than *nada.* To me he is just another *cucaracha.*"

She bit her tongue. Old habits died hard.

11

▲▲▲▲▲

There were two camp cots inside the tent. The major sat down on one and motioned Jorge to the other. Both of them seated, his eyes bore down hard on Jorge.

"You have had a difficult time with our Paco Durán, is that not so, *amigo*?"

Difficult? *¡Dios!* It had been a fair approximation of hell! But he surely couldn't say so. Durán would turn even more impossible if he knew the answer Jorge bled to give. And sooner or later he *would* know. But it surely would be more dangerous to lie to the man across the tent from him, on even the smallest matter.

"It has not been easy, *señor mayor. El sargento* does not ask the impossible. He demands it."

To Jorge's amazement, Álvarez burst into laughter. It almost sounded as if the major was laughing with *him*, the ignorant recruit, and *at* the tyrant sergeant. Not likely. No one could truly laugh at Paco.

"*¡Bueno!*" Alvarez said when the laughter stopped. His clean, dark features settled into seriousness. "The book was only one of the reasons Paco singled you out for 'special treatment,' Martínez. I hope you will eventually think it worth it."

Was he expected to say something about this, ask a question? No. He waited. In the company of men like the major or the sergeant the less he said now about the book—or anything else—the better. After all, no matter that Álvarez had talked about it earlier with something approaching approval, it still might be the book itself that had brought this trouble.

And it was trouble, wasn't it? The major's moment of affability shouldn't be allowed to fool him.

"For some time now," Álvarez said, "Paco, when he recruits, has been looking for someone for a special job. The exact man has been hard to find. Such a man must have certain qualities. Your abilities with *las aritméticas*, maps, and especially language, are *precisely* what is needed. Paco put you through all that misery to see if you were tough as well. He says you are. It may be hard for you to believe at the moment, but Paco has become very fond of you. I have never heard him praise a recruit as much. He says you are the quickest new man in Brigade Ignacio Zaragoza." He fixed Jorge now with the most intense, searching gaze he had ever felt from anyone. "I will be moving soon from the Dorados back to Regiment Bracomonte. I will need an aide. There are a few things more I must know about you, Soldado Martínez, and in the event you satisfy me, the job is yours—if you want it."

Jorge's brain filled like a balloon. Was he hearing right? An aide to an important officer such as the man across the tent from him? Such things didn't happen to *cucarachas*.

"I need someone with your background and talents, Martínez. But I need more than that from that someone, too."

He *had* heard Álvarez correctly. The balloon of his head grew larger. But something was very strange here. How and when could Paco Durán have told this calm, confident major everything the major said he had. Was it all in the file? And how could there even *be* a file? *Paco couldn't read or write.* He would have to think about that later, the major was going on.

"Why have you come to Mexico, Martínez?"

"To fight in the Revolution, *mi mayor.*" It was true, but was it enough, was it the whole truth? Should he tell the major about his being wanted for murder in Chupadera County?

Suddenly he knew he would have to tell this Dorado *everything*.

And he did, blurting it out, rushing the story into the close air of the tent.

Álvarez sat through it without a flicker of more than polite interest. "You did not come to us merely for glory and to satisfy some personal ambition, then?"

Would there be no comment? "I do not think so, sir."

"Do you have any idea at all of what the Revolution may require of true believers in the cause? Some things a revolutionary has to do are not precisely noble."

If anything, the gaze of Álvarez intensified.

It was good he had decided he wouldn't lie to this man. Lies would lead nowhere but oblivion. He nodded.

"I know now you can kill. Can you kill for Mexico? Without questioning an order you may not understand?"

"Sí, mi mayor."

There was a long moment of silence.

"All right, Martínez. Will you be my aide?"

He had to believe it now, or risk imputing deceit to this Dorado, which he wouldn't, from the look and sound of him, possibly allow himself to practice. No matter what Álvarez had said about a revolutionary having to do things that weren't "precisely noble," he couldn't conceive of the man across the tent from him acting in any other way.

Will you be my aide? Jorge Martínez's heart screamed a silent yes. He had to swallow it down. *¡Un momento!* He had to get one thing straight even if it meant risking everything. The major had said that he was moving back to Regiment Bracomonte. He would no longer be a Dorado officer. Something jabbed him. Dare he ask? He had to. *"Señor mayor . . .* if I become your aide, will I ever be a *guerrero?* Will I see fighting?" He held his breath. The question and its answer may have dashed the major's offer to the ground.

Trinidad Álvarez smiled. It was the same sad smile he had given Juanita when she and Jorge came to this tent before. *"Sí,* Jorge. You will fight. Even staff officers of Regiment Bracomonte fight. You may fight much more than you ever wanted to. I sometimes think there will be no end to fighting—ever." He sounded weary.

Jorge could hold nothing back now. "Then I will say yes, *señor mayor."*

"*¡Bueno!* Please call me Trini. But not where anyone can hear you tomorrow. General Villa wouldn't mind the informality, but El Primer Jefe Carranza is a fussy man about things like that. Now, let me find your book."

Tomorrow? General Villa? Carranza?

The answers came at once.

"I will need you in the morning," Álvarez said. "There will be another meeting at ten o'clock for commanders at the regimental level and above. You will accompany me and·take notes for me. Try to get the feel of things, even form opinions, although the opinions must be held for me alone, *por favor*. Venustiano Carranza will be meeting with our general, and so will General Obregón and many other *jefes*. The next phase of our struggle may well be shaped at this *conferencia*. Now, let us join the others, Jorge ... I may call you Jorge, no?" He stood. "One thing more. Within a month you will become a *lugarteniente*."

A lieutenant? An officer? It couldn't be. He felt dizzy. The balloon his head had become seemed ready to float right through the ceiling of the tent. Wait! Was this a trick? Another stage in Paco Durán's persecution of him? He searched the major's face. He had been right before. No deceit could ever make its way into that fine, open countenance. *¡Dios!* He would make the leap of belief. A dream come true? No. He couldn't have dreamed of this in this world or the next.

In front of the tent the soldier Esteban was serving Juanita and Margarita tin plates heaped with beans and some sort of meat, probably *carne adovada*. They both looked up at Trini Álvarez and then at him. They smiled. Juanita's smile, for the first time, didn't appear to be a completely contemptuous or teasing one. *¡Dios!* They knew! They knew everything that had gone on inside the tent. They knew what Álvarez had asked of him—and reading his face they surely knew his answer, too.

Then Esteban spoke to Trini. "*Perdón*, Trini," he said. "May I speak with the *señorita* here?"

"*Sí*, Stebbi, go ahead."

The soldier turned to the girl. "Juanita," he said. "I have owed *mi esposa* back in Casas Grandes a letter since before we took Torreón. Would you write it for me, *por favor*?"

"*Sí*, Stebbi," Juanita said. "It will give me pleasure. Come to Paco's tent sometime this evening."

And with that, Jorge knew, as surely as he had ever known a thing, just who had put the file together for Sargento Paco Durán.

He didn't have time to think about it.

From somewhere near La Pila, the sound of perhaps a dozen rifles fired in unison reached them. A deep, sick gasp from Margarita confirmed what he had already guessed.

12

"Don't splash the *mujeres* again, Captain Cockroach," Paco Durán said as they eased their horses into the Río Nazas at seven the next morning. "They will throw rocks at you this time, not mud. Paco Durán has no wish to be caught in the cross fire." There was a deep-belly rumble of laughter.

Jorge Martínez had known sleepless nights the past two months, some despairing ones, but the night he had just lain awake through had been one of pure joy, the stars shimmering jewels. Paco's gruff voice, stripped now of the bullying overtones of those endless days of training, could have been a lullaby for the sleep he had just missed without regret.

La Dama Fortuna hadn't merely smiled at him, she had gathered him in her arms and embraced him as if he were granting *her* some blessing.

Not the smallest part of his joy was that this morning he was on the back of a decent mount, a big dun somewhat like the Tennessee walking horse Ignacio had brought out for a younger Jorge Martínez once at the MacAndrews's D Cross A—in another country, another age.

What was it that Hattie Spletter, the Black Springs librarian who had ordered the Molinas book for him, was always saying? "It is always darkest before the dawn." *Sí,* the darkness he had journeyed through since he stabbed Jamie had now ended in a sunrise of expectation brighter than any real one he had known.

Captain Cockroach? He laughed, and Paco glanced over at him, smiled, and urged his horse through the current. *Sí,* Captain Cockroach. Yesterday when he guided his horse into this same brown, rushing water he had indeed been a cockroach, an insect to be reviled, stepped on, crushed. And this big, suddenly friendly man had surely stepped on him even if he hadn't quite crushed him. This morning the giant dynamiter-gunner had become an *amigo,* a comrade-in-arms, and Jorge María Martínez himself a man of some tiny significance at least. He was on his way to a meeting where events of great moment would take place, a council of all *los grandes jefes* of the war against tyranny: brave, strong men, thick fingers of righteous anger clenched into one vengeful fist to strike the enemy, Victoriano Huerta. And he would be there, would play a part in it. He would be a comrade-in-arms not just to Paco, but to the greatest revolutionaries of his time.

Paco said when they mounted that he was just to be Jorge's escort across the river, that he wouldn't be going on to the conference with him after they reported to Major Álvarez. "It will not be a place for such as Paco," the sergeant said without a trace of resentment. "I am a man of no education, and no importance."

Dios, how they had changed places! Jorge wasn't an officer yet, but Álvarez had said that within a month he would be. Paco was already acting subordinate in some subtle ways. It hardly seemed fair. This big, bluff old tiger was a veteran fighter, a true hero of the Division. He had spilled his blood countless times for the Revolution, and here was a tyro with no scars or even memories of battle, vaulting over him as if he were of no more consequence than the straw-filled dummy they had bayoneted to shreds on the blistering training grounds here at Torreón.

He should feel like a cheat, a mountebank. He tried to, couldn't.

All he felt was exhilaration at what this day would bring him.

Once again Juanita Durán waited on the far bank of the Río Nazas. She wore the same blouse and skirt as yesterday. This morning she carried a manila packet under a slim brown arm.

"*Hola,* Papá," she said, waving the packet. She smiled at Jorge. "*Hola.*"

She mounted behind her father, floating up to the back of the horse as she had on Jorge's the day before. Disappointment pricked him. What had he expected? That *everything* would go his way?

She was breathing hard, and although the morning was still cool, sweat had beaded on her forehead and upper lip, and her hair looked damp—but an even glossier, richer black than it had been yesterday. She must have run to the riverbank, run hard. Where from? Where had she slept last night? She had told the soldier Esteban to come to Paco's tent to have her write the letter for him, and Jorge had assumed she bedded down in her father's place. If she hadn't been with Paco, then where? A green worm twitched inside him.

"*Qué tal,* Juanita?"

"*Bueno,* Captain Cockroach."

Paco laughed. "It is really too early for *Captain* Cockroach, *querida,* even if Paco says it. Jorge is not even a *lugarteniente* yet."

"Have you remembered to bring a pad and something to write with, *amigo*?" she said to Jorge just before they reached the company street that held the tent of the major. "Trini shouldn't have to worry about little things like that."

He hadn't even thought about it. Would the major call him to account?

"*¡Que relaje, soldado!*" she said then. "And do not look so like a rabbit. I have a notebook and some pencils here for you." She thrust the packet across between the two horses, and as she did Paco's bay struck a hoof against a rock and stumbled. Her body shifted toward him and he had to put out a hand to help her regain her seat. His palm lingered for a second on her shoulder. He took the packet from her. She wasn't looking at him now; her eyes were straight ahead and fixed on her father's broad, khaki-covered back.

Álvarez was waiting for them at his tent, holding the reins of a fine-looking bay. He had buttoned his uniform tunic all the way to his strong chin, and this morning it looked bone-dry and freshly pressed. A row of colored ribbons flashed above his left breast pocket. He wore the broad-brimmed, embroidered sombrero of the Dorados, slanted forward above his eyes and a little to the side. He must have trimmed his full mustache. He had strapped on a holster holding an automatic pistol and held the same leather briefcase in which Jorge had carried his file to him. Perhaps it was the gun belted to his waist, but he seemed to have grown even bigger overnight, became even more of a *guerrero*. Jorge couldn't recall seeing a man look more magnificent. He must himself look the vagrant he had been in Juárez when Paco recruited him, his own clean uniform notwithstanding.

"Paco, Juanita . . . Martínez." A curt nod accompanied each of the names. These weren't yesterday's easy greetings. It sounded more like one of Paco's roll calls—dispassionate, abrupt. Clearly Álvarez was now the total professional and had already immersed himself in contemplation of the tasks at hand. "You and Juanita should not go any farther, Paco. You understand. But come to the plaza about noon. I may need you when this day's work is done. *Gracias, amigo*." He handed the briefcase to Jorge and then swung himself up into the saddle. "*Ándale,* Martínez!" The bay moved up the street at a trot that turned to a brisk canter in a matter of seconds, and Jorge had to dig hard into the flanks of his own mount not to be left behind.

He turned once to look back at Paco and Juanita. Paco waved. Juanita, now dismounted, didn't. But she watched him as he rode away.

* * *

Yesterday had opened his eyes to some of the extent of the Division's huge encampment, but only to some of it. When Paco trucked Jorge and the other new recruits down from Juárez they had arrived after dark, and with twelve-hour days of training he hadn't even begun to see it all. It engulfed the town of Torreón—so recently a hot, burning battleground and before that just a drab section point on the Ferrovía Central not appreciably larger than Black Springs—and it spread to the horizon, it seemed, in every one of the four directions. He wondered if Torreón would revert to type once this army moved out against the enemy.

The town was still there, of course, all but buried beneath a welter of equipment, horses, several more big guns like "El Niño," mounted on flatcars on the tracks running through the center of the small city—and more men, children, and busy women than he remembered even in El Paso. And what women they were! Every field and empty lot was filled with the ubiquitous, silent *soldaderas* with their cooking fires, piled bedrolls, pots, pans, tethered goats, chickens in bird-cages and tied to the legs of the tripods above the fires, and half-naked infants at play in the dust. But as they neared the center of the sprawling camp he realized he was seeing fewer and fewer of them. They were obviously kept at a distance from the heart of the Division by innate discretion or, more likely, orders.

Nothing, not discretion, sticks, stones, nor curses, would have kept the dogs away. They ran singly and in packs—panting, mange-plagued yellow curs gone feral, an occasional excited whippet or rangy, disdainful wolfhound, and scores more nondescript mongrels than could have been notched into a tally stick long enough to stretch from Torreón to Chihuahua City.

He urged his horse to a little more speed and checked it off when its head was almost even with the head of Trini's.

"*La conferencia* will be held in the railway station at the Division's headquarters," Álvarez said when they passed Torreón's whitewashed village hall. "It is the only building with a room large enough to hold us all. It is made of brick and will be impossibly hot by noon, but I do not think anyone will ask for a *siesta*. Not today. Do you know what this session will be about, Martínez?"

"No, sir."

"It will decide the next objective of our Division. General Ángeles's grand strategy says it should be Zacatecas. I do not think General Obregón or Señor Carranza are yet convinced. We shall know where we fight again by the middle of this afternoon."

At the railway station a crowd of horsemen, some up on their animals, some standing and holding them, blocked the area in front of the depot's big double doors. Two buses had parked alongside a half dozen motorcars, all of the open-topped touring variety like General Guzmán's Pope-Toledo that Jimson drove back in Chihuahuita. A small brass band with an old man leading with the bow of his violin was doing something horrible to "Cielito Lindo," and a dozen or so men who looked gringo were taking pictures with an assortment of cameras. Others with notebooks in their hands were talking to men in uniform. Of course the American press would be here in full force. The horsemen held Jorge's eyes longest and hardest. Dorados! All were armed. Their chests were criss-crossed with ammunition belts, the brass casings of the cartridges catching the sun like gold, while the peaked crowns of their identical sombreros sparkled like the whitecaps on the sea at Los Angeles so long ago.

One of the mounted Dorados stared at Álvarez and Jorge as they approached.

"Trini!" he shouted. *"¡Hola!"*

As if they had been waiting for just such a signal, the other mounted men in the shouter's group wheeled their animals about, and in the blink of an eye they were charging over the hundred feet still separating the major and Jorge from them, dust billowing behind them. Before he could let out the breath he had drawn at his first sight of them, ten or more of them had surrounded the major, their horses snorting, lifting their forelegs and then stamping their hooves down on the baked caliche, still others turning and whirling in tight circles like the trick horses of *charros* in a show ring, then rearing while their riders flailed the air and their horses' flanks with the great sombreros. Two of them edged close to Álvarez and thumped him on the shoulder, while some who had drawn pistols from belts and holsters fired into the already shaking air.

"Trini!" The Dorado who had shouted first called again over the din. One by one the other riders settled their animals down. The man was a captain, Jorge saw, with a short, thick, bulldog's body. "Tell me it is not true, Trini. You are not leaving us." It was a cry of almost monumental anguish.

"But I *am*, Navarro. I am sorry," Trini said. "Look, we will fight together again, *viejo*. I take command of Regiment Bracomonte Friday. The general has promised us first position in any new order of battle—right out in front with you. Don't look so sad. As the commander of the Dorados you will be a major soon. Teresa can surely use the extra money."

"Los Dorados will not be the same without you, Trini," Navarro said.

"In a week you will not remember I ever *was* a Dorado, old friend." The sad tone Jorge had heard yesterday was there again. "Is the general here yet?"

"Not yet. In a quarter of an hour we ride to the *casa* where he is staying and bring him to the meeting." He smiled. "I will swear I didn't say this, Trini, but I don't think he will come to the conference until after El Primer Jefe does. It is like a prizefight. The champion doesn't go in the ring before the challenger is there."

"So—Carranza isn't here yet, then. How about the others?"

"González from Coahuila has been pacing the floor like a frightened coyote since *almuerzo*, and that tough little *mierda* Obregón just got here, too."

"Any of our people?"

"General Ángeles."

"Felipe? *Bueno*. Is there a place for us to sit near him?"

"I think so. But I haven't looked inside for a while." He turned to the other Dorados with him and waved them away.

When they had moved off, he settled his gaze on Jorge. "Can I talk in front of this *soldado*, Trini?"

"*Sí*. Martínez, this is Captain Pablo Navarro. Martínez will be my aide at Regiment Bracomonte, Pablo."

The captain grunted and turned to Trini. "The next attack. Will it be Zacatecas?"

"I don't know. Felipe wants it. Carranza doesn't. Felipe has tried very hard to persuade the general. We will have to wait and see. It could go against us. But we still need Carranza's money. And there are political considerations, too."

"Money? Politics? *Mierda*, Trini! It *has* to be Zacatecas. The whole campaign might turn on it. Zacatecas is the key. We've earned it. Our blood has paid for it."

"I know. You know, and Felipe knows. Even cautious Obregón knows. Every *guerrero* in the Division knows. Unfortunately Carranza doesn't know, or if he does, has other *pescados* to fry today. Be of good heart, Pablo. Zacatecas is not lost yet. Where will you be sitting?"

Navarro looked as if he had been struck a blow. "I *won't*! Haven't you heard? Carranza refused to attend if so much as one Dorado set foot inside the door!"

"*¡Nombre de Dios!*"

"We have been told to leave here before the Carrancistas come."

"You will come back here *with* the general, though, will you not?"

"Of course. Only a direct order from Pancho himself could keep me and my men away."

"*¡Bueno!*"

Major Álvarez had been right about the atmosphere inside the depot. They found the air in the building already hotter than a *soldadera*'s fire, and as suffocating as that sandstorm in Doña Ana County when he eluded Corey Lane for a while. What would Lane think of Jorge Martínez if he could see him now?

The waiting room benches had been ripped from the bolts which had held them to the floor and pushed against the wall, and men in uniform were crowded into most of them, a number of others with rolls of paper under their arms, maps, standing or milling about. None of the men appeared armed. Trini had unstrapped his sidearm and given it to Navarro after they dismounted and hitched their horses to a rail near the buses. "Keep this, Pablo, *por favor,*" he said. "I may need it right after the meeting, so stay close by." There was an unmistakable note of earnestness in his voice.

The remark jolted Jorge a little. Why would Trini think he might need the pistol? The men gathering here were all *amigos*, weren't they, loyal comrades in a common cause?

The air in the station was murky with cigarette and *cigarro* smoke. "They will have to stop that when General Villa arrives," Trini said. "He doesn't smoke, and he doesn't like it much when people around him do. Do you smoke, Martínez?"

"Now and then, *señor*. Not very much."

"I think it is not so bad a thing for a *guerrero* to smoke, no matter what the general thinks, and I mean no disrespect. A smoke during a quiet time in battle or afterward can be like a leave with double pay. The general is such a strong *hombre*, so without nerves, that perhaps he doesn't need such solace. Men such as you and I are ordinary mortals." Something or someone apparently caught his eye. "It is time to go to work now. Get your notebook ready." He was looking at an older officer walking toward them. "*Cómo está*, Felipe?" he said when the man reached them.

General Felipe Ángeles!

It wasn't the first time he had been in the same room with a general. But what a difference! This man was no Epifanio Guzmán. He had heard much about General Felipe Ángeles, but even if he hadn't he would have known that greatness stood in front of him.

General Ángeles was of medium height, about the same as that of Jorge, but he held himself so carefully erect he seemed to tower, even over Trini, although Álvarez was an inch or two the taller. His uniform, as immaculately tailored as the one Trini wore, was bare of medals or ribbons. His face, smooth and passive, was marvelously attractive, handsome even, and held a pair of clear brown eyes which seemed to absorb everything they fell on. The eyes were surprisingly warm for those of a military man. If he reminded Jorge of anyone, it might be Douglas MacAndrews of the D Cross A north of Black Springs, Ignacio Ortíz's beloved employer.

"You are prepared, Trini?" the general said. The voice held every degree of the warmth the eyes promised, and an astonishing gentleness for such a lofty person. Was that such a big surprise? No. He remembered something he had read about this general. Tom Hendry, editor and publisher of the *Chupadera County News*, had called Ángeles "perhaps the most humane and principled leader of all the *insurrectos*."

"*Sí*, Felipe." The major reached toward Jorge and patted the briefcase he held under his arm along with the manila packet Juanita had given him. *¡Dios!* He hadn't yet taken out the notebook she said was in the packet, as Álvarez had told him to. But he couldn't reach for it at the moment. The general was looking at *him* now. Somehow he kept himself as still and straight as a post. It would be a disgrace to fidget, or betray how his nerves had suddenly turned to brittle straw.

"And this *soldado* is . . . ?" the general asked. He sounded as if he genuinely wanted to know.

"Jorge Martínez, Felipe. My aide. It is his first day with me." If Trini had noticed that the notebook was not yet in evidence, no impatience in his voice betrayed that he had.

"This will be an interesting—an edifying—experience for you, young man," Felipe Ángeles said. "Not many aides begin their careers with such advantages." He took his eyes from Jorge and looked around the room. "I believe El Primer Jefe will arrive any moment, Trini. Please find a seat where I can see you. What you report about the Division's strength when I call on you will be *muy importante*, as you know. And now I must find General Obregón and pay my respects to *him*. He is not so sensitive as is Venustiano Carranza; he is, when all is said and done, a capable, practical soldier, not petty, but I wish to take no chances. Much depends on what *he* says today, too. *Gracias, amigos*."

He took Trini's right hand in both of his and squeezed it. Then, to Jorge's amazement, he did the same with his. Jorge almost dropped the briefcase and the packet. "Remember, Trini," the general said just before he turned away, "that we must do everything we can to get General Villa to hold out for Zacatecas." With that last, he was gone.

Jorge wanted desperately to watch him find Obregón, the general whose army was making its methodical advance southward from Sonora. Obregón's force was the right wing of the offensive against Huerta the *El Paso Times* had reported on almost every day. He couldn't look. He had to get the notebook out. He fumbled, still shaken by his meeting with the hero of the Battle of Torreón.

General Felipe Ángeles—the genius artillerist, the architect of a dozen revolutionary victories, second-in-command of the Northern Division only to Pancho Villa, and Villa's master strategist—had spoken to Jorge María Martínez, *had taken his hand in his*!

Next to him, Trini Álvarez whispered, "*San* Felipe. He is a saint, *verdad*. I swear it!" Then, "Let's find seats, Martínez. Over there, where the Division's staff is sitting. Is the notebook still eluding you?"

As they walked across the room Jorge caught sight of General Ángeles talking with a shorter man with wiry, curly hair, a stocky man with "no-nonsense" written across his features, a man whose look seemed to breathe determination. Obregón, *sin duda*.

They found seats on the far side of the room, opposite the open doorway, where two other officers greeted Trini warmly and made a space on their bench for them. Although the pair looked questions at Jorge, there were no introductions. Once seated, Jorge saw through the open double door that the Dorados were mounting up. The voice of Pablo Navarro rang in the air, "*¡Vámonos, amigos!* Let us ride out and bring our general to this affair!" Horses with armed men swept past the door and out of sight.

Then something new and different stirred in the waiting room, already humming with conversations. Something outside had alerted the men standing at the streetside windows, and they were bunching up and looking out. One of them turned and shouted, "Carranza!"

Talk stopped as swiftly and completely as if someone had fired off a round.

Carranza! Jorge stuffed pencils in his shirt pocket, opened the notebook now in his lap, and leaned forward to catch his first sight of the Coahuilan politician.

He had to wait.

A file of men, some in uniform, some in business suits, came through the double doorway first. They looked about them warily, fanned out across the room and found seats, some near Álvarez and Jorge, others dispersing themselves to the different corners of the room.

An officer with the insignia of a colonel sitting next to Trini turned to Álvarez and growled, "The Coahuila people are trying to *pack* our meeting, Major. Who else is coming?"

"Gobernador Chao and González, Rodolfo."

"González? The bastard who won't even *think* about taking Saltillo?"

"*Sí*. Be more tolerant, Rodolfo." Even with his own excitement mounting and even without any real history of Major Trinidad Álvarez to guide him, Jorge was sure he detected a new, sharp tone in Trini's voice. "He does have problems."

"Not the least of which is Carranza himself." the colonel named Rodolfo said. He looked at the door. "Speak of the devil."

One of the more peculiar-looking men Jorge had ever seen had appeared in the open doorway. There was no one thing about him that made this so; it was the totality of him, a thing of posture and attitude as much as one of looks. Like some of the others in his group, he wore a suit, not a uniform. The suit flared unbecomingly at the coattails, and was buttoned tightly over a swollen, doughy chest and stomach. Perhaps the newcomer didn't feel the devilish heat inside the depot. A rolling white walrus mustache quivered above a beard that made him look a little like the gringos' Santa Claus, but there was none of the jollity of that oversized Christmas elf, no rosy face. His skin was a mottled, sick-looking yellow, marred further by a twisted, blackish vein at his temple. Bulging eyes peered into the room from behind a pair of metal-rimmed spectacles tinted a pale baby blue.

He took one tentative step inside the room and stopped.

Then the silence that had settled like a blanket when the man by the window had shouted "Carranza!" gave way to a low, barely heard, crackling sound coming not from the entourage which had entered just ahead of the "First Chief," nor from the soldiers near Obregón, but from the Villistas near Jorge and Trini Álvarez.

It was a soft but sharp flutter at first, the sound made when someone walks through a drift of cottonwood leaves in October or November. It grew louder, becoming as it did more the rustling of a flight of bats Jorge had heard once at the mouth of a cave on the *malpais*. Half a dozen heartbeats later he knew it for what it was. The Villa men were chanting a name in a breathy whisper: "Zacatecas . . . Zacatecas . . . Zacatecas . . . Zacatecas . . . Zacatecas . . ."

Behind the blue glasses the yellow face of Venustiano Carranza reddened, and the dark vein at his temple swelled. He surveyed the waiting room with the baleful look of an old bull wondering if he still rules his herd. He seemed rooted to the floor.

Two Carrancista soldiers holding rifles with fixed bayonets had come through the wide door behind him, and they now stepped forward and flanked him. He must have felt them there; he didn't look at them. His soft body stiffened.

The chant of the Villa men went on, but more subdued now.

"Zacatecas . . . Zacatecas . . . Zacatecas . . ."

Carranza had clearly borrowed strength from the armed men at his sides. He began a slow processional around the room, with the soldiers a pace to his rear, their eyes hard on the section where Jorge and Trini sat.

"We must not delude ourselves. He is not *entirely* a weakling," Jorge heard Trini say to the colonel.

The chant died when Carranza made a turn at the far corner and started for the benches holding the Villistas.

Then Jorge watched with fascination as he stopped in front of them.

The First Chief looked straight at Trini, and his face, from which the red flush had faded, suddenly turned purple. He stared hard at Trini's hat and then turned his head to the right.

"Archuleta!" It was a high, shrill voice, the voice of a woman, but a woman of anger and deadly purpose.

"¿Sí, jefe?" one of the business-suited Carrancistas on a side bench called back.

"Was it not in the agreement with General Villa that no Dorado would be present?"

"Sí, jefe."

Carranza turned back to Trini. "Leave this place at once, Dorado—or I will have you shot!"

Trini started up from the bench. His right hand streaked to his side, where the pistol had been before he gave it to Navarro. The two soldiers with Carranza brought their rifles to the ready.

"¡Trini!" It was General Ángeles. "No, amigo, no, por favor." Trini sank back, his face grim. Ángeles went on, "Major Álvarez is no longer a Dorado, Señor Carranza. He takes command of Regiment Bracomonte in two days' time. General Villa feels his presence here today is vital. The Bracomontes will spearhead any attack we make next week." He paused. "Whether Zacatecas or somewhere else."

Carranza kept his eyes on Ángeles for a moment, started to say something, stopped. He turned back to Trini. "All right. You may stay, I suppose . . ."

Trini smiled out of his grim face. It was an absolutely fearless smile. Then he reached up, grasped the brim of the sombrero, lifted the hat from his head, and with an easy, graceful motion, sailed it across the room. The Villistas shook the station's walls with laughter, but a glance at the colonel next to Trini told Jorge that one Villista wasn't exactly overjoyed at what the others apparently viewed as a minor triumph of some kind. The man's face was ice. "Gracias, Señor Carranza," Trini said now. "We are all *amigos* here, *señor, no*?"

Amigos? Jorge wondered. What was wrong here? Where was the revolutionary solidarity he had expected?

But there was no time at all to think about an answer to the question—if there was one.

The men at the windows were suddenly buzzing again, crowding each other for a better view of something happening outside. Dorado horses galloped past the door, and then another black motorcar ground to a halt in full view. A man in a tropical helmet sat in the backseat.

"It's Pancho . . . the general . . . he is coming. ¡Ya llegó Villa!"

One of the watchers turned toward the center of the room.

"¡Viva Villa!" he called. An echoing *"¡Viva Villa!"* became a roar. *"¡Viva Villa . . . Viva Villa . . . Viva Villa!!!!"*

Boots drummed the floor until the *vigas* in the depot ceiling shuddered.

¡Magnífico! If the Obregonistas and the Carranza people still sat like corpses, did it matter? This was the promised moment that had brought Jorge María Martínez down the burning length of the Jornada del Muerto and into the long-sought, true homeland of his *corazón*—Mexico. Even Trini was forgotten.

He heard his voice join the chorus.

"¡VIVA VILLA!"

13

▲▲▲▲▲

The man in the sun helmet settled into his place at the table in the center of the waiting room with a grace at odds with his top-heavy, ungainly body.

The Villa men leaned toward him as if they were iron filings drawn across a sheet of paper by a magnet. Carranza's people and the officers who had surrounded Obregón when

Felipe Ángeles spoke to him sat rigid and erect, but even in their resistance they seemed as affected by the pull of General Francisco Villa as all the others in the room. The shouting had died, but it still echoed in Jorge Martínez's head.

Venustiano Carranza, at the other end of the table from him, braced his two pale hands against its edge, as if he, too, were in danger of being drawn into the Tiger of the North's boundless field of force.

Obregón joined the group at the table, and so did Felipe Ángeles. Two other men sat with their backs to Jorge and the other Villistas. The civilian was probably the governor of Chihuahua, Chao, whom Trini had said would be here. If so, the one remaining man in uniform had to be González, Carranza's general leading the drive down from Coahuila.

The two riflemen who had toured the waiting room with Carranza positioned themselves on either side of the double doors. It pleased Jorge Martínez that *the* general, *his* general, had entered the room alone.

The first words of the chiefs at the table were lost to the turmoil inside him, and if the general himself had actually spoken he hadn't caught it. There were handshakes across the table strong enough to crush a Federalista skull, and the doubts which had chipped at him since Pablo Navarro and Trini talked together and after they took their seats, began to fade. In the rush of the moment he forgot the distrust of Carranza he had seen when the First Chief walked the room with his two armed men. These men at the table would form the one strong fist of revolutionary vengeance he had dreamed about.

The depot was fast becoming an even hotter oven now that the double doors were closed against the Dorados, the newspapermen, and the photographers gathered in the dust outside. The tatterdemalion brass band blasted a sour chorus of the national hat dance through the windows, with the lone fiddler's scrapings rising above the sound of the horns, and from somewhere in the great camp the odor of cooking oil and corn drifted through the room. The only thing relieving the closeness was that Trini's prediction had been right: no one had put a match to a cigar or a cigarette since the general entered.

"As soon as they begin discussing military or political matters, I want you to put every word said into that notebook," Trini said.

"*¡Sí, señor mayor!*" He sounded sure enough, even to himself, but could he do it? Carranza's and the others' words would be easy enough to capture if they stopped talking all at once, but how could he record those of the one paramount titan at the table, Pancho Villa? Even Holy Scripture only sparely reported the words of God. Mighty events would take place here today, and mighty utterances would fill the air. Would he recognize every single one of them?

The hand gripping the pencil began to cramp. *Relax, amigo. Do not tie yourself in knots. You cannot fail the major.*

The colonel on the other side of Trini cleared his throat. "When will someone talk about Zacatecas?"

The colonel had kept his voice barely above a whisper, but Carranza shot him a swift glance through the blue-tinted glasses. The colonel glared back at him. The First Chief's hands tightened their hold on the table's edge.

"There are some other, smaller things to be disposed of first, Rodolfo," Trini said. Again that edge in his voice.

All talk at the table stopped.

Francisco Villa smiled. He spread his arms. A braided leather riding quirt dangled from the left one.

"Welcome to Torreón and *la División del Norte*, Don Venustiano," he said. Carranza nodded but made no reply. Villa's eyes moved to the others at the table. "General Obregón . . . Gobernador Chao, *mi casa es su casa*." Chao started a little at the mention of his name. Hadn't Jorge heard somewhere that the governor and Pancho Villa were very close, almost *hermanos*? Obregón gave no sign he had even heard his name. González, a frail wisp of a man for the commander of an army, looked expectant. Had General Villa deliberately excluded him?

González leaned toward Carranza and said something Jorge didn't catch. The Coahuilan politician lifted a hand from the table and waved it in front of his face as if he were bothered by a fly. He looked at Villa.

"General Villa . . ." he said. "I have no wish to complain unduly, but General González tells me the officers in his delegation feel they have been insulted by some of your men since we arrived yesterday. Your *norteños* intimated that my Coahuilans were cowardly. The worst offenders in this regard were the ruffians who call themselves Dorados."

Villa leaned forward. His round face darkened. "My Dorados . . . ruffians, Don Venustiano?" Then he smiled like sunrise. "They might seem that way to someone who doesn't know them. They are simple fighting men, but they have *corazones* as big as all Chihuahua. If they are insulting"—a booming laugh seemed to blow the others at the table back in their seats—"remember they insult each other, too. To a Dorado a man is either as brave as a bull or he is a coward. Perhaps their standards are higher than those of other soldiers." He turned and looked straight at Trini. "Major Álvarez. Please have the *muchachos* try to mind their manners." His gaze was fixed on Trini, focused sharply, but it seemed to spread and encompass those around the major—Jorge, too.

"*Sí, mi general,*" Trini said. "I will speak with Pablo Navarro about it as soon as we are finished here."

"*Sí*, when we are finished!" the general said. "You remind us we have not yet begun, Trini. *Bueno.*" He looked the length of the table at Carranza. "*You* called this *conferencia*, Don Venustiano. *Por favor,* tell us what is on your mind."

Carranza's mouth twisted. It was several seconds before he spoke, and when he did the words came with difficulty. This was a careful man, but a determined one. "We need to review the whole strategy of this campaign, General. It is necessary to proceed very carefully in the next two months. If we go too far too fast, we could not be ready to turn around if the Americans try something like Veracruz on a larger scale."

"I keep forgetting you are worried about the Americans, Don Venustiano. I confess I am not. *Sí*, the Americans. There are a number of them outside the door. Shall we invite them in and have them tell us what their country's intentions are?"

"I do not think it wise to joke about things like this, General Villa."

"Oh? But nothing said here today goes beyond those doors, does it, *primer jefe*?"

Carranza glared. He lifted a fluttering hand and called, "Archuleta! My briefcase."

The man who had answered him about the Dorados earlier came from the benches at a run. Carranza dug into the leather case he handed him. "I would like reports on the particular situations and the readiness for battle of the three main divisions of the Constitutionalist army, General Villa. I have General González's right here. I presume General Obregón is ready, too. General?"

"*Sí, jefe.*"

It was a strong voice, stronger than Jorge might have expected from a man so small.

"Where are your forces now, General Obregón?"

"I regret to say that my army has stopped at Tepic, *primer jefe*. It is the end of the railroad to the capital. We will have to advance on foot and with mule carts until we make the link at Guadalajara. We need trucks, motorcycles, automobiles." The little man smiled. "Now, if General Villa would lend us his railroad genius Calzado . . ."

"Not Eusabio!" Villa broke in, his voice registering mock horror. "My division's infantry rides to battle on Eusabio's back. I will lend you some of my cavalry, though, Álvaro, perhaps those same ruffians Trini Álvarez will gentle later on today. When he is through with them even your Sonorans should find them pleasant *hombres.*"

The waiting room almost burst its seams with laughter, every peal seeming to thud against the soft body of Carranza. Obregón just smiled. He went on addressing Carranza over the laughter without looking at Pancho Villa. "We can move again in three weeks, *jefe*. Sooner, if you command it. We have every confidence in your leadership."

After the laughter had died away, Jorge found that a

number of men on the benches and all those at the table had turned and seemed to be looking at the man in a uniform without insignia of rank who sat at his right hand, unnoticed by him in his first confusion and excitement. This must be Eusabio Calzado.

"You have all the food, ammunition, medicine, and other supplies you need, General Obregón?" Carranza said. The petulant note in the high-pitched voice revealed he was still smarting from the laughter.

"As with other generals, Don Venustiano, I never think I have enough. But, seriously, *sí*, we shall be able to make do."

"General González is ready, too," Carranza said. "Is that not so, Pablo?"

González sat bolt upright in his place at the table, shaking his head as if he had just been abruptly awakened from a nap. "*Sí, jefe.* The Coahuila Division is ready for your marching orders."

At his end of the table Villa sighed a gargantuan sigh. "That is good to hear, General González," he said. "Then you can take Paredón and Saltillo for us, so the Northern Division can get on with the real work of winning this war. *Sí*, you will help us just as you helped when we came here to Torreón."

Jorge was scribbling furiously, his heart pounding for fear he would miss something Trini would need. It wasn't until after he put a period to Pancho Villa's last words that the ripsaw edge in the general's voice came as a small aftershock. He looked up, his pencil poised above the page. The depot had fallen to deathly silence.

The faces of the Villa men were hard. What had been said? He read his last line. "*Sí*, you will help us just as you helped when we came here to Torreón." Yes. Even Paco Durán's squad of ignorant recruits knew the Coahuilans *hadn't* helped win Torreón. Now he remembered. They had been expected to cut off Federalista reinforcements coming to the rescue of Torreón from San Pedro de las Colonias and the east, but they hadn't moved. That was why Brigade Ignacio Zaragoza had swung off the main line of march to cut the rail lines, in the action where Paco Durán had taken his latest three in a long line of wounds. González, according to Paco and the other sergeants, had stayed in his safe camp well to the north of Paredón. To any even halfway-proud commander, Villa's remark would be a blood insult. Would a challenge come from the Coahuilan general?

The silence stretched out. Then an angry, heated buzzing began among the Villa men.

"*¡Mierda!*" the colonel next to Trini said. "That *cobarde* González is bad enough. But the real criminal is that fucking, fake *jefe* Carranza. At least the asshole should have the decency to defend his own general."

¡Dios! Did one speak this way of a comrade?

Surely the colonel was wrong about El Primer Jefe.

But Carranza's face was not only suddenly bland—showing none of the agitation of a moment earlier—it wore the blandness of satisfaction. From his look, things were going well for the First Chief, although Jorge couldn't fathom why. The Coahuilan's most trusted general had been insulted, and so, by extension, had he.

"Do you have a report on the División del Norte, General Villa?" Carranza said now. *Sí,* he sounded almost smug. "Because of your request for your next objective to be a strongly defended city like Zacatecas ..." He paused. "We expect a report in significantly more detail than the ones we have just heard."

"Felipe!" Villa said.

"*¡Sí, mi general!*" General Felipe Ángeles's voice was calm and steady. "With your permission I will ask Major Trinidad Álvarez to report for me. Trini, *por favor.*"

When Trini stood, left the bench, and approached the table, Jorge felt bereft, a little naked, but there was no time to worry about it; if there was ever to be a moment to bend to his work and not miss a single syllable, it was this one. He should listen and write; he shouldn't look. Still, his eyes followed the major.

Trini had taken a position just off General Villa's left shoulder. He looked at Carranza at the other end of the table.

The First Chief was stuffing papers back in the briefcase, and taking his time about it, and Trini waited at the stiff attention Paco had demanded of Jorge's training squad. He looked prepared to wait all day.

At last Carranza lifted his eyes from the briefcase, and Álvarez began.

"With one detail yet to be attended to, the Division of the North has never been better prepared to undertake a major offensive, *jefes*."

Someone on the bench behind Jorge whispered "Zacatecas." Again Carranza turned his head, but the word didn't provoke him now as it had before. Something had set confidence soaring in the politician during the last few exchanges. There was no doubt he assumed himself in the ascendancy. Probably it was the deference shown him by Obregón and González in their reports, and in the case of the latter, fawning.

Trini went on. "We have found more than enough replacements to make up for our losses here at Torreón, and our training program has prepared the new recruits so well it is sometimes difficult to distinguish them from the veteran *guerreros*. The Division now numbers in excess of twenty-two thousand men, six thousand of which are cavalry with a plentiful supply of remounts. All soldiers, horse and foot, carry Spanish or Austrian 7.5mm Mauser or .30-30 Winchester rifles, with enough ammunition at their disposal to sustain them through ten or more days of intensive combat. Thanks to the crews of Eusabio Calzado, our means of transport is superb. We lost a locomotive in the attack on Torreón, but we now have two more than when we got here, with thirty-seven boxcars, twenty-two flats, and five tank cars, two for gasoline for our cars and trucks, three for water. Seven of the flatcars carry our artillery, twenty Schneider-Canet 75s, twelve St. Chaumond and St. Chaumond-Mondragón 75s, and enough Mondragón 70s to outfit four batteries. This country has never seen such accomplished gunners as those of General Ángeles before, not even when the French were here. Two more flatcars carry the siege guns El Niño and El Chavalito.

In automatic weapons we are well equipped with Madsen, Hotchkiss, and Rexer machine guns, and ten more are due here tomorrow from the Division's agents in Sans Antonio, Texas. Two of the boxes are fully equipped hospital cars, completely staffed. Food has been stockpiled since we took this city. Morale is at a pinnacle. We are ready for battle, *jefes. Sí.* Ready for Zacatecas."

The colonel Trini had called Rodolfo turned and talked across Jorge directly to Calzado. This time he held his harsh voice to a whisper, but Villa and the other five at the table, still fixed on Trini, wouldn't have heard him, anyway.

"Has Felipe gone *loco*, Eusabio?" he said. "Why the fuck is he having Trini tell them this much? They tell *us* nothing."

"General Ángeles has good reasons, Rodolfo. We have to prove we can *take* Zacatecas, don't we?" Calzado whispered back.

"*¡Mierda!*" Rodolfo groaned. "Let's tell Huerta, too."

Occupied with his duty to Trini, Jorge hadn't really looked at the colonel. He did now, and had a sudden cold feeling he had seen this man before, but not here at Torreón. A newspaper picture, perhaps? *¿Quién sabe?* No, even turning the colonel's square face with its pencil-thin mustache above a slit mouth into a black-and-white photo in his mind didn't bring any true recognition. It wasn't the set face with the keen, hard eyes that seemed familiar. It was the colonel's hands. Even idle in his lap they looked ready to chop or strangle. Killer hands. It would make even the strongest man glad the colonel was on his side in a fight.

Then he remembered where he had seen hands like these before—General Guzmán's bodyguard Jimson back in Chihuahuita had hands just like these.

Trini was still at attention at the table, but things were stirring at the end where the two Coahuilans sat.

"Major . . ." Carranza looked at some notes in front of him, ". . . Álvarez, isn't it? You mentioned one detail yet to be attended to. Would you care to enlighten us as to what this 'detail' might be?"

Trini looked at Felipe Ángeles. Ángeles nodded, but something in his face betrayed massive doubt.

"*Sí*, Señor Carranza," Trini said. He drew a deep breath. "Although we are well supplied with small-arms and automatic-weapons ammunition, we have a severe shortage of shells for our larger ordnance, the field and railroad guns. We would run out in half a day when we attack Zacatecas."

Carranza smiled. The soft white beard and mustache stiffened. There was a new gleam in the eyes behind the blue spectacles. He looked at Felipe Ángeles as if he had just turned up a face card in a game of stud.

"Perhaps we Coahuilans can be of help in this regard, General Ángeles. As you no doubt know, artillery shells are no problem with General González's Division. I believe he is actually *overstocked* with ammunition your artillery could use."

"We would be grateful if you remedied our lack, Don Venustiano. All of Mexico would share our gratitude."

"Then please tell us what you need, and we shall supply it without delay."

"*Gracias, primer jefe*. Major Álvarez will gladly outline our wants for General González's quartermaster people."

Pancho Villa was on his feet. "*¡Magnífico!* This has been a fine, productive *conferencia*, so far. Let us settle on the next place to feel the might of my Division, and then, Don Venustiano, I would like you and General González to come to my quarters for dinner. General Obregón and Gobernador Chao, as well. *¡Viva la Revolución! ¡Viva México! ¡Viva Carranza!*"

The "*¡Vivas!*" rolled across the waiting room only a shade less forcefully than before.

I was right! There has been too much at stake for this meeting to have ended in failure. These men will make the dream of Francisco Madero a reality, It is the fist, verdad! Jorge very nearly wrote it in his book after the last remarks of Pancho Villa.

Trini was returning to the bench with a smile on his face. The ovations for Villa and the other chiefs were still ringing all around them.

"A good morning's work, *no*, Rodolfo?" Trini said to the colonel.

"You think so?" Rodolfo said. "It's just too fucking easy, if you ask me. I smell a rat!"

It is only this one colonel who has doubts now, is it not? Villa was striking the tabletop with his riding quirt. The blows shattered the air like the reports of cannons.

"*¡Atención, compadres!* Our guest El Primer Jefe wants to speak."

No one else in all of Mexico could have hushed this crowd so quickly, Jorge Martínez thought.

"*Gracias,* General Villa," Carranza said. He was showing yellow teeth in the smile that now appeared behind the beard and mustache. "There is, of course, one small proviso attached to the gift of shells General González is prepared to make to the Division of the North."

"Proviso?" The quirt hung at Pancho Villa's side.

"*Sí.* It is not too much to ask. We must have your word of honor, General Villa, that our gift will only be used in an attack on the Federalist strongholds of Saltillo and Paredón. General González will join you in such an action."

Jorge had been wrong. The silence in the waiting room deepened—and darkened, too. But it didn't last.

"*¡No, no, Pancho!*" Rodolfo wasn't whispering now. "Don't fall for that *mierda*. He is trying to fuck us the way he did when we took Torreón!"

"*Momento,* Rodolfo," Villa said. He didn't look at the colonel, but kept his eyes on the sallow man at the other end of the table from him. "Paredón and Saltillo, *jefe*?" It seemed to Jorge that he almost choked on the *"jefe"* now.

"*Sí,*" Carranza said.

"Not Zacatecas?"

"No, General."

"*¿Por qué?* Paredón and Saltillo are two hundred kilometers to the east of my line of advance. When I have crushed Zacatecas almost nothing stands between my Division and the capital."

Carranza shrugged. "*Sí,* General. But perhaps you cannot

crush Zacatecas. What then? Believe me, we are only mindful of the welfare of your Division."

"Welfare? *You* are mindful of the welfare of *my* Division?"

"If you go south now, you go alone. You heard General Obregón. He is halted for the moment at Tepic. General González does not feel he can support your left flank if you move on Zacatecas before June."

Villa puffed. "My Division does not need them. We took Torreón without their help." He gave the white-faced González a scalding look before he turned back to the man across the table from him. "Give us those shells, Señor Carranza. If we attack Zacatecas your Coahuilan snail can crawl a few inches forward, leaving a trail of slime, while we *norteños* kill Federalistas by the thousands!"

"There is no call for you to insult a brave Constitutionalist general this way, General Villa."

"You think Pancho Villa ought to kiss his ass instead, Señor Carranza?"

Carranza put up his hands as if warding off a blow. "No Paredón, no Saltillo—no shells. That is my final offer. Do I have your word?"

Villa turned to Felipe Ángeles. "Can we reduce Zacatecas without your artillery, Felipe?"

Ángeles's face twisted. "I do not think so, *mi general*. It is a much larger garrison then Torreón, and their defenses are much, much stronger. General Barrón has entrenchments and embrasures of heavy timber and corrugated iron instead of the crates and carts we found blocking our way here at Torreón. He has scores of new machine guns, too." He paused. "No, we can*not* take Zacatecas without my guns."

"Will Paredón and Saltillo be a problem for my Division?"

"Only by virtue of the time we would then lose in moving on Zacatecas. Presidente Huerta is reinforcing General Barrón there with fresh troops on an almost daily basis. At this moment we have an advantage in numbers. We lose some of it every day. By June we will have lost it all."

Villa turned swiftly and left the table. The two Coahuilan soldiers at the door looked as if they wanted to break and run, but Villa veered toward one of the dusty windows. He put his hands on the sill and bent his head. The quirt swung back and forth like a metronome.

"I am sorry, Rodolfo," Trini said to the colonel. "I was wrong and you were right." The edge in Trini's voice was gone. It was a lament.

The colonel shrugged. "That bastard Carranza will do anything rather than let González fight. And even though I never did trust either of them, I admit I don't know why they want to wreck Felipe's plan. Two months ago they were all in favor of it. Don't they want to win this war?"

Calzado spoke from the other side of Jorge. "They're mortally afraid we'll get to Mexico City first. This is politics, pure and simple."

Trini nodded as if he were baring his neck for the stroke of an ax. "*Sí,*" he said. "I should have seen it. *Pobrecito México.*"

At the window Pancho Villa turned and faced them.

Whatever Jorge Martínez had expected to see on the general's face—anger, frustration, defiance, disappointment, none of them would have surprised him—he didn't see it. Instead, Villa was smiling. He struck his thigh with the riding quirt.

"All right," he said. "It will be Paredón and Saltillo, then. *La División del Norte* will attack next week! *La conferencia está terminada.*"

Carranza was smiling, too. He had been a big winner here today.

Jorge looked back at Villa. The general's smile was even broader now. He looked a winner, too.

But they couldn't possibly both have won.

Jorge left the railway station when Villa ordered the Northern Division men on the benches to wait outside with the people Carranza also dismissed, in order that the six chiefs—and Trini Álvarez—could make the final plans for battle. The colonel named Rodolfo had sneered at Carranza's two uncomfortable-looking soldiers as he and Calzado went through the door together.

"You won't be able to protect him forever, *niños bobos*!" he said. He laughed when they flinched.

Even the brilliant noon sun couldn't burn away the fog that filled Jorge's head as he walked across the diamond-hard caliche of the plaza. He would never understand the behavior of the mighty, much less their thinking.

The Dorados, all mounted, strangely silent, ringed the plaza. Pablo Navarro sat his horse like a statue, Trini's gun belt draped between his crotch and the saddle horn. The band was doing something utterly abominable to "Adelita."

At the edge of the crowd of photographers and reporters Jorge found Paco Durán and his daughter. Margaret Espinosa was with them. She looked troubled, but that was no surprise. Even the little he had seen of her yesterday had persuaded him that the captain-nurse would always hearken to a more mournful tune than even the one whose plaintive chorus the old fiddler was playing now.

Juanita was eating a tortilla wrapped around a chunk of meat. She wiped her mouth with the back of her hand and smiled at him. Thank God it wasn't a teasing smile. He badly needed a little simple warmth. These, surely, were the kind of people he belonged with, not the grand commanders inside the depot.

The girl was probably still feeling the contempt for him she had shown him from the outset, but Paco, at least, didn't let him down. He stepped to him and clapped his huge hands against Jorge's shoulders. His great strength was almost as reassuring as his open smile. "Captain Cockroach! *¡Hola!* Did it go well in there with you and Trini?"

Of course he didn't have an answer, but it didn't seem as if the big dynamiter-gunner would require one.

"I do not know, Paco."

When Margaret Espinosa spoke he knew there would be no need to tell them, anyway. "Paredón and Saltillo. I should be happy. There will be far fewer casualties to care for than if it were Zacatecas. Of course we'll have to face that, too, someday—more's the pity."

Yes, the word had gone out like an electric current when

the men who went through the double doors ahead of him reached the plaza. What an army! Did no one keep secrets here?

"Jorge . . ." It was Juanita. Jorge? No "Capitán Cucaracha?"

"*Sí,* Juanita?"

"Papá and I would like you to come to supper with us to-night. Will you?"

Would he? Oh, yes, yes, yes!

"I would be honored, *señorita.*"

"Right after retreat, then. Our tent is—" She broke off. Something over his shoulder had caught her eye. "Papá," she said now.

"*Sí,* Juanita?"

"Isn't that Fierro there?" She was pointing toward the steps of the railway station. Fierro! The man called "Villa's Butcher." Would he now see the same Fierro who had ordered the execution of the young *soldado* yesterday?

He turned. Juanita was pointing at the colonel Trini and Calzado had called Rodolfo. The colonel had settled his gaze on Margaret Espinosa. It took no special insight to see that his look wasn't one of idle curiosity. Margaret turned her head away.

The double doors burst open again.

González was the first one through, blinking against the sun with the furtive look of a whipped dog despite the fact that he and his chief were coming from this meeting with everything they wanted. Obregón emerged next, his face as passive as the Sphinx, and the still-mute Chao followed close behind.

Ángeles and Trini, their expressions impossible to read, came out next, just as the crowd swallowed Chao. Trini had rescued his sombrero and was holding it in his hand. He and Ángeles stopped under the depot's portico while Carranza, Obregón, and González climbed into one of the black touring cars. They were set upon by the reporters and photographers, but the car got under way and in seconds had driven through a gap in the ranks of the Dorados. Carranza looked straight ahead, as if making sure he wouldn't see any of the mounted men.

Before he could turn and look at Trini and General Ángeles again, a roar told him Pancho Villa had appeared.

When it subsided he saw Trini gesture at the driver of the car the general had arrived in.

"No, Trini, *gracias,*" Villa said. "I will ride back with my Dorados." He removed the tropical sun helmet from a head shaped like a cannonball and tossed it toward the backseat of the car. "Lend me your sombrero, *por favor, amigo,* and see if one poor, unfortunate Dorado will offer his mount to his general."

Before Trini could say a word half a dozen Dorados set spurs to their horses' flanks and were crowding the three men under the portico. Two, a hair's breadth faster than the rest, slipped from their saddles, and Villa stepped to a tall, beautifully configured roan.

Up on the big horse the Tiger of the North raised the hand with Trini's sombrero and brandished the quirt with the other. The quirt fell, the horse reared, its forelegs stretched against the sun. The man in the saddle pulled it down without any seeming effort. Then he shouted, "*¡A la causa, Dorados!*"

Pancho Villa swept out of the plaza with his Dorados on his horse's heels. The plaza shook from the drumming of hooves and the blasts from a score of pistols.

On foot perhaps just another human being when all was said and done, on horseback Pancho Villa was a god.

Jorge María Martínez forgot the trials and tribulations of the morning.

Villa rides. Sí. Pancho Villa rides! He will ride forever.

14

"Papá sleeps whenever he can. It's the only medicine he ever takes." Juanita laughed. "Except maybe for *cerveza* and tequila. He takes enough of them even when he isn't sick or wounded."

Paco was sleeping now. Jorge had mistaken the snores coming out of the tent for peals of distant thunder, but the night sky was alive with stars from the broken line of mountains in the east to the mighty Sierra Madre Occidental, and the snores had stopped. The sergeant had retired less than half an hour after they finished eating, when the sun was just touching the tops of the *sierras*, and when he left them Jorge felt robbed and pleased all at once. He wanted desperately to talk to Durán about what he had learned today, or—more to the point in his bewilderment—what he hadn't learned. There was enough of that to fill a book thicker than *Los problemas*.

But perhaps even more than wishing for the comment and advice of Paco, he wanted to be alone with Paco's daughter, even if she started that Captain Cockroach stuff again.

As darkness fell and the air grew chill, the girl cleaned up the remains of dinner and washed the tin plates and flatware in a bucket of water. She didn't talk, but once in a rare while he heard snatches of a hummed tune. He didn't know the song. At even more infrequent intervals she shot him swift, keenly searching glances. He didn't dare speculate on what if any message they might carry.

He hadn't gotten much out of Paco before Juanita served the supper: *albóndigas* which reminded him of those of his *abuela* back in Chihuahuita when he was a boy, and a chile stew hot enough to bring tears and make him forget for a few minutes the happenings at the railway station. No one, obviously, got much from the sergeant when he attacked food or drink. Jorge marveled at his appetite.

All right. So Juanita *wasn't* a *soldadera*. Feeding a stomach as cavernous as her father's was certainly training her to be one, though—and for a *brigade*, not just one *normally* hungry fighting soldier.

They sat on opposite sides of the small fire she had cooked the meal over, their backs against rolled-up bedding. With Paco surely wrapped in his own inside the tent, either the bedroll he was using for a backrest, or hers, had to be an extra. He wondered about that for a second, but he didn't let his wondering become a question. At the end of a day such as this he had no time for women, even in the unlikely event that this slim, graceful creature should become available here and now. But, *Dios,* she was lovely beyond words. The fire had burned down to coals, and although its dying glows still lent her face a cast of orange warmth, the dance in her dark eyes was hers alone.

He heard something like a rumbling sigh from inside the tent and really thought he felt the ground move as the big sergeant apparently turned over in his sleep.

Juanita looked toward the tent, her brow knit a little, turned back to him.

"Trini seemed pleased after he read the notes you took, Jorge."

He grunted. The major had seemed pleased with him, even though he was deeply somber, almost despondent, at the conference's outcome. But pleased about what? Jorge had only been a clerk today, not an "aide" in any way he understood an aide should be. All he had done was record what was said. And even if the words of the chiefs had been the "mighty utterances" he had looked for, there surely was no credit accruing to him simply because he could read and write.

Something was missing, something still eluded him. In the hours since he had left Trini in the plaza, he had come to terms with his first troubling sense of loss. He had been wrong to expect that even men fundamentally united in a great common cause such as the Revolution would see eye-to-eye on everything, especially matters of strategy and tactics. What had Jorge Martínez known before today? What had he done? *Nada.* And he had better keep that fixed in his simple mind. Even seemingly weak Pablo González, the reluctant commander of Division Coahuila, had risked his treasure and his life to oppose first Porfirio Díaz and then the only slightly less feared but even more universally hated tyrant Huerta.

Perhaps Carranza, Obregón, and Carranza's timorous toy general were right to insist on Paredón and Saltillo over Zacatecas, despite the gloom Jorge had seen on the faces of

Trini Álvarez and Felipe Ángeles when they stood with Pancho Villa under the *portal* of the railway station. Perhaps General Villa himself had come to the conclusion that the other *jefes* had the right of it.

That might explain why Villa had looked the unquestioned victor in those last moments of the conference. There had certainly been no sign of defeat or setback on the Tiger of the North's confident face as he made his tumultuous exit from the plaza at the head of his proud Dorados.

That, at least, would always be *un momento* for Jorge Martínez to remember. But he couldn't delude himself; the sense of loss had eaten at his bowels even before the sound of the cavalcade faded into the quaking air of Torreón.

A knot exploded in the fire, and the sharp, small detonation made him jump.

The girl smiled at him, and the blush that had begun to move upward from his throat receded. He smiled back at her. He had won a victory himself. Yesterday this sort of nervous skittishness would have brought still another scathing "Capitán Cucaracha." There had been nothing but "Jorges," spoken without seeming reservation, since he discovered her, Margarita, and Paco in the plaza.

"You and Paco come from Durango, no, Juanita?" That surely was safe, wasn't it?

"*Sí*, Jorge. From the village of Santa María del Oro. Papá was a blacksmith there in the old days."

Old days? How could there be old days for one so young? "*¿Y tu madre?*"

Juanita shivered and pulled a serape across her long legs. "My mother is dead." The pale words seemed to come from much farther away than just across the fire. Perhaps her family and her background didn't offer such a safe, easily handled subject, after all. "She died six years ago. When I was almost twelve." *Asique,* she was a year older than he thought.

Another knot burst in the coals, and a momentary brightening of the embers gave him a new glimpse of her face. The glow was gone. She looked as ashen as the edges of the fire.

Had his innocent question provoked this change? He felt himself a brute.

"Jorge . . . perhaps I should tell you about Papá and me—and Mamá." Something in her voice screamed silently beneath the words that this would be agony for her. "Mamá took her own life. On my saint's day. My birthday, too. I found her hanging in the storeroom behind Papá's forge. Her grave is in a field at the edge of town because the *padres* wouldn't let her rest in the churchyard where the Duranes have always been buried. Papá hasn't take Holy Communion since we left Durango. I don't think he ever will again. I go to church sometimes, not often; the last time was in Juárez—at Guadalupe."

She fell silent for a bit, then shook her head as if trying to shake a memory. Then it stopped, too. It must be too horrible for her to go on.

But something told him she was far from through. It seemed absurd, but he suddenly realized she expected him to encourage her, ask questions even.

"*Por qué,* Juanita? Why did she do it?"

"Shame." Another silence. "She was raped, Jorge."

Dios. Could he ask questions about something like that? Well, he had to. Her face insisted on it. "Do you want to tell me about it?"

"*Sí.* Yes, I do." She shuddered a little and drew the serape up to her neck. Seventeen as he now knew she was, she looked as she must have looked that terrible birthday six years ago. "No," she said now. "I don't want to tell you, but I have to."

She shed the serape, got to her feet, and tossed another stick on the fire. Back at her bedroll and wrapped to her chin again, she stared as if transfixed as the stick blazed up.

"Mamá worked as a maid in the big house on the *hacienda* of Don Sebastián López y Montenegro. No one in Santa María del Oro thought Don Sebastián a bad man as *hacendados* go. Papá liked him. He was not political back then. Doña Beatriz seemed almost a saint. They had three sons and four daughters. The oldest, Doña Luisa, was married, and had a *hacienda* next to Don Sebastián's. We saw little of her or her sisters, who were always in school in Spain or the United States, or traveling in Europe. Working at the house, Mamá saw a lot of the *muchachos*. And they saw *her*. She was just too beautiful, Jorge.

"Late that summer Don Sebastián and Doña Beatriz took the younger girls to Paris. Whenever they were gone like that, the boys would give big wild parties for their *amigos*. They would round up girls from the village to drink and dance with them—and do all the other things. Most of the girls were glad to be there. I can't blame them. They ate better there than they ever did at home, and they were given clothes they never could have afforded otherwise. No one in the village ever talked about *las diversiones*. It was the way of *los ricos*.

"The girls were pretty, and some of them were even happy. They were great, contented *damas* for a week. You would think *los caballeros* would have been content, too. They weren't. Perhaps it is the way of all men to want what they can't have. Mamá made it plain they couldn't have her. It didn't stop them.

"They went *loco* at this party. *Borracho* all day and all night. They kept Mamá in Doña Beatriz's room for three days and forced her to drink with them, telling her she should feel honored to 'take them' in La Doña's bed. Seven of them had her, over and over again—she couldn't count the times. Even once would have brought such shame she probably would have died from it someday, anyway."

Her litany of horror had been given in a dead-level voice completely devoid of emotion.

"When Mamá came back to *nuestra casa* after it was over, she didn't tell Papá for a while, but he guessed something awful had happened to her. When Mamá missed her next 'time' and knew that she was pregnant, she told him everything.

"In those days Papá was a different man from the terrible *sargento* you know now, Jorge. For all his great *fuerza* he was a gentle man. Oh, he believed in honor, *sí*, but he believed in God and the law even more. And there was only one 'law' in Santa María del Oro. Don Sebastián himself. When he came back from Paris with Doña Beatriz and the girls, Papá went to see him. Don Sebastián was *muy simpático*. He offered Papá fifty pesos and asked him to forget about it. Papa saw the *alcalde* of Santa María then, and the *padres*. None of *them* asked Papá to forget about it. They *told* him to!

"Then on my birthday, and saint's day, Mamá hung herself from a *viga* in the storeroom, and most of Papá died, too. He couldn't work. He hardly ate. The neighbors stayed away. Papá decided to close the blacksmith's shop. He only took care of one more customer.

"Don Luis, the oldest of the López y Montenegro sons, rode into the shop on a horse that had lost a shoe. It was on a Sunday morning, just as Papá and I were getting ready to go to mass. Papá was no longer religious, since the *padres* wouldn't let us bury Mamá in the churchyard, but he went with me sometimes. He didn't say anything to Don Luis, just took off his coat, put on his apron, and went to work. By the time he finished, our *calle* was deserted. The neighbors were all at *la iglesia*. Don Luis got back in the saddle and asked Papá what he owed him. *'Nada,'* Papá said. Don Luis smiled, said, *'Gracias, viejo,'* and started to ride away. He stopped, turned back to Papá, and said, *'Por favor,* Paco. Remember me to your *esposa*. Tell her we think of her often at the house.' He didn't even know Mamá was dead, Jorge, he didn't know!

"Papá dragged him from the saddle. He still had his big hammer in his hand, and when he had Don Luis on the ground he raised it above his head. Then he dropped it. 'No, *puerco*!' he said. 'It would be too quick, too easy.'

"Then, with only his fists, he beat Don Luis to death. Don Luis was young and strong; it took Papá almost twenty minutes. He kept begging Papá to tell him why until the very end. He thought he had done no wrong—ever. Papá didn't even answer him.

"We left for the mountains before any of the neighbors got back from church. We lived for a year and a half in a fishing shack Papá had been to as a boy—stayed there until Francisco Madero started the Revolution. Then Papá and I came out of *las sierras* and joined General Villa. We heard later that the *rurales* came to our *calle* and tried to get our neighbors to tell them where Papá and I had gone. They shot six of them. *Pobrecitos*. I am sure they would have told the soldiers everything if they had known. They all had a big regard for the law—like Papá did. I think that changed.

"After the first fighting broke out near our town, the people burned the *hacienda* of the López y Montenegros. They killed all the family except for the oldest daughter, Doña Luisa. She was visiting someone in Los Angeles, but they killed her husband, who was with the Montenegros. It gives me no joy. It didn't bring my mother back.

"Papá has never spoken Mamá's name since she died, never mentioned Don Luis or his family—and he has never cried. Neither have I, Jorge."

Perhaps not, but now something like a sob escaped into the night air.

The fire had expired while Juanita talked, but Jorge could still see her face by the light of the stars. Parchment. Smooth, unsullied parchment.

"But forget all this, Jorge, now that you have heard it. Well—maybe you can't forget it, but put it way at the back of your mind. Every *soldado* and *soldadera* in the Division has something in their past like this, or something even worse. What happened to Mamá, Papá, and me is nothing so very special."

She said the last with such an air of finality he knew he wasn't expected to ask her any questions about her mother now. Something told him it was time to move to other things.

"What will you do when we win the Revolution, Juanita?" he said. "Will you and Paco return to Santa María?"

"*Sí*. I still think of it as home, no matter what happened there. And what do I expect to do?" Her voice turned bright even as she talked, almost cheerful. The parchment gleamed with a life the starlight hadn't given it. "There will be so much more and so much better work to do than we did in

Santa María before. He says he won't do it, but I want Papá to be in politics. He couldn't be a statesmen, of course, but he is much wiser than he thinks. As for me—I am going to be a teacher. Margarita says she will arrange for me to go back to school, perhaps in that place she comes from in the United States. I have dreamed of becoming a teacher since I was a tiny *muchachita*." She laughed. "Of course, before the Revolution began it was only a dream. Village girls didn't become teachers then. Now I will have the chance."

Then he knew what had been missing from the conference today.

There had been much talk, and even more insinuation, of guns and attacks, of power and politics, of cowardice, courage, and personal pride. No one—not Villa nor Carranza, not Obregón nor even General Ángeles—had spoken of or for Paco and Juanita Durán or the shamed dead woman and six other lost villagers, back in forgotten, if ever known, Santa María del Oro, and not a word had been uttered about all the *soldados* and *soldaderas* whose sufferings Juanita had invoked, or whose hopes her own epitomized. The so-called butcher Fierro hadn't mentioned them, nor had Calzado the railroad man, nor Pablo Navarro. Trini had been silent about them, too. There hadn't been even one oblique reference to *Los problemas* or the serious and inspiring burdens of other books such as that of the compassionate Molinas. The name of good, great Francisco Madero hadn't surfaced once. Was it too much to ask that someone would remember? He could hope and pray that even if *los del abajo* or their ghosts hadn't been at the conference, their absence had been noted—if in silence. Had Jorge María Martínez remembered them? No, he, too, had been caught up in the "mighty events" taking place. In God's name, he must never forget again.

Juanita, still covered by the serape, rose and walked clear of the tent where Paco slept. She looked at the lights of the encampment across the Río Nazas.

"I can almost see Trini's tent from here. Margarita is with him tonight." He stepped to her side. She went on, "Did you see Colonel Fierro today? The one we call El Carnicero? He once wanted Margarita to be his *soldadera*. She turned him down for Trini. I don't think the Butcher has forgotten, but Trini tells his friends they mustn't worry." She fell silent, then she turned and looked at him. "You'd better get back to your own place, Jorge. Don't you have to be at the war council with Trini and General Ángeles in the morning? The Division moves out against Paredón and Saltillo next week, doesn't it?"

Within a week he would smell the smoke of battle. "Even staff officers of Brigade Ignacio Zaragoza fight," Trini had said.

He had better begin to learn the fear and other things he would need to know in order to survive. Paco Durán and Trini would still be his teachers for a long time. But battle itself would be the true, ultimate instructor.

Sí. Paredón and Saltillo, then.

"Jorge," Juanita said, "you do not have a *soldadera*, do you?"

"I haven't even thought about it."

"You will. Soon, I think."

She watched him ride off until he was lost in the darkness near the Nazas.

Had she said too much? Not about Mamá. Any man who came close to her would have to know about Mamá; her death had everything to do with what Juanita Durán had become.

Perhaps she had pushed things a little too far, too quickly, when she told him he would have a *soldadera* soon. If he had any sensitivity at all—and Jorge Martínez seemed to have it in abundance—he would know exactly what she meant.

Well, she *wanted* him to know, didn't she?—just as she wanted him to know about Mamá.

Where she really *had* said too much was in telling him that she had been at Guadalupe in Juárez that day.

She hadn't been exactly fair about that since she met him at the river yesterday. It was time to forgive him completely for an understandable lapse of memory. It was time to forgive him for anything and everything, except ... except that he was going off to war.

A woman, no matter how young, or how much a believer in the Revolution, should never quite forgive a man for that—no matter that she loved him beyond reason in every other way. It was even true with Papá. Margarita would understand.

She would have to face the frightening prospect that Jorge would be in battle within a week. It was good he would ride at Trini's side, although that wasn't an entirely unmixed blessing. Trini, wherever he commanded, always rode with the first attacking cavalry troop when the Division went into action; his reassignment from the Dorados to Regiment Bracomonte wouldn't change that in the slightest.

She rolled up her bedding and carried it inside the tent.

Papá was stirring, unusual for him after such a big meal and so much *cerveza*; even when sick or wounded he slept like a baby.

Undressed and in her bedroll she closed her eyes, only to snap them open when Papá spoke.

"A *soldadera*? Bah! You know nothing of being a *soldadera*. You should still be playing with *muñecas*."

"Papá! You are awake. You were *listening* to us!"

"*Sí*. To every word."

"For shame, Papá!" His great laugh shivered the canvas of the tent. She went on—furious. "I am seventeen years old. I have every right to—"

"—make an *idiota* of yourself? *Sí*. Go ahead. Become a widow even before you marry!" There was no laughter accompanying this last. "Think, *mi hija* ... Think! Wait at least until he returns from his first battle. His ... chances to stay alive ... will be a little better then."

There was something strangled about Papá's breathing now. He did love her, oh, *Dios* how he loved her. If only ...

Enough of that.

"I *will* think, Papá. But there are times when it is better to feel than think."

15

Corey Lane stretched himself across the gigantic bed in his room at the Hotel Mirador. He had two hours before he had to get bathed and force himself into his rented dress suit and go to dinner at the Ministry of Culture. Time enough to start on his first report to Henry Richardson from the capital of Mexico.

How much should he say to Henry in his letter? His friend at the State Department said they wanted him because of his insights, but surely he didn't mean *every* insight, every hunch. If he recorded all the impressions and guesses of the week, his report would be long-winded enough to blow a Spanish galleon all the way to the Dry Tortugas. The rumors that rippled from the Palace this past week had spread like the successive circles in the water when a fat trout jumped in Bonito Lake in the White Mountains; hard, reliable facts, on the other hand, had been precious few and hard to come by. And Henry and his superiors in Washington, as well as grouchy Agent Cobb in El Paso, were men whose currency was just that—facts.

It still troubled him that Jake Cobb at their last meeting before he crossed into Juárez and caught the first of the twelve different trains he had ridden to the capital, had put his foot down hard on his using the signal room at the U.S. Embassy to transmit his messages back to Boston.

"No! We don't want you anywhere near the place. Henry set up those publishers for you to keep anything you say out of the hands of State Department clerks. Even the marine guards at a U.S. Embassy—and the lady typists—can be Nosey Parkers, and they have mouths as big as the Holland Tunnel. And we sure as hell don't want your reports in code, anyway. You'll be just a historian down there, remember? Dummy it up like it was for that new book you're supposed to be writing." He looked sour at the notion of someone wasting time by writing a book. "Hell, nobody's going to be looking at it except some editor who won't know Carranza and Villa from Billy Sunday or Caruso, and he's not going to actually read it before it goes to Henry."

Easy for Jake to say. By insisting that his reports go through the Mexican postal service in "clear," he was sending Corey out to the end of a skinny limb, and the pen he was forcing into his hand might well turn out to be a saw. If his report got into the wrong hands, he could be on a train back to the border before he even had a chance to shake the dust from the clothes he had spent five days in on the trip down.

That journey of three times the crow's-flight distance between Juárez and the Federal District of Mexico here had been a waking nightmare. There hadn't been any real danger, but he had known several bad cases of the nervous sweats when he handed his passport and other papers to a seemingly endless succession of armed guards and suspicious railway conductors and inspectors, first in Chihuahua and Durango, and then during that ghastly detour through San Luis Potosí and on to Tampico and the coast. One ferret-eyed little bandit, a Villista from his uniform, slapped his shoulder with the barrel of his rifle a little harder than Corey liked when he asked him for his credentials. All the man really wanted was the pack of cigarettes he found in Corey's valise when he searched it. Another, a Federalist major this time, herded Corey and fourteen of his fellow passengers into the tiny ticket office of the station at Matehuala, kept them there for six hours until they could smell each other even above the reek of the chickens, fruit, and vegetables two of the women had with them as their only luggage, caused them to miss two trains on the direct line to León and the capital, and finally shipped them out on a freight-and-coach combination headed for Tampico. This train, a rattling, run-down toy which would have made a nineteenth-century Wells Fargo stage a luxury, stopped at every trackside hovel along the way, it seemed.

Fatiguing as the trip had been, in an odd way it had been marvelously useful to him. He could have read volumes on this puzzling war without coming to one-tenth the under-standing the trek down had given him—which was in turn only one-tenth the understanding he would eventually need were he to be of real use to Henry. The Great Revolution wasn't remotely like his own war in Cuba or any conflict he had studied.

Except for the territory immediately ahead of the armies of Villa and Carranza in Coahuila, through which his trains had threaded their way the first two days out from Juárez, there were certainly no well-defined fronts or clearly demarcated salients. A situation map of the states north of Mexico City must look like a checkerboard, and with not all the squares occupied by military forces of any description or torn by con-flict by any means. On one leg the train crew changed twice, from conductors and brakemen obviously in sympathy with the *insurrectos*, to those loyal to the government, and then back again. A nasty melee between the changeover crews broke out at the second switch of personnel, and that delayed them for another hour while the town's small garrison re-stored order. No train butchers sold food on board all that day, and he went without eating after almost choking on a stale, hard roll at daybreak—washed down with the *cerveza* which always seemed in plentiful supply at cantina stops along the way even when coffee wasn't—to a rolled tortilla just as stale at ten o'clock that night.

On this leg of the journey something happened that had nothing at all to do with the war or his mission for Henry, but which had everything to do with Corey Lane, the inner Corey Lane.

At one steaming stop he thought he spied a food vendor board the train a few cars ahead, and when the train rolled forward again his need for a bite to eat sent him through two coaches at the risk of losing his seat. He didn't find the ven-dor, but as he stepped through the vestibule of the third coach, a carriage fitted out marginally better than his own, the sight of one of the most beautiful women he had ever seen stopped him just inside the door.

The woman was napping, her head resting against the high

back of her seat, whose upholstery, a deep, midnight blue, couldn't have made a better background for her had it been deliberately chosen to display her silver-gray hair. Her smooth, wrinkle-free skin told him immediately that the gray was premature; she couldn't possibly have seen her fortieth year. She was dressed in a pale lavender full-length duster, with her hands folded in her lap. Perhaps it was her pastel appearance, her regular even breathing, her look of vulnerability, but *something* made him want to rush to her and take her in his arms. His heart swelled suddenly under his breastbone, and his breath caught. Then, even in the crowded carriage, he felt desperately alone.

For a moment he thought half-seriously of returning to his seat and bringing his luggage back here with him. The woman had a traveling companion, a *dueña* probably, sitting next to her, a birdlike older woman with dark, weathered features and a glittering, threatening eye he realized was assessing him keenly and, he had little doubt, to his disadvantage.

He returned to his own coach and was in his seat again before he realized that for the first time since her death the ghost of Lucy Bishop hadn't come to cloud his vision when he saw a woman who attracted him even in the slightest. He smiled in rue. *Ellen Stafford—take a note.*

He forced himself to survey the scene racing past his window. With what he faced in this country he couldn't daydream.

Twice he saw villages in flames, and on another occasion ragged troops, with a small antique fieldpiece pulled by mules trundling along behind horsemen on animals that looked a lot better fed than their riders, seemed to be moving to the attack against a collection of mud huts which couldn't be called a town or village by any stretch of the imagination. A fat man reminiscent of Sancho Panza was in the lead, brandishing a sword that could have been swiped from the museum wing of the Palace of the Governors in Santa Fe.

"Locals," an American businessman who had become his seatmate told him. "Those *hombres* probably haven't decided which way they will go yet. It may be just a neighborhood affair, to settle a grudge. Hell of a lot of vengeance being taken under the cover of the bigger thing." The man was originally from Cincinnati and was an oil broker with an office in Tamaulipas. "We ought to take this goddamned country over and give it a taste of Yankee order."

Once, and for the life of him now he couldn't remember on exactly which span of the trip it happened, a column of fifty or sixty riders, bristling with pistols and rifles, and with mordantly acquisitive looks in their eyes, paralleled the tracks, keeping up with the train as it struggled up a long grade. The conductor had shown something close to panic when the column first appeared and half a dozen rounds were fired into the air, but had finally smiled, and then breathed, *"Nuestras— gracias a Dios,"* as the column turned away, with the words meant more for himself than for his distraught passengers. Corey couldn't remember now, either, if the conductor and the train crew on that particular occasion had been of Huertista or revolutionary persuasion.

"Sort things out for us," Henry had said back in Black Springs. Hah! He hadn't even been sure of the loyalties of more than two or three of the hundreds of Mexicans he had ridden with during the five days. His few conversations with them had turned on crops and weather, or somebody's cousin or uncle who had emigrated to the States or was working there. Some of the men, in particular the soldiers on the trains, had been hostile, regardless of whatever allegiances they had. He seldom heard the word "gringo," but he saw it in all too many pairs of eyes.

Down the coast from Tampico they were shunted onto a siding to let a troop train headed north go by. He had been napping, and when the train's motion stopped he awoke and watched the Federalist detachment sprawled on the flatcars rumbling past his window. The soldiers looked even younger than the men he had commanded in his own Rough Rider company back in Cuba. With the oil port he had left that morning already in the hands of the Carrancistas, these infants would be in action in another day or two. When the government train at last cleared his line of sight, it gave him a new vista across the coastal plain. Scores of field *trabajadores* were apparently detasseling ears in a field of new corn. None of them so much as turned their bent heads from their tasks to watch the soldiers on the government train. It wasn't the first time he had seen such apparent indifference to the conflict that was ripping Mexico to shreds; north of Matehuala workers had been planting postage-stamp plots of ground within rifle range of a line of skirmishers advancing on what appeared to be a flour mill half-obscured by a pall of smoke. A strange, strange war. It was scarcely ever a case of "Here we was and there they was," as it had been in Cuba.

He never caught so much as another glimpse of the woman he had seen on the trip from Matehuala to the coast. Perhaps she had been a dream. He finally stopped looking for her.

He didn't stop looking for someone else.

At almost every stop long enough for him to stretch his legs on the platform he searched the faces of soldiers, villagers, and even the *campesinos* in their white cotton work clothes. Although he was nearing the capital now, there was still that one chance in a million his eyes might catch a glimpse of young Martínez. Jorge was somewhere in this troubled country, nursing troubles of his own, no doubt. Twice now Corey had let Henry Richardson's concerns come between him and what he had to do for the young man who probably still thought himself a fugitive, and Corey Lane had yet to keep the promise made to that young woman back in Black Springs.

But Henry's concerns were his concerns as well. After he had agreed to work for his old friend at the alcove table in the Cantina Florida, Henry had gone with him to Justice of the Peace Frank Foley, and had him swear Corey in as a State Department officer, practically threatening poor Frank with a lot worse than death were he to breathe a word about the uncomfortable little ceremony.

He had a job to do. He might as well get on with it. In his first week in the capital he had met all but two of the Huerta government men Cobb had listed for him as being the ones most likely to share confidences. The dinner tonight, however, arranged in part to fortify his "cover" and in part for his own reasons, wasn't likely to be productive. Narciso Trujillo wouldn't in all likelihood feel free to discuss things frankly, not with the gathering including three high-ranking Huerta men.

No, he didn't have much in the way of fact, nor was he likely to get it soon, certainly not tonight at the ministry. Henry would want what little he discovered, though.

He left the bed and went to the writing table in front of the high window overlooking the Paseo de la Reforma and its chestnut trees.

He picked up the pen. How did those lines go in Kipling's "Boanarges Blitzen?"

> Beg, borrow, steal
> But steer clear of ink
> That fatal, facile drink
> Has ruined many geese
> Who dipped their quills in it

He began his first report to Henry. How many more would there be before he returned to Chupadera County?

Hotel Mirador
Paseo de la Reforma
Mexico D.F., Mexico
May 10, 1914

Mr. Lemuel Cotter, Senior Editor
Ticknor & Fields, Publishers
Boston, Mass., U.S.A.

Dear Mr. Cotter:

This brief letter is just to inform you that I have arrived in the capital of Mexico without event.

In the week I have been here I have already made a number of the contacts you and Mr. J.C. of your staff suggested I make. The liaison with Señor Dr. Narciso Trujillo of the Ministry of Culture should prove invaluable in the shaping of the book you were kind enough to give me a contract for. Strangely enough, I was already acquainted with him. He was my guide when I spent time here in the capital six years ago doing the research for my first book—and is the man who initially made me aware of General Felipe Ángeles, at the time the commandant of the military academy at Chapultepec. I am having dinner at the ministry with the good doctor this evening.

Of course I am still having difficulty coming to grips with the vast subject you have encouraged me to explore, but I have an idea for the opening chapter you may well approve.

I think it should revolve around that same General Felipe Ángeles, who now is second-in-command of Francisco Villa's Northern Division, which has been refitting at Torreón in Coahuila state since the taking of that city more than a month ago.

General Ángeles is a strategist in the grand tradition of war-college graduates in Europe and the United States, and is a political scholar of accomplishment as well as a soldier. Please, do not for one minute think him another "mad attacker" as General Villa himself so often seems to be. The plan for three armies to advance southward toward the capital independent of each other is his. I do not think the government forces will be able to hold if Señor Carranza and General Obregón adhere to what appears to be Ángeles's strategy.

As a historian not entirely unfamiliar with military matters and operations, one thing puzzles me. There is an almost total lack of security among the several belligerent groups, a failure to keep secrets that would never be tolerated by American or European high commands.

It is well known here in the capital, for instance, that General Villa's forces are ready to take the offensive again, even if Carranza's González and Álvaro Obregón, whose Division is stalled north of Guadalajara, aren't. They, too, could make a major advance, however, if General Villa and Ángeles invest the city of Zacatecas in the state of that name. Zacatecas is well fortified, but to withstand an attack from Villa, the general commanding there, Barrón, would have to be supported by a large number of the troops now blocking the way of Obregón and Carranza. It would be a major undertaking, but Villa's army, a much more cohesive and modern force than is generally thought in the United States, is equal to the task.

It is common knowledge here, too, that the leaders of the three forces opposing the Federalistas had a big conference at Villa's headquarters in Torreón last week. Again that lamentable lack of security I mentioned. The international press was asked in to cover it! You may already know as much or more about it than I do.

There *will* be an attack by the Northern Division. That seems certain. I can't conceive of it coming anywhere but Zacatecas. To turn aside for any other possible objective would delay the Constitutionalist advance for a month and give President Huerta a breathing space in which to reconstitute his government and his army. Zacatecas would then become a more difficult problem for Villa and the Division. But my informed guess is that Villa, Obregón, and Carranza will listen to Felipe Ángeles and opt for Zacatecas now.

In any event, there will be a major engagement within the week, possibly in a day or two.

Sincerely:
Corey Lane

He laughed. He truly had meant to be brief, as he had written at the outset. It seemed to him his report held more wind than weight, but it would have to do for the moment. If he should prove right about the imminence of battle, he could chance burdening Henry with more of those vaunted "insights" in his next report.

But he *had* brought up the one insight he did feel he possessed. A small beginning, but perhaps he could direct the attention of Henry and his Washington superiors to Ángeles. The man they wanted, in Corey's opinion, might have been right under their noses for a long time.

Funny that his "cover" had prompted him to suggest putting Ángeles in the first chapter of an imaginary book when he was already committed to doing the exact same thing in a real one. Maybe it was a good cover, after all.

But he still had the sudden, sinking feeling that a Huerta security agent, reading the letter he had just composed for the eyes of his "publisher," would know it had little to do with any projected book.

The thin limb on which Cobb had positioned him swayed beneath his feet.

It would be good to see Narciso Trujillo again. He hadn't gotten close to the archaeologist when he was in Mexico City in 1908—they remained Dr. Trujillo and Señor Lane to each other all during their brief acquaintance—but there are some men you run across in life to whom you take an instant liking. Trujillo was one of them.

The doctor, whom he had called on to relay a message from an old professor friend at the University of New Mexico in Albuquerque, had been his guide through Chapultepec in the company of two other Americans and a clutch of assorted Europeans, and it was on that visit he had first met Felipe Ángeles. Strange feeling for an American to sit at luncheon with the commandant of the academy housed in the same fortress where the troops of Winfield Scott had slaughtered *los niños héroes*, the twelve- and thirteen-year-old cadets, in 1847. The commandant was apparently too gentlemanly to bring the subject up and risk embarrassing his American guests, not even when Trujillo, Ángeles, Corey, and the others at the luncheon strolled the rooftop, past the crumbling parapets and the crenellated gunports where Mexico's young future officers had wrapped themselves in their country's flag and leaped to their deaths rather than surrender. It was during that 1908 visit that the study of the general's life had first suggested itself to Corey.

Beyond Trujillo's introduction to him Corey didn't get to speak with Ángeles, and the general was reserved in his remarks to his guests, but what Corey saw of the academy itself, and the ambience of the tradition-bound old military school, spoke to him with singular eloquence. It was obvious that Ángeles—a handsome man with a grave countenance, but with luminous, perceptive eyes—was a superb administrator, and although running a small war college hardly, by itself, fitted a man for more encompassing office, the way it ran hinted at much more impressive abilities. A great man can often be more accurately assessed by how he is treated than by the way he performs or acts. Ángeles didn't stand much on ceremony; his simple uniform was free of decorations. That the general's aides and subordinates worshipped him—even though many of them addressed him by his first name—was abundantly clear. It was contagious, too. Corey found himself feeling the same way about his host, and thinking how undeservedly lucky that wicked old rascal Porfirio Díaz was, to have such a man working for him.

It came as no surprise when two years later Felipe Ángeles threw his support behind Francisco Madero, and a year after that left the service of that monster Huerta to serve with Pancho Villa, although Corey did wonder from time to time how Ángeles could not merely coexist but work in complete harmony with the rash Chihuahuan.

That the successes of Villa's División del Norte this past twenty-four months were due in large part—and perhaps *in toto*—to the thinking of Ángeles became more and more apparent to Corey Lane, following the war in the columns of American newspapers while he went through the motions of serving out his last term as the sheriff of Chupadera County.

Trujillo had seemed very close to Felipe Ángeles, but without the pressing urgency of Corey's mission for Washington there had been little cause for the archaeologist to open up about the Chapultepec commandant.

He wished he could ask Trujillo tonight to put him in touch

with Ángeles again, but did he dare do it without securing Henry Richardson's permission? He supposed not. His first tentative overtures on the general's behalf had been ignored. And was there any sense in trying until he discovered whether or not Villa's strategist was even interested? The best thing he could hope to reap from the dinner was that the Huerta people might leak something he could pass on to Jake Cobb or Henry.

At least Narciso Trujillo wouldn't take him for a spy.

When he finished dressing and went to the huge chest to put his father's gold watch in his waistcoat pocket he discovered the venerable timepiece had stopped. He didn't have the vaguest idea of how long he had spent laboring over his letter and had no notion of what the hour was. Then he remembered seeing a wall clock in the corridor, and he opened the door of his room and checked the time.

Good Lord! He had less than twenty minutes to make it to the ministry. He had looked forward to walking the mile and a half through the kaleidescopic early evening crowds, but now he would have to see if he could hire a taxi.

With his room on the third floor of the Mirador he didn't have time to await the arrival of the temperamental, cagelike elevator; he raced down the four flights of stairs, almost tumbling headlong as he set his watch to an approximation of the correct time, ran past the salon lounge into the lobby, and through the wide gilt doors opening on the Paseo.

Twenty-five or thirty feet up the Paseo from the Mirador portico a woman with her back to him and holding packages was standing at the curb rounding off the tiled sidewalk. The section of the broad avenue which served the hotel as a taxi stand was empty, but what appeared to be a car for hire was approaching at a distance of perhaps two hundred yards, followed by a stream of nondescript traffic. Damn it! If the woman took this first taxi, there was no telling how long he might have to wait. He didn't wish to appear rude, but on the off chance that she *wasn't* going to engage the vehicle now bearing down on them he stepped into the street and raised his hand. Then a shiny black Daimler touring car eased its way out of the *calle* which ran along the north side of the Mirador, turned directly in front of the taxi, and pulled to a stop in front of the woman with the packages. The taxi's brakes squealed, and the driver laid a heavy palm on his horn. The woman, with her back still toward Corey, stepped into the big car.

A somber man in a chauffeur's uniform had left the driver's seat and was holding the left rear door open. "*Gracias*, Tomás," the woman said. "La Posada Melgar, *por favor*." Even with the hubbub on the street, her voice cut through the din like a crystal bell.

Corey had no time to speculate on it. The taxi driver apparently hadn't seen him, and was backing up, preparing to swing back out into the Paseo traffic, loosing a stream of Spanish of a not too delicate sort through his open window. Corey stepped in front of the Daimler to hail him again, and as he did the touring car began rolling forward.

"Hey!" he yelled. "Watch it!"

"Tomás!" It was the woman, screaming from the rear seat of the Daimler. The big car only struck him a slight, glancing blow with its right front fender, and Corey moved away. As the car ground to a stop he caught a glimpse of its passenger, her face now just inches away from his.

He found himself looking at the woman from the train between Matehuala and the coast.

She bent her head over the side of the car. Her face, even in alarm, was, if anything, more lovely than in sleep.

"Are you all right, *señor*?" Her voice was the same bell of a few moments earlier.

He couldn't even check to see. "Perfectly all right . . ." He didn't know whether to add "*señora*" or "*señorita*," but he knew which he *hoped* it should be.

Now she was digging into a voluminous handbag. "Let me give you my card, *señor*. If you are *not* all right, I shall wish to hear about it, immediately." When she pressed the card into his hand he felt a charge of warmth from hers, even through her thin glove.

He wanted to say something more, anything—but he knew

that if he tried he would only stammer. He realized his mouth was hanging open and he closed it, feeling a fool and sure he looked one.

Then the Daimler pulled away and the taxi took its place. He read the card.

> Doña Luisa López y Montenegro
> La Posada Melgar
> Avenida Melgar
> México
> Teléfono 0801

He read the name aloud before he placed the card in his wallet.

Even in his undistinguished baritone it made music.

For Corey Lane the dinner at the ministry was, while not a failure, a thing he was sure would turn out to be a matter of no memory at all.

Narciso Trujillo was the same thoughtful, considerate scholar he remembered from 1908, but with fifteen people at his dinner he had no time for a private talk with Corey about Ángeles' or anything else, and the Huerta men, two in uniform—generals, of course; there were, Corey supposed, a plethora of these in the Federalist army—and one in mufti, drank a good deal, but gave away nothing useful.

Corey must have pulled the card from his wallet and read it five times during the course of the evening.

He fantasized about how "Luisa López y Montenegro" might sound coming from those full lips and that slender throat. Like a bell—surely.

16

As Luisa Montenegro and her driver Tomás pulled away from the Mirador she turned and glanced once more at the tall American she hadn't really looked at in the moment's instant fright. He was looking at her, too, and made a little bow when she turned.

From her first quick assessment he seemed an impressive man, a controlled, courteous man. A brush such as this with one of her own countrymen would have brought an anger-filled session of protest and probably vituperation, arm-waving, fault-finding, and even threats. She smiled. She wasn't being entirely fair. Yankees she had met abroad all too often acted that way, too, as dedicated as any Mexican to defending their persons and their presumed rights, if in less impassioned tones. If the man in the full-dress suit had wanted to make an issue of the incident it *would* have been his right.

There was no getting away from the fact that Tomás's skills as a driver left something to be desired. The old servant hadn't even learned to drive until he was well past fifty, the Daimler was still new and strange to him, and in all likelihood he hadn't taken it out on the streets of the capital in the month Luisa and Emilia had been in Durango at the *hacienda*. It would serve no good purpose to take him to task for this fortunately harmless second of inattention. She wouldn't tell Emilia about the near accident, either. Her *dueña* of twenty-two years was hard enough on her husband as it was. Away from Hacienda del Sol, Tomás didn't always function well.

There were times, not many, when Luisa feared she didn't function well herself away from home. Well, it wasn't a fear exactly; she did know she was a different woman here in the capital.

As she watched, the American climbed into the taxi which

pulled up to the hotel just behind them, keeping an intense gaze on her as he did. Which Luisa Montenegro did he see? The *doña* of the ranch, or the city-dwelling Luisa of Avenida Melgar? Sometimes, when she left the city for Durango, she was still the complete urban woman until she reached the *hacienda* gates well within the Montenegro rangeland; after her return she could remain La Doña until she had been back in the Mexico City apartment for a week.

Her mirror never distinguished between the two so different Luisas, why should she think the American might be able to?

She had never found men in Los Angeles or New York a particularly perceptive lot. How could this one differ?

The Massachusetts banker Farnum Bradley, with whom her hostess paired her at dinner that last night in Manhattan a year ago, after they all heard Geraldine Farrar sing Mimi in *La Bohème,* was a good case in point. As a matter of fact, the American she had just seen on the Paseo, tall, graying at the temples, elegant as only Englishmen and some few Yankees could be in evening dress, looked a good deal like Farnum. Her near victim's chest was bare of decorations, unusual for men wearing tailcoats and white ties in this city, particularly with Mexico fragmented by a dozen armies led by generals whose medals turned their uniforms into the *trajes de luces* of *toreros*. She had spotted him for an American when he shouted that warning "Hey!" He was surely an American businessman, an oilman or mining company executive. And yet . . . he didn't appear quite that ordinary. His steady gray eyes as he came to the side of the Daimler had looked at her as if from a great distance and across years of what? Pain? Perhaps. There was something else in the gray eyes, too, a flicker of what she might have called recognition had not the idea been so absurd. She had never seen this man before; he couldn't have seen her, either.

Idle to speculate about him. She wouldn't see him or hear from him again unless he required medical attention, which hardly seemed the case from the way he skipped out of the way of the big car, or with his erect bearing as he assured her he was all right, and the subsequent quick entrance of the taxi. She had given him her card, but hadn't asked his name. It would have scandalized Tomás had she done so, although he would never say a word about it, even to Emilia. Both old servants, inherited from her mother, thought they had unique claims on her which meant they had to keep her secrets as a matter of almost holy faith. She sometimes wondered if they didn't feel more loyalty to her than to each other.

The American who took the taxi outside the Mirador might look like Farnum Bradley, but it was only a minor physical resemblance; the deep-set eyes studying her when she handed him her card were the eyes of an entirely different man from the pompous banker from Boston with his prejudiced view of a Mexico he had never even visited.

Still, the man Tomás and she had almost run down was a *North* American, and probably as prejudiced in his own way as Farnum Bradley was.

Bradley had demonstrated a monumental ignorance of her country. As with most people she met in the United States he was fascinated by Pancho Villa, half believing in some assumed merit in the bloody depredations of the so-called Tiger of the North, half sure the revolutionary was just a glorified bandit, a picturesque character something like the Robin Hood of his childhood storybooks. Of the other figures in the struggle he knew less than nothing. He represented himself as a financier with vast international interests, but the names Madero, Huerta, and Carranza meant nothing to him.

"You seem untouched by the terrible happenings in your country, Madam Montenegro," the banker said at that dinner. "It's hard for an American to understand."

Untouched? Seething inside, she drew in her breath sharply and nearly blurted out the story of how the massacre of her family in 1910 had "touched" her, but gave the idea up in weary resignation. And an *American*? She knew she should take issue with the way he characterized himself—and by inference his fellow citizens—as the only legitimate "Americans," ignoring the fact that there were two huge continents in the Western Hemisphere teeming with millions of people who deserved the epithet as much as did any nephew or niece of that bony caricature Uncle Sam, but little as she liked it, she had finally grown accustomed to this particular conceit in her travels north of the border.

There were one or two more remarks before she divined that by "untouched" Farnum only meant that like most other Mexicans he had met, the sort who could travel to Europe and the eastern seaboard of the United States these days, she was still rich. She did offer an explanation of that.

"The Revolution has never touched Mexico equally or uniformly, Mr. Bradley. Not all the *insurrectos* hated people like me or wanted to get rid of us or strip us of our place in society. And what is going on there today is not one revolution, but many. Control of a district such as the one I live in when I'm not in Mexico City seldom remains in the same hands long. There was a big initial eruption in my state, of course, but it has swept on mostly to the larger towns and cities. The great *haciendas* are vital to our economy, and even if the Zapatistas don't realize this, the most devoted partisans of General Villa and Señor Carranza do. There were excesses to begin with, but now . . ." What was the use? The banker's eyes had glazed over. There was no way she could make him understand.

Yes, there were indeed two Luisa Montenegros. The American now speeding across her city in his taxi might have seen a little of each of them today had he known how to look. After the month's stay at the *hacienda* she was only now transforming herself back into the Luisa of the capital. Some of the Durango Luisa lingered. But "transforming herself" sounded as if it were a conscious thing. It happened to her willy-nilly.

The transformation would be completed by tomorrow without a doubt, when she returned to her work at the Ministry of Culture. She could put in a solid two weeks of studying and cataloguing the artifacts Narciso's digging team had unearthed at Cuernavaca before she left, again with Emilia in tow, for San Francisco. How many more "Americans" would she be thrown in with on this trip who would look on her as just another rich, frivolous woman "untouched" by the Revolution?

Perhaps the one she had just seen was different.

Stop that, Luisa. You will never know.

17

▲▲▲▲▲

"What is the date today, Jorge?" Trini kept his field glasses trained on the rolling desert and the blue-black smudges of the low hills surrounding Paredón, three kilometers east of the regiment's position just south of Estación Sauceda.

The morning sun still hadn't risen high enough to lift the smoke and haze cloaking the town, and its buildings shimmered and danced in the distance as if they had been cut loose from the Sierra Madre Oriental beyond it and were ready to slide into the Division's lap. If only it could be that easy. Jorge wondered what the major could possibly make out through the glasses the way things ran together in the haze, but perhaps his four years of almost constant combat had bred a special kind of vision.

"It is the seventeenth of May, Major Álvarez." No, he couldn't bring himself to say "Trini" yet, not this morning of all mornings, when he must be a soldier to the exclusion of all else. "Nineteen fourteen," he added.

"Mark it down. Remember it." Trini pulled the glasses from his eyes and turned to him. "Today you and I will ride in the greatest cavalry charge of *la Revolución*—with the brigade at the front of the first attacking regiment, Jorge. We should consider ourselves very fortunate, *honored*." Again the sadness settled around Trini's fine head, and with it a new quiet difficult to reconcile with the *commandante* he had seen as a steady stream of energy and controlled passion in the six days since the brigade boarded the troop train in Torreón. And—had a little bitterness seeped into the strong voice at the word "honored"?

It wasn't the moment to consider that too deeply. With only two hours left before the jump-off time, Trini's thoughts and emotions, as much as they meant to Jorge Martínez, had to take second place to his own. Paco, even if he hadn't been busy strapping the explosive charges to his two Kentucky mules, couldn't help him now, either.

"You are ready, Jorge?" Trini said.

¿Quién sabe? "As ready as I will be, I think."

"None of us are ever sure, *amigo*. It is new every time. Even the bravest have strange thoughts at the beginning of a battle, things we never tell each other."

"I understand, *señor mayor*."

Sí. At least he was beginning to understand—a few things, anyway. Even now, before the sound of the first shot reached his ears, before the first whiff of powder smoke hit his nostrils, he was learning the one thing all soldiers in history—from El Cid to the lowliest Castilian pikeman, from Alexander to the toughest, most battle-hardened, mercenary hoplite—had learned before him: the true, finite, physical dimensions of a war, any war, for the men who fight it.

A war was only two meters high, a meter wide, and half a meter thick—big enough to hold one man. And his fear.

Even with Trini and Paco and the men of *la tropa* close at hand, and with nearly six thousand other men and horses fanned out between burned-out Estación Sauceda and the breastworks of the enemy in the town, Jorge María Martínez was alone. No matter that thousands more guarded the section of the railroad to Saltillo, singled out for the fury of Brigade Ignacio Zaragoza, he was mortally alone. This new loneliness had announced its coming for days.

He felt cold all the time. Even in Torreón's scorching heat and in the feverish frenzy before the army's move from Torreón to Estación Sauceda, and during the move itself, inside a sweltering boxcar with Trini and the officers of the headquarters *tropa*, his body heat seemed to drop a full degree Celsius a day, and his toes and fingers became at times almost as numb as in the deepest Chupadera winter.

He didn't panic. There hadn't been any sharp or sudden

lurch of his heart, no extra beat or missing one. His stomach churned some, even when he was sure he wasn't thinking of the battle, but there was no nausea. He had functioned well in the frantic, busy days since the conference. But he never did get truly warm.

He wondered what he looked like to the officers and men he worked with as he logged in ammunition, checked rosters, brought Trini's files up to date, and listened to the major's intense but calm tutorials on the brigade's role in General Ángeles's battle plan for Paredón. But searching every face around him, he hadn't detected a glimmer in a single eye that his *compadres* found him any different.

If the old hands harbored resentment that he had come closer to their commander since the Torreón conference than any of them save Paco, he wasn't aware of that, either. Even if he still didn't know some of them by name, he discovered that he had begun to love them, and on the trip from Torreón he had also begun to learn something else every soldier learns—the fear of losing the good opinion of the men around him was as great as, if not greater than, his fear of the enemy.

But the big question still probed at him relentlessly here in the *barranca* where the horse *tropa*, the brigade, and the regiment waited for the flare of the Very pistol Trini said would send them out. If he hadn't known the white flash of panic yet, would it find him in two more hours? Would he prove a coward?

He didn't have time to frame an answer when Trini spoke. "I confess, Jorge, that although I have no reason to question our chances for success today, I would feel a little *más confianza* if Felipe's guns could talk to Paredón for a while before we ride."

The guns, *sí*. He had wondered when Trini would talk about the guns.

Every man in the regiment must be thinking about the guns.

There would be no artillery used in this attack. When the word leaked out it must have stopped the heart of the boldest of them. The guns had made the difference in the taking of Torreón. Would the lack of them today bring failure?

The decision that sobered the entire army had been announced last night at the meeting in General Ángeles's boxcar, and by General Villa himself, when he gusted in like a cyclonic wind, from Hipólito, where he and the main body of División del Norte's infantry had detrained twenty kilometers west of Estación Sauceda yesterday afternoon.

Rodolfo Fierro walked into the freight car a pace behind Villa. The smokers doused their *cigarros* and cigarettes. Ángeles took the pipe from his mouth and knocked it empty in a can of sand beside him.

Villa joked with brigade commanders Eugenio Benavides and Maclovio Herrera of "Benito Juárez," squeezed Trini's shoulder, even smiled at Jorge, and then he and Fierro took seats in camp chairs as Ángeles continued with his briefing. Fierro, Jorge noticed, only nodded to one or two of the officers; he didn't speak. He did fix his cold eyes on Trini for one long moment. In the light from the oil lamp on Ángeles's field desk and from those hanging on the boxcar walls, he looked even more threatening than he had at *la conferencia* in Torreón, if that were possible. Perhaps it was only because Jorge knew who and what he was now, and what his thin smile could mean.

Vito Alissio Robles had been giving Ángeles the report of the scouts he had led through Cañon Josefa to the end of the track here at Estación Sauceda the day before, and when Villa affably acknowledged him, he continued, but with a nervousness he hadn't betrayed a moment earlier.

"I swear the Federalistas don't even know we are here yet, Felipe. They are probably thinking we went south to Zacatecas—" Robles glanced with a little apprehension at Villa, then turned back to Ángeles. "Where we should be. Your guns are safe in their emplacements, General Ángeles." He doubled his right hand to a fist and smashed it into the curled palm of his left. The sound it made seemed to bolster him. "Velasco's garrison can't stand against them." A mutter of sublime, confident approval came from the other officers in the car.

"Felipe's guns, *sí*, Felipe's guns!" a colonel in back of Jorge said. "After the guns we can *walk* our horses in Paredón."

"*Gracias* for your excellent report, Vito," Ángeles said. He turned to Villa. "As Vito has indicated, my gunners are eager and ready, my general. They begin the first barrage at sunrise."

The Tiger of the North cleared his throat. He turned his great head from side to side, his eyes brightening as the lamplight caught them. He fixed them then on Ángeles. "*Momento*, Felipe, *por favor*," he said. "There will be one change in the battle plan."

"A change, *mi general*? At this late hour?"

"*Sí*. I want you to *save* your beloved guns tomorrow, *viejo*," he said. "There will be *no* barrage. We will not use them against Paredón—or even Saltillo when it is Saltillo's turn to fall."

There was a throaty gasp from someone standing at the boxcar's side, but except for that, the officers gathered for this last council before the battle, a moment ago outgoing and ebullient, seemed suddenly struck dumb. The oil lamps appeared to lose their power to illuminate. The car became a sickroom.

"I do not understand, *jefe*," Ángeles said.

"We can take this chickenyard *without* artillery, and when we wring the necks of its chickens and keep them from running to Maass's protection in Saltillo, we won't need the guns there, either."

He turned to Fierro. Had the man called the Butcher known of the general's decision? No. His tight smile had disappeared. He clearly was as surprised as the rest of them.

Ángeles alone found his voice.

"But *why*, General Villa? I have already moved three batteries of the 75s into position to destroy the railroad between Paredón and General Maass's forces in Saltillo. I feel it imperative that we loose the guns when he tries to reinforce

General Velasco from the south. I have also situated the lighter barriers where they can be moved up quickly to support the infantry as they attack the town itself. I feel my battle plan is sound." If he felt dismay or doubt, he didn't let either show.

Villa spread his arms as if to embrace them all. He laughed. "Of course your plan is sound, Felipe.. You are always sound. But I, too, have a plan. It will make it a little harder, but the cavalry and the dynamiters will be our artillery tomorrow." Then, his voice now trumpeting confidence, "We will use every horse and rider in the brigades of Herrera and Benavides. Not one man or animal will stay behind. We will hold none of them in reserve. We will ride to Paredón like the coming of the Apocalypse!"

"With respect, General Villa," Ángeles said.. "General Velasco has his troops dug into well-prepared positions all along the railroad. They have at least seven machine-gun companies along the tracks, and Vito's scouts have not been able to determine exactly where they are concealed. And they will use *their* field guns. Going in before my artillery softens them can cost us heavily. It is a great deal to ask of the cavalry."

"Sí. I know, Felipe," Villa broke in. "But we have asked a great deal of them many times before, *mi amigo*, and they have always answered willingly. They will tomorrow. Ask Maclovio and Eugenio now if they think their *guerreros* can do what Pancho Villa asks of them."

Benavides started to say something when Ángeles broke in again.

"There is no *need* to ask them, *mi general.* I know the answer they will give. They and their squadrons will do anything the general wishes done. *Pero con permiso,* may I ask instead why we brought my guns all the way from Torreón if we will not use them? It required a Herculean effort by Eusabio Calzado and his crews. They laid six kilometers of new track for me in just two days' time. It will break Eusabio's heart."

"Do not grieve for Eusabio, Felipe. His heart is strong

and it will mend. But you certainly have the right to ask why I have decided as I have." Villa's round face split with the smile of a big cat after a particularly satisfying meal. "I want that goddamned politician Carranza to think for the moment we are in complete agreement with him and that *bufón* Gonzáles he calls a general. His spies watched us load your guns at Torreón—*and* the ammunition they gave us out of their monumental generosity." The smile grew even broader.

Jorge, amazed at how this overpowering man could so quickly turn things one hundred eighty degrees, could feel how irresistible a force of nature the smile of Pancho Villa was! The general went on.

"But if we don't use those shells to take Paredón and Saltillo for them—something they should be doing for themselves—we can go after Zacatecas in another week— your guns all blazing gloriously—without having to plant more kisses on the asses of this so-called Primer Jefe and his timid pig. My mouth still feels smeared with shit from the ones they blackmailed out of me last week. Never again, I swear it!" He looked around the car. "How do the brave *hombres* of my Division feel about it?"

The roar shook the boxcar, the oil lamps flickered like lightning, and even Felipe Ángeles smiled.

And Jorge knew then why Pancho Villa had seemed as much a winner as had Venustiano Carranza in those final moments of the conference. He had made this decision then. And he had never doubted for a minute what the result would be when he announced it here tonight. He owned these men—every heart and soul among them.

Villa stood. The lamp on the wall behind him threw his shadow—even longer than he was tall—over the men sitting at the field desk with Felipe Ángeles like a blanketing serape.

"Until tomorrow, then, *compadres. ¡Viva la División del Norte!*"

"*¡Viva Villa!*" The explosion of it almost jarred the boxcar from the tracks.

* * *

In the last darkness before dawn, Jorge remembered that his own voice had joined the by now familiar chorus in the freight car last night with all the hot exultation he had heard in it in the depot back in Torreón.

But now, here in the *barranca* with Trini, he couldn't help wondering for a brief, well-nigh guilty moment if this kind of adulation was absolutely necessary whenever Pancho Villa so much as farted. He blushed. *For shame, Jorge Martínez! The great general is still your hero, isn't he?* If he had ever doubted this, Paco had driven his doubts into hiding one night at dinner with Juanita when Jorge asked, "Why are so many different kinds of men willing to die for the general, Paco? Don't mistake me—I have nothing but admiration for him myself—but he isn't what you could call a kind man or, the way the world judges these things, a civilized one."

"Paco can tell you why," Durán said. "Pancho is one of *us*. He is a bastard—but he is our bastard. *Nuestras*."

It must be this morning's jangled nerves that for that one moment had lured a shadow of a doubt out of hiding. Last night as Villa and Fierro left the meeting he had felt himself as fearless as a lion. When he was roused from sleep by a silent Paco, he found to his dismay that the insistent dread had returned. *Verdad,* he could use one more sight of Pancho Villa before today's charge.

The sun was now well into its full, soaring flight above the hills behind the town. The individual buildings had taken shape, but Paredón still looked asleep. Was Vito Robles right? Didn't its defenders know what was about to hit them?

Now only another hour remained before the attack began. *Dios*, but it was getting hot. *Bueno*. It might warm his frigid hands and let him grip his carbine better.

Trini had complained a little last night as they made their way from Felipe's freight car to the one with their bedrolls in it. "Without the artillery I wish we could have advanced the time for our attack. Los Bracomontes could be ready earlier.

I don't know why Romero and the other regimental chiefs can't be ready, too. It will be too damned hot by ten to sustain a full charge all the way to the tracks. We will have to walk the horses the first kilometer and a half. It will slow down Paco and the other dynamiters even more."

"Can the cavalry do it alone, *señor mayor*?"

"*¿Quién sabe?* General Villa thinks so. He is not sending us out without Felipe's guns because he wants to lose. If his judgment is good enough for Felipe, it will have to be good enough for us."

His admiration for Trini Álvarez had grown by leaps and bounds since five o'clock last Tuesday when the train pulled away from the yards and rattled eastward through the stench of month-old smoke still hanging over the wreckage of San Pedro de las Colonias, where the brigade had severed the rail lines and prevented General Maass from coming to Torreón's relief. He spent almost every waking hour at the major's elbow. As they crossed the searing griddle of the Desierto Laguna de Mayaran en route to Estación Sauceda, Trini talked about the war—the Revolution in general and the Division's part in it in particular. He was a walking text on strategy and tactics, and for a fighting Dorado as he had been until a week ago, an encyclopedia on the most esoteric military matters. His grasp of logistics and heavy ordnance was astonishing. He knew artillery tables and the rates of fire of the field guns and automatic weapons almost by heart, and his unabashed respect for the art of infantry warfare was something Jorge hadn't looked for in a dedicated *soldado de caballería*. Most Dorados, from what Jorge had heard in the weeks on the Río Nazas with Paco and the other sergeant-instructors, were reckless, cut-and-slash attackers like their adored general, with almost no concern or love for any other kind of combat.

Trini was a *student* of war as well as a practitioner-*querrero*. As the train swung through the curves beyond San Pedro de las Colonias the second morning out from Torreón, and he and Jorge sat with their legs dangling out of the boxcar's door, he talked a little about his past.

Unlike most of the commanders and almost all of the soldiers of every rank in División del Norte, who had joined Villa from civilian life as farmers, *trabajadores*, merchants, *vaqueros*, and sometimes even lawyers, Trini had always been a soldier. As a mere boy during the Porfiriato and until Díaz fell to the forces of Francisco Madero, he had been a cadet and then a teacher at Chapultepec when General Felipe Ángeles served as academy commandant. It took no leap of faith for Jorge to decide that Trini must have been a brilliant scholar-soldier, and that it was his time at the academy that had brought him to his worship of the general.

After graduating and accepting his commission, he had served first as a *lugarteniente* under the man whose armies they would fight at Saltillo and Paredón—Victoriano Huerta. It was normal, expected of a professional. "But when General Huerta had *el presidente* Madero murdered, Felipe joined the *insurrectos*. I followed him. I have never regretted it, Jorge. If Vito Robles got it right, the sector we ride into is defended by my old regiment, the 15th Mounted Guards. I fought with them and General Orozco when we took Juárez two years ago. I think I remember every man and weapon."

As he spoke he wiped his saber with a rag, looking it over from time to time, wiping it again. At last, apparently satisfied with its appearance, he brought the flat of the blade to his mouth and kissed it. "This is my graduation sword, Jorge. It was only meant for ceremonies, but it is a good, true blade. It anything should happen to me, pack it up and ship it to my father in Monterrey, *por favor*. It is an affectation for me to carry it in battle, but I truly believe it brings me luck."

There were other talks, mostly on strategy and tactics. He didn't confine the talks to Jorge. During the three last days aboard the train he held conversations with almost every *soldado a caballo* in the regiment, asking questions and listening hard, sometimes with one man alone, sometimes with groups of two or three, but never with more than five at any time. He had Jorge sit in on all of them.

If Trini's solicitations of opinions and advice from the men of his command, and his questions about their families and their spirits, were only an act, it was a good one.

Paco, on the other hand, talked little on the journey and hadn't said a thing this morning.

Since they reached this oven of a *barranca*, the giant had silently checked his blasting caps, cut fuses, wrapped a seemingly mile-long length of wire around his waist, and bound fagots of dynamite and half a dozen detonator boxes to the backs of the uncomplaining mules—all with as much deliberation as he might have shown hammering iron into shape in his blacksmith's shop back in Durango. He didn't look at all like a man headed soon into the mouth of deadly combat. As the sun climbed he became with each passing minute more and more an industrious, preoccupied worker packing his tools to move his means of livelihood from one job to another.

This line of thought, of course, led Jorge Martínez back to Paco's daughter.

He saw a good deal of Juanita in the two days following their talk by the fire.

She had come with Margarita to the siding where he and Trini, Paco, and the headquarters company of Regiment Bracomonte had boarded the train at four o'clock in the afternoon last Tuesday. A horde of women were climbing aboard the train, carrying their pots and pans, ammunition for their men—and in many cases for the rifles they obviously were prepared to use themselves, as Jorge knew they had used them in the past.

Margarita went straight to Trini's arms. Juanita tried to smile. •

"We will join you again at Saltillo, Jorge," she said. "Margarita won't, not or a while, at least. The hospital cars will move to Hipólito with General Villa as soon as they put the patients they have now on the train north to Juárez."

"You will not stay here at Torreón?"

"No. The women of the Division go almost everywhere the men go, Capitán Cucaracha. You should know that by now." *¿Qué pasa?* What had happened to him? The "Captain Cockroach" hadn't gone entirely in hiding, but the once galling epithet now seemed strangely pleasant. She went on. "I know you will be an officer soon, but, *por favor*, Jorge, listen to Papá when the fighting starts. He knows how to stay alive no matter how many bullets he attracts. And if he permits it, stay close to Trini. For all that he looks so sad, I believe his life is charmed. I want yours to be charmed as well. *Por favor*— come back."

He would stay as close to Trini as a second skin. If he wasn't yet sure of the difference between a defilade and an enfilade, he would follow Major Trinidad Álvarez even in and out of hell itself.

She had leaned toward him then and kissed him on the cheek. He reeled. No bullet from an enemy's rifle could have struck him with more stunning force. He felt it now, and rubbed his cheek . . .

Then he stopped thinking altogether.

He watched the men of *la tropa* check carbines, pistols, and saddle tack. He saw Paco Durán look toward the enemy lines. He couldn't even guess the sergeant's thoughts.

Dios. He couldn't now even know his own.

At ten minutes to ten on the morning of May 17, 1914, General Eugenio Aguirre Benavides raised his fist, dropped it again, and a thin stem of dirty, lazy smoke rose in the dry air three kilometers west of the village of Paredón in the state of Coahuila. A flower of green fire blossomed at the top of the stem, and the call to the saddle for the two main cavalry brigades of the División del Norte of General Francisco "Pancho" Villa echoed up and down six kilometers of line.

Then, seven minutes before the eleventh hour of the day, another shot from a Very pistol, blue in the blinding sun this time, brought 5,620 men and horses—if Jorge had added the figures Trini had given him correctly—together in full attack formation.

And in three short minutes more, a red flare from the pistol and the burst of a grenade sent them on their way.

Jorge María Martínez didn't know it, but a great poet, writing about a similar moment in history six hundred years before—and of just such men as those around Jorge now—had said:

"Cry havoc! And let slip the dogs of war!"

Major Trinidad Álvarez, a man with the simpler poetry of a soldier, his voice pitched low, only said, "*Vámonos*, Bracomontes!"

18

Down in the *barranca* Jorge hadn't really been conscious of how many were joining the assault.

The figures scribbled in his notebook were only cryptic ciphers. Reality was something else. When the major led them up on the mesa and the regiment closed on the right and left of them, the sight of the two brigades moving in full battle array would have taken his breath—had there been any left to take.

As far to the north as he could see over the rocky wastes and rolling sand, the attacking brigades made a rippling wall of men and horses, all advancing, but at a walk—not a gap anywhere along the line.

Except that a troop would occasionally move out ahead of its neighboring unit, only to fall back again when it reached the uneven ground of a mesquite-choked *barranca* or concealed arroyo, allowing another squadron or *tropa* to take the lead briefly before it, too, reached an obstacle, it could, for these minutes anyway, have been a parade.

Trini had said they couldn't sustain a full charge from this morning's position all the way to the railroad tracks. "We will not let them run until we close to within five hundred meters. See that the bugler stays close to me, Jorge." The bugler, on a horse almost as ridiculous as the one on whose dished back Jorge had crossed the Nazas when he was still a cockroach—*if* he no longer was—was a twelve- or thirteen-year-old boy named Tonito, unarmed, and naked to the waist.

Half a kilometer to the north, the big white hats of the Dorados bobbed above the ranks of the other horsemen of General Maclovio Herrera's brigade sealing the left flank of Regiment Bracomonte. Apparently they didn't give the smallest shit that they made themselves such a tempting target. Once Jorge thought he made out Pablo Navarro, right where Trini said he would be, well out in front of even the men of his own command. The Dorados, Trini said, were to swing to the north once the enemy at the tracks opened fire, and attack the southern edge of Paredón itself before the infantry, brought up by Calzado's trains from Hipólito during the night, sent out its first skirmishers. Trini's regiment had been posted almost on the southern flank, where the dynamiters could blow tracks, ties, ballast, and whatever rolling stock they found, and destroy a mile or more of the railroad well short of Paredón.

Behind Jorge, Paco and the two other dynamiters attached to Los Bracomontes were leading their loaded mules through the rocks and chaparral. Trini, with a smile, had told Durán just before Benavides's signal, "Don't pound along too close to our heels, *viejo*. I don't want you in the same *estado* with us if you and your toys take a direct hit." The big sergeant grunted. "Have no fear, *mi mayor*. I and my mules will stay well in back of you. Paco Durán does not relish swallowing the dust the exalted cavalry stirs up. Aagh!" It could have been the belch of a dyspeptic cougar.

They had covered something more than a kilometer by now, and he could make out the dark line of the railroad right-of-way, if they called it a right-of-way here in Coahuila. The tracks were down in a deep unscabbed gash in the desert, and the near embankment was a ready-made barricade for the Federalistas. "We can ride *to* them, but not on through, the way I would like, unless we jump the horses right down to the tracks themselves, losing some of them," Trini said. He had unfolded a map across the neck of his horse. "We may either have to rein up well short of them and fight on foot, or wheel fast when we reach them —attack once, regroup, and attack again. *Los caballos* are big, easy targets if they're not in a full charge. We have to think fast as we near them."

No matter what Paco had said, he, the other dynamiters, and the men of the battalion of infantry supporting Regiment Bracomonte were forced to chew a lot of dust. A curtain of it was rising behind the horsemen, lifted into the trembling blue of the sky to the west by a hot, tickling breeze that had slipped down the foothills beyond Paredón and the tracks. There would probably be clouds more of it when the two brigades began the charge.

In three places along the line where Jorge, not at all sure, had placed the railroad tracks, smoke was rising in thin columns bent eastward by the small wind. They must be the last flags of the Federalista breakfast fires.

Sí. There were *men* in the deep cut ahead of them, men with rifles and grenades, their chests crossed with ammunition belts exactly like the two sun-heated bands of webbing and metal now searing his own chest. The men at the tracks must be scuttling like land crabs to the rifle pits hacked out of the lip of the embankment Robles had described, checking weapons, probably steeling themselves for the artillery barrage that wouldn't come, gluing themselves to the raw ground until they were as flat as slanted cow turds. They must be praying and crossing themselves and clutching holy medals as they never had a woman. And every one of them must by now have taken that last precautionary piss he had taken himself just before Trini called them to their saddles, the one he had needed no one to warn him he must take. He had nearly forgotten that, too. It had been as if he were leaking hot drops of watery blood into the thirsty sand, his penis shamefully withered, his *cojones* swallowed up into his pelvic cavity. Had he really finished? His bladder was swelling up again. He reached down and loosened his belt a notch.

Yes, there were men waiting to kill them down there. Who had the upper hand now? In one of his lectures the major had said, "All other things being equal, the advantage lies always with the defenders of a well-prepared position. Surprise sometimes tips the scale a bit in favor of the assault. The enemy must never be granted too much time. Time, in the ultimate, Jorge, is not only of the essence, it is *everything*."

How much surprise was left? How much time had the canceling of the guns of Felipe Ángeles stolen from *this* assault?

The troop had been crossing a rare level, unbroken stretch of terrain, and for the first time had moved well in the van of the regiment and brigade. At this rate they would be at the breastworks before any other unit.

Trini called a halt and turned in the saddle.

"To arms, *amigos*," he said. "We have but another half kilometer to ride before Tonito will sound *al ataque*. It will not be the real charge, but make it look like one. I want their machines guns to open fire and begin using up ammunition even before we get in range. We will make a stop of half a minute on that sweep of white sand down there, and then go in." He leaned over, grasped the hilt of the saber jutting from the saddle scabbard, and drew it out. The blade sent the sun's rays into Jorge's eyes.

When they moved out again Trini and his mount set a brisker pace. *"Stay close to Trini."* *Sí*.

At the white sand Trini reined in smartly, and *la tropa* bunched up around him. "Spread out, spread out!" he shouted.

In a moment the horses and riders were a looser formation of dusty statues. Jorge Martínez saw everything at the enemy line in stark detail now: gunners behind the shields of field guns situated well beyond the far embankment, the heads of men in billed caps, the top of a boxcar down in the cut, and the flickering, faint blue, glinting signals that could only come from rifles in nervous hands.

Then, and he watched at the start of it with a detachment that amazed him, the first flashes from the enemy artillery on the far side of the tracks came as half a dozen quick, incandescent, miniature sunbursts. He stiffened. It was now beginning. He waited for the sound, and had to snap the reins down hard on his horse's neck to keep it still when the reports reached him. The sound wasn't what the artillery training range in Torreón had prepared him for. He was *facing* the guns now, not just listening through hands cupped over ringing ears as at Torreón when he watched from behind them, as gunnery recruits learned their trade.

The flashes had been so bright, so direct, he had been sure they were zeroed in on Trini's troop—on *him*, and he was surprised when the first shells, their explosive, angry rattle telling him they were shrapnel canisters—at least *they* sounded the same here as at Torreón—landed just short of the forward units of the brigade advancing on the left. As Trini had, Colonel Saturnino Romero had held his lead troop on the rise for perhaps the same length of time the major had halted the forward movement of Regiment Bracomonte. One quick glance told him none of Romero's men had fallen—yet. *Bueno.*

On the near embankment the Federalistas' smaller arms had begun to wink, and there was a crescendo of staccato racket. It all seemed out of kilter, with the sharp cracks completely out of timing with the flickers of orange that burned into his retinas. He could pick out the Hotchkisses readily enough. Nothing in either army could fire so rapidly. What had Trini said about the English weapon in that trackside lecture to the troop three days ago? "Hotchkiss 303. Since we use them, too, we know all about them. Good weapon for medium distances, but with an effective range of only about 450 meters. At 550 rounds per minute, it gorges itself on ammunition and overwhelms its cooling system. They jam too frequently. I can't understand the British using them in hot country like the Khyber. Heavier than our Rexers and Madsens, so not as mobile. Charge Hotchkisses straight on, as they quite often misfire when they are swung too high, as at cavalry right on top of them."

Uncanny how Trini had estimated the distance from the machine-gun nests. The Hotchkisses—there seemed to be three of them at the tracks—were stitching the desert thirty to forty meters ahead of them, spewing yellow dust and rocks up like the sandstorm on the Jornada. Safe as the troop seemed to be here on its patch of sand, could it ride through that? *No hay duda,* he would find out any second. Trini was raising the arm with the saber.

Another dazzling gleam caught Jorge's eye as Trini pushed the point of the blade down the slope.

"Tonito! *¡Al ataque, por favor!*"

Jorge lifted his reins in his left hand, and the index finger of his right slipped inside the trigger guard of the carbine.

The bugle didn't blast; it whimpered. The notes wavered in the hot air and died. He had hoped for something better from Tonito. This call would stir nothing in him.

Incredibly, the charge began.

The way the troop exploded into it made him think for a shaking second that an enemy shell had landed in its center. It didn't seem he had even set his spurs, but his horse was covering ground, *eating* it, with the rest of them. *"Stay close to Trini."* Where was he? Dust and smoke were drifting crazily. Riders surged past him, and one seemed to drive his horse into his with something almost like deliberation. *¡Mierda!* he couldn't even *find* the major.

But he found the enemy.

Things howled and shrieked past his ears. Useless to duck or dodge. Chance was everything, *ahora. Keep your eyes on that black line,* cucaracha. *Pick your spot, any spot. Ride for it!* By God he would be more than a *cucaracha* now. *Sí.*

The guns at the tracks were louder now, their reports melding into one impossibly long-lasting roll of thunder. The flashes from the muzzles of the guns he rode toward spread above the lip of the embankment like sheet lightning throbbing in the air, but throbbing red, an almost blinding red. Men fell. He didn't see them fall; he felt them. Was Trini one of them? Smoke burned his eyes, but he couldn't close them. Horses screamed. He had heard or read somewhere that the screams of battle animals sounded human. They didn't. Only the screams of men sounded human, and not all of *them.* He heard those screams, too.

Seventy-five meters short of the embankment he knew he was lost. Was this where Trini had said they might have to break off the charge? He needed no one to tell him it was a bad place to fight on foot. There wasn't a shred of cover anywhere. What had Trini been thinking of? He rode on. The carbine's stock was hard against his shoulder. He couldn't remember putting it there.

All he knew was that he hadn't fired yet. Would he do it? In the name of God would he find something to fire *at* before he died himself?

Then on the right a white gleam made a tiny slit in the wall of red. ¡Dios! Trini's saber! His left hand pulled the reins across his horse's neck, but the animal didn't turn. He twisted the reins with desperate savagery, the bit tightened in the horse's mouth and they veered toward the major.

Trini had risen in his stirrups. He kept moving toward the enemy. They wouldn't stop and fight on foot. Trini must have found a way to carry the charge right on through.

Sí. He saw it now. An arroyo hidden from sight where the troop had halted before the charge breached the embankment and opened on the tracks. It led on up the other side, a wide avenue straight to the field guns. The Hotchkisses positioned on either side couldn't be depressed enough to rake it with fire unless the gunners moved them. Once down in the cut the regiment would only have the riflemen to contend with, and even they would have to leave their positions to engage the attackers.

Trini, down in the saddle again, was riding straight for the deepest section. And then he saw what Trini planned. Once in the arroyo they could fan out and take the nests and the rifle pits from the rear. When the defenders turned on the Bracomontes, the rest of the brigade could continue the advance to the embankment head-on. And when that happened, the regiment could storm the guns on the heights across the tracks and get them out of action. With luck, Herrera's brigade could find a path as promising.

By all the saints Trini was good! It took more than studying a map to find this weakness. It took instinct—instinct, training, and those years of deadly, hard-won experience. Jorge Martínez could get there, too, couldn't he? *Sí.* If he lived. *Mierda.* He had gotten so excited he had forgotten that most of the fighting hadn't really started yet. If he forgot much more today, he *wouldn't* live.

In the arroyo the noise of battle dropped a decibel. It wouldn't stay that way long. The enemy had seen the troop and the first other units of the regiment ride in. They would move quickly to fill this gap in their defenses. Yes. Men with rifles were lining the upper banks of the arroyo even now, and at the top two Federalistas dragged a Hotchkiss through the rocks.

Trini had seen them, too. He was up in the stirrups again, and his horse was gathering its hindquarters on the lower slope. The reins were high in his left hand, and tight to the horse's mouth. It looked as if he were lifting his animal toward the struggling gunners. Jorge turned his own horse toward the narrow way. A cataract of falling rocks made him pull up short.

Trini reached the top of the arroyo just as the gunners did. The saber flashed, sliced downward on the shoulder of the nearest, a river of red gushed over the uniformed chest, and the man folded to the ground as if he were a limp, blood-soaked blanket. Trini turned his horse toward the other gunner, ten feet away from the first, and dug his heels in its flanks.

The second gunner had drawn a pistol. Could Trini reach him before he fired?

A shot rang out so close to Jorge it seemed as if it might tear his head right off his shoulders. The gunner dropped like a stone.

A wisp of smoke curled to the sky from the muzzle of Jorge Martínez's carbine.

He couldn't remember pulling the trigger. He never would.

Trini wheeled his horse around and guided it down the slope. His sword arm was crimson to the elbow.

"Don't stop now?" he shouted to the troop. "The guns. Ride for the guns!"

He didn't so much as look at Jorge.

It didn't matter.

In twenty furious minutes more—and after a thousand men had died—the División del Norte completed the conquest of Paredón, turned south to face General Maass and the Federalist forces at Saltillo, and Jorge María Martínez had become a veteran.

He still couldn't think of himself as one.

19

"Our Pancho was right as usual," Paco said. "It was easy. Too easy. I didn't get to set a charge either at Paredón or here. And where the hell are we, anyway?"

"This cow flop is called Ramos Arizpe. We're about seven miles north of Saltillo," the *yanqui* machine gunner Chambers said. "I seen better towns in China when I fought the Boxers." The gringo had been around.

"It isn't much," Paco agreed. "But Paco Durán is a fair man. He will admit their *cerveza* is of *primera clase. Sí.* First-class."

They sat at tables on the sidewalk outside an unnamed little hole-in-the-wall cantina on a side street that ran off from Ramos Arizpe's one main *avenida*—Jorge, Chambers, Paco, three other *soldados a caballo* from the troop, and the bugler Tonito, all meeting by pure chance as the Division, scattered by battle, tried to sort itself out.

Tonito, whom Paco said could have "*dos cervezas, y ya,*" had been the last casualty of the day back up the line at Paredón. It wasn't much of a wound, but the youngster was still hurting. Hurting, but proud of it. His upper lip was split, and as swollen as if he had walked into a stinging punch. He had lost part of a front tooth, too. One last stray bullet from the Federalistas had struck his bugle just as he lifted it to his lips to sound assembly for Trini after they had taken the surrender of the men at the field guns above the railroad tracks. The impact had jammed the bugle back into Tonito's mouth. For a moment they had all thought him dead.

For all his execrable bugling, it could have been the troop's most lamented loss. He had been a sweet, smiling puppy all the way to Paredón from Torreón. He reminded them every chance they let him get a word in that he was the only one of the seven of them sitting here to take any kind of hit. "Trini says I will get a medal after he tells the general all about me." Well, there was no harm in letting him revel in his ridiculous "wound" to the hilt. He probably wouldn't drink more than the two beers Paco allowed him, anyway, the way he winced when he lifted the first bottle to his tender mouth. They would have to find the kid another bugle somewhere.

A doddering old man was serving them another tray of beer and tequila. A pretty young girl had brought the first, three rounds ago. Chambers had made a lunge for her that she avoided as adroitly as a *torero* would a faulty bull, and one of the cavalrymen, Sena, had whistled and made suggestive gestures. They hadn't seen her since, nor had the man and woman who seemed to own the cantina put in an appearance. They had sent *el viejo* out to look after the tables filling up with straggling Villista *guerreros* while they were doubtless packing the girl off to relatives for the duration of the Division's stay. Smart. Even Jorge had looked at her with a healthy appetite, but only as a reminder of someone else. Not that he needed a reminder.

Juanita Durán hadn't been on any of the three trains he and Paco met. Hundreds of *soldaderas* tumbled out of the crowded boxcars, but the slim-armed, black-eyed daughter of Paco wasn't among them. The brakeman on the last one said there wouldn't be anything else coming down the line from Torreón, Hipólito, or Parras de la Fuente until morning. He didn't want another beer now, nor food, but what else was there to do?

There was, he discovered, lots to do. There was soldier talk to be made. He found he needed it.

"You just said it was easy, Durán. Easy for you, maybe, you big, stupid fat-ass," the trooper Jorge knew only as El Sapo said. "You didn't have to do any fighting at either place." With his bulging eyes and bloated, warty cheeks he certainly did look like a toad.

Paço ignored him. He turned to Jorge. "What exactly is going on, Captain Cockroach? What did Trini have to say before he went to see General Ángeles?"

"There will be no battle for Saltillo. General Maass has apparently decided to fall back on San Luis Potosí. His engineers are ripping up the railroad as they pull away."

The sergeant exploded. "*¡Mierda!* There won't be any work for me to do in the whole goddamned campaign. When do we move south to finish them?"

"We don't. We just occupy Saltillo."

"Mother of God! We're missing a big chance. How long will we stay there?"

"Only until General González and the Coahuilans march in and take over from us. Three or four days, maybe."

"What?" It was the American. "You mean a lot of good guys died just so we could turn everything over to Carranza and his bastards? Jesus! What a way to fight a war."

Jorge shrugged. "I suppose General Villa has his reasons. He must be thinking of Zacatecas now." *Sí,* a lot of "guys" had died. Enough in the Division; many, many more among the Federalistas.

The reports Trini passed along to him after the first postbattle meeting with the other regimental commanders were sketchy, but sobering enough. Herrera, whose brigade had fought off a flanking movement by the Huertista cavalry with a brilliantly smashing countercharge, had lost about 170 men, and Brigade Ignacio Zaragoza's dead numbered more than 220, the last Trini heard. Bad, but the figure wasn't expected to get much higher when all the units reassembled and totaled their losses up. The hoped-for surprise had been very nearly a complete one, and the infantry had gotten off almost scot-free of casualties.

Federalista dead were variously estimated as 1,100 and 1,300. With Maass taking in the few of Velasco's men who escaped the Division roundup, and absorbing them into his own demoralized army, it was unlikely anyone would ever know what the true number was. No one had as yet counted the wounded among those of the enemy captured. More than 2,000 other able-bodied, unscathed prisoners were taken.

And all this in thirty-seven minutes.

Easy? From a military standpoint he supposed it was. Trini had said so, too.

"Much better than I dared hope for, Jorge. We are in superb shape to move on Zacatecas in a week or two, or whenever Felipe and General Villa decide."

Villa himself had ridden to the high ground where the Bracomontes had secured the Federalista field guns and their crews: disconsolate, thoroughly cowed men who had simply stepped away from their weapons and raised their hands in the air when the troop and the rest of the regiment rode up and out of the arroyo.

"Splendid work, Major Álvarez . . . Trini," he had boomed. "After we do a little housekeeping here, we shall send another message to General Maass down the line." That, of course, had been before they learned that Maass didn't intend to make even a token stand at La Fortaleza in Saltillo. Jorge wondered what the general meant by "housekeeping," and he didn't find out until much later in the day. For the moment he was content to glory in the presence of Pancho Villa, the eternal victor.

But now, sitting in the sun with six other "victors," he began to learn still another lesson.

Few soldiers know exactly what they have done in battle, sometimes not even what they felt while doing it, until they have talked it over with the men they shared the action with and relived all the real and dream sequences of the nightmare it always is.

"You looked pretty fucking sure of yourself, the way

you rode, Martínez," El Sapo said. "Don't you have any nerves? Today was my fifth time out, and I still pissed my pants."

Nerves? Should he tell the toad that the first thing he did when the firing stopped was to check his own pants, front and rear? He could have filled them with shit for all he knew. He said nothing.

"I saw a horse take a direct hit from the field guns," Sena offered. "Never saw so much dog meat in one place in all my life—and not one dog to get it."

That must have happened well back up the last slope before the tracks. He hadn't see it, but he saw too many things that would come back to haunt him like the unhorsed *guerrero* in the arroyo, jerking around in circles with his hands covering eyes Jorge knew at once would never see any of the things *he* saw—ever again. Blood oozed thick ribbons from between the trooper's fingers and his mouth opened and shut and his throat worked as if he were trying to swallow a piece of gristle.

And there was the victim of Trini's saber—this was on the ride away from the assembly point and just before they started for Ramos Arizpe—lying in the gumbo his blood made of the sand, the wound as big as the raw mouth of Jorge's horse.

He looked in vain for the machine gunner he had fired his carbine at. Maybe he hadn't killed him, after all. No. He had been dead, all right. He needed no "experience" to tell him that. One of the gunner's fellow soldiers or a man detailed from the Division must have dragged the body to the pile of corpses on the lip of the embankment. He rode to the grotesque heap of dead, still looking. Would he even know him if he saw him? He saw two men from *la tropa*, a Corporal Luis Santander and a seventeen-year-old boy named Emilio whose last name he didn't know. Machine-gun fire, probably, had all but sawed through Emilio's upper torso. A Bracomonte had found a can of gasoline and was drenching the inert figures. He didn't hang around to watch him set a match to them.

Yes, they had to burn them, friend and foe alike. The sun began to cook men to a foul stew only seconds after life left their brains. As rapidly as the disposers of the obscene detritus of war worked, the field stank like a million untended, brimming outhouses by the time the sun reached its zenith.

Not one *norteño* ate so much as a *chorizo* until they had moved well south of the battlefield. A pull from a canteen was sickening enough, no matter how much a man needed water—and Jorge Martínez needed it a lot by then. He filled himself from his toenails to his throat. His desiccated tissues would sponge the lukewarm water up before a drop of it could turn to piss.

"Did anybody get a good look at the Dorados?" Chambers said. "Where I was, gunning down getaways, I couldn't see them at all."

"I did," Tonito said. Pride in the "wound" notwithstanding, his eyes had still been wide with fear and as round as baked tortillas ever since they got here. "*El capitán* Navarro used a sword like Major Trini's. He killed three soldiers with it when the Dorados reached the tracks. Slice, slice, slice. It was *magnífico*!"

Terrified as he must have been, the boy bugler had probably gotten a better overall picture of the fighting than any of the rest of them. Loping along well behind the attacking regiment, as Trini had made it clear he was to do, his vision would certainly have been more encompassing than that of men intimately, agonizingly involved—busy as insane army ants making up that picture. The more grisly sights perhaps blessedly blanketed out, it must have seemed just an adventure story come to life to innocent Tonito.

"Fierro must have been in seventh heaven by the middle of the afternoon," Paco said. "He led more than a hundred Huertista officers to the wall." He mimed a pistol with his hand and fanned it with his huge thumb. "Rodolfo Fierro is an *hombre* who truly enjoys his work."

"*Sí.* The 'housekeeping.' "

Before Trini had left him for his meeting with Ángeles and

the commanders of the brigade's other regiments, he had confided one last thing to Jorge. To his mild horror, it explained the general's use of the harmless-sounding word.

"General Villa has invoked the Law of Juárez, Jorge. Actually the Law was revived by El Primer Jefe Carranza months ago, but until today the general has not seen fit to enforce it to the letter."

There was no point in asking what the Law of Juárez was. Since Torreón the major had been forthcoming enough about everything without Jorge's questions.

"According to the Law," Trini said then, "all officers taking up arms against the Constitutionalist government of Don Venustiano pay the extreme penalty. No exceptions. Colonel Fierro will take charge of the executions. Thank God he had his own firing squads, so regular *soldados* won't have to do it." Trini, the stalwart soldier who had wielded the "true blade" of honor without a qualm, looked ill. "General Villa said that since Paredón was supposed to be the Carrancitas' fight we would do it *their* way. He said he wanted to make Señor Carranza happy."

The American Chambers had a word to say about that.

"Way I figure it, Pancho decided that if he shot them all, he wouldn't miss any of the Orozquistas. You don't fuck with Pancho Villa."

Orozquistas? Jorge looked at Paco.

"General Orozco's officers. Our Pancho has never forgiven Orozco for turning against Madero."

He remembered now. José Clemente Orozco had been the other general when Villa took Juárez—an age ago. Hoping for a loftier post in Madero's government than the new President offered him after the triumph over Díaz, Orozco had sat out Huerta's successful grab for power, refused to take arms against the usurper, and then, after Madero's death at Guzmán's filthy hands, had joined Carranza. Somehow the First Chief, until now, had kept Villa from killing him. Strange, Trini, Jorge remembered, too, had served under Orozco once. Things didn't stay the same in this *Revolución*.

The sun had dropped beneath the rooftop of the building across the *calle* from the cantina. Jorge still had to find a place to lay his head tonight—here in Ramos Arizpe. He wanted to meet every train as it came in. Somehow he had masked his elation at the way he had made it through his first embrace of combat. Of course he would let *her* know, *sí*. And if she knew, that would be enough. Paco and Trini would understand. It had happened to them somewhere along the line. It was a thing a man didn't talk about. But it was there.

"I've heard a rumor that we'll have a big parade when we reach Saltillo in the morning," Sena said.

Chambers spit out a mouthful of tequila. He rolled his blue *yanqui* eyes to the sky.

"Shit!" he said. "Almost makes me wish we lost."

20

Two morning trains arrived, the first from Parras de la Fuente. Juanita wasn't on it. When the second one wheezed in on the feeder line from Hipólito, and the girl still didn't appear, Paco found one of Eusabio Calzado's men eating his breakfast on a flatcar while the locomotive—which looked like something out of Jorge's grade school history book—took on water. The man greeted Paco with a hearty *abrazo*. Every man in the army seemed to know the Bracomonte dynamiter.

"That Nuevo León railroad sergeant says she is at Hipólito with Margarita and the hospital cars," he said when he returned to Jorge. "I might have guessed. *Mierda*. She is playing nurse again, instead of looking after her helpless little father." He smiled at Jorge. "Hector says no more trains will stop here at Ramos Arizpe. They'll roll right on through. Let's get aboard this one and get down to Trini in Saltillo. He will skin us alive if we're not back with *la tropa* when that goddamned parade begins. One of the hospital cars will move to Saltillo this afternoon. Hector thinks it will be the one with her and Margarita. *Vámonos.*"

They found their field bags on one of the three battered trucks that ferried the regiment's smaller gear across the desert, swung them aboard the flatcar with the Nuevo León sergeant Hector, and hoisted themselves up beside him. Jorge checked his over. Nothing seemed missing. The book, he was relieved to find, was still where he had tucked it under his extra shirt. Sergeant Hector, sounding disappointed, said he hadn't seen anything of the battle for Paredón. "I was so far back, loading ammunition, I hardly heard the Federalista guns." He had a million questions. Jorge let Paco answer as they rolled south toward Saltillo. He had his own thoughts. He only glanced at the countryside they passed through, a section of small farms crowded against each other for the full ten kilometers to the yards at what would be his first real Mexican city since Juárez. Workers waved to the train. The crew of the Madsen machine gun mounted at the back of the flatcar fired a burst in the air in reply, laughed like fools when three *campesinos* in a spring-green field flattened themselves against the soil with the reflexes of trained *guerreros.*

He was getting a headache, and his face was burning. He had taken a lot of sun these past few days. He pulled himself up to walk a few unsteady paces and stretch his legs. Back near the Madsen six *soldaderas* huddled around their few belongings, the familiar enameled pots, red and blue bandanas stuffed with maybe one change of clothing and tied to sticks like the pokes he had seen hobos carry along the Southern Pacific tracks south of Black Springs. Three of the women had the inevitable chickens from the flocks wandering the encampment at Torreón. All of them were singularly ugly women, none of them, he supposed, truly old—in years. But they looked *aged*, like the meat hanging in the butcher shop in Mex Town. One had a mustache nearly as heavy as his own. Crones like this sad half dozen couldn't possibly share the same sex with . . .

For shame, Martínez. Uncharitable . . . unworthy of a man who claimed the same cause as these *pobrecitas* did.

Stacked crates split most of the flatcar down its middle and he sank down with his back against one of them, on the other side from the *soldaderas*. He had no strong wish to go back and listen to Paco tell Sergeant Hector-whatever-his-last-name-was the story of the battle. For the moment all he wanted was to be left alone with his own banked but burning thoughts. None of the women appeared to have noticed him. He put his head in his hands.

The women's voices rose above the grinding of the wheels.

"You are sure he's dead, Rubia?"

"*Sí.* There is no doubt. His *amigo* Ricardo came and told me."

"*Bueno.* They don't often bother. *Falta de tiempo,* they always say. How did he die?"

"A sniper. Ricardo says he felt *nada.*"

"He was your fourth?"

"*Sí.* And the second longest. Six weeks. Since before Torreón."

"We should keep score, Rubia. I am on my fourth, too, *if* I find him at Saltillo." This was a third voice. Laughter.

"Urbino was the best." The one called Rubia again.

"We always say that when they are gone."

"He was the best, *verdad.*"

"He never beat you?"

"Of course he beat me. But he *was* the best. I say it—and I know. He was kind. And he wasn't always after my cunt the way the first three were. And when he was he said nice things about me in the night."

"You will find another. Maybe that *niño* who got on at Ramos Arizpe with the big sergeant. He looks serviceable. He might even last a few months. Sometimes they do. If not . . ."

He could feel the woman's shrug almost as much as he felt his own shiver of embarrassment. He turned over to his hands and knees and started to crawl to the front of the car. *Dios,* how his head hurt. One last exchange reached him.

"What will you do after the war, Henriqueta?" A new voice.

"There will be no 'after the war.' Such thinking is for *los hombres.* For us there will be no such thing." Henriqueta didn't sound bitter—just practical.

Paco and the railroad sergeant Hector were laughing about something when he reached them.

He didn't feel much like joining them. His stomach felt a little queasy, and when he put his hand to his forehead it was like a stove. Sunburn or fever? *¿Quién sabe?* Things would be better when they reached Saltillo. Things would be much, much better when Juanita got there, too.

The same cacophonous brass band with the old fiddler which had committed such mayhem on the music at the conference in Torreón led the Saltillo victory parade. Nothing, not the train trip, the ten days during which they presumably could have practiced, nor the echoes from the triumph of Paredón, had done a thing for their musicianship. No onlooker complained out loud, but there were mouths twisted in sourness as the violinist tried to play while marching, the bow popping off the bridge of his instrument with each lurching step, and the horns lagging lamentably behind even this faltering lead. Jorge thanked his *estrellas* that when the Bracomontes finally rode into the line of march, they would be so far behind they would be almost out of earshot. Tonito, if he could find another bugle, would fit in nicely with these dismal minstrels, who had added a disastrous drum to their ensemble since Torreón. Every beat of it brought back the headache that had started on the train.

A second band stepped smartly in to the *avenida* just before the regiment took its place. A purple banner with a message in silver script proclaimed that this was a local outfit, the absolute pride of Ciudad Saltillo. They were pretty good. Trini remarked that Villa partisans in the town said they had played as well for General Velasco six weeks earlier, when the general and his Federalista forces had entrained for Paredón for their ostensible resistance to Venustiano Carranza's Coahuilans. "Fierro wanted to shoot at least some of them this morning, as an example," Trini said, "and General Villa was inclined at first to let him have a trumpeter or two, but when they auditioned for him and played 'Adelita' to perfection, he relented. Good thing. The trumpets are the only relatively weak second of this band." He laughed. It all seemed one great *burla*. This wasn't the same Trini who looked so sick yesterday in speaking of the executions of the Huertista officers. Perhaps he had less affection for musicians than he had for soldiers of any uniform.

Pancho Villa hadn't as yet appeared for the parade. Another black touring car, not from the motor pool at Torreón, but commandeered here in Saltillo in all likelihood, the engine running, was parked at the parade marshaling point, awaiting the arrival of the general.

"Any second," the word went out. The resplendent Dorados waited near the motorcar.

The brigade commanders were already riding with their men down the *avenida*, which was surprisingly wide and graceful for a city the size of the Coahuilan capital. There were ceramic tile inlays in long sections of the sidewalks, and two lines of ancient chestnut trees stretched all the way to La Fortaleza, the medieval-looking stronghold that was the town's biggest structure—larger even than the cathedral—where the parade would break up and where Villa planned a dinner for his staff—and the international press, who had swarmed to Saltillo from every point of the compass.

Every general, colonel, and major of the Division had cheerfully answered Villa's call for a command performance this morning—with one exception. Jorge hadn't caught so much as a glimpse of General Ángeles. He mentioned it to Paco, and Trini overheard him.

"Felipe is on his way back to Torreón with his artillery," the major said. "Apparently General Villa wanted him to get everything ready for Zacatecas. He doesn't care much for parades, anyway. Nor do I, if the truth were known."

Dislike for parades ran from top to bottom and through the middle, then. General Felipe Ángeles, the *yanqui* Chambers, and the otherwise dedicated Major Trini Álvarez, all had at least this much in common.

The journalists and photographers invited to General Villa's dinner weren't the only ones covering the parade for a watching world. As Jorge rode the parade route next to Trini, he saw motion-picture cameras with their tripods up on platforms or anchored in the beds of trucks, with men in riding breeches and boots, their soft caps turned backward, cranking away like mad. The legends on the black, metal-bound boxes that were stacked around them said that most were from American newsreel production companies. One of the cameramen suddenly swung his camera straight toward Jorge. His heart stopped. He was still a wanted man. He turned away in a flutter of uneasiness, slid his sombrero from his head, and covered the side of his still-burning face.

¡Dios! What sort of foolishness was this? There was no cinema theater back in Black Springs, and if Corey Lane did happen to see the film someday, somewhere, what in the name of God could the sheriff do about it? The Jorge Martínez whom Lane had chased the length of the Jornada del Muerto, and finally cornered momentarily in Chihuahuita in El Paso, was now almost a thousand miles inside Old Mexico, a soldier in a foreign army locked in combat, as safe from Chupadera County law as if he were fighting on another planet. Safe, *sí,* but not feeling too damned strong at the moment, in spite of the adrenaline loosed by this morning's celebration. Something ticked painfully in his head, and his face and neck were even hotter than before.

Along the parade route men and boys were waving the flags of Coahuila, and women—two out of three in the throng *were* women and not grim or sad-eyed *soldaderas*, either— were dancing on the sidewalk, cheering, blowing kisses, swaying hips and swinging skirts in time to the sounding brass of the Saltillo band. Brown legs flashed gold in the morning sun. Little girls ran to the horses of the officers and offered up bouquets of flowers. Had all this happened six weeks ago when the stylish band now jaunting along in front of them had blared its way up this same *avenida* ahead of the troops of General José Refugio Velasco? Had they decked his *soldados* with posies, too, and had the women almost throwing themselves at the Bracomontes now made the same advances to the Federalistas?

Behind him the cries of *"¡Viva Villa!"*—repeated over and over again, rising gloriously in the air above all the other cheering, and even topping the heavy drumming of the horses and the insistent booming beat of the music—told him Pancho Villa had come in sight. He turned to look, but he couldn't see through the squadrons of cavalry on his and Trini's heels.

The headache was more penetrating now.

His head swam suddenly, and his eyes blurred. *Dios*, was he going blind? He closed his eyes hard, forcing his upper lids down into his fevered cheeks.

When he opened them again, he opened them on sights and sounds he knew at once he could never talk about—to anyone.

The dogs of Torreón raced into sight.

Not dogs *like* the dogs of Torreón, but the *very* dogs, the same dogs he had seen as he and Trini had ridden to the conference in the railway station his first day as Trini's aide. It seemed impossible, but he recognized the silky whippet and the imperturbable, aristocratic wolfhound of the encampment, could recall with perfect, crystal clarity the markings on the slavering, spotted cur his horse had nearly trampled into the plaza's dust. Scores of remembered mongrels of all shapes, sizes, and canine inclination ran between the horses' legs, became hundreds suddenly. How had they gotten here? Some powerful *brujo* had been at work, one who could summon with his black magic an instant transport far more complete and effective than Eusabio Calzado's ever were. It was crazy, but there they were. He must be going *loco*. He closed his eyes again. He had to blink all of this away.

When he opened them the second time nothing had changed—except that the dogs had multiplied and were now running out of doorways all along the *avenida*. They dropped like hairy leaves through the branches of the chestnut trees and jumped snarling to the street from rooftops. They streamed from *calles*, poured out of alleys in twos and threes and packs of fifteen, twenty, thirty, fought each other in savage struggles, pissed on the women dancing on the sidewalk, rammed their noses up each other's asses, and fornicated in frenzied couplings. Some bit children, others worried chunks of bloody meat they carried in their jaws. They foamed purple at the mouth, and they howled and yapped and barked and bayed, and hunched their yellow, mangy backs in contortions of seeming agony as they shit in legions, dropping oleaginous green turds into the placid flower beds between the trees . . .

Not a soul in all that crowd save Jorge María Martínez saw them. The men and boys kept right on waving. The urine-soaked legs of the dancing women flashed with even wilder gaiety and abandon than before, smiling children patted the flea-infested heads of vicious beasts even as they sank their teeth in their tender flesh . . .

The chants of "*¡Viva Villa!*" rose to rhapsodic heights, ringing in his ears like the doom tocsin peals of a monster *campana encantada*.

His vision dimmed again. He felt himself sliding from his saddle, powerless to stop the fall.

Before he hit the ground the world went black . . .

The whispers came to him through a long, dark tunnel where inky water dripped into unseen pools.

"The fever broke late this afternoon, Juanita. While you napped." It was a moment before he knew the voice. Margarita.

"Why didn't you wake me, Margarita?"

"You needed *your* rest. You were up with him all night."

"He is well now?"

Silence. Then, "Yes. It wasn't all that serious. He is almost at full strength again."

"But he raved so, and for so long."

"Only part of that was from the fever."

"Only part?"

"Yes. I have seen this before, Juanita. Men pretend it doesn't happen."

"Will he be all right?"

"Yes, if he understands what has gone on with him. Rest will help, of course. But the only real, lasting medicine would be for him never to have to fight again. Too much to hope for, *cariña*. They never stop."

"But you just said he is no longer sick."

"He isn't. Not in the way we think of sickness, anyway. But in a way, it's worse than malaria or dysentery. Physically, he is as strong and well as ever. You might call it an exhaustion of the soul. He fought his fears even harder than he fought the enemy. It must have begun many days ago. He probably had no way of knowing it was coming on. Do not think badly of him. He possesses the highest kind of courage. Something like this may never come again."

"What can I do?"

"You love him, don't you? I sometimes think love is the *only* cure." Silence. Then, "I must get back to the hospital now. I will come back here in the morning. Paco was lucky to find a place so quiet for him."

He heard a door close, and it was a jolt against the wall of shame that had risen in him. The highest kind of courage? He felt weak and craven—worse and despicably lower than a cockroach. What was old Paco's assessment of him now? And Trini's? Even young Tonito would spit upon him through his cracked, bruised lips and swollen mouth. El Sapo had wondered if he had no nerves. In a way the toad cavalryman was right. He had nothing.

But he would have to face them—and Juanita.

He forced his eyes open.

She was standing by the door. He wanted to look about

him and determine exactly where he was even before he asked, but first he had to look at her, even if he dreaded it. Their eyes met, and he saw in hers the things she had hidden in those few times when she turned away before. She was letting him see them all now.

Then she was walking toward the bed he was lying on.

"Can you move over a little, Capitán Cucaracha," she said, "and make room for your *soldadera*?"

He trembled—but he moved. He watched her lift the blouse above her head, heard the skirt rustle to the floor. She slipped beneath the coverlet.

And the war, not the war outside this room, but the war in the mind and soul of Jorge María Martínez, *soldado de caballería*, went into hiding for a while.

PART 3

▲▲▲▲▲▲▲▲▲▲

THE
RISING
TIDE

21

"I have them right here in me wee hand, laddie!" Fergus Kennedy shouted to Corey Lane across the crowded dining room of the Hotel Mirador. It was the first tremor of excitement he had seen in the little Scotsman in the week they had known each other. Heads turned as Kennedy ran half the length of the room, but the diners turned discreetly back to their plates as he took the chair across from Corey. His sharp, bony face was flushed. "General Tenorio signed our permits an hour ago. I would have been here sooner, but I stopped at the railway station and booked our berths. Ye'll want to pay me for yours right away, of course, won't ye?"

Corey smiled, reached inside his coat, and brought out his wallet. Fergus Cameron Kennedy was almost a comic-strip rendering of the thrifty Scot.

He handed Kennedy a pair of banknotes. As the Scot made change to a centavo from a small leather purse with a clasp rubbed down to the brass, Corey said, "When do we leave?"

"Ten o'clock in the morning. If we can believe the booking agent. He says it will be a straight-through train, no changes all the way up to Zacatecas, and no long delays. I'll believe that when I see it. Tenorio's aide telegraphed Medina Barrón's headquarters and they'll be waiting for us. I went by the Ministry of Security, too, and got permits for our handguns."

"Do you honestly think we'll need guns, Fergus?"

The Scotsman patted the side of his bulky Harris tweed jacket, and Corey thought of how sweltering it must be inside such a horse blanket on a day like this. His own light gabardine coat was uncomfortable enough in the June heat of the city. "I always carry a gun, Corey, permit or no permit. But since we'll be up beyond the relatively civilized environs of the capital, it might be nice if I was a wee bit legal for once.

Suit yourself about whether ye'll want a gun or not. I thought ye might, since ye come from the wild West."

Fergus's weapon was probably a Webley, or one of the other small English makes, with nothing like the bulk of the Colt .45 automatic Cobb had pressed on Corey in El Paso—and which he had stuck in the bottom of his valise under his writing case, wondering which of the two was more likely to get him into trouble. He certainly hadn't needed a weapon of any sort till now. With luck he never would. He didn't doubt for a second that the thorny Scottish thistle sitting across from him knew how to use one.

Right now the thing that most occupied his mind was the question of whether or not Henry Richardson would approve of this junket if he knew about it. He couldn't very well telephone Henry or Cobb and ask. Sending reports, even by the circuitous, if so far secure, routing through Lemuel Cotter at Ticknor & Fields, was risky enough. To place a call he would have to go to the Mexico City telephone exchange, make his report within the hearing of a horde of eavesdroppers, probably.

Actually, Henry should be overjoyed Corey would now monitor the battle for Zacatecas from the close-in vantage point he would have as a guest of Huerta's General Medina Barrón. He might feel a touch sticky about Corey's being there in the company of Kennedy. The British were friends, sure, but to be spending a week or more in close quarters with a man Corey had now identified as a full-fledged agent of His Majesty's Government? "Simply not done," Henry would be bound to say.

He had met Fergus at the saloon bar here in the Hotel Mirador several days ago. The Scot represented himself as a buyer of Mexican beef for a meat broker in Liverpool. Corey had, at first, bought the man's story readily enough—come to think of it, he had bought every one of Fergus's Scotch and sodas at the bar that night as well—and he had been pretty damned sure Fergus had swallowed *his* cover story, even as he swallowed the whisky that seemed to have absolutely no effect on the vinegary little man.

His first clue Fergus was other than he claimed came in the lounge of the Mirador an evening later, when the Scot inveigled him into a game of whist with two guests of the hotel—for stakes so minuscule they might as well have wagered matchsticks. The other two players were an elderly couple up from Morelos, a *hacendado* named Don Fernando Salazar and his wife, Celestina, burned out of their *estancia*, Salazar said, by a splinter group of *insurrectos* who were linked to the "Attila of the South," Zapata.

As Don Fernando offered the deck for the cut, Fergus apologized for his lack of Spanish. "Never have learned a word of it, I'm ashamed to say. We're terrible with languages in Ayrshire, and I'm the worst. No skill with tongues at all."

The Scotsman kept score, and in the middle of the third rubber, Corey, the least accomplished player, asked to see the pad before entering his bid. *"No skill with tongues."* Perhaps. But Fergus had noted the names of their companions, and the score, in a distinctive, graceful hand, a "bonnie bit of copperplate" Kennedy himself might call it.

It was a pleasant game. When they finished and the Salazars said *buenas noches*, Corey and Fergus repaired to the bar for a nightcap. Fergus ordered his "wee drap," excused himself, and headed for the men's room. Corey paid the check, not too terribly put out at how the little tightwad had slickered him again. Then he noticed a scrap of paper in front of Fergus's barstool that must have dropped from his pocket. He bent over and picked it up.

It was a scribbled note *in Spanish*, with several names and addresses of people who all appeared to be high muck-a-mucks in the Ministry of War, written in the same unmistakable hand Corey had seen on the score pad. Fergus had appended remarks, also in Spanish, after each of the names.

There was nothing particularly damning about it—except that the Scotsman had denied any facility with Spanish. Certainly he would need the native tongue in his dealings with Mexican beef suppliers. But why the lie, if it was one?

He felt himself a sneak, but he watched Kennedy like a hawk the next day and a half, wondering how much of an effective spy he could be if he still harbored such fastidious aversion to looking over someone's shoulder. The second morning, when he found Fergus getting his pebble-grained Peale's boots blacked by the *mestizo* shoeshine boy in the hotel's side arcade, he slipped behind a potted palm and watched him for a second. When the boy finished with him, Fergus dropped the copy of *La Prensa* he was reading—obviously the property of the shoeshine stand—and began haggling over the price of his services, in Spanish of an easy, arcane, and comfortably colloquial fluency.

Corey's first instinct was to maneuver Fergus into an inadvertent or outright admission that he did speak Spanish, and find the reason for this perhaps harmless duplicity, but decided, no; that might prompt questions in return *he* wouldn't want to answer. So he kept watching.

The day after the "great surveillance at the shoeshine stand," as he called it in his mind, he spotted Fergus at the bar with Antonio Encínias, one of the Mexican government "sources" Cobb had told him to look up when he arrived in the capital, and whom the El Paso agent said was "about fifty percent reliable. Officially he is an information officer for one of Huerta's top people. Only use him as a last resort, but introduce yourself only under your cover as a writer, Lane, and give him about one-third the pesos he asks for. You won't like him. An amateur such as you won't like many of the people I put you in touch with." Corey hadn't. The informer struck him as a sleazy cutpurse. He paid him the expected retainer, but to date had not availed himself of the man's services—and hoped at the time he would never have to. Pity he had to now.

He waylaid Encínias on his way out of the bar. He held a twenty-peso note out to him, but kept a tight grip on it.

"Who was that *hombre* you were talking to, Antonio?"

"Señor Kennedy? A friend. He buys beef cattle for the big English market." Encínias fidgeted but eyed the money lustfully. Corey pulled out another bill and put it with the first. Encínias gulped. "I think perhaps he is a spy for the British."

Corey held the money fast. "What did he want of you?"

"He wanted to know about you, Señor Lane."

"What did you tell him?"

"*Nada*. That I knew nothing." A lie, of course, but it told Corey as much as would the truth. He let Encínias have the money, and the Mexican hurried off like a footpad.

So Fergus had suspicions about him, too. Not too disquieting—in this case. Despite Woodrow Wilson's passionate neutrality about European politics, Henry had let slip a couple of things about how Washington and London worked together, even in matters only concerning the Western Hemisphere. But it meant that any minimal trust he had put in Encínias's discretion would have to be withdrawn. If he guessed Corey was anything but the historian Corey had told him he was, Encínias would sell him to Huerta as quickly as he had sold him to Fergus, and as cheaply. The next bidder for information about Corey Lane might not be a *British* agent.

He forgot about any possible bearding of Fergus Kennedy. It was enough that he knew the exact status of the Scotsman, and perhaps could turn the knowledge to his advantage— once he knew where his advantage lay. And if he eventually tried, he had better not forget that Kennedy was in all likelihood an experienced player in this game, certainly in possession of skills far more professional than the meager gifts of a backcountry peace officer turned foreign agent overnight.

After the talk with Encínias he sought Fergus out with even more regularity than he had before, and gradually it became apparent that the "beef buyer" had constructed a similar strategy for dealing with the American "historian."

At dinner two nights ago Fergus said, "I've been giving a wee bit of thought to something that might interest a historian like you, laddie. I've got to go a few miles north of here Monday to see a rancher about a shipment of cattle I've bought, and I thought it might be amusing to poke along a wee bit farther and see what Pancho does to the Federals at Zacatecas. Fancy tagging along?"

"Couldn't we get caught up in the fighting?"

"Don't think so. Barrón has a clear line of safe retreat even if he takes a bad whipping, something that's by no means certain. It will be the big battle of the campaign. I should think ye'd not care to miss it."

He promised Fergus an answer in the morning, but before the two of them finished their brandy and cigars he made up his mind, and he told Kennedy he would like to go. Fergus promised to see to the details.

Now, with the arrangements made for the next morning's journey, and with tickets in hand, he decided he had better fire off a report to Henry. He had already had a reply from the State Department man to his first, mildly taking him to task for the leg up in Washington's thinking he had tried to give Felipe Ángeles.

In his room he pulled his writing case from his valise. He picked up the Colt automatic, stared at it for a moment, and replaced it in the satchel.

At the desk he pondered how much he should tell Henry. Nothing substantive for the moment, just that he was going to Zacatecas.

Henry had picked up his allusion to, and admiration for, Ángeles in the first report made through Lemuel Cotter, but had differed with the inference Corey drew. "We here in the editorial department," Henry had replied over Cotter's signature, "are not sure of your assessment of Ángeles as the strongest character for this chapter. He does not, in our opinion, have the ready recognition required to make a solid history—either with general readers or the scholarly community—and in particular the 'principal scholar.' Would welcome your suggestions of others. Perhaps the unfamiliar surroundings have induced a kind of fever in you. Please get well soon."

So much for Washington heeding the first advice of the "Special Foreign Service Officer."

He wrote his letter.

Hotel Mirador
Mexico City
June 17, 1914

Mr. Lemuel Cotter
Ticknor & Fields, Publishers
Boston, Mass., U.S.A.

Dear Mr. Cotter:

Thank you for the concern for my health expressed in yours of 2 June 1914. I hope all is well with you, too, although I fear you also have suffered a slight catarrh.

Yes, I certainly was wrong about General Villa's attack. That it was Paredón and Saltillo rather than Zacatecas seemed to surprise everyone here in the capital as much as it did me. The most experienced foreign journalists were taken aback as were the chaggrined military men in General Huerta's government. It still confounds anyone who can read a map of Mexico. It took the Division of the North two hundred miles out of its way and delayed its advance to the south for a month— and without furthering the progress of either Obregón or González an inch.

It seems that Carranza is still almost suicidally intent on upsetting what appears to be the grand strategy of General Ángeles, whom I wrote about before. After Paredón and Saltillo, apparently believing Maass and Velasco couldn't get to Zacatecas in time to reinforce Barrón, he sent a sizable force under General Natera to attack the city, and steal a march on the Villistas, his "allies." It caught the press napping, and the ensuing battle went largely unreported. It was a disaster for the *insurrectos*. Unlike some other Federal military leaders, Barrón is a capable commander. He will not be dislodged from Zacatecas easily.

Now, however, it is General Villa's force, ably led by General Ángeles, which is investing Zacatecas, and the real battle for that city is beginning. This might well be *the* crucial showdown of this stage of the Revolution.

I still think that Ángeles should be the pivotal character, not only in the first chapter but perhaps in the whole book.

Sincerely:
Corey Lane

P.S. I am leaving in the morning for the battlefront, where I will be the guest of General Barrón. This should provide additional material on Ángeles, as the men fighting him see him, and perhaps some that might even persuade the "principal scholar."

C.L.

He felt slyly wicked, throwing his biggest news into the report in the form of a postscript.

One of these days he was just going to have to chance getting Henry on the line. Perhaps if they gave him a short leave after Zacatecas he could stop in El Paso on the way north to Black Springs, and he and Agent Cobb could put through a call. If not he would simply have to do it from here, maybe on his return to Mexico City from Zacatecas.

But did he really want to leave for north of the border after Zacatecas?

The answer to that question would have been an unequivocal yes two weeks ago, before the automobile of Luisa López y Montenegro brushed against him. Her card, its faint scent of lavender now completely gone, was dog-eared. He had looked at it incessantly for three days after Narciso Trujillo's dinner before he finally placed a call to La Posada Melgar, telling himself that assuring her there were no ill effects from the inconsequential mishap was the ordinary, decent thing to do. He telephoned three times altogether, getting no answer at all on the first two occasions, but hearing a male voice on the third. Fearing it might be a husband who would demand explanations, he hurried through his reason for trying to contact the *señora*.

"*Soy el superintendente de la Posada Melgar, señor,*" the man at the other end of the line said. "*La Doña Luisa no está aquí ahora.* I speak English, *señor.* You would like that?"

"Is it possible, and are you permitted, to tell me when she might return?"

"I do not know, *señor*. She visits now in San Francisco *en los Estados Unidos*. Sometimes such visits take a week, sometimes a month. May I inform La Doña who has called for her when she returns?"

What good would it do? She hadn't asked his name. "I am sorry, no. She does not know me." There was a vast silence, a silence that seemed to accuse him of impertinence, if not intrusion.

The feeling that he was perhaps aiming too high at a target he wasn't even dead sure it was wise to draw a bead on didn't stop him from hiring a taxi and having the driver take him by the inn on Avenida Melgar, a leafy street that broke away from the Paseo opposite Chapultepec Park.

La Posada Melgar turned out to be an attractive dove-gray building with balconies and shuttered windows, styled in the French manner seen so often in this section of the city, the sort of apartment hotel which had counterparts in Paris and New York. It spoke of wealth—old wealth, quiet wealth, but wealth nonetheless.

Then he was shaken by a thought. San Francisco! Even if she took ship on the west coast she would have to go north first right through the core of the war zone, well beyond the same Zacatecas which was his and Fergus's destination in the morning, and on the same rail line they would have to take. The papers were reporting heavy fighting everywhere along the Ferrovía Central's northern route. Was she courageous or merely rash? Well, she had certainly given the impression of self-confidence. But wasn't there also an afterimage of something like melancholy as well?

But what business was it of his? He would likely never see her again, and she doubtless was out of his class in any event.

He would this time have welcomed the ghost of Lucy Bishop.

There was a mild fever raging in Fergus Cameron Kennedy when they boarded the northbound train next morning.

"I can smell powder smoke, laddie."

Corey examined his ticket again. It was straight through to Zacatecas. "Fergus," he said, "where do we get off this train to see your *hacendado*? And how long will your business with him take?"

"That's been canceled. We're just a pair of footloose trippers on a lark. It will be a bonnie do, aye. Did ye bring your gun?"

22

▲▲▲▲▲

General Medina Barrón's sad eyes showed no sparkle at all when he greeted Corey and Fergus, although the words of the stocky, gray commander of Huerta's garrison at Zacatecas were welcoming enough.

"You must be *hombres* of great courage to visit us at this time," the general said. He looked weary, glum, not at all like a man who had just driven off the formidable army which had assailed his position a week ago. Carranza's General Natera had pressed home an attack surprising in its intensity for the same army so reluctant to fight at Torreón and Paredón, but Barrón's had been more than equal to the task. Corey had expected the stolid general to be at least mildly exhilarated.

The staff officers at dinner in the general's headquarters shared none of their leader's gloom. Corey hadn't seen so many ribbons and medals since a visit to the Imperial War Museum in London, but even the candlelit glitter on every tunic in the room was nothing to that in the eyes of these colonels and majors.

Barrón's men seemed sure they could deal with the Northern Division's advance every bit as well as they had dealt with that of Natera. Reports now indicated they would get their chance.

There had already been minor skirmishes with Villa's patrols for two days, with both sides testing each other. Although a small number of Barrón's forward positions had been overrun and a few men had died, the lethal jabs of the Chihuahuan's outriders hadn't lowered the spirits of the defenders of Zacatecas. Still flushed with their victory seven days ago over Natera, even if their general wasn't, they boasted about what their soldiers would do to the Villistas when their turn came—some of it with graphic reference to the genitals of the enemy. Judging by the talk around General Barrón's table, they couldn't *wait* to face the *insurrectos* across open sights—or better yet with swords in hand. Several of them expressed puzzlement that Villa's forays had been merely small-unit actions. Clearly they had expected another pell-mell cavalry rush like the one at Paredón, and were disappointed that the Division of the North hadn't accommodated them by pouring through the valleys north of their battle lines.

Fergus was having the time of his life. Whatever the supply situation for the Federalistas might have been, there was no shortage of Scotch whisky. Lord, how the Scot could toss them back, and with almost no visible effect. Tough as he was, and as seemingly limitless his capacity, Corey still half expected him to cave in any minute. He had already caved in on one thing. Since reaching Zacatecas he had abandoned any pretense of not knowing Spanish, even if he still intended Corey to know him only as a cattle broker.

In the afternoon, an arrogant, talkative captain named Morales—no more than five feet two inches tall, not happy about wasting his valuable time on a pair of foreign rubbernecks—had been their guide on an automobile tour of a small part of Zacatecas's defenses. Remembering Cuba, Corey was impressed by what he saw. Barrón obviously had a reliable corps of engineers. The strong positions they were shown by Morales, tied together by a good network of field telephones, gave clues to the general's plan for defending this last stronghold.

Zacatecas lay in several connected valleys formed by small but steep hills linked to even more valleys and hills north of the city. Morales drove them past dozens of field and mountain gun emplacements manned by crews who looked well trained and alert. The rocky hills would channel the enemy cavalry—expected, the captain said, to be even more reckless after its gaudy triumph in the great charge at Paredón—into narrow streams right under them when they attempted to force the inner citadel, streams the guns could dam or divert with ease.

"This is not the best terrain for Pancho Villa's horsemen, but that has never stopped the fat, stupid pig before," the dwarfish captain said. "I suppose he is waiting for the trains to get his infantry in position. Of course, we have no fear of the bandit's infantry. They will fade like the sunset when they face General Barrón's real *soldados*. This will not be Paredón or Torreón." He almost grew taller as he spoke, and his eyes sparked until Corey thought his pomaded head might go up in flames.

Fergus, when the captain dropped them at the hotel where they had been quartered, agreed. "Nasty as the wee mon is, he may be right. If Villa's infantry can't clear those slopes of guns, the 'invincible' Northern Division could be stalled here for a month with no decisive victory. Barrón must have about thirteen thousand troops tucked in on these bonnie braes. And what our escort, silly beggar, said about Pancho's infantry might be true enough. They're surely not up to the standards set by his cavalry, certainly not like the Bracomontes and Dorados."

"Thirteen thousand? How did you arrive at that figure, Fergus?"

"Part of my job consists of estimating numbers of livestock, laddie. I'm very good at it. It's not much different with the two-legged kind."

The "beef buyer" again. How long would Kennedy carry on this charade?

But more to the point at the moment, how had he really arrived at the thirteen thousand he seemed so supremely sure of? The captain hadn't mentioned numbers, and he certainly hadn't shown them nearly enough of the disposition of

Barrón's forces for Fergus to make any such assessment. The Scot must have other lines of intelligence. And "Bracomontes"? Corey knew of the famed Dorados, of course, but he had never seen or heard the other name. Damn it. If Cobb would only permit him to contact the military attaché at the American Embassy, perhaps he might be as well armed with information as Kennedy was. Henry was keeping him on too short a string.

"What do you think the size of Villa's 'herd' might be?"

"Weel, lad. He took fifteen thousand to Paredón, but three or four thousand foot soldiers weren't with him there. They stayed in Torreón. He'll need every one of them for this fracas. He's been recruiting hard all spring. He's got money now, or Carranza does. As much of a 'guid Scot' as the First Chief sometimes appears to be, he has to make a ha'penny or two of it available to Pancho, or he'll risk losing the whole Revolution. I would say Villa must have significantly more than twenty thousand men by this time."

Oh, yes, Fergus knew things. "Barrón is pretty well outnumbered, then."

"Aye. But, as our ridiculous Captain Morales said, this isn't Paredón or even Torreón. And Barrón isn't Velasco, either."

With the dinner finished—an excellent one of *cabrito* and a fine red wine Henry would have liked—Barrón told the orderly who served them to bring another bottle of Scotch, pointed to Fergus when the man brought it, and said, "Would you two gentlemen do me the honor of staying on with me a few moments longer—*por favor*?" Old Hispanic *cortesía*, warming.

The other officers took this as their signal to retire.

"You have questions, *señores*?" the general said when they were alone. The voice was marvelously gentle, but with an underpinning firmness that reminded Corey that above all he was a tough old soldier. He pushed a decanter of port toward Corey.

"When will the fighting begin in earnest here at Zacatecas, General?" Fergus said as he poured himself two more stiff fingers of whisky. "I would have thought Villa would have made his first serious attacks by now." My God! He still sounded as sober as a Methodist preacher. "Pancho is not a man to hold back."

"No, he isn't. *Generally* speaking, the way of the man they call the Tiger of the North is to go on the offensive without pause. He is a very bold, impulsive captain. Sometimes to the point of recklessness. And until now he has always been utterly predictable. I wish he would have attacked already, Señor Kennedy," Barrón said. "We could cut them to pieces in these narrow valleys. I confess I counted on it."

Unlike the wine-fueled boasts of his staff, this wasn't braggadocio. He meant it. "*Asique.* General Villa's way is not, however, the way of Felipe Ángeles, and I think I see *his* fine hand and keen intelligence in this delay. If I know Felipe—and I do—he has personally looked over every one of my forward positions and fairly accurately judged my strength to the last man and the last round of ammunition. There are some things Felipe delegates, but he gathers most of his intelligence himself. If he is charged by General Villa with ordering the attack, he will only do so when he is completely ready. I hope to be ready, too. My biggest problem, as I am sure you see as well as I, will be to cool the hot blood of my young commanders. They all say they despise General Villa, but secretly they admire him—and his battle tactics. They will fight well for me, *sí*, but I fear sometimes they think me too slow for this kind of war. I must not allow their courage and impetuosity to result in rashness. Our predicament is not hopeless by any means."

"You do expect to win, don't you, General?" Fergus said. It was just shy of offensiveness. Perhaps the flood tide of whisky had begun to sweep over the dikes of prudence, after all.

Barrón made a brief, feeble try at indignation, then gave it up. "Of course I expect to win, Señor Kennedy. I would submit my resignation to Presidente Huerta *immediatamente* if I did not. *Verdad.* We must win. Should we not. . . ." He shrugged and put his hands in front of him, palms up, as if in supplication. A breach in the tough hide?

Regardless of the sympathy for the Revolution which had been growing in Corey since he came to Mexico, he liked the courtly, soft-voiced Barrón. Enough to hope he could save Zacatecas? No. But how had an unsavory tyrant such as Victoriano Huerta kept the loyalty of an honorable officer such as Medina Barrón? And what kind of soul-searching had Barrón gone through?

"Felipe is delaying for reasons of his own," Barrón said now. "Do not think for one moment that he is wasting time. Do you have any questions, Señor Lane?"

"Just one, sir. Why did you permit Mr. Kennedy and me to visit you? We must be an unnecessary burden at a time like this."

The grizzled fighter's sad eyes became even sadder. He turned first to Fergus. "I trust you will not take offense at the way I answer Señor Lane, Señor Kennedy. None is meant." The Scot didn't look the least bit chastened. He merely shrugged, and Barrón turned to Corey again. "I know who and what you are, Señor Lane. I regret to say that even Presidente Huerta knows who you are."

The delicious *cabrito* and fine red wine congealed as ice in Corey's stomach. "General Huerta knows who I am? I'm sure I don't know how he could, sir."

"You don't? Well, I am not surprised at your modesty now that I have met you, Señor Lane. We know you as more than an insignificant historian."

"Modesty, General? Now I most certainly am confused."

"It is this way, *señor*. Señor Dr. Narciso Trujillo of the Ministry of Culture is my very best *amigo* in the capital. When we meet, our conversations are wide-ranging. He told me about the dinner you and he attended at the ministry when you came to Mexico. He was much impressed with the book you wrote. Unfortunately the security police somehow knew about it, too. They took it to General Huerta. *El presidente* was perhaps the greatest Indian fighter in the history of our country. Narciso tells me you used those very words. That part pleased General Huerta. But he took offense at the way you described his conduct of the campaigns against the Apache and the Yaqui, and for a while considered expelling you from Mexico. He seems to have forgotten that for the moment.

"I did not *permit* you to visit me, Señor Lane. I invited you. I do not feel that in doing so I am being disloyal to my President. The battle that will begin here soon will be the most important of this tragic conflict. *Ahora,* if you are not yet a notable historian, my *amigo* Narciso feels certain that you will be one on a not too distant day. He and I both want a truthful, accurate record of what happens here. All we ask is that you be fair when you write your book—*por favor.*"

Corey only nodded. Words wouldn't come. Barrón turned to Fergus once again. He smiled broadly at the Scotsman. "Of course we know who and what you are, too, Señor Kennedy. A buyer of beef? Well, I suppose any *hombre* who eats beef buys it at one time or another. It is not free even in Mexico. And now, *señores,* I must bid you *buenas noches.*"

After the car dropped them off at their hotel Fergus suggested a nightcap. He had been silent on the trip across town from Barrón's headquarters. At the bar he stared into his glass.

But then he began to laugh. The laugh started somewhere down around Glasgow and rippled northward to John o'Groat's like a pipe band doing a wild Highland fling.

"Eee—this is rich, laddie," he said when he caught his breath. "Ye're just a newcomer in the great game—and ye fooled them. Old-hand Fergus came a cropper." There was no laughter now. "I'm a professional, Corey, but I've never scored too well in my profession. That's why I'm doing this wee stuff here in Mexico, instead of playing the greater game in Europe." There was hurt in the scratchy voice. He brightened, "But I suppose ye ken the humor in a' of it."

It was funny, all right. But even funnier to Corey was the discovery that he had almost been kicked out of Mexico, not for being the spy he was, but because of the cover his master back in Washington had devised for him. So much for experts. Would Henry laugh? Most likely not.

What wasn't funny was the sad case of General Medina Barrón.

Fergus was snoring only minutes after they reached their second-floor room, undressed, and climbed in bed.

Sleep wouldn't quite come for Corey. He left his bed and went out on the balcony. The beam of a huge searchlight situated on a hilltop north of town was sweeping the underbellies of heavy, sullen clouds and then dropping to the hillsides even farther to the north. Down the street from the hotel men in uniform and women with their heads swaddled in *rebozos* were entering and leaving Zacatecas's magnificent old baroque cathedral.

Rain pelted the windows as he fell asleep.

He awoke to hear the guns of Felipe Ángeles hammering the soaked hills of Zacatecas.

When he went to the window he saw that a downpour must have lasted through the night. Now there was just a discouraging, mucky drizzle. In the street a line of trucks was moving toward the sound of the distant firing. Columns of infantry and a squadron of cavalry crowded the sides of the street to let the trucks go by. It was a deathly gray morning.

Fergus was still snoring.

23

"The enemy guns were shelling us from the hill at Mina la Plata ten minutes ago, *mi general,* I swear it! They have vanished!" Captain Tito Morales said.

The diminutive captain—not so arrogant here on the summit of La Bufa as when he picked Corey and Fergus up at their hotel after breakfast, or when he guided them yesterday—pulled the field glasses from his eyes and turned to

Barrón in the staff car that had just arrived with a motorcycle escort. It was as if he was imploring the Zacatecas commander to rescue him from some folly peculiarly his own. Corey, regretting that he had left his own binoculars in Morales's car, looked through the drizzling rain toward the promontory called Mina la Plata on the map the captain had given him. Morales was right. Moments before Barrón arrived on soggy La Bufa, the hill the Villistas occupied across the narrow valley had erupted with flashes. The hill was just an unrelieved, waterlogged gray now. The guns had vanished. It was almost dark enough to bring into play the big searchlight whose stanchion Corey had leaned back against until the general's automobile shuddered to a stop in front of him, probably the same beacon whose wandering beams he had spotted from the balcony last night.

"Do not despair, Capitán Morales." Barrón was eyeing the boulder-strewn slope across the valley. "Steel yourself. This will not be General Ángeles's last surprise for us today—or for as long as this battle lasts—but it is amazing, *verdad,* that he could get those clumsy Schneider-Canets out of sight so fast. I hope our gun crews can learn from Felipe today. If they do not, there will be no tomorrow." He glanced through a sheaf of papers Morales handed him. "Get Colonel Ruiz on the field telephone and tell him to cancel his assault on La Mina. The Villistas will have left riflemen hidden in those rocks, and there is nothing to be gained by men dying to take an otherwise empty hill. See if they can save Loreto, but tell Colonel Ruiz that he must hold La Sierpe at all costs! No, do not telephone, go there yourself." He scribbled a note and handed it to Morales.

He turned to Corey and Fergus. "Unless you have a strong wish to remain here on La Bufa, please join me, gentlemen. Captain Morales will not be able to escort you any closer to the action. He has to get to La Sierpe now. I wish nothing ill to befall you while you are my guests. I do not think you will want to be on La Sierpe today."

Corey started to say something, but stopped when Fergus shook his head slightly.

They retrieved their gear from Morales's car just before the captain left, and climbed in beside the general in the backseat of the larger automobile. As the car pulled away from the forward command post Barrón turned to Corey. "You have known war, have you not, Señor Lane?"

"Yes, sir. I was with Colonel Roosevelt in Cuba. My experience, though, is like some fine wine. It does not travel well. This might just as well be my first time in combat. Cuba was a long time ago."

"And you, Señor Kennedy?" Barrón said.

"I went with Roberts to Pretoria against the Afrikaners. One of the few Scots seconded to the Royal Welsh Fusiliers. It's been a long time for me, too, I'm afraid."

They bumped down the small hill toward the road, and the general stopped talking until they reached it.

"From time to time I read the reports in the press of both your countries with considerable amusement," he said when the sounds of shelling and distant small-arms fire died away a little. "Or rather, it would be amusing were it not so deadly serious. The journalists who have followed affairs in Mexico seem to think I am facing a bandit leader who knows how to rob banks and trains, butcher civilians, and accomplish little else. They seldom mention General Ángeles. Pancho Villa captures almost all of their attention. I believe you both can see that today I face a formidable army—well equipped, well trained, and above all, well led. My troops may be the last barrier between *los insurrectos* and the capital. If I fail here, General Obregón in the west and the Carrancistas coming down the eastern coast will find little opposition. Felipe Ángeles has planned well. The diversion of General Villa's forces to Paredón and Saltillo merely delayed matters here."

"General . . ." Fergus broke in. "Has the hill at Loreto fallen?"

"By this time? Probably. The enemy infantry was halfway up it twenty minutes ago. We did not really intend a firm stand on Loreto. Colonel Ruiz will fall back on La Sierpe now. We will make our fight there."

Infantry? No sign of Villa's cavalry yet? Yes, Barrón's enemy was a formidable psychologist as well as a soldier.

In the broken conversations with Barrón's staff, overheard remarks made by brigade commanders as they toured the forward positions this morning, and in his talks with Fergus, Corey was gradually beginning to form a different picture of the size and capabilities of the División del Norte of Pancho Villa now hidden in the smoky valleys and behind the hills north of Zacatecas.

As Barrón had pointed out, this wasn't Coxey's Army he was facing. Corey had been surprised at the strength of the artillery on the other side, and even more surprised at the extent and duration of the cannonading. As was the case with so many of the Federalist officers they had dined with last night and met this morning, he had more or less expected to see the cavalry of Villa first, had looked forward to seeing another wild ride to glory. The fact that it hadn't happened yet didn't mean, of course, that it wouldn't. Barrón's problem, and indeed the problem of any commander fighting the revolutionaries, was that he could never be sure which Pancho Villa he had to fight: the Pancho of the rash, hell-for-leather charge, or the Pancho guided by the classic military judgment of Ángeles. If the northerners had a secret weapon in this battle, as in all the earlier ones, it was just this doubt. Despite Medina Barrón's superb surface calm, Corey could feel the tension in the general.

"General Barrón," Fergus said as they rolled into the center of Zacatecas with other vehicles frantically getting out of the way of the staff car and with masses of uniformed men parting in front of them like the sea, "could you have your driver laddie drop us off at our hotel?" It surprised Corey. He would have thought Kennedy would want to stay with the general, in the thick of things.

It must have surprised Barrón as well. "You won't be able to follow the battle from a hotel room, Señor Kennedy. But as you wish."

Once in the small lobby the Scotsman scurried to the desk, checked for messages, and was handed one he merely glanced at before stuffing it in his pocket. Only then did he turn to Corey. "We'd better get our gear packed, laddie. I don't like the smell of things. For all that he seems in tight control, Barrón talks like a beaten man. He has given up on that hill called Loreto, even before he knows for sure he's lost it. I don't know how long it will take, but this city is going to fall to the other side. We should be ready to leave once that starts happening."

It didn't seem like the same man who had boarded the train in Mexico City with such anticipation. In the room, he turned to Corey. "I'd keep your gun handy if I were you, historian. When things break down here, we'll be fair game—just another two gringos to be victimized. Let's get everything else to the train station and start it back toward the capital. We'll have to arrange for transport out of here for ourselves, too."

This was a different Fergus, too, from the greedy toper of the night before or the slightly bemused observer of this morning. Had fear brought on the change?

"I'm not sure I want to leave until it's over here, Fergus," Corey said. "I'm surprised you do."

"Didn't say a thing about *leaving*, laddie." Fergus winked, and the eager man of the journey north was back again. "Just want us to travel light in the next day or two. For all that talk about you writing history for him and his doctor chum Trujillo, I think Medina has already started hiding things from us. He certainly doesn't want us to see the situation from La Sierpe, but we'll take our own look from there, if that sits all right with you."

"Sure, but how? We've lost Morales as an escort."

"Not to worry. There's a colonel up there I know pretty well who will give us the fourteen-carat 'gen.' Barrón didn't exactly forbid us to go to La Sierpe. All we have to do is get there. Give me five minutes with our host here at the hotel and I think I can promote a car and a driver. Game?" Fergus eyed him shrewdly. "Since I'm making all the arrangements, laddie," he said, "I think it only fair that you pay for the car."

Corey broke into laughter. What the hell was he laughing about? This was nothing short of insanity.

"I'm game," he said.

"I was certain you would be, laddie."

The car was a shabby old Daimler as big as a battle cruiser, but reminding him sharply of that of Luisa López y Montenegro outside the Mirador. Apparently Fergus hadn't been able to find a driver willing to risk his neck too close to the roaring guns, and Corey took the wheel. The canvas top was ripped in three places, letting in steady drips of water that ponded a quarter of an inch deep on the floorboards, but that was only a minor inconvenience. Something weird had happened to the gearbox or the clutch; Corey couldn't force the shift lever into any gear above second, and unless he kept a death grip on the gearshift knob, and hung on to it for dear life, it popped out with maddening regularity. Damned hard work. He would have insisted that Fergus drive, but a glance at the miniature Scot's short legs told him Fergus would never be able to reach the pedals from the high bench seat. Besides, even if he hadn't as yet pulled the silver flask from his kit bag, odds were fairly heavy Kennedy would have it to his mouth at any moment. Corey was fairly sure Henry would be scandalized at his "Special Foreign Service Officer" keeping such dissolute company, agent of a friendly power or not.

"Who is this colonel and how do you know him?" he asked Kennedy as they jolted out of Zacatecas's northern limits.

"He's a mercenary Frenchman formerly of the Legion who calls himself Dupont, although I hae me doots that's his real name. He's been a source of mine for a year now. He's as shrewd a military analyst as I've found in Mexico, and he won't have any 'patriotic' ax to grind. He'll tell us what the real situation is. Knows war inside out, Pierre does. Won the Croix de Guerre in Indochina."

Source? Well, since the remarks in the bar last night, Fergus's status as an agent hadn't exactly been a secret. "Have you been in contact with him since we've been here?"

"That message I picked up at the hotel came from Pierre. I did telephone him from Mexico City when we decided on this trip."

"What's his military job?"

"He's a sapper. Designed most of Barrón's hard defenses here. As I recall, ye looked impressed by his work yesterday."

"I was. But an engineer officer? That's not exactly a 'front-line' occupation."

"Pierre likes combat more than most sappers do. He's never far from the fighting."

"Why didn't we try to look him up him yesterday?"

"We're guests here, laddie, remember? I wanted us to see what Barrón wanted us to see before we struck out on our own. We don't owe him anything now."

"And you didn't want Barrón to know you knew this Frenchman."

"Aye. That, too."

"He'll know now."

Fergus smiled. "He'll be pretty busy generaling today."

The hotel had packed them a lunch, and Corey wheeled the Daimler off into a shallow arroyo and suggested they eat it before they reached the front. It was a Hobson's choice as to whether they should feed themselves outside in the rain or remain in the swamp the car was fast becoming. They stayed inside and ate in silence. When they finished, Fergus dug his kit bag from the backseat, rummaged in it, and came up with two small flags: the Union Jack and the Stars and Stripes. Without a word he stepped outside and to the front of the long hood of the automobile, affixed the tiny sticks with their patches of bright cloth to the radiator ornament, and yelled back to Corey. "Don't know if this will do us any bloody good, but at least our countries will be in evidence at the great battle for Zacatecas." Amazing fellow, Fergus.

The sound of the guns had moved much closer to them. Lightning or reflected gun flashes lit the pewter sky above them. Things were definitely heating up. He had told Medina Barrón that his combat experience didn't "travel." Not quite true now. He was back in Cuba again, and what *did* travel across the years and miles was his anxiety—not fear, at least not yet, but close enough.

When Fergus rejoined him, Corey fished out the map Morales had given him and spread it across his knees. The captain had penciled circles around five small hills which held the Federalista forward command positions.

"Where are we most likely to find this Colonel Dupont?"

"He said he would be on La Sierpe until two o'clock." Fergus jammed his thumb at a spot on the map. "Here."

"Isn't that the hill where this Colonel Ruiz is commanding? The position General Barrón said was to be held at all costs?"

"Would ye rather not go up there, after all, Corey? As they say, discretion *is* the better part of valor."

Corey studied the map again. La Sierpe was the most forward of any of the circled hills except for the one he now identified as Loreto, by this time fallen to Villa's infantry, if Barrón's reply to Fergus's pointed question about it turned out to be correct. "It will be the best place to see these early stages of the battle," he said. "Of course I'd rather not go up there, but we'll have to, won't we, if we want a good look at what goes on? All we can hope for at the moment is that the *insurrectos* don't get there before we do."

"Ye're a braw, bonnie lad, Corey. Let's not muck about here any longer, then." He hopped outside, and went to the front of the car's long hood. It took a dozen turns of the crank before the engine fired.

They had to wait a bit before they could get back on the road. What looked to be the same trucks he had seen in the early morning as they lumbered past the hotel and headed toward the fighting were now coming back down the road from La Bufa, which also—if indeed they had picked the right road—forked off to both Loreto and La Sierpe. Even though Villa hadn't yet turned loose his Dorados, or the Bracomontes Fergus had spoken of, there was a damned good chance he would see them soon. He could forgo that pleasure for the moment. Until the Daimler was on the switchbacks leading to the heights, and relatively safe from being caught in a cavalry charge, flying Fergus's two brave but pitiful little flags would be like pissing against the wind. Pancho's savage riders wouldn't have time to sort out "just another two gringos" as noncombatants. Perhaps they wouldn't even care to sort them out.

The trucks rolling by the arroyo had been pressed into service as ambulances now. Bodies were piled inside like cordwood. With the Daimler's engine clattering away, and with the steady pounding of guns coming from hills barely seen through the drizzle, no sound reached them from the trucks, but he could imagine with exquisite remembered pain the moans, groans, and cries of anguish from the broken men inside them. Yes, Cuba traveled, after all. Experience of war was as peripatetic as death itself.

"By the Lord Harry," Fergus said. "They've already taken a fearful beating. And the real killing hasn't even started yet."

A break came in the line of trucks and Corey steered the car up to the road. In the next mile he had to turn off on the muddy shoulder a half dozen times to let more trucks, teams of mules dragging small field guns and ammunition caissons, and a few genuine ambulances pass through. By the time they reached a sign reading "La Sierpe" that pointed to another set of switchbacks indistinguishable from the ones which had led up La Bufa earlier, a trickle of foot soldiers soaked to the skin was coming down the valley road. He stopped the car for a moment before he made the turn. The soldiers looked derelict. An officer brandishing a revolver was trying to divert the sluggish stream up the road Corey would have to turn into, but the beaten men kept plodding back toward the town. The officer was shouting something. The men didn't look at him. They weren't exactly fleeing; this was no headlong rout. They just kept moving along the road to Zacatecas, heads bent down, their faces as gray as old adobe.

The officer's revolver flashed and one of the shuffling men pitched forward to his knees and then eased himself down full length on his chest and face. Once in the mud he didn't move. Strangely, his collapse seemed to have nothing at all to do with the shot the officer fired. He didn't even look dead. It was as if he had simply decided to get a bit of sleep. None of his companions looked at the fallen man any more than they had looked at the pistol-waving officer. And none among them so much as quickened that slow, steady pace. The gun flashed again and another fell. This one at least twitched a few times in the roadbed. Again no one looked.

All of the men in the ragged column were still armed; none had tossed their rifles. Corey half expected them to turn them on the officer. It didn't happen. The officer's shoulders sagged. He turned toward Zacatecas himself and joined the column. His face was as gray as any Corey saw. Within fifteen or twenty seconds he couldn't pick him out from the others making this disconsolate retreat.

"Do you suppose Barrón has ordered a general withdrawal?" he asked Fergus. "Will we find anyone left at that command post up there?"

"Aye, laddie. This lot must have come from Loreto. The Villistas have probably crossed the ravine from there, maybe have reached the foot of La Sierpe already. We'd better get up there in two shakes of a lamb's tail if we're going to see what we want to see before *it* goes, too."

Corey put the Daimler in gear again, hoping against hope that they wouldn't snap an axle in the canyonlike ruts they bounced in and out of.

As they climbed higher the sound of the guns grew louder, and now, too, they could hear shells landing somewhere beyond the summit of the hill. Halfway to the top of La Sierpe three rain-streaked soldiers huddled against a sentry box to which ran telephone wires. They stepped into the ruts, stopped the Daimler, and held trembling rifle barrels above the hood, pointed straight at Corey's head. A fourth, a corporal, he guessed, emerged from the box, came to the driver's side, and stuck his head in under the canvas top. His breath reeked of garlic.

"*Sus cartas. ¡Pronto, pronto!*" He had a flat, *mestizo* face. Corey and Fergus handed over their papers and with a silent snarl the corporal, or whatever he was, returned to the sentry box.

"Do you suppose he'll turn us back?"

Fergus laughed. "Not a ghost of a chance, laddie. He'll either let us pass or have his three nervous beasties ventilate our skulls."

After a three-minute wait during which Corey was sure he had aged a decade, the corporal stepped out of the box, waved Corey forward, and handed him back his and Fergus's papers.

"*¡Gringos locos!*" he muttered as the Daimler pulled away.

"From the sound of things we'd likely be better off if he *had* turned us back," Fergus said as they made another sharp turn. Sporadic reports of small-arms fire had joined the echoing bursts of the heavier ordnance. There was no way of telling where it was coming from.

At what appeared to be the last hairpin turn before the top, a burning truck blocked the road, and Corey had to swing the Daimler dangerously near the lip of a chasm to get around it, holding his breath and heart against the possibility that the flames would reach the truck's gas tank and engulf them, too, in the resulting detonation. The driver of the burning truck, dead, but with his hands still on the wheel, was a boy. Even as Corey watched, flames licked up from under the dashboard and set fire to the youngster's khaki cap. His hair flamed next. Corey turned his eyes to the road. His lunch wasn't sitting well.

Smoke curled up and blew away from three other places in the rocks on the hillside. The guns from the *insurrectos'* batteries were targeted on the valleys and ravines on the other side of the hill, but some of them were intent on taking out the command post on La Sierpe. The jagged, smoking holes with blackened edges on either side of the road must have been caused by errant shells which had cleared the summit and landed far down the back side of the hill. It might be pretty bad on top. The Daimler, too, would become a red flag when they reached the top.

The idea occurred to Fergus, too.

"Why don't ye stop here, Corey? We can do the last wee stretch on shank's mare. It will give us a way back out if things get intolerable." He sounded wary enough, but he looked like someone off to see a football match.

Corey stopped the car and turned it around. It took half a dozen passes in the narrow road to get the long car pointed down toward the main highway that led back to the center of Zacatecas. Fergus wouldn't have to crank for him to start the car from here. A glance told him the city itself hadn't yet taken any artillery fire, but the roads in and out were clogged with traffic—machines, animals, and men. As they left the Daimler, Fergus spoke again. "Don't forget your gun, laddie."

Corey grunted. The last thing he wanted to carry the rest of the distance up La Sierpe was the heavy automatic Cobb had given him, but he supposed Fergus had the right of it. The Scot certainly had known what he was up to until now. Corey dug the belted weapon from his bag, strapped it on, eased the pistol from its holster, and charged the top slide back to get a cartridge in the chamber, the way Cobb had shown him. The slab of blue-black metal wasn't anything like the sidearm he had carried up San Juan Hill. Until El Paso he had only heard about these "forty-fives" Colt had developed for Jack Pershing after the Filipino Insurrection. It felt as uncomfortable in his hand as an outsized Stillson wrench—or a small, metal headstone. "Not much for fine target work," the agent had said, "but it will knock a moose over like it was a rabbit." He reached back into the rear seat of the car and got the binoculars he had forgotten on the ride up to La Bufa with Morales.

As he put the automatic back in the holster and snapped the flap he realized the rain had stopped.

The sun broke through the clouds for a fleeting second, ducked back as quickly, and the gray washed over the stony road again. He wondered if the sun had been appalled at the sights over the brow of the hill, and if he would be, too, when he and Fergus got their first look at the principal battleground.

Fergus had already started walking, and he hurried along in his wake.

The sun made another, longer try at lighting the scene again, hid itself as abruptly as before, but then came out apparently to stay. To the north and west the sky turned clear and blue all the way to the mountains, and as Corey and Fergus reached the top the last clouds scudded off to the southeast well past Zacetecas. Whatever happened during the rest of this day wouldn't happen in the shadows.

Far from being empty, as Corey had speculated, the hilltop was crowded, covered with men in batallion strength across the crest, and, yes, some of the enemy fire had hit its mark. A tent with an open front revealed medics working over wounded. There were three bodies lying behind the tent.

They made their way through at least two companies of riflemen hunkered down and leaning forward into rifles and carbines held hard against the rocky ground, and then skirted a squadron of cavalrymen dismounted and holding their untethered horses' heads. Lancers. All the animals were saddled. Neither the foot soldiers nor the horsemen looked as if they had been in action yet, but they looked like hardcase veterans. This hill would be no easy pickings for the Villistas if and when they stormed it, although as he looked down the steep, convex slope that led to the valley between La Sierpe and the Loreto hill, he couldn't help wondering what earthly good cavalry would be in terrain like this. He wondered next if any of these men knew of the partial retreat already taking place.

There was a scattering of trucks, military cars, and motorcycles, too, all of them pointing back down toward Zacatecas the same way he and Fergus left the Daimler. They weren't the only ones up here admitting the high possibility of rapid, probably ignominious, exit.

He spotted Morales first, in earnest conversation with a harried-looking colonel he took to be Ruiz, the unfortunate warrior Barrón had said was to hold La Sierpe "at all costs." When Morales saw Corey his mouth dropped open.

Fergus disappeared, but before Corey could even wonder where the Scot had gone he was in sight again, with a slight, stoop-shouldered, older officer in tow.

Colonel Pierre Dupont, former French Foreign Legionnaire, veteran of jungle warfare in Indochina, holder of the Croix de Guerre, was the last man on this hilltop Corey would have taken for a tough mercenary soldier. He looked more academic than soldierly, even in his superbly tailored uniform.

Fergus made introductions, adding, "I hope you have a wee bit of French, Corey. With Morales and Ruiz eavesdropping like old back-fence wives, Pierre will be more comfortable in his own language. More forthcoming, too."

The colonel looked Corey over through horn-rimmed glasses with lenses so thick his eyes looked large enough for a head three times the size.

"*Comment ça va*, Monsieur Lane?" Dupont said. "I think we may not have much time together."

"*Je vais bien, colonel, et vous aussi?*" This might prove awkward. How well would the French he had studied at Amherst, but never truly mastered even in Paris on his "Grand Tour," hold up now? "Not much time, sir? Then you don't think this position can be held?"

"*Je ne sais pas*. It may have been lost when General Barrón brought his cavalry to the heights, as he did here." He made a small gesture with his thin hand toward the waiting squadron. "General Villa will not be so foolish as to ride to the top of every little butte to meet them. He will attack, of course, but only after his artillery and infantry have done their work. General Ángeles recognizes that Zacatecas is not Paredón. He has planned his assault impeccably. Even the little Corsican would approve. *C'est une bataille classique, vraiment!*"

Ángeles again. Henry Richardson, please take note.

Without another word the Frenchman turned and walked to the rim of the hill overlooking the valley separating La Sierpe from Loreto. Fergus touched Corey on the elbow and they followed. Out of the corner of his eye he saw Morales and Ruiz move along after them, but at a distance of perhaps fifty feet. Would they order them off this hill?

"Ruiz is running Barrón's show from here, Pierre?" Fergus said.

"*Oui, mon ami.*"

"And ye have no command responsibility?"

"*Non.* They pay me for what I build for them. Anything else would be *de trop.* I do not regret it entirely, however. I will not have to take the blame for what may befall them here today. General Barrón's officers are good fighters, of great courage—perhaps *too* much courage—but as for strategy and tactics . . ." He shrugged in a monumentally resigned Gallic manner.

At the rim the view astonished Corey. It was like looking at the terrain sandbox in Colonel Roosevelt's Cuban head-quarters, a far more encompassing look than the one he had gotten with General Barrón back on La Bufa in the morning. The general, competent as he seemed, would have served himself and his army far better if he had come here. Corey had called Captain Morales a toy soldier. The figures he saw in the valley were *all* toys, but what deadly toys. He pulled out his map and began to orient himself.

Dupont leaned over and tapped the map. "*Permettez-moi, monsieur.*" Corey swung it around so the colonel could look at it, too. "Your map is not to scale," Dupont said. "It is a much greater distance, by perhaps as much as a kilometer, from Loreto to La Sierpe here. The *relative* locations of the different vantage points are accurate enough, however. Were I in command here . . ."

Whatever he tried to say was lost in the shrieking whistle of an incoming shell. Corey held his breath until the projectile cleared the hilltop, as had those which had made the holes seen on the way up. Good Lord! The Daimler. Well, he and Fergus would just have to find out about the car when they finished here. Two more rounds gave warning of their arrival just before they exploded a hundred or more yards down the slope, behind the rifle pits which were probably the work of this Frenchman and now filled with squads of well-dug-in defenders. There must have been a dozen of such manned positions, entrenchments for the most part, but also some cleverly built-up breastworks which took full advantage of the natural rock outcroppings. Ingenious design.

Suddenly he realized something was missing. In him. Where was the fear that had seized and shaken him in Cuba?

If anything, he was in more danger here on exposed La Sierpe than on San Juan Hill, and back then he had known many moments of something close to paralysis, even though he had somehow kept right on walking up that deadly slope with his company. Why didn't his hand tremble as he held the map? He hadn't turned any braver in the intervening years. He remembered Tom Hendry's coolness under fire that day. The *Chupadera County News* man had nothing to defend himself with save his ubiquitous notebook, a bundle of pencils, and the penknife he used to sharpen them—and *he* had walked the hill with the Rough Riders, not out ahead of them, but not lagging, either.

Loreto, which until this moment had been alive with the flashes of field and mountain guns, it had turned in the wink of an eye to a pastoral, peaceful hillside from the look of it. Was Ángeles moving his artillery again, as he had so magically whisked it away from Mina la Plata this morning? Or was it just the misleading lull before a redoubled storm? He trained his field glasses on the distant slope and detected movement. Men? Guns? No! A small herd of cattle was grazing in the high pasture just beneath Loreto's summit. It was much the same ludicrous juxtaposition of peace and war he had witnessed time and again on the long train trip from Juárez. Some scenes hadn't really been rewritten in the six hundred years since Agincourt, when some French peasant, possibly an ancestor of Pierre Dupont here, had plowed a field parallel to the line of mail-clad knights advancing against King Harry's archers, those Welshmen from whom Fergus's mates at Pretoria had descended.

But the fact remained that Ángeles was using ordinarily unwieldy artillery with the precision of a fencing master with a foil; the saber strokes of Villa's main brigades of infantry and his incomparable cavalry were yet to come.

"Have you any idea, Colonel Dupont," he said, "why we haven't seen the enemy cavalry yet?"

"*Oui*, Monsieur Lane. It is not down there."

"Not down there? Forgive me, I don't understand."

"If you study your map carefully you will see that those

valleys aren't wide enough for an advance of cavalry across the broad front General Villa can best turn to his advantage. But he can bring up his infantry on Calzado's trains and send them up the heights faster than horses could ever do. We've already seen a few of them. The main force has still to arrive. I imagine it will arrive shortly. We have reports of two trains coming into the valley from Vetagrande."

Fergus nosed into the conversation. "It's a new dimension in the warfare of movement, laddie. At least one *I* haven't seen before, and I saw some bonnie tricks by the Boers. Calzado doesn't merely *transport* Villa's and Ángeles's forces in the way of your Civil War and the Franco-Prussian do. The trains themselves are tactical devices. Ángeles's infantry doesn't march. They're not the world's best, but thanks to Calzado's ingenuity and industry at laying and repairing track, they're almost always in the right place at the right time. They can spill troops right onto the battlefield fighting."

"But that still doesn't answer my question about the cavalry. You don't hold six or seven thousand tested men out of a conflict of this importance."

Dupont again. "You are right. You do *not* hold back such a weapon." He placed a delicate finger on Corey's map. "I believe General Villa's cavalry brigades are east and west of here, bypassing the entire battlefield below us. Some of them will ride into Zacatecas as General Barrón attempts the withdrawal I fear may come. The rest will cut off any possible retreat to Guadalupe, southeast of Zacatecas. Ángeles and Villa will not be content with mere victory today. They want annihilation. If all this happens as I think it might, *ce guerre-ci est finie*. Even the capital will fall."

"The situation for the Federalists is truly that desperate, then? Is there nothing Barrón can do?"

"*Oui* and *encore, oui*. It is desperate, yes. And yes, there is still one thing General Barrón can do. He can *win* here. On this ground—La Sierpe."

"Just how will that save things?"

"If Colonel Ruiz can repulse the enemy here and counterattack, he can drive Villa's infantry back up the valleys toward. Vetagrande here." He shifted the finger he had kept on the map. "The enemy's two main bodies will be isolated from each other then. Taken in turn they can be crushed."

"Then Ángeles has undertaken an enormous gamble?"

"Indeed. But war always entails such gambles. Let us turn our attention on the valleys now. I believe things will get most interesting in the next few minutes."

Then, as if the Frenchman had willed it, the deep V of the valley beneath them suddenly rippled with cannon fire across a mile of front. Ángeles had indeed stripped his guns from Loreto's sloping side, and repositioned them.

"Regardez, messieurs!" Dupont whispered. "The trains. They have entered the valley. It begins now."

24

▰▰▰▰

Corey expected the top of La Sierpe to take the first salvo, and began counting the seconds between the flashes and the landing of the shells as he had as a boy when he marked time between a bolt of lightning on Sierra Blanca and the thunder that rolled across the rangeland of the X-Bar-7. He had gotten pretty fair at it back then. Of course, in the Ojos Negros he knew the distance between any two points. Here he had no such knowledge, nor did he know the speed of the shells and canisters the gunners beyond the railroad tracks were hurling at them. But they should begin hitting now.

This was just another exercise in that busywork designed to keep fear away, not a great deal different from Tom Hendry sharpening his pencils back in Cuba. So far it had worked.

And at any rate, he had been wrong. The first barrage wasn't targeted on the command position. Ángeles was directing his fire only a thousand yards up the slope, where the first of Pierre Dupont's entrenchments creased the ground.

Debris rocketed into the air and hid the line of trenches. Clouds of smoke drifted over the defenders' heads.

Dupont had called their attention to the trains just nosing into the valley. The first of the two had stopped already and men were pouring from it, to "spill" directly onto the battlefield as Fergus had described the Villista habit of deployment, moving quickly then into the lowest sections of the right-of-way and gathering in attack formation. A few skirmishers were already climbing the railroad embankment, joining units which had crossed the tracks from the bottom of Loreto in the early morning. Some of these were drifting back through the ranks of the detraining units. Apparently their commanders were giving these a little rest. The second train was snugging in behind the first.

Corey lifted the field glasses to his eyes just in time to see the first shells from the Huertista batteries on La Bufa and El Grillo, nearer town, land on the run-out from Loreto, beyond the trains. There was no damage he could see. General Barrón's gunners would have to do a lot better than they were doing at the moment if they were to save the day for him.

He lifted the glasses from the cut of the valley and swept them across the hilltops to the east.

On almost every ridgeline, on barely seen roads, and in the broad fields such as the one where the cattle still grazed the high side of Loreto, something was moving like a tide. As the Frenchman had predicted, Pancho Villa's cavalry was ignoring the battle shaping up under Corey's gaze to move into position on the southeast heights above Zacatecas. If and when Barrón lost La Sierpe here, the Dorados and their comrades would cascade into the main road leading into town and out of it toward Guadalupe, avalanche down on retreating columns of infantry along a lengthened flank almost impossible to protect.

Morales and Ruiz had come to the vantage point now, but stayed a stone's throw away from Corey, Fergus, and the colonel. They had maps and glasses in their hands, too. The diminutive captain shot the three of them a wicked glance and then engaged Ruiz in conversation. The Federalist colonel said something to the captain, and Morales left him. Ruiz stared back at his reserves of infantry and horsemen, a man suddenly terribly alone.

Dupont cleared his throat. "The issue will be decided in the next ten or twenty minutes, *messieurs*." Dupont seemed detached, almost as though there was for him no personal involvement in the outcome.

"But we can't know in that time if the attack from the tracks will succeed or fail, Colonel," Corey said.

"No, we cannot. But Colonel Ruiz must make a decision soon. If he holds his reserves here on La Sierpe out of the battle he will have the makings of his counterattack. If he sends them down into the lines below us too early, whatever advantage might accrue to him at first will slip away. You were looking at the riders on the hills to the east of us, Monsieur Lane. We can forget them *pour le moment*. It will all happen here."

Corey pulled the glasses down toward the tracks.

The second train had stopped and was disgorging men and weapons in even greater numbers than had the first. Closer, the fire against the first line of breastworks had intensified. In one shattering explosion bodies were hurled into the air like dolls. At the embankment, the infantry from the first train began flowing over the top, stretching out then into a skirmish line three and sometimes four men deep. There was no hesitation. They began to climb the slope as the ranks of the men from the second train massed in the right-of-way behind them.

The gunners on El Grillo had shifted their attention to this new and more pressing problem, and shell bursts plowed the lower slope of La Sierpe. Men fell all along the advancing line, and the line itself began to waver. Machine guns firing from the Federalists' stone and corrugated iron battlements cut down attackers as they came in range.

From deep in the valley a bugle sounded. The line of advancing infantry stopped. In one or two places gaps were showing, and men leaked back down toward the railroad trains. Across the tracks the field guns of the insurrectionists had fallen silent, but surely they would speak again, and quickly—would have to. Villa's infantry needed their support now as perhaps they never had.

When the guns did find their voices again, he discovered how much he still had to learn—and how much he had already learned this morning.

The next flashes from Ángeles's artillery lighted the lowest reaches of Loreto like an incandescent wall. The earlier barrages hadn't been half the magnitude of this one. The big 75s Ángeles possessed were joining the action with a vengeance. Pancho Villa's master gunner, until now, had been playing with his enemy.

When he and Fergus had hiked to the top of La Sierpe from the Daimler, he hadn't been able to tell where the guns in the valley had been pointed by watching their intermittent blinking. Now he could. The full weight of the Northern Division's heaviest ordnance would be unloaded not on the Federalists' lower defenses, but on the hilltop. Here. And it would fall as a mammoth sledge in—he counted as he had before—no more than seven seconds. He dropped the binoculars, flattened himself against the ground until he felt no thicker than a flounder, clapped his hands over his ears—and picked up his count at "four . . . five . . . six . . ."

Through his hands the blasts came only as heavy, rolling flutters ascending to muffled thumps which echoed inside his bones. It was a long, attenuated moment before he was sure he was still alive. With the way the enemy shells had seemed to blanket the entire crest around him, it seemed beyond belief he hadn't been touched at all. He lifted his head. The mingled screams of horses and men pierced his eardrums. When he struggled to his feet he saw Fergus getting up, miraculously untouched, too.

Dupont was sitting with his back against a boulder, holding his side. Blood was oozing through his thin fingers and spreading over his otherwise spotless tunic.

"I'll get a medic for ye, Pierre!" Kennedy shouted above the din now building on the hilltop.

"*Non, non, mon ami*. It is not a wound of great significance. Besides, if you look to the rear, I think you will find the medics are no longer with us. The guns found their tent. But I cannot see the battle while sitting here. Tell me what is happening."

Fergus peered over the edge. "The troops from the second train are on the hill. The Villistas are resuming their advance. The first of them are almost at the trench line."

"This barrage was not merely clever, *mes amis*," the Frenchman said. "It was diabolic. Let us see what *le bon colonel* Ruiz decides to do." He pointed at Ruiz, who was now moving back to where the field telephones were. "I fear he is about to make the one fatal mistake Ángeles is counting on."

Barrón's commander on La Sierpe had been lucky, too, but he looked shaken.

Ruiz raised his left arm before he reached the telephones. His right hand pointed down the hill.

"*¡Apúrense!*" he called.

Horses and men began pressing forward. In seconds the reserve battalion was at the ridge to the north of Corey, Fergus, and Pierre Dupont, and in only seconds more it had cleared it and was starting down.

"Are they reassembling below the ridge?" Dupont asked.

"No, Pierre. They're moving right on down," Fergus said.

"*Mon Dieu!* Then Ruiz has been tricked. He fears another bombardment will finish them. He should not concern himself. There is no possibility that Ángeles could bring such a weight of fire to bear again for at least twenty minutes. He fired too many rounds. His Schneider-Canets and Chaumonts must have time to cool. With Ruiz's reserves spreading out on the slopes beneath us they have lost their cohesion as a fighting force. What are the Villistas doing now?"

Fergus took another look. "They've overrun the breastworks now, and their field guns are firing up the slope again."

The Frenchman winced and pressed harder against his side. His wound was deeper and more serious than Corey had thought. "I think it is now time for you and Monsieur Lane to leave this hill. You will learn nothing more of value here today. This battle has now passed into history for all intents and purposes."

"Aye, Pierre. Corey?"

"I've seen enough, Fergus." He bent over Dupont. "Let us help you to our car, Colonel—provided it's still where we left it—and take you back to town."

"*Non, merci,* Monsieur Lane. I will stay here until General Ángeles's vanguard reaches me. It seems I have just now lost my job. I wish to submit my application for a new one—if the Villistas are taking applications. *Je suis heureux avoir fait votre connaissance, monsieur. Au revoir.*"

"Don't, Pierre!" Fergus sounded anguished. "Let us get you out of here. Villa shoots captured officers out of hand these days."

"Perhaps. Some applications for employment *are* rejected. In any case, I do not think I would enjoy very much the motor trip Monsieur Lane was kind enough to offer."

They found themselves part of a line of cars, trucks jammed with men, motorcycles with and without sidecars, men on horseback, and walkers and runners crowding the road down to the highway leading into Zacatecas. The horror they had left behind seemed to stretch out tentacles to drag them back. Ruiz was in the rear seat of the car ahead of them, a man battered into shock. Morales's little car had a new driver now. Corey had almost tripped over the tiny captain's body, what was left of it, when he and Fergus exited the hilltop.

One of the first shells to land must have destroyed him along with most of Ruiz's headquarters company and the men in the medic's tent. His legs and half of one arm were gone.

The sentries who had stopped them on the way up were nowhere to be seen. The box was empty, but Corey heard the ring of a telephone as they passed it.

Just above the junction with the highway Fergus reached over and grasped his arm. "Pull over, laddie. I think we had better do a little thinking. We won't get far at the moment, anyway."

True enough. The road into Zacatecas was choked with all manner of vehicles, horses with riders and even more without, and the hordes of survivors streaming around the shoulder of La Sierpe. A lot of these men had thrown away their rifles. The retreat from La Sierpe was a full-scale, mindless rout.

"Well, Fergus? The railway station?"

"No real point, lad. Pancho's cavalry surely had dynamiters riding with it. They will be south of town by now. In a couple of hours there won't be an inch of track unblown between here and Guadalupe. I do hate to leave the gear we took to the station, though. There were two bottles of bonnie Glenlivet in my duffel bag. But we're as safe as anywhere for a wee bit. Besides, we still have a show to see if Pierre, bless him, was right. The dynamiters may have been sent south, but Pancho's geegees will fall on what's left of Medina's army in the next half hour."

"I'm not sure I want to see it."

"Nor do I, come to think of it. But we will, I fear."

"And after that?"

"I don't want us to actually steal this car, Corey, but we had better keep it for the next day or so. There won't be any trains for the south. I suppose we'll have to find more petrol somewhere and then head for the capital when the roads are safer. Or would you rather chance throwing ourselves on the doubtful mercies of the victors?"

"Don't know. I suppose we could do worse than going back to the hotel and sitting things out there tonight."

"Aye, laddie. We'll just have to travel whatever back roads into town we find, and get to it when we can, hide the car in a stable or barn until morning, and tell our host we lost it on the hill. He'll want to be paid for it, of course." Yes, and Corey was fairly sure who would be called upon to make the payment.

Petrol. Corey turned the engine off. He immediately wished he hadn't. They were on a flat pull-off, where Fergus would have to crank again to start it.

The sound of heavy guns was still rounding the rocky

shoulder of La Sierpe, but with none of the concentrated fury or frequency of the earlier barrages. The Villista artillery was merely finishing things off. In the valley below them a third train was inching toward Zacatecas. The first two must have been shunted to a siding to let this one pass. Flatcars teemed with fresh troops and held machine guns. Some of the stragglers on the highway looked the train over and quickened their pace, and although the entire road was out of small-arms range from the moving troop train, the frayed column veered to the opposite side of the roadbed as if the twenty or so feet they gained would give them more protection.

Zacatecas itself still seemed untouched, and must have beckoned to Barrón's mutilated soldiers like a haven of security and rest.

Then something happened that ripped that hope to shreds.

At first Corey only *saw* it.

In the center of Zacatecas an entire city block of rooftops lifted into the air as if they had been pulled skyward by unseen ropes. A stupefying flash of orange almost as bright as a second sun lit their undersides. Then the roofs settled crazily as walls blew outward, filling the streets with mud bricks, and scattering shattered timbers that from this distance looked like jackstraws. In a second, monster billows of oily, ugly smoke covered everything.

Then the sound came rolling up the valley—the most deafening sound Corey had ever heard. It made the remembered noise of the battle for La Sierpe the mere blowing of a string of Fourth of July ladyfingers by comparison.

"They've hit the arsenal." Fergus's voice was a throaty, awestruck whisper.

The men on the road to the highway and those on the highway itself had stopped, transfixed and frozen on the crowded road as if they might never move again.

But they somehow did.

Some only sank to their heels and stared toward the city, others ran into the chaparral on the high banks at the side of the road and began climbing the rocky hill. Some resumed their slow march toward the town. Corey had seen such walks once before, at Chupadera County's sole execution during his terms of office.

And three on the road near the Daimler turned, detached themselves from a splintered column, and began moving toward the car. Each of them still had his rifle, but slung to the backs of shirts stained dark from rain or sweat—or blood. The nearest had his thumb hooked under the leather sling strap.

"The crank, Fergus," Corey whispered. "They want our car."

"No time, laddie. Ease your gun out slowly. Don't let the buggers see it."

The first of the men stepped to the front of the car. His free hand reached for Fergus's little flags. He pulled them from the Daimler ornament, lifted them to his face and sniffed them, then threw them down into the drying mud. The other two fell in beside him.

The automatic felt even heavier and more unwieldy in Corey's hand than it had when he hefted it before he strapped it on.

The man at the front of the car unslung his rifle, laid it across the Daimler's hood, reached up and rubbed his chin. He patted the hood of the Daimler. Then he touched the brim of his cap in a contemptuous salute.

"*Buenos días, señores.*"

"*¿Qué tal, amigos?*" Fergus said. "May we offer a ride to town?"

What an actor! His voice wrapped friendly silk around the Scottish burr.

The man smiled at him and shook his head. "You may do more than that, *señor*. You may offer us *el auto* if you wish." The smile vanished. He banged the hood hard. The rifle started to slide away and he put a big hand out to stop it. "Or even if you do not wish."

The man at his right levered a cartridge into his rifle, pointed it above his head, and fired a shot into the air. The third man was grinning like an idiot, but he hadn't freed his rifle. None of the stragglers down the road even turned a head.

"*Sí, amigo. El auto es el suyo, con respeto.*" Fergus still sounded affable. "Perhaps you will permit us to ride with the three of *you.*"

The first man laughed. It was the threatening laugh of a hyena. Then his eyes narrowed and his mouth worked as if he were chewing something tough and tasteless.

"*Pero* you will have nowhere more to go today, gringo. A ride for you will not be necessary. *Por favor,* get out!" He looked at the other two as if he expected some applause. The man with the rifle aimed at the sky began moving past the hood toward Corey.

The Scotsman's Webley was now in his left hand. He put his right hand on the handle of the door beside him and turned his craggy head toward the back of the car. "We can't negotiate with these sassenachs, laddie." His whisper wouldn't have stirred a speck of dust. "I'll take the talker first and that smiling cretin second. Empty your fucking big pistol at the other one as you leave the car. Don't rely on a single shot. Keep firing until there's not so much as a twitch." He turned back to the speaker at the hood. He pushed the handle down, keeping the pistol in his left hand hidden by the dash. He lowered his feet to the roadbed just as the first man reached for his rifle.

It was over in five seconds, but it could have been a year. Fergus pushed the first man from where he had fallen across the Daimler's hood. The smiler had made a break away from them, but was now lying in the ditch. It had sounded like the firing range at Fort Bliss before Cuba, and Corey, even after he had replaced the automatic in his holster and stared down at a red-blotched heap of laundry at his feet, still heard echoes from it and from the Scotsman's Webley, but then he realized it wasn't echoes, but more firing, coming from somewhere else. Comrades of the three dead men? Had they killed these three only to die themselves?

It was a frightening second before he realized the shots

weren't meant for him and Fergus, but were off in the middle distance, down the highway.

He lifted his eyes from the body of the man he had killed. Far down the road every last one of the retreating Huertistas still in view was being ridden into the ground, gunned to death and sabered by cavalry that had appeared while Fergus and he were occupied with the three dead men. A full squadron of riders had boiled up from the direction of the tracks. Ten or twelve of the attackers had now split from the others and were pounding along the highway back toward the Daimler.

"We did splendidly in the frying pan, laddie," Fergus said. "Let's see how we sizzle in the fire."

The little Caledonian rogue sounded downright cheerful.

Their escort handed them over to a sergeant and a squad of riflemen at a roadblock at the northern edge of town. Three of the soldiers slipped into the backseat of the Daimler. Everything was done with gestures. A suspicious-looking young officer took the .45 and the Webley from them. Neither they nor their captors—if such they were—said a solitary word. One of the men in back prodded Corey's shoulder with the muzzle of his carbine and they drove through more carnage than he had seen in all his time in Cuba.

Brief bursts of rifle and pistol fire sounded from an alley or from behind a building from time to time.

When the street opened into the cobbled plaza of the cathedral, the carbine-carrying watchdog behind Corey thumped him on the back with his fist, reached a hand across the seatback, and signaled for him to stop.

Out in the plaza's center a slit-eyed colonel in the uniform of the División del Norte sat in a high-backed, brocaded chair at a small round table that held a bottle of wine. Three other officers sat with him, two on wooden chairs, one on what looked to be a barstool. The plaza was filled with riflemen in Villista uniforms, and at the edges of the plaza, tables outside restaurants and wineshops held another horde, eating, drinking, laughing, and hurling catcalls and insults at the line of vacant-eyed men in front of the colonel's table.

Federalist officers and men stretched from the table to the broad steps of the cathedral, where still more of them waited. The colonel or one of the other officers spoke with each man who reached the table, and after a few moments the men they talked to were waved to the right or left. Most were turned left. A few men in the line wore civilian clothes. It was all marvelously efficient, orderly, and businesslike. Corey soon figured out that the ones sent to the left were being taken by soldiers carrying rifles around the pinnacled corner of the cathedral's walled cemetery. He didn't want to believe what his eyes, and his ears especially, were telling him, but volleys were erupting once a minute and belief came willy-nilly. He couldn't see the stretch of wall where the executions were taking place. He was grateful. None of the men the colonel or the other three officers talked or listened to—there were only a few who were allowed a word—made a sign of protest as they were turned to the left and led away. None of those sent to the right, and presumably back to life, seemed especially relieved or happy.

Then a man he recognized reached the head of the line. Colonel Ruiz of the hilltop. Ruiz's hand flew to the brim of his cap in a crisp salute. He didn't wait for the colonel's wave, but turned and marched toward the wall as if he were on parade. A guard fell in behind him. Corey couldn't suppress a low, pained gasp.

"Don't concern yourself, laddie," Fergus said. "The worst part of Ruiz's day was when he lost La Sierpe. Barrón would have shot him, anyway."

"*¡Silencio!*" one of the men in the backseat shouted. The colonel turned and looked at the Daimler. Corey heard the back doors open, and in an instant the man who had sat behind him was alongside the driver's seat, waving him out with the barrel of his carbine. At the table the colonel beckoned to the guard.

"Well, at least it appears as if we won't have to wait in that dreary long queue," Fergus said. "My puir wee feet are killing me."

There was another cry of *"¡Silencio!"*

Their guards prodded them across the cobbles toward the table. When they reached it, the man who had sat behind Corey in the car saluted and then fished a scrap of paper from his pocket. The colonel looked it over and dropped it on the table. Some wine had spilled, and the paper turned red as blood.

"Sus cartas, señores, por favor," the colonel said as one of the other officers refilled his empty glass. "And while we examine them, allow me to introduce myself. I am Colonel Rodolfo Fierro of the Northern Division of General Francisco Villa."

Corey handed over the papers he pulled from the inside pocket of his jacket. It was better to let them do his talking for him—for the moment. Fergus must have decided much the same. He was as silent as Corey when he handed the colonel his.

The colonel looked at Corey's first, studied those of Fergus next, went back to Corey's. After perusing them for the better part of a minute, he closed his eyes. Narrowed as they were, it didn't take much effort. At last he opened them.

"Much as I do not relish shooting foreign nationals, *señores,* I am afraid I must make an exception in your two cases." He plucked the wine-soaked scrap of paper from the tabletop. "This note is from Lugarteniente César Luna, the officer who placed you under arrest. Lugarteniente Luna says you were found leaving La Sierpe in the company of Federalista officers and men—that you both were armed—and that your weapons had been fired."

"We took no part in the fighting on La Sierpe, Colonel Fierro," Corey said.

Fierro's smile was thin, his lips bloodless.

"Will it surprise you, Señor"—he glanced at Corey's papers—"Lane, that we have heard that kind of denial many times already this afternoon?"

"I suppose not, sir. But Mr. Kennedy and I will gladly give

you our word of honor that we were observers, and observers only, on La Sierpe." He should go on. He should plead, fall to his knees and beg for his life. This was not a matter of cowardice or courage. It was not a matter of indifference. But although belief had come to him that men were being shot around the corner, it wouldn't come that he could be one of them.

He said nothing further.

Fierro put his wineglass down, placed the tips of his fingers together, leaned back, and gazed upward to where the cathedral's spire soared above them. He looked as if he were praying.

Then his two hands separated. One was clearly pointing. To the left.

Bodies were being hauled away in mule-drawn carts when Corey, Fergus, and the three guards rounded the corner of the wall.

Well, Henry Richardson. I can't very well blame you for this. I came to Zacatecas here by my own free choice. And I haven't even fought to save myself as I should have. Perhaps the seeds of death in my character have been germinating far too long. Pity I won't see you again. I could give you some insights now, old friend. That they wouldn't be the ones you hoped for scarcely matters.

Ruiz's riddled red corpse was still slumped at the foot of the wall. He looked as if he were merely enjoying a *siesta*.

A peevish, put-upon-looking sergeant seemed to be in charge of the firing party, whose members were lounging against the side of the building across the narrow alley from the wall. He fairly screamed at Corey's guard.

"For Christ's sake, Enríquez! Will someone find enough guts to tell El Carnicero Grande Fierro to slow things down? We've run out of fucking cartridges. I've sent for more, but it will be fifteen or twenty minutes before they get here. It's easy for him, filling himself with wine while we do all the goddamned work! *¡Mierda!* The Revolution won't fall apart if we let a few of these bastards live until tomorrow."

"Don't take it out on me, Pérez," the guard protested, his tone petulant. "I only follow orders. I will, however, go back and respectfully inform the colonel of your *problema*." He turned to Corey and Fergus. "I am very sorry for this unfortunate delay, *señores*." He shrugged his shoulders, nodded to the two other guards, and started for the plaza.

Fergus's laugh filled the alley. "I thought it entirely too good to be true when we didn't have to wait in that bloody line," he said when it subsided.

The two guards motioned Corey and Fergus to the side of the building and the riflemen in the firing party moved aside for them. They sank to the caliche and leaned back against the adobe bricks. Just in time. Corey knew his legs wouldn't have held him upright many moments longer. His throat was dry.

"It's been a bonnie life," Fergus muttered. "Not long enough by half, but bonnie."

Then the tough little man began to sing.

> "Gie me a wee doch an' doris
> A wee drap, that's a'
> A wee doch an' doris
> Afore ye gang awa'."

Corey suddenly felt sleepy. Impossible. He couldn't, *wouldn't*, sleep away the last quarter of an hour of his life. But, damn it, his eyelids were leaden. He let them close. At that it was perhaps better not to see too well right now . . .

The sound of hoofbeats brought them wide again. A horseman trailing two other mounts had rounded the corner and was entering the alley. The rider reined up sharply in front of the firing-party sergeant.

"Sargento Pérez!" The young man's voice was all cold command. The sergeant dropped a tortilla he had dug from somewhere.

"¿Sí, lugarteniente?"

"I have a release order from General Ángeles for these two prisoners—countersigned by Colonel Fierro." He waved a sheet of paper at the sergeant. "I am to take them to the temporary headquarters of the general *ahora!*"

He handed the piece of paper down to Pérez, and while the sergeant looked at it, it dawned on Corey who the young officer was.

He had seen him last in an alley just like this in El Paso, Texas. But that had been outside a whorehouse, not in the shadow of a Mexican cathedral.

Jorge Martínez had changed considerably since then.

25

"You did *what?*" Paco Durán had been attacking an enormous plate of tortillas and beans, and washing it down with a bucket of beer in a cantina where Jorge found him a street away from the plaza. His full spoon stopped in midair. "You took a terrible chance, *amigo.*" The dynamiter looked more worried than Jorge had ever seen him—and for the first time, frightened.

"I know, Paco."

The spoon dropped into the plate. "Why did you do it? You owed the gringo *nada.* If Fierro finds out, you'll take this *hombre* Lane's place at the wall."

"I know that, too. I couldn't help myself."

"Does Trini know what you did?"

"No. I haven't seen him since we rode into the plaza. I don't think I'll tell him. I couldn't get him involved."

"*¡Bueno!* I don't want to lose him, too. Fierro could easily find a wall big enough for both of you. But how in *el nombre de Dios* did you ever get that release from General Ángeles?"

"I didn't."

"Then what was that paper you showed Pérez?"

"A menu from the cantina in the plaza I was in when they brought Lane and the other gringo to Fierro. It was all I could find."

"*¡Chihuahua!* How did you know Pérez couldn't read?"

"I didn't. But so many men in this army can't, I thought it worth the risk."

Durán's big face flushed and Jorge bit his tongue. The sergeant growled. "So Pérez and I can't read. Maybe it would be better if *you* had never learned. Juanita, too. Reading grows no beans. What about Ángeles's and Fierro's signatures?"

"I forged them."

"This gets worse, Captain Cockroach. Why didn't you at least let them shoot the *other* gringo? If you owed nothing to the tall *yanqui*, you owed the little one less than nothing."

"I didn't know how long it would be before Pérez was resupplied with ammunition. I was afraid *el pequeño* might start yelling when I took Lane up the alley without him. Even misery like that loves company."

"It will have even more company if Fierro ever sees the two of them again and asks why they are not dead. And have you considered, *amigo,* what will happen if Pérez ever shows that 'release' to anyone?"

"I didn't let him keep it. I burned it once the two gringos were on their way."

"You did one thing right, at least. None of this tells me, though, why you committed this *muy grande* asshole stupidity to begin with."

Why had he done it? Jorge had asked himself that question a thousand times since he rode away from Lane and his companion at the edge of Zacatecas.

Paco was right. His grudging respect for Corey Lane wasn't enough reason for saving him. Were the tables turned, would the gringo have stirred himself for *him*? But perhaps that was it. Given the opportunity, Lane would have. The stories about his fundamental decency, the kindness he had shown even to fugitives and criminals in the Ojos Negros, must have been lurking close beneath the surface of Jorge's muddled thinking as he drank his *cerveza* in the cantina in the Zacatecas cathedral plaza, and watched Fierro's ruthless, drumhead mockery of justice.

But, aside from merely respecting him, was the character of Corey Lane enough for Jorge to risk his own life this way?

No, there was something more that prompted him to action when he saw Fierro wave the two gringos to their death. He hadn't hesitated long enough to think or breathe. It was as if he had long ago prepared himself for the moment the car carrying Lane and his companion stopped fifty feet from the cantina—or as if *something* had prepared him—or rather someone.

He knew now, if he hadn't known at the moment.

The casual way Pancho's "Butcher" Fierro had extinguished life—so different from the more fully understood mayhem of battle—had begun to tell on him, roiling his insides with a disgust that turned his beer to wormwood as he watched.

At first he found himself reluctantly approving. All of the men who faced the firing parties were enemies of the people. When they took up arms against the Division of the North they surely must have known they would die if they lost. But then one of the men Fierro sent to the left turned out to be the same colonel whose surrender brand-new *lugarteniente* Jorge Martínez, leading a squadron into action for the first time, had accepted when he and his riders reached the road into Zacatecas. The captured officer saluted his judge with such simple dignity and walked so serenely to his death that revulsion welled up. *Basta.* Death simply could not be this casual. If it were, this whole cause might well be lost no matter how heady today's victory had been.

And, oh, what a victory it had been!

"Nothing can keep General Villa from getting to the capital first now," Trini said when the regiment regrouped in the southeastern precincts of Zacatecas after the last skirmishes in the city's streets. "That does not mean, of course, that all our fighting is behind us, nor that men will not die in the next few weeks, but the biggest battle has been won. The First Chief's tricks before Paredón and Saltillo came to nothing."

Paredón and Saltillo. He knew himself to be a different Jorge Martínez since then. He had still felt needles of fear stab his belly here at Zacatecas during the fighting on El Grillo, but they weren't the cold, deadening icicles of shock they had been when he had first ridden by Trini's side into the flaming mouth of the unknown—and afterward, in his failure of nerve in the parade at Saltillo. What he had felt yesterday and today was now a controlled, reasonable—and sometimes useful—fear, something surging steadily in his veins and arteries, something he would get used to, could live with. *Sí.* He had to. From here on out it would never be any different.

He had handled his first small command well, if not with spectacle or bravado. After the assault on the last manned field guns on El Grillo he had gathered his men around him to ride in tandem with Paco down to the road clogged with fleeing Federalists almost falling over each other in their eagerness to surrender. Paco had helped him restrain his riders from killing every Huertista they saw, not merely the few who still resisted.

How lucky he had been when Trini assigned the dynamiter to him permanently.

His respect and liking for the giant had deepened. Jorge would never voice his feelings for the sergeant, and it was unlikely that Paco would ever let his for Jorge slip out. *Bueno.* Men didn't do that.

One thing between them had changed, but only in part. Ever since Jorge became Trini's aide, and even after General Ángeles had commissioned him an officer when they returned to Torreón from Saltillo to mount the offensive against Zacatecas, Paco had never abandoned the tough, faintly derisive way of talking to him he had used in those painful days of training. Jorge was still, and would probably always be to Paco, Captain Cockroach, as he had been just now when the sergeant took him to task for his rescue of Corey Lane. But the nickname, and even more, Durán's mock derision, was only apparent when they weren't in combat. Once the shooting started at Paredón, and in the last five days at Zacatecas culminating in today's signal triumph, he was "sir," "señor," or "mi lugarteniente"—even in the worst heat and blast of battle. He hadn't expected the ursine former blacksmith to display such an impeccable military manner—not with him.

And *of course* Paco was right about Lane.

Once Lane had swung into the saddle, he and Jorge stared at each other wordlessly, until the little one shouted, "Are we going to muck about here until they pipe in the haggis?"

Strange accent, but Jorge had heard it once before. Angus MacAndrews, Jamie's dead uncle. The little gringo came from Scotland. He looked like a jockey on the big horse Jorge brought him along with the one for Lane.

Jorge laid the reins across his horse's neck, jammed his spurs into its flanks, and led the way at a trot the length of the alley leading from the plaza. He didn't dare let his horse out to so much as a canter, couldn't risk appearing in too much of a hurry while the still-baffled Pérez was gazing after them, but once he found a *calle* leading to the southern side of Zacatecas he yelled *"¡Vámonos!"* back over his shoulder, beat his animal with his quirt, and at a full gallop guessed his way out of town.

Pure luck kept them away from Villista roadblocks.

Then the enormity of what he was doing settled on him like a leaden serape when they reined up at the crossroads.

"I think this is the road to Guadalupe," he said, pointing south, "but if I were you I would make my way through the hills for the next few miles. Perhaps you can catch up with whatever is left of *los Federalistas puercos*."

Lane opened his mouth, but Jorge held his hand up.

"Go! *¡Ahora!* There is no time to talk. And I have no wish to hear what you might have to say, anyway. *¡Vamos!*" Panic was rising, almost choking him, panic he hadn't known in battle.

He turned his animal and rode back to the plaza and the cantina without looking at Lane again.

The sun was slanting over the cathedral, and the shadows of Fierro and the others at the table were growing long. The colonel was still waving men to the left. Even fewer went to the right now. Volleys echoed from the alley every five or six minutes.

"Eighty-seven," a bearded sergeant in the cantina said. "I think El Carnicero wishes to set a new record this afternoon. According to the Law of Juárez he can only shoot traitor officers and *políticos*, but if he runs out, I suppose he can promote some of Barrón's *soldados* and hold elections for the civilians he wants to kill."

Paco had finally resumed eating, and his plate was empty. He pushed it away from him, tossed off the dregs of his *cerveza*, and belched. "How will you account for the two *caballos* you took for the gringos, *amigo*?"

"I told Luis and Ernesto that Fierro wanted them. They found others somewhere."

"*¡Mierda!* You have the nerve and soul of a *gitano ladrón*." His huge face sagged into sorrow. "The worst part of this foolishness, Captain Cockroach, is that your two fucking gringos probably won't live out the night in spite of what you did. Fierro has given orders that our patrols are to kill anyone they find in the hills between here and Guadalupe. No exceptions." He belched again. "You do not wish to eat, *amigo*? Your *soldadera* will rip off my *cojones* if I let you get thin when she is not with us. Perhaps you can take comfort from the fact that she will do the same to Fierro when he shoots you."

26

▲▲▲▲▲

Until now Corey had let Fergus take the lead in nearly everything about this junket, but he knew that for the rest of the journey it would be up to him. As Jorge had suggested, and before they had ridden half a mile from where young Martínez left them at the crossroads, he turned the two of them up and away from the road into a dry watercourse easy enough for the horses to negotiate, and in minutes they were in high scrub country well above the highway to Guadalupe.

Intermittent gunfire still echoed from the town in back of them and from the valley.

He wouldn't let himself think about Jorge Martínez now; that would have to wait until they extricated themselves from the lesser but still precarious fix they were in. But he did wonder what Fergus had made of Jorge's *deus ex machina* rescue of them.

The Scot, while an adequate if not accomplished rider, was city-bred—Glasgow, hadn't he said—and he clearly had no feel for hill or mountain country, his evocation of his "bonnie Highlands" notwithstanding. He was having a tough time of it guiding his mammoth animal up these rocky slopes. To Corey, the rugged terrain of this ridge south of the Zacatecas—Guadalupe road seemed little different from the trail from Black Springs to Blazer's Mill back on the Mescalero. This was no time to relax, though. Without weapons, food, or, to his dismay when he checked the canteen in the saddlebag, water, it could turn awkward before morning— more than awkward, downright dangerous. His present sense of relative easiness wouldn't hold up through the night. This ridge might look like a *hundred* places in the Ojos Negros—it wasn't any one of them. Every growth of scrub and every jutting rock could hide a fugitive Huertista soldier, still armed, as he and Fergus no longer were, and covetous of his and Fergus's mounts. They were still locked tight in a land of killers—and helpless now to fight them off.

The sun had dropped behind the high hills on their right, but it was still glowing orange on the far side of the valley. Here and there smoke rose from wrecked trucks. Ángeles must have moved some of his guns to La Bufa to bring the Federalists fleeing Zacatecas under fire.

From where they were riding they could look down into the gorge separating Zacatecas and Guadalupe, catching occasional glimpses of both the road and the railroad tracks. Stragglers moved along the road and from time to time squadrons of cavalry issued from the depressions on either side of it, rounding up individuals and small groups and turning them back to the city Corey and Fergus had left behind.

Once or twice puffs of smoke from small arms rose in the fading sunlight, followed after a delay of seconds by the reports. Once a man fell, as he watched, twitched a little in the now darkening road, then lay still. Then he made out more bodies in the ditches running beside the road. None of it seemed real.

What would soon become real was the aftershock sure to hit him about what had happened in Zacatecas.

They found water. He thanked his lucky stars they came across the thin soundless trickle staining a rock wall while it was still light, in the dark they would have ridden past it and begun the next morning with an already burning thirst. As it was they had hell's own time filling their canteens, holding them tight against the wall until their knuckles ached. It took five long minutes to get enough water inside the canteens to make a splash.

Back on the horses, Fergus gestured toward the valley.

Where the gorge ran out into some sickly yucca flats southeast of Guadalupe a stream of black smoke too heavy to be from rifles was rising above the railroad tracks. A long freight train of alternating flatcars and boxcars filled with soldiers pulled into the main track from a siding in the marshaling yard south of the smaller town, and inching toward the horizon like a reticulated snake. "Must be the last of Barrón's army—if you can still call it an army, laddie," Fergus said. "I don't recall seeing a battle end so decisively. The Federalists won't be able to make another real fight this side of the capital—and probably not even there."

"Then it's all over now?"

"Aye, lad—except for what's going to happen in the next ten seconds. Look!"

The Scot pointed some distance back up the main track. Half a mile to the rear of the freight with the load of troops, a lone locomotive with only a tender and no cars behind it had emerged from the gorge and was racing toward the point where the spur from the marshaling yard was feeding the flatcars into the main line and over a trestled bridge.

"My God!" Fergus said, his words thick and his voice

hoarse. "We're about to witness one of Eusabio Calzado's famous *ferrovía* torpedoes. There's probably a long ton of dynamite in that tender."

Men were jumping from the cars of the freight and scurrying up the gravel embankments on either side. Some fired rifles and a lone machine gun spat flame at the battered, black engine bearing down on them. The gap closed.

The locomotive made an almost playful hop where the closed switch tried to bar it from the troop train, then tipped forward on the cowcatcher, and vaulted crazily into one of the slow-moving boxes.

A broad streak of cadmium yellow with vicious red flashes blotching it broke and shattered for a hundred yards on either side of the point of impact, and then it was as if a giant hand twisted the track and right-of-way like a huge belt, spilling three, no, four cars of soldiers into the cut yawning under the trestle, flipping other cars at both ends of the bridge on their sides like toys. Then the roar of the explosion reached Corey's hillside. It was only his imagination, had to be, but he could swear he heard screams inside the larger sound.

"And that," Fergus said, "puts an exclamation point on the Battle of Zacatecas. Calzado's a proper thorough brute. How did the bugger know which of those cars carried what was left of Barrón's heavy ordnance and its ammunition?"

A thousand feet below them more clots of cavalry appeared on the road between the larger town and Guadalupe. At intervals of a quarter of a mile groups of three or four horses and riders peeled off and began fanning into the hills ahead of them. There must have been fifty or sixty of them all told.

"Fergus, we don't dare try for Guadalupe now, or even south of it. There's no way we could make it through those patrols."

"Aye, laddie. But what do ye suggest? We've got to catch a train for the capital."

"We're going to have to hole up on this side of the road until dark and then try to make it across. San Luis Potosí is

262 ▲ Norman Zollinger

straight east of us, isn't it? That's Carranza territory, last we heard. Damn it! I wish we had a map."

"Aye, but it's a couple of hundred kilometers, at least. Nasty-looking bit of terrain down there, and I don't suppose it gets much better as we go east."

"I know. I don't see that we have much choice, though. It looks like Villa's people are going to follow Barrón on this rail line all the way to Aguascalientes. West of us it looks bone-dry and maybe not even inhabited. We've got to find food pretty quick, and water for the horses. What we found is enough for a day, maybe, but if these animals don't drink soon, they'll quit on us."

"Ye're the clan chief noo, laddie. I'm only along for the ride."

Crossing the road turned out to be the easiest of their problems. By the time they reached it there were only a few of what appeared to be captured trucks heading back toward Zacatecas to avoid, and no Villa cavalry appeared, and once on the far side of the highway and on their descent toward the river, Corey found himself facing the same question which has plagued commanders since the first march soldiers ever made. Should they cross the river now to make the next day's start easier, or make camp on the near bank and cross it in the morning when they were rested?

The question became rhetorical at the river. The ride down the hillside, and the race across the road leading the horses into the scrub beyond it, had put them both in a fair sweat and their mounts in a heavy lather. It was too dark to look for a shallow ford, and he feared the shock effect if they stumbled into a deep, cold pool. They had no bedrolls and nothing else to retain body heat except their thin jackets and the skimpy blankets from their horses, and while he toyed with the idea of going upstream until they found corpses they could strip for extra clothing, and perhaps food, the thought proved too grisly to hold for long.

He called a halt. Fergus looked grateful. They tethered the horses to some stunted trees that in the light of a half-moon looked hauntingly like the piñons of the Ojos Negros, and collapsed on the bank of the stream. A cold wind rose, and the rushing water at their feet sounded like ice breaking up on the Rio Concho in March. The horses drank deeply from the stream. So did they when they drained the warm water from their canteens and dipped them full again. His stomach cramped after the first swallow. It was going to be one hellish, miserable night. Fergus coughed his way through a shiver.

Then the lights of fires and lanterns began to appear in the hills back toward Zacatecas, and a few more winked on the slopes above the road leading to Guadalupe. The cavalry patrols must be making camp for the night and postponing the search for stragglers at least till daybreak. Their quarry, if any was left, must be hiding in the folds and on the ridges of the land, too, defeated Huertistas as much on the run as he and Fergus were—and as much in the dark.

They would have to lie as low as slugs themselves.

Then rebellion and resentment rose in him like a fountain. The hell with it. It was a long time until sunrise.

"Do you have any matches, Fergus?"

"Aye, lad. A whole box of Lucifers. Why? Do you have a smoke or the makings?"

"No. I want to build a fire."

"Bonnie!"

It wasn't a roaring fire; there wasn't much available in the way of fuel. What they found—spindly, tinder-dry squaw wood stripped from the scrubby trees at streamside—blazed like kerosene, but dwindled in seconds to a faint punk glow. It warmed their insides at least, if it did little for their flesh.

Clearly, though, sleep wouldn't come very soon.

"That beastie Fierro is quite a piece of work, isn't he?" Fergus said.

"Fierro?"

"The colonel in the plaza. Rodolfo Fierro."

"That was the Butcher?"

"Aye. He didn't remember Fergus."

"Why should he?"

"I arranged a shipment of Hotchkisses for Pancho a year ago in Chihuahua City. Fierro and I had a drink together. There were a lot of Villa's other cronies there at the time."

"For Pete's sake, Fergus! Why didn't you speak up?"

"Fat lot of good it would have done. Didn't want Fierro to hear my brogue, anyway. He hates the English with a passion, and although I'm a Scot, anyone from the British Isles is a sassenach as far as he's concerned. He might not have sent us around the corner, but just done the job himself."

Corey looked hard at him. His bony features were russet in the weak firelight. "You ran guns to Villa?"

"Aye. I've run them to Obregón and González, too." He fell silent, then, "And on occasion I've armed Huerta in my own wee way. Haven't for a while, though. Not since Whitehall decided he would lose."

"Fergus, when are you and I going to come clean with each other? Exactly what are you and your government up to here in Mexico?"

Fergus's smile matched a sudden feeble flicker of the flames. "The usual, laddie. It's minerals and food, ultimately a matter of money. And above all, petroleum. The Royal Navy is going over to oil for fuel. So are the Germans, not to mention the little yellow beggars from Japan."

"You have no real interest in this country for itself?"

"Of course not. This is just a side road of history for a great power. Important, aye, but if it were really big, they wouldn't trust it to an insignificant wee mon like me, now would they? But what about you Yanks? You lot are playing the very same game."

"All Washington wants is stability here. President Wilson—"

"Aye . . . Wilson. The principled pedagogue of Princeton. There's the rub, laddie. It isn't that your President's public morals are low, not at all; just that his perception of what everybody else's should be is so bloody high. At bottom, and he won't recognize this, the 'stability' he wants is identical with Perfidious Albion's greedy self-interest. The only difference is that Britain doesn't bother to disguise it. Now, look ye. No one doubts that you Americans are good people. Ye're sincerely generous, and your devotion to democracy isn't just talk. But ye're also like the rest of us in looking after yourselves. If ye'd just admit it, we could get on with the business of great nations without all the fussy meddling you colonials seem to cherish. In the long run the Mexicans would be better off, too. Woodrow Wilson can't remake this country in the Yank image."

It wasn't as if the same thoughts hadn't occurred to Corey, but it was mildly irritating to hear them voiced with such offhand cynicism.

"The real trouble with you Yanks is that ye've never learned to compromise. The red-white-and-blue blinds ye to shades of gray. Perhaps it has something to do with all that space ye've been able to fill up. If things didn't work out for you, ye simply went West. It's an attitude that might cost ye more than tuppence ha'penny someday. *This* miserable fucking country, on the other hand, has lived by compromise. Blooded Spaniards or *mestizos*, they're distilled Europeans at bottom. That's not so bonnie, either. I'm willing to bet those two bottles of Glenlivet that this Revolution will fail because of it."

"You think Huerta still has a chance?"

"No, laddie. He's through. This battle will finish him. But the people the Villistas call the *perfumaderos*—the politicians in it just for themselves—will take over. London doesn't trust Carranza, but it feels it can use him. While we use him, he'll break the heart of youngsters like that cavalry officer who got us out of Zacatecas." Even in the weak light Corey could see Fergus's eyes twinkle suddenly. "By the bye, there's something odd about that rescue. If Ángeles ordered our release, why did that laddie sneak us out of town the way he did? Why didn't he take us to the general as he told that sergeant he was ordered to?" Fergus laughed. "Ye said something about us coming clean with each other, Corey. Why did I get the foolish notion that boy and you know each other?"

"Yes. We know each other, Fergus. Perhaps it would be more accurate to say we *knew* each other."

* * *

He found a ford and they crossed the river before the sun cleared the hills northeast of Guadalupe. They bushwhacked for the better part of a mile before they found the dim beginnings of a trail.

His first impulse was to set the spurs to the horse and strike out for the east and San Luis Potosí, but he knew if they didn't get food soon the rising morning heat could bring about a debilitation no amount of the sweet water in their canteens could keep at bay. They couldn't be profligate with the water, anyway. Even full canteens wouldn't last forever, possibly not even until they found another river or a spring. Fergus hadn't complained of hunger yet, but it might well be the only time in his adult life the Scot would have preferred to fill his belly with food instead of whisky.

Remembering the cattle he had seen grazing across the valley from La Sierpe at the height of the battle, he thought of making a detour to the north. The presence of the herd on such small upland pastures, rather than on wide, open range, hinted at a nearby farm or *estancia*. If they rode to the ridge where he had seen Villa's cavalry moving to the flank attack on Zacatecas, they could probably spot a house or line shack before the sun was high enough to punish them too brutally. He discarded the thought as far too risky. This close to the battlefield that stretch could still be infested with *insurrecto* troops, and although he and Fergus might be able to bluff their way through or past them, he wouldn't stake their lives on it. To begin with, all their papers were still in the hands of Villa's hatchet man, Fierro. They were fortunate their guards hadn't relieved them of their wallets. In all likelihood they would need every peso they had for food and bribes before they reached the capital.

They had to go east, then, and take their chances.

One thing: they heard no gunfire in the entire length of the valley. The Battle of Zacatecas was indeed history.

The map he had studied before Fergus and he left Mexico City had placed Zacatecas at 2,446 meters above sea level. Since they left the river they had climbed perhaps another five hundred feet and were still gaining altitude with every clop of the horses' hooves. In the Ojos Negros he could always fix the elevation pretty accurately by the vegetation, but here he had no such knowledge to rely on. He did know that at more than 9,000 feet their chances of gleaning any nutrient from the trailside vegetation were next to nothing. It was still too early in the year for berries or nuts he might recognize and be sure were safe. Most of the plants he saw could be toxic, anyway, as bad as Chupadera County's jimsonweed. He had to fight his horse from time to time to keep it from grazing the suspect grasses bordering the trail. He cautioned Fergus to do the same.

They had moved up through rounded *lomas* bare of any growth taller than waist-high scrub, and the top of each of the small hills they crested was even devoid of that. Now the trail was petering out. He looked in vain for cattle droppings, or any other sign of something connected with human life. The sere, brown hills rolled to the horizon in endless waves. Without a compass and with the year near the summer solstice, the sun would be so close to straight overhead at noon that he wouldn't be sure which way was east for a while. They could travel in circles for a couple of hours without knowing it. He fixed his eye on a *cerro* more sharply pointed than its neighbors. That would keep them going straight—if he didn't lose sight of it when they dropped into the arroyos separating the stretches of higher ground.

"Don't go to your canteen too often, Fergus. We'll need water more when the sun gets higher. And if things don't change by late afternoon, we may have to kill one of the horses for food."

"With our bare hands, laddie? That will take a wee bit of doing, won't it now?"

"We can manage. Then we'll take turns riding and walking. I don't think either of them has the strength to carry us double."

"Forbidding-looking country this," Fergus said. "Brings to mind the 'clearances' beyond Ben Lomond and in Glen Coe."

So Fergus was thinking of home ground, too. "Clearances?"

"Where the sassenachs stripped the forests off the Highlands after German George defeated Prince Charlie in the '45, to make room for their bloody sheep. We Scots weren't always shepherds, ye ken."

The talk was good, superfluous as it might be. It might go some little way toward keeping their minds off their predicament. Even more than the weakness sure to come if they couldn't find something to eat soon, he feared the delirium that could accompany it in these shadeless hills. Better not to think about it.

"I always thought Kennedy was an Irish name," he said.

"It is. But Ayrshire is full of Kennedys. We're a *bona fide* clan, Corey."

"Never heard of it."

"Not many people have. Clan Kennedy is a sept of Clan Cameron. We take orders from the Lochiel in war and aboot other such bonnie matters. Back in the 1400s our clan chief, the Fourth Earl of Carrick, wormed his way into the history books by roasting the Abbot of Crossraguel in the dungeon of his castle at Dunure to get the abbey's lands. As a secular mon I take a wee bit of pride in that."

"And I suppose it's nice to have a notable criminal in the family."

"Aye. I'd always thought my ancestors were only sheep thieves."

"But as a 'guid Scot,' how do you square working for the British? Aren't the sassenachs, as you call them, the ancient enemy?"

"We're practical people in Ayrshire, laddie. Made that way by the dour reality of living on the border. We don't forget, though. We do a little for the Crown, but in our canny Scots way we do a lot more for the Thistle—on the q.t. of course." He growled. "I'm not too keen about Clan Kennedy's motto at the moment."

"What is it?"

" *'Consider the end.'* "

It wasn't working. Corey couldn't keep his mind off his stomach.

There wasn't another word between them for an hour. They passed the pointed hill, and he marked another distant one to serve them as the next guide.

At two in the afternoon, with Fergus nodding in the saddle, they came to the foot of a ridge that seemed even in the heat haze a shade more green than the rest of the slopes around them.

Beyond the top line of the ridge, terraces holding growing things stepped down to a flat-bottomed valley half a mile below them. Whitewashed buildings, stone rather than adobe, dotted the valley floor. Several dozen clustered around a little church.

A boy with a stick was chasing a squealing young pig through a plot of corn in the third terrace down. He caught the pig as they watched.

A church bell broke the hot silence.

The boy looked up and waved to them, and as he did the pig broke free and the chase began again.

"The train comes to our village every week or two, *señores*. I think it comes next Monday, but perhaps a week from Monday. I forget when it was here the last time," Segundino Silva said. He shook his white head. "We can ask *mi niña* Dorotea or her *esposo* Juan when they come in from work in the fields."

"And the railroad goes from here to San Luis Potosí?" Corey asked.

"I am not sure, *señor*, but I think so, *sí*."

"Is there a station agent we can ask, Don Segundino?"

The old man looked apologetic enough to cry. "There is no station, *señor*, consequently there is no agent. There are just the tracks at the east end of the village, where *la ferrovía* drops off freight and picks up the things we grow. I have never ridden the train myself." He brightened. "Juan has. *Sí*, perhaps he knows these things."

"And there are no *soldados* here?"

"No, *señor*."

"Do *los soldados* ever come to San Gabriel?"

"No, *señor*, what would *soldados* want with us?"

Corey sighed. Incredible. A mere seven-hour ride from the greatest battle of the Revolution, and Segundino and his fellow villagers didn't even know it had taken place. In the twenty-seven hours Corey and Fergus had been here in San Gabriel de los Árboles, they hadn't found a soul who knew much about the Revolution, and damned few who even knew one was going on. There wasn't a telephone in the village, as Fergus discovered when he went looking for one to call the British Embassy, and no telegraph, either, Corey supposed, now that Segundino had informed them there was no railway station. Fergus smelled as if he had looked for more than a telephone.

"Is there an automobile in the village we can hire?" the Scot asked.

The old man shook his head. His rheumy eyes actually did fill with tears now, as if he was taking personal blame for the difficulties his two gringo guests seemed to be having. "We are too poor in San Gabriel for such things, *señor*."

Corey had feared Fergus might also check the availability of weapons for the two of them, but he apparently had sized things up much as Corey had. Aside from a shotgun or light rifle for hunting, there probably wasn't a gun in the entire valley.

"We'll just have to be patient, Fergus. The empire can struggle along without you for a bit."

"It won't be easy, laddie. A' the local offers besides tequila is Kentucky whiskey. Small wonder your ancestors beat the sassenachs in your rebellion. That bloody stuff turns a tabby to a tiger."

"Scotch wasn't such an effective tonic for your ancestors at Flodden Field, *amigo*."

He left Fergus discussing cattle with Segundino and wandered the village. He saw the boy who had chased the pig yesterday as they rode in. The boy smiled shyly, ducked inside an archway, peeked out again. Sombreros were doffed when he entered the same cantina whose stock of liquor had disappointed Fergus. A young, smooth-cheeked priest nodded to him from a quiet, leafy *santuario*. He didn't hear a shot, or a shout, or a hurried word anywhere he walked.

The tiny hamlet put him in mind of San Isidro on the upper Concho, back in Chupadera County, a place out of time and certainly out of mind unless a man was stranded in it as he and Fergus were.

Last night, when the bells in the village's tiny twin-towered church tolled a soft, dulcet angelus as he sat with Segundino on the adobe's small patio, feeling the warmth of the beautiful old man next to him come over him like a gentle breeze from secret, blossoming orange groves, he had mused to himself that *here* was where Jorge Martínez belonged—not in the van of a rampaging army disguising the work of hell as that of heaven.

Then shame burned him. What right had he to make such a decision for the idealistic young man from Black Springs, even if he phrased it in silence as mere suggestion? He was no better than some of the missionaries—not all, of course—who came to the reservations thinking that the proud people they were working with were children.

Jorge was no child. He was a believer. He was doing what he had to do. And in that he was light-years ahead of Corey Lane.

Could he ever bring himself to believe in what he had to do for Henry Richardson? Would it remain only an academic exercise?

The train did come on Monday. They left the two horses in payment for Segundino and Juan and Dorotea's hospitality. Corey tried to press money on the trio, but the old man fluttered his brown hands and protested strongly.

"We do not need much *dinero* here in San Gabriel, *señores. Los caballos* are more than enough payment for the little things my family was happy to do for you and your *amigo.*"

Corey and Fergus rode out of San Gabriel de los Árboles in a boxcar filled with melons. A few of the train crew regarded them with idle curiosity, but for the most part ignored them. They might have been just two more pieces of freight.

27

MEXICO CITY—DECEMBER 3, 1914

"What you seem to be forgetting, Corey," Henry Richardson said, "is that Ángeles in just the past month has lost most of the high political ground he occupied after Zacatecas and at the conference at Aguascalientes last summer. I'll grant you it's not his fault, but I would say his star is not in the ascendancy." Henry couldn't have slept for more than three hours after the long trip from Washington, but he looked fresh and ready to do business.

"It isn't ground he couldn't reclaim, Henry. Particularly if we provide some kind of support, even if it's only of the moral sort. Can't we at least talk about this?"

"Certainly. If you are so sure about Ángeles, I want all your thinking, particularly now that Huerta has left the country."

Henry had knocked on his door unannounced, and had held his finger to his prim lips when Corey opened it. "I'm not really here, Corey," he said when the door closed behind him. "We still shouldn't be seen together."

Well, Henry's willingness to listen held hope. Corey had looked forward to seeing him, sure Henry would see things his way when he was here in Mexico City where things were happening, give Corey a chance to make his plea for Pancho Villa's chief lieutenant and strategist. He had of course expected Henry to be somewhat stiff-necked about his championing of Ángeles, but even more frustrating was the State Department man's brushing away his request that he be allowed at least limited contact with the American Embassy.

"If I'm to be effective for you, I need more up-to-date information on Washington's intentions than what I can get out of the week-old *New York Times* I buy at that magazine kiosk in the Zócalo. I've been operating in the dark for six months, especially since war broke out in Europe. Is that the only thing on State's mind now? You've only answered one of my reports since August. I feel useless."

"Don't fret, Corey. Your work here is important. I've been pretty busy, as you can imagine. But I'm simply not authorized to give you access to Washington's dispatches. I'm sorry. And yes, we are spending most of our time watching Europe now. My budget for Mexico has been cut again. I don't like it, either."

"Damn it! Things may happen too fast for me. If I have to continue sending my reports through Cotter, anything important may get to you too late to do you any good. Do I at least have your permission to try to get close to Zapata, then?"

"No. Not yet. I *will* promise to try and get it for you, though. We would still like you to concentrate on Carranza. Villa, too, of course. At the moment Washington is content that what's-his-name, Carbajal, is President, even if it's a short stay. Carranza won't back him long. Carbajal's not apt to rock the boat with too much vigor while we unload it. We want you to cozy up to the Carrancistas, but we haven't completely given up on Villa or his undisciplined lot."

"You've cut off their purchases of arms in Texas."

"They can begin again if Villa furnishes proof of continued good intentions toward us. Now, give us your view of the whole situation."

"You already know most of it from my reports."

"I'll risk being bored by hearing it again."

"All right. After Zacatecas, which, you may recall, Villa and Ángeles took against Carranza's wishes, the Division stopped its advance to the south. It was an overwhelming victory, but it took a lot out of the Northern Division. They had to regroup and resupply. The Huertistas had stripped forces from the east and west to face Pancho, and Obregón had a clear path to the capital. Zapata was already threatening the city from the south. When Huerta collapsed, Obregón filled the vacuum and kept the Morelos army from occupying it. Then, just before the conference at Aguascalientes, Carranza and González joined him. Of course the Obregón-Carranza armies had stretched their lines pretty thin, too. They pulled back to the east coast, where they are at present. Then Zapata and Villa moved in from the south and north."

"Villa is in control here now, then?"

"Not exactly. He runs everything north of the capital, but in the city itself he shares power with Zapata. Obregón has token forces here, too, but I don't think he has an agenda of his own—yet. It's a sort of tacit truce at the moment."

"Where is Villa's army?"

"The bulk of the Division is at León in Guanajuato."

"Why has he kept it there?"

"The break between him and Carranza is an open one now, particularly after the way Carranza ignored the Aguascalientes resolutions even Obregón agreed to. They'll be in open warfare soon. Carranza and González have cut off Villa and Ángeles's access to coal and munitions. That's what stalled the *norteños*, and that's why they need guns and ammunition from Texas more than ever."

"He could still fight, though, couldn't he? And could he form a government?"

"Yes to the first. The División del Norte is still the biggest and best army in Mexico. Word has it that Ángeles is restraining him from moving south. My informants"—should he tell Henry that his "informants" consisted largely of Fergus and the people Fergus had put him next to? No—"tell me that Ángeles wants to move straight east and attack the Constitutionalists on the coast. I think it's a good idea myself. Putting aside my feelings about Ángeles for the moment, why aren't we backing Villa *unreservedly*? You said he had to furnish proof of good intentions. He supported us on the Veracruz occupation thing, when no one else in Mexico did, Carranza in particular. As for Pancho's forming a government, I just don't know. Unlike Ángeles, he only regards himself as a fighter. He reveres the memory of Madero, true, and he's immensely popular here, as well as in the north, but he apparently has no political ambitions of his own, at least none to be President. But even if he doesn't *want* the presidency, I should think that sort of self-denial would have great appeal for Woodrow Wilson. The 'office seeking the man' kind of thing."

"Didn't I tell you once that President Wilson has turned a mite more practical? He has leaned toward Villa on occasion because, as I told you in Black Springs, he's fascinated by him. But he found Pancho's recent pronouncements infuriating. Oh, it was understandable when the general called for his own and Carranza's resignation, but the sham theatricality of his suggestion that both of them be taken out and shot revolted Mr. Wilson. Carranza seems more stable."

"He doesn't care much for the United States."

"True. But we're not in a popularity contest. Carranza at least has a national policy—and the makings of an international one we can deal with even if we don't like it. Villa doesn't really have either."

"Ángeles does."

Henry ignored that. "Let's get down to cases, Corey. Anything new to report since your last message to Boston?"

He had to recognize that he was beaten on Ángeles for the moment. "There's one piece of what might be news. Rumor has it that the Germans are more active here in the capital now. My understanding is that they are interested in Carranza. So far they haven't made any moves on Villa or Zapata. It's a funny situation, Henry. Zapata seems to have no more lust for the presidency than Villa does. Between the two of them they have complete military control over the entire country outside the capital, except for the east coast and that pocket south of Guadalajara which Obregón's lieutenants still hold, but they haven't been acting much like conquerors."

Zapata and his people in particular, he might have added.

Since Victoriano Huerta had taken ship at Veracruz for exile in July after the defeats in the north and Morelos, the Zapatistas had drifted in and out of the capital for five months, sometimes seeming like a true occupying army, sometimes withdrawing silently—as they had when Obregón moved in from the northwest and blocked them—flooding and ebbing like a tide of white in the loose cotton field-hand clothes they wore, men who would have looked more at home tending crops in serene San Gabriel de los Árboles hidden away east of Zacatecas than here in the capital's uneasy counterfeit of calm.

When Huerta ran to the coast like a thief in the night, Zapata's *obrero-paisano* army moved into the terrified capital from the south like sheep nibbling at spring grass rather than as the rapacious horde the press predicted they would be. Instead of indulging themselves in the pillage even the city's underclass had braced for, the Zapatistas had acted more like country bumpkins come to town to take in the sights. Hungry, of course—what army in Mexico, save Obregón's, wasn't these days?—they had gone from door to door in the capital's southern districts begging food, bowing like servants to householders and merchants, with their big straw sun hats in their hands and hiding the cartridge belts across their chests—obsequious and humble. Camped out in the parks, quietly filling the *calles*, museums, and streetcars, they looked more like refugees than conquerers—until one saw the occasional stained machete that had been used against machine guns.

There had been, of course, the tragicomic occurrence of three nights before Henry's arrival, when a fire broke out in the warehouse district where two brigades of Zapatistas bivouacked in sheds by the railroad tracks. What happened next could have come right out of a picaresque penny dreadful. None of the farmer-revolutionaries had ever seen a pumper engine racing to a blaze before, and with the clanging of the bells and the sight of ax-wielding, helmeted firemen, they had been sure that either Obregón or some left-behind Huerta loyalists were attacking them.

They shot and killed twelve of the firefighters before residents of the district could explain things to them.

Perhaps Henry hadn't read or heard about it. Corey wouldn't tell him. He wouldn't tell him either that his own feelings about Carranza and his attitude toward the United

States had come from Fergus. It hadn't seemed prudent yet to mention his liaison with the diminutive British agent. Henry had assumed that the trip to see Medina Barrón was entirely Corey's idea, and it hardly seemed important to disabuse him of the notion now.

"Washington hasn't changed its mind about Zapata, then, I take it?" Corey said. "There's favorable talk about him in fairly influential circles here. And his people worship him. He could be the small-'d' democrat Woodrow Wilson wants."

"No. He's only a nine-day wonder in our view. For heaven's sake, Corey, he and his Morelos crowd weren't even present in the first round of talks at Aguascalientes."

"I know. Obregón kept them out at gunpoint—at Carranza's insistence—until Villa demanded they be allowed to attend. When they did show up, though, Zapata's delegates made the only substantive contribution to the discussions."

"You mean that ridiculous Plan de Ayala?"

"Why is it ridiculous?"

"Taking a third of every *hacienda* for the peasants? It's a dreamer's plan, Corey. Devised by a dreamer who can't even read or write. It would turn Mexico's economy upside down."

"Perhaps that's what it needs. Actually, the plan is surprisingly modest in its demands. I expected something much more vengeful, and I sure would have understood it—and sympathized."

"*Misplaced* sympathy, Corey. Political configurations must be based on something other than vengeance. That's one of the principal troubles with this benighted country. These people could do with a lot less emotion. Calm reason is what's needed here. The sort Washington could provide."

Vexing as it was at times, he could take Henry's supercilious dignity; this sudden smugness was something else. He exploded. "For Christ's sake, Henry! Do you have any idea what things were like in this country under Díaz and Huerta? Mexico was the most oppressive slave state since ancient Egypt!"

"Come now, Corey! That's a rather wild, irresponsible charge, isn't it?"

"Is it? Perhaps. But consider this. Now, I'll confess I'm not in possession of precise figures, but did you know that in 1909—six years ago—every last inch of the land between Brownsville and Tijuana that abuts the United States was owned by fewer than two dozen families? The *hacendados* had their own armies, backed by those killers the *rurales*, and their own private courts and jails. They executed people on their own warrants. The peasants were tied to the land as securely as any medieval serfs. And what the rich didn't own, foreigners did."

"Corey, Corey . . . you're beginning to sound like Emma Goldman or some IWW agitator."

"Be that as it may—it's true. And except where Villa and Zapata—and in some few cases the peasants themselves—took a hand at righting matters, things haven't changed much."

Henry stood up and moved to the big window looking out over the Paseo de la Reforma. His straight back looked a bit less rigid than it usually did. Perhaps a tiny bit of what Corey felt had reached him. He wasn't a bad man. He turned back to Corey.

"Let's be realistic. Granted that some things need changing, you still can't turn a sovereign twentieth-century nation over to unskilled illiterates with no experience of governing. Why, when the Zapatistas finally did show up at Aguascalientes, the newspapers said they arrived like hobos. They begged transport from truckers as if they were vagrants, stowed away in mule trains, and even rode the rods under railroad cars, wearing little more than rags, and, I'm told"—Henry shuddered—"no underlinen." Yes, that would horrify fastidious Henry Richardson. "Once there, they couldn't even look after themselves. General Obregón, an enemy, mind you, had to set up Bowery-style soup kitchens to feed them. Do you honestly think such incompetent ragamuffins could actually rule?"

"I suppose not. But an intelligent, politically sophisticated man who understands their needs—and damn it, their importance!—could."

Henry smiled. "Someone like Felipe Ángeles?"

"Exactly."

"Have you actually met Ángeles yet, Corey?"

"Once. Years ago. Can't say I really know him."

"Since he's such an idol of yours, perhaps you should get genuinely acquainted. I'm probably going against my own better judgment, but I might be able to arrange it."

Corey's heart skipped. "How? Villa's people have turned down every overture I've made so far to visit the Division. It's almost as if they knew what I was doing in Zacatecas."

"That was good work, Corey. We appreciate it. General Ángeles is coming into the capital a week from Saturday. The embassy is giving a ball for the provisional government notables and the diplomatic corps, and we think he can be persuaded to attend. There will be others present I'd like you to look over, too—Álvaro Obregón, González, perhaps the First Chief himself. Apropos of what you just said about the Germans, you'll be interested to know that we've invited them, too. No Zapata or Pancho Villa, of course. I don't think they would fit in at this sort of gathering. Ángeles will be the only one from the Villa side. Look now, just because we don't see eye-to-eye on some things doesn't mean we don't value your opinions. If I can wangle you an invitation you'll have to attend under two constraints, though. You're not to mingle with members of the embassy staff, and you're not to come anywhere near me. It will be full soup and fish, of course. Will you come?"

"Absolutely." Something occurred to him. "Could you get an invitation for Dr. Trujillo at the Ministry of Culture, too?"

Henry looked doubtful.

"The man you spent time with when you first got here? I suppose I could. If you think he would be useful. I'm surprised to find he still has his job. Maybe I should be more surprised that he had his job in the first place. He didn't seem to fit in with Huerta's crowd." Henry pulled his watch from his vest pocket. "Well, that's as far as I feel we can go for now. Please check the corridor for me, Corey, so I can make my departure without being seen." Anyone but Henry would have said "so I can sneak out." At the door he stopped. "When you come to the ball, I'd appreciate it if you would keep some of your radical notions to yourself. You are an American, remember."

"I know what I am, Henry."

Five minutes after Henry left, he found himself fuming. Henry seemed as narrow in his view of Mexico as most of Corey's countrymen were.

As elated as he was at the chance of meeting Felipe Ángeles, the feeling left him like a breath of air held too long when he considered that Henry probably only meant it as a sop. No one in the chain of command above him had the slightest intention of listening to him seriously. He fought the feeling that he ought to pack his bags and get back to Black Springs.

But he knew he was being much too hard on Henry.

Even though he had irritated Corey during this disappointing meeting, Henry was still one of the most admirable men he had ever met, reserved, certainly—oh, hell, call a spade a spade, stuffy—but secretly warmhearted and generous almost to extremes. He had been that way in Cuba.

Although the regular army sergeants poked fun at Henry's unflagging, lofty dignity, his fairness with everyone, regardless of rank or position, had made him perhaps the most respected American officer in Havana.

Corey smiled. The clerks in the office hadn't even tried to hide their amusement with the Bostonian, mimicking his speech and manner almost before his back was turned; a lesser man would have called them to account.

And it wasn't just this tolerant reserve which had drawn Corey to Henry back in those Havana days.

For several months Henry seemed to verge on bankruptcy between paydays, borrowing money from Corey for small purchases, something that didn't square with his usual spartan habits.

Then the two of them made a routine visit to an orphanage on the outskirts of the city where the army had sent food and medical supplies in the days immediately after the fighting. Regulations required that their office inspect such places from time to time to see that U.S. goods were indeed reaching the intended recipients, and Corey assumed this was Henry's first time there, as it was his. But almost every one of the sisters of Las Hermanas de la Merced seemed to know him.

As they fussed around him, Henry acted even more businesslike and crisp than in the office.

He didn't reveal any particular concern for the orphans' plight, and they were a pitiful, malnourished lot whose looks made Corey feel a little sickish. At a nun's behest, one stunted youngster, a mulatto with a bad cast to his eye and a nasty skin condition, tried to thank Henry for what the American army was doing for the home. The child extended his hand. Henry shrank from it, shuddered then, much as he had a few moments ago when he talked about the Zapatistas' reputed lack of underwear at the Aguascalientes convention.

But when he and Corey said goodbye, the sisters crowded around Henry again and beamed on him as if he were their order's patron saint. "And for the money you have been sending us, Señor Richardson," the mother superior said, "you are foremost in our prayers—and in those of *los niños. ¡Gracias, gracias, muchas gracias!*"

When Corey pressed him, Henry—blushing, and as discomfited as if he had been caught exposing himself on a public street—finally admitted he had been sending the orphanage most of his army pay.

From that day on it cost Corey a pretty penny in gifts and money, too, even though Henry never once asked his help.

Henry couldn't have changed all that much in the years since Havana. Not unless Plymouth Rock itself had changed.

Still, the Henry Richardson of Havana and the almost cynical, manipulative Henry Richardson of the last half hour hardly seemed the same men.

Was it the task of Corey Lane to reconcile the two of them? It was a task that might be well beyond his Chupadera County capabilities.

Fergus's low-key but critical assessment of Americans and

their inability to compromise came to mind. Damn it! Corey couldn't be expected to reconcile the two warring natures of his countrymen, either. What was that clan motto of the strange small Scot? *Consider the end.* Until something blasted Corey out of his present despairing mood, he had to consider that the end justified the means. And he would have to go on with this business, his frustrations about it swept aside by his own approximation of the sense of duty that drove Henry Richardson.

Narciso Trujillo had become a good friend since Corey looked him up again after Fergus and he got back to the capital, and the times spent with the mild-mannered doctor had been a sometimes welcome relief from Fergus and his persistent gadfly buzzing.

After resting at the Mirador after the train ride to the capital from San Luis Potosí, Corey had gone to the Ministry of Culture and found Narciso Trujillo cataloguing a collection of onyx Aztec artifacts in his musty office.

"Señor Lane! It is good to see you. I feared for you at Zacatecas."

"I came by to say *gracias*, Dr. Trujillo."

"¿Gracias, señor? ¿Pero por qué?"

"For the undeserved kind words you said to General Barrón about my work."

"It was only the truth, Señor Lane. I am sorry your views also got to General Huerta, but it came to nothing. I was happy to discover."

They lunched together at the Hotel Reforma, plunging immediately and deeply into a discussion of Mexico's troubles. It wasn't a two-way talk. Mostly Corey just asked questions and listened to Trujillo's surprisingly candid answers. Together they probed the country's history, and the economic problems Corey finally felt emboldened enough to suggest were caused by bad government and even worse management. To Corey's surprise, the doctor came out squarely for Zapata's Plan de Ayala. "It, or some variant of it, particularly Emiliano's ideas about the return of *los ejidos* to the peasants, is the only long-term hope for peace. *La tierra,* the land itself, has always been the soul of Mexico. That soul should be reunited with the bodies of *los pobres* who work it."

"I suppose it's not for me to ask, Dr. Trujillo, but do you think Zapata could form a government for Mexico?"

"No. Emiliano is a spirit, not a statesman."

Trujillo obviously concerned himself with much more than old bones, ancient trinkets—and graves. "What Zapata's 'plan' does *not* address, however," he went on, "are the things which must be done if this country is to join the twentieth century. We are not all peasants or *vaqueros*. My countrymen are gifted people. We must find other enterprises for our many skills, not just the ones provided by petroleum and silver, which only take things *from* the land. And we must tell the world that *madre* Mexico is not for sale."

Then, as they neared the end of the meal, the conversation turned from politics to something resembling philosophy.

"I think sometimes, Corey"—it was "Corey" and "Narciso" before the coffee arrived—"that my countrymen and I have an excessive preoccupation with death, a passion for it. You have seen our Day of the Dead, have you not?"

"Yes, I have. In Chihuahua, some years ago. It fascinated me. I won't pretend to understand it fully, but I found a strange beauty in it."

"*Sí.* If we could only hold it to a feast day, a religious ritual, it would be *magnífico*, but I fear there is a strong current of the profane running with the sacred in this stream of celebration, and it clasps our emotions in little ways *every* day of the year. We do not always succeed here in separating death from life, and I do not mean from spiritual life, but life as it is lived in the town and city streets, and in the fields. Death draws my people as the moon draws the tide. It tugs at us always, even when we are sure it has no claim on us."

Corey had never seen a man betray more profound sadness than the one who sat across the table from him.

Now he wondered, as Henry had, how Narciso had held his position under the tyrant Huerta, and why, since he apparently had more in common with the long-suffering middle class and the scorned intellectual elements in the capital, Zapata hadn't demanded his resignation. Or why Villa hadn't. The Tiger of the North, for all his martial genius, was politically a lowbrow populist at best. He might ask for more than Narciso's resignation—his head.

Perhaps the answer was a simple one. With confusion reigning everywhere in Mexico these days, and absolutely triumphant here in the capital, it might be that no one had looked at Narciso. He commanded no divisions.

"Narciso," he asked, "is there a man on the horizon who could pull Mexico from the mire?"

"Sí. Felipe Ángeles." It jolted Corey like a nearby lightning strike. He only half heard Narciso go on, "But I believe you have already come to that conclusion yourself." Shrewd guess on the part of this strange little man. Corey hadn't mentioned the artillerist in any of their talks.

On the way back to the Mirador he had his driver swing by Avenida Melgar. He hadn't tried calling since he and Fergus returned to the capital. What was the use? The lady on the train and in the black touring car was more ephemeral than ever. He should just forget her. He wouldn't see her again, and it probably was just as well.

Shortly after his luncheon with Narciso Trujillo, a fever to do something more lasting than espionage had seized him and he had begun to make notes for a serious study on the things that were happening to Mexico—and him.

Now, Henry gone at least until the ball, he went to the *escritura* by the window and took out his writing case.

Words wouldn't come. Damn it! He lacked the talent or the background for work like this. He was just a simple, and probably simpleminded, peace officer. He ought to leave such endeavors to his betters.

There was a knock at the door. Henry again? Had he forgotten something? Something as simple as giving his Special Foreign Service Officer the well-earned boot?

He opened the door and found a bemused Fergus. It was the first time the Scot had ever visited his room.

"Guid morning, laddie." He looked past Corey. "Bonnie

digs, these. His Majesty's Government doesn't put me up like this. Is there a drop of something potable in these elegant premises?"

"Isn't it a bit early for a drink, Fergus?"

The Scot's answer was a crinkle of his craggy face Corey could only characterize as winsome. He went to an ornate Spanish highboy and picked up a decanter of Cuernavacan cognac and one crystal glass.

Fergus took a seat by the window. He chuckled. "I saw an auld acquaintance as I crossed the lobby," he said. "A laddie from your American State Department. Name of Henry Richardson. Now, just what do you suppose he's up to here at the Mirador?"

"Haven't the foggiest." The little bastard. Corey had better duck any conversation that might come from Fergus Kennedy's spotting Henry Richardson; he had never been too damned successful at keeping things from him. Perhaps it might not prove too difficult this time, though. Fergus's short legs were twitching with what looked like happy agitation. "What brings you here besides your thirst, Fergus?"

"Pour me that drink and I'll tell ye." The cognac Corey doled out disappeared in one swift, easy toss, followed by a slight grimace. "Since ye seem to have nought else, I suppose this will have to do."

"Except for that look of disgust at my feeble attempt to be hospitable, you seem inordinately pleased with yourself."

"And well I might be. Just gleaned a bonnie bit of news."

"Oh?"

Fergus winked the wink of a conspirator at him. "Would ye have any interest in seeing Pancho Villa and Emiliano Zapata meet each other for the first time, lad?"

"For Lord's sake, Fergus, are you serious?"

"Wouldn't joke about something as big as this."

"When? And where?"

"Tomorrow. Xochimilco. They intend to wrap the whole Revolution up. Don't know if we can actually get into the meeting, but we can try, if ye don't feel ye'll be bored by a lot of silly speeches. I don't think the press has even heard about this yet."

28

▲▲▲▲

He stood outside the Mirador on the broad sidewalk inset with blue and white Puebla tile, waiting for Fergus and his rented car and driver to pick him up. Without a doubt he would have to pay for this ride, too, but even if the driver gouged them with the universal cupidity Corey had grown used to in Mexico, it would be worth every last centavo. This could well be the happiest trip he had made since he went to work for Henry Richardson. His euphoria at Fergus's news still enveloped him in a warm mist.

If Villa and Zapata joined forces, and if both still spurned the presidency, it could position Felipe Ángeles precisely where Corey thought he should be. Maybe Washington would listen then.

The Paseo de la Reforma was filled with people, and more flooded over the lawns and through the eucalyptus trees and ragged palms of the Alameda Central, just visible behind the hotel. Band music was throbbing through the *avenidas* leading to and from the Zócalo. No *siesta* now. He wondered how many of those stopping to buy an *helado* from the canopied stand a city block down the avenue from him knew what would happen in Xochimilco today—the fourth of December 1914. He could hardly restrain himself from shouting the news out to them in a *grito* like the "*¡Viva México!*" of the President on each September 15 when he rang the Campana de la Libertad in the belfry of the cathedral in the Zócalo. He couldn't remember now whether Carbajal, the Carranza-backed president Henry had mentioned, or earnest, decent Eulalio Gutiérrez, named to the office by the Zapata and Villa delegates at Aguascalientes—but not even here in the city, never mind the Palacio Nacional, at the moment—had performed the old liberation ceremony this year. He had gone to dinner with Narciso that night, and to a lecture on Spanish colonial art afterward. It wasn't the first time he had felt like a cheat with the doctor, parading himself as a historian with no other ax to grind. Well, at least he *was* trying to be a historian now, as well as a middle-level secret agent. And his new deep sympathy for the people of this land was certainly sincere enough. He wasn't cheating Narciso about that.

It was a bright, cool, invigorating morning, but as grateful as he was for the seemingly never-failing sun and the tonic of the *tierra templada* air blowing lightly across his cheeks, he knew he would have felt the same euphoria in a downpour or a hurricane. Something seemed about to burst inside his chest, something surely heightened by the prospect of today's trip, but something which had been swelling there all along.

Lord, how he had fallen in love with this most marvelous of cities!

Except for Boston and New York, most American cities he had seen looked new to him, raw and temporary, and even the best of them—vibrant and stimulating as they were, but presenting an almost enervating metropolitan sameness from their dockside slums to the diamond circles of their opera houses—lacked the kaleidoscopic, *a lo reina* charm of the Mexican capital. Largely a matter of age, he supposed. They were urban infants compared to this sprawling, complex *pueblo grande*—so supremely unconcerned with the storms raging around it.

In some ways even Rome, Paris, and Madrid, remembered from that peripatetic summer after college, still wore the blush of youth by comparison.

Mexico, Distrito Federal, had been a genuine city when the great European capitals of today were only primitive mud and stone hamlets, or crude timber stockades barely holding beasts and barbarians at bay in the antediluvian gloom. Funny that he had mentioned Egypt to Henry in his lament for this country and its ancient pain. The canal-laced Tenochtitlán of the Aztecs that Hernán Cortés and his Iberian thugs battered into submission with their "civilized" engines of destruction—before it was overlaid through the centuries with the mellow Churrigueresque building triumphs lining the Paseo today, and the nineteenth-century French imitations of the dove-gray façades of St. Germain de Pres that fronted on the *calles* running off it—must have looked a lot like a Karnak in miniature.

He didn't delude himself, though. Queenly countenance or not, the comely wrinkles of character on the face of Mexico City had been won at an ungodly cost. And that face would be scarred again before all this ended, in spite of its present sublime indifference.

"Penny for your thoughts, laddie." It was Fergus at his elbow.

"Where's the car, Fergus? I expected you to pick me up here in front of the hotel."

"Around the corner. The driver *muchacho* I hired doesn't have a permit for his wee buggy. He doesn't want to be caught on the Paseo."

"That's just great. The last thing we need is to get ourselves arrested before we reach Xochimilco."

"Afraid Henry Richardson won't let you play with Fergus anymore?"

"He doesn't know we've *ever* played together."

"Then ye haven't told him what we're up to in this bonnie jaunt today?"

"I did tell him that. I called him at the embassy last night. But I didn't mention you."

"There's a canny laddie. I'm not sure Henry trusts me and my lot, particularly now the Empire is at war. What did the old fusspot say?"

"He was pretty upset. But he didn't forbid me to go."

Upset? Henry had smoked as Popocatépetl never had, permitting himself a rare blasphemy. *"God damn it. Don't you even try to talk with Zapata!"* The only reason he hadn't forbidden today's trip to Xochimilco was that Corey hadn't stayed on the telephone long enough for him to do so. It would be easy to obey orders and avoid Henry at the ball, and probably wise—if the invitation still arrived.

But outraged as Henry was, the State man had let something hopeful slip about today's meeting. "If Villa and Zapata really want to, perhaps they could stabilize things to Mr. Wilson's liking. And even if they don't want power personally, perhaps they could settle on someone stronger than what's-his-name? Eulalio Gutiérrez. Just listen, mind you."

The car was a dilapidated British Leyland some *barrio* mechanic had mongrelized by the addition of parts from a number of other makes, looking in much worse shape than the Daimler they had used at Zacatecas, with a jury-rigged canopy of orange and yellow canvas much like the one over the *helado* vendor's stand floating ridiculously above it. Ludicrous as it might appear, it did somehow reflect his ebullient mood. The driver, an Indian or *mestizo* boy even tinier than Fergus, looked confused and nervous; his hands shook as if diseased. He managed a shy smile, and Corey struggled into the cramped backseat, where he sank through worn leather cushions almost to the floorboards. Every spring in the heap must have been shot to hell long ago. Damn Fergus. If only once in a while he didn't feel he had to remind the world that he was a thrifty Scot. Hell, it wasn't his or His Majesty's money, anyway. He laughed. Nothing could dull the golden light that could shine on this excursion, no matter how uncomfortable he was. And at least this time he didn't have to drive.

"*Vámonos,* Luisito, laddie!" Fergus shouted in the front seat beside the boy at the wheel. He sounded every bit as elated as Corey felt.

With the Leyland coughing as if consumptive, they took backstreets away from the Paseo, twisting through narrow, congested alleys crowded with the ubiquitous burros—and the other, human, beasts of burden—zigzagging like a cutting horse moving through a herd of Herefords at branding time, with washing hung on lines between the buildings almost touching the Leyland's flapping canopy, until they reached the broader thoroughfare leading to the south and Xochimilco, a wide street called the Avenida de los Niños Héroes, named for those valiant teenaged cadets of Chapultepec, if he remembered rightly. Surprisingly, for all that Luisito's palsied hands gripped the wheel with such pressure his knuckles whitened, the boy was a competent driver, and it gave Corey enough confidence to look around him. He hadn't visited this part of the city before, despite Narciso's urging him to stir himself to go down and see the famous floating gardens. He couldn't give them more than a glance today. They weren't *turistas*, he and Fergus.

In the middle of a solid block of shops the Scotsman turned and tapped Luisito on the shoulder. "Pull over and stop for a wee bit, laddie," he said. He turned back to Corey. "Could ye find it in your heart to lend old Fergus a fiver? I seem to have left me wallet in me digs."

Corey fished out his own wallet and extracted a bill. He shook his head in mock sadness as Fergus took it and stepped from the car. They had stopped directly in front of a tobacconist's and Fergus disappeared through a louvered door. In a moment he reappeared with a paper sack in his horny little hand.

He handed the sack back to Corey, said, "Put these in your coat pocket, lad," and with a nod signaled Luisito to get under way again. Corey peeked in the sack and found perhaps two dozen small black *cigarros* of the ugly twist kind that raised such an awful stink. He thought of asking, *Who the hell is going to smoke these horrors?* then thought better of it and fixed his eye on the route, a trifle vexed, but amused as well, that Fergus hadn't offered him any change.

Ahead of them the wooded slopes of Ajusco, the dormant volcano brooding over the Valley of Mexico, seemed close enough to touch, and to the east, their soaring hollow heads lost in the clouds, the much more imposing massifs of Popo and Ixta—Smoking Mountain and Sleeping Woman to the Indians—leaned toward the city as if they were ready to fall upon it.

From time to time he spotted armed soldiers on the sidewalks—coming in and out of shops and lounging around statues, or pissing insolent streams into the fountains that studded the center of the boulevard—Villistas from the

Northern Division, judging by their sweat-stained khaki uniforms. There weren't many of them in evidence. Not surprising, since they were nearing the precincts still partly occupied by the Morelos men of the "Attila of the South." Pancho's followers and the Zapatistas might become allies today, but there was no way *los del abajo* were ready to forget how easily friends fell out. The two leaders might crush each other with the heartiest of *abrazos*; the rank-and-filers would keep their distance.

"When exactly is Villa expected in Xochimilco?" he asked Fergus.

"Noon, lad. And I don't think he'll be late."

"Have you any idea who he's bringing with him?"

"None at all, but I expect we'll be treated to the sight of more Dorados than we laid eyes on in that whole week we spent at Zacatecas. Zapata will have a sizable Praetorian guard riding with him, too. He and Pancho might become chums today, but they'll want to impress each other first."

Corey didn't really care if they saw one Dorado, or a thousand. It was Ángeles he wanted to see. Sometime during their escape from Zacatecas, Fergus had mentioned that he had met the general once, not that Corey was likely to talk with him in this setting, even if the opportunity arose. That could wait until the ball at the embassy next Saturday.

And he realized, too, that there was someone else he wanted to see, possibly more even than Ángeles.

Jorge Martínez.

The young man from Black Springs had never been too far from his thoughts in the past six months. As a matter of fact, he had come to mind every time Ángeles had.

If Jorge had changed so much in the short time between El Paso and Zacatecas, what sort of metamorphosis had he undergone in the half year since the battle in the north? That is, if young Martínez was still alive. Not all the fighting against Huerta had ended at Zacatecas.

There were no more Villa soldiers to be seen on the avenue now, and in fifteen more minutes the Niños Héroes itself narrowed to a country road. Once in a while they passed companies of cotton-clad men bivouacked in the cypress groves at roadside. They didn't look it, but these men were soldiers no less than were the Division men they had passed earlier. Numbers of them stepped to the edge of the road to watch them as they passed. They were all armed. At another, still narrower road into which Luisito turned the car, a sign read, "Xochimilco—3 KM."

The Leyland protested, its small engine popping and cracking erratically. Luisito looked worried when he glanced over his shoulder at a group of Zapatistas who had backfilled the road behind them. Apparently the good behavior of the Morelos men over the past several months hadn't allayed his fear. He had probably seen more than enough soldiers in his short life.

Then the dirt road they were traveling became a cobbled street vibrating the Leyland's skinny wheels, the flora at its side suddenly lush and of a startling green. The lake must be close at hand. They rattled into the village itself. Walls of men in white rose on either side. One sullen look from them blended into another.

An alley between a corral and some kind of empty animal shed opened on the right, and Luisito turned the car into it with the mightiest wrench on the wheel his thin arms could make. They braked to a stop with the dust from the alley roiling up and over them.

"*¡No más!*" he cried, his voice half an octave above hysteria.

"We're on our own, laddie," Fergus said as he bolted from the car. "Could ye pay the bairn?"

Luisito didn't even say *adiós* as he sped away with Corey's banknote held against the steering wheel with one of those white-knuckled hands.

It was only twenty paces back to the entrance to the alley, but by the time they reached it the gap had filled with Zapatista *guerreros*. Rifle muzzles made black circles against the white cotton suits. It only took a quick survey for Corey to decide that *obrero* clothing or not, these weren't men of the exact same stamp as the peasant fighters who had roamed the city like curious kindergarteners for the past several months. These brutes looked capable of killing for pure sport. Luisito had sensed a real threat.

"The *cigarros*, lad," Fergus whispered. "Get them out."

It worked like a charm. Hands left the hilts of machetes, and fingers came out of trigger guards to fondle the smokes Corey passed out while Fergus moved at his side, lighting one of the black cigars after another. Under the cloud of reeking tobacco smoke that lifted over their heads, Corey was relieved that the black looks were fading. There were even smiles on a face or two.

"I think we might just have recruited our own honor guard, Corey," Fergus said.

"I wonder how long we'll have to wait." He reached for his waistcoat pocket to get his watch.

"No, laddie, no!" Fergus yipped. "I don't think they'd rob us, but let's not be putting any ideas in their heads."

One by one the smokers turned their backs on them. Two had stepped a bit in front of the others and were gazing with keen interest toward the center of the village, talking to each other in low, electric mutters.

"Something's up," Fergus said.

Then, from far down the village street, the cry came.

"*¡Viva Zapata!*"

The sound broke along the street like the relayed cracks of a thousand blacksnake whips. "*¡Viva Zapata . . . Viva Zapata . . . viva . . . viva!*"

He knew he shouldn't push himself through the pressing rank of white-clad men in front of him, but he couldn't help himself. Fergus's hand was on his shoulder. He shook it off.

The cry changed in tenor, became a low, rolling chant.

"*¡Emiliano . . . Emiliano . . . Emiliano!*"

Men beat their feet on the cobbles and in the dust at roadside. The dust billowed toward the village rooftops in thick, sepia clouds, veiling everything in sight. Rifle reports split the air. As they died away, the dust settled some, finally cleared completely.

A hundred feet down from Corey's forced vantage point a

white horse with a silver-mounted, jet-black saddle was striking its hooves on the cobbles. A man who must have just slid from that saddle was standing by its side, holding a head trying hard to toss. Slim, not tall, he stood beside the big horse easily, as still as a reed in a placid *ciénaga*, his black coat and tight, black *charro* trousers with silver buttons down the side dark and exclamatory against the snowy purity of the animal's flank. At his throat a pale blue neckerchief, filmy as a cobweb, fluttered ever so slightly in the small breeze wafting away the last wisps of Xochimilco dust. The silver on the saddle and on the elegantly fitted pants caught the warm winter sun and distilled it to a delicate liquid coolness.

Corey strained to see Emiliano Zapata's eyes, but even had he been closer he couldn't have; the brim of a giant sombrero was tipped far forward, hiding them.

The men at the sides of the cobbled street were still chanting. *"Emiliano . . . Emiliano"* but the object of this hummed adulation seemed not to hear it. If he heard voices at all, Corey knew to a certainty they came from some secret inner recess.

"Bonnie entrance, eh?" Fergus said, his voice breathy with an awe Corey had never expected from the sardonic Scot. "Villa will have his work cut out for him to match this mystic wee beggar."

Corey had been so intensely focused on Emiliano Zapata he hadn't noticed a man on horseback riding toward the lone figure from even farther down the village street. The rider pulled up beside the Morelos chieftain, leaned from the saddle, and said something to him. Zapata nodded slightly but didn't look up, and the horseman urged his animal forward and in a second had ridden past the alley entrance.

"Otilio Montaño," Fergus whispered. "I've never sorted him out exactly, but he's very close to Zapata. I expect he'll greet Villa. Someone must have spotted Pancho and his mob coming into town."

Sure enough, a low buzz was beginning at the north end of the cobbled street, and the men in white were pushing into it back along the way they had come with Luisito.

"*¡Los norteños!*" a man smoking one of the *cigarros* they had passed out exclaimed. Horses hooves drummed faintly in the near distance.

Montaño had stopped about a hundred yards from them and had risen in his stirrups as if to get a better view. He looked strangely more like some kind of scout than a welcomer, some sort of sacrifice to attack. Was this to be a meeting of allies or adversaries?

The hoofbeats grew suddenly a bit louder, but despite Fergus's confident prediction, there couldn't be very many riders in General Villa's escort.

Then, just as suddenly, Pancho Villa rode into view. There were perhaps a dozen horsemen with him, certainly not twenty. They pulled up just five feet short of the man Fergus had identified as Otilio Montaño. Montaño brought his hand to the brim of his sombrero in a salute that betrayed just the slightest sign of nervousness.

"Eee, laddie," Fergus breathed. "El Caudillo certainly doesn't pay much mind to the dictates of revolutionary fashion, does he? He still looks more like a mule driver than a general."

Indeed, contrasted with Zapata, Villa looked outlandish, dowdy. A sun helmet straight out of Kipling's British India topped his big round head and florid face, and a loosely woven brown sweater with a rolled collar covered his barrel chest. He looked tall in the saddle and probably still would when and if he dismounted, but it was hard to picture the victor of Juárez, Torreón, Paredón, and Zacatecas on foot like ordinary men. Corey's first impression was that everything about the Tiger of the North ran to excess: the cavernous mouth, the teeth in the broad smile that broke now, the thick, simian arms with the brutal hands so sure and powerful on the reins.

"The first heat of the impress-the-other-chap sweepstakes goes to Pancho by a nose, laddie. The bloody nerve of the man! Riding through the capital and its Obregonista snipers with only a tenth of a troop like that," Fergus said. "Emiliano must have expected the whole Northern Division to come with him, as Fergus did."

"Is Ángeles with the Villa people?"

"I don't see him anywhere. This kind of do is hardly Felipe's style, anyway. One other face is missing. Fierro's. I'm not too bloody disappointed."

Corey looked back down the street. Zapata hadn't moved. There was something Kiplingesque about him, too. What was that line? *He trod the ling like a buck in the spring ... and he looked like a lance in the rest.*

Montaño was saying something to Villa now, no doubt making some probably graceful speech of Latin welcome. Villa nodded through it, from time to time peering past the speaker's shoulder at the slim, dark, unwavering wand of a man standing with the white horse. Montaño finished. He wheeled his horse around and started down the street. Villa got under way as well. The horses and riders behind pressed on the heels of their leader's mount, but one of the huge hands left the reins, flattened against the air, and they stopped as one.

As Montaño and Villa neared Zapata, Montaño turned his horse aside and the two improbable strongmen faced each other. Neither spoke before Villa left the saddle. A Morelos man dashed from the side of the street and took the reins of the northerner's horse. As he started to lead it away, Zapata held the reins of his out to the man, and the man took it, too.

Villa towered over the man from the south, and yet it would have been apparent to a blind man that in everything that counted for anything at all they were of a size—giants both, if of vastly different and unlikely sorts.

"Bienvenido, mi general," Zapata said. "It is good to meet an *hombre* who knows how to fight the enemies of the people." The voice was an odd blend of fire and ice, a voice that could cut through stone.

"Gracias, General Zapata. We have fought for a long time, you and I."

Fergus was right. If he was no longer a muleskinner, he

had the booming manner, the strength, and probably the un-relenting, driving instincts of the breed.

Improbable that these two men held the future of Mexico in their hands.

Impossible to tell which might be the more dangerous of the two in combat.

They stared at each other in utter silence now, and although they gave no outward sign, it was as clear as the bright December day that a process of shrewd assessment was going on.

Then—and Corey knew he would never afterward be sure who moved first—they stepped toward each other and embraced.

The cries of *"¡Viva Villa!"* *"¡Viva Zapata!"* and *"¡Viva la Revolución!"* fairly shook the village of Xochimilco from its rocky base.

The two generals broke apart, turned, and with their arms about each other's waist, started down the street away from Corey.

Corey found himself moving willy-nilly as the Morelos men to whom they had given the *cigarros* poured, flooded, into the street, pushing him along as if he were caught in a heavy tide. Fergus, his small body caroming off one cotton-clad peasant after another, somehow freed one of his arms from the crush and tapped one of the cigar smokers, a mammoth, sweaty, hoglike man, on the shoulder.

"The two great *jefes* will go somewhere to talk now, no, *amigo?*" he said.

"Sí, señor. En la escuela municipal."

"Who may go to the school to hear them?"

"Their revolutionary staffs—and any true *guerrero* who can get inside."

"Do you suppose my *amigo* and I—"

The Morelos man's great laugh cut Fergus off. "Are you *loco, señor?* Gringos? I do not think so."

"Fergus!" Corey called. He had to shout to make himself heard above the raucous concert of noise rising on every hand, and he had to wedge himself hard through the jostling, aromatic bodies squeezing Fergus away from him to keep the Scot in sight. The narrow street had become a raging sluiceway of humanity. "Fergus!" he called again when he gained the Scot's side, hoping against hope the men around him knew no English. "We've *got* to get in there!"

"Dinna think more free smokes will buy us seats, laddie."

"Will money, then? This could be the most important meeting of the entire Revolution."

"It could well be the end of it for us. Hang on to me jacket. I'm not big enough for this sort of work."

The moving crowd stopped, and it was as if they had been dropped on a beach by a receding wave. They were outside a two-story stone building, and the mob had left them, rushed an open double door at the front of it, and was trying to force its way inside, body by hurtling body. Inside the door a staircase was filling with still other men pounding their way up. Men with machetes and rifles stood guard on either side of the doorway. A half squad of men with cameras tried to brush past them, but rifle barrels dropped in front of their bodies like a port-cullis.

"No sense in trying here, Fergus," Corey said. "But we know now that they're on the upper floor. Let's duck around the school and see if we can find a back stair or something."

"Ye're mad. Stark raving mad!" Even with the heavy clamor Corey could hear him clearly. "But I am too, lad. Must be contagious. Let's go!"

A number of men in the crowd must have had the same idea, and several were already in the wooded schoolyard when they rounded the farthest corner. Three were standing by the back wall looking up at a fire escape like those Corey had seen in Boston and New York. These simple farmers had obviously never seen a tangle of ironwork quite like this, and clearly had no understanding of its purpose or how it operated. One by one, faces glum with disappointment, they left the backyard for the building's front again.

Corey waited until they were all out of sight and then bent his back. "All right, Fergus. Climb on top of me and reach up for that lower section."

It took two tries for Fergus to get balanced on his shoulders, but at last Corey heard the fire escape grate and groan as the Scot hung from it, and in another moment they were climbing the iron stairs. It seemed incredible, but there wasn't a soul down in the schoolyard watching them.

"I hope there's no nervous laddie up there with a rifle or a grenade he's wondering what to do with," Fergus said.

At the top of the fire escape they reached the window intended for the exit. They went to their knees and peered through it. Men in white had backed up to it, but a space between the two closest gave them a partial view of what seemed to be some kind of assembly hall, although to view it meant they would have to jam their heads together and almost press their noses to the dusty glass. So much for sight, but after taking this risk, would they be able to hear a word? At the moment too many men were moving about the room, talking, drumming their feet on the wooden parquet floor he saw. Surely they would settle before Villa and Zapata began to talk.

Amazed at their luck, he found that he and Fergus were no more than twenty feet from where the two generals had taken places at opposite ends of an oval table that held Pancho's sun helmet and Zapata's pearl-gray sombrero. The Morelos men and Villa's lieutenants from the División del Norte hemmed them in, but none had taken any of the half dozen empty chairs at the table. Lucky, too, that a pane was missing from the window, so that Fergus and he would probably hear anything spoken above a whisper.

At last the men inside found seats if they could—there were a few chairs and benches away from the dark table with the two hats. Most of them remained standing or leaning against the walls—and the room quieted.

Villa spoke first, or tried to; Zapata interrupted, then stopped and said, "I am sorry, *jefe. Verdad*, I am sorry . . ." There was an awkward lapse that lasted for several seconds. The two men looked at each other almost shyly. Someone in their audience coughed. It sounded like a pistol shot, but neither of the pair at the table looked away from the other.

"Great Scott," Fergus whispered. "They're like bashful newlyweds who dinna ken how to get to the fucking part."

"Shut up, Fergus! We can't miss any of this," Corey whispered back.

Villa had taken the floor again.

"We in the north have thought about you and admired you for a long time, General Zapata. I myself am not one to fawn upon people, but you and your followers have fought the common enemy so well."

"And in Morelos, General Villa, we feel you are a man we can count on. You are *muy guerrero*."

A good beginning, Corey thought. But in the next ten minutes there were fifteen or twenty more exchanges just like this, with sometimes the same sentences repeated almost word for word. Hoping for more, for something solid, Corey began to wonder just whom they were talking to—each other, their listeners, or themselves.

"I think they're a lot better with guns than they are with talk," Fergus offered.

Corey agreed. This morning, waiting for Fergus in front of the Mirador, he hadn't known what to expect from today, but whatever it was, this wasn't going well. The words of the two men who had fought so long, so hard, and so damned well were fine enough, but something was lamentably missing. Where was the fire? Where was the grand design?

The men in the room seemed to grow listless as these soporific exchanges continued. But Villa and Zapata knew their people, didn't they? Maybe these predictable bromides were all the rough fighters within these walls could handle. Maybe this was the only way to keep the struggle going.

As far as Corey could tell, no one had turned and looked through the window, but if they had, they probably couldn't see through the dust that Fergus and he were gringos. His knees must by now have deep corrugations in them from holding the place on the fire escape into which he and Fergus had crammed themselves. Worse than the hurt, though, was the thought that perhaps they had wasted time and energy climbing up here.

Only once did flame blaze in the conversation between the two men at the oval table.

"Carranza," Villa said, "is a man who is very—"

The rest was lost in the angry buzz that ran the length of the room like a prairie fire. The first of whatever reply Zapata made was lost, too, but the rapid nodding of his dark head showed that the name of the First Chief had touched him like a spark falling on a powder train. The shouts and cries filling the room died in time for Corey to catch the last of it. "Carranza is a scoundrel!" Now perhaps they were getting somewhere.

Villa spoke again. "He is a person who has come—from God knows where—to turn the Republic into an anarchy!" His big voice throbbed with rage. Perhaps their abiding hatreds of the Coahuilan would weld them into a new unifying force. Villa hated El Primer Jefe in a deep, visceral, animal way, a way of ecstasy. The dark man from Morelos hated him as part of a bulging packet of much larger hatreds; Carranza was for him only *one* of those arrayed against him and his people and their hunger.

The talk moved to the men Carranza had surrounded himself with. "Men who have always slept on soft pillows; they do nothing but massacre and destroy. With them we shall never have progress or prosperity—or a division of the land," Villa said.

Zapata leaped to that. "It is the land—always the land, *mi general.* We cannot ever forget the land. The land must be returned to the people."

The remark held both the passion of prayer and the harsh urgency of command.

"*Sí,* General Zapata—the land!"

There followed another quarter hour of discussion about the *ejidos*, and it gradually came to Corey that Zapata had but one thrust in his character. That it was pure and fierce, with a classic simplicity and nobility about it, mattered little. Henry was probably wrong about him being a "nine-day wonder"—his star would shine for a long while yet—but he was right in judging him, as Narciso had, as not a man to lead a great country to its dreams.

As the talk settled almost to trivia piled on trivia, Corey searched the other faces in the room. Both the Villistas and the Zapata men seemed satisfied with the bone their leaders were throwing them. Why? Why weren't they demanding richer food than this? They weren't stupid. These were men whom Francisco Madero had stirred with ideas *alone* to march against Díaz four years ago, with all the fearful results that cataract of courage brought down upon them.

Then he knew why. These men had fought so long they could only respond to the rhetoric of violence and anger. They were getting what they wanted here today. No thought was being given to what they *needed*.

What they needed was a man to articulate the future for them. They needed Felipe Ángeles.

And the most tragic thought was that of all the men in this room that could well have held hope, the two men at the table knew what they needed least of all. They were merely weapons.

All talk ceased. Zapata made an almost unseen motion with his hand and one of the men broke from the side of the room. In his hands were a bottle of cognac and two tumblers.

Alongside Corey, Fergus chuckled. "Emiliano will have to drink alone. Pancho doesn't tolerate the stuff. Perhaps old Fergus could step inside and help him out."

"*No, gracias, mi general,*" Villa said. "*Solamente agua, por favor.*"

Had Zapata heard him? It seemed not. He poured the two tumblers full and pushed one of them toward the northerner. Villa stared at it. The assembled *guerreros* stared at him. Expectancy filled the room like marsh gas ready to explode.

Then the fearless Tiger of the North, the dauntless, resolute rider of the winds of revolution, picked up the glass and drained it off in one mighty gulp.

His face turned florid and his eyes swelled out as if they would leave their sockets. His breath stopped, and when at last it came again, he uttered a weak, choked cry. "*Agua . . . agua.*"

The same *paisano* who had brought the liquor hurried to the table with another glass and Villa swallowed as if his life hung in the balance.

He got to his feet, steadily enough for a man who had just swallowed such a mammoth dose of powerful spirits, but perhaps it wouldn't hit him for a few minutes. Zapata rose as well, rounded the table, and extended his hand.

As he did so, he turned and looked at Corey and Fergus's window, and for the first time Corey saw his eyes. It would take a strong man to return that gaze for any length of time.

Arm in arm the two generals walked toward the stairwell at the front of the room.

"Seen enough?" Fergus said.

"More than I wanted to," Corey said.

They clambered down the fire escape, and as their weight pressed on the lower section and it lowered them toward the schoolground, he felt as if he were making some despairing descent into a swamp of gloom.

Why should this be? Nothing had been done wrong here today, no wickedness committed; the statements and sentiments the two leaders had shared were fine and noble, and their listeners, by and large, had approved, had even lifted their hearts and voices in agreement—and yet . . .

A precious moment, a golden chance, had been lost.

There was more firing of weapons from the street in front of the school and by the time they got there themselves, Villa and Zapata were standing on the steps surrounded by the men who had been in the room with them. A brass band had appeared. The air was alight with more than flashes from the rifles; the photographers were in a frenzy of picture-taking. Villa, still the more ebullient of the two men, was trying to speak, but the band and the noise of the crowd drowned his words. The great meeting of Xochimilco was a thing of the past. Finished.

They bought a ride from a trucker heading across to the Cuernavaca–Mexico City road and from there took a trolley into the heart of the capital.

"Not a word about how they're going to fight Carranza and Obregón, did ye notice, laddie?" Fergus said at one point of the poky journey.

"Not a word about how they view the future, either."

"Nay. It's a sad day for this puir fucking country. They held that future in their hands, and they've let it slip away."

"Those hands have held guns too long to get a grip on other things, Fergus."

"Aye."

He hadn't expected the Scot to be so perceptive—or as caring as his voice suggested. There was more to his companion than a professional capacity for intrigue and trouble.

When they reached the bar in the Mirador Corey was sunk in a deep well of gloom. Someday, he feared, Mexicans would look back in regret and anger at what hadn't happened in Xochimilco.

And one other thing kept erupting in his mind. He hadn't seen Jorge Martínez.

29

"I despise doing this, Paco. I am like Trini, only I wasn't noble enough or strong enough to say no to Fierro," Jorge Martínez said as he watched the train prepare to get under way again. A shriek of the locomotive's whistle rattled his horse and he patted the animal's neck. He slid his carbine back in the saddle holster and signaled *la tropa* to fall back from the tracks. "I didn't join the Division to hold up trains."

"The next time it will be easier, Captain Cockroach," the dynamiter said.

"¡*Mierda*! There should be no next time. Robbing poor people of their few miserable pesos will never come easy for me, *amigo*. For you either, from the look on your big stupid *frente*."

"Colonel Fierro says that everyone who rides this railroad

supports Obregón or *el primer bufón* Carranza, Jorge. They are not all poor. And the Revolution certainly needs the money. Trini, even more than you and I, knew this."

"That old *viuda* from Morelia in the next to last car—the one with her two grandchildren and the load of chile *ristras*—doesn't support *anybody*. She thinks only of *familia* and *iglesia*, and doesn't even know what the Revolution is all about. *She* is poor."

"*Sí*. But she must contribute her *pequeño* share to the cause, too. *¿No, amigo?* We make this fight for such as her—and *los niños*."

"If we keep robbing them, they will starve—and we will make this fight for no one."

There had been one personally disgusting, scary moment during the robbery.

Trooper Carlos Sánchez had lifted a gold chain from a well-dressed woman traveling with her husband in the one first-class carriage, and for a tight moment Jorge María Martínez, son of honest Andreas, had been tempted to become a thief and somehow get the chain for himself. Christmas would arrive in less than three more weeks, and for a moment his imagination had gone wild as he pictured the chain circling Juanita's slender neck and drooping between those firm breasts. He watched Sánchez drop it into the bag and forgot it.

Jorge grunted. The day wasn't a total loss, even if he had decided to forgo the chain. It turned a little better in the next to last car, due to the old widow.

Sí. The wrinkled *mujer* with the diamond-black eyes and cheeks like brown, petrified apples had been wonderful, the only bright moment in a day of dull anger that began when Fierro, over Trini's objections, sent them into this deep, rocky canyon after the train.

As they went through the third-class car where she huddled with her two tiny charges, her eyes glittering with terror, she had whimpered a few weak, futile words of protest and finally offered up a number of small coins. Trooper Juan Gallegos, a pompous ex-policeman from El Sueco in Chihuahua—a good *guerrero*, but too often a stickler for following orders to the letter—had spotted the wedding band on her left hand when she dropped her money in the gunnysack he held. It was *his* first train robbery, too, and his eyes gleamed as if he had stumbled on El Dorado.

"El anillo, madre, por favor," he said.

The whimpering old crone with the apple cheeks vanished in an instant and in her place sat a woman of blazing righteousness.

"No!" she screamed, rising on frail legs. *"¡No, puerco, no!"* Corrosive spittle sprayed from her wrinkled mouth.

Gallegos was knocked back by the force of it and almost fell into the lap of a trembling businessman cowering in the seat across the aisle from the old lady. Gallegos righted himself and placed his collection bag on the floor of the car, looking as stern as only a tough Chihuahua cop can look. Jorge, watching from the vestibule at the far end of the carriage, started for them just as Gallegos began to speak again.

"¡Por favor, señora, el anillo!" His rigid back declared that a *soldado* of the División del Norte and former big-shot policeman would brook no nonsense from an insignificant *abuela pequeña*. He stepped toward her, unslinging his rifle.

As Jorge moved quickly down the aisle he was treated to the sight of the old woman drawing a knife with more blinding speed than he had ever seen one drawn in a cantina fight or at a regimental card game where someone cheated. The old woman had it at Gallegos's throat, and although the trooper held his ground stiff as a board, his Adam's apple was bobbing and jerking in a frantic effort to escape the point.

"Gallegos!" Jorge shouted. *"¡Basta!"* The woman looked to the sound of Jorge's voice and that gave Gallegos time to move away. He had evidently forgotten about the rifle. Jorge wondered if the dumb sonofabitch realized he had just saved his life. Gallegos wouldn't have come anywhere near bringing the weapon into play before his throat was opened wide.

"Buenos días, vieja," Jorge said when he reached the old woman. He smiled and spread his empty hands wide. "May I have *el cuchillo, por favor*? No one will take your ring." He

turned to Gallegos and gave him a hard shove. "Move to the next car, *soldado. ¡Pronto!*"

She handed him the knife, but with a suspicious, guarded look still lingering on her corrugated face. He stuffed it in his boot top, leaned over, and kissed her on the cheek. The ancient eyes softened, and she cackled like a giddy young hen.

Now, with solid, reliable Paco next to him on the railroad embankment, it came to him that with such a spirit burning everywhere in Mexico, the Revolution should never fail— unless the Carrancistas had more people such as the old woman and powerful, dedicated Paco on their side than Pancho Villa and the man the general went to see two days ago, Emiliano Zapata of Morelos, had on theirs.

"If collecting 'taxes' from our countrymen who ride trains bothers you, Captain Cockroach," the giant ex-blacksmith said, "perhaps the bank we go after next week will please you more. No money in the banks belongs to *los pobres.* Only the rich keep their money in the banks."

Sí, he had thought of that himself, but it didn't make today's work sit any easier on his conscience. It was still robbery. He had to banish such feelings. Trini was already in deep, deep trouble over this sordid business.

The major had flatly refused to obey Fierro when he came to Bracomonte headquarters yesterday and asked him to lead a squadron of cavalry on three small attacks: the one this morning on this rusting branch of the Ferrovia Central, one next week on the bank at Texcoco northeast of the capital, and one on the offices of a silver mine near La Laborcilla in northern Querétaro state, the last to be carried out when spies told Fierro the payroll was coming in. Fierro hadn't *ordered* Trini to lead the attacks, but the implication was clear. Trini had tried to persuade the Butcher, quite civilly and almost with deference at first, that such actions, aimed primarily at civilians—although some of Álvaro Obregón's infantry were said to be guarding the mine—were inconsistent with the honor of a professional officer, and so repugnant to him personally that he, Major Trinidad Álvarez, would not take part.

"Not even if you give orders to have me shot, Rodolfo." It was said softly, with no bravado.

Fierro had smiled thinly, shrugged, and left.

Jorge had laughed when the deadly colonel was out of ear-shot.

"Do not gloat, Jorge," Trini said. "He will return with an order from General Villa."

"What then, Trini? You can't disobey the general."

"I'll try not to, my friend. I'll see General Ángeles, of course, but I won't do what Fierro wants. I am afraid you will have to lead this criminal nonsense about the train tomorrow morning. I am sorry, *amigo*."

"Me? Trini! *Por favor.* If you will not do this thing, I will not, either!"

"Don't be foolish, Lieutenant Martínez! You will not help me by getting shot yourself."

In the end he persuaded Jorge, or perhaps Jorge let himself be persuaded. Well, it was different in his case. Trini was an officer and a *gentleman*, as was Felipe Ángeles, not just a jumped-up cavalry recruit, a rough and not yet altogether ready revolutionary such as Jorge Martínez was. The lofty code that defined and refined the distinguished general and, in Jorge's view, the no less distinguished major, didn't even apply to underlings like him.

Trini would have had no decision to make about something like the gold chain; the idea of taking it for himself would never have occurred to him in the first place, but Jorge Martínez was a lesser man. He would have to find something else for Juanita for Christmas.

The thought of her now made him rue how long this business with the train had taken. The sun was dropping behind the far embankment, and it would be well into the night before they reached the Division encampment. Juanita might be asleep, and he never liked to wake her. He needed her badly at this moment, and when he reached her he didn't want to just lie beside her and watch her as she slept. Not that he hadn't done just that for long blissful hours often enough.

Enough of that! It would make a man too crazy to be a soldier. He would have to get the *tropa* on the move.

"Get the troop together, Paco," he said now. "We'll ride for camp as soon as the train clears the canyon."

"*Sí*, Captain Cockroach." The big man rode on down the line.

The carriages were passing Jorge now, leaving the canyon at a snail's pace.

The old woman waved to him from her open window, a tiny brown face on either side of her.

"Lugarteniente!" she yelled.

"*¿Sí?*"

"Come closer, *hombre*." He urged his mount right beneath the window, walked it alongside the moving third-class coach. "If I had slit the throat of your *soldado*, would you have shot me?"

He laughed uneasily. "No, *vieja*—but . . ." *Tell her the truth. She's safe now.* "I think perhaps one of my men would have shot you without my ordering him to do it."

"I thought so." Her forehead wrinkled even more. "I want to give you something. Hold your hand up near this window. Hurry! The train is starting to move faster." She pushed her brown claw over the edge of the sill. "I think you know I would have died before I let someone *take* my wedding ring. But at my age I really do not need it anymore. Give this to someone you love someday—and remember me. Now catch!"

He felt something plop into his cupped hand. When he looked from the ring resting in his palm to the old woman she had already closed the window and was grinning through it. The two brown faces were still on either side of her, button noses pressed against the glass. He opened his mouth in protest. No use. The train was picking up real speed.

In another twenty seconds it disappeared beyond the far cut of the canyon.

He hadn't counted the money or the jewelry and watches, but he felt sure it had been a moderately good haul. *Sí*, as nasty as the task had been, it had gone well. No one had been hurt. Perhaps it would satisfy Fierro and turn aside whatever wrath he still felt for Trini, but knowing the predatory nature of the Butcher as he did now, chances were the brutal bastard would be happier if someone *had* been hurt. The old woman's ring burned his chest through his vest and shirt.

They rode out of the canyon single file, the same way they had come into it to stop the train on its laboring ascent of the western grade, but this time with their weapons holstered. He had let Gallegos carry the two bags stuffed with the loot they had garnered from the passengers and the ransacked mail car, to perhaps soften the man's memory of the push he had given him. A commander never knew where such an *hombre* might find himself in a battle, and there was little point in letting him carry a grudge behind eyes that could sight a carbine in on that same commander's back. *Sí*, he had learned a thing or two in the past half year, a thing or two that probably weren't anywhere in Trini's code.

When they stopped for their cold *fríjol* supper he would have to count and list the contents of the gunnysacks in front of the men, and get them to make their marks on his tally sheet. And for all that Gallegos was by all indications a strict adherent to the "book," he would stay close behind the Chihuahuan all the way to the finance office back at camp. That attention to detail *was* in Trini's code, and he was thankful the major had spelled it out for him with such insistence. He wouldn't have thought of it himself. The lessons on how to stay out of trouble never seemed to end. Pity Trini couldn't have exercised such wisdom on his own behalf, led this harmless if disturbing raid himself, and stayed out of whatever shit he now found himself in with Fierro and probably Pancho, too.

He still wanted to keep his eye on Gallegos, and he sent Paco to the front to set a brisker pace. The ex-policeman couldn't very well dip into the sacks, of course, with his *compadres* all around him, but if he eased to the rear of the *tropa* on the high, brushy trail they were now riding, and then slipped even farther back, there were any number of arroyos he could turn his horse into and be out of sight in minutes. It would take a perfect first guess at his route and hours of tracking to find and shoot him then. Since Zacatecas, desertions from the Division had begun to be a problem. So *much* had changed since Zacatecas.

¡Dios! Where was his head? He was getting paranoid. No one under his command, save Paco, had been as reliable as Gallegos had; for all his stuffy egotism he was a paragon of a soldier. Jorge had no wish to make an *amigo* of the man, but he could use another twenty *guerreros* exactly like him.

He looked at Paco riding at the head of the column. He could use another twenty Pacos, too, but there weren't a score more Paco Duráns in all of Mexico—or in the world.

In the nine months he had known Paco, Jorge had discovered a whole new set of dimensions in him almost every month of the nine. It was now virtually impossible for him to even remember the tyrant who had abused him so mercilessly at Torreón right after he joined the Division. Working and fighting together, it was just as hard for him to remember he was Juanita's father.

Before the Bracomontes moved from Zacatecas to their present bivouac at León in Guanajuato, the dynamiter had discovered a blacksmith's shop abandoned by the owner, a well-known follower of Victoriano Huerta. He had prowled the smithy with eyes as wide and a smile as big as those on the faces of anglo kids in Black Springs when they went through the penny-candy section of Stafford's after a new shipment came in from Chicago or Kansas City.

Paco moved in. Juanita and Jorge had found two rooms above a cantina a block away from the smithy, but Paco chose to sleep in his bedroll in a cubicle behind the forge, a cluttered room so small he couldn't extend his cedar-trunk legs. With only sporadic fighting going on and not much need by the regiment for his services as an expert on explosives, he had spent not only his nights but almost every one of his waking hours in the shop. His ordinarily sober countenance was wreathed in smiles from morning to night and, Jorge suspected, even when he was sound asleep.

Word got out that Durán was hammering and firing iron for next to nothing: *"Whatever you can afford, good lady,"* he would say to a *soldadera* who asked what she owed him after he fixed a cooking pot or mended her *soldado*'s saddle tack. *"Just drop your* dinero *in the cigar box by the door."* A tide of customers soon flooded to his borrowed workshop. It was sheer magic how his time spent in the smoky, noisy, forging shed transported the huge sergeant back to happier times. The clang of his hammer was like joyous laughter.

There was one unsettling moment in Paco's idyll of labor, though.

Jorge and Juanita brought him supper one night, and a *lugarteniente* with whom Jorge had ridden at Zacatecas accosted him. While Juanita delivered Paco's meal Jorge and the other young officer chatted, close enough to where Paco worked that Jorge could hear as well as see when Juanita walked up behind him. A long bar of glowing iron was in the vise on the bench Paco was working at, and he was twisting it with a wrench and a pair of pliers, the muscles in his broad, naked back stretched and swollen to hawsers with his efforts, and sweat running like a river. Juanita set the tray with his supper at the end of the bench and the big man turned, glanced at her, said, *"Gracias,* Florencia," and went back to his work.

Jorge remembered Juanita's words that night across the fire at Torreón. "Papá has never cried, never spoken Mamá's name."

Now the giant realized what he had said. He turned to his daughter again. Tears filled his big, dark eyes. He didn't put his hand up; just blinked them away. Juanita pretended nothing out of the ordinary had happened, and none of the three of them ever talked of it. But from then on, Paco didn't seem to set to his work in the smithy with the same energy and fervor he had shown.

Paco, too, had run up against Rodolfo Fierro with a display of insubordination as reckless as Trini's, and even more heart-stopping—considering that the dynamiter was a lowly sergeant—but with a result so astonishingly mild Jorge could nourish some hope that yesterday's fright would be resolved as readily.

Fierro came to the blacksmith's shop one busy Saturday, and ordered him to fabricate three dozen sets of manacles and leg irons. "Some of my prisoners are miners," he said by way of an explanation Jorge was amazed to hear him make. "We need these *perros* to work a pit at Mina la Plata, so I can't very well shoot them as they deserve. Since the mine won't be ready for a week I want to keep them under lock and key."

Paco stared at him for several seconds before his face turned hard and heavy.

"No!" he said. "Paco Durán does not forge chains for *any* man."

Fierro smiled that same thin, sharp smile and his hand started for his pistol. Paco didn't move. The Butcher's hand stopped. Without another word, but with the smile still a razor blade, he got back on his horse and rode away.

Jorge lived on the edge for a week, sure that Fierro would send a squad of men for Paco, but nothing happened.

Why? Rodolfo Fierro had unblinkingly killed hundreds of far more important men than Paco Durán: colonels and generals, *alcaldes,* assorted ministers almost up to cabinet level, bankers, merchants, *hacendados* without number, and, it was rumored, even some highly placed men of the cloth. Pancho Villa, to Jorge's knowledge, had never once taken him to task for his red-handed arrogance, had, insofar as anyone knew, encouraged it or at the very least looked the other way. Why not Paco? There had been more than twenty witnesses to this burning humiliation for Fierro. He could have shot the dynamiter with a yawn, between sips of wine.

Jorge finally came to the conclusion that the killing of Paco would have been an act completely different not only in degree but in kind from Fierro's customary slaughter. Paco must possess an importance for El Carnicero all out of proportion to his rank. Over the years since Francisco Madero began the Revolution, the somber giant had trained hundreds of the ablest fighters of the Division, and while those men might have hated and feared Paco as he beat and bullied them into becoming tough *guerreros*, just as Jorge had, almost every one of them came to look on him as a second father, also as

Jorge had. In the corridors of power the colonel might have slashed about him with impunity; perhaps he felt he had to move with more caution through the tunnels of the humble. Colonels could take a bullet in the back as easily as could junior officers.

Gradually, as time went by and Fierro, by the look of him in meetings Jorge attended as Trini's aide, apparently wasn't going to revive the matter, Jorge forgot the incident. But now, in the wake of Trini's contretemps with Fierro, the fear of the Butcher's vengeance returned.

Toiling with his hands was something like a religion with the man from Durango. While he was an accomplished worker in the more mundane tasks asked of him as the temporary master of the smithy, Paco played with wrought iron with surprising delicacy and art—an altar screen he made for a small church in neighboring Guadalupe was a vision in lacy metal—and he was a gifted woodcarver as well. He carved *santos* much like the *bultos* that came down to Latino homes in Chupadera County from the hill towns north of Santa Fe, two of which were kept in special niches in the whitewashed walls of Andreas and Ismelda Martínez's bedroom at the rear of the Cantina Florida. Jorge thought Paco's mute but eloquent figures much closer to being genuine works of art.

To watch the mammoth left hand caress the blocks of pine with so much love, while the sharp knife in the right sought the saint hidden inside the wood, was almost as much of a tactile pleasure for him as doing it clearly was for Paco. It wasn't all pleasure. The San Sebastiano bristling like a hedgehog with cruel barbs, begun in Zacatecas and finished at the Division's next encampment at León, was painful to look at, with the saint's tortured face distorted in lifelike agony.

Jorge, remembering what Juanita had told him of Paco's bitterness toward the *padres* resulting from their denial of a burial ground to lost Florencia, once asked him, "Why do you spend your time and skill on these religious things, *viejo*? I thought you hated everything about the Church."

"I don't hate God, *amigo*. And I do not hate those who act

and die for Him and His children as *los santos* did. I have many doubts about those who pretend to *speak* for Him."

Jorge and *la tropa* rode into the Division camp well after the supper hour. By the time Paco, Gallegos, and he handed the proceeds of the train robbery over to Capitán Ernesto Salazar at headquarters it was almost ten o'clock.

As he and Paco made their way to the Bracomonte sector to see if Trini was there, he wondered if he should have listed the old woman's ring with the other loot. No, damn it! It wasn't part of the haul. It was a gift!

They didn't find Trini. None of the *soldados* they questioned had seen him all day. None had heard from him, or a thing about him. It troubled Jorge, but he knew there was little he could do about or for the major tonight. He put Trini and his predicament completely out of mind, although not without a little twinge of shame at how callous he was getting about other people's troubles, but by then he was almost frantic with the thought of getting to town to the room above the boot shop he shared with Juanita, making the little speech beginning to run through his head, gathering her in his arms, and taking her to bed. Food could wait till morning.

He knew he somehow had to cap his impatience until Paco had said hello and then *buenas noches* to his daughter, but he also knew damned well he wasn't going to ask the sergeant to stay for a *cerveza*. Juanita had started her time four days before this train thing came up, but by now she should be fine again, perhaps as eager for him as he was for her. He prayed she had stayed awake. Sometimes she did, no matter what the hour.

He bounded up the stairs to the room, with Paco plodding slowly up behind him.

There was a line of light at the bottom of the door. *¡Bueno!* He almost kicked it open.

Any other time he would have welcomed the sight of Margaret Espinosa. The nurse had been a good friend to both of them.

She sat on his and Juanita's bed, with Juanita in the one

rickety chair, facing her, and his first thought was not a charitable one.

But when he got a better look at Margaret's pale face the second thought came as a cry. "Trini?"

"He is with General Ángeles, Jorge. He's been holed up in the general's headquarters since late yesterday. I saw him this afternoon."

"Fierro?"

"He has men out searching for him. Trini says General Ángeles will see General Villa tomorrow, before he leaves for Mexico City and some meetings. He's pretty confident El Caudillo will tell the Butcher to call his men in. General Ángeles is taking Trini with him to the capital, so Trini says he'll be safe until Fierro forgets about all this. I wish I could be so sure. Even if things work out the way Trini thinks they will, I know from bitter experience what a long memory that killer has."

She didn't want to tell Margarita to leave, with the nurse looking worn in her worry over Trini, but the air in the room had turned to poison, with only the fresh draft of Jorge's arrival as an antidote. Trini could be standing in the way of a danger his principles wouldn't allow him to step away from, and everyone in the little room knew it—if *he* didn't. Something was turning sour in the Great Revolution which Margarita's man—and hers, too—were fighting, even if Jorge hadn't recognized it yet. It came as no surprise that Trini had turned morose; it staggered everyone who knew him that he had turned almost suicidal in his resistance to the wishes of that animal Fierro. Margarita had every right to agonize about her major.

Juanita Durán was luckier. Jorge didn't want to do the Butcher's dirty work any more than Trini did, but at least Trini had been able to talk the sense into him he couldn't talk into himself. As Margarita had said just before Jorge burst through the door, "Men! The ridiculous obstinacy they insist on calling honor sickens me. I swear I don't know why I love him."

The little changes in Jorge, too, over the past few months had piled up into one huge one, and the only time he seemed able to forget the hateful things duty was forcing him to do, now that the more satisfying great battles seemed to be behind the army, was when they were alone. But even after today's distasteful chores he seemed in an especially buoyant mood tonight.

Yes, she wished Margarita would leave now.

She could see in Jorge's eyes that although he was too polite to ask, he was wishing the same thing, wishing, too, that Papá would leave with Margarita.

That, of course, would be nicest, but Papá didn't really count. Jorge and she had gotten used to his presence and could talk and act almost as if he wasn't with them. The fear that her father might look with disfavor on their being together had disappeared miraculously in less than a week after Saltillo; his big open countenance actually signaled approval even while Jorge was recovering from the fever, although Papá never put it directly into words. It was a relief, of course. She would have become Jorge's woman then whether Papá blessed their sharing the same bed or bedroll or not, but it made it immeasurably better that he seemed to.

Sí, even with the disturbing news about Trini, Jorge was a little brighter tonight than he usually was in the wake of forays such as the one he had just returned from. The kiss he gave her after he listened to Margarita promised even more than usual.

¡Dios! Let them leave, por favor.

Papá was smiling. She hoped it wouldn't trouble Margarita that someone, anyone, could smile while *she* worried over Trini.

Then Papá stood up. "Capitán Espinosa," he said. "*Por favor,* let me escort you back to your quarters. After that, Paco will listen for news of Major Álvarez. When I hear something I will come to you with it immediately."

"And come to me with it, too, Paco," Jorge said.

Juanita smiled inside her. It wouldn't do to let Papá know how she had *prayed* him into leaving.

When the door closed on her father and the nurse she leaped into Jorge's arms. To her surprise and sharp if tiny disappointment he pushed her away.

"Wait, *querida*," he said. Well, at least his voice was as loving as it had been. He was holding his fist out in front of him. "I have a gift for you."

"A gift?"

"*Sí*. But first you must give *me* one."

"I am sorry. I have none for you, Jorge."

"Ah, but you do. You just do not know it yet."

"What is it, then?"

"You."

"I made myself a gift to you long ago, *cariño*."

"Not the way I am asking now." *Dios*. He was smiling the oddest smile, not looking straight at her, but down at his closed hand. "I have been thinking. I no longer want you for a *soldadera*."

He was joking, and she knew it, but her heart dropped like a stone.

"Jorge . . ." It was the weakest of whispers.

He opened his hand. "Here is my gift." She stared at a small golden band. His next words overpowered the beat of her heart. "What I would like from you is that you become *mi esposa*. A great officer of Regiment Bracomonte should have a wife, not a mistress."

30

Even had the disaster at Xochimilco—as he still perceived the meeting between Villa and Zapata—not been haunting him, the evening at the U.S. Embassy would have begun badly for Corey.

The baby-faced marine lieutenant who took his and Narciso's invitations spent a long time checking their names against the guest list, glancing with undisguised suspicion at the Minister from time to time. The glances embarrassed Corey for Narciso's sake. The marine only made it worse when he found them on the list. "Never any question about *you*, Mr. Lane," he said, "but there are so many big-shot greasers we got to look after here tonight, we got to check everybody who looks funny to us. He's a doctor? In the Ministry of Culture? What the hell is that, and who's sick there?" He acted as if Narciso were deaf or not there at all. Didn't the superior young shit think it a possibility Narciso spoke English better than he did?

Of course, the dark, almost swarthy Trujillo was not exactly a prepossessing sight in his fifteen-years-out-of-style full-dress suit with the slightly frayed sleeves, his shaggy hair in need of a trim, and his gray mustache drooping and yellowed with coffee and tobacco stains.

Corey had been surprised to find a rental evening suit that fitted him as if it were tailor-made, and shoes that went with it. So many small shops were failing nowadays here in the capital he had feared the one he rented from when he first came to Mexico might not be in business any longer.

Henry, of course, were they to talk tonight, would chastise him for not wearing the decorations gathering dust back at the X-Bar-7 in Chupadera County. Corey hadn't really looked at them in a dozen years. He glimpsed his well-starched friend across the foyer soon after he and Narciso had their credentials examined, talking with a group of obviously mixed origin and nationality. Henry's noble chest was a splash of colored grosgrain ribbon and bright metal, the DSC prominent alongside the gaudy sunburst of gold a grateful, newly independent Cuban government had awarded him just before he and Corey left Havana. In fairness, Corey's hyper-dignified boss wasn't overly impressed with his own trove of medals; he was just a faithful believer in protocol and manners. "You do honor to your host, Corey, by wearing your decorations," he had chided Corey at a function much like this in Cuba, when Corey showed up in a service uniform whose khaki tunic was as bare of color as his jacket was now, although he at that time possessed every honor Henry did except the Cuban one. Lord only knew how many more such trinkets the State Department man had picked up in the fourteen years since then. Corey, following orders, had no intention of getting close enough to him to see.

The strains of what he thought he identified as Moussorgsky's "Celebrated Waltz" were drifting into the foyer from the ballroom.

"Let's find the bar," he said to Narciso when they finished going through the receiving line. Henry, off to the side, peered at them out of the corner of his eye. "I've a hunch we'll need a drink before this affair is over." Corey led the way.

"There is *mucho dinero* in evidence here tonight, Corey," the little doctor said as they walked past Henry and his gathering.

Corey thought the implication clear. "Mine is a very rich country, Narciso. Our great wealth sometimes clouds our judgment."

"I meant no criticism of your nation or its citizens, *amigo*. I was speaking *primeramente* of my *own* obscenely rich countrymen in attendance here. They do not look much like people threatened by a revolution."

They crossed a section of the ballroom to a bar in an alcove. There were a few early dancers courageous enough to put themselves on exhibition. The floor reeked of big money, but, as Narciso had pointed out, not all of it Yankee or European. Corey could bet some of the dress-suited and uniformed men waltzing with women who swept long silk skirts across the floor, and who glittered with diamond tiaras and breathtaking necklaces and pendants, were indeed the cream of Mexican *criollo rico* society. He supposed, too, that if he inquired into their antecedents closely enough, he would run across more than one latter-day *gachupín*, a Mexican national born in Spain, as were most of the original *conquistadores*. These more recent arrivals were as predatory as the first had been. He couldn't warm to them as a class, but he had to admit they made up a race of remarkable energy and enterprise, inheritors of the genes of the arrogant adventurers who marched with their halberds and crosses into his own land four long centuries ago and who had laid their mailed gauntlets on every inch of the alien soil of Nuevo México in less than a decade, leaving handprints it would take an eon of fierce winds to wear away.

In the bar a small shock awaited him: Fergus Cameron Kennedy in dress kilts hung with an ermine sporran!

He almost laughed. Although the embassy's huge rooms were certainly warm enough, the skinny limbs rising from the white spats, together with the bony, hairy knees, looked blue with cold. The "wee, braw Scot" simply didn't have the legs for kilts. The Scotsman would never lose the capacity to surprise him. Henry, at least, would approve of the way Fergus had decked himself out. He wore *his* decorations. Unless Corey was mistaken, one of them was the Victoria Cross, won at Mafeking or on some such bloodstained Boer War field.

Fergus was standing next to a tall man who wore as many decorations as Corey had ever seen. The Scot, when he caught sight of Corey, looked right through him as if he weren't there, but then he winked. The wink was more warning than invitation. Corey turned Narciso to the bar several feet from the British agent.

Before Corey could order a drink for himself and Narciso, an enlisted marine barman placed a pair of tulip-shaped champagne glasses on the mahogany in front of them and filled them. Fergus had turned his back on Corey and was paying close attention to the tall, richly decorated man. His companion was powerfully built, but not bulky, blond as late autumn grass, and with eyes of an almost Baltic blue.

Somehow, despite the sea of obligatory champagne being poured into glasses the length of the bar, Kennedy had promoted a large tumbler of what looked to be Scotch whisky. Corey wondered if it was his cherished Glenlivet.

The tall man spoke to Fergus in low, muffled tones, but once in a while his voice rose and a German word spilled out. The man glanced at Narciso. He nodded to the Mexican.

"The man two places down seems to know you, Narciso," Corey said.

There was a split second of hesitation on Trujillo's part, then, "*Sí*. He does," Narciso whispered. "That *hombre* is Wolf Kemper, Corey, a marine engineer from Frankfurt. He is making studies for a new deep water port in Baja California and one at Mazatlán."

"I should think the Germans would be too busy with the war in Europe to get involved in such projects now."

"It's not the Germans, Corey. He is in the employ of a Japanese consortium the Huerta government brought into Mexico."

Corey heard a fairly heated word or two directed by Fergus at the German. "There's no bloody excuse, Wolf, for the way the German Army is carrying on in Belgium!" Corey heard him say, his voice as stringy mean as he had ever heard it. The nervy rogue! Bad enough that he was using the U.S. Embassy as his personal spying ground tonight. Must he use it to fight the bigger war raging across the ocean, too? Of course he must. Fergus Cameron Kennedy, for all his comic appearance and behavior, never stopped working or fighting for a second.

"Let me know the moment you see General Ángeles, Narciso, *por favor.* I'm not even sure I will recognize him after all these years," Corey said. Fergus's ears perked up in midsentence. Remarkable. He hadn't missed Corey's words even as he talked. He had the receptive sensitivity of the aerial of a Marconi wireless machine.

"*Sí, amigo,*" Narciso said.

A new waltz began in the ballroom and the other drinkers at the bar, all men, drifted off in search of partners. The barman was busying himself polishing glasses a dozen feet away, and the four of them were now quite alone. The music was the boisterous overture to "Die Fledermaus," not the most danceable tune the orchestra could have selected, in Corey's view, and it almost drowned the two conversations. Then the German turned abruptly from Fergus and marched to the far end of the long bar, his back rigid. Once there, he stared back at the Scot. He wasn't a happy man by the look of him. Fergus lifted his whisky to his lips and gazed out across the room with a look of studied indifference on his face. He didn't even turn toward Narciso and Corey. Then, still without looking at them, he began to mutter something out of the corner of his mouth. "Narciso"—*he knew Trujillo, too?*—"introduce me to Corey."

"But Señor Kennedy . . ." Poor Narciso seemed baffled out of countenance. "You and Señor Lane already know each other." Strange. How did Narciso know that?

"Aye, Narciso. But he and I can't very well start talking seriously with Wolf looking on until he's seen us meet. Make it look real. There's a bonnie lad."

They made their way through the charade of introduction, with Corey forcing a smile and hoping he didn't look as grim as he felt. Why this damned comedy? And why was Fergus dragging Narciso into it? Narciso was out of his depth and looked as if he knew it. It suddenly dawned on Corey that there was some connection between him and the British agent that one of them should have told him about before tonight. Mild and sweet as the little doctor was, like Fergus he knew far more people in the game than his arcane profession alone could have led him to know—General Barrón, this German Kemper, Huerta, Henry, Fergus here, and Felipe Ángeles. Archaeologists simply didn't deal with people like that. Come to think of it, how had Narciso known he was backing General Ángeles that day at the Reforma? Wait. Hadn't it been Jake Cobb who sent Corey to Narciso in the first place?

Fergus's crooked smile wasn't just a pose for the watchful German at the end of the bar. As had been the case in all their adventures together, he was enjoying himself immensely.

"What game are you playing now, Fergus?" Corey said.

"No game, laddie. Fergus has never been more serious. Keep smiling. The Wolf mon is still watching. I had to turn a wee bit rough to get him away from us at all. Try not to look at *him*. Narciso, have you told Corey here who Kemper is?"

Narciso jumped. "*Sí*, Fergus. The part about him being a marine engineer."

"You mean there's more, Narciso?" Corey asked. The doctor fell silent. He looked sheepish, as if he had been caught doing something dirty. Corey bit his lip. Could no one be trusted in this labyrinth? Probably not. Narciso Trujillo had lived a lie with him. But in fairness Corey had performed his own masquerade with Narciso and by rights should feel *some* shame about it.

Fergus growled. "Wolf Kemper is no more a 'civilian' than any of the three of us. Actually, Kemper's not his real name. He's a Junker baron of some sort and he was a colonel in the German Army until he caught one in the shoulder fighting the Russkies at Tannenberg last August. Now he's been secretly—or so the Jerries suppose—seconded to their embassy here. Nice chap, for all the scowls he's giving me at the moment. Not a very clever agent, though. Oh, I daresay his business with the Japs is legitimate enough. But most of the time he works with von Rintelen here in Mexico and reports directly to the Kaiser's Foreign Office."

"Von Rintelen?"

"Good grief, mon! Doesn't Henry Richardson tell ye *anything*? How can ye possibly do your wee bit of work? Von Rintelen is the German government's chief spy and *agent provocateur* here in this bloody, wicked, but lovable country. Actually, he's in New York at the moment, but he'll be back."

Corey turned to Narciso. "And did you know all about me from the start, *Dr. Trujillo*?" That was cruel, addressing the little man like that.

Pure misery twisted the Minister's sad brown face. "*Sí*, Corey. Your own people . . ."

Fury ripped Corey. Henry Richardson had a lot to answer for. But anger now would serve no good purpose. He turned back to Fergus. "Putting aside for the moment that I feel I've been passed around from hand to hand like an unwanted orphan, you sneaky sonofabitch, aren't you putting your mission, whatever it is—and mine, although I now doubt I have one—in jeopardy, by standing here in the open and getting damned close to confidential business? This man Kemper might not be clever, but he can't be an utter fool."

"No, he's not a fool, lad, but he's a pitiful amateur. Like most Jerries, he has an arrogant faith in secret meetings, *noms de guerre* like Kemper, and fancy codes. Romantic buggers, the Kaiser's lot. They don't seem to know that the best disguise an intelligence agent can have is the clear light of the bonnie day, not false whiskers or elaborate covers. Blind trust in codes will come back to haunt Germany someday, mark Fergus's words. When you write your secrets in invisible ink, everybody wants to read them. He knows about me, of course. Whitehall wants him to. But not to worry about his tumbling to you now. With his fine, Teutonic mind-set, the Wolf mon can't conceive that I would be silly enough to operate right under his aristocratic nose."

As if Fergus had prompted the German to forgo suspicion and watchfulness for the moment at least, Kemper had engaged the barman in conversation, and was no longer watching them. Handsome man. Athletic-looking.

Then Narciso gave a low, almost inaudible cry. He was looking toward the foyer of the embassy. Some sort of satisfaction had evidently replaced his anguish of a moment earlier. "General Ángeles . . ." he breathed.

Corey turned and looked across the ballroom floor to the foyer himself. Three men, two in the uniform of the División del Norte, were standing just inside the wide entrance to the foyer. He didn't need Narciso or Fergus to tell him that the shorter man was Felipe Ángeles, even if the other had not been younger and wearing the insignia of a major. Ángeles hadn't aged or changed a jot since 1908. He still wore leadership like a cloak.

"Here's your chance, laddie," Fergus said. "Now, don't take Fergus's advice about conducting things in the open to some ridiculous extreme. Let Henry Richardson find a quiet, secluded place for the two of you to talk."

That did it. But Fergus was right, as usual. He would have to beard Henry now, orders or no orders. "What if Ángeles won't meet with me, Fergus?"

"Don't worry your head aboot that, lad. He's already agreed to listen to you. He wants a witness, though. That's why he brought that *norteño* major chap, Trini Álvarez. I had a little talk with Álvarez this afternoon."

No—Fergus hadn't lost any of his capacity for surprise.

"But I could not push myself forward the way you seem to suggest, Señor Lane," Felipe Ángeles said. "And by that statement, do not, *por favor,* assume for even a moment that I am being coy, that I am asking to be seduced."

"I would never push you, sir. I have no wish to do so, even if I had the authority. These have just been thoughts. Thoughts which I must admit no one in my government has led me to have. They are my own. I realize they can't carry any particular weight with you, but I beg you to consider them."

"I am happy, then, that I am not speaking with someone who is just a messenger for someone else. I admire your forthrightness, Señor Lane, but I caution you, my first inclination is to resist your blandishments with all my power."

They sat together, the three of them, in a small private library where they had been ushered by an embassy official assigned them as a guide by the shocked, indignant, but finally—when Corey demanded his help with an insistence he could hardly believe himself capable of—grudgingly acquiescent Henry Richardson.

The problem of Henry's pique would have to be dealt with later, perhaps even before he left the ball tonight. It didn't worry Corey. This might turn out to be his last day of duty as a Special Foreign Service Officer, but it was too late to lament that now.

To Corey's utter amazement, Ángeles remembered him from the luncheon six years earlier. "Ah, yes, Señor Lane. You came to the academy's little affair as the guest of Dr. Trujillo, did you not?" He picked up his brandy snifter, rolled it in two steady palms, and lifted it to his nose. It was apparently all the general was going to do with the fine Napoleon Henry's aide brought them, and it didn't look as if he was abstaining with any concentrated effort. He had refused the embassy man's offer of a cigar, too. Major Álvarez, a keen-looking man of about thirty, a warrior if Corey had ever seen one, had turned down cognac and the smoke, too, and faded into the background, but Corey knew he wasn't missing anything.

And since Narciso Trujillo reintroduced them, Ángeles hadn't smiled, either. That had been half an hour earlier. But he hadn't evidenced any enmity or suspicion. The general was the eye of the storm, with a serenity about him that made it hard at the moment to remember the cyclonic winds raging about his country. Seldom had a man impressed Corey as much in so short a time. He felt he had known Felipe Ángeles a great deal longer than the six years since their walk together on the rooftop of Chapultepec.

Fifteen minutes into this talk he had taken one of the bigger gambles of his life. He told the general exactly what he had been put in Mexico to do, and what he wanted from Felipe Ángeles, and he didn't ask that Ángeles hold the information in confidence until *after* he told him. He had put himself completely in Ángeles's and the major's power. More astonishing than the gamble was the satisfaction his sudden faith in these two men afforded him. To his relief, the general nodded, and he knew this signal was better than a written contract or a pact signed in blood, and that it would be binding on the major, too. He knew, too, that if Henry Richardson were a *Mexican* official he would have his Special Foreign Service Officer against the wall and shot before the sun came up.

"I would think someone has to step forward and pull things together, sir."

"*Sí.* There is no question about that, *señor.* There is a question as to whether or not I am that someone. *I* have a question, señor. What makes a *norteamericano* such as you feel that I am the man my country needs?"

It might sound too much like arrant sycophancy to tell this great man of the study he was doing of him, but *something* had to be said. "I am a historian in my life north of the border, General. I have already published one book on the Revolution. I have followed your career, when I could, ever since I first met you. I think I've read every word you've written that has appeared in English translation in the United States, and quite a bit in Spanish that has not."

"Some of your countrymen who have read me seem to think I endorse anarchy, *señor*. Do you not share their view?"

"No, sir. I feel, as you seem to me to feel, that new ways must be tried in Mexico, if it is to take its rightful place in the family of nations. A day will come, and soon I think, when your proposals will never again be thought of as extreme. The world, as well as Mexico, is changing. When the conflict in Europe runs its inevitable course, there could well be a reordering of society everywhere. Mexico"—would what he was about to say come out with as much sincerity as he meant it to?—"could lead the way."

Ángeles smiled. "Perhaps someday you will find yourself the target of the same criticism at home I often feel here."

"I'm not an important target, General Ángeles. Never will be, I expect."

"History may make some surprising judgments on the importance of men of goodwill." He fell silent for a moment and Corey glanced at Álvarez. The major nodded ever so slightly at him. By God, the man was urging him to continue his courting of the general.

"I cannot state too strongly how much I, and many others, feel your country needs you."

The smile turned to a frown. "You give me, I fear, entirely too much credit, Señor Lane. I have another question, one perhaps even more pressing than the one you answered so flatteringly—and so graciously. How might my saying yes to you be viewed by those at whose side, and largely on whose behalf, I have fought my battles?"

"I see no one else, sir. I do not think the mantle would fit well on either General Zapata or General Villa, even supposing they wished to wear it, which I doubt." Did Ángeles wince at the name of Villa? "If it is not you, General

Ángeles, I am afraid that Venustiano Carranza will be that someone—by default."

That remark brought the only ripple to mar Ángeles's superb calm. "Ah, I see, Señor Lane, that unlike your government, you have discerned the greatest danger facing Mexico since Generals Díaz and Huerta were deposed." There was considerable heat in his voice, heat at odds with his comportment during the rest of the interview. Out of the corner of his eye Corey detected a flare-up in Major Álvarez as well.

Then, in the softest of voices, with the calm once again restored, and with nothing in the words themselves to indicate their portent, Felipe Ángeles put forth the biggest challenge Corey Lane had ever faced.

"I might be persuaded, Señor Lane, just might, were the right person to be consulted, and were he to offer unstinting approval and support."

"And just who is that right person, sir?"

"I believe you already know, Señor Lane."

With that, the meeting with General Felipe Ángeles ended as swiftly as the flip of a light switch.

"I think ye're doing your chum Henry a disservice, laddie," Fergus said. "On balance it was a good idea to keep you in the dark for a while. I don't think he wanted to put too much of his own brain weight on your thinking. Take it as a compliment."

If only he could. Best to ignore that until he had done a lot *more* thinking. Corey looked around the ballroom and out toward the foyer. He had sat alone for a full fifteen minutes after the general and the major left the library, partly in order that they wouldn't be seen together, but mostly to consider the decision he had made in the wake of Ángeles's last remark. "Didn't Ángeles stay?"

"Not even for a wee moment," Fergus said. "He left the library looking like he might, but when he saw Carranza and Obregón had put in their appearance at this do, he and Álvarez headed for the door like a pair of carrier pigeons. Ángeles is a proper grand gentleman, lad, and he doesn't want to embarrass you Yanks in the slightest. He'll be fighting those two with every gun in the Division in a matter of weeks. He and his major will take no part in the counterfeit games the rest of us are playing here tonight. By the by, Álvarez is an interesting specimen, too, Corey. He has a bonnie future if the Villistas come out on top. Remind me to tell you all about him sometime. Did he do any of the talking?"

"Didn't say a word."

"Not surprising. Good subordinate. Good leader, too. He's the interim commanding officer of Regiment Bracomonte. Led the charge at Paredón."

Regiment Bracomonte? Álvarez was Jorge Martínez's commander, then! Had Corey's history since last April been only one fumbled opportunity after another as far as the young man he had chased down the Jornada was concerned? Was that still important? It had to be, if Corey Lane had not climbed so high on the ladder of abstraction he had been dizzied out of his own humanity by the altitude.

Fergus was going on, "Are ye going to let old Fergus in on your conversation with Ángeles?"

"Not yet. I don't want the weight of *your* thinking, either. Tell me something, though. Just how afraid of Rodolfo Fierro are you after that little episode in Zacatecas?"

"Absolutely terrified, laddie. Why?"

"I somehow have to get to Pancho Villa, Fergus. Want to tag along?"

"Wouldn't miss it for the world, lad! When do we go?"

"I'll have to clear *this* jaunt with Henry. I'll let you know." Arrant nonsense, all of it. Henry would approve of no trip for him ever again, except one back to Chupadera County. Still, he would play the string out until he got his marching orders. "Now, take me to Carranza and Obregón and introduce me." He didn't have to ask the Scot if he knew the pair of them.

Fergus tried to pick a time when the two Constitutionalist leaders were alone and approachable, but the time didn't come. Officials of the embassy, among them the ambassador himself, kept Obregón and Carranza hemmed in. A line of men, some with their ladies on their arms, waited their turns to speak with them. The line moved slowly. In the end Corey had to content himself with assessing them from a distance.

His early studious distrust of the First Chief voiced to Henry was, at this first real look, distilled into an intense, purely personal, visceral dislike, and he questioned the fairness of making a judgment on the unreliable evidence of his eyes and his academically formed prejudices, especially after his respect for Ángeles had been so thoroughly reinforced at the meeting in the library. He couldn't deny his immediate reaction. There was something malignant about Carranza, despite a weak smile meant to reassure the men and women he was meeting. When he looked at him a moment longer, something he had heard recently came to mind. "Men who sleep on soft pillows," Villa had said of the men around El Primer Jefe at Xochimilco. The politician himself was the pillow. Carranza had that softness about him that supported nothing. Still, Pancho hadn't served himself well when he dismissed his nemesis with that contemptuous wave of his powerful hand. What Corey saw in Carranza was a *Machiavellian* softness. Soft men, underrated, can often turn more dangerous than the hard men their enemies are ready for. They take their deluded opponents unaware. The faint smile under the white beard—looking as if it had been tacked on as a last-minute ornament meant to disarm—gave the Coahuilan away as did nothing else. Hamlet was right. *A man can smile and smile, and be a villain* . . .

Corey turned his eyes next on Obregón.

The short stocky revolutionary chieftain was an entirely different matter. There was nothing seemingly devious or underhanded about Carranza's general, but there was also nothing given away in the steady gaze he bestowed on each of the dignitaries who shook his hand. *He* wasn't soft. He stood close enough to Carranza for them to appear as Siamese twins at a glance, but, strangely, for all that recent events said otherwise, they didn't seem to be together. Something clicked in Corey's head. He couldn't prove it, therefore couldn't say it, not even to Fergus or Narciso, but he knew, with a certainty he had known about very little else since he came to this confusing city, that tough, capable Álvaro Obregón wouldn't be *Carranza's* general for too terribly long. This confident, quiet, compact tiger would never, in the ultimate, be anybody's general but his own.

Carranza was engaged in conversation with a man of imposing appearance, whose dress suit carried as many decorations as brightened the chest of Kemper. Fergus tugged at his sleeve. "That's the German ambassador, Admiral Paul von Hintze," the Scot said. "We know something about him he doesn't yet know himself. We intercepted a Foreign Ministry signal to the Jerries' Washington embassy. He's the next envoy to China. They're putting him there to woo the Japanese. He would have been sent straight to Tokyo if the Japanese weren't pretending to be at war with Germany."

"Is he here with Wolf Kemper?"

Fergus laughed. "Not that anyone is being told. They meet three days a week on a public bench in the Zócalo, on a typically clockwork German schedule, but tonight they'll pretend they don't even know each other. Unlike us, they won't even risk being introduced here. Silly buggers. An ambassador is *supposed* to know prominent businessmen from his own country. The attempted secrecy of these meetings was what set us to looking at the Wolf mon in the first place."

"Who's that waiting to speak with Carranza next?"

"Lord Cowdray. Big British oil. Arrogant old monster, even if he is one of ours. He was rich to begin with, but he's far richer now that he's sold the Royal Navy this country's oil."

"And the next one in line?"

"Yours, laddie. Francis Bentley. Lawyer for the Guggenheims. Wants to keep all that free San Luis Potosí copper available to his New York clients. Mexico's a grab bag, lad."

"The oriental behind him?"

"Don't know his name. The Japs run people in and out of the capital through a bloody revolving door. Can't tell, of course, how important this one might be. We might learn something about that a bit later by whether he puts his head next to von Hintze or Kemper. We don't have the foggiest about what the Mikado's chaps are up to. One of my jobs is to find out." He broke off. Thirst had come over him again. "Eeeh, lad, look! They're getting ready to serve the supper. Let's get to the bar and toss off another wee drap before your punctual beggars force us to the tables. There will be nothing to drink but that insipid bubbly when we sit down to eat."

"I think I'll pass, Fergus. I suddenly don't feel much like drinking or eating." What had happened to him? What he had felt at the conclusion of his talk with Ángeles—if not elation, certainly what was by all odds well-founded hope—had left him after his scrutiny of the Carrancista present tonight. The image of vultures circling a rotting, bloated carcass which had visited him before here in Mexico had suddenly come again. "Where did you leave Narciso, Fergus? I think I'll say good night to him if he doesn't want to leave, and be on my way myself."

"He stayed in the bar after he introduced ye to Ángeles and Álvarez. I think he's drowning his sorrow that you Yanks are making such a bloody fuss over Carranza at this do. I think ye ought to hang around a bit longer, laddie."

"Nothing can keep me here another second, Fergus."

The Scot shot him a swift, sharp look. How much of his mounting despair had the quick-thinking, perceptive Kennedy fastened on?

He headed for the bar. He didn't even wait to see if Fergus followed.

Two sets of double doors had been opened between the ballroom and the banquet hall. Servants were still setting places on the gleaming white tablecloths. The bulbs in the chandeliers were alight, but no one had as yet set a match to the candles on the tables. There would still be a waltz or two before supper was announced, and Fergus would have time for more than one "wee drap." Yes, he was ready to leave.

The bar was crowded again. It took him several seconds to find Narciso, and when he did, the doctor had already spotted him. Poor, miserable little guy. His small face was a mix of eagerness and sorrow. He was probably even more ineffectual in the sort of machinations a conspirator had to indulge in than Corey was himself. He would have to take him off the hook.

Narciso was facing him, and apparently had been listening to a woman whose back was turned to Corey. When he moved in closer Narciso returned his sad eyes to her and gave her almost his full attention.

". . . and only if I am still here in the capital, Narciso," the woman was saying. "I will of course eventually return to Durango as soon as I am sure the fighting is over." He only heard the words. Any overtones were lost in the hum of nearby conversations.

He tried not to listen as she went on. Until he caught Narciso's eye again he would feel like an eavesdropper, which was precisely what his government was paying him to be.

Idly, his eyes took the woman in, her back at least.

She was slender. A richly brocaded lavender gown cut very low in back displayed flesh of almost glowing warmth. Old ivory. Not that *she* was old. Mature, surely, but by no means old, despite the silver gray of the hair piled atop her head, a head tipped slightly backward toward him in what? A display of pride? A necklace of pearls was fastened at the nape of her neck. Elbow-length gloves which matched the gown covered her slim arms. Another rich *criolla* woman, twin to a dozen others he had noticed here tonight, even if he hadn't really looked at any one of them.

"But you have excited me with the invitation to the lantern show, Narciso," she said, "Tenochtitlán . . . I sometimes dream of it, until the terrible present wakes me up. Yes, I would be honored if you will have me there . . ."

Narciso looked at Corey across her bare shoulder.

"Corey," he said. "I would like you to meet one of my dearest friends."

The woman turned and faced him. He saw her eyes first, and in their irises the reason for the selection of the gown. Their lavender and the lavender of the dress had been dipped from the same narrow liquid sliver of the spectrum. Steady eyes, for all the dance of light they made in the iridescent face with the straight, thin nose and the delicately arched brows.

It was the woman of the train and the touring car.

"*Señora*," Narciso said, "may I present *mi amigo* Señor Corey Lane. Corey, this lady is Doña Luisa López y Montenegro. Doña Luisa was a student of mine a few years ago, when I was still at the *universidad*. Then, when I moved to the ministry, she became a volunteer research assistant in my department. A very dedicated one, I might add. You two share a common love for history."

"No need to introduce us, Narciso. I have, so to speak, run into Señor Lane before," she said. Again the bell. She put her gloved hand out. He almost panicked. With a lady like this did you lift an offered hand to your lips? He had never kissed a woman's hand—not in this fashion, anyway. He took the hand in his, and he felt the heat of hers through the thin fabric of the glove as he had that day in front of the Mirador. He mumbled something. What a gauche clown he must appear to her.

Thank God Narciso was going on. "I have just invited Doña Luisa to a lantern show on Tuesday about a dig one of my crews has just finished down near Cuernavaca. She has graciously consented to attend. I wonder if you, Corey . . ."

He wondered? He needn't have, unless he had suddenly gone blind.

Doña Luisa began to laugh. "My hand, *por favor, señor* . . ."

He was saved from dying right on the spot by another, unfamiliar, voice.

"Luisa, forgive me. But I do believe the dance just beginning is mine, *ja*? And I am to take you then in to supper, is that not so, *Liebchen*?"

Corey turned and looked into the blue eyes of Wolf Kemper.

"I am sorry I did not get to make an introduction to the German, *amigo*," Narciso said.

"No matter, Narciso. I feel sure Herr Kemper and I will meet again."

He followed the pair with his eyes as they made their way onto the ballroom floor. She looked back at him once and smiled. Was it a smile of genuine warmth or one of curiosity? Was it less than either—mere *cortesía*?

He watched them until they disappeared in the swirl of dancers.

31

"General Villa has relieved me of the command of Los Bracomontes," Trini Álvarez said to the young officers gathered round him at his first—and now last—regimental staff meeting after his return to Guanajuato from Mexico City with Felipe Ángeles. "I have no standing with the regiment any longer, so this meeting is dismissed. Your new commander will call you together within an hour, so stay close by, *por favor*."

At his words murmurs and groans came from his listeners like a small, dark wind, but one man in front, Jorge Martínez, didn't make a sound. The announcement left him too sick at soul to even breathe. Trini's face was as sad and ruined as the crumbling side of an Aztec pyramid.

"Fierro, Trini?" Jorge asked him when the two of them stayed behind after the others left. "El Carnicero did this, didn't he?"

"One would think so, *amigo*. But then he asked General Villa that I be placed in command of his new squadron, Los Diablos."

"That is not the place for you. The unit is too small to be worthy of you. Only twenty men as of the report this morning."

"That is not important. I will serve wherever I am assigned. There are no small commands—only small commanders. Were you on the list for Los Diablos, Jorge?"

"No."

"I will ask for you, then. Paco, too." He gave Jorge an inquiring look. "That is, if you will both come with me. Perhaps you and I and Paco can make something of them."

"Of course I will come with you. And—although I should not speak for Paco—I don't think anything would keep him from joining you. But is it true Los Diablos will be attached to Fierro's headquarters now that he is a general?"

"*Sí*. I think perhaps he wants them to become for him what Los Dorados are for General Villa."

"*¡Mierda!* We will no longer serve under General Ángeles, then?"

"I am afraid not, *amigo*. I made a request that you and I be left somewhere in Felipe's command structure, but Rodolfo was adamant, and General Villa turned me down. He said I was the only officer in the Division Fierro would trust with the new squadron. I should feel honored, I suppose." He smiled, but the smile had to force its way into his drawn face.

"What does General Villa plan for General Ángeles now?"

"That is the only good news. After a year of being only the strategist for the Division, while other generals claimed all the glory, General Villa has given him command of his own army. I am happy about that at least. The bad news is that General Villa will not allow Felipe to move on Veracruz as he wishes."

"What are his orders, then?"

"He is to take Paredón, Saltillo, and then Monterrey."

"Paredón and Saltillo? We have already fought for those places once. Must *los hombres* of the Division die for them again?"

"*Sí*, Jorge. This time we must take them from the Carrancistas. We should never have turned them over to González and the Coahuilans. But even though we need them back eventually, it is not a battle we should be fighting now. And after Felipe takes them, the next battle, for Monterrey, will not be easy, now that Herrera and Villareal have joined forces and gone over to the new enemy." For the first time since Jorge had known him, Trini sounded bitter. It was a deep, poisonous bitterness, ugly to hear and feel, particularly after the even darker than usual sadness moments ago when he said goodbye to his Bracomonte officers. "I confess I do not like the feel of things, Jorge," Trini added, "but it is hardly my place to question General Villa's orders concerning Trini Álvarez. I am, after all, his *soldado*, his *contrato*, to do with as he wishes, but I wish he would listen to Felipe about Veracruz."

For Jorge's part, confusion had fragmented his thinking about the struggle. He had no idea what he felt. After Zacatecas he had taken it as an article of faith that save for a few minor skirmishes the Revolution was over, won, that the ideas and ideals of Francisco Madero had triumphed, and that Pancho Villa would rise like the sun and lead Mexico to the good life for all its people. At the time he had been sure that even El Primer Jefe, hiding now behind the guns of General Obregón at Veracruz, would see it this way, too. The disagreement between Carranza and El Caudillo at Torreón was a *pequeña* thing—a tiny aberration, wasn't it?—something which would be resolved to the joy and satisfaction of Mexicans from the Baja to Quintana Roo when they remembered the great, and at that time supposedly final, victories of last summer. General Villa had met Zapata, and both had avowed their common purpose. Certainly there had been talk all fall and in the early winter of Villa's and Zapata's distrust of Venustiano Carranza, but it truly seemed, until this last month, only the clash of personalities, and that it wouldn't last, not when they all considered what they had already won—what Mexico had won. The convention at Aguascalientes had voiced with one mighty shout the intent of all of them to keep their armies in check now that Huerta had been defeated and driven into exile, and Eulalio Gutiérrez, a good, sincere man and soldier, had been named President there. Gutiérrez should have his chance. General Obregón had agreed to that. Surely even Carranza would fall in line.

But then Obregón had sent an army to occupy Monterrey,

and two weeks ago Zapata had marched on Puebla in a countering show of solidarity with General Villa. Everything had changed. Well, not quite everything. There was still one thing they all could hold on to.

"There is still nothing our new enemies have that can stand against the Division, Trini." There was a note of pride in his voice, but pride was all he had to sustain him at the moment.

If Trini's bitterness and sadness had dismayed him this morning, it was nothing compared to what he saw now on the major's face: a sudden, fast-closing cloud of doubt.

"Don't be too sure of that, Lugarteniente Martínez," he said. "I think perhaps we have lost our fine cutting edge. We are still the strongest military force in Mexico, but we cannot remain so if we dissipate our strength by robbing banks and trains, and bullying the towns where we are stationed. Our ability to deploy our army has been severely limited. Without the coal the First Chief has denied us since Zacatecas we cannot run our trains."

"But we can *ride* to battle, Trini! Nothing the enemy can do can stop the Dorados and Bracomontes."

"*Sí.* If it *comes* to that again. In the saddle we are *magníficos*, but on foot we are not the overwhelming striking force we were, and although I am a cavalryman by training and inclination, I will be the first to admit that horses have limits in modern combat. Felipe says that the day of the cavalry in warfare has passed forever, and while that saddens me, I must agree with him. Artillery and infantry won the day at Zacatecas."

"But at Torreón and Paredón our horses made the difference."

"True. But the graveyards of history are filled with generals who insisted upon fighting the last battle over again. Felipe has urged for three months now that we use our remaining precious coal and move against Obregón at Veracruz with big guns and rifle brigades, but General Villa fails to heed his wisdom. He still views everything from horseback." Jorge wondered if Trini was thinking about *his* nearsighted vision. "And in all *respeto*, I must say that General Villa has weakened us in ways which do not yet show. He has sent his best commanders and advisers, like Felipe, Urbina, and Chao, to the corners of the country, and only kept close to him those of undoubted courage but of no vision—men like Fierro and Contreras. They and the *porros* under them understand *nothing* but guns and killing. I think sometimes El Caudillo is intent on just going home to govern Chihuahua, fighting small actions along the way that only bleed us. The move from Guanajuato to here at Irapuato was not wise in my opinion. It takes something from the Division's spirit every time we move a foot farther from the capital of our enemies. Álvaro Obregón is not doing these things. He marshals his army on the coast, sits tight, heals what few wounds he has, and gathers strength. He knows the Revolution is not over."

"But he fell back in retreat at Puebla when the Zapatistas marched up from Morelos, Trini. They took the city almost without a battle."

"Exactly. But Obregón's army is still intact. He will resupply at Veracruz, where he expects more arms from the merchant *extranjeros* to arrive. Zapata is strung out over hundreds of miles of country he doesn't understand. And he has no transport, either. It is only a question of time before Obregón regroups and marches on the capital again. He will sweep Emiliano before him, since we are now too far to the north to help, and if he doesn't destroy him completely, he will keep him penned up in the sugarcane of Morelos for a year."

"How did we get in this predicament?"

"Because General Villa is not a true *político*. He is *muy guerrero*, but he has no great plan. General Ángeles could give him one, but he seems inclined to listen to no one but Fierro at the moment."

"Could not the great *jefes* of the Revolution all just stop fighting each other and talk again?"

"Such a course, *amigo,* would require a great deal of common sense—not a plentiful commodity in Mexico these days."

Jorge wondered what Molinas would have to say about the state things had fallen to. ¿Grandes problemas? Sí.

More than such important worries, though, were the sharper, closer ones Jorge had about Trini Álvarez himself. Had the major's refusal of Fierro's request for him to lead the attack on the train himself really been forgotten? Margaret Espinosa certainly didn't think so. In talks with Jorge and Juanita she had seemed to blame herself. "Rodolfo has no designs on me now, but he never forgets when he thinks someone has taken what he has decided belongs to him." Paco was noncommittal, but Jorge could guess at the dynamiter's thoughts. Durán worried for Trini, too. He was a monumental worrier. Jorge Martínez was getting to be one himself.

But surely the major's new appointment as leader of the embryo Los Diablos signaled an end to their concerns. It made sense. Major Trinidad Álvarez was far too skillful an officer for Pancho Villa to lose. No general with an ounce of brains would send such a man to the wall. No one could accuse the Tiger of the North of being stupid—rash and reckless yes, but not stupid. Even Rodolfo Fierro would agree that Pancho Villa was right. Fierro, for all the other things which might be wrong with him, wasn't stupid, either.

Rumors passed along by some of the junior officers in Division headquarters had it that Fierro had certainly *wanted* to make an example of Trini right after the business about the train, and that for a day or two Pancho had considered giving him Trini's head. Ángeles's taking Trini with him to the capital must have given Fierro time to cool off, and probably saved the major in the bargain. Then, too, Villa might have soothed the Butcher by passing Trini over for the promotion everyone who knew him said was long overdue. After Zacatecas Jorge had thought he would be working for *Colonel* Álvarez in only a month or two.

When they shook hands and left the stable which had served as Regiment Bracomonte's nerve center since coming to Irapuato from Guanajuato, Jorge knew the blackest moment he had known in months, as he watched Trini stride away from him, obviously heading for the hospital car and

Margaret Espinosa. At a glance his walk was as firm as ever, his shoulders as square as they had always been, and his head as high—but it wasn't the Trini Álvarez he had known till now. This was an automaton. He wouldn't bend or break. He would keep moving forward until the parts wore out.

Jorge hitched a ride in a truck loaded with worn-out tires being hauled to the dump for burning. This afternoon he had to look over some horses driven into camp yesterday from Sinaloa, and see if he couldn't secure half a dozen remounts fit enough for the depleted remuda of his *tropa*. By the time he found a wrangler and went to the corral to get his share of the new herd, he wouldn't be with Juanita again for hours. As always, his suddenly drumming pulse almost shook him, as it did every time he thought of her.

In Irapuato they had rented a shack with a dirt floor on the edge of town, actually the worst living space they had occupied since Saltillo. It made no difference. Although the dirt floor swarmed with beetles, and although the shack smelled of every animal that had called it home for half a century, it still was home after Juanita went to work on it. Somehow, somewhere, she managed to find fresh flowers almost every day that brightened the dark, dank hut to something of the muted brilliance of their rooms in Saltillo, Torreón, Zacatecas, and Guanajuato. She mended old furniture scavenged from burned-out houses in the town, showing some of her father's skill with wood and metal, and the few things he had bought her with his meager lieutenant's pay were always on display.

This time, with no smithy to lure him away to quarters of his own, Paco lived in the shack with them, separated from them at night only by a bed sheet hung from the ceiling. His closeness created a problem for a while.

They had made love often enough with the sergeant under one roof with them in the earlier towns, but this was the first time they had done so within the same four walls, and she had to persuade him to even try.

It seemed it would be a disaster to begin with. He couldn't force away the image of Paco wide awake and listening behind the sheet. But in the end they had gotten it done. She had helped him, doing some strange things with him and to him which had shocked him to the core, but which had almost blown him outside his skin. She had fumbled awkwardly at first, but had come on with an eagerness that took his breath, along with every other thing inside him. "I've wanted to do those things with you for a long time, Jorge," she breathed when they finished, "but I was afraid you might think I learned them with someone else."

That particular thought had never once crossed his mind, but he did wonder a little about the rightness of the things she did to him, and the things her body began to ask of him. Gradually, though, rightness no longer mattered, goodness and richness did. Then he discovered for himself how she had discovered them. His first attempts to please her weren't easy, but to his surprise not one thing he did seemed strange or unfamiliar. They must both have wanted it this way for a long, long time—if only in their most secret dreams.

They would begin by whispering to each other, but she couldn't hold her whispers down, and near the end she would fairly shriek her joy, and it pleased and frightened him all at once.

But splendid as it was, Paco's presence still bothered him from time to time, and he feared another failure, one from which he might not recover no matter how she ministered to him. He told her so. It got so he told her everything. In the end she gave in laughing to his nagging worry, and they only began with each other after Paco's snores resonated through the darkened room. They would lie together hardly breathing until the dynamiter started rumbling, then they would fall on each other as if each of them was a banquet to the starving.

At the Division's cavalry depot he found the horses he wanted, signed the requisition papers, turned a string of five over to his *soldado de caballería* wrangler, and rode the sixth to the shack. He let the animal out to a brisk canter as he went through the farm gate, steeling himself to the task of passing the news about Trini to Paco and Juanita.

Juanita was waiting at the front door with her father. She was beaming.

Paco's big face wore a smile that made him look like a friendly jack-o'-lantern.

"*Hola,* Capitán Cockroach!" Paco bellowed. "Or I should say now Capitán *Martínez.*" For the first time since he had known him, the giant was saluting him.

"What are you talking about, *viejo?*"

"You do not know, Jorge?" Juanita said.

"Know what?"

"Papá heard it at headquarters. You have been promoted. You are a captain now!"

She lifted her skirt above her knees and shook it back and forth across her brown legs as she had the very first time he saw her, on the bank of the Río Nazas at Torreón. He couldn't spoil the moment with his troubling thoughts about Trini now. *Dios,* how he wanted her.

"We must not delay our marriage any longer, *querida,*" he said.

"I am ready anytime you are, *mi capitán.*"

At dinner he urged *cerveza* after *cerveza* on the sergeant. Paco always went to bed early when he had drunk more than usual. Jorge couldn't wait to hear his snores. This bad day might yet be saved, in part at least. Juanita smiled across the table at him.

They did not make love that night.

Just before they turned in, a rider arrived with a handwritten message for Jorge from Trini Álvarez.

Amigo Jorge—

I regret to inform you that my request to have you join me in Los Diablos has been turned down by General Fierro. You are to stay with Los Bracomontes. My appeal for a transfer for Sargento Paco Durán has also been denied.

Buena suerte
Trini

* * *

Devastated as she was for Trini, Juanita Durán feared more the effect it would have on Jorge. Even before the news that Trini would leave the regiment he had shown moments of deepening despair.

The tasks he had been assigned lately by the Butcher and the other *jefes* of the Division were taking a terrible toll on his ideals. He no longer spoke with such passion of the Mexico they both would know after the Revolution. His talk now was only of men, horses, guns, and how the three could be used against the inconsequential targets El Carnicero was assigning him.

She was pleased about the promotion, of course; it would mean a bit more money, perhaps even enough to put some by for the day the war ended and they could begin a life together. The day the war ended? Did she still believe it would ever come? Yes, she had to.

In the meantime all she could do was hope and pray that things would turn better for Trini Álvarez.

She saw how her betrothed, her *prometido* (wonderful word), was modeling himself on the major. She saw, also, how much like Trini he had become, and in fact how much like him he had been to begin with.

If the end was coming for Trini Álvarez she didn't want a similar end for her man. He had to transcend all this bloodshed. He had to—for her sake, for his own, and for the sake of . . .

No, she couldn't tell him yet of what she knew was stirring in her. Men being the way they were, this was hardly the time to tell him how much she wanted to begin a child.

It certainly wasn't necessary for them to marry before she became pregnant, but it would make Papá happy. It was only Papá's feelings about this that concerned her, wasn't it?

Do not try to fool yourself, Juanita Durán. It is important to Jorge, too, and because it is, it is doubly important to YOU.

32

Corey's second trip down to Xochimilco was entirely different from the first, but in its own way even more disappointing than the one with Fergus.

It shouldn't have been.

The gardens were lovely—an unexpected burst of summer in the mild January air and pale but brilliant sunshine. The picnic lunch of pâtés, croissants, and some kind of Mexican game fowl, served by Luisa López y Montenegro's mute old servant couple, her *dueña* Emilia, and Tomás—who had driven the touring car to the Mirador the day Corey saw Luisa for the second time—was sumptuous and delicious, the gentle boat ride a voyage of minute but marvelous discoveries. Luisa herself was a vision, the fulfillment of the fantasies which had visited him the night after the ball and again more strongly still after Narciso's lantern show and the late supper Luisa gave him at the tiny, sedate residence hotel in Avenida Melgar just outside Chapultepec Park, where she and her two servants occupied the entire second floor.

It wasn't Luisa's fault the day didn't turn out as she planned it. It was his, caused in part by his jealousy of Wolf Kemper, and by agonized awareness of his own inadequacies.

All he could hope for when it ended was that she hadn't guessed at his misery.

The morning after the ball at the embassy, even before his second sight of Luisa at the lantern show, Henry Richardson came to the Mirador, sat openly with him at breakfast in the dining room, and put emphatically to rest the fears Corey had harbored about his mission being canceled. This desire for such an outcome had disappeared completely when he had held Luisa's gloved hand in his the night before.

"Yes, it was a test, Corey," Henry said just before they

parted company. "You've passed it admirably. I now think it would be more than merely useful if you do go to see General Villa about Felipe Ángeles. Carranza didn't leave many of our people at the embassy enamored of him. Nor did Obregón. You'll have to give Washington some time, of course, to accustom itself to thinking about Ángeles's chances and his possible value to us. We move slowly at State. It's our stock-in-trade. Yes, see Villa. But wait until we give the signal. We'll be in touch."

He felt good about Henry permitting him to stay on board, but Henry's remarks troubled him. Would his masters here and in Washington only think of backing Ángeles because of his "possible value" to the United States? What about the general's value to his own people and to Mexico?

Then he saw Luisa again at Narciso's lecture and lantern show . . .

The doctor's audience was quite a different mixture from the one Corey and Narciso had sampled at the ball. Except for Luisa, the people in the lecture hall at the ministry could hardly be numbered among *los ricos*. Men outnumbered women about four to one, and while some of them were young students he judged to be of military age, but by no means of martial inclination, most were mature if not elderly, and almost all of them looked as genteelly shabby as Narciso did himself. Luisa shone in their midst with a nearly blinding glow, even when—especially when—the room was darkened for the little Minister's presentation.

He would be embarrassed all out of countenance if Narciso ever asked him his reaction to the lecture. He scarcely heard it. As the shadow of the doctor's pointer flitted across the screen, and as the insistent tip tapped ripples into it, he kept his eyes fixed on Luisa, two chairs away. One of Narciso's students had escorted her to her seat, and he knew a swift pang of disappointment that she apparently hadn't even noticed him before the evening's program got under way. She certainly had no difficulty keeping *her* attention on the sepia images or Narciso's words. Then Corey was embarrassed when the white-haired fat man sitting next to him smiled and moved his chair back a few inches, obviously to afford him a better look. He felt his face flush, but he didn't stop looking at her. Couldn't.

She sat absolutely motionless, erect in the straight-backed chair, intent on Narciso, her slender neck slanted forward like that of Nefertiti on the model of the famous bust he had studied in the Metropolitan in New York City on a trip down from Amherst as a student a quarter of a century ago.

The platinum-silver hair was unaffected by the amber wash reflecting from Narciso's screen. Nothing could dim or discolor the argentine purity of it. Her mouth opened in little gasps of appreciation during the rare exciting moments in Narciso's lecture—as when one of the slides showed the broken bits of stone Narciso speculated might be a carving of the Aztec moon-goddess, Coyolxauhqui—revealing even white teeth, with now and then the tip of a tongue just barely touching and moistening her delicate but full upper lip, and above it the straight nose showing the merest hint of irregularity, something that only added to its perfection, if that were possible.

She wore a severe, dark maroon dress—threaded with silver in some seamstress's skillful, but in the ultimate, futile attempt to match that matchless hair—with a high mandarin collar and sleeves that reached to her wrists, fastened there with a row of old ivory buttons each of which seemed a small treasure of antiquity. Another woman in the same garment would have looked forbiddingly prim. On Luisa the gown evoked a picture of an inviolable solitude he, of all men, could probably never breach. The ivory buttons reminded him of his first sight of her graceful back in the much more daring gown she had worn at the ball, and he wondered why his thoughts had turned so immediately to ivory then. Yes. He remembered. In that stunning scene in *Anna Karenina*, Kitty, arriving at another ball, had spied the more mature, confident Anna in a dress very like the lavender Luisa had worn at the embassy, and the thought of ivory had struck young Kitty, too, to disquieting effect. Luisa must be just about the age of Anna at that time in Tolstoi's novel. He felt a sudden let-down. Was there a Karenin for Luisa López y Montenegro somewhere in the offing?

Then Narciso's magic lantern winked out, and in the thick, impenetrable darkness he felt bereft and cheated for the half minute or so it took for the doctor's projectionist to find a replacement bulb. When the light came on again he found her face turned toward him, and her eyes full on his. The shock of her utterly frank gaze addled him so that for a second he was thoroughly persuaded that she had been able to see him clearly in the dark.

"*Buenas noches,* Señor Lane." She hadn't actually spoken the words, just formed them silently with the richly shaped mouth, but he would have sworn he heard her voice.

He heard it clearly at the brief reception after Narciso's program ended. He stood behind her while she conversed with two novice archaeologists who had taken part in Narciso's Cuernavaca dig. She then turned to him and without preamble or warning said, "It is delightful to see you again, Señor Lane. Would it be possible for you to share a modest supper with me when this affair is over?"

He accepted, but could barely remember, a second later, what exactly he had said.

She went on to tell him she had invited Narciso, too, but that the doctor had begged off with regret, claiming a previous engagement. He tried to keep his pleasure at this from showing on his face, finally decided he didn't really care much if it did. He wondered again about the possibility of a husband somewhere. Would one be at the "modest supper," too? She wore no gloves that night, and although a massive ruby on her right hand heightened the color of her long dress, her left held no rings at all. Perhaps . . . but he wasn't at all sure what indicated the married status of a woman of Luisa's world.

A taciturn Tomás, as he later learned was the name of the elderly, uniformed servant who waited beside the Daimler, drove them down the Paseo to Avenida Melgar, past Chapultepec Park, where *el palacio* was almost hidden behind the lush, green-black branches of the ahuehuetes, and on to the *posada*, set in its own small park. Neither spoke during the fifteen-minute journey.

There was more than enough talk at table, too much he feared, since almost every word of it was his. The lecture and lantern show were disposed of in four or five brief sentences, and he was glad about that; he didn't want her to discover how little attention he had paid to Narciso's efforts in his intense absorption with her. Much too soon for any such admission. But she subtly drew out of him a recitation of things he hadn't thought about in years.

He finally brought himself up short, blushing. Narciso had remarked that he and Luisa shared a common love for history, but the old scholar surely hadn't meant the history of Corey Lane.

When he left, she held the naked left hand with the tapering ivory fingers out to him, and to his surprise and satisfaction, without any clumsiness at all, he lifted it and brushed it with his lips.

Standing in the cool night air of Avenida Melgar while silent Tomás brought the Daimler around to drive him to the Mirador, he put his hand to his mouth. The breeze he heard rising in the trees in the park across the *avenida* could never be allowed to cool the warmth lingering on his lips.

He might have expected Fergus would know a thing or two about Luisa.

"She's thirty-seven or thereabouts, laddie. No children or other close kith or kin. Family nearly all dead, butchered by local *insurrectos* when Pancho roared out of Chihuahua four years ago, the husband, too. Luisa still owns and runs a monstrous grand *estancia* near Santa María del Oro in Durango, but she spends a lot of time here in the capital. I've bought cattle from her manager from time to time. I do send the odd haunch or joint to what these days is a not so Merrie England. I *am* a buyer of beef, ye ken, a bonnie one, Medina Barrón's suspicions notwithstanding. As they say here, *buena suerte,* lad. The lass is comely enough to be the consort of an Ayrshire laird. I'm past this sort of thing meself, but I think ye might need a lady like Luisa."

Then, prompted, Corey admitted to himself, by the slightly shameful joy that there was no "Karenin" in the offing, his eagerness swept him away, and it began.

In the next week he saw Luisa almost every day. She inducted him effortlessly into the cultural life of the city which Narciso had only pointed him toward, and visits to art museums and monuments were sandwiched between long walks in the park, with Emilia two dozen paces behind them. Although Luisa slipped her arm easily enough into the crook of his arm wherever they went, he was never truly alone with her; the old maidservant Emilia a constant companion, and when they took the Daimler it was Tomás in evidence, stony as a Toltec statue. Corey somehow capped his longing to have her exclusively to himself, but it wasn't easy. He finally decided it was the best thing, after all. He had no notion of how he might go about getting any closer to her than he did on these pleasant winter afternoons and evenings. This lady could not be rushed.

She could not be read easily, either. While her conversation sparkled, particularly when she was commenting on an exhibit in one of the museums, or on a trip to the ministry to pay their respects to Narciso, there were times when she would fall silent for long moments. He couldn't reach her at all when this happened. It wasn't hard to guess a little of what might be going on in her mind, if not her soul. Fergus's story haunted him. Losses of the magnitude of hers would drag anyone into a pit of gloom.

But the only truly disturbing moment of the week came eight blissful days after their supper, on the Friday they visited the Zócalo so she could show him the Aztec ruins of Teocalli behind the cathedral. When they left the ancient stones Luisa wound a gossamer scarf around her head and they walked through the old church to return to the plaza where Tomás waited with the car. She suddenly broke away from him, took a few steps toward the main altar, knelt on the bare stone floor, crossed herself, and bowed her head. It was the same dark, withdrawn pose he had seen her in from time to time all week long. This time, fortunately, it took only seconds.

When she joined him again, and they started toward the mammoth carved doors at the front of the nave, she spoke without looking at him.

"You are not Catholic, are you, Corey?"

"No, Luisa, I'm not."

"You have a church, though, do you not?"

"Yes—but I can't claim to be a regular communicant, Luisa."

She looked at him more searchingly than she had in any of their times together. "It must be difficult not to have a strong faith in terrible times like these." The corners of her mouth turned down, and she kept her steady gaze on his face for half a minute. It wasn't an entirely unpleasant look, but it was an hour before he could shake it from his mind, and then only when she proposed the picnic at Xochimilco, brightening like a child at Christmas as she talked about it. On the way back to Posada Melgar they stopped near the Mercado Merced to pay their respects to the moldering bones of Hernán Cortés. It seemed for Luisa a moment well nigh as reverential as when she had bowed her fine head before the Virgin. Common love for history, indeed.

At the teeming market he smiled with amusement—and relief—at her delight in racing from stall to stall and piling sack after sack of delicacies for the picnic into his and Tomás's arms. On the drive through the backstreets leading down toward Avenida Melgar the Daimler was redolent with the aroma of fruit, baked goods, and potted meats, overpowering to senses becoming more alert than they had been in years.

"I'll go to the earliest Mass Sunday morning at San Fernando. It's close to the Mirador, and I can pick you up straight afterward," she said.

She sent him back to his hotel early that Friday night, and when they parted at her door he searched her face for any disaffection with him the interlude at the cathedral might have caused. He didn't find it.

"Tomorrow night, Luisa?"

Her face fell a little then. "I am truly sorry, Corey, but to-morrow night I have something on I cannot possibly get out of. I am going to supper and the theater with a friend. You saw him at the ball at the embassy. His name is Wolf Kemper. It is something planned weeks ago." Then she turned distraught, almost close to panic. "*¡Dios!* I forgot! I promised Wolf the whole weekend, Corey!" Now she searched *his* face. "Would you mind too terribly if he came with us to Xochimilco?"

Mind? He said, "Of course not, Luisa," but he very nearly added a bitter *the more the merrier.*

He didn't exactly run to Fergus for comfort, but he had hoped for something a little more in the way of solace than what he got when they dined Saturday evening at the Mirador.

"Bonnie, laddie, absolutely bonnie!" The Scot was beside himself with glee. "Old Fergus has been racking his wee brain for days trying to dope out a way to put you next to Kemper without him and von Rintelen getting the wind up, and now the beggar has fallen right into our hands. I must have been bloody well fey when I said you needed a lassie like Luisa."

Damn Fergus's ratlike little eyes. The last thing in the world he wanted was for Luisa to be even an approximate accessory to espionage. Still, it was, after all, his work for Henry Richardson that kept him in Mexico and close to her.

That work was held in abeyance by things other than his preoccupation with Luisa.

The impatience to see about Ángeles he expected to erupt like boils before too many days went by—after the breakfast when Henry told him, in what amounted to reconciliation, that he had to wait for a "signal"—didn't quite. And now he felt no urgency in his plan to see Pancho Villa about his general.

He did a lot of thinking about Luisa after he left Fergus at his customary post at the bar of the Mirador. Unfortunately, he did a lot of thinking about the other woman with a bell-like voice he had known. The ghost of Lucy Bishop had failed to appear again, but something in him made him summon it.

It was now almost sixteen years since he lost Lucy without so much as a goodbye or a farewell kiss, and almost eight since she died of consumption at Fort Sill. She had long ago released him. Had he truly released himself? The Mimbreños and other Apaches under close arrest for twenty-six years were back on the Mescalero and in Arizona now. He had seen Lucy's mother Ana twice up on the reservation just before the messy business with young Martínez came about. "Lucy begged that you forget her, Corey," Ana told him. "She said to tell you that her life had been a good one. Her work with the Chihende Apache children at the fort brought her all the rewards she needed. But I know she loved you until her *dahitsaah*, as I believe she once told you she always would. Get married. Lucy would want that. You need a woman. You are not as good alone as you think you are."

He needed a woman? He had faced that question over the years without anyone having to tell him to. And he had tried. He had tried hard with Ellen Stafford, and bless her, Ellen had tried, too.

But now? Yes, he needed a woman now—a certain woman. Did he still have too much work to do?

Perhaps he could find an answer at Xochimilco tomorrow. It would be a good place to ask himself again, in the company of what he now knew without the slightest doubt was *the* woman—and with the challenge of at least some of his work also there in the person of the German agent, adversary now in more ways than one.

But at Xochimilco he could have done very nicely without the presence of Wolf Kemper. Not that the tall German was bad company, far from it.

His manner was engaging, as crisp and dazzling as the white linen suit he wore, and as impeccable, if a bit stiff and formal. All the same, stiffness or not, Kemper exhibited that seductive European charm bred by centuries of brushing against other expert charmers of every class and background. As Corey had noted in his brief glimpse of him at the ball, he was a spectacularly handsome man, surely devilishly attractive to women. Corey felt overmatched. Fergus had predicted that Wolf Kemper would be a hard man for him to dislike. Should he try? Woodrow Wilson's vaunted passion for neutrality notwithstanding, the United States might be fighting this German someday soon.

After the boat ride, Tomás spread an acre-sized quilted lap robe on the grass in a grove of eucalyptus trees near the waterways, but in a spot decently distant from the docks.

"Luisa has been to my country, Herr Lane," Kemper said as he opened a bottle of champagne, his surprise contribution to the party, one which had brought a cry of pleasure from Luisa. Corey felt like a country bumpkin. Why the hell hadn't *he* thought of bringing wine? He had tried to pay for the food she had purchased at Mercado Merced, but this was different. This lofty Junker baron had opened a lot of champagne in his time, and with the same accomplished, sommelier dexterity he demonstrated now. A large diamond caught the sunlight as the man's powerful thumbs eased the cork from the bottle. "Have you ever visited Germany in your travels, *mein Herr*?"

"Once, many years ago, Herr Kemper."

Kemper looked a bit surprised, but he didn't pursue the when or where of it. Small wonder. Corey must look to the suave German precisely the uncultivated hick he suddenly felt himself to be.

"Where are you from, Herr Lane?" Kemper asked next as he filled Luisa's glass.

"New Mexico." He knew it would serve no purpose to mention Black Springs or Chupadera County; certainly the obscure place names would elicit no recognition. "New Mexico" wasn't any better. He might just as well have said Alpha Centauri or Patagonia.

"*Ja?* You do not look or sound like a . . ." Kemper fumbled for the word he wanted, and Luisa came to his rescue, laughing.

"Corey is a *norteamericano*, Wolf. From *New* Mexico . . .

in the United States. I don't believe you caught the *New.*" She turned to Corey. "I only know Santa Fe in New Mexico myself. It is quite a famous place." With that explanation she somehow seemed to come to Corey's rescue, too. Perhaps she was unaware of what a backwater the Ojos Negros Basin was, or how far it lay from his state's colorful and comparatively cosmopolitan capital. He felt a bit of a fraud letting her link him in some accidental way with a "famous place."

"When we left Mass this morning," Kemper was saying now, "Luisa told me you are a historian, Herr Lane."

"A very minor historian. I believe you could stand on the New Mexico state line and throw a rock and stand a good chance of hitting someone who has never heard of me—or my work."

"You are far too modest, Corey," Luisa said. "Narciso told me your work is excellent, and much more widely known than you seem to think." Coming from her he wanted to believe it.

"What sort of history?" Kemper said.

Corey told him of the book on the beginnings of the Revolution, adding that he was now working on a biography of one of the figures in it. He could have bitten his tongue. Henry would be outraged that a German agent would discover that *any* American was interested in Felipe Ángeles. Fergus would hoot at him as a "bloody amateur." He waited for the expected question as a condemned man waits for the ax.

"There is much interest in the United States about this struggle, *ja?*"

A near miss, thank God. "Indeed there is, Herr Kemper. We share a long border with this country." Out of the corner of his eye he saw Luisa nod. "Is there not interest in the Revolution in Germany?" Careful. Let this "marine engineer" tell him what interested Germans.

"Another, bigger struggle interests us much more these days, Herr Lane. The war we are fighting against almost the entire world occupies all of our attention." There was something a little edgy in the words.

"¡Por favor, señores, por favor!" Luisa's voice quivered. "Let us not talk of such ugly things as war on a lovely day like this."

"I am sorry, *Liebchen,*" Kemper said. "You are right, of course. Let us now devote ourselves to the wine, *ja?*" He tipped the bottle toward Corey's glass, apparently so skilled at pouring he could keep his eyes on Corey's as he did. Not a drop spilled. "That was a very *gemütlich* affair at your country's embassy, Herr Lane, and an extraordinary gathering for other than social reasons. It was *Weltpolitik* such as I have not seen since leaving *Deutschland.*"

"Are you involved in *Weltpolitik,* Herr Kemper?" Corey's question should sound innocuous enough. After all, it was the German himself who had brought the subject up.

"Nein, nein, nein!" It was a clamor of low-keyed but vehement protest. "I have no concern with *Politiken* of any kind, except as a loyal citizen of the fatherland. I am a man of business, an engineer. I make studies for the construction of port facilities for only the *civilian* authorities in Mexico." The emphasis on "civilian" might have made the disavowal a little too transparent even for someone not in the "game." Corey decided he had better not show any more curiosity about what the German was engaged in, but apparently Kemper wasn't quite through. "You see," he said, "I am not fit for military service." His strong right hand had moved to his left shoulder and was kneading and rubbing it. Tannenberg? "I had a bad fall on the polo grounds at Baden-Baden a year ago."

Luisa, sitting to the left of Kemper, reached for him and gently stroked the shoulder. "Does it still give you so much trouble, Wolf?" she said.

Corey started, pricked by a needle of envy. Be honest, he told himself, the sensation was one of jealousy, plain and simple, not just lukewarm envy.

A bright macaw was croaking from its sunlit perch on a low branch of the nearest eucalyptus. It was mocking him.

It mocked him through the rest of the afternoon and on the long ride back to the Mirador.

No—on balance the second trip to Xochimilco wasn't a bit more satisfying than the first.

33

"I don't think you can make your way north to Villa's army for some weeks yet, Mr. Lane," Major Will Hendricks said. "Rail lines are out, here and here, and these are just the disruptions we know of." He put his index finger at two spots on the map of Guanajuato. "Your chances of making it by motorcar are even worse. It's a purely personal opinion, but I think Pancho's big Northern Division is beginning to feel the wear and tear of four years of fighting. While the Division is still a significant force, it hasn't the cohesion it had when he took Zacatecas. With Ángeles off in the north meeting the Constitutionalists with his new army, all the military activity Villa seems to be directly engaged in at the moment is sending out small units to raid and rob. Maybe Pancho can't handle success. It happens."

Corey had seen the first hints of a tendency to rest on the laurels of past victories when Villa met Zapata at Xochimilco.

One thing had taken a turn for the better. Henry, before returning to Washington, had opened up the embassy to him, and it looked as if Major Hendricks, the assistant military attaché, would be invaluable. He seemed bright, capable, and to this point cooperative. Tough, too. Corey's only doubts now were about the extent to which the major's superiors backed him and how much he had behind him in the way of current intelligence. The embassy of a fabulously wealthy nation sat in the capital of a country in the throes of the greatest revolution of the still-young twentieth century, but all they had given Hendricks and his boss for a situation room was a cubbyhole hardly larger than Corey's bath at the Mirador. The map of Guanajuato that Hendricks had spread on the desk in front of him, and the larger one of Mexico on the wall, were dated 1903 and 1905. They were both crosshatched with corrections and additions sketched into the print in ink and pencil by a dozen different hands and styles, with enough smudges on both to make them look like badly kept Bertillon fingerprint files. Corey had looked in vain for San Gabriel de los Árboles on the larger map. The hamlet was too small to attract the attention of the cartographer. Perhaps not attracting attention was a blessing for San Gabriel in today's Mexico. The innocent villagers there should be allowed by any of the contesting forces to grow their melons in peace.

"Where are General Ángeles and his command now, Major? And can I get north to him?" As much as he liked Hendricks, and as helpful as the man was trying his best to be, Corey was impatient as hell. Didn't this major, or Henry for that matter, understand that time was of the essence? A declaration of support for Ángeles, coming from Pancho Villa, might stop Carranza and the Constitutionalists in their tracks. Even Obregón might swing away from the Coahuilan and toward the new contender. His choices would be either that or facing him in battle. At the ball the little bulldog general hadn't looked entirely sold on Carranza, not to Corey, anyway.

"Ángeles is operating considerably north and east of Villa at the moment," Hendricks said. "I don't think you would have much luck in reaching him at all. Obregón's forces lie in a big semicircle southeast of Ángeles, and although they're not heavily engaged with the *norteños* at the moment, the country between the two main bodies is in a state of virtual anarchy. We couldn't help at all if you got yourself marooned between the two of them."

"Is Ángeles winning?"

"Whenever he takes the field. That, however, isn't often. He has logistical problems. Carranza and González, here"—again the authoritative finger jabbed the map—"have effectively cut him off from the coast. He has to pick his battlefields pretty carefully. He did win decisively at Saltillo and Monterrey, but although they were well-planned and well-executed actions, they took a lot out of him."

"When and where do you think Villa and the Division will take the field again?"

"I don't think he will *take* the field. The field will be brought to him. That doesn't mean he will lose, however."

"What do you mean 'the field will be brought to him'?"

"Obregón is rolling Zapata back down toward Morelos. He doesn't seek battle; he just moves in and occupies whenever his enemy tires and draws back a bit. Interesting strategy. It's a war of attrition, but with a difference. He moves forward to a defensive position and lets Zapata break himself against him. When Zapata falls back to regroup, Obregón moves forward again and the process is repeated. I think he'll move past the capital—probably not even really try to occupy it—then turn north and attempt the same sort of thing against Villa. He'll face a different enemy in the Northern Division, of course. Zapata's forces are guerrillas, good ones, but not the kind of army to fight well on a clearly defined front. Obregón won't have things his own way quite so readily when Pancho brings Ángeles back from the northeast to do his planning for him."

"You'll let me know when you think it's time for me to try to get to Villa, then?"

"Count on it, sir."

The political briefings the embassy staff members gave Corey proved just as edifying, but more because of what the striped-pants crowd *didn't* tell him than because of what they did.

Before Henry left he had fully persuaded Corey that he wouldn't struggle too hard against Corey's championing of Felipe Ángeles. "Personally, I still think he's a touch on the radical side. His writings seem to indicate some Fabian thinking, but perhaps he's the best we can get. I do know I don't care for Carranza. He's capable as a politician, but as a statesman he falls short in Washington's opinion. He's devious, and he plain doesn't like us. Zapata's out—completely—but I guess you see that now, too, Corey. Frankly, I still think Villa's our man. With all his faults State could sell him to Mr. Wilson a lot easier than we could sell Ángeles. Villa's no statesman, either, but we could provide all the statesmanship Mexico needs on the q.t. I know how committed you are to Ángeles, but don't be too surprised if we stick with Villa. I would, were I Mr. Wilson." Henry paused for a moment then, lost in thought. "Damn it!" he said at last. "I hired you because I had faith in your judgment. Regardless of my personal outlook, I think now that you had better make an all-out effort with Villa on behalf of Ángeles." Corey's feelings soared.

Henry had made his position clear, but Corey soon discovered it was strictly his. At the embassy now, Corey found surprisingly little criticism of the First Chief, and, not so surprising, faint sneers whenever Villa's name was mentioned. It wasn't too difficult to fathom why. The American businessmen who drifted in and out of the embassy had an unadmitted influence on the staff's thinking, from the ambassador himself down to the most junior clerk. The oil and mining magnates and their front men, when he got to talk with them, didn't sneer at Villa. But he discovered in conversations at the Mirador and the restaurant bars on the Paseo where many of them took dinner that they accepted Carranza as an unalterable fact of life.

They felt to a man that they had to deal with him as the least of several evils. Most of them still longed for a return of Victoriano Huerta, but Carranza was sitting on Mexico's oil and was securing a lock on the henequen trade centered in the largely peaceful southeast, and he was doing it by political maneuvering, not with guns, getting solid support from the *alcaldes* and petty governors of the gulfside states. The lawyers and professional men representing American interests were unanimous in wanting Villa beaten, driven out of the near north and away from the copper and silver his Division and its satellites were camping on. They felt they had a good chance at dislodging him. Guns were easy to come by, and easier still to ship to Obregón, with Carranza controlling the gulf ports.

Longing for Huerta, they would have canceled the First Chief out, too, but buying all the people now rallying to

Carranza and his crafty general would require a Herculean effort, and, more to the point, too much money. Their agents, traveling unhindered in Durango, Guanajuato, and the other middle Mexican states, knew of Villa's every move, and were in many ways the best sources of raw intelligence available to Corey. Will Hendricks conceded that they were his principal sources of information, too.

"If they can move about so freely, why can't I?" Corey asked him. Again he hoped Hendricks would hear the *I can't wait* in his voice.

"They're right there on the scene, Mr. Lane, have been since the Porfiriato. Most of them are as Mexican as Pancho is himself. You would come to Villa from the capital. He has an abiding distrust of anyone coming north from Mexico City. Gringos above all. Those roving bands of his shoot first and ask questions only later, if they even bother. You'll need ironclad safe-conduct guarantees before you go, something validated by Fierro as well as Pancho. We'll have to somehow satisfy them about what you were doing with Barrón in Zacatecas."

Fergus, when Corey told him of the enforced holdup on the trip to Villa, and how it was chafing him like a burr under the saddle, agreed with Hendricks.

"Your soldier laddie is absolutely right, Corey. We'll just have to bide our time."

It occurred to Corey that he had never really asked the Scot what his assessment of the larger picture was. He did now.

"I don't take the larger view, laddie. I just do my job."

"Surely you have a personal opinion, don't you?"

"It's not worth tuppence ha'penny."

"All the same, I'd like to hear it."

"All right. In the main I agree with you about Ángeles, but only if we're thinking about what might be best for this puir suffering country. I'm taking the King's shilling, though. Can't bloody well afford to think of what's best for Mexico. Can't afford to care."

The impish grin left Fergus's face. Damned if he didn't look almost sad.

"You do care, though, don't.you?"

Kennedy sighed. "I suppose I do. I've been in this country for nine years now, lad. Made friends. Ye'll not be surprised to learn I've made most of them over a glass of whisky, but that's beside the point." Plaintiveness, but not of the wheedling sort, smoothed and softened his scratchy voice: "I'll be a pensioner in four more years, and I've pretty well made up my mind I'll take my pension here. Most likely I'll die in Mexico. In the meantime I'll do me best by the crown as long as it's paying me. Aye. I still have a secret hankering to strike one big blow for King and country, although it seems unlikely that I ever will. When old Fergus is his own wee mon again it might be a different yarn. I might sell my services to someone like Ángeles, and if he doesn't make it and if the mystic bugger's still around, to Zapata. I would never back Carranza." He broke off, eyes bright again. "We'll wait until this canny major of yours says it's time to go."

Oh, yes, Fergus cared. It gave him a new and even more appealing dimension. With his words some magic hand slipped the burr from under Corey's saddle. If Fergus could wait, so could he. Kennedy wasn't quite through.

"Your boss Henry cares, too, Corey. I think perhaps your understandable anger at how he tricked you might have clouded your view of him. I've known Henry Richardson five years now, from a distance, of course, but I've a bonnie pair of eyes. For all his starch and silly worship of protocol he's a decent mon. He and I just have to be practical for the mo'. We can't muck about trying to do the impossible. Whatever pranks we engage in have to *work*."

One other thing Corey could console himself with: he would have more time with Luisa now. But with Wolf Kemper cantering well ahead of him on the inside track to the lady, it brought the barest minimum of consolation.

He was with her most weeknights and either Saturday or Sunday, without fail, but when he wasn't, he was convinced the German was dancing attendance on her. Of course he couldn't ask. There were quiet suppers with Luisa at Posada Melgar—with the ubiquitous Emilia hovering about—

interspersed with dinners at the big hotels on the Paseo, and a succession of visits to more museums and galleries than he ever would have thought even the sprawling capital could boast. Once she had Tomás drive them to the high saddle between Popo and Ixta. He scarcely gave the breathtaking view of the Valley of Mexico more than a moment's thought. He couldn't take his eyes from her. The silver hair had rippled in the wind, and the crisp air brought a flush of pink that livened the ivory cheeks. He knew what was happening to him, knew the probable futility of it, but he couldn't stop his wishful thinking from running wild. He had to fight a sudden urge to take her in his arms and crush away any possible resistance.

He found that squiring her about the city was depleting his money at an alarming rate, but just as he began to despair of being able to continue the ineffectual pursuit of her that she didn't seem to realize he was making, there came a beneficial, just-in-the-nick-of-time spin-off from Henry's rescinding his edict against Corey's trafficking with the embassy; he collected almost $1,700 in back pay. Money had been slow in arriving from budget-strapped Cobb in El Paso, who had doled out a few pennies now and then, the notes accompanying the payments almost whimpering out loud. The embassy's bursar also handed him a check for $470 for the out-of-pocket expenses incurred on his and Fergus's pilgrimage to Zacatecas. He needed every cent. His account at the Stockman's Bank of Black Springs was anemic to say the least, and he hated to go to his mother, Virgie; three years of bad and sometimes no rains at all in the basin had severely cut back the earnings of the X-Bar-7, and she was almost as short of cash as he was.

As happy as he was to get the money for purely practical reasons, he was happier still that it seemed to indicate full support on the part of Henry.

Luisa gave a dinner party in her apartment at the Melgar, and as Corey feared and expected, Wolf Kemper showed his handsome face. Narciso Trujillo was there as well. Kemper arrived in the company of another German, a man almost as tall as the putative marine engineer, with shrewd eyes that took in everything. No one introduced the stranger to Corey; Kemper's companion left after making apologies to Luisa while Tomás was still passing through the gathering with the preprandial hors d'oeuvre and wine.

"Von Rintelen," Narciso said. "You will recall that Fergus said he was an important *hombre* for Germany in Mexico." This, then, was the super-agent Fergus had mentioned, Kemper's chief.

To his mild surprise—and despite his trepidation when Tomás had admitted him and he discovered a generous sampling of the capital's old *criollo* society in attendance—it promised to be a not unpleasant evening, except for one small thing. It disturbed him beyond what he might have expected that the twenty-odd guests, from the look of them, seemed unaffected by what was happening in and to their country. The hurricane winds of the Revolution seemed to have left them unruffled.

They were all resplendent: fashionably dressed women, men in black ties and dinner jackets, and with a king's ransom of gems and pearls adorning the coiffures, earlobes, fingers, and bosoms of the women. Corey had finally invested in a dinner jacket himself with part of the money he had received from Uncle Sam, but he felt no more at home in it than he had in the white tie and tails he rented for the ball. The men and women he saw wore evening clothes like second skins. Their laughter was the sound of some still-quiet triumph of class and wealth. Looking around a room where credenzas were alive with massed banks of cut flowers whose sharp petals were dulled by the waxy haze from dozens of candles, the same thoughts came to him that had come to him at the embassy affair. Can this be Mexico? An impoverished land lying under the cruel and bloody hand of war? Didn't these dedicated sybarites care, or were they just whistling as they danced past a graveyard with a million plots waiting to be filled?

In the situation room that morning Hendricks had shown

him a collection of picture postcards, scenes of the struggle here in Mexico, spawn of a small but vigorous commerce which had come to life in the United States in this past year of the Revolution. Scores of American photographers had aimed their cameras at what was happening, squeezed their shutter bulbs, and rushed their plates to processing laboratories along the border, fixing sights of the bloodbath for posterity. "These things are selling like hotcakes as far east as New York City," the major said. At first Corey had been heartened by what he took to be keen interest on the part of his countrymen in Mexico's troubles, but then he realized the appeal of the cards was merely that of the macabre.

The biggest sellers, according to Will, were ones of firing squads, corpses in various states of gruesome decay, the maimed and wounded. As a subject, horses, dead or alive, brought a brisk trade according to Hendricks, as did the views of cocky U.S. Marines occupying Veracruz and herding captives at bayonet point. Except for an image of Venustiano Carranza looking like a malevolent Kewpie doll, the only revolutionary leader whose photograph was printed on the postcards was that of Pancho Villa; there were dozens of El Caudillo. They portrayed him as a kind of unwashed Robin Hood—or as a bloody-handed butcher. He found no cards with the fine face or erect, commanding figure of Felipe Ángeles.

Staged as the scenes on many of the cards were, there was a grisly truth to them as well. What was the reality of Mexico? The shadows in the silver chloride that coated the glass plates of the itinerant photographers? Luisa López y Montenegro's guest list? Both? Neither? Either way, he felt an urge to pass the postcards out in this cheerful, insouciant gathering.

He somehow knew he wouldn't find any persuading answers among these handsome, anachronistic creatures living right on top of the volcano. He wondered how many of them concerned themselves at all about the future, and he drew Narciso into a corner and voiced his perplexity.

"*Sí*, Corey. There is much of the warning noise of *el*

destierro abroad in my country, but the capital sleeps and dreams right through it. Perhaps nothing will awaken it before it dies." Narciso looked troubled, but by something more than what he had just said.

"What's gone wrong, Narciso?"

"Disturbing news. Carranza has just this afternoon entered into *una alianza* with Casa del Obrero Mundial."

"The labor organization? That surprises me. He's never been a particular friend of labor. Why on earth would they support him?"

"Perhaps because it is the first time *anyone* has asked them to the dance. They do not wish to sit alone at the wall forever."

Corey would have to dig more deeply into this, but he couldn't now. Tomás was announcing dinner.

Luisa, at the head of the table, placed Wolf and him next to her and across from each other, Corey on her right. A priest in a jet-black cassock occupied the chair at the other end of the long table from his hostess, to the obvious discomfiture of the guests seated near him. Perhaps they didn't perform their religious duties as faithfully as Luisa seemed to, and feared the *padre* knew it. It was only a momentary suppression of their spirits, though. Even before Tomás and Emilia served the soup the priest's companions were laughing and chattering with the rest of them. Corey bit his tongue. For a second he had wondered if Luisa was like some of the wealthier and more powerful Catholics he knew in Santa Fe, the sort who kept priests on tap for every social outing as if they were family retainers. She hardly glanced at the clergyman.

The German scintillated all through the meal, dropping celebrated names and places into the conversation with radiant charm. Luisa sparkled at every sally. Kemper apparently had taken heed of her gentle chastisement at Xochimilco when he broached the subject of the wars raging in Mexico and abroad. He confined much of his talk tonight to matters of art, sport, and the theater, with only one lapse about that clearly unsavory topic for her, the war.

"The thing to perhaps be regretted most about the conflict in Europe," he said, "is that now it is impossible for me to travel to London's West End to see the plays. The theater in Berlin is *sehr gut, ja,* but it has yet to rise to the level of the English stage. If Englishmen could make war the way they make drama, my poor country would not stand a chance against them. The same excellence is found in their horse racing and their fox hunts." He looked across the table to Corey. "Do you ride to the *Hunden,* Herr Lane?"

"I'm afraid not, Herr Kemper. My time on horseback has been spent in far more utilitarian pursuits." If only he had the wit and daring to throw Oscar Wilde's dictum about foxhunting at the German.

"Ah, Then, Herr Lane, you are perhaps what you Americans call a cowboy?"

Corey studied Kemper's smiling face. No, the man wasn't trying to insult him. He looked as innocent as Buster Brown. "I have been a cowboy in my time, Herr Kemper. Not the easiest of professions."

Luisa burst out laughing. "When are you two going to stop this Herr Kemper–Herr Lane nonsense? At Xochimilco I thought at times I was attending a session in the Palacio de Justicia."

Corey was chagrined when Kemper beat him to the punch with an apology, first by what he had to say, but more with the graceful stage business he employed as he said it. The German reached over and took Luisa's hand and brought it to his lips. "Forgive me, *Liebchen.* I will make an intimate of our good friend here *sehr schnell.*" He looked at his rival again. "Tell me . . . *Corey.* You look like a man who would be formidable at sport. Do you by any chance play tennis?"

"I did at one time, but I haven't for many years. There's not a lot of it where I come from."

"There is a club with two excellent courts near my hotel that extends guest privileges to foreign visitors, Corey. Would you someday care to . . . ?"

Damn it again. If Fergus heard about this, the Scot wouldn't rest until Corey and Wolf Kemper faced each other

across a net. He could almost hear him now: *Do it, Corey!*
Ye've got to move in close to Kemper. The Stars and Stripes
forever, laddie.

He managed to stammer, "I'd be delighted," and then,
weakly, breathed out, "Wolf."

It got worse.

"Perhaps," Kemper said now, white teeth flashing at Luisa,
"you would join us, *Liebchen*?"

Corey hoped neither of them heard his groan when Luisa
agreed.

"You were a cowboy once, Corey?" she said after they
made a tennis date for Wednesday afternoon.

"My family has ranched in New Mexico for three generations, Luisa."

She smiled. "The López y Montenegros have been in the
cattle business for a long time, too. But you are nothing like
the *charros* of Durango. They are not historians, nor do they
have your love of antiquity, or your . . . sensitivity. Are all
norteamericano cowboys like you?"

"No," he said. "Nor do they wish to be."

She penetrated him with the blue-black eyes right to the
back of his head, she kept on looking at him for several seconds after his words died in the air, and then she shook her
head from side to side, almost imperceptibly, and it devastated him.

He was among the very last to leave the party, with
Narciso right beside him. Kemper stayed behind, and for a
moment jealous anger flashed inside him, but he resigned
himself to the probability that this was the way it would always be.

He asked Narciso to the Mirador for a nightcap, and the
doctor agreed.

He had extended the invitation to Narciso because he had
questions about Carranza and the labor group, and about the
old scholar's place in Henry's scheme of things. He hoped,
too, that Fergus would be at the Mirador bar. Perhaps he
could get them both sorted out, once and for all. He could

bounce his questions from one to the other and keep after them like a ferret until he was sure of his own place.

Fergus usually was at the bar at this time of night, alone and with a drink clutched in his horny fist, but when Corey and Narciso settled at a candlelit table in a tiled alcove in the smoky barroom, the Scot was nowhere to be seen.

The questions Corey had on the tip of his tongue never got asked.

Apropos of nothing definite, just as an opening and almost idly—or so he thought—he asked a different question.

"Tell me something, Narciso. What is this Revolution all about? I was pretty clear about it when I came to Mexico almost a year ago, or thought I was. Now I find I know less than I did then."

"Your asking, Corey, says that your thoughts are far ahead of those of some of my own people. It means that in spite of your modest disclaimer you already know the Revolution is about much more than beans and corn for the poor, more than freedom and justice even, certainly more than politics." He stopped when a waiter came to the table, ran a rag across it, and stood in silence waiting to take their order. When the man started back toward the bar, Narciso went on. "Did you look at our waiter? He is like me, a *mestizo*. *Sí*, I have Indian blood. How much of it and where it came from, I do not know, but it is there nonetheless. On the other hand, the people at Luisa's tonight were all *criollos*, of pure Spanish ancestry, and I am sure that if I stepped outside the doors of this fine hotel into the Paseo, I could find for you, within five hundred meters of where we sit, a man, a woman, or a child who is Indian *solamente*. Although each of us was born to a different station in life, we are all the same, this waiter, Doña Luisa, the *obreros* traduced into the camp of Don Venustiano today, and I. We have lived together, and yet apart, for almost four long, rigid centuries now. We cannot shake those centuries from our souls. Each of us, under the skin that your great *poeta* Shakespeare called 'the paste and cover for our bones,' is a special metaphor for Mexico. That is what this Revolution is all about."

"I think I understand. It is time for you to stop living in the past."

"No, no, no! Forgive me if I correct you, *mi amigo*. We here in Mexico do not live *in* the past. In a very real sense there is no past for Mexico, only an ever-recurring present. In your country—and I mean no criticism—you take a different view of time than we do here. Time, I think, is a straight line for you *norteamericanos*; its arrow flies in one direction only. What is past is done. I think this is what you mean when you speak of progress. Here time is a circle. We here in Mexico constantly return to our beginnings, not in memory or flights of fancy, but in the flesh. Tomorrow is today, and yesterday tomorrow—*y ayer es mañana, y son también hoy, siempre.* Sadly, it teaches us what we can expect. What is history for you, for us is ritual. In essence, we Mexicanos *are* the ritual. Our lives, our souls, our very beings, are repetitive, unbreakable, perpetual ritual. Not ritual of thought and action, however, but something bred in the bone, coursing through our veins, and licking up our blood with tongues of flame. We are, as your *poeta* said in *Lear*, 'bound upon a wheel of fire.' "

The waiter returned with tequila for Narciso and a cognac for Corey. He was a short, burly man running to fat as he aged, and he moved slowly, placing the glasses in front of them as if it was the last task he would ever do in this life, but also as if his motions were the first mute offerings in a Sisyphian eternity of serving. His face was a flat, wooden mask; the only sign of life in it came from the flickering light of the table's lone candle. Corey pressed a bill on him and told him to keep the change. He mumbled *"Gracias,"* his voice dry as dust, as he turned away.

"Sí," Narciso said now. "Everything has happened before, is happening now, and I fear will happen again until our planet is a dismal cinder. It is what I believe Nietzsche called the 'eternal return.' The great figures of our Revolution are not named Villa and Madero. They are Cuauhtémoc and Montezuma. There is no Zapata, Carranza, nor Obregón, but Huitzilopochtli the warrior-god and Tezcatlipoca the devilish

trickster. The names matter little. They have been here before, every one of them, and they will come again. Even today Hernán Cortés burns his ships on the beach and begins his conquest. This time, perhaps, he calls himself Carranza, although I hope his new identity will be that of Felipe Ángeles or someone else as noble. Do you remember Luisa telling me the night you met her at the ball that she dreams of Tenochtitlán? She does not dream. She *sees* Tenochtitlán, not Mexico, every time she awakes and takes her coffee out to her balcony at Posada Melgar to gaze at *las sierras*."

"But this Revolution?"

"*Un momento, por favor.* I have just now come to that.

"We have something here I do not believe you have in your country, Corey. *La fiesta.* Certainly you have celebrations, holidays, but there is a vast difference between a *función*—a mere party—and a true *fiesta*. A *fiesta* is an explosion of the soul, an orgasm, a death—and a *concepción*. It is the one thing that breaks the ritual, but even in breaking it, it renews it.

"The Revolution is such a *fiesta*, a festival of blood and death and life. It is a great howling *grito* of joy and sorrow, a release that perhaps eludes you in your Calvinism." He raised his worn, brown hands and fluttered them before his sorrowing face. "But I am an old fool. I talk too much. I must say *buenas noches* now, *amigo. Gracias.*"

He left the table after shaking Corey's hand and made his way toward the door. He looked as burdened as the waiter had, but there was something free and strong in his careful steps.

You, my good friend, Corey thought, *are no old fool. You are probably as close as I'll ever get to that "reality of Mexico" I speculated on.*

34

"I am glad to see you back at work with us, Luisa, We missed your skills while you were gone," Narciso Trujillo said. How long had the old scholar been standing behind her at the workbench? He still worried about her, even now, four years after Francisco's death. "There is, however, not a great deal to do these days. I am afraid the dig at Cuernavaca will be my last expedition until the war is over."

She looked up from the table where Narciso's two young students and she had been trying to piece together the shards of pottery the younger of them had found in the excavations she had seen in the lantern show. "That's just one more thing to blame *la guerra* for, Narciso. It prevents us from doing so many things we wish to do." *¡Nombre de Dios!* She must sound to the two students as if she were just another rich woman who looked on the Revolution as a matter of personal inconvenience, nothing more. Thank heavens Narciso knew how deeply the things happening in and to her country troubled her. He knew her better than any of her friends and acquaintances in Mexico City, and his opinion outweighed any but that of the newest one, who might not feel he had enough to go on yet to form one. Narciso, of course, only knew the Luisa of the capital, not the Luisa of Hacienda del Sol. No one in Mexico City knew *that* Luisa, not even Tía Sofía, who in her gargantuan conceit thought she knew everything.

"Have you seen our mutual friend Señor Lane in recent days, Luisa?" Narciso asked now.

It brought an odd, warmly pleasurable excitement that he should mention Corey Lane at the very second she thought of him.

"*Sí*, Narciso. Actually, I have seen quite a bit of him."

Ah, yes, the picnic at Xochimilco had been a *very* satisfying experience for Luisa López y Montenegro. So had the dinner she had given in her apartment.

She hadn't wanted or expected a competition between Corey and Wolf Kemper—two men vying for her attention and affection had never excited her, had never even been a girlhood fantasy—but she might have known that was exactly what it would turn out to be . . . more or less. There was no denying there had been a little womanly thrill in watching and listening to the two of them at Xochimilco and the *posada* as they talked about everything except what was uppermost in their minds. Was she giving herself too much credit? No. There were some things a woman could be sure about. It was her secret for the moment that it had been considerably less of a competition than either of them knew, and prudence demanded she keep her secret a bit longer. Blurted out too soon, it could come to nothing.

She had known men with the continental flair of Wolf all her adult life; Corey Lane was still a new and largely unknown quantity.

The German, of course, knew what he probably assumed was her entire world as well as she knew it herself. That he was a consummate charmer by the rules of that one world went without saying; his manners, even with their touch of arrogance, were impeccable. In many ways he reminded her of Francisco, although he was much younger than her husband had been when he died at the *hacienda* that hideous day in 1910 when the villagers came storming out of Santa María del Oro. As was the case with the dead husband she hadn't really mourned, she was sure that if Wolf was indeed the marine engineer he claimed to be it was the first work he had ever done in his life.

Corey Lane was different, all right. Shy. No, it wasn't truly shyness. He met people without diffidence, conversed easily and readily with those she introduced him to at the theater and at their dinners together either at the hotels or at the affair she had given at the *posada*—to show him off, although he didn't seem to realize it—asking questions with unfeigned interest in the answers, but volunteering few opinions of his own.

He was quiet. Yes. It was a bone-deep quiet, but not silence: something about him resonated in a way she had never before known in a man, or if she had, had never felt, not as she was beginning to feel it now. His quietness was one of the soul.

His one flaw—if it was a flaw—was that he didn't seem to know his own worth. It was a more encompassing denial of his intrinsic human value than mere modesty or self-effacement would have been.

How much of her assessment of him was her own, and how much sprang from the things she had learned about him from Narciso?

According to the little doctor, leaning over her now in a quite transparent pretense of interest in the pottery reconstruction she was working on, Corey had been more than a scholar and writer in his life in the United States. He was, Narciso said, a highly decorated veteran of his country's war with Spain, a civil administrator in Cuba after the war was over, and in recent years a longtime law enforcement officer of great if only local reputation in one of New Mexico's more remote counties. "Not a *político*, but a student of politics," Narcisco said, "and strangely, for so peaceful and gentle a man, a man capable of fierce action, a serious man, a man of purpose. *Muy hombre* in every way." Narciso was as taken with him as she herself was fast becoming. It did not occur to her to wonder just how the doctor had learned so much about this "gringo," as he might have called Corey in some other context, and it disappointed her mildly that she couldn't ask him the really important things about Corey she wanted to know. And was she becoming only *taken* with this quiet, sad, *norteamericano*?

Be honest, Luisa Teresa. It amounts to a good deal more than that.

How far was she willing to let it go? More to the point, how far was she willing to push it? The way Corey silently—and, she prayed, unconsciously—demurred at each of her tries for intimacy left no doubt *she* was the one who would have to somehow bring things to what might prove to be a frightening head.

She only knew she was now feeling things she hadn't felt since that foolish episode in Rome a year after Francisco's death, the weekend involvement with the young Italian poet which resulted in the most embarrassing confession she ever made, followed by an absolution she still couldn't claim she had really earned. Her repentance then had come from the head, not the heart. Yes, the short affair with Luciano Visconti had been a foolish one, but not without rewards. She had needed it desperately as she emerged from shock only to find what was worse, loneliness, almost everywhere she traveled in that dead year after her *hacienda* world was swept away, perhaps forever. The rewards, though, such as they were, were short-lived; she had plunged right back into a well of loneliness, staying deep within it until that secluded supper after the lantern show. Something happened there in the candlelight. Even Emilia, who had long ago given up on commenting on her moods, had noticed and remarked on the change in her.

Even if the Church hadn't forgiven her for Luciano, she could have forgiven herself, had indeed done so very quickly, but she was still vaguely disturbed by her other, possibly more important dereliction: she had never yet made the confession and repentance she should have made after the death of Francisco, not even to old Padre Juan at the family chapel at the *hacienda*.

Padre Juan had married her and Francisco twenty years ago, after her father, Don Sebastián had picked their wealthy neighbor as her husband when she was seventeen and Francisco was already forty-two. She had accepted the arrangement without protest or dismay. It was exactly the kind of marriage generations of Montenegro women before her had known, made the best of, and even thrived in.

To be sure there had been an occasional inner lament for the Luisa she had put behind her after the marriage vows; the reckless, sometimes feckless Luisa who had ridden as well as her brothers; the spirited Luisa of the convent school here in the capital who smoked an occasional secret—sometimes not secret, but defiant—*cigarrillo* at the parties the teaching sisters were never told about.

By and large she had settled without misgiving into the *hacendado-hacendada* life she was raised to live. That it was a life and married state devoid of the romantic love she had read about and that even the nuns somewhat reluctantly pictured as the ideal of Christian marriage was something her training would not allow her to complain about. She hadn't even wanted to complain. Don Francisco López was a generous, decent man, if lacking in excitement. The physical side of her union with him wasn't a total failure, either, although the brief episode in Rome opened her eyes, and her body, to the possibility of far more satisfying transports. *That*, however, wasn't part of the confession she made in Rome. She had confessed the act itself, but nothing about how it affected her.

If she hadn't been deliriously happy with Don Francisco—white-haired by the time he was murdered, and suddenly old after sixteen years of marriage, and defeated by the knowledge that he would never be able to give her children—she certainly wasn't miserable. Travel, work at the ministry here and in the field, the great parties at the *hacienda* and in the capital: these things had filled any real or imagined wants or needs.

Then, when the pastoral world of Hacienda del Sol was sucked with such sickening finality into the first vortex of the Revolution, and her husband was hacked to pieces along with her mother, father, sisters, and brothers, she discovered that she scarcely missed him. She grieved for the rest of her family almost to the point of madness—but not for the man whose bed she shared. The discovery horrified her. The firestorm of an ensemble rage she couldn't understand and probably never would had raced over the *hacienda*, and although things had returned outwardly to a semblance of the way they had been by the time she returned from what proved a fortuitous trip to Los Angeles, the scars and chars remained—if visible only to Luisa Montenegro.

No, she had never confessed her surely sinful lack of grief at Francisco's death even to Padre Juan. It was as if her husband of sixteen placid years had been no more than one of the gilded mirrors in the great hall of the *hacienda* the mob had smashed in its frenzy, or the antique desk chopped to kindling and burned, setting fire to the two-hundred-year-old Spanish tapestries which had been her mother's pride. Was she an unfeeling, wicked woman? Someday some priest—but not Padre Juan—would have to tell her, heed her pleas for absolution, and then send her on her way to grace again with some truly agonizing penance.

Would some priest also tell her she had done wrong in falling in love with a North American Protestant? There was no doubt what Padre Juan would say. The adulterous adventure with an Italian poet adhering to the true faith would be a very minor matter by comparison.

But—could she deny the things she was beginning to feel for Corey? She needed advice, and not necessarily the kind of advice she could get from priests or even from old Sor Rafaela in the convent.

Didn't she owe herself at least a major fraction of what she owed the Church? Was her soul any more important than her entire being. Or her heart? *Careful. You are listening to the Luisa of the capital and the wide world now, not the Luisa of the* hacienda.

Well, if she went on listening to *that* Luisa she knew where to go for counseling of a sort. Counseling? *Do not lie to yourself, you want encouragement, not counsel.* She knew where it could lead. It was a risk she suddenly knew she had to take . . . wanted to.

One of the potsherds she was trying to find a mate for fell into place as if some other hand had guided hers.

"Bueno," Narcisco Trujillo breathed over her shoulder. "As I said, Luisa, we have missed your skills here in the workroom." He patted her shoulder. "When you are finished, could we take lunch together in my office?"

Narciso, her dear old friend, would be glad to provide advice, but it wasn't *his* she needed.

"I am sorry, Narciso," she said. "There is someone I must visit on my way back to Posada Melgar. Another time, perhaps."

Tomás waited in the Daimler outside the ministry.

He left the driver's seat and held the rear door for her.

"Back to *la posada*, Doña Luisa?"

"No, Tomás, not directly. Drive me first to the home of Doña Sofía, *por favor*."

PART 4

▲▲▲▲▲▲▲▲▲▲

PLOUGHING
THE
SEA

35

Two more banks, three trains, and today, with the senseless, brutal rape of this peaceful community, an entire town.

Jorge María Martínez could no longer persuade himself that he was a *guerrero*, a revolutionary, a *soldado*, or a courageous fighter in a sacred cause; he had become in his own mind, at least, a common criminal—a *bandido*, a thieving *ladrón*, and in a sickening distant echo of the not forgotten stabbing back in Chupadera County, an *asesino*, a killer. And he couldn't blame his dereliction entirely on the fever that had dogged him for the past three days, leaving him weak, tired, and desperately in need of sleep.

The worst of it was, until the fiasco in this town today, he had been getting good at what he did.

When Rodolfo Fierro ordered the attack on this secluded place he had welcomed the idea. He wouldn't be holding up a bank or robbing a train or victimizing helpless civilians. Fierro said at last night's briefing that the town was held by two companies of Carrancista infantry. "They have terrorized the villagers for a month. You must liberate them, Capitán Martínez."

Doubts began when he discovered that in taking the town he would have more help then he really needed. Too much help. Fierro had seen to that. Jorge's troop alone, if Fierro let him have just one machine gun, could have reduced the town and brought the small garrison to a sensible surrender in the same half hour it eventually took, but two other troops had gone along at the insistence of the Butcher, one to join them when they were on the road, with no Hotchkiss or Madsen, but with a 55mm mountain gun rattling along behind them. He would rather have had the *yanqui* Kimball and just one marginally reliable Hotchkiss, but with the small cannon to breach whatever solid position the enemy might have prepared, one other troop at the most would have been enough. Jorge commanded all three units. Until the attack began. Command went to hell in a hurry even before Tonito blew his bugle.

The tiny, twenty-man garrison stationed in the town—nowhere near the full two companies Fierro said were there—had fought stubbornly through the pall of smoke from the shelled granary, but when the mountain gun sheered off one of the towers of the church and the next round landed flush on the stone casing of the plaza well, smashing it to shards, the defenders broke for the hills. That's when things fell apart. That skinny maniac Correa, Fierro's nephew, hadn't waited for Jorge's signal. He and his troop burst from the line with Correa screaming like a banshee, charged down the main street, jumping their horses over the barricades, and firing at villagers trying to find shelter even in blazing stores and animal sheds. None of Jorge's and Paco's shouts could stop them.

Jorge's third troop, led by a rodent-faced *lugarteniente* named Salazar, who seemed every bit as *loco* as Correa, had chased after the fleeing Carrancistas while Jorge was trying to catch and stop Correa. On foot, the Constitutionalist riflemen couldn't outrun Salazar's riders, who trotted back into the town fifteen minutes later, while Jorge was grimly trying to establish some sort of order, their ratty asshole of a commander grinning like a candy skull, the hacked-off heads of three of the town's erstwhile occupiers impaled sloppily on bloody saddle horns, strips of flesh-and-blood vessels already turning black trailing from them. On one of the heads, the still-open eyes were blank, bulging white marbles, the pupils rolled completely out of sight. Even so, they stared a silent accusation at Capitán Martínez. He looked away, but everywhere he looked his eyes fell on burned and riddled bodies of the townspeople.

He almost lost control. Drained by fever and exhaustion, he almost lost his stomach, too. *Dios*, he dreaded telling Trini Álvarez about this disaster of an attack.

He should have sniffed this ugly farce in the making at the

meeting with Fierro last night, when El Carnicero gave him and Correa their orders.

"The people of this village are loyal to General Villa," Fierro said. "Or will be when you drive the oppressors out, Capitán Martínez. Kill anything that moves when you begin your attack." Correa, listening by Jorge's side, had nodded as if he were taking holy vows. The man was a certifiable lunatic. Brave, sure—who in the Division wasn't brave when the fighting started?—but without an ounce of sense, a smiling cretin. Jorge had seen him in action in the hills southeast of Zacatecas, blowing the heads off Federalistas pleading to surrender.

None of this excused Jorge, though. He should have kept command.

The Butcher had sown the seeds of Correa's rashness at the meeting when, ignoring Jorge, he said to him, "Capitán Martínez is in command, *lugarteniente,* but in the Division we prize initiative above slavish obedience to orders. Set these people free."

Set them free? Well, Jorge supposed they had. But they had only set them free to bury innocent neighbors, free to try to douse the fires—bucket by ineffectual bucket, since their main well was gone—and free to rake over the sad ashes of what had been their town. It would take a month of afternoon spring winds to blow away the stink already rising. The winds might not begin here for a week. Then the villagers would have to haul timber from the distant hills, pull the steaming stones from the rubble, and rebuild their ruined village not from scratch, but from far *back* of scratch. Amazing what one small field gun could do when there was no artillery to answer it.

Twenty bad minutes after the fighting ended, he looked for Paco, who had tried to get the third troop to break off its pursuit of the running Carrancistas. He finally found the big sergeant, dismounted, talking with a group of smoke-blackened village men in front of the town's one miraculously untouched building, a seed and feed store. At Jorge's call Paco left them and walked his horse toward his captain, no reproach at all on his wide face.

"Get a detail to clear those bodies off the street, Sargento Durán," Jorge said. "Then find out about our losses and report back to me. And if you see Lugarteniente Correa tell him I want him now!"

"*Sí,* Captain Cockroach. But first, *mi capitán,* those *hombres* standing there are the elders of the town. They beg a word with the great Villista *capitán.*"

"Great Villista *capitán*? Horseshit! I suppose they want to complain about the way we wrecked their town, not that I blame them. It was far too much of an attack, *amigo.* I am not proud of this morning's work."

"They have not spoken of that, *mi capitán.* They only want payment from us."

Jorge snorted. "Payment? What the hell can we pay them with? I'm not a finance officer. I have no money."

"They don't want money, Jorge."

"No? Then what the hell *do* they want? We can't get food or medicine here for another week, if then. With the Division moving south toward Celaya in the morning Calzado won't have a train free to come this way for days. In the name of God there isn't a thing I can do!"

"They say they don't need food, either, *mi capitán.* And they say there *is* something you can do." The giant looked nervous, odd for the implacable, usually easygoing man from Durango. "They . . . they want the captain to . . . shoot some people for them."

"For Christ's sake, *what*?"

"They want you to execute some traitors. Some of their fellow townsmen worked too well with the enemy *soldados* while they were stationed here. Some of their women went with the Carrancistas, *también.*"

"*¡Mierda!* I have done all the killing I intend to do today! And I sure as hell am not going to send *women* to the wall. If they want their neighbors shot, they can fucking well do the job themselves."

"I told them that, Jorge. They fear that might look like

murder to the families of the guilty ones. They will have to live here with the traitors' surviving relatives, who will not forget anything that happens today. If the captain does it, they feel it will be justice. *Con respeto, capitán,* it might not hurt to listen to them."

"Tell them the answer is no, *sargento!* Then move your ass and get those bodies out of my sight and find out for me how many men I've lost. *¡Pronto!* I want to ride out of this grave-yard at four o'clock, before it starts to smell. I don't want to stay here overnight."

"Sí, mi capitán." The sergeant moved back to the group of somber villagers. They looked at Jorge as Paco talked to them.

He decided to move out of earshot, but just as Paco fin-ished, mounted, and moved off up the street, Lugarteniente Jesús Correa rode up to the petitioners who had listened to Durán. After only a glance at Jorge, Correa bent toward the man who seemed to lead the group, an old man with a gray beard and thinning hair under his sombrero. Leaning from his horse, Correa looked like a vulture. Soon arms were waving, soot-darkened fingers were pointing up and down the street, and that sonofabitch Correa was smirking like an ape. What the hell was the bastard agreeing to? Jorge could guess. Hadn't Correa seen and caused enough death today to last him for a while?

Now all of them fell silent and looked to Jorge. Correa was staring at him, too. This reckless killer wouldn't rest until he reported the weakness of Capitán Jorge Martínez to Fierro.

Paco might be right. Maybe it wouldn't hurt to listen. But, *mierda.* Even to listen would be dangerous. For himself he didn't give a shit, but Rodolfo Fierro probably already knew Jorge María Martínez in his heart of hearts would always be the faithful follower of Major Trini Álvarez. This might bring Trini's now merely simmering troubles with the Butcher to the boil again.

He set his spurs and reined his horse toward Correa and the knot of villagers.

"Qué pasa, Lugarteniente Correa?"

"These good *hombres* wish you to convene a court for them, *mi capitán*. Many crimes have been committed by traitors in their village."

"And what did you tell them, *amigo*?"

"I told them the captain would do it, that he is a man of wisdom and great insight, *verdad*. I told them no one can lie to the captain, and that his sword of justice cuts deep and true."

¡Mierda! As little as he liked it, Jorge had to keep in mind that it took all kinds to make a revolution.

He would have to end this insanity here and now, but with care. "How many 'traitors' do they have evidence against, Lugarteniente Correa?"

Correa looked down from the saddle at the gray-haired, bearded man standing slightly in front of the others. The man removed his hat and held it across his chest. He had a thin mouth and eyes like coals. "Seven, *mi capitán*," he said. "There would have been nine, but two of the worst were killed in the fight today."

"What is the evidence against these men, *viejo*?"

"Evidence, *mi capitán*? We have no 'evidence.' We do not need 'evidence.' Every man, woman, and child in the town *knows* what they have done." He pulled a scrap of brown paper from his pocket. Clearly he had been made spokesman because he could read and write. He might well be the only one in the group who could. "We have here the names of the guilty ones. Five men and two women." He held the paper up toward Jorge, who shook his head. Shit! It was true. Women, too. "All the captain has to do is shoot them. Everyone in the village will swear on the head of our *santo* that they deserve it."

"Everyone?"

"No one will dare swear they *don't*."

¡Chihuahua! This business was getting stickier by the second. He would have to think fast, and talk faster. If only his head didn't hurt so much. "You have a priest here?"

"*Sí, mi capitán.*"

"Does not this *padre* preach forgiveness?"

"*Sí.*"

"Well?"

"In this case we cannot listen, *mi capitán*. Two of the traitors are his *hermanos*. Even a *padre* will lie for his brothers. He was friendly with the *soldados*, too. Some in our town have even said *his* name should be on this list."

¡Dios! If these ignorant, superstitious villagers were even for a moment considering killing a *priest*, this was far more serious than he could possibly have imagined. He didn't have to turn his head to see if Correa was watching as he spoke. Best to keep all expression from his face.

Somehow he had to impose whatever authority he could summon up, but now, with the small sickness still plaguing him, he feared for a second he might pass out, as he had in the parade at Saltillo, after Paredón.

"Look, *viejo*. To do what you want to do there must be a trial. That is the law. And those accused must be tried by your court."

"We have no court, excellency. Until the Revolution the *hacendado* held all our trials. He and his family ran away when war came here the first time. A year ago. The last government never bothered with such things as courts—not here."

"Where is your *alcalde*?"

"We have no *alcalde*, either."

A faint ray of hope. Perhaps he could stall long enough to get out of town. "*Orígenes*—beginnings—must be made, *viejo*. You need an *alcalde* and a judge before we can even *talk* of executions. Round up your people when they've put out all the fires and buried their dead, and hold an election. This is the legal way."

The gray-bearded old man pushed his scrap of paper at Jorge again. "If we hold this election and a trial, will the *capitán* promise to shoot these criminals then?"

Why not? What he had just suggested would never come to pass in this benighted mountain village. He made his decision. "*Sí,*" he said. "You have my word as an officer of the División del Norte of General Francisco Villa. But it can't take forever." He reached in his shirt pocket and pulled out the watch with the snap cover he had taken from the banker at San Esteban two weeks ago, and which Colonel Toma had told him to keep when he turned it in at headquarters with the rest of the haul. It was half past twelve. "You have until four o'clock. I and my soldiers will be leaving then."

That should hold them. They couldn't possibly invent the machinery for what would probably be the first election in the town's history in little more than three short hours.

The old spokesman started to say something, but Jorge held up his hand and cut him off. The old man shrugged and turned to his delegation and with sweeping motions of his big hat herded them away. The smile had fled from Correa's face. He looked about to fume.

Paco had returned by the time the group disappeared behind the feed store.

"We have lost three men, *mi capitán,* and seventeen of the villagers have died. Six of the enemy, here in town. I don't know how many in the hills and on the road. There are another dozen wounded, four of them ours. I have assigned a detail to clear the dead from the street and bury them. It looks like only three, maybe four, of the enemy escaped. Men from all three troops are helping put out the fires. I'll relieve the fire detail at two o'clock, and at four we'll be ready to leave, as the captain wishes. Have you any further orders, Capitán Martínez?"

"No, Sargento Durán. Our dead and wounded: are any of them old *amigos?*"

"No, *mi capitán.* At least Paco did not know them." He glanced at the other troop commander, who looked now sullen, if not quite mutinous. Paco went on, "All of them are . . . were . . . in Lugarteniente Correa's *tropa.*"

The last made him throw caution to the wind. He turned to Correa, who still hadn't taken his eyes from him. Correa's goddamned itchy trigger finger was nothing compared to his disregard of his duties as a troop leader. "You and I must have a little talk tonight, Lugarteniente Correa. You won't like what I have to say. It can't escape even someone as stupid as you that I am not satisfied with your part in the attack. But right now I want you to see to your wounded men and give your dead a decent burial. Why the fuck haven't you done this on your own instead of sticking your filthy nose into this ridiculous meeting? You are a disgrace to the other officers of the Division! *¡Vamos!*" Correa's eyes, still bloodshot from the smoke he had ridden through during his insane charge, flared in hot anger for a second, but he said nothing, shrugged, and urged his horse away from them. He looked back at Jorge once. He didn't even try to hide a sneer. He sure as hell showed no fear. The bastard probably felt he was locked in pretty tight with his fucking uncle.

"All right, Paco," Jorge said. "*Ahora,* let's get something in our *estómagos*. It's been one hell of a time since breakfast."

"What have you decided to do about those traitors?"

"*¡Nada! Un momento, amigo*. That is not quite true. Find us a place to sit down before I fall off this horse and I'll tell you all about it."

They found a corral with a solid wooden fence to lean their backs against, pulled beans and their canteens from their saddlebags, and ate. Or Paco did. Hungry as he thought he was, Jorge found he could hardly get a mouthful down. The horses and mules inside the corral behind them were restless from the smell of the smoke still drifting across the street.

Neither of them mentioned Jorge's fairly stiff tonguelashing of Correa, but as Paco shoveled down his beans, Jorge told him of his demands on the old villager and his delegation.

Paco looked doubtful. "*Bueno*, Jorge. That was *muy diestro* of you, but I think that before the sun sets you'll have to send some people to the wall."

"No, Paco!" He laughed bitterly. "Before the sun sets, the way I feel, I might walk to the wall myself. I was very firm with *el viejo*. No election and trial—no firing parties. They can't possibly comply. Besides, is there a wall left standing in this smoking sewer to send anybody to?"

"I know what you are like, *amigo*, and I admire you for it, but in this case I am not sure you are being wise. Is it not possible that the people they want shot really *are* traitors? Men die on suspicion every day in Mexico. Think about yourself."

"I *am* thinking about myself. I joined this army to be a soldier, Paco. Let someone else do this kind of thing."

"Good idea. Let *me*. I will handle all of it for you. You don't even need to be there. You know Correa will run right to El Carnicero, don't you? The blood of the Fierros runs as thick as axle grease."

"I can't think about that right now. Forget about this, Paco, and let me get some sleep. The ride back to Division will probably take all night."

Paco sighed. "I suppose you know best, Jorge. But if you do not shoot these people, maybe then you will let Paco see to it that Jesús Correa never reaches the Division. That much can be done. Even officers with maps lose their way in these dark hills from time to time."

"Do you think Fierro would believe that of a missing nephew?"

"Why not? Some of the best men tire of fighting, desert, and are never heard from again. Lugarteniente Correa looks like just such a man. In fact, he looks like a man with a *grande* headache."

"A headache? What's that got to do with the price of beans in Tamaulipas?"

"You know the story, *amigo*. If you don't, it goes like this: a general, I never caught his name, in one of the Revolution's armies, I don't know which one, was at supper with his staff. One colonel wasn't eating. When the general asked why, the colonel said he had a headache. The general went on stuffing a tortilla in his *boca*, but with his other hand drew his *pistola* and blew the colonel's brains out. No more headache. No officer on the general's staff ever had a headache after that. I don't *know* if this is true, but I believe it. If Correa has the headache I think he has, it would be a kindness to—"

"Paco . . ." Jorge slumped against the fence, pulled his sombrero down over his face, and closed his eyes. "I think at bottom you are just an incurable romantic. The aspirin you suggest giving him would be too loud. Three troops would hear it.

"There are much quieter medicines, *amigo*," Paco said. "Try to sleep, *por favor.* Do not take offense, but to Paco you look like hell. My *niña* will think I took bad care of you."

He awoke to Paco shaking his shoulder. The dynamiter was holding the reins of his and Jorge's horses in his hand as he bent above him. "Jorge! Jorge!"

Jorge looked at his watch: 3:47. *Sí.* Paco must have the three troops ready for their four o'clock departure. Then he realized his sergeant was intent on something else.

"*Qué pasa*, Paco?"

"We have what I think you are going to call big trouble, *amigo*. For Paco it is *nada*, but for you . . ."

"Spit it out, *viejo!*"

"These slowpoke farmers somehow rubbed their asses with chile powder. They've run an election—I couldn't believe it—named an *alcalde*—that old fart you talked with by the feed store—and he's appointed a judge. They're holding a trial for their 'traitors' at the feed store right this minute." Paco paused. His face was as dark as midsummer clouds above the high Sierras.

"There's more, isn't there?" Jorge said.

"*Sí, amigo*. You will not be happy about the man *el viejo* picked to be the judge."

"*¿Por qué?*"

"It is Jesús Correa. He is acting just like his fucking bloody uncle."

Jorge was on his horse in a second, and in another they were galloping the length of the still-smoke-shrouded main street even faster than Correa and his troop had overrun it as they charged the other way this morning. God damn it! He had not only botched the attack which should have been so simple, he had gone to sleep when he should have remained on watch. Trini would never forgive him for this criminal delinquency in a million million years. He had joked blackly about it before he fell asleep, but now he truly felt he should be shot himself.

There were half a dozen *soldados a caballo* at the storefront, all from Correa's troop. He leaped from the saddle even before his horse stopped, and tossed the reins to one of them. He didn't look to see if they were caught. He almost sprawled across a sack of grain or seed just inside the door when he entered it. The room was jammed.

At the far side of the room Correa was sitting at a table. Five men and two women, one of the women a girl who looked as if she could be a younger sister of Juanita, stood in front of him. Correa was speaking.

"... and it is the judgment of this court that you be put to death by rifle fire, and that the sentence ..." He looked up, saw Jorge, looked at the prisoners again. "... be carried out immediately."

Jorge's legs gave way, and he sank to the floor beside the sack of grain. His vision blurred, but he couldn't pass out now, couldn't ... couldn't ... couldn't ...

"Lugarteniente Correa ..." The intended shout came only as a whisper. He could barely hear the words himself ...

The dark shadows along the rocky trail leading to Irapuato clutched at him. Only the strength of hate and anger kept them from dragging him from the saddle. From time to time he groaned against the night.

"Do not abuse yourself so, *mi hijo*," Paco said. "You were one sick *hombre*, still are, although you do look a little better. There was nothing you could have done. Besides, you gave your word of honor as an officer, remember? And they all died well. Even *las mujeres* and the *padre* made no fuss."

"The *padre*, too?"

"*Sí*. The people didn't ask for him. It was Correa's idea."

Correa was up in front of the column, at the head of his troop. His laughter floated back over the heads of twenty-five or thirty riders, rising maddeningly above the echoes of hooves clattering from the blackest hillsides Jorge María Martínez could remember.

"But if you will forgive my saying so, Jorge," Paco said, "you should not have tried to stop Correa. He will have everything going for him now when he reports to Uncle Butcher."

He had tried to stop him? He didn't remember that.

In that case, there was something he had to do, something every fiber in him cried out to do, but he knew he was still too weak to do it himself. Still, it had to be done tonight, in another hour, when they halted to make the camp they would have to make after getting out of the village so much later than he planned.

The niceties of personal honor would have to be forgotten just this once. There was far too much at stake. It was time to be practical.

"Paco," he said, "I believe you were right this afternoon. Lugarteniente Correa has a vicious headache. He only laughs to hide his pain. Do you suppose . . . ?"

They bivouacked in a deep canyon where the bend of a small *río* had carved out a deep, quiet, inky pool.

As on the ride to the attack on San Gabriel, the three officers bedded down together, and Paco herded their troops ahead and out of sight.

It must have been two in the morning when Jorge was awakened by a sound no stronger than a drawn-out whisper or the sigh of a child. Salazar, across the fire from him, was sound asleep. Jorge turned on his other side, and in the faint light of the fire's last dying coals he saw the immense bulk of Paco Durán dragging someone away from the area near the fire. It was Jesús Correa, his legs trailing limply, barely twitching. The ex-blacksmith's powerful right hand covered Correa's mouth and chin like an iron pillow, and his left arm encircled the lieutenant's toothpick-thin arms and bony chest, which was struggling to draw breath in the crushing anaconda grip of the dynamiter-sergeant—and failing. His crazed eyes were rolling from side to side as if they were trying to leave the sockets.

They disappeared into the rocks at the side of the trail. The sighing sound died away.

In about five minutes a splash from the *río*'s pool broke the silence. Salazar stirred, but didn't awaken. Lucky for him. He might very well have come down with a headache, too.

Jorge returned to sleep, knowing he would never forget the day he led the attack on San Gabriel de los Árboles . . . the day he killed a town.

36

"No two ways about it, Corey. Carranza's stock with the President has risen rapidly now that he has the support of that big union, what's it called? Casa del something or other?" Henry Richardson's voice on the telephone from Washington was muddy and chopped up with static, stripping away its customary confidence and authority, but it was still better talking with him over Mr. Bell's bothersome instrument than reporting in writing through Cotter.

"Casa del Obrero Mundial, Henry. The President's recognition of Carranza's government isn't imminent, is it?"

"I don't know. Mr. Wilson owes a great deal to American labor, and his friends in the unions, men like Sam Gompers, seem to look with favor on the First Chief because of this latest move. The only thing going for us at the moment is that labor leaders in Detroit, Pittsburgh, and Chicago don't spend a great deal of time thinking of Mexico at all, but you never know when they might, and bring pressure on the White House. We can't delay too long."

"I'll go north the moment Will Hendricks gives me the word, Henry. Incidentally, thanks for letting him work with me. In the meantime, I've got something else to report." It was time to tell the Bostonian about Wolf Kemper. He did, at length, including to his minor embarrassment the tennis at the club near Kemper's hotel.

"Well . . ." There was a long silence on the line from Washington, then something as close to a chuckle as staid Henry ever permitted himself. "A contact like that might prove useful. We do know that von Rintelen, your fellow Kemper's superior, has been in constant contact with Carranza in Veracruz. That the Germans are paying court to the Constitutionalists is probably all to the good. Perhaps then we can persuade the President to hold off on going with Carranza. Do von R. and this Kemper spend a lot of time together?"

"Some, but not recently, to my almost certain knowledge. Just once that I know of, and that was weeks ago." Weeks ago? Luisa's party seemed years ago—and only yesterday. So did the damned tennis match, which had turned out to be exactly the fiasco Corey had expected.

"Is your German in the capital now?"

"Not at the moment. He's somewhere on the Pacific coast with his Japanese employers' people, using that 'marine engineer' cover of his."

"The Japanese connection worries me a little. The Hearst papers are starting another round of that Yellow Peril scare stuff. But I don't think in the ultimate the Japanese present nearly the danger Germany and the Central Powers do. Either way, keep an eye on Kemper, and see if you can find out who if anyone he has been seeing in Carranza's crowd, and what they might be saying to each other. Narciso Trujillo might be of assistance in that regard. He must have an informant or a disaffected Constitutionalist somewhere in the capital or on the coast who'll keep an ear cocked for him. What else is stirring down your way? I mean the military picture in particular."

"Hendricks seems to think things will heat up between Obregón and Villa pretty quick. So do I." So did Fergus, but perhaps it would be better not to mention that. Corey still hadn't told Henry about his now long-standing liaison with the Scot, and although he wondered why he hadn't and why it troubled him, it didn't seem wise to tell him now.

"Things will heat up? Genuine war?"

"There's a big battle shaping up in the near north. Obregón is moving up toward Celaya. Villa's been as quiet as a church mouse, but he won't avoid action there."

"Are you planning on taking this one in, as you did the one at Zacatecas?"

"Only if I can see it from the other side this time. I'd like to observe General Ángeles in action, although he's still in the northeast and may not even taken part."

"Careful, Corey. We could ruffle Pancho's feathers if we tell him we want to give our support to a subordinate. Villa must remain the backup candidate—for both of us."

Villa as a *backup* candidate? This was a switch. A good one. Henry had, of course, abandoned his categorical "no" on Ángeles. Now it almost seemed he was ready to back him all the way. It looked fairly good for the future. If Corey could get the Tiger of the North's nod of approval for the former commandant of Chapultepec, Henry might come all the way over to Ángeles's side, too, and of his own accord.

"Keep an eye on Kemper," Henry said again just before ringing off. He hadn't appeared a bit interested in Corey's recital of what turned out to be high comedy on the tennis court.

Kemper had walloped Corey 6–1, 6–3, and then teamed with one of the club member wives, another German as gifted an athlete as he was, to beat Corey and Luisa 6–0.

The tall German was an all-out competitor who fought for every point as if the world would end if he lost it, and not only when he faced Corey across the net. He unleashed a gigantic serve against Luisa, too, and although she didn't complain by word or look, the German's partner did, making pointed remarks in German about whose meaning Corey couldn't be sure, but in which he thought he caught the equivalent of "bully," defusing Corey's own anger with the powerful Kemper. Wolf looked perplexed, but remained every bit as affable as he had been on the three previous occasions Corey had been in his company; it seemed he had no inkling that he was behaving as anything other than a perfect gentleman. And he was almost too magnanimous in victory.

"If you went back in training you would present me with great difficulties, Corey," he said when the four of them relaxed with lemon squashes in the club's pavilion afterward. Corey noted he didn't go so far as to say that he would actually lose. Clearly this Teutonic knight didn't feel he could ever be a loser to Corey Lane—at anything. *Keep an eye on Kemper.* He would have preferred that he never saw the tall German again. Well, he wouldn't for a while, at least, and he breathed more freely in the days following the tennis match.

Fergus was satisfied. "Ye and Luisa have taken Wolf from his job quite nicely, Corey. One of these days old Fergus will have a nasty surprise for him and his boss, von Rintelen." He didn't elaborate, and with his own concerns in the forefront, Corey didn't press him, not even when the Scot added, "Henry appears about to get most of everything he wants out of both you and me." Henry? How did he figure in what Fergus was working on? It didn't seem important at the moment.

With Kemper now off to Mazatlán or some other undisclosed port on the west coast, and with not a word from Hendricks and consequently no pressure from Fergus to play secret agent, Corey felt as if he had just been let out of school, not that it promised to be a trouble-free vacation.

"*. . . the capital sleeps and dreams . . .*" Narciso Trujillo had said.

True. Although he discussed the political and military situation with Fergus and Will Hendricks nearly every day, almost no one he met at the Mirador or at the Ministry of Culture, certainly none of the Mexican nationals, so much as spoke of the battles impending in the north nor of Obregón's grinding advance down toward Morelos. The contending armies were all avoiding the Federal District and there was a somnolent air about Mexico City in these soft spring days that drifted over Corey's moods and wants like a cloud of perfume.

He had all the time in the world, and in the company of Luisa, all the world an infinity of time could ever need.

That he was now deeply and irrevocably in love with her was no longer a matter of conjecture. What still bothered him was whether he should tell her, when he should tell her, and if he did, what he was prepared to do about it. The old saw that "true love conquers all" was just fine in storybooks, but this was no storybook romance. He wasn't an ardent young swain; he would be forty-three on his next birthday. Was it marriage he was after in the long run? Why ask? Nothing short of marriage would ever do.

But what kind of marriage could it possibly be? Luisa, at least on the face of it, appeared to be a woman of enormous wealth; her apartment at Posada Melgar had all the accoutrements of luxury that surrounded a woman who didn't have to consider cost. And there was more to it than money. The china on which Tomás and Emilia served their dinners bore the crest of the López y Montenegros. All Corey Lane had in the way of heraldry was the crude brand of the X-Bar-7. One of the paintings on the beige walls carried the signature of Camille Corot. Photographs in silver frames—and two or three in solid gold—stood on tables and chests he could be reasonably sure were of authentic Louis Quatorze or Chippendale or some other equally priceless antique provenance. The pictures showed scenes from around the globe, and although Luisa herself appeared in only a few of them—no surprise that she was not a woman to leap into a pose at the removal of a lens cap—they clearly had been taken on her travels abroad both long before and since her husband's death. Almost all of them were of the haunts of the rich and mighty and of the rich and mighty at play: at Monte Carlo aboard a steam yacht as big as the *Lusitania*; a snow scene with an enormous sleigh in what he thought was probably St. Moritz; Paris, London—and Rome, of course. One photo in which Luisa did appear showed her kneeling in front of the Pope in a fairly intimate room somewhere in the Vatican. Yes, it was only fitting that Luisa would have something very close to a *private* audience with the Holy Father. An event like that would certainly not be "caviar to the general," but one expressly arranged for her. The total effect of her present surroundings and her past could prove insurmountable if he let it. She knew the world and its corridors of power as well as he knew every ripple of the Rio Concho back in Chupadera County.

Could he find comfort—and collaterally, confidence—in the fact that he wasn't exactly a pauper or an entirely ignorant provincial himself? The X-Bar-7 would someday come to him. But the Lane treasure was a pittance compared to that he saw stitched into the mantle of fortune Luisa wore with such casual grace. And if he had been to town to "see the elephant" it was probably too many years ago.

Where would they live as man and wife? In none of his attempts to imagine what life with her might be like could he place Luisa in Chupadera County. Who in that enormous, empty stretch of barren land and humdrum, workaday existence would be acceptable associates for this lady? Oh, Corey's mother Virgie and his old hero Jim McPherson would fill the bill while they lived; with their inner decency and sincere, unaffected manners they would be welcomed by, and comfortable at, the Court of St. James itself. And bright, cosmopolitan—for Black Springs, anyway—Ellen Stafford could come to be a good friend for Luisa, too, in spite of her past intimacy with Corey, but beyond those three there would be no one else.

Could he and Luisa make a home together here in Mexico City, then? Or at that *hacienda* in Durango Fergus had described with something approaching awe, surprising for the ripsaw iconoclast the Scot normally was?

No. Mexico was out. And that would be *his* shortcoming, not Mexico's or hers. For all that Corey had also fallen in love with this mournful country and its people, he was an American. Life as an expatriate would still be a low-grade, defeating exile. He doubted that in the long run he could do the writing which had become even more important to him since he signed on with Henry Richardson were he to settle anywhere but in the Ojos Negros Basin. Its mountains, its corroded alkali flats, and its vast, melancholy sweep of sky— forbidding as they were to some—defined him.

Here in Mexico he could never be Corey Lane, and to make himself over and offer a contrived new man to Luisa would be a monstrous sham. He would become every bit the "squaw man" Lucy Bishop feared he might have become in Chupadera County if he had married *her*.

In spite of all the obstacles looming in front of him, there was one photograph in the collection in the Posada Melgar apartment that held promise. Somehow it made things possible. It drew him like a magnet every time he called for her. This one *was* of Luisa.

It had been taken a dozen years before, when she was still Narciso Trujillo's student. Narciso was in the photograph, too, looking as if he had just walked up to her. She was standing in front of a dig like the one at Cuernavaca in Narciso's lantern show, holding an immense potsherd. From the look of the flat-topped pyramid in the background, he knew this picture had been taken somewhere in the Yucatán. Under a large straw hat, the silver hair looked darker than it did nowadays, but the premature gray had been making its first incursions even then. She was dressed in expedition khaki, with a shirt open several buttons down from the throat, with sleeves rolled almost to the elbows. Her armpits were dark from perspiration, a smudge of dirt covered the high left cheekbone, and the nails on the hands holding the clay-caked fragment of old pottery were black, one of them seemingly broken. There was nothing deliberately posed about the picture; it was as if Luisa had just arisen from her work as Narciso and the photographer approached. In the darkroom the developer had scratched lettering into the negative, and on the print the resulting white legend read, *"Doña Luisa López y Montenegro y Profesor Narciso Trujillo para Kinich-Kakmo. 7 Julio 1903."* A blithe disregard for what appeared to be a nasty, ragged gash in her right forearm, as well as a look of quiet joy, suffused Luisa's face. He hadn't seen it hold such an expression since he had known her. Wait. The joy had been there briefly that afternoon in the Mercado Merced when they shopped for the picnic at Xochimilco, and earlier that same day, as she knelt on the bare stones of the cathedral and turned her face up to the Virgin. He wanted to ask her for the photo, but of course he didn't.

Luisa had already been married when she and Narciso had made this trip to the Yucatán, a trip which must have consumed considerably more than just a day or two. Travel alone from Durango or here in the capital to the peninsula would easily take a week. And how long had they spent at the digs themselves? A voluntary separation of such a probable length of time from home and husband wasn't usual for a woman of her station in almost any country, never mind here in Mexico, where traditional forms were followed as slavishly as anywhere on the planet, nor did it square with the way Emilia tagged behind them on their walks through the park. It raised so many possibilities he decided he had better not let his racing, wishful thinking carry him to where it seemed to be carrying him; he might well win the Olympic gold medal for the conclusion jump.

But above all, the photograph said some things about Luisa herself that satisfied him deeply. In spite of her regal delicacy, the light-footed grace she had shown in her flowing seersucker skirt on the tennis court in their losing effort against the two Germans, and the willowy, almost ethereal, easy dance of her body in those walks, Luisa was no gently nurtured orchid. Yucatán in July was by all reckoning a green hell, an unrelenting, debilitating hell even for the strongest and most dedicated diggers for the past. The woman in the picture had fought it to a standstill.

But this was a different woman from the Luisa of today. The eager face showed nothing of the dark moods which still came from time to time, and which still continued to trouble him. Not difficult to determine why. This Luisa hadn't yet suffered the hideous blows of the massacre of her family in Durango. He wondered if she would ever speak of those events.

He was surprised to find that nowhere in the apartment at *la posada* did he see a picture he could identify with any surety as that of Luisa's dead husband, not even in the ones showing groups. He tried not to think about that at all, but it was perhaps this that made it so difficult to attach the word "widow" to her. Fergus had known Don Francisco, and he had described López y Montenegro, but beyond the fact that the man killed in the first risings had "a bonnie snow-white head of hair, like a bundle of Highland thistles," nothing of the description stuck. Sure. We only remember the things we want to remember.

Perhaps, but there was one thing he didn't want to remember, but couldn't keep out of his mind. That first glimpse of her utter piety and devotion in the cathedral, and her questioning of him afterward, haunted him. There had been no talk since then about her Catholicism—or of his own possible persuasion, or lack of it. The apartment had one crucifix, a small one, hung above an antique mahogany credenza. The look of her kneeling before it was as real to him as if he actually had witnessed it.

After the picnic, rankled by the fact that Kemper had gone with her to Mass that morning at San Fernando before they picked him up at the Mirador, he decided that if she ever asked him to go he would join her, but the invitation hadn't come. She had never mentioned it, but he was pretty sure Kemper was a regular Sunday morning escort. Except for that one time, Corey never saw her before three o'clock any afternoon after church. He knew jealousy on those Sunday mornings and early afternoons in a way he had never known it before. It gnawed at him, but he also blushed to find that he enjoyed the feeling. He only hoped Emilia was in attendance those Sunday mornings, too.

The matter of her religion, if he ever confessed—no, not confessed, *professed*—his love for her, would become something he would never be able to run or hide from. It wouldn't turn on a mere question of the form of faith, but of faith itself.

What would his reply be when she asked, as inevitably she would, "What are *your* beliefs, Corey?" It wouldn't be an unfamiliar question; he had certainly asked it of himself times without number.

When he served in Cuba the metal tags he wore around his neck read "Protestant," for religious preference, but it was as much a ploy to avoid unwanted conversation as it was any genuine declaration; in fact, when he enlisted he had been tempted to write "infidel" into his records, but realized the U.S. Army hadn't yet cultivated a sense of humor. Virgie and Jim went into Black Springs for services once in a rare while, but he hadn't attended any kind of church himself since the mandatory chapel convocations in his college years. If anyone in Black Springs looked askance at his truancy, they never made him aware of it.

He wasn't an atheist, that much he knew. He probably wasn't an agnostic, either, although he leaned toward it. That there was "something," if not someone, out or up "there," he was willing to concede, but of the nature of that someone or something, and his or its possible plan or purpose, he had little idea, and perhaps even less in the way of interest. As far as Corey Lane was concerned, the jury was still out on such matters; he had been content, until now, to let it languish in the jury room and declare the court in recess until new evidence came to light. The blunt truth of the matter was, unfortunately, that he could not believe, nor could he put any great trust in what he had always felt to be a perfectly reasonable disbelief.

He shouldn't speculate so. He should let her speak for herself about what she believed, but there was no need to hear her voice. He had been looking at and listening to her soul ever since they met. He saw and heard it in a thousand small, half-obscured visions and sounded and soundless utterings: he saw it in the anguished look she gave the statue of St. Sebastián in Chapultepec Park; in her breathy gasp as they stood before a painting of the Ascensión in the Museo Nacional; more clearly in her delicate, echoing footfalls on the tiled walkways of the convent near the Church of Loreto during their visit to Sor Rafaela, a friend and sometime teacher from Luisa's childhood, a withered, terminally ill old nun who had once been assigned to the mission at Santa María del Oro which the López y Montenegros had attended and supported for generations. He heard Luisa's soul in the almost fierce whispers of comfort she breathed at the coldly silent sister sitting in a reclining chair under a *portal* in the convent's death-shaded cloister.

But most of all he heard it in remembered words, not, strangely, any Luisa herself had spoken, but in those of Narciso Trujillo in the candlelit bar of the Mirador the night after Luisa's party.

"What is history for you, for us is ritual . . . repetitive, unbreakable, perpetual ritual . . . something bred in the bone . . . licking up our blood with tongues of flame . . . We are . . . 'bound upon a wheel of fire.' "

No matter that Narciso had been speaking of something in a separate province from the technicalities of theology, it was all inextricably tied together, and much of what he said that night was an overlay for Luisa that blended with her ivory skin, not that it was only skin-deep; it reached to the core of her.

"*. . . a* grito *of joy and sorrow.*"

No, he didn't need to be told about the beliefs of Luisa. They weren't, when all was said and done, merely beliefs; they were passionate urges of faith, faith to an unplumbed depth he had never known. They didn't come from the slight and undemanding exercises of the mind which had governed *his* life till now; they pulsed in her blood, had pulsed there for long centuries before she breathed. Nothing like it raged in him. Were they then to remain forever at the farthest ends of some spectrum of inner life in this, and, consequently, in other things as well? . . . with him at the cool, detached ultraviolet edge, far from her banked but burning infrared? Would the parade of intervening colors keep them separate from each other?

Narciso was right. The soul of Luisa López y Montenegro and the ritual soul of Mexico were one and the same. And what would *la fiesta* be for her? Could he ever come to a true, visceral understanding of any of the things Narciso said?

Understanding. Yes, he needed a plentiful supply of it.

A week after he talked with Henry he called for Luisa at La Posada to take her to dinner at El Gavilán and on to an evening listening to a string quartet play Mozart and Schumann. She had arranged for their tickets, and was to send Tomás to pick them up, and when he left the taxi at the door of the Melgar, he was still tossing a mental coin as to whether he should offer to pay for them or not. He smiled ruefully. Fine worldly type he was if he couldn't determine the protocol for as simple a matter as this. A tiny thing, but again further evidence as to just how far apart they were in so very many ways.

Expecting Tomás or Emilia, he was surprised when Luisa opened the door herself.

"Come in, Corey. I am terribly sorry, but Tomás discovered the concert has been canceled. The cellist has run off to Veracruz to join Don Venustiano's army." She didn't look sorry. As a matter of fact she looked strangely impish. He hadn't seen such dancing lights in her face before. "I hope it will be all right with you, but since we have nothing else to do I called my old maiden aunt, Sofía, and persuaded her to give us dinner. She is my only relative here in the capital, and I have neglected her very badly since . . . since you came along."

Only relative? For some reason he had thought there were none at all; she had seemed so alone, so splendidly solitary.

But an evening with an "old maiden aunt"? As happy as he was to be with Luisa in any circumstances, the prospect didn't exactly make his heart beat with expectation.

Tomás drove them to a small but ornate house in the baroque residential district in back of La Ciudadela, where Luisa told the taciturn old servant to return for them at eleven. Since it was now but a few short minutes after seven Corey groaned inwardly. Four hours? In all likelihood they would make the planned concert seem like a Roman orgy by comparison.

Doña Sofía Mendoza de Tenerife would never see her eightieth birthday again, Corey decided after a half minute in a sitting room filled with gilded and bejeweled bric-a-brac that looked as if it belonged more in a booth in the midway of a carnival, and after a mere half hour there he decided, too, that at least sixty of those eighty-odd years must have been spent in self-indulgence of a spectacular order.

In that half hour the gaunt little wraith in the Mandarin sheath and with hair that matched Luisa's downed four glasses of amontillado, threw five sticky chocolate creams into a mouth that looked like the slash of a knife, smoked a twisted *cigarro* as black as original sin down to where she could barely hold it even with her clawlike, painted finger-nails, and started on another. Perhaps it was the smoking that kept her thin; if she catered to all her appetites in the way she just had, she should have been a butterball, as rounded as that monument to bad taste sitting on the mantle, a marble nude with a clock in its belly.

But how on earth had he managed to take all this in, reeling as he still was from the shock of her first words to him?

"So-o-o-o . . . you are the *yanqui* bull who wants to mount the López y Montenegro's last prize heifer? *Buena suerte, amigo.* You look like you might be able to do the job. A little lean, *pero muy hombre!*"

Good Lord! It couldn't be that he heard Luisa laugh; she never would have laughed at anything so crude. Were his ears playing tricks on him?

A servant named Pablo—nearly as skinny and ancient as Doña Sofía, and as talkative, domineering, even bullying, as Tomás and Emilia were silent, withdrawn, and obsequious—served a dinner consisting almost in its entirety of what looked like native grasses. There was a tiny portion of some kind of tasteless but formidably spiny fish for each of them, and little else save the parboiled vegetation. Oddly enough, Corey got the feeling that as dismal as the meal was, a special effort—for this particular bizarre household—had been made this evening. Dessert was one of Sofía's chocolate creams for him and Luisa, but three more for their shrewlike hostess. The coffee was execrable.

He almost gasped when Luisa crossed the room and took one of her aunt's *cigarrillos* from a canister. He did gasp a little when she lit it. The smoke curled around her platinum hair.

If the food left something to be desired, the amount and caliber of the wine didn't. It was a Montrachet le Bâtard, a label Corey hadn't seen since before Cuba, and at tall Pablo's peremptory insistence, he drank more than he was used to. A truly fine cognac accompanied the bad coffee. He drank too much of it as well.

The next round of conversation began innocently enough, with the usual, expected questions from Sofía about Corey's antecedents, his work, and what he was doing in Mexico, but in accents that revealed her Spanish was as much that of a foreigner as was his, within hers a good many words and phrases in French mixed in. She had, it turned out when she talked about herself, something she seemed to revel in doing, lived most of her life in Paris, and still sorrowed for the City of Light. She was only back here because she thought it proper somehow that she eventually die on native soil. As old as she appeared to be, there was a hot, youthful flame raging through the desiccated body, and it didn't seem likely to him that death would pay her a visit until it was invited. Her fierce, narrow gaze assured him it wouldn't dare.

Then, just as he began to relax into a belief that no more jolting comments such as the one she made when they arrived were forthcoming, the tenor of her talk changed again.

For an hour, as he squirmed and twitched like a sausage frying on a chuckwagon griddle, she treated him—if it could be called a treat with Luisa listening—to a tale of amorous adventuring that made the life of Ninon de Lenclos seem the "short and simple annals" of a nun. Her yeasty chronicle of conquest—he could think of no other word—was a catalogue of the great and near great of Europe in most of the last quarter of the dead century: the commandant of St.-Cyr "*pauvre Henri* died at Verdun three months ago;" a sculptor he guessed had been Rodin himself; assorted French industrialists and financiers; and one famous chef who said she was a "*pièce de résistance, nonpareil.*"

"It was more *non*resistance, I assure you, Señor Lane." He wasn't imagining Luisa's laughter now. "What about you two?" Sofía went on. "Have you made love yet? No. You haven't. I can see it in your faces. Don't waste time."

"Stop it, Tía Sofía!" Luisa was still laughing. "You're embarrassing Corey."

Good grief, wasn't the old harridan embarrassing *her*?

Then Tía Sofía turned very, very serious. "You two think I made jokes, *n'est-ce pas*? Not so. Nothing is ever wrong when two people love each other. Perhaps you do not yet realize how much in love you are, but I can see it also. I repeat—*don't waste time!*"

The ride back to Posada Melgar was perhaps the most silent time they had ever spent together. She insisted he come in when they reached the door to her apartment.

"Emilia will fix a decent cup of coffee. You have earned it."

No, they hadn't spoken during the ride back from Casa Tenerife and they didn't now, as they waited on the balcony for Emilia, but when the sleepy *dueña* brought the coffee service out and said good night, Luisa looked up from the rim of her cup.

"Of course you realize I subjected you to Tía Sofía for a reason, don't you, Corey?" She went on. "I couldn't think of any other way to get myself off the pedestal you have placed me on."

"A pedestal? I really didn't think of it that way."

"I am, after all, a woman." She held her hand out to him. "What Tía Sofía said was true for me, Corey. Was it for you?"

Something other than the wine and brandy made him suddenly dizzy.

He put his cup down and crossed to where she was standing beside a wrought-iron table. She put her own cup down and came into his arms.

Their lips met, and to his utter astonishment her tongue found his.

* * *

In the morning a note from Hendricks at the embassy brought him on the run.

"Time to go north, Mr. Lane," the major said. "I've secured for you the closest approximation of a safe conduct I could sweat out of Villa's people here in the capital. No iron-clad guarantees, though. Are you ready? I'm afraid it might be now or never."

Corey nodded, eagerly enough, he thought, but something seemed to stick in his throat.

Now? Must he go *now*?

Nothing stuck in the throat of Fergus Cameron Kennedy when he found the Scot, as he expected, with his elbows on the bar at the Mirador, and told him of his talk with Hendricks.

"Tallyho, laddie! Let's have a drink to good hunting—gin the buckle bie!"

"What, Fergus?"

"Gin the buckle bie. Guid Scots. Motto of the Robisons. Means 'if the buckle holds.' "

37

▲▲▲▲▲

The tall, sad-looking gringo Corey Lane, who was now walking away from the shack, had just put Juanita Durán in the most difficult position of her nineteen years.

Jorge would be home from the meeting at headquarters soon, and before they went to bed tonight she would have to reach a decision. She sat down at the stacked dynamite boxes Paco had tacked together for her to use as a dressing table, and picked up the mother-of-pearl hand mirror Jorge had bought her last payday.

The face that looked back at her in the dim, waning sunlight didn't please her as it sometimes did, although it was some relief to find that she didn't look as old as she felt in the wake of the *norteamericano*'s visit. She put the mirror down on the scarf covering the boxes and ran the palms of her free hands down the sides of her face, feeling for the wrinkles she almost expected to see. Unless she was deluding herself, her brown cheeks were as smooth as ever. She picked up the mirror again. It was the eyes: the *eyes* were old. Strange that Jorge had never once mentioned it. He must have noticed. He still looked deeply enough into them to burn her soul every time they faced each other. That was one thing about him which hadn't changed.

Perhaps she could talk to Margarita about Lane and the other things troubling her. *Sí.* The captain-nurse was a *norteamericana*, for all that Juanita sometimes forgot it, and although no more of a woman than Juanita was, she could perhaps understand things about Juanita's *guerrero* that would elude a simple village girl with no real experience of men— and no real experience of *yanqui* men at all. And Jorge at bottom was a *yanqui*, no matter that his name and all his ancestors on both sides were as Mexican as she was. There were times when he seemed even more gringo than did this Corey Lane who had first come into camp three days ago. Juanita knew it even if Jorge didn't.

On second thought she couldn't talk to Margarita, who had worries enough of her own about Trini now. If anything, Trini was an even more perplexing problem in these first humid days of April than Jorge was. He had hardly spoken to any of them, even Jorge and Paco, since he took command of Los Diablos. Margarita must feel even worse than she did.

And could one woman give another answers about *her* man? And what questions could she ask her? After this length of time, a real woman, a woman who had known a man every way she thought a woman could possibly know a man, shouldn't have any questions. But was she truly a woman yet? *¿Quién sabe?* Just to lie with her man, his tough fingers gripping and kneading the back of her neck while his hungry lips seared hers and his tongue moved like a flame inside her mouth didn't make a girl—*en realidad*, a child—into a woman. It took far more than that.

It took more than that to make a man of a boy, too. She had seen it happen to him, seen him move from wild, intense, passionate idealism to the steely toughness of the *capitán* Paco respected as much now as he did Trini Álvarez. Paco Durán had patience with boys, none at all with men. Paco looked only for results from men, and she knew her father had found what he had looked for in Jorge even in those early days at Torreón.

Jorge had paid a terrible price for that toughness, first to her father, then to the war itself, and finally to the cruel demands his command made on him. Had she to pay a price now as well? Would the tall man Lane exact a payment she couldn't bring herself to make?

She had no doubt at all about Jorge's love for her; if anything, it was stronger now that they were married than it had been in the beginning. Strong enough to almost frighten her at times. When they made love now it still began with the same somewhat hesitant tenderness, but unlike the secure joy of the early days it more often than not ended with a fierceness that bordered on desperation, as if he feared it would be the last time ever. It was ecstasy, oh, *sí*, but it sometimes left her feeling like a length of metal hammered razor-thin on her father's forge back in Santa María del Oro—more so in the three nights since Lane's arrival, even though she knew for a fact that neither Jorge nor the gringo had spoken a single word to each other in the two times they had been together.

But in some ways, though, it had begun long before Lane, and had grown insidiously worse during these past weeks when there was no real fighting, only the dirty little jobs General Fierro assigned the Bracomontes. After an attack on a bank or a train, or on some unknown town the Butcher decided needed a bloody lesson, Jorge seemed as dead as stone for days on end, only rousing himself when they reached their bed in the shack. At least there had been a revived hot spark in his dark eyes since Lane had come. But not always. After Lane's arrival he took to walking to the small hill beyond the corn patch and climbing to its low top soon after supper. He never took her along, something at odds with her memory of their evening walks together at Saltillo and Zacatecas. Now he stood as solitary as a marmot, looking north as the setting sun played over his bearded face. When he returned to the shack even lighting every candle in the room wouldn't have brought a flicker to his eyes. He never picked up the Molinas book anymore. For all she knew he might have thrown it away.

Between those times of furious love he was nearly as silent as Trini was, but if anything, kinder to her in a thousand small ways than he had ever been, and she surely had no complaint about any of his behavior in that regard, never had.

The aspect of him that troubled her above all else was that most of the gaiety, the teasing, the soft, sweet banter of their early days together had fled.

¡La guerra! Of course it was the war. But at least it hadn't turned him into the brute so many of the *soldaderas* said their men became, accepting it as their part of the struggle against the enemy. Perhaps he was brutal when the guns talked, but it was unlikely she would ever have to watch him then. Margarita *had* said something once about that side of both Jorge and Trini. "We can never have the whole man, *niña,* no matter how much love we give them, nor how much they love us. There is a part they will never give us, never let us see, even if they want to. We give everything, but I suppose it has been that way since the first man and woman touched, and certainly since the first time men fought wars. And it's not just war they keep from us. Even when the fighting is behind them, they have a secret side to them they may not even know they have."

Well, there were no raids now. The regiment was readying itself for the next great battle, the one that in her quiet desperation she almost welcomed. Jorge only shrugged when she asked him when, but Paco said it would be within a week. She drifted back and forth between the relief she felt that Jorge was safe for a few more days and strange doubts she didn't dare face, but which she knew she had caught from him. *Sí,* he had doubts; they came most persistently when his day's work with *la tropa* was behind him. He always seemed so much more sure of himself when he was with the soldiers under his command, in the corral near the shack working with new horses, or having the rare *cerveza* with Paco. At night he apparently had too much time to think.

Still, she had much to be thankful for. More than once, listening to the horror stories of the camp women whose men had beaten them senseless in drunken rages, she thanked the good Dios that Jorge hardly ever drank, and never touched hard liquor of any kind. He had never been one to hang about in the town's cantinas, either, not with the men of his own troop or with the other young officers of the regiment.

All of this was *nada* after the visit Corey Lane just made.

At first she thought the gringo had made a mistake, that it was Jorge he had come to see; certainly he wouldn't want to talk with a mere woman. He wouldn't differ in that from any of the men she had known—except Jorge.

"I've about given up on cornering Captain Martínez himself, *señorita*," Lane said when she stood in the doorway facing him in the late afternoon sun, "but I simply must talk with someone close to him."

She didn't like the sound of the word "cornering," but she backed away from the door and motioned him to the shack's one chair, suddenly ashamed of a place she had delighted in for weeks, shabby and smelly as it was. The hand she pointed with shook a little. Perhaps he hadn't noticed. Foolish thought. This man was too keen. Those gray eyes wouldn't miss a thing like that. She folded her hands in her lap and pressed her legs together to hold them steady.

"I'm sorry, *señorita,* but I'm afraid I don't know your name." His voice was soft but firm, and his accent in Spanish wasn't the usual gringo one that fell so harshly on her ear.

"Juanita Durán, *señor*." She might as well get one thing straight from the very start. "I am the Captain's *esposa*." It was the first time since the small wedding a week ago she had said aloud that she was Jorge's wife.

"That's what I was told. My friend Jorge is a very lucky man." Friend? Jorge hadn't acted as if this man and he were friends, not in the way he avoided him since he drove into the compound with the other gringo, an ugly little *hombre* who seemed to know everyone in the regiment.

The gringo went on, "I must pass along some information for *el capitán*. It is *muy importante*, and I haven't been able to get a word with him. Would you give him a message for me, *por favor?*"

"*Sí, señor.* But I do not know for certain just when he will return." Would he guess that she was lying? Jorge could show up any moment. Would he be angry if he found the gringo here?

Lane looked around the shack and she cringed as the gray eyes seemed to be pulling secrets from everything, all the tiny evidences of her life and love. Something warned her that this man, for all his seeming decency, was a threat to her, and that she shouldn't like him—but she couldn't help herself. No woman, no matter how slight or distant her interest in a man might be, could totally resist such a look of essential, ineffable sorrow. This was a man life had treated with indifference, perhaps with cruelty, and yet . . .

There was sadness in him, *sí*, but no self-pity. The eyes were alive with hope. Juanita Durán had deep experience of just such a look. Jorge Martínez, even these days, and even in his darkest moods, wore such a look.

Corey Lane was a man in love. And unless she was mistaken, the love was new. Strange, this sudden knowledge— not vouchsafed by anything this gringo said, but which she could never doubt for a moment—gave her such a feeling of ascendancy that fear left her as a shadow does when a cloud slides past the sun.

"*Esta mensaje, señor.* What shall I tell Jorge?" Her voice seemed to startle him; he had been so deep in thought that he had obviously blotted out everything in the shack for the moment, even her.

"Forgive me, *señorita.* My mind wandered for a moment." He knit his brow. "How much has Jorge told you of his life in New Mexico?"

"*Muy poquito, señor.* Just about his family."

"Has he ever spoken of a young man named James Mac-Andrews?"

"No."

Lane looked perplexed. "That makes it a bit more difficult for me. Forgive me if I don't tell you why I asked that. I don't want to betray a confidence of Jorge's in any way. As a matter of fact, I wouldn't go on with this at all if it weren't so vitally important that he hear what I have to say." He drew a deep breath, smiled, and her fear lifted even further. "I would appreciate it if you would tell him that all the charges against him in Chupadera County have been dropped. Tell him he has my word of honor on this—I do think that counts for something with him, at least it did at one time."

"Charges, *señor*? I do not understand."

"He will, *señorita*. What is important is that Jorge knows it is completely safe for him to come back home."

She was scarcely conscious of his leaving the shack, not knowing when he was gone if either he or she had said another word. That terrible pronouncement was all that remained: "it is completely safe for him to come back home." The fear attacked from somewhere deep inside her.

The words echoed in her head again, and the mirror fell from her hand, shattering as it struck the hard-packed floor. No matter. It couldn't possibly matter now. The looking glass had kept its own counsel and would have gone right on keeping it. But how about all those years of bad luck the shards at her feet would bring her? Seven or a hundred, did the actual number matter? Only the one black web of clinging misfortune could possibly have any meaning now. The rest by comparison would be less than *nada*.

She was sweeping up the bits of broken glass when Paco and Jorge rode into the field in front of the shack. There was no way she could face Jorge now, before she had time to think over what the tall man had said, and she hurried the chore. One sharp piece brought a gush of blood from her thumb when she picked it up, and bright, heavy drops fell to the floor. She grabbed a rag draped over the edge of the porcelain washbasin on her makeshift dressing table and let herself out the shack's back door, wrapping her thumb as she moved on through it.

Outside, she leaned her back against the rear wall. In only seconds her thumb began to throb with as much insistency as her brain was throbbing, and she twisted the now crimson rag even tighter.

". . . must have gone to the well, Paco." Jorge's voice drifted to the rear of the shack as if it had crossed an ocean.

"No, *amigo*. The bucket is still here—and full. Wherever she is, it gives me time for another *cerveza* before we eat, without her giving me that look of hers." His laugh boomed, but there was an unfamiliar strain in it. "One for you, too?"

"*No, pero gracias, viejo.* The way I feel now it would poison me."

Silence fell, broken only by the impatient bleating of the goats in the pasture beyond the cornfield. They needed milking.

"Why is he here?"

"*No sé,* Paco. Hard to tell if he still wants to take me back to hang me. He seems to be very welcome with the generals of the Division. Do you suppose Fierro does not remember him from Zacatecas?"

"Not a chance, Jorge. He might have forgotten just Lane himself, but he couldn't forget him *and* the little one. They make an unusual-looking pair."

"Then something has changed Fierro's mind about sending them to the wall."

"Maybe it's because Lane has suddenly become an important *hombre* for General Villa."

"That makes sense, if it should turn out that way. We will have to wait to see until our Pancho returns from El Paso, though."

"When will that be?"

"Tomorrow—the day after at the latest."

"Well, we won't fight Obregón until he gets here."

There was more silence before her ears picked up the sound of Paco opening a second bottle of *cerveza*. Even with her thumb still paining her, and with the turmoil raging in her head, she couldn't help smiling at what a wonderful, sneaky old rogue her father was at times. If only his giant thirst was all she had to concern herself about.

"The worst thing about today, though, Paco, was the way Trini looked, sitting there."

"*Sí.*"

"I sometimes think it would have been better for him if Fierro had simply had him shot. This must be torture."

"But he still has command, Jorge."

"Command? *¡Mierda!* The scum El Carnicero has given him to lead into battle can't be called a command. Trini must feel dirty just having to associate with them. Every one of them is some kind of criminal. They are not *soldados*!"

"Maybe it will change when General Ángeles returns."

More silence. These were two deeply troubled men. Poor Papá couldn't be enjoying his *cerveza*. She had forgotten her aching thumb.

She wanted desperately to run back inside the shack, gather both of them into her brown arms, and cradle their heads on her chest. No. Their pride wouldn't let them stand for that.

"The gringo wouldn't dare take you away by force, Jorge," Paco said. "He knows he wouldn't live to reach the edge of camp. And anyway, your gringo law doesn't reach down here." It was clear Papá knew a lot of things she didn't know.

"I don't think that's what he has in mind, Paco. He probably wants to talk me into going back of my own free will."

"Do you want to go back? Things are not as good here in the Division as when you joined it. Even Paco Durán thinks of quitting from time to time. After all, even with your affection for Mexico, this is not your country."

Waiting for Jorge's answer was like standing on the edge of a cliff with a strong wind at her back.

"I do get homesick, Paco."

She ran. She streaked across the cornfield. By the time she stopped at the fence, blood was dripping from the rag again.

She couldn't stand here long. The sun was almost down to the mountain rim. Jorge might come out any second to take up that lonely vigil on the brow of the hill.

It wasn't hard to imagine what his thoughts would be if he knew what Lane had said.

38

▲▲▲▲▲

"I ken how bloody frustrated ye must feel, laddie," Fergus said, "but ye'll just have to muster up all your patience. Pancho's been pretty busy. He'll be even busier in the next few days."

Thank the Lord for the little Scot and his counsel. Fergus was right, of course; there was nothing for him to do but wait, and no good purpose to be served by tearing himself up with anxiety while he did. But waiting was hard. He had never particularly considered himself a man of action, but now he realized that back in Chupadera County he had a good deal of leeway in making decisions, and had more than once taken matters into his own hands and forced a conclusion to events seemingly careering out of control.

Here in Irapuato he felt handcuffed. With Ángeles still with his new army in the northeast, and Villa either in El Paso or Ciudad Juárez, meeting with the few Americans of prominence who had backed the Chihuahuan all the way down the line from the very start—Corey's mission was stuck on dead center and with no chance it would budge until the Tiger of the North returned to his Division. It was particularly irritating now that he had at last gotten Henry Richardson's full support. "Tell General Villa that important elements of the United States Government will come through for Ángeles, Corey," he said in his last call before Corey left the capital. "The President, of course, has to be won over yet, but an announcement by Villa now might just do it."

There had been a tense moment when Corey and Fergus arrived at Division headquarters three days ago to find that Villa had gone north. In the absence of El Caudillo there was no question who was running things.

Rodolfo Fierro, the Butcher himself, examined the safe-conduct signed by Gutiérrez which Will Hendricks at the embassy had provided, with only his narrow eyes showing over the top of the already much-handled document they had dragged out for every pip-squeak quasi-official and squad leader they came across since they left the capital. At last, lowering it from his lean, wolfish face, Fierro had smiled a knowing and grotesquely sardonic smile.

"*Bienvenidos*, Señor Lane . . . Señor Kennedy." Oh, yes, he remembered the two of them from Zacatecas, sure enough. It was a dangerous, dicey moment. Will had said there would be nothing ironclad about the safe-conduct, but no test of its minimal guarantees would have a higher acid content than this one. "You cannot, of course, see General Villa," Fierro said next, his voice turning from amused coldness to deadly fuming, "for the simple reason that the general is not here in Irapuato at the moment. Since you are here now, you may stay until his return. You may look the Division over, and you may have the run of Irapuato's cantinas. You will report here to headquarters every morning to get a new pass for the day. It will accord you a certain amount of freedom here. It will *not*—however—allow you to leave! I have no guarantee that your next stop won't be the headquarters of General Obregón. I did not ask you to come here; I must be asked before you go away!" The statement with its sudden heat at the end left no doubt about his real feelings about Corey and Fergus, despite the quite broad smile which accompanied the words. He stood up to dismiss them, and Corey had to stifle a gasp when he saw the .45 automatic their guards at Zacatecas had taken from him strapped to the Butcher's waist.

His thoughts went racing down a stream of nasty possibilities.

Fierro, by some fairly reliable accounts, had personally dispatched as many as seven hundred of Pancho Villa's enemies, and there were only guesses as to how many of his own—real or imagined. Some were rumored to have been North Americans, although Corey had never heard any names. It would be the irony of ironies if Fierro shot another unknown gringo with the gringo's own gun. What the hell—would it matter whose gun he used?

But the arrogance of General Rodolfo Fierro as he waved Corey Lane and Fergus Cameron Kennedy out of his presence as casually as he had waved them toward death in Zacatecas was an enigma.

If anything, he was even more arrogant and sure of himself than when he sent them to the alley wall and supposed execution in that grim comedy in the cathedral plaza, and now he was showing as well the ebullience of a victor, despite the fact that since Corey and Fergus had seen him last he had suffered two disastrous, and personally humiliating, military defeats.

In late December, Villa, after assigning Ángeles to the northeastern sectors of the erupting war against Carranza's Constitutionalists, had given Fierro command of a well-equipped army, fully supported by artillery, and sent him into Jalisco to deal with the Constitutionalists' Juan Dieguez, with the aim of splitting Obregón away from his supporters in Sonora. Dieguez, a little-known Carrancista general, with no particular reputation of tactical brilliance, and commanding a much lesser force, had bloodied Fierro's nose badly at Guadalajara, driving him back in disarray, taking the city, and capturing most of the field guns Ángeles had employed so skillfully in the reduction of Zacatecas. Villa, shrieking curses, had left Guanajuato and retaken Guadalajara—and Ángeles's guns—in a furious daylong battle. But when Villa went south to the capital and the meeting with Zapata at Xochimilco where Corey had gotten his first glimpse of him, the Butcher had made a rash, unauthorized attack on Tuxpan on the Caribbean coast and lost two thousand men. The conduct of the first and third actions had been marked by tactical stupidity on Fierro's part so patent it drew criticism in the Mexico City press, usually loath to offend any soldier in any position of authority on either side. In almost any other army, Fierro would have been retired in disgrace, if not court-martialed. Indeed, in *this* army, Corey wondered why he hadn't been summarily and swiftly shot.

Yes, even if he hadn't been blown out of command, one would have thought to find Fierro chastened, or at least much more subdued than he seemed nowadays. It did raise a small, nagging doubt in Corey's mind about the judgment of Pancho Villa. The book on Villa was that he never tolerated fools.

Why would he keep a proven loser close to him in Irapuato while he sent Felipe Ángeles out to capture backcountry rail centers and benighted towns of something less than high strategic value? Was the Tiger myopic about this fellow Chihuahuan Fierro, or just unlucky?

"They go back a long way, Corey," Fergus said. "They were both among *los del abajo* when all this began. Fierro's no general, but he's a braw fighter. In the early days, his gun cleared the way for Pancho, and for all his flaws, he's passionately loyal to him. Pancho Villa prizes loyalty above all else."

Was Francisco Villa, like so many leaders before him, living in the past? Perhaps Corey could make a judgment about that when he finally met him. But when would that happen? It was difficult to be as patient as Fergus advised when they would have to await Villa's return, with no guarantee that even then would he get the ear of the flamboyant revolutionary.

Had he thanked Providence for Fergus? Yes, but he had better do so on a daily basis.

It was the first time the Scot had used his entire bag of intelligence tricks where Corey could see him perform.

Lord, how Villa's people talked to him. Most of Kennedy's forays into the confidence of the *norteños*, of course, revolved around his capacity for liquor, and his willingness— hell, manic Caledonian joy—in testing that capacity to the outer limits. Corey followed him in and out of bars as long as his own ability to withstand the assaults of tequila and mediocre rum would let him. There was virtually no Scotch whisky to be had, but Fergus kept imbibing his way toward glory of a sort, saying, "I suppose I'll just have to gag this cactus piss down for King and country, laddie."

It fascinated Corey to watch him engage the men they met

in the cantinas of Irapuato. No one could have been more unlike these tough, battle-hardened revolutionary fighters than
Fergus was, but they opened their minds and hearts to him as
if they were in the gloom of the confessional. It revealed an
entirely different Fergus than had the visit the two of them
had paid to General Medina Barrón just before the Battle of
Zacatecas. There they had been confined to associating with
highly placed Federalist officers. Here in the Northern Division's stronghold city Fergus almost ignored anyone above
the rank of sergeant. Clearly, it was a milieu to his liking.

"The lads in the pits always ken far more about digging
coal than their superiors think they do," he told Corey.
"More, in fact, than they themselves ken they ken."

True enough in all likelihood, but no clearly focused picture of what they knew emerged until Fergus sifted, sorted,
and collated the tiny grains of information gleaned from solitary drinkers and the more frequently met groups of dedicated topers. It was uncanny how the bits and pieces could be
made to tell a plausible tale. One of Calzado's railroad men,
for instance, spilled the news that he had just come down
from Chihuahua on a train loaded with artillery shells.

"*Dios*, it was a heavy load." the man confided. "We took
a whole *semana* coming down. We had to break up in sections on the steeper grades."

Fergus laughed. "Did you make the guard detail get off
and walk?"

The man laughed, too. "I would have liked that, *amigo*, but
we didn't have a guard detail on board."

"Did the train make up in Ciudad Juárez, *amigo*?" Fergus
asked.

"No, in Chihuahua City."

"Ah, yes," the Scot said then. "That was the train I saw
pull in yesterday, the one with fourteen flatcars. *¿Otra
cerveza, sargento?*" Corey's eyes widened. Neither of them
had been anywhere near the Irapuato marshaling yards since
they arrived. As a matter of fact, it was the one place in the
city their passes weren't valid for.

"*Sí, gracias.*" Calzado's man nodded eagerly and Fergus

signaled the cantina owner to bring him another beer. The railroad man went on, "*Twenty-two* flatcars. You gringos do not count so well."

"And you made a side trip to the coast, no?"

"Where did you get that idea, *amigo*? We rolled straight down the *muesca central*."

When they left the man at the bar, Corey asked, "Why those questions about the route and all?"

"He didn't know it, laddie, but he just told me the shells he carried came from munitions works in Chihuahua rather than ones in Europe or the United States. Your Yank stuff would come across at El Paso or Laredo, and English or French arms by ship through the northern ports."

"What difference does it make?"

"It will make a *hell* of a difference in the way the gunners will have to situate their larger artillery pieces. They'll have but a fraction of their usual range if they're using Mexican-made ammunition. They may not even know it. Ángeles would."

There was more. The fact that the train carried no guard told Fergus that Villa's people in the far north had faith that the "central slot" was still firmly División country, and breaking the train into sections in the *sierras* meant "it was truly loaded, laddie. All the flatcars must have been carrying Chihuahuan shells. That means there's a bonnie big do in the offing." The Scot grinned and sniffed the air like a dog after a bitch in heat. "We got here in the nick of time."

There were a great many more deductions very much like this one, made after similar exchanges with medical corpsmen, teamsters, and clerks and soldiers in the Division's supply depots. Fergus didn't confine his information-gathering socializing just to the men. He had long, earnest talks with the *soldaderas* at their cooking fires and at the stream where they did their wash. "A wee bit more dangerous talking with the lassies, Corey; a knife I might not see could come my way. But I learn a lot about the way this army might move when we're talking food."

Other sources, also tapped for the most part in the drinking places, were the men returning from the small raids the Division had been carrying out after Zacatecas. Their talk revealed the nature of the opposition then encountered, the strength of it, and sometimes the actual identity of the units Obregón had deployed throughout the Bajío. It also gave Corey his clearest picture of the deadly nature of the more remote arenas of the conflict, and the savagery which seemed uniquely peculiar to it. The raiders described a war that even in its smallest manifestations was so brutal, so primitive, it made the one he had fought in Cuba a drill-ground exercise by comparison. He didn't even try to count the civilians they reported killed.

Much as he wished it were otherwise, Jorge Martínez wasn't one of the men Fergus cornered at La Rosabella or Cantina Mimosa, or at any of the half dozen other watering places they regularly monitored. He saw the young man, twice, at headquarters when they went there to renew their passes for the camp. He had made an attempt to get Martínez off by himself, but Jorge proved as swift and elusive as a pronghorn in the Chupadera grass. A girl, or should he say a young woman, a creature of extraordinarily fresh young beauty, had accompanied him both times. It took little in the way of intuition to know they spent their nights together. The second encounter gave birth to the idea that he could send his message to Jorge through the girl. It didn't please him, but he knew he would have little rest until he had discharged the responsibility weighing even more heavily on him since he had seen his erstwhile quarry again.

Seeing Jorge made him realize once more what a pitiful secret agent he was; no matter how much he wanted to talk with him himself, he was relieved Jorge wouldn't fall into the clutches of the little Scotch ferret. There was a good possibility that Martínez might tell Fergus something truly vital, and that it would reach Fierro that he had. Bad enough that the Butcher could still learn about how Jorge engineered his and Fergus's escape from Zacatecas.

Aside from Fergus building up a fairly accurate assessment of the order of battle of the Division when it took the field again, one other thing the Scot learned about the Villistas was absolutely paramount to future operations.

"The morale of this army, what our French friends call *esprit de corps*, is at a low, rock bottom, Corey," Fergus told him. "Logistically they're in passably fit condition, save for the fact that they don't have enough coal to move their locomotives the length of a football field. They do have plenty of what you Yanks have nicknamed ammo, and more than enough food and medical supplies—and what's still the best cavalry in the world. But the recent inaction, the ineffective, mucky wee raids they've carried out all fall and winter, and the belief that allies like that wraith in the South, Zapata, have let them down, might have sapped the will to fight. Now mind ye, that can change when Pancho gets out in front of them, but above all I think they need Felipe Ángeles. Weel, that's *your* task. Villa may not be inclined to listen to you, but you should try to persuade him to bring Ángeles back here in a hurry. It's no secret here that Obregón is digging in at Celaya. It's a fight Pancho can't very well duck, and it could be the one that ultimately settles everything. Aye, he'll need Ángeles again, as he did at Zacatecas."

As a miniature of Fergus's glum painting of the current psychic state of the División del Norte, there was the alarming case of Major Trinidad Álvarez.

Corey, so sure that the major—who had impressed him only slightly less than had General Ángeles himself in the meeting at the embassy—would be wherever the general was, had not expected to find him at Irapuato, and hadn't even asked about him.

On their second morning at the Division Corey turned from the desk where he had gotten the day's renewal for his and Fergus's passes and found Álvarez behind him.

He didn't recognize him for a second, and even when he did he couldn't be altogether sure that the man facing him wasn't a sad-eyed older brother of the one he remembered. This couldn't be the superb soldier who had sat with Ángeles and him in the embassy library, the strong, quiet man who missed nothing, and who had filled Corey with confidence and hope for any future dealings. But it was Álvarez, all right. Something terrible had happened to him in just a few short months. His face was drawn and almost haggard, and it seemed as if he had lost weight. That tremendous core of strength and rectitude was still fully visible, perhaps even more so now that the outer man seemed to have been burned away.

But what was he doing here? In the capital he seemed tight as a tick with the great Villista strategist, as if he would never be out of call for Felipe Ángeles. He must agonize to be with the general now.

He seemed to look right through Corey, and for an awkward second Corey feared the major was deliberately avoiding talk, and, suddenly wary, he withheld his own greeting. Perhaps they weren't supposed to know each other. Perhaps the two of them were still the only souls, save for Ángeles, Henry, Narciso, and Fergus, who knew about the brief meeting at the ball.

But Álvarez put that idea to rest for the moment with a wan smile. "*Cómo está*, Señor Lane?"

Then his face froze. He turned about and strode away from the line with something like the same purposeful movements he demonstrated at the embassy. Behind him Corey heard a strange sound, something like the growl of an animal. He turned toward the desk again and saw Rodolfo Fierro leaning against the back wall of the office, staring at the major's retreating back as if his eyes would drill holes in it.

Was he imagining it, or was the air suddenly heavy, charged with a malevolence he had seldom felt in all his life?

Fergus again, when Corey told him about the encounter, "No doot about it, laddie. Our upstanding major chap has somehow gotten on the wrong side of the Butcher. He'd have gone to the wall long ago, according to the gossip, but his connection with Ángeles is too strong for even Fierro to ignore."

"We'll have to talk with Álvarez before Villa returns."

"*Ye'll* have to talk with him, Corey. I've me own porridge to stir."

The Scot was indeed deep in his own intelligence work, and while Corey wondered about just what that might entail, he didn't ask. Asking might draw him into something he didn't want to be involved in, not with his own agenda to attend to.

At supper with Fergus on their third day in the encampment, he tried to make sense of what he had seen and heard, and to assess the intricate canvas the Scot had been working on. The imp seemed to be bubbling to tell him something, but Corey couldn't keep his mind on any matter larger than his talk with Juanita Durán in the late afternoon. The relief he had expected to feel at finally passing along to young Martínez that he was no longer wanted in Black Springs hadn't come. He couldn't rid himself of the memory of the girl's stricken face. It took no amount of genius to figure out what had hit her with such harrowing effect. That she was deeply in love with Jorge wasn't a matter of mere guesswork. It had glowed even in her troubled, suspicious countenance all through their talk together, and had flared to incandescent splendor whenever either of them spoke Jorge's name. It was a look very like the one he had seen in his shaving mirror every morning since his last night with Luisa.

His reflection, however, didn't carry the cast of fear he saw in Juanita's face. Not hard to fathom. She was hiding it well for one so young and essentially vulnerable, but she was deathly afraid of the very thing Corey hoped in his heart of hearts would indeed occur.

Corey wanted Jorge to return to Chupadera County; she needed him here with her in Mexico, forever. She had probably long since despaired of ever crossing the Rio Grande with him, either as wife or lover, and his possible desertion of her would leave a burning wound. The mere prospect of it had already deeply wounded her, and he felt genuine guilt for causing her such pain. What other course had been open to him, though?

He knew, too, that *she* knew what he wanted for her *soldado*. If anyone ever had the right to have the messenger put to the sword, Juanita Durán most certainly did. Strangely enough, considering that he had spent less than a quarter of an hour with her, and had absolutely nothing but that first— and very likely only—purely superficial assessment of her to go on, he didn't doubt for a solitary second that she would give Jorge his message, no matter how she wished she didn't have to, and no matter how tragic the results for her. He in turn wished fervently that he had a chance to know her better. He wished Luisa could know her, too. Small chance of either.

Was Luisa facing a similar choice, one he couldn't help with any more than he could help with this one?

Funny that he had considered what might become of the two of them with such searching care *before* she told him that she loved him that last night, and hadn't allowed himself a thought of it since then.

"I'd offer a penny for your thoughts, Corey," Fergus said, "but being a proper thrifty Scot, a ha'penny will have to do."

"My thoughts aren't worth even that, Fergus." Thoughts about Luisa were beyond price.

Thoughts about Luisa, yes. And not all of them comforting. It had been a sticky moment when he went to Posada Melgar to tell her he had to leave the capital for a "meeting."

"How long will you be away, Corey?"

"I don't know yet."

"Why must you leave now? Is this meeting so important?"

"Yes, it is, Luisa. Perhaps the most important of my life." He bit his tongue. Would she ask what the meeting was about? No, she wouldn't. His rushed goodbye, rushed because he feared questions, seemed to stun her.

Then the question he had asked himself on the taxi ride from the Mirador brought a hollow feeling. How could he possibly leave her, even for a moment? If she asked, his failure to answer so soon after the discoveries of each other they had made the night before could bring ruin, and he almost abandoned all caution and told her everything. But he said nothing. He didn't check his tongue because he didn't trust her, but rather because of the same feelings that assailed him at Xochimilco and countless times since: he didn't want her even remotely involved in his mission here in Mexico.

"Hurry back, Corey," she said at last, peering at him as if she suddenly knew what dangerous ground they might be entering. "We've just begun—and there's so much for us to talk about."

There were no questions in the embrace she gave him, nor in her kisses. Both were echoes of the night before—and rhymes to what had passed between them then.

How would he make it through the next week, or two or three—or whatever length of time this suddenly onerous job demanded of him—without her?

Now, on this third day with the army of Pancho Villa, and at breakfast with Fergus, he wondered again if any of what he was going through—his preoccupation with the hoped- and prayed-for ascendancy of Felipe Ángeles, his worries over Jorge Martínez and now the girl Juanita, and the fortunes of Mexico itself—was worth the candle he was burning at both ends. It certainly hadn't escaped him that it might well turn out to be a *Roman* candle; it could blast him to emotional shreds if and when it went off.

"Did ye get to see that captain laddie who shepherded us out of Zacatecas?" Fergus asked.

"No. I talked with his young woman, though." The Scot would be too shrewd to ask what about. "Have you found out anything about when the Division might take the field, Fergus?" Kennedy seemed full to the brim with something.

"No, Corey. Villa's due back tonight, although ye and I, of all people, aren't supposed to have tumbled to it. I expect he'll take the Division into action quickly after he arrives. My guess is that the shooting will start in earnest before the week is out. Now, lad, are ye ready for my biggest news?"

"Spill it."

"Wolf Kemper drove into camp yesterday afternoon."

39

Jorge María Martínez stood on the hilltop and looked to the north as he had every night for nearly two weeks, staring at the distant heights as if he could see through them. In a way he could. For well over a thousand miles. The imagined sights didn't warm him, and there wasn't much heat left in the setting sun. The Division was settling in for another fretful night, and the last of the supply trains was grinding to a halt in the marshaling yards across the *río*, brakes squealing, and with the last thrown switch crashing like a round of cannon fire. Familiar noises, but somehow new and different and not at all reassuring in this chilly April evening.

He shivered, but not from the cold. Would he ever reach a full understanding of what war and revolution were all about? If he did it would probably be an understanding he could never share. Certainly it wouldn't resemble in any real way the spangled dreams he had dreamed back in Chupadera County, nor would it bear much resemblance to the tales of combat he had heard when he worked the bar in his father's Cantina Florida, not the wild yarns of the few old Indian fighters still hanging around Mex Town, nor those of the Rough Rider veterans like Corey Lane who wandered across the tracks from time to time. He had grown to something resembling manhood with the firm belief that war, while not to be sought deliberately, was the proper province of that manhood. It was a splendid belief, growing up. The reality was something else.

He had discovered as early as Paredón, of course, that fear was a highly personal, nontransferable experience, and now at last he knew that one man's war was not exactly that of any other man—in almost *any* respect. And no two *guerrero* leaders had the same idea of how to face the enemy. *Sí*, this was true not only for lowly line officers such as Jorge María Martínez but for the great commanders, too.

General Villa was coming in from the north tonight, and General Fierro had called regimental meetings the length and breadth of the Division for the morning. *Dios,* how he wished General Ángeles would be here, too. Without the clear, calm judgments of "San" Felipe, as Trini called him, there was the very real danger that General Villa would approve the idiotic battle plan for Celaya and the rest of the Bajío that El Carnicero had laid out in the last two weeks. "Cavalry, cavalry, and more cavalry! We will sweep them into the sea!" the Butcher was reported telling his staff night and day.

No one had asked them to, of course, but Jorge and Trini had worked out a strategy of their own weeks ago, one Trini said would meet with the approval of Felipe Ángeles, and they agreed that Fierro's route was a high road to disaster. Worse. Jorge must now admit the possibility that the former Chihuahuan muleskinner he had worshipped for longer than he could remember had learned nothing from the Butcher's failures at Guadalajara and Tuxpan. The troop's bugler, Tonito, could have devised a better plan.

He knew pretty well what Trini thought about the course Fierro, and Contreras, too, seemed intent on taking, even if he hadn't spoken to his former commanding officer in weeks. And he remembered all too well what the major had said about the role of cavalry for the rest of the campaign, and knew in his heart how right he was. Like Trini, he had regrets. He wondered what was going on in Trini's fine mind these days as they readied themselves for battle yet another time.

He knew a little bit about what was going on in his own—and in Paco's. He wished he knew what was going on in Juanita's.

At supper she had been as silent as this rocky hillside. Every other time the fighting was close at hand, even in the blackest of nights before the small raids the Butcher had sent him on, she had been bright and gay, even if the gaiety had been only a forced one to keep his spirits up—and to float her own. He had delighted in it, although he always sensed the deep-seated fears she harbored for him and Paco whenever battle loomed.

Had he been a superstitious man he might have seen tonight's taciturn behavior as an omen. He had forgotten it when he saw her lacerated thumb. He had helped her bathe it gently, and wrapped it better than it had been in the red rag she had discarded when she began his and Paco's supper.

"Foolishness, *mi cariño*," she had said when he had asked her how it happened. "It will be all right." She had said no more about it, and it slipped his mind as well.

There was a lot for him to think about on this hillside, beyond just the chore facing the Division.

The reappearance of Corey Lane had brought the same knotting inside him he had known when he had seen the tall lawman in El Paso and again in Zacatecas, and no matter how often or with what conviction he told himself that Lane could no longer be pursuing him this deep in Mexico, the thoughts of what he would still have to face back in Chupadera County—supposing he ever got there again—weren't pleasant ones. In all probability he would go to his grave with that still hanging over his head. *Dios,* he could find that grave quicker than he wished. There was nothing to be gained by thinking about that tonight, though. The perils of war were faced better, he had found, if you only faced them once. No sense in practicing something which you had to do perfectly the first time it was tried.

"I still think you should have let Fierro shoot the tall gringo and his *amigo*, Captain Cockroach," Paco had said in their moment alone after dinner.

"Too late to worry about that now, *viejo*. But see if you can find out what the hell Lane is doing here. He is not just a *turista*, I know that much."

Paco had sniffed around headquarters mightily, and returned to him with the word that Corey Lane was some sort of scholar-journalist, with solid credentials from the Americans at the U. S. Embassy, validated by Villista agents in the capital, and with a safe-conduct signed by President Gutiérrez. "El Presidente's signature does not mean all that much these days, of course, but someone, somewhere, thinks very highly of this gringo, Jorge. I also get the strange idea that Trini Álvarez knows more about him than El Carnicero does."

He found Trini, and asked, but got no satisfaction whatsoever, except that the major's uncharacteristic evasiveness persuaded him that Paco was right, as usual.

"I do not think it would be good for you to know too much about this *norteamericano* and what he is doing here for the moment, Jorge," Trini said.

Although he had long since told Paco the bare bones of the sordid story of what had happened in Black Springs, he had never breathed a word of it to Trini—nor to Juanita.

It seemed certain, though, that Lane was in Irapuato as something other than the principal law enforcement officer of an obscure New Mexico county tracking down a young killer named Martínez; it didn't, however, mean that there were no others back there in the Ojos Negros looking for that same young killer. Nothing had changed. He couldn't go home. Not yet.

Did he want to go home? *¿Quién sabe?* The Revolution he was fighting in was far from finished, perhaps wouldn't be finished for many years, but if what was being said all over the Division was true—and he was sure it was—the battle shaping up to the south of them would be the crucial one of this phase of it. Winning now wasn't the most important thing; it was everything. No matter what numbers the dice were showing now, he had to wait until they stopped rolling. He could make no decisions until then. But what he told Paco an hour ago was certainly true. He did get homesick now and then, and never more so than on the three occasions when he had seen Corey Lane.

Now he was consumed by the desire to talk with the man from Chupadera County, and get answers once and for all. And yet something held him back. Was it that such a talk would offer choices he had no wish to make? Nonsense.

Nothing Lane could possibly tell him would have anything to do with his situation here. Was it, after all, the homesickness?

Admit the likelihood and have done with it, amigo.

But there was something else, too. He blushed to think it, but he wanted to talk with Lane for still another reason, one that had little if anything to do with Jamie MacAndrews except in a very distant way. He wanted to impress the lawman, and as a result impress Chupadera County when Lane got back to Black Springs someday. He wanted to present to him a fighting revolutionary as hard and tough as any the sheriff was apt to run across here in Pancho Villa's army. Jorge María Martínez was an *hombre* of significance here in Mexico. He was a *capitán de caballería* of Regiment Bracomonte, a veteran of the great, hot charge at Paredón, the gloriously bloody Battle of Zacatecas, and scores of smaller skirmishes just as dangerous and deadly. It was petty of him, he supposed, but he wanted the high and mighty gringos of the Ojos Negros to know it.

Sí, he was homesick, but he wasn't ready to cut and run, wasn't ready to return to a life of doffing his cap and bowing and scraping, of crawling in the dust before men who had never known the fierce pride that comes from being shot at without fluttering the white feather of cowardice. No, he wasn't through here in Mexico, not by a long shot.

The night wind was rising, and because of it he didn't hear the rustle of Juanita's skirt. The first he knew that she had joined him on the hilltop was when she placed her hand on his shoulder. He turned from facing northward and took her in his arms. She buried her face in the crook of his neck and pressed hard against him.

¡Dios! He could never be cold again, not when that warm, soft body was next to his.

Warm? Her body brought him more than warmth tonight. Tonight it raged with a heat that almost frightened him.

Her breath, sweet as it was, was feverish, too. From the cut perhaps? He held her a bit away from him and looked at her.

"¿Qué pasa, mi amor?"

"Jorge," she whispered, "I have something important I

must tell you. A man came to see me today. That tall gringo who is new in camp. He had news for you. Good news. From your home."

From the look of her, whatever Corey Lane had said to her, and no matter how she had just now characterized it, it couldn't possibly be good news.

She stared upward into the darkness above the bed.

Jorge lay deep in sleep beside her, and so far through the long—and for her tormenting—night, hadn't stirred or made a sound.

He had taken the gringo's message well, *sí*, but he hadn't uttered a word himself.

It didn't matter. She knew what was in his mind. He would leave her. He would stay for the battle he and her father agreed was the battle that could make or break the struggle, but he would leave.

There could be no beginnings of a child now.

When she first decided he would leave, during their silent moment on the hilltop after she gave him the news from Lane, a wild cry he couldn't hear came from deep within her. *"Now! Juanita! You must bear his child. It will be something of him to keep when he is gone, something to remember."*

Then her heart turned to ice. No. It couldn't be.

A child would make him a prisoner. She couldn't do anything to keep him with her against his will.

She would have to go back to being as careful as she had been in the early days.

Strange that she had never gotten pregnant yet.

And if she did?

Margarita would help. He would never know. Margarita would be here long after he was gone.

40

"Ye can't bloody well be engineering a deep-water port here in the heart of the Bajío, Wolf," Fergus said. "What exactly has von Rintelen sent you to Irapuato for? Does auld Kaiser Bill have a sudden hankering for chile peppers?"

The German stiffened. "Von *whom*, Herr Kennedy?" It had been "Fergus" until now.

"Have it your own way, laddie. If you say you don't know von R., I'll believe ye, though thousands wouldn't."

Kemper rose from the table he shared with Corey and Fergus. He bowed rigidly to Corey, and although he didn't exactly click the heels of the *charro* boots he was wearing, it was almost as if he had. "You will excuse me, *bitte*, Herr Lane." Perhaps the familiar "Corey" was to be reserved only for Luisa. Small of him, Corey supposed, but from Kemper he actually preferred the formality of "Herr Lane." It kept his mind on the fact that they were adversaries, not easy to do, given the man's usual affability.

Corey nodded as Wolf did a curt volte-face and marched out of the cantina without another word to the Scot.

"Sensitive bugger, isn't he?" Fergus said.

"Why did you tell him we drove up here together?" Corey said. "He's bound to suspect we're working in tandem in some fashion."

"Aye, I suppose he will. Bonnie. The actual truth is, of course, that I'm now working on something quite aside from what ye're up to, and moreover it hardly matters any longer, laddie. He can't very well stop your audience with Pancho tonight, and if you're successful with the Tiger, he'll damned well know everything in the morning, anyway. And by that time it will be too late to make a difference."

"Do you have any idea what he's doing here?"

"Aye. He wants Pancho's ear, too."

"Can he get it?"

"If German offers of money and arms count, and they do. The Jerries can be more miserly than Scots, though." He tossed off the last of his drink, making a sour face as he did. "Ye'd better get yourself ready for your presentation at court, laddie. I'll stay on the track of our German friend."

Corey half wished Fergus were coming with him to headquarters, but decided no, this was better. He couldn't rely on Kennedy forever.

Still, he needed him for just a little longer.

"Any last-second advice for me, Fergus?"

"Ye need no advice from the auld mongoose, Corey. Ye're a big lad. What ye're up to is the right thing for everyone."

"But you've met Villa. I haven't. I'll admit I'm more than a little scared."

"Don't apologize. I've been in the game eons longer than you have, and I'd have quite a fright at the prospect meself. Look at it this way. Ye're in for a rare treat."

"Well, I've gone over everything I've learned about Francisco Villa. I guess I'm as prepared as I can expect to be."

Fergus stuck his callused hand across the table. "Guid luck, laddie. Oh, I suppose I do have one wee bit of counsel. I know ye're scared—in a healthy way. But don't show it. There's nothing our Pancho despises more than the look of fear."

With his riding boots laid across the top of the mahogany desk General Francisco Villa impressed Corey slightly less than he did the day he entered Xochimilco, but only because he wasn't on horseback now. Pancho Villa dismounted wasn't truly Pancho Villa. The riding quirt he tapped into the palm of his left hand was a constant reminder of the fact. He didn't look armed, nor did the American Carruthers seated to his left, whom Corey knew from newspaper photographs. The man on his right, Rodolfo Fierro, however, still carried Corey's .45 strapped to his hip.

"Señor Lane! Welcome to the División del Norte."

"*Gracias,* General Villa."

"They tell me you are a writer of history. Have you ever seen such history to write about as you are seeing now in Mexico?"

"I am not here as a historian, General." It was time to open up. "At the moment I have come to talk with you as an officer of the U.S. State Department."

The dark eyes narrowed. "You have kept that a secret from my staff. That is not a good thing for a guest to do, *amigo.* What do you want from us, *hombre*?"

"I don't know if I can speak freely, *jefe.*" Corey looked as pointedly as he dared at Carruthers, and held his gaze even longer and more searchingly on the saturnine countenance of Rodolfo Fierro. A little tickle of apprehension ran through him. Villa had asked these two men to be present. Was he pushing things too far too quickly to reveal his uneasiness with the general's *compañeros*?

He felt marginally better when Villa's cannonading laugh shook the office. The Tiger of the North turned to the Butcher.

"Rodo, *mi amigo.* I think our *norteamericano* writer *hombre* wants you to leave." Fierro winced but said nothing, and Villa continued. "You are right to worry about Rodolfo, Señor Lane. *Sí.* He remembers you from Zacatecas. Does it surprise you that I know about that? My people keep no secrets from me."

It did surprise him, but it didn't seem to call for an answer. He waited. It was a warm evening, with no breeze stirring, but the office would have been close and oppressive on the coldest winter night, such was the heat the Chihuahuan generated. If Fergus and Will Hendricks were right, and he didn't doubt for a moment that they were, the long months of inactivity might have sapped the strength of the Division; they hadn't drained any from its leader. Corey's pulse quickened. Armies reflect the qualities of their commander. This man could still fight. That ability would outlast a thousand enemies like Venustiano Carranza. The initiative could be restored to the Villista cause as speedily as it seemed to have been stripped away. Villa's endorsement of Felipe Ángeles, coupled with bringing Ángeles back from the northeast to fight at his side and direct the traffic of the next looming battle, could blunt the advance of Obregón, drive him back toward the coast, and in the bargain erode the political gains Carranza had made in the past few months. The situation was critical, surely, but far from hopeless if this man acted.

But—as he had told Villa moments earlier with such temerity—there was no way he could speak candidly and openly while Villa's two companions flanked him, and at this present delicate moment, the Tiger didn't seem inclined to send them off.

Somehow he felt no pressure from his fellow countryman, Carruthers. What the lean, silent soldier of fortune's position was with Villa and the Division he had no way of knowing, but Fergus had volunteered that Carruthers might be the liaison with Pancho's remaining American friends and supporters north of the border. If such was indeed the case, the American posed no threat; might in the long run become an ally. Carruthers had scarcely looked at him since they all sat down together. He sat now picking at his fingernails with a splinter of wood, seemingly oblivious to what was going on.

The Butcher's distrust of, and enmity for, Corey Lane was as readable as if it were a legend printed into a balloon above his head in the manner of dialogue in comic strips. Urging Villa to dismiss Fierro could only redouble the danger he presented. Still, were Corey to avoid failure at this juncture, the man had to go. He took a firm grip on the arms of the chair he was sitting in. It would be disastrous to have his hands show the slightest tremor at a time like this.

"General Villa . . ." He gulped down apprehension. "I can't say the things I would like to say until I can say them to you alone."

Villa snorted. Hard to tell if it was a snort of anger or amusement, or of equal parts of both. "Careful, gringo. You are very close to telling me what to do. Do you remember I said my people keep no secrets from me? I keep none from them."

It was time to take a chance. "What you choose to tell them when I am done is, of course, your affair, General." He swallowed hard. "I do not think either Mr. Carruthers there or General Fierro is important enough or wise enough to hear any of it before you have a chance to edit it, sir." He very nearly shook as he said it.

Villa pulled his legs from the table and his boots hit the floor with a thud Corey could feel in the soles of his own. Then the general stroked his cheek like a man checking to see if he needed a shave. He did. Corey almost laughed aloud at the utter absurdity of such a thought at such a moment. The laugh didn't come, but he knew he hadn't been able to suppress a smile. Had he lost everything in the past two seconds?

Then *Villa* smiled. The smile was reflected in the quizzical look of Carruthers and met by absolute fury and hatred in the face of Rodolfo Fierro. Corey had made an implacable enemy of the latter, but what the hell, he hadn't been exactly a friend to this point. All that mattered now were El Caudillo's next words.

They weren't long in coming.

"Rodo," he said, "take our *amigo* Carruthers and wait for me outside. And Rodo, take off Señor Lane's *pistola* and leave it with him."

No. His people *didn't* keep secrets from him!

If he had thought he had made an enemy of Fierro before, he knew that now and in the future the Butcher's enmity would know no bounds. He thought Fierro might shake himself to pieces with rage when he stood, unbuckled the belt with the .45, and held it out toward him. It was more than an awkward moment. Villa's lieutenant was a dozen feet from him, obviously expecting Corey to rise, walk to him, and claim the weapon.

He almost made the mistake. He started up from his chair, but he caught Villa's eye and sank back into it. Pancho might not be the master strategist or brilliant tactician Ángeles was, but in the games where one man proved his will was stronger than another's he probably had no equal in Mexico, or in the world. He certainly hadn't missed the silent contest between

Corey and Fierro. He was grinning from ear to ear. Corey remained motionless. Carruthers had moved through the door at the back of the office, but Fierro stood with his arms extended and the gun belt draped across them, looking for all the world like some khaki-cassocked priest of death.

Finally, Villa cleared his throat. "I don't think he will move, Rodo. Take him his gun, *por favor.*"

Fierro came toward him, dropped the gun in Corey's lap, then spun around and left the office before Corey could so much as blink. When the rear door closed behind him, Villa spoke again. "Are you prepared to kill my General Fierro at your first chance, Señor Lane?"

"No, sir, I'm not. I didn't come to Mexico to kill anyone."

"That is unfortunate, *señor,* because Rodolfo most certainly intends to kill *you*—at *his* first opportunity. Killing is Rodo's business, and there is no one better at it."

"When do you suppose that 'opportunity' might come, General?"

"*¿Quién sabe?* But I think he will kill you the very second I say he can." If the earlier laugh had been the report of a cannon, this new one came as a barrage of an entire battery emptying its barrels all at once. When the last crashes of it died away the room was filled with a silence so heavy, so palpable, so viscous, Corey felt it must be oozing through the windows and under the doors, filling the encampment to the farthest bivouac. He had the unreal feeling that every man, woman, child, and animal in the Division was wondering now about that silence. He could well wonder himself.

Never before, despite all the doubts and misgivings dogging him every foot of his strange, often dreamlike journey here in Mexico had the full enormity of the task facing him been so apparent. What on earth made him think he was equal to it?

He had told Fergus he had gone over everything he knew about the man sitting behind the desk, and he had. He had almost memorized every word in the file on the Tiger of the North that Will Hendricks, showing unusual daring and trust for a man in his profession, let him take back to his room in the Mirador, and when he was through he compared it with the similar one the major dug up for him on Carranza. Through with both, he almost called Henry to ask if anyone in Washington ever *read* these dossiers. Even on the simple face of it, anyone with half an ounce of brains studying them would be hard put to pick the First Chief over Pancho even for a second or for the most suspect of reasons. As he had pretty much expected, there was only a skimpy file on Felipe Ángeles. The lack of a fuller one seemed almost deliberate.

Well, there wasn't much time to speculate on any of that now. He was going to have to deal with the man he was looking at.

The dossier had only told him the known facts about this untutored mule driver from Chihuahua who had been born Doroteo Arango. It didn't tell him what the man really was. Many of the facts, admittedly, were damning. Some weren't. There was agreement on the part of observers at opposite ends of the political spectrum that no matter what crimes Pancho Villa might have committed on his wild ride to power, there was nothing small or venal about him. There was a consensus that even if he had cast money to the winds on behalf of the Revolution, he was singularly free from personal corruption, had never enriched himself by so much as a lone centavo. According to the gossip mills of the capital, and fairly trustworthy sources in the embassy, too, the same couldn't be said for five other generals on either side. Strange that two of the honorable ones, at least where money was concerned, were the twin titans of the División del Norte, Ángeles and Villa. Strange—but perhaps no coincidence.

Pancho's reverence for Francisco Madero was real, too; it had brought him to his bitter, unrelenting enmity of Venustiano Carranza early in the revolutionary game. Yes, behind the wanton savagery, behind the ruthless sacrifice of friend and foe alike in Pancho Villa's holy cause, there was a strange, complex human being Corey suspected *no one* knew—not even the women he pursued so single-mindedly.

Now, in this dim, musty office, its air murky and foul from the oil lamp guttering on the desk and throwing the bold, round features of the guerrilla leader into larger than life relief, Corey came to still another conclusion.

As a historian devoted to his field of study, and as a dedicated believer in history as guide and teacher, he suddenly felt depressed; history, no matter how it tried, would not be kind to Francisco Villa. Certainly it would not be fair—and hardly accurate.

The hard-line assessors of the Revolution would doubtless deliver him to the future as a buffoon and charlatan, albeit a dangerous one. The romancers—and they were hard at work already in the United States—would make of him a Mexican Dick Whittington. Corey wondered which of the two camps *he* would eventually find himself in when he wrote about him. In a way Villa, with his incomparable swagger, had asked for both portrayals. He surely would have served himself much better without such posturing, but . . .

It was that very swagger which had brought three quarters of northern Mexico together under the ripples of his battle standard. Narciso had spoken of the idea of *"fiesta"* in Mexico. Doroteo Arango—Francisco Villa—was the embodiment of that idea. He wasn't a man so much as a threatening volcanic eruption. How had Narciso put it? An *"explosion . . . an orgasm."*

He might erupt now, when Corey had his say—or as much of his say as the man across the desk would allow. Well, there would be no more waiting.

"Tell me about the history you write, Señor Lane," Villa said. "Do you write about Pancho Villa and the fight he makes for Mexico?" The strong, subtly insistent note was clear. From another man it would have fallen on Corey's ear as pure egotism, not so with this one. This was the far more colossal, but strangely still ingenuous, narcissism of mythology. Villa had dressed that narcissism in the modern technology of sycophantic journalists, claques, and movie cameras, but it was as ancient as the land he had rampaged across. Corey couldn't suppress a smile, hoping against hope it wouldn't be misread. Villa's patterned self-aggrandizement hadn't put him off. He understood at last why men would follow Francisco Villa in and out of hell.

"I have written about you, sir, and I will again. But I am not in Irapuato as a historian."

"No? Then what *is* your business in the Division's camp?"

At last. As in the *corrida de toros*, the moment of truth was at hand. This was no blind bull, though, but a fully alert, dangerous animal, in spite of, perhaps because of, the hurt mask his face had become.

"I am a Special Foreign Service Officer of the United States of America, General Villa. I am here on behalf of my country's State Department."

What would he do if El Caudillo asked to see his credentials? He didn't have a single scrap of paper identifying him as anything other than Corey Lane, historian.

Villa leaned forward in the chair as if he would push the desk ahead of him like a bulldozer, and the bright, wide, chocolate-brown eyes bulged. "*¡Mierda, hombre!* You are a spy! Perhaps I should call Rodolfo back."

"I hoped you would listen to me first, sir."

Corey could almost see the mental coins being tossed.

"Pancho will listen, *señor*," Villa said at last. "But you must talk *rápidamente*."

Yes, it was imperative to speak quickly and with brutal directness. Corey spilled his message down a sluiceway of desperation.

"I—and the people in my country I represent—would like to see General Felipe Ángeles become President of Mexico, not just President in name as Señores Gutiérrez and Garza have been, but in absolute fact, with the wholehearted backing of the great Francisco Villa!"

In the silence that followed, Corey became even more conscious of the immense force of the ungainly man across the desk from him. Would Villa call for his Butcher and have done with this minor nuisance? These were bad, bad moments.

The general placed his two big hands flat on the desktop. It looked as if he could hold a world down with them. Corey remembered him once being quoted as saying, "I use the ocean for a gargle." He looked as if he could.

"You have come here, *amigo,* to knock Pancho from the saddle?"

"Not at all, sir. We want someone to ride *with* you."

"I am frankly amazed, Señor Lane," he said, "that any of you gringos have even heard of Felipe."

"It is true that only a few of my countrymen know of him, but those who do prize him highly."

"Surely you must know that I do myself, *verdad?*"

"I'm counting on that, General."

"Hah! You think me easy to predict?"

"Not at all. I said that because of what I see as your abiding love for the people of Mexico. Next to you, General Ángeles is the best hope they have."

"If Felipe is only *next* to me, why are you not asking me to be *el presidente?*"

"Because I don't think you truly want the office, General Villa." Should he tell him how he came to this conviction at the meeting with Zapata in Xochimilco? Not yet. But Villa was looking at him open-mouthed, and he had better seize the moment and move along. "With General Ángeles as President and you and your Division to give him the authority he must have, Mexico would be in the best of all possible hands, *las manos de Dios.*"

Villa growled. He held his two hands in front of him and clenched them into rocklike fists. "These are the only hands I trust to hold Mexico and make it well, *señor.*"

"I understand." If he only trusted his own hands, how could Corey persuade him to deliver Mexico into those of Ángeles? He began marshaling in his mind all the tidy arguments he had practiced on Fergus as they drove to Irapuato from the capital. It was all solid, and he knew it. But he wouldn't know for sure how credible they might sound until he saw the looks on Villa's face as he went over them point by point. Suddenly he was unsure of any of it. This was not a rational human being he was facing; Pancho Villa was a creature of almost pure emotion. The pat debater's ploys which had sounded so convincing with the Scot might seem bloodless and barren in this yellow-lit little office with its smell of burning oil.

"You see how it is, Señor Lane?" Villa said now. "*Sí*, I think perhaps you do. It is strange to find such understanding in a gringo. I think perhaps you love Mexico almost as much as Pancho Villa does."

Corey took a grip on the arms of his chair and readied himself to speak again. He didn't get a chance.

"Señor Lane," Villa said, "you are the first *hombre* who has ever suggested to me that I make Felipe President of Mexico."

"Forgive me, General—but someone had to. I don't know why someone hasn't long before now."

"I have made myself very hard to talk to about some things, my friend. Do you understand that, too?"

"I think I do. When command is at stake, a leader cannot let those under him see any doubt, any other plan save the one at hand."

"*Sí*. With such understanding, perhaps *you* should be President of Mexico."

Risky as it might be, he had to push on. "Is there a chance, sir, that you agree with me about General Ángeles?"

Now came the most frightening silence of Corey Lane's life. Each throb of the pulse in his temple was a distinct hammerblow. It lasted a full half minute, then broke under the mammoth sigh of Pancho Villa.

"Not only a chance, *señor*. I agree with you completely. I have thought for many months that Felipe is the best leader we could offer the people of my poor country." Great Scott! Would this prove at the last to be easier than Corey had dared dream? Wait now. Villa looked suddenly troubled. "*Pero, mi amigo,* such things are more easily said than done. I pretend in public there are no limits to my power, but this is not quite true. I think I must now give you a lesson in Villista politics.

"The men closest to me in the Division—like Rodolfo— and the generals of the other armies which fight with us, think Pancho Villa is a god. They are like *niños* in this regard. Whenever someone says that someone else should rule this country, that man becomes their enemy, someone to be eliminated. It is even true with our good friend in the south, Zapata. I think this would be true even if I named the man myself. They would think that man had tricked me. This is why I have tried to move the Division back toward Chihuahua in the past half year. One or more of *them* must call for General Ángeles. To persuade them to decide on him, I have given Felipe his own command. He will never rise to the top as *número dos* in the División del Norte. But with the victories he has made in the northeast now, perhaps they will see his real value to the Revolution, not just to me. And they will only see him this way when they think Pancho himself is through with fighting. At the moment Álvaro Obregón will not let Pancho stop. He must be destroyed before anything else is done. You must be patient, Señor Lane. Your *amigos* must be patient, *también*. Let Pancho drive Obregón from Celaya and we will talk again." He stood up. Clearly, Corey was dismissed, or close to it.

"*Gracias,* General Villa," he said. Why didn't he feel good about what Villa said? He had done what he had come to Irapuato for—the Tiger's endorsement of Ángeles. True, Pancho had some people he had to persuade, but that couldn't be an insurmountable task for so powerful a leader. It was now only a question of time. But that was one of the rubs. *Was* there time? It would be up to Henry and Secretary Lansing to hold the President off on recognition of Carranza. Something else dug at him. If Villa intended keeping Ángeles in the northeast with his own army, it meant he wouldn't be at Pancho's side in the battle for Celaya now shaping up, the battle Corey suddenly realized had to be won.

"Señor Lane," Villa said next, "in your time in the capital, have you been able to enjoy the favors of its *señoritas*?"

Corey walked back to the hotel with light feet, and with a head that threatened to float away at times. He had garnered more than he had dared hope he would in the meeting with

Pancho Villa. It wasn't the *end* result he had hoped for—but it was a start.

The great weight of the gun belt and the .45-caliber automatic bothered him some, but he decided he would have to wear it for the rest of his stay with the Division of the North. He was going to have to meet with Villa again, and he knew now that Villa felt more at home around armed men—and, from his parting comment, made with a smile but in all seriousness, around men who shared his love for women. Could he wish Luisa here?

He had smiled back at the general, said, *"Sí,"* and wondered if this could be considered a betrayal of her. Lord, how he missed her, and longed to be back at Posada Melgar with her.

He found Fergus in a mood as ebullient as he had ever seen the Scot, for once spilling his own news out with no apparent interest for the moment in what Corey had to say. It piqued him just a little.

"It's been a bonnie night for auld Fergus, laddie. Perhaps my days as an also-ran are done, or will be."

"How so?"

"Wolf Kemper has been receiving a lot of cable messages, and some of them are from Berlin. Surprised me. I thought he took every order from von R. I dinna think I would have found out how they were reaching him if we were all back in the capital, but from up here in Irapuato the trail is easier to see. The forest and the trees sort of thing."

"What *are* the messages, Fergus?" Had Fergus even been quite this excited in their times together? No. This *was* something new.

"The usual stuff, lad. Nothing of real importance at the mo'. Actually, I dinna care *what* they are right now. It's been the *route* of them that interested me. I didn't think the Jerries were up to what they obviously are in spite of what London has been thinking. But what I discovered in the Division's telegraph office tonight is exactly what Admiral Hall's bright lot in room 40 predicted it would be. Signal intelligence is only trustworthy when you can follow every twist and turn of it."

What the hell was Kennedy talking about? He would have to pursue this with him sometime, but not now. He was too full of his own accomplishments.

"Ye're done guid work tonight, laddie, aye," Fergus said when Corey finally more or less forced his news on the Scot. "Henry Richardson and his bunch should be proud of ye."

Then everything else was forgotten when Fergus spoke again.

"One other thing I learned tonight, Corey. I don't suppose the Tiger told you, but the Division moves on Celaya and Obregón tomorrow."

41

▲▲▲▲

The Bajío of Mexico, north of the capital and lying between Irapuato and Celaya, is a broad flat plain deep with black soil and crosshatched with mile after countless mile of irrigation ditches separating lush fields into squares rich with corn and beans. Small farms nestle cheek by jowl and reach almost from the southern boundary of Irapuato to the north edge of Celaya itself.

Corey Lane, while not fancying himself a strategist nor a tactician, knew at a glance it was not ideal terrain for the deployment of cavalry, even if he couldn't see very much of it from the railyards of the city. He had gotten a good look at the Bajío on the drive up four days ago, but since then rains had turned the hard dirt roads he and Fergus had bumped over to gumbo. Off the roads, the soft earth would mire horses and drag the strength from their legs. It wouldn't make a good platform for positioning field guns, either. On the other hand, the ditches would be superb for the stubborn use of infantry, and the battle for Celaya could become one much like those going on in Belgium and France—those agonies of grinding attrition, where advances and retreats were measured in feet and inches, and the master strategist was "General Mud."

Álvaro Obregón, laying out his defense forty kilometers down the line, must be pleased as Punch to be facing Pancho Villa today on such a soggy carpet, one that couldn't have suited his army and his tactics better had he designed and rolled it out himself. It was tailored for the war of dedicated caution which was the Carrancista general's trademark.

Fergus had cast doubt on the Division's morale again at breakfast, but Corey didn't think it at anything but peak strength as he watched he advance cavalry squadrons moving out of Irapuato this morning. Pennants were fluttering at the head of several of the horse *tropas*, and here and there a bugler piped into the misty air. The animals and riders moved smartly through the exits from the city. What a difference in their mood the arrival of Pancho Villa had made! If only the Division's foot soldiers were up to the standards of this splendid cavalry and the artillerists trained by Felipe Ángeles, few armies in the world could stand against them, mud or no mud.

But this wasn't Zacatecas with its panoramic views from La Sierpe. Unless the young lieutenant named Gómez whom a surly major at Fierro's headquarters assigned him as a guide and driver showed a little more eagerness to move closer to the action, Corey wasn't going to see a hell of a lot. The boy officer didn't look afraid; he just seemed intent on staying near the battery of news photographers and movie cameramen also being held away from the fighting for the moment. In the gray sky above them a biplane cut lazy didoes and graceful swoops at odds with the erratic coughing of its engine. The sound of it reached him before he saw it, and at first he thought he was hearing small-arms fire. He knew airplanes were coming into more and more use in the Revolution, but this was the first one he had seen. Aside from some value as spotters for artillery, he wondered what a commander might use them for. The airplane finally straightened up its wings and soared southward toward Celaya. He heard distant bursts of fire as it winged out of sight. Could that fragile bundle of metal tubes and fabric hold up against a really concentrated fusillade?

He missed Fergus. The Scot had told him as they left the hotel that "I willna be taking this one in today." It was uncharacteristic of Kennedy, missing out on major action this way, but when Wolf Kemper, carrying a huge briefcase, emerged from headquarters just as Corey and Fergus reached it, and then climbed in a car with the German flag at the radiator ornament and a nondescript civilian in the driver's seat and sped off to the east, he knew why—Fergus was going to stay on Kemper's tail.

Corey hadn't seen Villa yet, but Fierro had left headquarters on horseback with a clutch of junior officers at almost exactly the same time Kemper had, heading south, his small cavalcade threading its way through the columns of infantry massing in the railroad yards and awaiting the departure of the main body of the Division's cavalry. As far as Corey could tell, the Butcher hadn't spotted him. Of course he must have known of the escort the bad-tempered major gave him. Say what you like about the man, Fierro clearly intended to be at the van of the attacking units.

"Twenty to twenty-two thousand, laddie," Fergus had said the night before when Corey asked for an estimate of the troops at Villa's disposal. "Obregón must have about the same number, but most of his are infantry and I imagine he's tucked them away in the ditches pretty neatly. Villa has far more big guns, but with those Chihuahuan shells he'll have to advance them to badly exposed sites to do him any good, and it may take him a while to discover that. His enemy outnumbers him in machine guns almost four to one, too. It will be a verra interesting operation, to say the least."

Corey chafed. He wanted to get forward to a better position for observation as quickly as possible, but as long as the picture-takers weren't moving toward the front his escort showed little inclination even to start the car. The boy plainly was hoping he would become a movie star. He had a tiny hairbrush he used to tidy a silky mustache whenever a cinema crew came anywhere near the two of them. A steady stream of officers seemed to be paying even more court to the small army of cameramen than did the lieutenant. At first he thought they wanted to be recorded for posterity as did the youngster at the wheel of the motorcar, but then he realized they were only killing time, waiting for something—or someone. Perhaps he wasn't missing anything, after all.

He knew it to be the truth when three more units of cavalry swung around the corner of the warehouse holding Division headquarters and filled the main south road. Lieutenant Gómez beat on the automobile's horn with his fist until Corey thought he might go deaf.

"Los Dorados!" Gómez shouted over the noise of the horn as the first of the new squadrons cantered by the car.

Of course!

The battle would not truly begin until Pancho Villa's famed strike force was in position for the first attack. He might have known. The Tiger would go with the tactics which had subdued Chihuahua City, Ciudad Juárez, Torreón, Paredón, and even more recently Guadalajara in Jalisco in the wake of Fierro's and Contreras's sad performances. But this performance could be as sad, if Villa tried to use the cavalry against Obregón's fixed positions in the same, now possibly outdated way.

He wondered what Felipe Ángeles would be thinking now.

As if the thought of the great artillerist had pulled their lanyards, the field guns far to the south began to talk. They must have been moved up during the night or very early in the morning, and with the advance squadrons now there to protect them they were signaling the beginning of the conflict. The barrages continued for perhaps half a minute and then stopped. Why? The firing certainly hadn't been sustained long enough to soften up the cavalry's objectives or to cut supply lines at Obregón's rear, and surely the enemy couldn't possibly have overrun the batteries yet. When a full minute had gone by without any further sound from the distant guns, Corey decided the forward observers had now seen that the Chihuahuan shells were landing far short of their targets, just as Fergus had predicted. How long would it take to move them within range? Would Pancho wait?

The second group of cavalrymen were now moving past the car. Compared to the resplendent Dorados, this bunch was a rabble, with a hodgepodge of arms and equipment, poorly mounted, and only wearing the rudiments of the uniform of the Northern Division. "Los Diablos," Gómez said. His tone was one of contempt.

Los Diablos! This was the leper squadron to whose command Major Trinidad Álvarez had been banished. Yes, there he was, rising at the far side of the ragged column. Corey waved, but the major either didn't see him or was too occupied to reply. Perhaps too ashamed? If such was the case he was hiding it more or less successfully. His head was high and his left hand was sure and steady on the reins. A firm right hand was curled around the hilt of a saber in an ornate scabbard. Corey thought about shouting to him, thought better of it immediately; you didn't intrude on the private mental processes of a man riding out to meet the enemy.

As it turned out, it was fortunate Corey hadn't called to him.

Rodolfo Fierro was riding back up the line, his eyes wide and white. He turned his horse when he reached the major, rode tandem with him for a pace or two, and then both men reined in their horses. Fierro was doing all the talking. After a moment Álvarez lifted his hand from the sword and saluted. He set his spurs deep in the flanks of his mount, and the animal bounded forward. Fierro was smiling now.

Orders had just been given. Corey had no time to think about what he had seen, but it sank into the back of his mind. The first units of another, much, much larger cavalry force than either of the other two were brushing past the car, and this outfit he recognized from Zacatecas as the Bracomontes. Jorge Martínez commanded a troop in this regiment.

He searched the faces of the riders, but with no result. Perhaps the young man from Chupadera County wasn't to fight today. But that didn't seem likely, either. From everything Corey had been able to see, smell, and hear this morning,

Villa was holding no troop, no carbine or field gun, no single *guerrero*, in reserve. The lame and halt would fight today. Jorge rode somewhere in that pushing, pulsing mass of animals and men, even if Corey couldn't see him. It was just that the war had suddenly become faceless, as all wars eventually do when both the alluring and the ugly masks are ripped away.

Fierro, after leaving Álvarez, had ridden to the front of the warehouse-headquarters building, and the photographers were swarming on him. Again something positive about the Butcher struck Corey. He seemed discomfited by the attention he was getting, impatient to have done with it, and the flaring of the magnesium flash pans seemed a nasty irritant. This violent man was no glory hound. Indeed, this was a man content to remain in the hulking shadow of another; he was a man with no genuine identity of his own. Rodolfo Fierro was the dark-side *doppelgänger* of Francisco Villa. Was there a light-side equivalent somewhere? It wasn't Felipe Ángeles; Ángeles was his own man. No. If Pancho had a light-side counterpart it was Mexico itself. Remembering Narciso Trujillo's words again, Corey wondered just how light that side could be in this age that turned itself back on other dark ages in the Nietzchean "eternal circle" Narciso had spoken of.

But now the reporters and photographers abandoned their wooing of Fierro and were gathering around the main door of the warehouse, almost fighting each other in their efforts to get close to it. He knew why.

The shouts shivered the air. "*¡Viva Villa! ¡Viva Villa! ¡Viva Villa!*"

The door to the small office where Corey had met the general gaped open and the Tiger of the North came through it. Dressed for riding this morning, he looked as if he would have taken the doorjambs off if they hadn't been wide enough. He raised his two thick arms above his head and the flashes from the cameras turned the gray spring day into a summer storm, but his wide grin outshone even the magnesium-fired lightning.

From nowhere a *muchacho* no bigger than a copper centavo coin, and as brown, appeared, leading a magnificent white horse. When Villa swung up into the saddle the roar erupted from the crowd again, the big horse reared, and its rider waved his sombrero in triumphant circles above his head. Yes, this was Pancho Villa!

With the animal's feet firmly on the ground again, Villa rode the few yards to where Fierro sat his horse. The photographers tried to follow, but a swift swing of the strong free arm stopped them cold. Villa bent his head toward the Butcher, spoke at some length, then clapped his listener on the shoulder. Fierro wheeled his mount and at a touch the horse moved into a gallop, heading south on the heels of the now disappearing Bracomontes.

Villa turned and settled his gaze directly on Corey. In the blink of an eye the white horse was at the car.

"*Buenos días,* Señor Lane. It is a fine morning for a battle, no?"

"It's a bit wet and cloudy, General, but I suppose it's as good a morning for it as any."

"You are a fatalist, then, *hombre?*"

"Not precisely, sir, but I do believe a victory is like gold—it is where one finds it."

"*¡Bueno!* I like your way of thinking."

"General Villa?"

"*¿Sí?*"

"Will General Ángeles join you for this battle?"

Villa's heavy lids drooped into a soft squint. "You think Pancho cannot fight a battle without Felipe?"

Bad mistake. Corey wasn't home free by a wide margin yet, nor was Ángeles. There was still some tiny, residual resentment of the strategist, apparently. "No, sir. It's just that it might be a different fight without him."

Villa shrugged. Good. His pique had only been a momentary thing. What was it that Henry had said about President Wilson's characterization of the strongman? "That natural animal." True enough. One thing about Francisco Villa he could trust. He harbored no duplicity. Every emotion he showed, no matter how dangerous or wrong, was an honest one.

"*No, amigo.* Felipe will not be with the Division today, nor for the duration of the battle. His horse fell on him last week, and he cannot walk or ride. Great man though he is, Felipe does not ride like Pancho does."

"Do you intend to go immediately over to the offensive, General Villa?"

"*¡Sí!* My enemy Álvaro Obregón has already played into *mis manos,* Señor Lane."

"How so, sir?"

"Scouts have reported that he has foolishly moved General Maycotte's cavalry brigade west of Celaya in a stupid attempt to flank our positions. I have sent Rodolfo to fall upon them with the full weight of Los Dorados, the Bracomontes, and even his personal ruffians, Los Diablos. They will attack within the hour. In the meantime the main body of the Division will move into the center to prepare for the truly big offensive. This front will stretch for seven miles. Our cavalry will ride circles around Álvaro's pitiful riflemen. They cannot cover ground as horsemen can."

He was close to making a believer of Corey. If Pancho Villa wasn't invincible, who in this struggle was?

"May Lieutenant Gómez and I drive down to watch, General?" Gómez, who had been gazing worshipfully at Villa, snapped his head around, eyes alight with expectation. Good. He wanted to get near the fighting as much as Corey did, perhaps more. Playing nursemaid to a silent gringo must have been bothering him since the major turned Corey over to him. Villa burst into laughter, and then nodded.

"*Sí, hombre.*" He turned his dazzling smile to Gómez. "Take very good care of this gringo, *lugarteniente.* Keep him alive for General Fierro. The man I know you all call El Carnicero may want to shoot him someday soon. Rodolfo would not be happy if General Obregón did it first."

And without another word, Pancho Villa rode off to join his army.

42

"It's *loco*, Paco," Jorge said. "Why does Trini stand for it?"

"Because, like you, Captain Cockroach, he is a *soldado*. But don't ask me, ask him."

"He must have lost twenty-five or thirty of his men already, and half the day is left. I don't think the rest of his riders will follow him into another attack."

"Oh, they'll follow. *Sí.* If they don't, El Carnicero will have them shot. They know they have less chance with him than they do with the Carrancistas. Perhaps *el gran general* Fierro has a plan he hasn't told us about."

"Plan? *¡Mierda!* What kind of plan has less than a hundred men charging the same dug-in positions twice without a rest? Their horses can't take it, never mind the men. The least he could do would be to send us in to support them. The brigade has made one attack, with more than five hundred riders, and we only reached the first line of ditches. Trini and his lousy Diablos were lucky to get within a hundred meters. They were even luckier that they didn't lose a lot more men than they did."

"Well," Paco said, heaving a gargantuan sigh. "We weren't really after the machine guns, anyway, Jorge. We were only supposed to destroy Maycotte's cavalry. And we did that. El Carnicero only sent us after the guns then. Even the small damage we did there is *salsa*. And maybe it's all he will ask Trini to do today."

"*Dios,* I hope so. I never saw such insanity, sending our most ineffective unit against Obregón's best time after time. If that is a plan, then I'm La Virgen de Guadalupe!"

"I know, I know, Jorge. But orders are orders. I didn't see Trini hesitate when Fierro sent him in alone. If it was you, you'd do the same."

"Don't be too damned sure of that, Paco. I'm not an idiot. Can you see Fierro's messenger?"

"He rode toward Los Diablos just a minute ago."

"For Christ's sake! Is he sending them in a third time?"

"Fierro is a stubborn man." He put his hand on Jorge's shoulder. "Look on the bright side, *amigo*. We have gained much. And even if Trini fails we've softened the gun positions for tomorrow."

"One more ridiculous charge and Trini won't see tomorrow. Look to our own wounded now, Paco, and report back to me."

The dynamiter moved his horse out from under the eaves of the farm shed Jorge had decided would be *la tropa*'s rally point.

Damn it! If it hadn't been for the mad waste of Los Diablos in this early afternoon, it would have been a splendid day, perhaps his very best as a Bracomonte captain. Until the ridiculous attacks on the machine gunners, the troop had been superb, catching fire from Los Dorados cascading toward the enemy on their left when they surprised Maycotte's careless squadrons in open country, a kilometer away from their supporting infantry and more than half that distance from the protection of the ditches. The cavalry action had become a one-sided affair after that first attack. Fifteen minutes and complete success. *¡Magnífico!*—if he could *ever* make himself feel good about the bloodshed and waste. More than a hundred prisoners, many of them dying, and three times that number of the enemy slaughtered outright. Division casualties, while not inconsiderable, were but a fraction of Maycotte's. Since Paredón the sight of dead men and blasted pieces of men, dead or barely alive, hadn't become a bit more appealing, but now he did somehow manage to feel something very close to good. The madness and mayhem was better than the apathy of the winter months and the corrosive effect of robbing trains and banks. He was a *guerrero* once again. For an hour he was as buoyed up as a man in combat could ever be. And for another hour, until Fierro ordered the first big charge on the ditches, he had mused more than once that perhaps Trini wasn't right; perhaps the days of horses in warfare weren't numbered, after all. They had been irresistible and terrible this morning.

None of this, though, were he to be completely honest, was the *main* reason for his euphoria.

The Division, the brigade, the regiment, *la tropa,* and Jorge María Martínez in particular, had been blessed with a special audience.

Before they had swung into action, and from the shelter of this same dilapidated shed, he had spotted Emilio Gómez and his passenger, Corey Lane.

His heart had swelled to the size of a *calabaza* under his cartridge belts, and for the first time he realized how much he wanted the good opinion, not just of Chupadera County, but of this particular Chupadera County gringo. This had been before the first attack on the machine guns sobered him.

Knowing Lane was watching the Bracomontes, he had fought his own personal war almost to the point of foolhardiness, riding nearly up the backs of a half dozen fleeing Maycotteros, praying that the enemy horsemen would turn about and make a fight of it; he had no wish to shoot any man—even the most evil Carrancista—in the back, not with the tall lawman looking on. Thank the good *Dios*, the Maycotteros did turn, fighting with *mucho coraje*, if firing wildly. He kept himself forward in his saddle, and his horse on a direct line for their panic-blinded guns. The confusion which had ridden with him in every fight since Torreón was curiously absent all through the charge. His targets were crystal clear. Two of Maycotte's men fell to his carbine before the others turned tail again and galloped back toward the Obregonista lines. Halfway through the short fight he found himself wishing he had Trini's sword, even if he had never wielded one in combat. It would have been something marvelous indeed to cut and slash under Corey Lane's gray eyes. Never mind. He had done well, and Lane had seen him, he was sure of it. The sun had come out briefly while they came to grips with the enemy, and when the *tropa* broke off that first engagement and he wheeled his horse around, the reflection from Lane's binoculars had blinded him for a second. When his eyes cleared he saw the man from Chupadera County standing in the rear seat of the automobile. *¡Bueno!* The sheriff or journalist or whatever Lane was had gotten an eyeful, or two or three. Had Lane then waved at him? He couldn't tell for sure, but he waved himself, and got an answering wave from Gómez.

Sí. In the main he was satisfied. He hadn't lost a man in the sally, although six took wounds, but with only one sustaining more than scratches. It was an almost picture-perfect cavalry operation. When he rallied the *tropa*, and galloped them to the comparative safety of this empty shed, he hoped Lane would have Gómez drive him over. He hadn't the faintest idea what he might say to him, but he knew he was ready to talk with Corey Lane at last, and he could talk with him as a highly successful *capitán de caballería* at the moment, a quietly proud victor.

But the euphoria faded as quickly as a dream when a rider came to the shed and told him that General Fierro had ordered a full attack on the machine guns in the ditches, and that Los Diablos instead of Los Dorados were to lead the way. Pancho's pets under Major Navarro Ruiz would make up the right wing, with three *tropas* of Bracomontes on the left, one of them Jorge's own.

"At ten o'clock exactly, *señor capitán,*" the messenger told him. "You have a watch, no?"

"*Sí,* I have a watch. But is Fierro out of his fucking mind? The artillery hasn't worked those machine guns over yet. And there is nothing but a kilometer of mud and *vaca* shit between here and the enemy lines! When we reach them we'll be moving about as fast as sick *tortugas.* This is work for big guns and infantry, and we have neither."

"Do you want me to tell General Fierro you decline to fight, *amigo*?"

His stomach soured, and he hawked up a gob of bitter-tasting spit. He wished he could spray it in Fierro's wolflike face. His back stiffened, and heat rose in him like a fountain.

"Tell our *loco* general that Tropa Martínez of the Bracomontes will be happy to oblige him in this formula for disaster."

The messenger shrugged his indifference, saluted with a faint look of derision, said *"Hasta luego,"* and rode off.

Jorge checked his watch. Fierro hadn't left him but three and a half minutes until the jump-off. Precious little time to let his riders finish licking wounds, less for him and Paco to check weapons and ammunition, still less for them to herd *la tropa*'s exhausted riders and their horses into line again. Nervous as the prospect of the attack made him, he felt only half the concern for himself and his men that he felt for Trini. The major had engaged the Maycotteros, too, in that first furious outing. He and his motley command had ridden a course against the enemy five hundred meters closer to the machine guns than that of the Bracomontes, not right at the apex of their deadliest cross fire, but still well within lethal range, and Jorge, just before his own attack rolled up the enemy's flank, had seen three Los Diablos riders swept from the saddle. It was hard to make out individual riders in the melee that followed, particularly after the sun went behind the clouds again. Only the pale flashes from Trini's sword reassured him his friend was still alive and fighting.

Trini and Los Diablos had regrouped in a grove of stunted trees just two plowed fields away from Jorge's *tropa* while fresh squadrons, the main force of the brigade held in reserve at the beginning—the only sensible move Fierro had made so far—roared out and harried the remnants of Maycotte's cavalry streaming westward in disarray. Even when the battle moved some distance farther off, the screams of horses rose above the rattle of the Villista rifles and the drumming of Obregón's machine guns.

There wasn't time for him to ride over and meet with Trini before the five squadrons set out again across mushy green fields stretching away to the machine guns in the ditches. It was a pitiful attack from the outset, and all he could hope for was that when they ran into the hot wall of lead sure to rise in front of them, they would be too far away for Lane to see, even through his glasses. God forbid the tall gringo should think this disgrace typical of the way the Division fought an important battle. He forgot about that when the first bursts came from the ditches. The Obregonista gunners were good. Deadly. They set up a withering enfilade that stripped the leaves from the new bean plants in a wide swath in front of the attacking squadrons. Trini's Diablos, well ahead of Los Dorados and the three Bracomonte troops, caught the worst of it, but through the smoke he could still see the saber urging the Diablos on. "*Viva*, Trini," he muttered to himself as he raised his right fist for the all-out charge.

He left four of his own men lying in the new green stubble of the trampled, muddy bean field, and when they rallied at the shed again, Paco told him that three of those who had made it back after Tonito sounded the retreat had fought for the last time today, one of them, a fat corporal named Herrera, doubtlessly forever, his huge stomach laid wide open by the ripping fire from the ditches, the wounds gushing blood where he lay in the mud at the corner of the shed. Regrettable losses, every last one of them, but the attack wasn't quite the calamity for the troop it might have been. His instincts had served him well when he sniffed failure and signaled back to Tonito to trumpet an end to it.

Well, he, Paco, and Trini had finished with their fighting for the moment, too; surely even a commander as rash and stupid as El Carnicero would see the futility of going on until the artillery could zero in on the enemy positions.

Then, to his consternation, he heard the bugler of Los Diablos blow *al ataque*, and saw Trini lead his riders across the field again. The major was a miracle worker, nothing less. Los Diablos to a man were misfits, worse, the dregs of the army, but you couldn't tell it now. They were riding like genuine *soldados a caballos* today at least. He might have known. What was it Trini had said once? "There are no small commands, just small commanders."

When he looked to see if Lane was still watching, he discovered Gómez had run the car down a path alongside an irrigation ditch two or three hundred meters closer to the enemy positions, just barely out of rifle and machine-gun range. *Muy valiente,* this gringo. He felt a tiny surge of hometown pride.

All by themselves now, Los Diablos were drawing four times the fire they had in the first sally. The attack had no hope of success at all. Trini was pressing it toward the Obregonistas a bit farther now, but a glance told Jorge he couldn't possibly get as much as twenty meters closer than the first time, not with any living riders. At least half a dozen more Los Diablos men fell as they neared the breastworks, and by the time they turned about to seek the haven of the grove of trees, riderless horses were running helter-skelter across the field. Men on foot were running, too, some of them taking wounds in their backs that seemed to be sawing them into bloody halves. One of them, staggering like a blind man, looked like Trini at this distance, and Jorge Martínez's breathing stopped.

Fierro's messenger was waiting for the ruptured Los Diablos formation when it reached the trees. Then Jorge saw Trini slip from the saddle, unharmed from the way he moved, and he drew a breath at last. That should close off combat for the day.

But then, and this time to his horror, not mere consternation, he saw Trini mount again, raise his sword, and begin walking his horse southward toward Celaya. Los Diablos filed in behind him, and in half a minute they fanned out into another attacking skirmish line.

There were a dozen fewer of them when they returned to their cover in the trees this time.

¡En el nombre de Dios! They didn't even dismount before Trini turned them and formed them up again. Surely Fierro wouldn't send them in yet again without the field guns, but where in hell *were* the guns? Jorge's blood boiled up, threatened to blow right out of his ears. Someone had to stop this.

Then his mind focused hard on exactly what was taking place.

"Paco," he said, "I want to send a message to the general. Who can we spare?" He took his pad and pencil from his shirt pocket and began to scribble a note.

"If you're writing what I think you're writing, Jorge, I don't think it's such a good idea. General Fierro doesn't like advice."

"It's not advice, *viejo*. It's a formal protest."

"Then it's an even worse idea than I thought, Captain Cockroach. Protest? It is an accusation, too, no?"

"*¡Sí!* But don't you see what this really is, Paco?"

"*¿Qué?*"

"*It's murder!* You were right. Fierro does have a plan. But it has nothing to do with the battle we are fighting. *He wants Trini killed!* He planned this a long time ago." Was he seeing things, or were there tears in the big sergeant's eyes?

"You are probably right, Jorge. *Sí*—I know you are. El Carnicero has not forgotten. But don't you see that if you interfere he will arrange something just like this for you? And you don't have General Ángeles to buy you even the little time he bought for Trini."

"We can't just let this *happen*, Paco! Assemble *la tropa*! We're going in, too."

"*Sí, amigo*. But we can't help. By the time we reach him, there will be nothing left of Los Diablos. We'll be as alone as they are now."

"No, we can't help him. But with luck we can *stop* him!"

He didn't wait for Paco to mount the troop. He gouged his horse with his spurs. The mud sucked at the horse's hooves.

Half a mile away another man recognized the criminal folly of General Rodolfo Fierro's plan of attack.

Corey Lane had held the binoculars to his eyes for so long and with such unconscious, fierce pressure his forehead felt as if a vise had gripped it for a year. The physical pain was nothing, though, compared to the despair growing within him. He pulled the glasses from his eyes.

It was only one battle, important surely, but not Armageddon, and it hadn't been lost yet. As a matter of fact, on the face of things, the morning's astonishing action had been one of singular success. The Villistas had smashed Maycotte's brigade to pieces, routed it, inflicted harrowing casualties, and if their own had been heavy in the subsequent ridiculous and ineffectual charges on Obregón's machine gunners and infantry, they certainly hadn't been insupportable.

And yet—he knew as surely as he knew his own name that Pancho Villa had lost the battle for Celaya. He knew it before he and Lieutenant Emilio Gómez had swallowed the last dry, tasteless morsel of the lunch they had brought with them. It would take days yet, but the outcome was as sure as death. And there would be a lot of that.

Corey Lane had never been privy to the thoughts of Major Trinidad Álvarez on the subject, but he knew as well as did that exemplary officer that the day of cavalry in warfare had long since waned. That day had ended at Zacatecas just as it must have ended one day in the first few months of the war in Europe. It was a lesson he had learned himself in Cuba, when his own Rough Riders left their saddles with reluctance, to make the dangerous but victorious walk up San Juan Hill. In that walk they had become, willy-nilly, infantry—the Queen of Battles.

This morning the daring riders of the Bracomontes and the Dorados had performed with brilliance, as had even the less skilled and soldierly Diablos—whose fight had been a tribute to their commander, Álvarez—but the engagement was really and truly only an echo from the past. If only they had stopped after they defeated Maycotte. What would transpire before the week was out on these green and crimson fields would break the hearts of old horse soldiers everywhere. It was already transpiring. With a deepening sense of foreboding, and a little sadness, he knew he had witnessed in the repeated attacks on the trenches of Celaya today the beginning of the destruction of the finest light cavalry army of the twentieth or perhaps any other century.

Easy enough to blame Fierro. But the fault was not his alone. Pancho himself should answer, too. Fierro for all his multiple faults was only waging war the way he thought— hell, *knew*—his chief wished him to. The horse that fell on General Felipe Ángeles should share the blame as well. Only the cool head of the great strategist of Zacatecas could have turned Pancho and the Division aside from the mad path they were galloping along.

Ángeles. A defeat for Villa here at the gates of Celaya might mean the end of his ascendancy, a far more crushing blow both for Mexico and Corey than the loss of a single battle, no matter how crucial it might be.

But by two o'clock Corey persuaded himself that the day's events had probably run their course. The day of reckoning had been postponed. He felt relief and satisfaction that Jorge Martínez and Major Trinidad Álvarez would live to fight more battles. A blessing. They had both taken enough losses to last them for a while, Álvarez far more than just enough.

Then, at the same instant that Jorge Martínez was shaken with horror that his friend and teacher was making yet another attack, the same shudder rippled through Corey Lane as he watched Los Diablos move out from the grove of trees. Not again! With only a handful of riders well behind the major, there was no way any of them could survive an assault on the fixed positions which had erupted in flame time after time during the gray, muggy afternoon. He stared at Álvarez's slowly advancing squadron in disbelief. Was the major crazy? Even disoriented by those foolish, futile charges, Álvarez couldn't have suddenly lost *all* his senses. He heard Lieutenant Gómez gasp. Yes, even a soldier this young would see someone *else* had ordered this insanity.

When he lifted the glasses to his eyes again, he saw the major had spurred his horse into a clumsy counterfeit of a charge. The animal must be verging on collapse. He swept the glasses back toward the rest of the Diablos and found that just beyond them another lone rider was spurring his mount full tilt toward Álvarez. Jorge Martínez! His carbine was pouring fire at the distant ditches. He must have known it was useless. Good man, young Martínez. He must have set out only to turn Álvarez back. But in another three seconds the major would be beyond help or turning. He had somehow coaxed some speed from his bone-tired horse and had now outdistanced his command by at least a hundred yards. There was now no way the young man from Chupadera County could reach him before he stared right down the barrels of the waiting guns. Álvarez, his saber pointed at the enemy, closed to within a hundred and fifty yards of the first line of ditches. The riders behind him had reined up sharply.

Then, as Corey swung the binoculars back on him, Major Trinidad Álvarez took a direct hit from something of considerably larger caliber than a machine-gun shell.

The horse crumpled under him. His body arched into the sky above the horse's head. The sword spun through the air, light winking from it as it twisted and landed tip-first in the ground a dozen feet past the point where the major fell, the blade vibrating then in the severed bean plants like a tuning fork. Nothing stirred in the limp body of Major Trinidad Álvarez.

"Turn, Jorge, turn," Corey implored, hurling the words into the noise of battle with all his might. "You can't help him now!"

"¡Basta, Jorge, basta!" Gomez shouted.

But Martínez didn't turn. He was beating his animal with the reins in his left hand as he stuck his carbine back into his saddle holster with his right. Was the young fool so unhinged by what had happened that he intended finishing the major's futile charge himself?

The ground in front of him and at either side was stitched with death.

He rode straight for the saber, leaned from the saddle at a frightening angle, and jerked it from the ground.

Only then did he turn his horse.

Juanita Durán watched in silence as Jorge laid Trini's sword in Margarita Espinosa's lap, shuddered as Margarita shuddered.

"I am sorry, Margarita," Jorge said. "I could not get the scabbard. It was under the body of Trini's horse. I will look for it if we go that way again tomorrow."

The captain-nurse, her eyes as dry as the Chihuahuan desert, looked down at the bright steel blade with its golden inlays. She put out a trembling hand toward it, drew it back as swiftly as if the blade were glowing red. "No, Jorge, *por favor*. Do not try. You must keep your mind only on staying alive yourself. That is all that matters now."

Juanita's heartbeat slowed.

Jorge spread his hands. "Trini once told me he wanted his father in Tamaulipas to have his sword if anything happened to him, but I think he would be even happier knowing it was in *your* care."

Margarita looked surprised. "Oh, I don't want it, Jorge. I don't even want to touch it. I will, however, take it to his father if someone will wrap it for me. I can do it on my way back to the United States. I leave the Division on the first train north tomorrow. I am going home."

A faint sob broke from Juanita's mouth.

"We will miss you," Jorge said.

"Jorge . . ." Margarita said. Her face, dead as stone and white with shock until this moment, turned hard and angry. At least the anger made it seem touched with life. "Why don't you come with me?" She turned to Juanita. "Forgive me, *cariña*." Then, to Jorge again, "We don't belong here, you and I. I'm not sure this country even wants us. Yes, it is long past time for you, too, to go back home."

Juanita Durán's heartbeat now seemed to have disappeared altogether. She closed her eyes. Would her *soldado*'s answer kill her?

"No, Margarita," Jorge said. "I cannot go back home. Not yet. Perhaps I can never go back home. There are still some things in Mexico for me to do."

"Things to do? You mean more killing."

"*Sí.* I suppose I do. But there is much living for me to do here, *también*. And as well as living myself, there are some other things I must keep alive."

43

▲▲▲▲▲

Corey finished packing and took a last look around his room in the Mirador to see if he was forgetting anything. The high-ceilinged room with the faded, slate-blue and off-white wallpaper and the gilt-framed mirrors had actually been home for a long time, and he would miss it—for a while. The hotels on the Paseo were jammed, and by dinnertime Señor Gabaldon would have a brand-new tenant in residence; five minutes after the new occupant unpacked there would be no sign that Corey Lane of Black Springs, New Mexico, Special Foreign Service Officer of the United States, had ever lived here. He would leave virtually no sign he had ever known the capital. He had certainly left no imprint on it in the half year that had passed so swiftly since the Battle of Celaya.

Just as well. His sojourn in Mexico had been a sad sequence of failure after failure. With Luisa persuaded that the troubles in her home state were almost over, going back to Durango on the afternoon train, no one in Mexico City save Narciso would remember him, much less lament his leaving.

Wait, he had forgotten Fergus. Fergus would miss him. But only for the briefest moment, and he didn't know where Fergus was operating now, anyway. He hadn't seen him since six weeks after they left Irapuato, when the two of them drove down through the somber, smoking, and deathly silent battlefield of Celaya, where the dreams of Pancho Villa and Felipe Ángeles had gone glimmering. The tough, resourceful, and for two months now strangely absent and secretive Scot apparently had enough to keep him occupied these last days of 1915 with what he had uncovered about Wolf Kemper and that *éminence grise*, von Rintelen. It was idle to speculate about what Kennedy was up to now, but the British agent's look of triumph back in Irapuato—about something he still hadn't as yet disclosed—continued to puzzle Corey, please him, too. If only *his* mission in the north had been a tenth so successful. It hadn't been, and it would be better not to dwell on it—just leave here with "modest stillness and humility . . ." Humility, yes, he had humility in plenty.

In the larger sense there was nothing so new or different about this departure. Root-bound in the rock-hard caliche of the Ojos Negros as he had been almost all his adult life, his history had been one long goodbye to many things other than that forlorn but deeply loved landscape, things not regretted so much as twenty minutes after they were put away from him. Had the steps he had taken since boyhood always been away from things, not toward them? Had his history been nothing but a closing in of himself, and on himself?

It wasn't true with Luisa. He was still moving toward her. His love for her, even now growing by leaps and bounds, and her full-hearted response, were the only suns smiling on him in the shadows of his losses here.

He would board the train with her for the journey north. He had mixed feelings about the trip. As elated as he had been at the prospect of a time alone with her apart from the concerns, troubles, and defeats of the past year and a half, and as much as he looked forward to seeing her home in Durango, and making the discoveries about her childhood she had expressed an almost compulsive desire to have him learn, part of him sickened at the thought of crossing still another time the field north of Celaya where nearly a third of the División del Norte had fallen in the two weeks of fighting following the death of Trinidad Álvarez. The flat green landscape was still smoking when he and Fergus left it; it would smoke in his mind forever. Some of the smoke would take the shape of Felipe Ángeles and Corey's dreams for him. Yes, smoke was all that remained of that. And the winds of chance were fast blowing it away.

He had come down from Celaya as beaten as any Villista, but not quite yet defeated in his hopes for Felipe Ángeles, and still a firm believer in what he had told himself that first day, when he had held the field glasses to his eyes and watched Jorge Martínez lead his troop into the thickening heat of conflict. At that moment, hazardous as things appeared, the battle hadn't yet been lost, much less the war. He had deluded himself in the ensuing days that Ángeles would ride in from the north as a *deus ex machina* and save the day, but even when that failed to happen he had somehow been able to hold despair at bay. Perhaps he still had some of that faith in Francisco Villa that made otherwise reasonable men throw themselves toward death the way they did.

For two days Villa had hurled his horse brigades against Obregón, trying to tempt the Carrancista cavalry into battle in the open, but Carranza's stubborn, tenacious, irritating little general had held fast to the trenches Bajío farmers had dug over the generations for altogether different reasons, cutting down the riders of even the brilliant Dorados as swiftly as those farmers had scythed their fields to stubble in more peaceful times.

During the week following the attacks Corey witnessed, the Division regrouped, resupplied to the extent that Calzado's coal-deprived freight trains would permit, patched up the wounded, and prepared for another assault. He tried to see Villa, but high-rankers—particularly the hate-filled Fierro himself—and minor staff members alike, rebuffed him at every try. The Chihuahuan must have been hiding away from any possible criticism of the conduct of the battle, an improbable Achilles sulking somewhere in an adobe tent.

Corey finally tracked down Jorge Martínez, but their exchange was as short, sharp, and final as a pistol shot.

"I think you should go home, Jorge. You know it's safe now. Juanita did tell you, didn't she?"

"*This* is where I belong, Señor Lane."

He wanted to ask Jorge about the sword he had rescued, wanted to tell him what an act of courage it was, but the young man walked away.

Corey kept looking northward for Ángeles while the Division gathered its strength again, almost praying for the sight of him, but the general never came to Irapuato.

For a week he still didn't abandon hope. Even without his great lieutenant at his side, Corey felt sure that Pancho Villa must have learned *something* from the first two disastrous days of Celaya.

But when the Division went over to the offensive again after five days of rest, it was immediately clear such wasn't the case at all.

Squadron after squadron broke themselves against the machine guns, riding across fields turned to swamps when Obregón's engineers flooded them, abandoning attack formation and picking their way through the bodies of men and horses still not removed after the first days' fighting, seeking death almost intentionally, it seemed. The carnage was ghastly, the smell when the sun finally came out an evil, all-pervading, rotting presence. When the buzzards finished with the corpses, the fields would be ossuaries: scattered bones and bleached, grinning skulls white accents on the muddy green. *Fiesta,* Narciso had called the Revolution in his sad, weary voice. Corey Lane had another word for it.

One battle, only one battle, he kept telling himself in a litany of fading expectations. But two more like it and Pancho Villa, Felipe Ángeles, the legacy of Francisco Madero, and the hopes of Mexico would be memories.

When a month had passed, those two more battles had also been fought and lost.

It was time for him to leave, but more memories struck him.

He and Fergus had talked but little as they drove south from Irapuato and then veered westward to give Obregón's patrols a wide berth, but the Scot's spirits seemed irrepressible. He sang snatches of songs in Scots Gaelic as they made their way through the desolation of the bean fields and then on through the emptier deserts sloping upward toward the mountains. Corey grew mildly vexed from time to time that Kennedy could be so cheerful in the face of such a monumental setback for the cause he had supported, tacitly at least.

When they pulled up to the entrance of the Mirador two days later, and as they unloaded Corey's gear, Fergus finally said: "It should please ye to hear, laddie, that while ye were trying to help Pancho and Ángeles stay alive in this bloody

Revolution, auld Fergus discovered exactly how von Rintelen and Kemper get their instructions from Germany. It might amuse ye, but then again it might not."

"The German Embassy?"

"Nay, lad. Zimmermann, Kaiser Bill's Foreign Secretary, runs the two of them personally. For all of his more important moves he trusts *them* more than he does his own ambassador. Signals reach them from Berlin by way of Buenos Aires. Bonnie arrangement."

"Why?"

"Take a guid grip on your tam-o'-shanter. They cross the North and South Atlantic by ordinary cable."

"What's so unusual about that? I'd expect it, sure."

"What ye wouldn't expect, though, is that the cable lines are owned by the *United States* and run by Henry Richardson's bosses in Washington. You Americans are babes in the woods in the great game. Strangely enough, I find it a wee bit lovable. As I said, it's amusing."

It didn't amuse Corey, but it didn't particularly trouble him. He had enough other worries at the moment. He had to report to Henry without delay.

"It was terrible, Henry," he said to the Bostonian when he got him on the phone a week after his return to the Mirador. "Can you and Secretary Lansing still hold the fort and keep the President from making his decision for a while?"

"We'll try, but frankly, Corey, time is running out. He now wants stability in Mexico more than he wants a fragile imitation of democracy. Unlike him, but Europe's on his mind to the exclusion of almost everything else these days." There was a pause. "Thanks for trying, old friend."

He had already rushed to Luisa's arms at Posada Melgar, feeling an overwhelming surge of passion when he reached them, but something else as well. Healing. He wasn't entirely sure which he wanted more.

Oddly, she didn't ask where he had been for the past two weeks, and when he tried to tell her, she cut him short.

"Never mind, Corey. I don't want to hear about it. You're

back. That's all that matters. Let's just enjoy each other while we can."

In spite of the downturns of fortune in every other thing, he was happy. Delirious. The act of love with Luisa astonished him. What a dolt he must have been when he first tried to imagine what it might be like on those silent rides back to the Mirador after a late supper or an evening at a concert, back when he was so sure Wolf Kemper was so much closer to her than he would ever be. He had suppressed his fantasies with ruthless determination. Now he found their intimate life together far more wonderful than the fantasies ever could have been had he allowed them.

Somehow he had conceived the notion that her cloistered Catholic childhood, a lifetime surrounded by luxury and wealth, where the everyday pedestrian occurrences of life were stately, formal promenades, would build a wall of physical reserve around her that would defy entrance by any suitor, no matter how skilled—as he most surely wasn't—or ardent—even as he most surely *was*—and deny any exit she might try to make herself. No wall of any kind stood between them. Their times together in the huge four-poster in her lavender-scented room at the *posada* left him giddy, satisfied until dawn took him back to the Mirador, and then more yearning and voracious as another day without her wore on, more in love than he had ever dreamed he possibly could be. She was absolutely free and generous with that breathtaking ivory body, totally uninhibited, her firm, soft flesh knowledgeable and sure.

No matter that he felt twinges of guilt, luxuriating in her love while Mexico broke and shattered, or that there wasn't world enough and time left for this unfortunate land.

When he had reported to Henry and settled in five months ago he saw Will Hendricks at the embassy.

He gave the major his impressions of Celaya.

Hendricks took in Corey's assessment in grim silence. Then, "Sadly, it was the same at León, Mr. Lane. General Ángeles joined Villa there, but it was far too late. Even he couldn't mend things by then. Fierro left most of Ángeles's guns on the field at Celaya. Almost all the Division had left in the way of effectives was the cavalry Obregón didn't hack up in his infantry counterattack in the second Celaya battle. I think it's all over but the shouting. I suppose it will drag out for another year or so, but Villa's finished."

"Ángeles?"

"Finished along with him."

Corey fought against the rage mounting within him. It was small comfort Hendricks looked devastated. He must himself. He said nothing. The major wouldn't, of course, know the answer to his other one-name question: Jorge Martínez?

"Where are the two forces now?"

"Obregón is doing exactly what he did with Zapata. He advances and digs in, then he outlasts his more impetuous enemy and counters. The French and Germans could take a lesson from him. Villa is moving back to the north. He's cleared out of the states of Guanajuato, Zacatecas, and all but a fraction of Durango. Looks like he'll set up shop in Chihuahua and try to do it all over again from his old power base. I don't think he'll make it. For one thing, he's out of money. He'll probably go back to banditry to refill his war chest, but the law of diminishing returns is at work with a vengeance. As things stand at present, if Obregón doesn't want it for himself, he's almost in a position to hand Mexico over to Carranza, lock, stock, and petroleum barrel."

"How do you feel about that, Will?"

"It's a prescription for catastrophe for this country. For the United States, too. Carranza hates us. But no one cares much about my opinion."

"I don't suppose it's much consolation, but I do."

"Thank you, sir."

Two nights ago Luisa had proposed the trip to Durango. "But I won't go unless you come with me, Corey." Yes, a respite from the turbulence of the capital had a powerful appeal. He could return to the fight for Ángeles, if one could still be made, renewed and vigorous.

Then, this morning, Henry had called.

"I'm sorry, Corey . . ." The heavy voice of the State Department man was an unmistakable warning gun for what he would say next. "It's all over. President Wilson has decided to recognize Venustiano Carranza and his government."

Even half-expected, it was a lethal blow.

"I'll get my resignation to you in Will Hendricks's next packet to Washington, Henry." It was the voice of another man from the one who had come to Mexico so long ago.

"No, no, Corey! Please. I don't want your resignation. I'm dreadfully sorry if it looks to you as if our government has wasted almost two years of your life to no good purpose. Don't resign, I beg of you. Go on back to Chupadera County for a rest, but keep in touch. We may not be quite done in Mexico, you and I."

"No, Henry, damn it! I'm through here. It's not just my failure about Ángeles, either. In these past six months I've gotten sick of my arrogance, and that of my country, too. What right have we to try to fix things here?"

Now, as he was almost ready to leave the Mirador for Posada Melgar to pick up Luisa for the train, he looked out the window into the teeming rush of the Paseo. Would he ever see this city again once the train left the station?

Yes, he would—if *she* came back here.

And despite Henry's well-intentioned advice, if she did, even Chupadera County would have to wait.

44

"There it is, Corey! The village lies just beyond those low hills. Those are the little towers of Iglesia de Santa María peeping up back of that jagged ridge." Luisa's almost child-like excitement was the same as on the day they shopped the *mercado* for the picnic at Xochimilco. This typical, sudden shift of mood from her deep quiet on the long, sticky journey through Guanajuato and Zacatecas no longer had the power to surprise him, but his delight in it was new every time. "We didn't go there often. Our family's chapel is on the *hacienda*, six kilometers to the west. In the old days we would have had the train stop here. There's no station here, but the López y Montenegros could stop even the first-class express trains back then. We had our own semaphore to signal the engineer. My father or our *maestro de caballos* would have been waiting by the track with horses for us. It's a lovely ride to the *hacienda*." As suddenly as joy had seized her, the last subsided into soft tones of bittersweet lament. Then, in bitterness with none of the sweet remaining, she went on, "Now we have to go all the way into Ciudad Durango and take a car back out to the *estancia*. It's another thirty kilometers up the line to Durango." He understood the drop in her spirits. Sorrow for lost times; some anger, too. Yes, he understood, but the darker times on the trip gave him pause, particularly as they came with more frequency with every additional mile separating them from Mexico City.

The train began to labor up a long curved grade cut through tawny granitic rock. From the little he could see of the steep roadbed ahead it would have to slow even more. "Why don't you nap for a bit, Luisa? The way we're poking along it will take another hour at least to reach Durango."

"Yes," she said. "I think I'll try." She closed her eyes. "I love you, darling." In less than a minute she was asleep. He hoped her dreams were good ones, untinged by regrets for the way things were.

As much as her waking, heady presence stirred him, he was grateful for a few moments alone with the thoughts brought on by the three days' train ride. The thoughts had attacked and troubled him, but he felt he had hidden it pretty well. Nothing should be allowed to spoil this trip. A descent of his own into a discernible black mood was the last thing he could permit himself.

But the sight of the Bajío just north of Celaya a day and a half ago had blasted him, brought everything that had happened there back in a sickening rush. He should have wiped it from memory by now, but he hadn't.

After the passage of six months, the smoke was gone, drifted out over the Caribbean on the breezes of history. But the smoke in his memory still rose and swirled, and, as with real smoke, clouded his eyes and left them burning, smarting—teary. Across the field of his blurred vision he saw the doomed attacks once more, the mud-hindered gallops of the Bracomontes and Dorados, and the earnest but stumbling advance of every rider of Los Diablos save their leader. He saw that leader fall again, and he blinked his eyes against the sight, blinked hard. He rubbed away whatever it was that turned his eyelids gummy.

When he opened his eyes again he saw no bleached bones, no skulls, no pale, inert skeletons of men or horses. No mud. No sign of slaughter. He should have known. The *campesinos* of the Bajío would have dug them into the rich soil months ago. The way had to be cleared last April for the year's second growing season.

Here and there small crosses lifted their arms inches above the vegetation, crude wooden affairs not unlike the *camposantos* that spiked the secluded hills north of Santa Fe and the stark Concho heights of Chupadera County. On the *lomas* of the Sangre de Cristos and the outcroppings of the Ojos Negros they were limned against the sky. Here they nestled in the leaves of bean plants. The crosses looked as if they had been staked into the earth many more seasons ago than the one just past; the invidious Guanajuato sun had weathered them to streaky gray, sweated the moisture from them, and twisted them until they looked as if they were tortured fossils of a primordial age.

It was harvest time, and the bean fields were browning out. When the yard-high plants were cut and mattocks skinned the earth again, more crosses would appear. Until then, the fields, partitioned into hectare squares by the all but invisible ditches which had hidden Obregón's machine guns, would remain what they were: shag-haired graves.

Graves or no graves, the charges of the Villista cavalry

were beginning again in his mind when Luisa touched him on the shoulder.

"You were here, Corey." It wasn't a question.

"Yes. How did you know?"

"Narciso."

"Narciso is a gossipy old woman sometimes."

"Did you *fight* on the side of the Villistas?"

"No, Luisa. I was only an observer."

"But like Narciso, you believe in their cause?"

"Yes."

She said nothing more about it.

After changing trains at San Luis Potosí they reached Zacatecas in the middle of the night.

He had awakened at Guadalupe, cramped and miserable in the raffia seats of their day coach. Luisa was sleeping peacefully beside him. She had been absolutely wonderful about their poor accommodations, never complaining, smiling as she remembered aloud that before the Revolution, during the Porfiriato, the coaches on this line had been rolling grand hotels, with European-style sleeping compartments and restaurant cars with chefs to rival those of any railroad in the world. The car they occupied today was fitted out no better than the coaches of the trains that made every stop between Boston and Springfield when he was in college in Massachusetts, not much better in fact than the one behind the engine, hardly more than a cattle car, where Tomás and Emilia were traveling with the luggage, jammed in with families transporting household goods, the ubiquitous pigs and chickens, and all the gatherings of stoop-labor lifetimes. His and Luisa's carriage bulged with men who looked like fairly prosperous shopkeepers, perhaps a lawyer and a doctor or two, and several small children with two stern women who could be governesses, one a nun. There was an obese *padre* in a full cassock snoring in a seat near the vestibule. When Corey and Luisa boarded the train at the capital's marble railway station he had guessed the priest was of considerable rank from his aloof, self-satisfied bearing, and Luisa had confirmed it, mur-

muring "Monsignor . . ." along with the slightest of curtsies, when they passed him to find their seats.

Did any of these assorted wayfarers know, and if they did, remember, what had happened on this jolting stretch of track?

An orange moon had exploded over the rounded tops of the barren hills to the east that Fergus and he had hungered and thirsted across before they rode into the plenty and peace of San Gabriel, and by its light he could see far down into the gorge that connected Guadalupe with Zacatecas. He picked out a dozen places as the one where they had bivouacked through that freezing night, and two dozen fords which could have been the one they used to cross the *río*. He was sure of each of them as the train approached it, and then just as sure it was somewhere else when they had passed. It was too long ago.

They stopped for the train to take on water in Zacatecas City. Luisa didn't awaken, but Corey stepped down to the platform and gazed upward toward the cathedral plaza. Hard to tell that little more than a year ago this city was a shambles. Harder still to remember Colonel Ruiz, the *calle*, Sargento Pérez, and the wall.

As they pulled away from the station, the moon, silver now, bathed lofty La Sierpe. Did phantom riders with carbines at the ready prowl its silent slopes even as others had raced across the Celaya fields just yesterday, or what seemed like yesterday?

At daybreak the conductor came through the coach and told them they were crossing into Durango state. With each passing mile Luisa's eyes grew brighter. "I am taking you home with me, Corey. You will love it as I do, I promise you."

Then without warning something pulled her down into one of those somber moods.

It was becoming a wearing day. For him, too. Her nap took her now into a deep sleep, and it didn't appear she would awaken for a while; the louder noises of the wheels on the grinding upgrade showed not the slightest sign of disturbing her.

Perhaps he should try to get forty winks himself. He probably couldn't . . .

He was fifteen years old and riding the high Mescalero with young Harold Bishop, Lucy's brother, racing the Apache youngster to Blazer's Mill, and losing as usual. It was hard to beat Harold anywhere in the big, close timber when he was on the bare back of the spotted pony; impossible when his sweet tooth was in full cry and there was a new shipment of hard candy waiting for him in the bins at the ramshackle general store. Hotchkiss School didn't teach you to compete on horseback with a son of a Red Paint warrior.

"Darn it, Harold!" he shouted against the wind. "You had an unfair head start!"

Harold looked back over his shoulder, his black hair a glistening flag. He grinned, slipped his rifle from his saddle holster, and fired shot after shot into the bright summer sky . . .

. . . the train convulsed to a shuddering stop.

The coach echoed with the sound of small-arms fire, and outside the sooty window uniformed riders were galloping along the right-of-way, firing into the canyon air. The volleys rose in a crescendo of staccato racket.

"What is it, Corey?" Luisa was upright, fully awake in an instant.

"Someone's stopped the train. I think it's a holdup."

"Tomás and Emilia! All my jewelry is in the bags they have with them in the car up front! They'll be in danger!"

"Maybe they'll be all right. If it is a holdup, the bandits probably won't want to take the time to go through all that stuff in the coach where they are. I expect they'll work this carriage over pretty hard, though, thinking that *here* is where the money is." He turned from the window and looked at her. "Will you be all right?"

She nodded. Her face, still soft from sleep, and with tiny pearls of moisture at the silver hairline, was changing. He saw no fear, but knew she must feel at least some apprehension. At a moment like this fear could be a valuable thing to have. Her head lifted, and her features firmed into a look he had never seen before.

"I won't let bandits think me afraid, Corey. Yes. I'll be all right." She slipped her slim hand into his.

The heavy tread of boots rang from the metal steps of the carriage. Faint, distant shouts threaded through the close air, but were drowned by the apprehensive rising talk among the passengers.

The seat they shared was well toward the back, but the man now blocking, totally filling, the door to the vestibule would have looked gigantic at five times the distance. He held a gunnysack opened wide at the mouth, his cartridge bandoliers crossed over a chest of magnificent proportions, and on the sleeve of a Villista uniform he wore sergeant's stripes. The excited mutterings in the coach faded swiftly into silence.

As he stepped inside, revealing two men with rifles following him, Corey realized he had seen this giant before, but he couldn't remember where.

The sergeant stopped at the seat holding the monsignor, and the fat clergyman struggled to his feet, lifted the skirt of his cassock, and pulled a wallet out of whatever garment he wore beneath it. One of the two riflemen rapped him smartly on the arm with the muzzle of his gun and then poked it at the monsignor's pink, puffy hand. The priest tugged at a large ring. He struggled with it. It must have graced that third finger so long fat had grown around it. The soldier who had nudged him with the rifle pulled a knife from somewhere, just before the ring came free. The *padre* dropped it in the sergeant's sack. Bills extracted from the wallet followed. The sergeant and his two soldiers moved along the aisle, passing right by the nun and her terrified woman companion. The huge sergeant stopped and smiled at the children, and then began taking what appeared to be willing offerings from the other passengers. They pressed money on him, thrust rings and watches in the sack. One dark-suited man reached into a valise and held up a bottle of wine. The sergeant shook his head, then smiled and nodded, and the bottle found its way into the sack as well. Not a word was spoken. It was as orderly a procedure as passing a collection plate at a Sunday service.

Corey felt Luisa's hand tighten in his, and as the sergeant neared them her nails dug into the palm of his hand. With every step the huge man took toward them they cut more deeply.

The locomotive let off steam, and from here near the end of the train the long, drawn-out hiss seemed like an ironic sigh, a small, misleadingly plaintive whisper of regret or resignation.

Then another uniformed figure appeared in the doorway at the far end of the car.

Corey didn't have to pick at his memory about this man. The slim, erect body clothed in the khaki of the Northern Division was that of Jorge Martínez.

Their eyes met. He remembered now where he had seen the sergeant. He had ridden by Jorge's side on that grisly field south of Irapuato. Lieutenant Gómez had pointed him out to Corey. His name was Durán. Yes Durán . . .

Now Jorge started down the aisle behind Durán.

The sergeant, still intent on gathering his loot, moved much more slowly and they both reached Corey and Luisa at the same time, with Jorge partly behind the big man with the gunnysack. Young Martínez had walked deliberately enough, but he hadn't taken his eyes from Corey's.

Jorge had changed again, even more than he had changed between El Paso and Zacatecas, or between Zacatecas and Irapuato. He looked even tougher, more steel-like, but that wasn't the sum of it. There was a weary cast to his face that verged on cynicism. The Revolution had used this boy hard. Boy? Yes, damn it! He was a boy. No matter that he had probably been through a man's share of hell since he left Black Springs a year and a half ago.

"Ladies first, *señora*," the big sergeant said to Luisa, pushing the sack across Corey's lap and in front of her as he looked warily at Corey, his eyes sending a mild warning.

Even in this moment of threat the sergeant's countenance was not unpleasant. He smiled at Corey.

Luisa's nails sank even deeper into Corey's palm. He took his eyes from the sergeant and looked at her, to find a face carved from ice.

"Paco," she said. "Do you not recognize me?"

The sergeant looked straight at her for the first time. His mouth dropped open. The sack fell at Luisa's feet.

"Doña Luisa!" It was somewhere between a gasp and a roar, the sound of a man startled out of his wits. Then the smile he had given Corey made way for something Corey couldn't read. The sergeant drew a breath so deep it bid fair to suck the air from the carriage. "Paco Durán," he said, "would recognize a López y Montenegro in the blackness of *el purgatorio, señora!*"

Jorge Martínez surged forward. "Paco," he said. "Did I hear you right? This woman is . . . ?"

"*¡Sí, mi capitán!* This *señora* is Doña Luisa López y Montenegro of Hacienda del Sol."

Jorge's right hand swept downward to the flap on the holster of his revolver. A low, throaty, animal sound spilled from his mouth. Corey rose from the seat. Good Lord! Jorge's weapon was halfway out when Sergeant Durán's tree-limb left arm slammed across his chest.

"*¡No, no, mi hijo! Por favor*, this is the business of Paco Durán, and of Paco Durán *solamente!*"

"*Pero,* Paco . . . I have *sworn* . . . I promised Juanita, long ago . . ."

"I know, *amigo.* But I have first right here. Paco alone must make any decision about Doña Luisa." Was it an order or a plea? His face was infinitely harder than the rocks strewn along the right-of-way, and the big body trembled as if warring armies were at work inside it.

Time stretched almost beyond its elastic limits. Then the broad face softened. He bowed. "I think it is now time to be a human being," he said, his voice a rumble, "not a beast. *Hasta la vista,* Doña Luisa." He turned to Corey. "*Señor.*" He leaned over, his great bulk no longer so menacing and heavy, retrieved his sack, turned, and pushed Jorge gently back up the aisle.

They were at the vestibule before Corey could bring himself to move.

"Jorge, Jorge!" he called as he raced after them.

Martínez didn't stop.

When Corey reached the top of the metal steps, Jorge was already in the saddle alongside the train.

"Stop where you are, Señor Lane!" He was all command now. "I advise you not to leave this train. If you do, I cannot be held accountable. I am not in sole charge of these *soldados*. General Fierro has sent another officer along to watch me."

Two middle-aged men Corey remembered seeing board the train at San Luis Potosí were being herded down the railway embankment by three mounted Villista troopers. One shuffled and lurched as if drunk, the other pressed his chin down hard against his chest. Both had their hands tied behind their backs. He didn't want to see any more.

He raced back to Luisa. What a despicable failure he was as lover and protector. Strangely, he hadn't felt even a touch of fear during the whole of the encounter, just a draining weakness. Luisa had been in mortal danger for a moment there. Paco Durán and Jorge Martínez were two superb fighting men at the peak of their killing power, not the simple, already defeated Federalist soldiers he and Fergus had blown away on the shoulder of La Sierpe. And this time he didn't even have a gun. The automatic Fierro had returned to him was packed away in the luggage with Tomás and Emilia. He sank into the seat beside Luisa.

She was staring out the window, her face a mask.

Outside, the three troopers had draped *riatas* tied to their saddle horns over the crossbar of the nearest telegraph pole. The other ends were tied around the necks of the two prisoners he had seen. He took Luisa's hand, a hand suddenly as cold as snow. He didn't want her to see what was going to happen next.

"Luisa," he said. "Will you tell me what that was all about?"

She turned to him. Her look was blank, hollow. Her lips moved, but she didn't speak. Then, with another terrible effort, and in a voice he didn't even know, she said: "Six years ago Paco Durán murdered my twin brother. He beat him to death with his brutal fists."

45

▲▲▲▲

It was more than the misadventure with Paco Durán on the train, but it would, Luisa knew, bring on the change she feared.

As her foot hit the littered cobblestone platform in the Durango railway station, Luisa López y Montenegro of Posada Melgar became Luisa of Hacienda del Sol, and for an instant she feared the cold stones would shrink the first Luisa to nothing and she would disappear forever.

Sudden doubts about this trip—which had seemed such a happy idea when she proposed it on the balcony of the *posada* apartment back in the capital—assailed her with gale force. Perhaps the only way to save herself would be to wait right here on the windswept platform and take the next southbound train back to the life she had only begun to live with him.

But the damage had been done, even if he didn't know it yet. She would have to make repairs, but how? There was little she could say or do. She couldn't, unfortunately, turn the clock back or forward no matter how much she wanted to. The stay at the *hacienda* would have to run its course, minute by tortured minute. In fairness, the man she had come to love so deeply must be given a good long, searching look at the *hacendada* he didn't yet know and perhaps never could. Would he—or more to the point *could* he—love *that* woman as he had loved the woman of Mexico City? Could the woman of the *hacienda* love *him* as the Avenida Melgar woman had? On the second question the answer was an un-equivocal yes. It had to be. There was more than enough love in her for a dozen women of even greater differences than the ones tearing her in two at this frightening moment.

Why in *el nombre de Dios* did there have to *be* two such different women? The answer lay somewhere in the black history behind the meeting on the train with Paco Durán, but that wasn't the sum of it by any means. Paco and her brother were just a part of the answer, just one of a myriad of things which had shaped the Luisa of Hacienda del Sol. Full disclosure of all those things would turn on each of her thirty-seven years of life there—and on two full centuries before that.

Yes, Corey would have to know them all; no matter what the risk.

Tibo Vergara's sixteen-year-old son, Gilberto, waited in the open-topped car parked beside the luggage room a stone's throw up the tracks, standing behind the wheel and waving to Tomás and Emilia as they descended from the coach behind the engine. The boy turned to her next, made a deep bow, and straightened up with a broad smile on his face.

His shout of "*Cómo está*, Doña Luisa?" was mostly lost in the blast of the locomotive whistle as the train began pulling out again.

Behind Gilberto and the car, seventy-six-year-old, wrinkled Martín Chavez perched on the seat of a wagon with the *hacienda*'s name emblazoned on the sides, burned a half inch deep into the wood, and drawn by four black Montenegro mules. The old man beamed even more broadly than did Gilberto. Tomás, Emilia, and the luggage would ride with Martín. Surely Corey would see the happiness with which she was greeted by her people, the strong, warm sense of family even in this small group gathered on the breezy platform. Perhaps at least some of her fears would come to nothing.

She glanced at him, permitting *herself* a smile.

Corey was frowning. He looked hard in the direction of Martín and the wagon. Behind the wagon three mounted men dressed in the familiar mauve jackets of Montenegro *vaque-*

ros cradled rifles across their saddles. Martín was armed, too.
He had strapped a pistol which looked as old as he did to his
waist. She had forgotten that Tibo Vergara now insisted on
such escorts whenever she came to the *hacienda* or whenever
guests or *estancia* people went to Santa María. Corey turned
to her.

"Do your people expect trouble, Luisa?"

"Just a precaution, Corey."

"Makes sense, I suppose, particularly after the thing on the
train."

There was, in his usually calm voice, an unspoken plea for
her to talk more about that meeting, but she couldn't. Not yet.
She knew he wouldn't press her.

Once loaded, the wagon started first, and Gilberto swung
the big car close in behind it. He wasn't a truly accomplished
driver, no better than Tomás, and the car jerked in the lower
gear he had to use to keep from overrunning the wagon and
its three-man mounted guard.

"*Con permiso,* Doña Luisa," he said over his shoulder.
"My father says we must stay close behind Martín and *el
convoy* until we leave Durango and reach Montenegro rangeland. Just in case we see *bandidos*." He sounded as if he
might welcome them. Youth! She had seen a pistol on the
front seat when she and Corey entered.

"Don't we have to go through Santa María del Oro before
we reach the *estancia*?" Corey asked.

"Yes, *querida,*" she said, "but the village lies wholly
within López y Montenegro land." He looked surprised, and
without knowing why she suddenly regretted having told him.
It wasn't what she wanted him to know about her home, not
so soon.

The *avenida* they took to leave Durango for the road to
Santa María del Oro and the *hacienda* she said was nine kilometers beyond it led through a seamy *barrio*, not the raw
slum of the meaner sections of the capital, but bad enough.
She had seen it dozens of times in the past few years on her
travels down to and back from Posada Melgar, but had she
ever truly looked at it? No.

She didn't look now—but she *saw*. Even keeping her eyes on the street ahead, images intruded. What she saw now in the eyes of people on the street was hate. *Face it, Luisa. Your vision has been sharpened simply by the fact that Corey is with you.* His great compassion, evident everywhere they went in the capital, must be contagious. But yes, her vision *was* sharper now. She would see more hate as they rolled through Santa María.

But then she would be home, at least Luisa of the *hacienda* would be home, surrounded by the people who had cared for her and cherished her all her life. Her first task would be to go to the chapel, find Padre Juan, and make that confession she had never made. Would she make still another? One to follow the one she made at San Fernando in the capital just before they left?

A sudden, unreasonable and yet palpable fear took hold of her.

Could her love for Corey, and his for her, take all the battering it could receive?

46

His first three days at Hacienda del Sol were curiously defeating ones. He never quite came to grips with Luisa's revelation on the train, or the tale of horror she told him their first night in the *hacienda*—not only of Paco Durán and her twin brother but of the killing of all her family and the partial destruction of her home by fire when the Revolution exploded in earnest—but even without those shocks he would have been uneasy and, he hated to face this but he must, slightly distanced from her.

Fergus's recounting of what had happened here, so hard to credit her in this place of peace and plenty, had carried nothing of the agony in her voice when she spoke her brother's name. *Nothing*.

The grandeur of Hacienda del Sol and his first real look at Luisa in it staggered him. The richness of her apartment at Posada Melgar had been but the hint of enormous wealth; Fergus's report on the great *estancia* had failed miserably to prepare him for what he saw on his walks with Luisa or his wanderings alone. Hacienda del Sol wasn't a home. It was an entire village, a way of life—a world. A world unlike any he had known. And more than a world, it was a state of mind, a state he had no hope of coping with, much less attaining.

Even Tres Piedras on the upper Concho, the great show-place ranch of Gideon Bainbridge back in Chupadera County, burned to the ground these many years, couldn't in its best days compare with the vast complex Luisa had known as home. If the Revolution had taken something from its splendor, he failed to see what it could have been.

Spectacular as Hacienda del Sol was, though, the drive from the station in Durango had been a picture of Mexico's ills in miniature.

Their route to the *estancia* in still another Daimler touring car, driven by a pleasant Mexican boy of sixteen or so whose hand was heavy but unskilled on the throttle, whisked them across open rangeland once they left Durango and pulled around the wagon, but not nearly speedily enough to erase from his mind's eye the last lower-class *barrio*, a section that appeared as ill-used as some of the towns he had seen wrecked by war in this country: with filthy streets whose gutters ran as foul-smelling open sewers, and with even filthier naked children playing in them. Playing? The urchins who turned their great, haunting black eyes on the *hacienda*'s car as it passed seemed to have no idea of what was meant by play. His eyes sought it, but all they found was bloated bellies and shrunken dreams.

Luisa and Corey rode straight through the *barrio* in silence, but once in open country her eyes darted from left to right as she pointed things out to him. They rolled through low russet hills blanketed by grazing livestock, cattle which she told him all carried the brand of the Montenegros. In the thirty-five-minute journey he was sure they passed enough beef on the hoof to nibble every pasture in the Ojos Negros to caliche waste. Fergus could have bought a dozen hundredweights of meat here every week for a year without making a noticeable dent in these monstrous herds.

A road of finely crushed white gravel that sparkled like a high snowfield led into the *estancia*, winding through clusters of stone buildings where the *hacienda*'s servants and field workers lived in luxury—compared to what he had seen in Durango.

"Hacienda del Sol had three hundred twenty-seven people when I was here last," Luisa said as they pulled through a fieldstone and wrought-iron gate that was itself an architectural marvel. "I don't know how many souls call it home now. Some have been born and some have died while I have been in the capital. There are families who have been here for five generations."

A sprawl of a compound off to the left of the road, entirely separate from the other buildings, was apparently the heart of the ranching operation. The Lanes' X-Bar-7—main house, outbuildings, and all—would have been lost inside it. He spied a bunkhouse as large as any barracks at Fort Bliss and a smithy bigger than the Lane tackroom. The branding and holding pens of the *hacienda* covered three or four acres, and a corral with a remuda of perhaps sixty horses abutted them. He had no idea how many *vaqueros* might be on the Hacienda del Sol range today, but there were probably enough of them to make an army by the standards of Chupadera County.

The family chapel Luisa mentioned on the train, nestling in a grove of eucalyptus, was larger than San José in Black Springs's Mex Town. It was built of solid stone, not adobe. As they drove past it, an old priest sitting on a bench in the parklike setting leaped to his feet and waved to them.

"Padre Juan . . ." Luisa breathed. "He heard my first confession."

Corey couldn't help wondering, and blushed as he did, if the good father would hear another one soon.

But no surprise at Hacienda del Sol had a tenth of the impact of his first sight of the house itself.

The style was pure, graceful Nueva España, with none of the French influence—the heritage from the time of Maximilian and Carlotta—so visible in the capital today. The forebears of that "three hundred twenty-seven," or whatever the number now was, must have built it for some long-dead Montenegro feudal baron. Clearly, though, an artist in stone and wood had been brought in for design and supervision—perhaps as much as a century ago.

A massive carved door shaded by a portico that seemed to run around the entire structure opened into a foyer the size of a squash court from both of whose sides curved balustraded staircases that swept up to a second-story balcony. The walls alongside the stairs and at the back of the balcony were hung with portraits, one of which—Luisa said it was of the first Don Sebastian, the family patriarch, done in London in 1783—was of a genuine grandee in a tricorn hat, mounted, with a sword held triumphantly against an inky blue El Greco sky. It made Corey think of another, more recently sighted sword.

"The west wing is at last completely restored. It's taken almost four years," Luisa told him. "When the mob came out from Santa María and Durango to destroy my family, they got drunk and set that side of the house afire. ¡Estúpidos! They had to call the *hacienda*'s people to help put out the blaze. In their drunken insanity they forgot they intended to camp here for a while. They infested this side of the house like maggots!"

"How long did they stay?"

"A month. It took almost a year to get the smell of them out of the drapery!"

"Why did they leave at all?"

"General Villa offered small fortunes to new recruits. When they left, our people here at the *hacienda* just went quietly to work—without orders, since all my family and the overseers were dead and I was gone—and put everything to rights." She fell silent. She obviously didn't want to talk about it anymore, not now, at any rate. Truth to tell, he didn't want to hear more. All he could think about was how grateful he was that Luisa hadn't been at Hacienda del Sol at the time of that first rising.

His room—and it didn't surprise him that he was quartered away from her, some proprieties had to be observed—was large and sunny, with leaded casement windows opening on a view of the chapel in its small, tailored woodland in the middle distance. The first morning, raucous birds awakened him, and when he went to the window he saw Luisa walking toward the chapel, her head already bowed and swathed in a black lace *mantilla*.

She looked lovely, but something about her appearance shocked him. There was something faintly resembling *new* widowhood about her in her looks, walk, and manner. She wasn't the cosmopolitan woman of Posada Melgar or of the cultural whirlwind of the capital. His breath stopped. The woman he was looking at was not the woman who had carried him to those undreamt-of heights in Xochimilco, on the high slopes of Popo and Ixta, and in the mystical walks in Chapultepec Park.

They didn't make love that first night, but he hadn't really expected they would. She would have to shake out all sorts of memories first.

Hacienda del Sol, in its way, was as pastoral and idyllic as San Gabriel de los Árboles had been—and as unreal. But somehow the bright sun flooding it cast darker shadows than he had expected. Why?

There was, for all that the household ran as smoothly and punctiliously as a Swiss watch, an edginess about some of the servants which amused him when he finally doped it out.

Tall, morose Tomás moved quietly and effortlessly into the top position of authority at the *hacienda* almost the moment they arrived, displacing a man named Fabiano, who apparently was *mayordomo* only when Luisa and her two old servants weren't in residence. The shift in command smacked a little of the way things might be ordered at a "royal progress," and although nothing was ever said, Fabiano's broad Indian nose was certainly a bit out of joint during the first two days at least.

But if there was any deep-dyed resentment of Tomás and Emilia—who had assumed the role of head maid even as

Tomás took over the management of just about everything else—it didn't extend to Luisa.

Once, when Corey was a boy, Grandmother Alicia had told him—apropos of absolutely nothing, her customary way of doling out homilies of any sort—"You can't tell a lady by the way she acts, Corey, but by the way she's treated." Perhaps that was where his similar idea about great men had come from. Imperious Alicia Lane would have done superbly herself as the chatelaine of Hacienda del Sol. Her dubious yardstick for assessing ladyhood was far less dubious when he remembered the respectful, at times fearful, manner in which X-Bar-7 hands and the shopkeepers and professionals of Black Springs treated *her*. Alicia had overseen the Lane properties and affairs with a scarcely concealed iron hand—a sometime fist—from the time Corey's father died until Virgie took over after Alicia's death.

Applying Alicia's dictum when he and Luisa met members of the *hacienda*'s tremendously extended "family" as they strolled the house and grounds together told him she was not only a lady but a great lady, beyond any question. Of course he already knew that, but the fresh evidence soon amounted to proof. The bows and curtsies, the doffed caps and hats, were the sort of gestures given royalty. And none of it was feigned. These people, from the household staff to the gnarled old gardener rising and smiling from his rose beds, *loved* her. A round dozen recounted some specific recollection of kindnesses she had done: a dying grandmother visited and cheered, an infant nursed back to health from diphtheria, a pregnant young girl steered safely and blessedly into marriage. Yes, they loved her. It wasn't, however, love for a friend or equal; it was love for a queen. The reaction surpassed anything he had seen Alicia receive in Black Springs—in degree or kind.

Once again he wondered how Luisa and he would fare as husband and wife in basically egalitarian and certainly "just plain folks" Chupadera County.

One big disappointment deepened his discomfort.

He and Luisa spent less time together in the first three days than they had in any similar span since he returned to the capital from the disaster at Celaya.

She closeted herself for hour-long sessions with the *estancia* manager, a retired Federalist major named Vergara, a conspicuously unfriendly, hard-bitten, muscular man she said had fought Villa at Torreón and in other battles before Huerta collapsed. "Tibo was a *rurale* in the district before the Revolution, a policeman." He was faintly disappointed at the harmonics of approval that seemed to underlie her brief recital of his police and military service. The word *rurale* had sent shivers up and down his spine.

He was disappointed even more that he was never invited along when the two of them made long inspection rides across the rangeland.

There was a wonderful old handmade mahogany desk in his room, reams of paper, and a plethora of pens. "You can work on your book while I attend to the affairs of the *hacienda*, Corey."

He tried to write, couldn't.

The highway of history along which he hoped to entice some imagined reader had too many sideroads enticing him, and of course he could invest no more of himself in the biography of Felipe Ángeles. There would be no return on such an investment for a long, long time—if ever.

He had pretty well put to rest the idea of Ángeles becoming the paramount strongman of Mexico, President if one wished to give it a more palatable taste. He didn't even know where the general was at the moment, and hadn't a much better idea about the whereabouts of Pancho Villa, except that he was somewhere in Chihuahua, not active, but reportedly swearing vengeance for the object of his erstwhile love, the United States, for recognizing the patchwork government of Venustiano Carranza. In any event, Corey was now off Henry Richardson's payroll, so whatever interest he had in either of the two revolutionary leaders was purely academic.

The sideroad that forced *him* to turn was clearly marked: Jorge Martínez.

Luisa's story had fixed the giant sergeant on the train in the terrible scheme of things here at the *hacienda*, but where exactly did Jorge fit, and why had he looked so murderous until his sergeant held him back? He had still been in Black Springs when Luisa's family was killed, and in 1909, when Luisa said her brother died at the hands of the village blacksmith in nearby Santa María del Oro, Jorge was in high school, shocking Corey's neighbors in that riotous forensic contest.

Paco Durán. Not an uncommon name in Mexico; he must have heard it fifteen or twenty times over the past year and a half. But something nagged at him. Durán . . . Durán . . .

Then he remembered.

The dark young beauty in the shack at Irapuato, the wife of Capitán Jorge Martínez of the Bracomontes—*her* name was or had been Durán.

It was a far cry from all the explanation he needed, but it was a start.

Why was he spending so much time thinking about it? There were other things.

Or were there now? He shouldn't take himself to task too harshly about his failure in the mission Henry sent him to Mexico to accomplish; all along odds had been against success. Better men than Corey Lane, with far more tangible armament at their disposal, had failed in just such missions all through history. Besides, the ultimate decisions had been ones few people even in his own camp had wanted him to make. It broke his heart for this country he had come to love, but he would have to live with it.

But the problem of Jorge Martínez was one he should have handled without a hitch. It took no special powers beyond the ones he already had as sheriff of Chupadera County to accomplish a simple thing like bringing a boy back to his home and family. He wasn't an inch closer to it than he had been when standing at the window of the wineshop back in Chihuahuita, spying on General Epifanio Guzmán for Agent Jacob Cobb.

This morning, with Luisa and Vergara out on still another ride across the pasturelands, Corey persuaded Tomás to get him a horse, and he rode the eight miles in to Santa María.

The mid-December highland air was crisp and clear, the horse was as fine an animal as any he had ever ridden, and he felt a stab of regret that he was making the ride without Luisa. Actually, he was a little jealous of the manager, until he came to his senses and realized how childish he was being. Patience. It had been a year since she had last visited Hacienda del Sol. She had work to do. There would be more than enough time for him after this first week's chores were put behind her, and she had already told him her duties would be mostly finished by Christmas Day.

In Santa María he found the office of the *alcalde* and the *alcalde* himself ushered him into an office not much larger than a broom closet. The official was a small round man all smiles, anxious to please a visitor to his town, even a gringo.

Pancho Villa might have abandoned virtually all of Durango state, but he had left something of himself behind. The *alcalde* was a Villista. A tattered recruiting poster for the Division still adorned the office wall.

"How can I be of help, *señor*?" the little mayor said, beaming.

"*Por favor.* I am looking for relatives of a onetime resident of Santa María del Oro, *alcalde*—a man by the name of Paco Durán—or anyone who knows or knew him."

"You are a friend of Paco's, *señor*?"

"I have met him."

"You are staying in Santa María del Oro?"

"I am at Hacienda del Sol, the guest of Doña Luisa López y Montenegro."

The air of affability left the office with the speed of light. Things were churning in the *alcalde*'s round head from the look of him. He trembled, but his mouth was set hard. "I fear I cannot help you, *señor. Por favor,* excuse me now. I have a very busy morning."

Corey found himself in the street with such swiftness it was almost as if he had been thrown out bodily.

The morning sun was warm now that it had cleared all the hills and rooftops, but he felt chilled to the marrow. The *al-*

calde's reaction to the name of Montenegro had dropped the temperature a fistful of degrees.

He unhitched his horse and had his foot in the stirrup when he decided he couldn't give up that easily, and he mounted and eased the animal into the center of the street.

Half a block down toward the railroad, hidden from view by the ridge Luisa had pointed out from the train on the journey north, he saw a tiny, weathered sign above a doorway whose wooden frame had settled into a lopsided parallelogram. Had he been riding with more purpose he would have missed it.

ISABEL DURÁN—SORTÍLEGA

A fortune-teller named Durán might be exactly what he needed at the moment.

Maiden lady Isabel Durán was a match for the sergeant in size and appearance, and it didn't surprise him at all when she told him she was Paco's sister.

"I have not seen *mi hermano* for seven years," she said.

She took the news that Corey was a guest at Hacienda del Sol with a good deal more equanimity than had the *alcalde*, but she didn't really relax or open up until he told her he was trying to find Jorge Martínez rather than her brother and then gave her in brief Paco's connection to Jorge—and his own.

"¡*Sí, señor!* I know this Martínez—at least I know *about* him." Her niece Juanita had written about her *capitán*, Isabel said, and although she had never met him, the mere fact of Corey's knowing Jorge established minimal credentials for him.

He almost told her of seeing Paco and Jorge on the train, decided against it. It might not have a good effect were she to discover that her brother had been but a few miles from her just four days earlier. Worse, she might think Corey was only tracking them down to do them harm because of the robbery.

Then she said, "If you see Paco before I do, tell him it is safe for him to come back home, *por favor*."

Unfortunately, the fortune-teller could give him no help at all in determining the whereabouts of Jorge now.

"I am sorry, Señor Lane. Juanita's last letter came from Irapuato, and I know they're not there any longer. ¡La guerra!" She shrugged her huge shoulders and the room seemed to shake.

"Gracias, anyway, señorita." He made to leave, "Señorita Durán, would it hurt too much to tell me exactly what happened here in Santa María and at the hacienda during the bad times?"

On the return ride to the hacienda the horse revealed what he thought of Corey several times by trying to stretch his canter to a gallop. He wished he could let it out a little and capture some of its spirit for himself, but he wanted time to think before he joined Luisa and her ranch manager for lunch. It would have been better if the ride had been one of fifty miles instead of eight.

The story Luisa told him at that first hacienda supper, with one or two things missing, was the same in most details as the one he had heard from the lips of Isabel Durán, yet they could have happened in two different countries and in wholly different epochs. They were distinct and differing tales—as told. Both were horror stories. Both women believed their versions to be gospel. Both had the ring of essential truth.

When he left Isabel and stepped into the street again, he found it filled with silent villagers. They stared at him. In a few pairs of eyes he saw hate as strong as any he had ever encountered—and no little amount of fear. The word about him must have gone out from the alcalde's office like ripples from a stone tossed in a pond.

One thing had come out of the morning: the villagers of Santa María del Oro didn't join in the worship of the Montenegros which was the universal aura of the hacienda.

"You rode in to Santa María, señor?" Major Tibo Vergara asked at lunch. "Perdón, Señor Lane, it is not my place, I suppose, to offer you advice, but the village is a good place for anyone here at the *hacienda* to avoid."

"I confess I got that impression." Corey glanced at Luisa. Out of the corner of his eye he had seen her nod at the manager's words.

"I do not understand what is wrong with those people," she said. "They have prospered because of the Montenegros!"

Prospered? What was Luisa saying? Santa María, while not the run-down *barrio* of Durango, hadn't looked prosperous by any stretch of the imagination. "How long has it been since you were *in* the village, Luisa, not merely driving through it?" he asked.

"Seven or eight years, Corey. But why do you ask? Nothing takes me there."

He tried to content himself with that. She didn't *know*.

The subject of Santa María didn't come up again for the rest of the meal.

What did come up was politics—in fits and starts—but only after Vergara and Luisa had hashed over the state of the *estancia*'s cattle business. Once again he was nonplussed by the immensity of the Montenegro operation.

Fergus Kennedy wasn't the only buyer of beef making purchases at the *hacienda*.

Japan, Germany, and the United States, of course, were all heavyweight customers. The conversation turned on a herd of three hundred fifty head to be shipped to Veracruz, ultimately bound for the stockyards in Chicago.

"We are fortunate, Doña Luisa," Vergara said, "that Obregón has chased the Villistas out of the territory between us and the coast. Pancho took five of our shipments last year—without paying us, of course."

"There's not a great deal to choose between General Obregón and that *bandido*."

"Agreed, *señora*. But as long as Venustiano Carranza runs things in Mexico, Obregón will behave himself. Carranza is not *el presidente* any thinking Mexican would choose, but I shudder when I consider that Pancho Villa or one of his hand-picked cutthroats might have been the alternative."

"I suppose you're right, Tibo. Still—things were so much more orderly under Don Porfirio. If there were only a truly good man on the horizon."

She couldn't have been a supporter of Díaz, she simply *couldn't*. Not the intelligent, *simpática* woman Corey knew.

He took the plunge. "How would General Felipe Ángeles be as a choice for President of Mexico?" It was like diving into Bonito Lake in January, the freeze no less apparent on Luisa's smooth features than it was on the hard face of Tibo Vergara.

"Corey! General Ángeles is little more than an anarchist. He would give Mexico to the *paisanos* and *obreros*. There would be no more Hacienda del Sol. No! I fear, too, that General Ángeles is an enemy of Holy Church."

"Sorry, Luisa." He *was* sorry, but he couldn't back down. "I met and talked with the general the same night I met you. I was impressed. I know he has the interests of all Mexicans, high and low, very much at heart."

"He fooled you, darling."

It ended the talk—and the lunch. Vergara claimed urgent business at the bunkhouse before he joined his mistress for their afternoon ride. He bowed to Corey before he left the room, but fixed him with a hard, contemptuous look. Luisa left without a word.

Her inspection of the *estancia* with Vergara that afternoon would be the last before the holidays, she had said. Guests she wanted Corey to meet were arriving in two or three days' time, and she wanted her plate cleaned, cleared, and washed.

"I'm sorry I've not been able to spend more time with you, Corey."

It left him with five hours to kill before dinner with her. Writing didn't work. He put the work aside after only two desultory sentences and pulled a sheet of stationery from his writing case. He began a letter to Fergus he would send in care of the British Embassy, but he scarcely got started on the first paragraph of it, either. He tried to nap, but a half hour of trying ended the attempt.

The December sky had clouded over, the wall of the *sier-

ras seemed to move closer to the *hacienda* before they became obscured, and a brisk, cold wind, threatening heavy weather, was rising in the northwest.

He closed the massive shutters at the casement windows, fastened them, slipped on the heavy sheepskin Tomás had thoughtfully placed in the antique armoir in his room, and went for a walk through the compound.

He had pretty well explored most of the grounds of the *hacienda*, but he hadn't really seen anything of the ranching operation Vergara ran.

It was almost a mile and a half to the first of the outbuildings, the mammoth, barrackslike bunkhouse, and when he reached it he saw behind it another, smaller building which he could never have seen from the road.

It was a squat, plain building built of squared-off, dead gray stone, with tiny windows quite high up in the blank walls. Thick iron bars securely bolted to the stone crosshatched the windows. In the packed dirt between the bunkhouse and the block a post a foot in diameter and sunk in the ground reared its blunt head like a sentinel. Lengths of heavy chain hung down from near the top of the post.

Something twisted inside of him. Hacienda del Sol had its own jail! His lecture to Henry Richardson about Mexico came horribly to mind.

He wanted to turn and retrace his steps to the house, but something moved him toward the grim little building.

At a distance from it of thirty feet or so he heard voices. Feeling himself a grubby spy again, but powerless against a suddenly overwhelming curiosity, he moved closer.

What seemed to be two men inside the jail were talking. Their voices, one indistinguishable from the other, drifted through the bars dim and distant.

". . . she does know, *amigo*. She is like all the rest of them. ¡*Verdad!*"

"No, no, not the *señora*. He never tells her what he is doing."

"Will he have us shot?"

"Not this time, *amigo*. This time it will just be a flogging, but it will not be pleasant. Damn that gringo! Any questions asked in Santa María about the Duráns always get back to that *puerco* Vergara. He will round up every one of old Paco's *primos* he can find."

"Who told him the gringo was asking about Paco? And how did he come to act so fast?"

"Does it matter? He has spies all over town. Two of them are old *rurales* who got away five years ago. And he has the backing of that General Méndez who is in Carranza's pocket. I don't know if the señora knows about *him*. She should. He keeps the Montenegros rich in return for Vergara's bribes."

He didn't stay to hear more. He went back to the main house at a dead run, and collapsed in exhaustion and anguish on the bed in his room.

She had never looked lovelier than she did in the candle-light at dinner, but her ivory reflection in the polished dark wood of the long table was that of "things seen darkly, as in a mirror."

And even the real Luisa facing him was now becoming as veiled as the reflection.

He had posed his first questions as gently as he could, but with a persistence that he feared might sound like bullying. He didn't tell her what he had heard at the jail behind the barracks—the military appellation for the bunkhouse now seemed the only way he could think about it—but he did tell her of his talk with Isabel Durán.

If he had expected hysteria, or heated denials of the fortune-teller's version of the dreadful events of half a dozen years ago, he would have been disappointed. Her long silence was worse than either. The silence in his heart echoed it.

At last she spoke.

"Believe what you must, Corey." Her voice was firm, without a quaver, but he heard the deep hurt in it, and he wished with all his heart that the tile floor beneath his end of the table would fall into a bottomless pit and take him with it.

Then, with shame burning his cheeks, he told her everything: why he had come to Mexico, his wooing of Felipe Ángeles and Pancho Villa, his hopes for the people of Mexico, everything he had thought and done in the past year and a half. The only things he held back were the parts Fergus and Narciso had played in his apparatus of deceit. The shame deepened as he told it. Then she said something that brought a feeling far worse than shame.

"Did you become involved with me only to get close to Wolf Kemper, Corey?"

He was as shaken as when Felipe Ángeles's big guns had nearly taken the top off La Sierpe.

"Good heavens, no, Luisa! Please, please—don't think that for a moment. I love you!"

The only color in her face was what the candlelight lent it.

"If you say so, Corey, I believe you without reservation," she said next, "but there is something between us suddenly that looms much larger, isn't there?"

Suddenly? Not so. It had been building for longer than he had admitted. He had evaded and avoided it, but now it was here, as inevitable as he had feared. He waited. It was more frightening than when he had waited against the wall in that deadly *calle* in Zacatecas.

"You are an outsider here at Hacienda del Sol, Corey, and a foreigner in my country. No matter how much you love Mexico you might always be an outsider. Things are so much simpler for North Americans. I didn't think that mattered, but I only deluded myself. I think I have as much sympathy for the lot of the poor as you do; I just think there is another way to care for them than by chaos and killing. Our way of life has gone awry, but the system just needs fixing, not discarding."

Yes, it was a sentence of death—or it amounted to it. He could no more duck or dodge than if he had reached the wall in Zacatecas.

"Can we go on together, Luisa?"

"I . . . don't know." Her face now was as waxen as the candles. It was both an eternity and no time at all before she spoke again. "At the very least I think we need some time away from each other. I love you, but I need time to think. A lot of time, I fear . . ." A lot of time? The word "forever" seemed to hover in the air and poison it.

She paused again. Her voice and breath had been so low and light they wouldn't have flickered a candle held an inch from her mouth, but they echoed inside his head as an anguished scream. He waited for the final words that would bring despair. They came.

"Corey . . . I can't love you here as I did in the capital . . ."

He left Hacienda del Sol next morning.

She saw him to the portico, but she didn't accompany him when Tomás drove him to Durango. Just as well. It would be a journey through the meanest streets of hell.

It was raining, but he stood outside on the empty platform and waited for the train to take him to Ciudad Juárez and the border.

Everything was gone.

He would leave Mexico without even a tiny victory. Ángeles was gone, Jorge Martínez was gone.

Luisa was gone.

If there had ever been a *fiesta* for Corey Lane, it was over now, the celebrants fragmented, blown to bits . . .

A dog-eared calendar flapped its pages on the station wall. It was December 21, the winter solstice.

She didn't leave her room—the room she had shared with Francisco—for three long days, forcing herself into sleep she didn't want and which failed to heal, hardly looking at the trays of food Emilia brought her.

"Corey . . . I can't love you . . ."

Padre Juan called at the big house every afternoon, but she had Emilia turn him away.

The old country priest had given her an exacting penance, his kind but unyielding face when he whispered from behind the grille as dimly ravaged in the shadows as the one she saw etched sharply on the hard glass of her gilded mirror, but she had agreed to it in a sudden rush of shame and guilt—almost begged for something even worse.

She made it worse herself. *Mea culpa . . . mea culpa . . . mea culpa . . .*

". . . and I can't love you here . . ."
Here? Did there have to be a *here*?

She left Hacienda del Sol on Christmas Day.

Tomás found her the key to her bedroom door, the key that hadn't been used for twenty years. When she turned it in the lock the heavy click was like a knell.

But she knew exactly where she had to go and what she had to do. She would wait for him in the *posada* if it took a thousand years. Somewhere she would find the strength to do every penance God asked of her, forever, if necessary.

She wouldn't seek him out in that Chupadera County he talked about. There was another place for them, and she knew what it was, or at least where it would begin.

She knew something else.

There were things that mattered far more than her immortal soul.

47

Las Palomas, Chihuahua—March 9, 1916

Major Jorge Martínez couldn't sleep. He wasn't sure, but he didn't think he had slept an hour in the last three.

He hauled himself from his bedroll, wrapped his poncho around him, and reached for his canteen.

He had closed his eyes from time to time through the early dark, but sleep stayed at a distance, taunting him from somewhere out in the desert wastes that stretched away in four directions, a teasing phantom flitting through the cactus and cholla surrounding the arroyo where the troop was bivouacked.

It was just past midnight, and the Little Dipper had already made a quarter turn around the North Star. An hour must have passed since the train from the east had rumbled by somewhere beyond the barbed-wire fence to the north of his small camp, sounding, in the biting cold night air, as if it were running right through the arroyo itself, its whistle the hollow call of a *tecolote*.

He took a pull from his canteen and decided there was no sense in closing his eyes again. In little more than an hour it would be time to have Paco rouse the troop and get them mounted, ready to move to the attack.

In his twenty-one months with Villa's army, attacks had never gotten easier for Jorge Martínez—never again as easy as his first one as a Bracomonte, the one at Paredón. The ridiculous attack they would make today would be the worst.

He would have called the general *loco*, except that in the past year he had come to realize how resourceful Pancho Villa was, how he could wriggle away from one defeat only to suffer and survive yet another, and in spite of fiascoes which would have stopped a lesser man, still hold an army together. There was a reason for today's assault, even if it was hard to see how it could help the Revolution, and even if most of them died while making it.

The general had told his officers at the meeting just before *siesta* that the attack would be punishment for merchant brothers in the town beyond the wire. They had never delivered the guns and ammunition and above all the horses he had paid them for three months ago, the general said.

Horses? *¡Mierda!* It had little if anything to do with horses. Major Jorge Martínez knew it was political. Everything was political with Pancho Villa, except the never-ending parade of women through his quarters, and even some of the women were instruments of politics.

But it wasn't fear of the attack, or the thoughts of the bodies, the blood, the flies, and then the stink, that kept sleep away—although the fear was surely part of it. It was the question he had asked himself for a week now, ever since the general had promoted him to major and hinted at his plans for this attack. *Sí*, the persistent, nagging question. The question the general, too, had silently asked with his fierce, black-diamond eyes when he fixed them on Jorge at the meeting.

No answer had come in the dark of night. Six months ago one would have come so easily—unbidden.

A dozen feet away, separated from Martínez by a patch of stunted ocotillo, lay the mountainous bulk of Sargento Paco Durán, dynamiter for Martínez's understrength command. *He* was having no trouble sleeping. No question plagued Paco: he wasn't a man given much to questions.

As with almost everything else he did, the big man even slept like a mountain—heavy, rooted to the earth—his barrel chest rising and falling no faster than the tide at Veracruz, belying the speed he showed in a fight of any kind, with fists, knives, his cherished explosives and blasting caps, or, as today's fury on horseback would demand—guns.

In today's attack, there would be no time or necessity for Paco to ply his special trade. Today no bridges needed blowing, there would be no adobe walls or breastworks to blast to rubble; he would launch no locomotives skyward with his destructive artistry. Today he would be just another rider with a rifle. Still, the major would need Paco today more than ever.

The older man—at forty-eight almost twice Jorge's age—had been the major's first teacher when he joined the army in the Frontera, when the División del Norte was winning everywhere it fought. An unrelenting tyrant *sargento* then, bullying his raw recruits into becoming soldiers, Paco now was an ungrumbling, if rarely smiling, subordinate who had never once shown the resentment some of the others had at the major's sudden rise from the ranks just before Paredón. He never complained, either, not even when Jorge had broken him to mere *soldado a caballos* for two long weeks after the drunken affair at Casas Grandes in January, when Paco had beaten the owner of La Cantina Flores half to death.

Sí, he would need Paco today, but not to protect him from the enemy. He would need him to keep an eye on Crestino Bautista, even as General Fierro's spy was watching Jorge.

Just before supper Bautista had checked into Jorge's camp three kilometers north of Las Palomas and five from the cow town that would be their target in another hour now, bearing a letter from the Butcher's aide-de-camp.

By old custom field-grade officers could turn away transfers once the order of battle had been announced; this letter made it plain that in the case of Crestino Bautista the custom would be disregarded; Jorge's hands were tied. He either took the new man into his troop or relinquished his command.

He could have kicked himself for begging headquarters for replacements for the men he had lost to the Carrancistas in the disaster last month at Agua Prieta. Bautista was one of the three replacements Fierro sent him.

It had been Paco, of course, who had confirmed Jorge's feeling that he was now saddled with a spy, maybe an assassin.

"Es un espía, verdad," Paco had said when he and Martínez had left Bautista and the others to huddle together and talk about the attack while they downed the *orina de vaca* Jaramillo's *soldadera* Chita claimed was coffee. *"Es muy peligroso, mayor.* I have seen the work of this one at Ciudad Juárez, before your time. Four of my *compadres—muy guerreros* and loyal—went to the wall because of a word from him that *maybe* they were Porfirianos. He was an officer then. Maybe he still is, no matter that he claims to be just another soldier. His nose is in Fierro's ass, and his tongue is in his ear."

The anatomically laughable picture had almost taken the chill from Paco's warning.

"I'll be careful, Paco. But maybe El Carnicero has only sent him here to watch me. I can understand his doubts. This is probably just a warning. If he wanted me to die tomorrow he wouldn't have sent an *asesino* either of us had any chance of knowing. He would have paid someone here in *la tropa* to do the job."

"Maybe Fierro has done that too, Capitán Cucaracha. Some hired piece of *mierda* kills you, and then the spy kills *him*—and gets a medal."

Jorge sighed. *"Muchas gracias,* Sargento Durán. What would I do without you to look on the bright side for me. *Someone* should get a medal."

But the veteran wasn't in the mood for joking, and Jorge put his hand on his massive shoulder. He tried for a squeeze, but it was like clamping his hand to a boulder. "Seriously, Paco, if it will make you feel better, watch the *marrón* before the attack begins. I'll be too busy then. If he so much as looks cross-eyed at me, kill him. But wait until we return the first volley from the other side."

¡Dios! How casual he had gotten about ordering a death. It must be something he had caught from Fierro and all the other butchers he had known. Not surprising. Hadn't some wise *hombre* once said, "Lie down with dogs; get up with fleas"?

They hadn't spoken of Bautista again, but Jorge watched him carefully. He *was* a spy or a killer, *sin duda,* far too eager helping Chita get the supper, much too friendly with the other men for a new man in camp, obsequious—and nervous, the coffee mug shaking ever so slightly when he lifted it to his mouth. Just before the company laid out their bedrolls he had looked at Jorge for a second, smiling at him from across the tiny fire masked from the enemy by a serape stretched between two poles. As Jorge returned the look, but without the smile, the spy's face seemed actually to shed its flesh, become a death's-head—a trick of the firelight, *sí.* The major shifted his gaze to Paco. He was watching Bautista, too; no smile on his face, either.

Crestino Bautista might breathe easily and regularly for the next few hours, might eat, drink, smoke, and even fart like a living human being, but he was already dead. Jorge's dynamiter had lain with this spy's dog of a general—and other high-ranking dogs—four years longer than Jorge had. The fleas Paco had gotten from those killers were scorpions.

Now the camp was stirring. Unkillable Tonito, the *muchacho* who played the bugle, was poking up the fire. The boy probably hadn't forgiven Jorge for his order that there would be no call this morning, and very likely none once the troop was in position. He would have told the youngster to stay on this side of the barbed wire while the rest of them rode out to battle, but he knew it would do no good. Tonito would follow them across the line, anyway. He would stand a better chance if they took him with them. How old was this *niño* now—sixteen? It must be in the records somewhere. Jorge hoped he wouldn't have to look for the records and search them to find where he must send his things.

Somewhere to the east, the main body of the army had bedded down in arroyos just like this. They must be getting ready, too. Jorge's small unit was to swing a kilometer west of the town, bypassing the cantonment of enemy *soldados* just north of the railroad station and start the attack on its exposed right flank. The plan was to let General Villa deploy his three old French fieldpieces—all the artillery left to the Division now—in the time bought for him by Jorge's men. Then, after the cannonade stopped, the stronger force would hit the town from the east and south, while Jorge and his riders turned about to face the two troops of enemy cavalry stationed at the ranch three miles west, according to the scouts who had crossed the line a day ago—just blunt whatever charge *they* made while the general did his butchery—and then fade back across the wire, drawing the enemy with them. It was a good plan, simple—if Jorge could indeed turn or break the enemy charge with but little more than half a troop and no time for Paco to set a minefield.

But even if the plan worked the way the general had drawn it up, no one, least of all *el mayor* Martínez, would be singing "Adelita" while this morning's work was under way. Well, perhaps little Tonito would, since Jorge wouldn't let him play it.

Only one chore remained before he mounted and led the troop out across the flats. And it would have to be done before the others were out of their bedrolls to see him do it.

He went through his saddlebag, found the letters from Ignacio and Concepción he had carried all through this bad campaign, tore them to shreds, and scattered the pieces to the dark breeze. He did the same with his army paybook.

It seemed fitting. For a long time he had suspected he had no identity at all.

There was now nothing in his kit that would identify him if he died today and his body was left behind when the troop withdrew. And no matter how heavy the fighting got, he would save at least one cartridge from the garland of them hanging about his neck like a noose of brass and leather.

The likelihood of the authorities in the town or anyone else back home discovering that Major Jorge Martínez had been in on this attack was remote in the extreme, but he couldn't take even the smallest chance. It could go hard with his family if it did. After this morning the soldiers and civilians across the wire would look for vengeance everywhere.

There was, of course, no way to protect the woman waiting for him from the vengeance of what he now realized were his enemies on *this* side of the wire.

Would he see her again? Would he live to see the child she carried? He smiled, thinking of how he had worked to persuade her to try for it. He knew now why she had been so reluctant, why she kept on shaking her head.

She should have known he would never leave her.

He wheeled the troop sharply to the right at a small roadside sign he couldn't read in the dark. No matter. He knew what it said.

"Columbus—New Mexico—1 mi."

They were on United States territory now . . . and the question that had kept him awake all night came again.

"How will you feel and what will you do, *amigo,* when you find a fellow American in your sights?"

There was still no answer.

48

"How does it feel, *viejo*?"

"Like the fires of hell, Captain Cockroach."

The right shoulder of Paco Durán wasn't a boulder now; it was a rotting *calabaza*—soft, swollen, and as yellow as a pumpkin, too, where it wasn't purple and sickly green, but he was riding passably again.

It was a near miracle how he was recovering, and even more miraculous how he had managed to stay with the troop as they rode from their pursuers in the first week following the attack. He had vomited up every meal for three long days.

Jorge had tried to link up with one of the units of the Division that carried a *cirujano* or any kind of medic on its roster. Paco had been lucky, but he still could use skilled care. If the gangrene had set in, as Jorge was sure it would, it wouldn't have done a bit of good to cut. Lower down the arm Jorge could have done it himself—he had discovered long ago there was no particular trick to that, although one of his three patients had died after amputation—but the shoulder with its complicated bones and muscles, *¿quién sabe?* This kind of operation would have required the services of a genuine surgeon, to save his life, never mind the shoulder and the arm.

But where *was* the rest of the army? And where were the riders he had dispatched to find them? He had looked for General Villa and the Division every rock-strewn inch of the trek south, but the horizons, when the troop reached them, were as flat, empty, and desolate as the ones they had left behind.

It was even closer to a miracle how Paco had been able to go on fighting at all after he had taken the wound in the first fire from the American cavalry thundering out of the darkness west of Columbus—fully ten minutes before the scouts had led Jorge to believe they could possibly reach him.

He had just loosed the troop's opening blind volley into the west end of the town when the gringos hit them. The troop hadn't even dismounted yet, never mind turned to face the attack they knew would come eventually.

"They can't get to your position before the sun comes up and blinds them, Jorge," that Sonoran sonofabitch Romero had said at the meeting. He had smeared his greasy thumb all over the one map Jorge had. "Look, *amigo*. You'll be here—in the town. They're at this ranch, here. You'll have plenty of time to take cover in the big arroyo south of town or even build a barricade. I give you my word as Chief of Scouts."

Scouts? *¡Mierda!* Romero and his *marrones* must have been soaking up tequila and pulque like *esponjas* instead of scouting. It hadn't always been this way. When Jorge first became a Bracomonte, the reports of Pancho Villa's scouts had been fourteen-carat gold. Now they were like the entire army—as rotten as Paco Durán's shoulder. His only consolation was that if the rest of the Division had taken anything like the bloodying his small detachment had, the general would have shot Romero and his scouts or hung them from the first cotton-wood they reached after they left the town. But they would have been the wrong ones to die for this idiotic blunder; that fate should by rights befall whoever ordered this insanity in the first place. Fierro or Villa himself. It made no difference.

Fever had wrung big Paco dry even in the saddle. The horse he had always handled with such mastery had, as he worsened day by day, gone its own erratic way with him—cantering ahead of the column, falling well behind from time to time, and then wandering off into the mesquite at awkward moments. The sergeant had listed perilously in the saddle whenever the desert was level enough to move forward faster than a walk, and Jorge had finally detailed Tonito to put Paco's animal on a lead.

It kept the dynamiter a little safer, and with Tonito also fixing the food Paco couldn't hold in that mammoth stomach, and lifting the canteen to a mouth that looked sewn shut, only to see the water run crazily off Paco's beard and down his chest, it had taken the boy's mind off the fact that his friend Pepe had died in Columbus.

The fevered face of the sergeant didn't show the pain he must be feeling, but even if he lived, as it now seemed he would, it surely had taken a terrible unseen toll.

The only good thing about their situation now was that the gringo cavalry had apparently given up the chase. They must have run low on water the second day out from Columbus, and since they didn't know Chihuahua as even Jorge's poor excuses for Bracomontes did, they couldn't find the holes and wells the troop circuited at a distance during the daylight hours and doubled back to only after night had fallen and Jorge had seen the fires the Americans had set.

Their enemies must have run short of ammunition, too.

Small wonder. They had used enough of it when they rode him down in town. It was the only thing about the fight the gringos made he could, as a professional, find to criticize. The waste, *Jesús*, the waste. Trini, if he were alive, would be appalled. It must be nice to be so rich. Obregón's army, not so rich as the Americans, but richer than the Division nowadays, would never be guilty of it.

Thinking it over, there was one other small thing he might be critical of: the Americans didn't move so well, not nearly so well as the disheveled, poorly mounted men Jorge led now. The gringos would have shit at the speed of his command a year ago. Even now he had only had to fight them three times in the two-day hunt they made for him, and only at the times and places he had chosen.

But in the town the Americans hadn't needed to be swift, just early. And that they were.

He had led the troop in from the west and down the wide, empty main street of Columbus. One signpost was dimly lit by the beams of a lamp shining through the window of a store or office of some kind: *Broadway*. He smiled, almost laughed. This wasn't the Broadway his sister Concepción dreamed about after reading the eastern magazines Ignacio brought to the Cantina Florida. It looked a twin of Estancia Street in Black Springs, but the Estancia Street across the tracks on the anglo side of town.

He halted the troop where small sheds and open-front half-stables assured him they couldn't be taken from the sides, motioned Paco to him, and together they rode another hundred fifty meters or so, guiding the horses with soft hands. So far, so good. It was comforting that their mounts moved quietly, although dead silence wasn't absolutely necessary. None of the citizens in bed along this street would do much more than roll over grumbling if a horse whinnied or a shoe rang against a rock. They had lived all their lives with the night sounds of animals.

He and Paco rode as far as the huge square building with the big sign reading "Ravel Bros. Mercantile Co."

¡Magnífico! By guesswork alone he had stopped his force

at exactly the right place. This was the building the general wanted for himself. He had said at the meeting that it was the two merchant brothers here who had taken his money and not delivered. Pancho Villa vowed he would collect the debt in person. Jorge was to stay just far enough west so the field guns could be wheeled down the street from the east and positioned where they could blow the Ravel warehouse to kindling from point-blank range. It was the only reason the guns had been bumped across half a thousand miles of desert. You didn't need artillery to destroy a wooden town like this. Rifle fire for the defenders and torches for the buildings would do the job. This town had a lot of soldiers in the camp on the other side of the railroad tracks and even more at that ranch somewhere behind them, the ones who had to be kept at bay long enough for the general to take his revenge.

"Jorge," Paco whispered. "We were right about Bautista. He hasn't taken his eyes from your back since we rode through the cut in the wire."

¡Mierda! He had forgotten the general's spy. Bad sign. What else was he forgetting? "Then you'll just have to keep him off it, Paco."

"He will be on his own back soon enough. *Prometo.*"

They turned and rode slowly back to where the troop was waiting.

Jorge's eyes scanned the three ragged lines of riders filling the street from hitchrail to hitchrail. Bautista was in the second rank. Could he order him back to the other side of the barbed wire on some pretext? No. He hadn't become a spy and an assassin by being stupid. He would certainly sniff Jorge's intentions out. Better to keep him on the inside of the tent pissing out than on the outside pissing in, and infinitely better to rely on Paco's two hands, his trench knife, or one well-aimed shot than to trust in trickery. For the moment Bautista posed no threat. As Jorge had told Paco, El Carnicero's killer would wait for enemy fire before he made his move.

But now it was time to forget him. It was time to be a soldier.

Jorge turned his horse and looked down the street toward

the warehouse. He raised his left fist over his head and then leaned over and pulled the carbine from his saddle holster. Behind him breechbolts clicked in the darkness. Somewhere off to the left a rooster crowed. Ignorant bird. It was still more than an hour until sunrise. He hoped the timing of this attack wasn't as bad. He pushed his left hand under the webbing of the rigid bandoliers crossed over his chest and pulled the gold watch he had taken from the body of the banker in San Sebastián from his pocket. It was still too dark to read it. With the carbine in his right hand he couldn't strike a light, but Paco had seen his predicament. A match flared, and the odor in the cold air was like that of the gunpowder and cordite they would soon smell.

Five minutes after four. Another ten minutes yet. Damn it! In spite of his misgivings of the last fourteen hours, he wanted battle now. Let the answer to the haunting nighttime question come if it decided to; he had worked on it all he could.

Lights began to flicker in some of the buildings down toward the warehouse. Could he take ten more minutes? He would most certainly have to give the order to fire if so much as one figure stepped into the empty street. "Men, women, or children, kill them all," Fierro had said.

Then he knew for a fact that the Division had reached the jumping-off place. It wasn't anything he heard or saw, but something he just felt. It wasn't a shudder of the ground or any shaking of the town's wooden buildings; it was a tremor of his instincts, instincts turned sensitive by almost two years of war. It was time.

He raised his left fist in the air again. Beside him he could feel Paco straighten himself in the saddle. *"Pronto."* It was just a whisper, but he knew it carried.

He felt the rifles of the troop fan out, seeking doors and windows, heard the slight metallic rustle as the weapons brushed against the bandoliers, heard one trooper curse his restless horse.

He dropped his fist.

"¡Fuego!"

When the last report died away and the last shard of glass

had tinkled into silence and the last echo had rebounded from the slab side of the warehouse, he could hear the Division.

It was a low rumble first—a thousand and more boots pounding the gravel and caliche as the general's force fed itself into a skirmish line, then the sounds of horses pulling the wagons loaded to the sideboards with cans of kerosene. Perhaps he could hear, too, the guns being cocked, but at three quarters of a mile away it was probably only his imagination. He would hear the heavy grinding of the carriages of the artillery soon, without imagining it.

How long would it take the storekeepers, waiters, lawyers, drunks, and householders who had just been blàsted from the last sleep they might ever know to spill from the doorways or thrust their heads through the shattered windows? And how many of them would be stupid enough to do it?

"The general won't open fire until he hears our second volley, Paco," he said. "When we've made it, dismount Porfirio's men. I saw hitchrails in that alley fifty meters back. They won't be in any possible line of fire, and we can use the alley to break away to the south when we're finished here. Have Porfirio take his men to cover in strong positions facing down the street. Once they're secure, do the same with the other half. Then turn the first lot around to secure our rear. You and I and Gómez will fight with the second bunch."

"I won't be able to keep an eye on Bautista then, Jorge. He is riding with Porfirio."

"We'll have to chance it, Sargento Durán," Jorge said. "I want you with me. Gómez and his asshole *manzana* pickers never did take orders well. They'll leave the street before I want them to if you and I don't hold them here.

"*Sí, señor mayor.* But I go respectfully on record that I don't like it."

Jorge laughed. "I'm not worried, Paco. You've gone 'respectfully on record' in almost every fight we've made together."

His fist was aloft again.

"*¡Fuego!*"

Again the crash of the volley died away without a soul appearing in the street. Two rounds of fire and still no enemy in view. This was more like drill than battle.

But the answer to the question that had plagued his night had come. He was a professional fighting man, a revolutionist, not a milksop. When a head snugged into the V of his carbine's sights, he would fire.

Now the guns of the Division barked to life, and then, surprising him with its quickness, the reply of the gringos roared from somewhere near the tent city beyond the railroad station. A bugle call rose above the gunfire. Smart work—or had their enemy been somehow warned? It seemed unlikely with this still-empty street in front of him.

Porfirio's men were out of the street now. He could see the first of them filing under the *portales* of the buildings on either side of them, with the good, reliable *guerrero* from San Luis Potosí named Guil Jaramillo out in front of the group on the right. Lucky for Paco and him they weren't all *bufones*. Guil settled in behind a tractor parked at the edge of the porch of some sort of store and laid his rifle across the seat. Two other men slipped in beside him.

From the sound of the gunfire on the eastern edge of town the Division must be closing with the *yanquis*. The din was mounting. Any second now the general would turn loose the Dorados, the last few good ones he always kept with him. Jorge frowned. It was the charge of this very unit which had fooled him into thinking they had won against Obregón. That was just before the machine gunners cut them down like mechanical ducks in a carnival booth.

On the opposite side of the street, other men were hunching down behind barrels and wooden crates. They wouldn't need an order to fire now.

Some of Porfirio's men were hauling boxes and what looked to be bags of feed to the center of the street behind them and just west of where the tethered horses were now making all kinds of racket. Lights were beginning to appear in the frame shacks on both sides of the street ahead of them.

Paco was gone now, and Gómez had eased his big bay

alongside Jorge's Appaloosa. Someone fired a shot—at what, Jorge couldn't tell.

Then he saw his first target. A nightgowned figure had broken from a doorway leaving the door ajar behind him. The light pouring through the door made the figure a perfect target as he started across the street.

Jorge lifted the carbine to his shoulder.

Then the figure turned its face straight toward him, and he saw that the long white nightgown covered the body of a boy. Eight or nine years old. No, make it ten. Even in the dim light he could see the bright staring eyes as the boy brushed a shock of wheat-colored hair away from them.

Jorge lowered the carbine.

But as he watched, the face became a red blot of blood, and the boy pitched forward to the hardpan of the street like a rag tossed away.

"Mayor Martínez! Look out!" Gómez yelled beside him. He turned and saw the lieutenant raise his rifle. In an upstairs window on the left another rifle glinted and then disappeared when Gómez fired.

Jaramillo and the two men with him were firing down the street. Shadows, which as he peered into the darkness turned out to be men with guns, his men, were flitting under the roofs of the porticos halfway to the warehouse. Some of Gómez's men had begun to fire, too, the reports melding to a roar.

Where was Paco? By now he should have gotten all of Porfirio's troopers in position to cover the men still in the street as they, too, dismounted. Bautista? Had he beaten Paco? Was he even now sighting in on Jorge's back?

The now steady rifle fire was getting strangely louder; not only louder, it had changed its pitch, sounding now as if it were coming from another place.

Beside him, Gómez suddenly exhaled a great brushy sigh and slumped over the neck of the bay with his arms hanging limp and a dark stain spreading down his back—and Jorge knew in an instant that hell had stolen a march on him.

The shot couldn't possibly have come from up ahead of them. Bautista? Had it been meant for him?

He turned. Back up the street, just beyond the place where Porfirio's men had begun to build the barricade, he saw three bodies. His men! But *how* in the name of God?

Then flame blossomed in an almost solid bar across the street behind the feed bags and the boxes scattered on the caliche where the dead men lay. The sound of the fusillade filled his ears with the scream of white-hot metal.

The Americans from the ranch!

"*¡Vámonos!* Take cover!"

Two more of his men fell as they broke for the sides of the street. One of the horses just kneeled down and laid its head on its side as if its rider were a *charro* guiding it through its tricks.

The flames from the gringos' guns ripped the blackness apart again.

Now the street this side of the partial barricade was empty save for Jorge. Time to think of himself. He dug his spurs into the Appaloosa's flanks and rode for the alley where the other horses were.

One of his men was kneeling at the corner of a shed facing on the street, keeping up a steady counterfire. What the man could possibly see in the darkness escaped Jorge, but it was good he was doing something.

Fifteen feet into the alley he found Paco.

His sergeant was squatting in the dirt with his huge rump resting on his heels and his right hand clasped to his left shoulder. Blood soaked his shirt and cartridge belt. He looked up at Jorge with flat, dead eyes.

"I am sorry, Jorge," he said. "I didn't get him."

"Never mind that now, Paco. How about you?"

"He rode out already, Jorge."

"*Es nada.* We have other things to concern us now. Let me see that." He reached for Paco's hand.

"He will try again, *amigo*. Watch for him."

"*You* will watch for him, Paco. Did he do this?"

"*Yanquis*, Jorge, *los gringos*. What are they firing—cannonballs?"

Jorge turned and beckoned to the man kneeling by the

shed. The man held his fire and looked down the street and then faced Jorge.

"Come here and take care of your sergeant, *soldado*," Jorge called to him.

The man took one more look down the street, then turned and crawled to the two of them. Jorge saw now that it was Zirco, the one Yaqui Indian left in the troop from better days. Good. He could leave the big man for a moment and get his fight in order.

By the time he went to the Appaloosa, took his field glasses from his saddlebag, and then went to the corner of the shed himself, the gunfire had diminished, become intermittent.

The faint light from the east was marching westward, and in a quick scan of the buildings well beyond the barricade he saw the Americans, now some distance back of where they had blasted the troop with those first two devastating volleys. They must have withdrawn a hundred meters or more and were now regrouping out of range. It was a good tactic on the part of their commander. The American captain or major, or whatever he was, couldn't know Jorge was there only to hold him up long enough for the general to wheel up his antique guns, and he couldn't know how few men Jorge had. For all he knew Jorge could be leading a thousand. And for the moment at least he was as ignorant of Jorge's intentions as Jorge was of his.

From the American's point of view there was no sense in rushing matters. When the sun came up, both he and Jorge would know a great deal more about each other. *Sí*, sound thinking. But it also served Jorge well. The gringo leader should have been preparing to grind Jorge into the caliche, but he couldn't know that. The American wasn't cowardly, but perhaps he was careful, and that alone might buy the general as much time as would Jorge's fight.

Across the street he could see more of his own men. They, too, had sensed that things would go easier for a little while. A couple of them even had *cigarrillos* going. Porfirio, grinning like a fool, waved to him. Jorge patted his hand against the air in the signal to hold things down, and the *lugartenien-*

te from Hermosillo nodded. Porfirio wasn't a gifted soldier, but he was marginally better than Gómez was . . . had been.

Gómez, *sí*. Jorge took time now to look at the street itself.

Two . . . three . . . seven . . . nine bodies, counting that of his dead lieutenant. And those were only the ones in sight from where he hunkered down next to the shed. There could be several more. He knew of one. The boy.

With the building corners in the way he couldn't see much of anything at all on his side of the street. All of the ones in view looked dead. Two horses were down as well, and one other poor beast wandered in crazed, drunken circles. Nine gone at least, ten with Paco out of it. It reduced his force to twenty-seven at the moment—maximum. And this business was a long way from being over with.

The firing had died away to nothing now.

But only here where Jorge was. It was getting noisier and heavier where the Division was advancing. The general must be dealing out severe punishment to the *yanquis* who had bivouacked near the depot.

The sky to the east was yellowing. Any second now the sun would pop up above the cottonwoods at the eastern end of Broadway, and then he could pretty well be sure the American would not attack for almost another hour, when the sun was high enough to keep his gunner's sights sharp and clear. He stood up, stepped into the street for a better view. Porfirio waved at him frantically. He almost shouted to the lieutenant not to worry. The gringos' withdrawal had put Jorge out of range of them, too. Down past the warehouse men were filling the street, but also beyond carbine range. Civilians, but all carrying weapons. He almost felt a twinge of pity for them. They were right in the path of the general's intended final push against the warehouse.

He took two more steps toward the center of the street, and from here the steeple of a church came in view. There was movement in the belfry. He took his binoculars from their case and trained them on it.

Three men in those ridiculous flat-brimmed, pointed hats he had seen on the soldiers at Fort Bliss were readying a machine gun. He shivered. He prayed that his personal opponent back up the street didn't have one or more. He remembered Obregón and Agua Prieta, and what just four of them had done to the Division there. Celaya had been the beginning of its pitiful decline, Agua Prieta had been the cascade into complete despair.

He returned to the alley to find Zirco holding his canteen to Paco's lips. The dynamiter's shoulder was bound with rags. Zirco's shirt was gone and his cartridge belts hugged his naked chest.

"*¿Cómo estás, viejo?*" Jorge said to Paco.

"*Bien*, Jorge."

"You wouldn't lie to me?"

"No, *amigo*. And if I did I would confess it, *verdad* I would—if we ever meet a priest. Will there be priests where we will go if this turns out the way it started, Jorge?"

"*Sí*, Paco—or better still, angels. Trini always said angels rode with you and me."

"*Con respeto*, I think I would rather have Trini himself riding with us. He was *muy guerrero*, Jorge."

Jorge turned to Zirco, who had discreetly moved to the corner of the shed, rifle in hand again.

"Zirco."

"*¿Sí, mayor?*"

"Cross the street, *por favor*, and tell the lieutenant to come over here. Have him bring five men with him."

While Zirco ran, Jorge walked to the back of the alley. Yes, his first glance when he had ridden in here had told him what he wanted to know. There was nothing out there to the left of the arroyo but an immense stretch of flatland stretching to the wire and Chihuahua. This would be their exit route.

"You wanted me, Jorge?"

"*Sí*, Porfirio." The man would probably think him *un idiota* when he told him what he wanted. "Send three of your *soldados* back across the street and have them send six to us. Three should be walking and three running hard. And see if someone else can catch that riderless *caballo*. Then send two across and bring four, some riding if they can get their horses, some on foot."

To his surprise Porfirio was nodding and smiling. *¡Por Dios!* For once he understood.

Jorge made one of the trips himself, to the feed store straight across from the alley. He found two more bodies. Eleven gone.

In twenty minutes the exchange was completed and what was left of the troop was in the alley. He wondered if he had fooled the American commander. He doubted it. He wouldn't have been fooled himself. But there was a chance, and he did want all his men on this side, anyway. Even after finding the two dead men he hadn't seen, he had been too sanguine. He counted twenty-one. Twenty-six horses stood at the hitch-rail and two more were tethered to rings in the wall across from it.

The shed on the one side of the alley and the store or office building on the other both had pitched roofs. Too bad. What he wouldn't have given for just one of the solid adobes of Chupadera County with its parapet. He couldn't put snipers up on these flimsy, slanted affairs. He had Porfirio detail three men to guard the back end of the alley. Then he sent half a dozen men into the shed to knock planks from the western wall for gunports.

Fire erupted from the east. He raced to the street with his field glasses. The machine gun in the church was jumping in the belfry. Clouds of smoke rose in half a dozen places at the eastern end of town. The general's arsonists were busy. Small-arms fire broke out much nearer than he had heard it from that quarter, and the civilians he had seen earlier were gone from where they had assembled east of the warehouse. From the sound of things they would soon be coming back. Not long after that the artillery would be trundled into place.

He turned and put the glasses on the gringos he would have to delay or stop. Yes, they were getting ready. They had seen the smoke and heard the machine gun, too.

He pulled his watch from his pocket. *¡Dios!* They had been here for an hour and forty minutes now.

Back in the alley he found Paco on his feet. The sergeant had his rifle in his huge right hand.

The guard at the street end of the alley signaled Jorge. As he ran to him, he heard the first of the rifle fire. It was just a covering fire, but the riflemen had moved close enough that chips and splinters flew from the shed and the building across from it. Inside the shed, and from the porch of the other building, the troop opened fire.

The gringos were advancing along both sides of the street to the west of them, covering each other and making runs of fifteen or twenty feet. The nearest of them weren't firing, just moving into position. Disciplined fighters, all of them. But two of them fell as he watched.

He had to stop them before they established themselves in the buildings opposite the entrance to the alley. This was a pathway to escape, not a fort. He had known that when he had chosen it, of course, and had decided escape outweighed defense. The general had demanded an hour from him. He had given him almost two.

Then he detected a change in the timbre of the battle raging in the east.

There was no more from the machine gun in the church, but the sound of rifle fire seemed a bit more distant.

It was a second or two before the meaning of it hit him.

The general was retreating.

From the pall of smoke now beginning to obscure the sun it seemed that many more fires had been set. This little tinder town could burn to the caliche. But the general was retreating. The once invincible División del Norte was suffering the most humiliating defeat of its history. Merchants, lawyers, clerks, stableboys, schoolmasters, probably housewives, too, along with a not terribly large force of American cavalry with no heavy ordnance, were beating the mighty Pancho Villa, Tiger of the North.

And the now tiny command of Major Jorge Martínez was on its own. "Paco," he said to his sergeant, "let's get the hell out of here. I want to live long enough to see my son born. Juanita won't wait for me forever before she gives birth to him."

PART 5

▲▲▲▲▲▲▲▲▲▲▲▲

EL
RECOBRO

49

Acting Sheriff Corey Lane sat at the desk in the office in Black Springs, New Mexico, with his head in his hands.

If he had any sense at all he would forget about everything here in town, get back out to the X-Bar-7, and sleep for a week. Fighting the fires across the tracks with the people in Mex Town through that long night last weekend had taken more out of him than he had thought at first. He had recovered well enough physically, but in other ways . . .

Why hadn't he expected the attack on Mex Town? A fool would have guessed that the anger over Columbus would erupt in some way.

At daybreak four days ago, with the fires all under control at last, a momentary euphoria had lifted him, despite the fact that Mex Town was a smoking grave. It was the first time he had been busy in the more than two months since he returned to Chupadera County from Mexico. The crisis over, he was back in the doldrums once again.

With the exception of going over the weekly report for the county commissioners there wasn't anything on the desk that had to be done this morning, and even had there been, it could wait for Ben González to get back on the job. The newly elected sheriff was due back from the hospital in Albuquerque this afternoon, with his broken leg mended at last, according to the message from Ben's wife three days ago. If he had arrived back in Black Springs last week, Ben would have had to deal with the conflagration and its sobering aftermath. As things stood, he would still have to run the investigation into just who the night riders were who stormed through the *barrio* with their torches in the small hours, when every possible witness was asleep or drunk or both. It wouldn't be easy. The questions Corey had asked since Mex Town burned hadn't elicited one answer worth a damn.

A lawman started with motive on a hunt such as this one. It wasn't hard to find in this case. Pancho Villa's monumental stupidity in making his Draconian attack on American soil, either out of pique or twisted revolutionary politics, had provided just about every man and woman, and most children in the .Ojos Negros, with all the motive they needed.

Last Wednesday, even before the news of Villa's raid on the border town flashed up the line from El Paso, he had heard Abe Gibbon, the brutish telegrapher in the Western Union office at the depot, tell a drinker at the bar in the Sacramento, "Greasers are all alike—anywhere. The ones over there in Mex Town would cut our throats in a second if they thought they could get away with it. We ought to skin every one of them before they try. They ain't good for the U.S. of A.; even *ours* ain't real Americans."

The listener had nodded as if he were hearing gospel. It was the same sentiment Corey had heard in too many places on the anglo side of the tracks over the years. Now the bad blood had boiled over, and Ben would have hell's own time mopping it up and tracking down who was responsible, unless the night-riding cretins who had burned the *barrio* bragged about it to someone who would actually tell the sheriff. The mounted arsonists had planned well and organized quickly. Burning the mud of Mex Town wasn't easy.

Corey hoped Ben would take the help he intended offering. He might not. Decent Ben might feel awkward about giving his former boss any kind of orders. Corey would have to persuade him that he could be almost as good a subordinate as Ben had been himself in the eight years they had worked together. He wouldn't mention how much he needed some new responsibilities to take the place of the ones he had evaded by coming home. Perhaps shrewd Ben would guess. Corey could relieve him of some of the paperwork around the office at the very least.

Could he? He wasn't doing too well with the report lying accusingly on the desk.

When he stepped in for ailing Ben a month ago, happy for the chance to be jolted out of his depression by the prospect, he had been secretly pleased when he discovered how few were the changes his good friend and fellow peace officer had made in the department's operations while he had been out of the country those two years that now were but a dream. He took it as a compliment, whether Ben meant it that way or not.

For the first week, with his old badge pinned to his shirt again, he had been charged up and almost carefree, but the lassitude which had dogged him since he came up from the border settled over him again, even more blanketing than before.

He swiveled in the chair and it squeaked. It had squeaked for years, but it had never bothered him back then. In those days the sound was *only* a squeak. Now it rasped at him like another conscience.

In his two months back there had been no letter from Luisa, but he hadn't truly expected that there would be. It was over. He had been ten times a fool to think they ever had a real chance together.

There had been nothing from Henry Richardson, either, so that was over, too. He still scanned the *El Paso Times* for any news of Ángeles, but with Pancho now not much more than a harried leader of guerrillas instead of the commander of a superb modern army such as the one the Division had been at Torreón, Paredón, and Zacetecas, Ángeles seemed to be permanently in exile, or at least relegated to the shadows. No news story, editorial, or feature article mentioned him. Perhaps it was all to the good. If the great strategist were ever to come to the fore again, it couldn't help his cause were he to be too closely identified with the imitation Pancho Villa marauding ineffectively in Chihuahua and Sonora nowadays. If the American press now looked on the Tiger of the North as a ruffian bandit and little else—as some segments of it had from the outset—the picture they were painting for their readers was beginning to be a more faithful likeness by the day, or at least a more fitting caricature. And Pancho was sitting for this only slightly distorted portrait almost willingly, it seemed.

What had once been news of heroic battles had now become an expected litany of bank and train robberies, orgies of wanton killing for no discernible purpose, broken only by the disaster at Agua Prieta when Obregón crushed what remained of the Division as a fighting force to be feared—and then this mindless attack on what Pancho must have considered a helpless town, an action which should have been a piece of cake, but wasn't. The Division had scattered itself across half of Chihuahua's desert reaches, and the War Department of the United States had now ordered General Black Jack Pershing to cross the border to pursue and punish Villistas wherever he could find them.

Why had Villa done something so manifestly stupid? What could he possibly have gained even had the raid succeeded? Pride was the only conceivable answer. Corey understood Villa's outrage at Woodrow Wilson's recognition of Venustiano Carranza—shared it. But this was where someone with a better understanding of how men and nations shifted loyalties to serve what they determined to be their own best interests would have forgone this thoughtless act of vengeance. Someone like Ángeles. It hurt to think of that.

He should get back to the damned report. He picked it up, put it down again. In his present, clinging apathy perhaps he wouldn't be of much help to Ben no matter what his intentions were.

Sure, El Caudillo had found himself trapped. But like the futile thrashing of a caught ferret, the strike at Columbus had been an act of manic desperation. He had gnawed his own paw to shreds to get free, but he had gnawed the wrong paw, and remained surely in the clenched steel teeth of circumstance, and now was too weakened by the resulting hemorrhage to ever free himself.

Not the biggest, Columbus was still the worst defeat Pancho Villa had so far suffered.

But at least the world was taking note of the generalissimo's defeats. Those of Corey Lane were going unremarked—as they should.

He picked the report up again. Feeling sorry for himself wasn't taming the bulldog. He should get back over to Mex Town and see how the job of rebuilding the Black Springs *barrio* was coming. The work had begun while the smoke was still rising and most of Estancia Street was a morass from the water the bucket brigades had spilled as they fought the fires. *Campesinos* from the upper Rio Concho had swarmed into the smoldering town to work shoulder-to-shoulder with the now homeless residents there even before the sun had risen to cut the gray pall over the charred timbers and soaked adobe brick.

He should go over there even if it meant he had to look yet again into the beseeching eyes of Concepción Martínez, Jorge's sister, look at her once more and remember how he had failed her, too. When he saw her first, after his return, she had never once voiced criticism for his failure to bring her brother back, but he had atoned for that with a hair shirt of his own making.

He decided to make the trip as soon as he finished touching up the report for the commissioners. Ben would be too tired from the bus trip down from the city to do the boring, time-consuming chore himself.

He had rewritten half of it when Jimmy Lee Babcock, Ben's number one deputy, entered from the outer office. "Corey, that foreman from the D Cross A, Ortiz, is out here looking to have a word with you."

Ignacio Ortiz, the slender, earnest, intelligent man who had fought the Mex Town fires with him so valiantly, was Jorge's best friend in Chupadera County.

"Give me five, if he'll wait, Jimmy Lee."

Douglas MacAndrews was a lucky man to have Ortiz, if only to balance the agony his son Jamie brought him. Although he had heard good things about Ortiz, Corey hadn't known the foreman well until the night of the fires, but he got to know and value him pretty *damned* well in the glowing crucible Mex Town became as it burned to the caliche.

The looks and deeds of two people, Ortiz and the Martínez girl, would stay forever in the foreground of his memory of that night: her swirling red skirt as she hauled buckets of water up and down Estancia Street as well as any man; the foreman's dark, intent face when carrying out Corey's orders, directing the amateur firefighters from blaze to blaze with a quiet word or two. It had almost made him forget how much hatred for their anglo neighbors must be mounting in the hearts of the miserable, decent folk who watched in silent despair as everything they owned went up in flames. The girl had let some bitterness show as she worked, but the slim foreman had simply gone about the task of saving what he could. Never once did he even slow or pause in his rescue efforts to try to place blame for the tragedy. If ever there lived a man who embodied the idea of that French saying, *il faut d'abord durer,* that man was Ignacio Ortiz.

It wasn't a quality he hadn't seen before. He had seen it in the simple, long-suffering *soldados* and *soldaderas* of Pancho Villa's now doomed army. It didn't at all diminish the sight of it in Ignacio Ortiz.

He finished correcting the report in a haste he didn't regret and called out to Jimmy Lee to show the D Cross A rider-foreman in. He stood to wait for him.

"Sit down, Señor Ortiz, *por favor. ¿Qué pasa?*"

"I have come to speak with you about *mi amigo* Jorge Martínez, Sheriff Lane."

"Yes?" Damn it! This was the last thing he needed.

"I believe you saw him when you were in Mexico." How on earth did Ortiz know this? Concepción. Of course. "The people here in Black Springs who love him want him home."

"I more or less told him that, Mr. Ortiz. He said he wouldn't come."

"Perhaps it will be necessary to tell him again, in stronger terms. His father, Andreas, is dying, *señor.*"

Old Andreas dying? The man Corey owed his life to? "What's wrong with him, Ortiz?"

"Consumption, Señor Lane. I think it is quite advanced. Jorge is needed here. There is also the other compelling reason for his return. Jorge Martínez can never be himself anywhere else on earth."

Strange statement. There wasn't any basis for it in any fact Corey knew, and yet . . . Ignacio Ortiz was right.

"I don't know where Jorge is now. And I haven't the faintest idea how to find him."

"I don't know where he is, either, Señor Lane—but I know where he was last week." He pulled something from his shirt pocket and placed it on the desk carefully, as if it were something delicate or dangerous. It was a letter in one of the flimsy, gray, speckled envelopes like the ones Corey had bought himself in Mexico to use for his reports to Henry. "Would you read that, *señor, por favor?*"

Corey picked it up. The postmark read: "Las Palomas, Chihuahua 28 FEB 16." He looked at Ignacio and slipped the letter from the envelope.

The first part of it was what one might expect: the usual queries about the health of someone's family and that of the friend to whom the letter was addressed, the assurance that the writer's own was excellent, and then . . .

. . . and I have been given special work because I am an *americano.* Someday I will be able to tell you all about it. I can tell you that soon—very soon—something will happen to open the eyes of every gringo.

Jorge

Corey feared the letter might burn his fingers as it had just seared his eyes. He dropped it on the desk and pushed it at Ignacio.

"Put it away, *please,* Mr. Ortiz." Douglas MacAndrew's foreman stuffed it back in his pocket. His eyes held Corey's. There should be a least a flicker of fear in them, but there wasn't. "Don't you realize what this letter means? Jorge was at Columbus with Villa! If our American authorities discover that, he could *never* come back home."

"Will they discover it, Señor Lane?"

"I am a sworn law officer, only temporarily, of course, but nonetheless—"

"*Will* they discover it?"

Ben González's office began to close on Corey. He fought the pressure of the walls with every ounce of strength he could summon up.

"No," he said. There was no sign of triumph on the foreman's face. "You knew what my answer would be, didn't you?"

"*Sí, señor.*"

"How did you know?"

Ortiz shrugged. "Partly because *mi amiga* Concepcíon Martínez says she would trust you with her life, but mostly because of the things I saw in you the night we fought the fires."

"You could have talked to me about Jorge without showing me that letter."

"*Sí.* But Concepción and I didn't want you to do anything for Jorge without knowing the risks you might be taking." He stood up. "*Gracias* for your time, Sheriff Lane." Like a wraith, he was gone.

He sat for an hour, trying not to think. Jimmy Lee peeked in through the door once and pulled his head back out as if someone had taken a shot at him.

Ignacio Ortiz had asked no promise. Perhaps he despaired of getting one. Perhaps he was also as wise a man as Corey had ever met.

He pulled his watch from his pocket—12:17. The county clerk's office upstairs would be empty for the rest of the lunch hour, another forty-three minutes. He could use the telephone in private.

"Good to hear from you, Corey," Henry Richardson said. "What's on your mind?"

"When does General Pershing go into Mexico, Henry?"

Henry laughed. "You don't seriously believe I would tell you even if I knew, do you? Come now, Corey!" There was a pause. "Why do you want to know, apart from nosiness?"

"Because I want to go with him."

"What?"

"I've got business to attend to in Chihuahua. I feel I can do it better if I'm with the general's expeditionary force. Get me assigned to him, Henry, seconded or whatever you people like to call it. I'd prefer to be with him as a civilian without any duties holding me too tightly to him, but I'll go back in uniform if I must."

"You're coming back to work for me, Corey? That's good news!"

"No! Disabuse yourself on any such idea, Henry. This is a strictly personal matter."

"In that case, I don't know, my friend."

"Henry! I think you owe me."

Henry's voice carried a good-sized portion of suspicion when he spoke again. "Are you going to make another try for Ángeles? If you are, please keep in mind that if I don't *reappoint* you, you'll be strictly on your own. Washington won't help you in any way. You would be fully exposed, with no *bona fides* of any kind."

"But you'll do it? You'll get me posted to our forces on the border?"

"Did you think for a moment I wouldn't, Corey?"

Corey restored the receiver to its hook and rang off.

After a quick bite at Carmi's, he would go over the weekly report he had revised so halfheartedly this morning and do it right this time. He owed Ben another afternoon's honest work. Henry Richardson would understand such niceties of duty, and approve.

Outside, he could still smell the stale smoke from Mex Town. Not remarkable. It might stay in his nostrils for a long time yet.

"Jorge Martínez," he muttered to himself. "You'd damned well better be worth all this. And you, Ignacio Ortiz—God damn your melting, mystic eyes . . ."

He decided against having lunch at Carmi's. Concepción would find him something when he saw his old friend Andreas, and talked with him about his son.

▲▲▲▲▲

50

"We have been beaten badly this last year, Paco, but this is the first time we have been hunted," Jorge said.

Paco only grunted pitifully, compared to the seismic growls of other days. His shoulder was healing decently at last, but the ordeal must have stripped thirty pounds from the massive body. Flesh draped from his limbs like a worn, brown coat.

"Have another *cerveza*, Papá," Juanita said.

"There is no more, *mi hija*."

It was one of the few times Jorge had heard her urge her father to drink. She obviously believed that getting the weight back on him was worth the risk of a few more ounces of alcohol. Her bright face belied the worry she must be feeling for him. At least *she* looked good. The extra pounds and inches around her middle were far from unbecoming. She had laughed at him when they reached this cheap *posada* in the tiny railroad town of El Sueco in central Chihuahua after they fled Columbus. "Oh, of course I'm glad you hurried to be with me, *cariño*, but it is nowhere near time yet. Another month at least."

"Last night he kicked your belly hard. It made my hand jump. He wants to be born soon."

"Trust me, Jorge. It is not yet time."

"You know, of course, just when he started?" he scoffed gently.

"*Sí*. Why would you think I wouldn't?" She lifted her head and smiled a defiant smile. "Do you remember that night in—"

"Juanita!" He nodded toward Paco, scowling a scowl he didn't truly mean. Paco was smiling. *Bueno*. There hadn't been many smiles from him during his recovery.

"I wish Margarita was still here," Jorge said next.

"Well, she isn't. I miss her, *sí*, and she would be good to have around, but it is not of great importance. The women in my family gave birth for hundreds of years without nurses—and without doctors."

"This is the twentieth century, Juanita!"

"That makes a difference? Women's bodies haven't changed. I am strong. And I've never felt better in my life. I have been able to do everything I had to as a *soldadera*—and as a wife."

He couldn't argue with that. She hadn't flagged, either in caring for her father or in looking after Jorge. They had picked her up at Moctezuma where they had left her before Columbus, and she had ridden as well as any man in what was left of the troop as they moved south to El Sueco, out-distancing the Americans under that general with the big reputation from the Philippines, Pershing.

Paco stirred himself, rumbling, "What is all this *mierda* about us being hunted? *Sí*, we are hunted, but it can't be worse than the things we faced at Celaya and León." Every word took a special effort. He was better, but he wasn't quite Paco Durán yet.

"True. But the thing about our present fix, *viejo*," Jorge said, "is that we will be hunted from two directions. By the *yanquis* moving down from Texas, and the Carrancistas under Obregón from the south. My guess is that the Obregonistas will reach El Sueco here in force in two, no more than three days. We'll be in a vise we won't enjoy. This is still a Villa town. No matter who reaches it first, this Pershing or our main enemy, they'll tear it to shreds."

"Not that it matters, Jorge, but we are hunted from *three* directions."

"Three?"

"*Sí*. You are forgetting the spy Bautista."

"Why are you still harping on him, Paco? He made no move to kill me in the fight at Columbus. That was the best chance he could hope to get, if he truly wanted one. And he behaved just fine on the ride south. He fought as well as any of our men in that skirmish against the Americans. If he intended to kill me he would have done so by now. *Es nada*."

Paco sighed. "*¿Nada?* A knife in the back is *nada?* A pistol shot from an ambush in the rocks is *nada?* I know you are now *un mayor muy grande*, but sometimes you are the same *estúpido* recruit I tried to teach at Torreón. Bautista has been asking a lot of questions about that nephew of the Butcher, the one who had the fatal headache. His bloody *jefe* never forgets. You must remember how he waited to get Trini at Celaya. Waiting is for him an enjoyable part of the games he plays. If he has decided he wants you dead as much as he—"

There was a small, pained gasp from Juanita. She stood up and pressed both hands to her lower abdomen.

"*Basta*, Paco! Enough!" Jorge said. "*¿Qué pasa, cariña?*"

"Do not stop talking, Jorge. Either of you. I know what we are facing. I am not a child," Juanita said. "And no, you will not become a father tonight. It's just that I must make water again. It is the only thing I don't like about being so *encinta*." She moved toward the door, her walk an ungainly waddle compared to the sinuous, easy stride that caught and held his eye the day he splashed across the Río Nazas astride that shameful, shitting nag, on the way to his first meeting with Trini Álvarez.

"Now that she is gone for the moment," Jorge said, "I can speak more freely, Paco. Look, old friend. Perhaps you are right about there being some danger from Bautista, but it serves no good purpose to alarm *tu hija*."

"*Sí.* You are right. I should have known you weren't asleep altogether, Captain Cockroach."

"Then quit talking about how I might get a knife in the back, *por favor*, and let's think about what we should do about him."

"Why don't you just let me kill him, Jorge?"

"Not yet, Paco. Fierro would know something is wrong in this *tropa* if you did. I may be stupid, but I think I can make use of Bautista. I want to find out if Fierro is still with General Villa or is operating somewhere on his own. I have an idea, but there are other things worrying us at the moment. How many men did we have left this morning?"

"Nineteen. At the rate they're deserting, I think that in one month we will be down to you, me, Bautista, and our inde-structible *chico* Tonito and that fucking bugle I could do without. I think *el asesino* is now just waiting until you have fewer men on hand to look out for you. By then we'll all be walking. When Bernardo Griegos ran off last night, he took three horses with him. We've lost a dozen mounts in a week."

"Do any of the other men know where Griegos went?"

"If they do, they're not telling me."

"Then there is no point in the whole troop chasing after him. Have any of our scouts learned where Pershing and his *yanquis* are?"

"Only that they are somewhere in the northern deserts try-ing to find Pancho and the Division."

"I hope they don't have any better luck than we have had, *viejo*."

"They wouldn't have any chance of finding Pancho at all if they didn't have those aeroplanes looking for him. I don't know what those ridiculous kites could ever do in a real war, but I will admit they are better than binoculars. Did you see that one flying over the railroad yesterday?"

"Yes. Nothing for him to see here in El Sueco. The *tropa* is no longer big enough to attract anyone's attention. Maybe he was counting pigs and chickens. Americans get just as hungry as Mexicans."

"There won't be many pigs and chickens to count by to-morrow. The villagers are leaving as fast as they can and tak-ing their livestock with them. How long will *we* stay in this sinkhole, Jorge? And where will we go from here? Don't you think it is time for us to find the rest of the army? The gen-eral must be planning a big attack on the *norteamericanos*, maybe as early as this month. He will need us."

The questions were ones Jorge had dreaded hearing for a week. Well, he couldn't hide the decisions made piece by piece in the last three sleepless nights from the big dynamiter much longer. "I'll give you some answers in just a moment, Paco. First, I want you to tell Bautista tomorrow morning that he is to take a message to Fierro. I would bet my last centavo he won't ask where the Butcher is. He already knows. And he won't refuse a chance to get more orders from him."

"Won't he smell a trick?"

"I want you to tell him he is to pick up our pay. Tell the other men that's why he's going. Even if he doesn't want to, they will make him go. We haven't seen a peso in more than two months. Pretty soon we'll have to start robbing trains just to feed *ourselves*. *Sí*, he'll go. Then, when he is on his way ..." This would be the painful part of it for Paco, *and* for him. "We will leave El Sueco ... we will ride hard for *las sierras* ... and we will not even try to find the army."

"Jorge! Isn't that desertion—just as much as our men leaving us?"

"*Sí*. That's exactly what it is."

"But why, Jorge? *¿Por qué?*"

"There will be no attack on the *yanquis*, Paco. Not this month, not this year ... not ever. General Villa's war is over."

"*¡No, no, amigo!* Don't say that. It cannot be!" As violent as the protest was, something in Paco's voice gave away the fact that his giant heart wasn't in it. Jorge hated hearing the tacit surrender as much as he hated bringing it on, but it did make it easier to continue. "Your war is over, too, old friend."

A faint cry came from the doorway. "What about *your* war, Jorge?" It was Juanita. He hadn't noticed her return.

"I think now that my war has been over for a long time, *mi amor*. This past year I have been fighting a war that belongs to someone else."

She looked away quickly, as if an unseen hand had slapped her. He would have to make it right before they slept tonight. He watched her cross to the bed and sink down on the edge of it. He felt moisture in his eyes and blinked it away.

"Do you have a map of Chihuahua, Paco?"

"*Sí*, Jorge. One that Trini gave me once."

"Get it, will you, *por favor*?"

The giant struggled to his feet. No, he didn't move nearly as fast these days. He went to the saddlebag he had hauled inside the dingy room the first night in town, pulled out a grease-mottled map, and handed it to Jorge.

"Who is the best tracker in the troop, Paco?" Jorge said as he unfolded the map.

"*El indio,* Zirco."

Marvelous. If he could really trust anyone left in his shriveled command, it was the Yaqui, secretive and withdrawn as he might look. "¡*Bueno!* I want you to send him out on Bautista's trail an hour after the spy leaves. He is just to follow him until he finds out where Fierro is, and then he is to join us again. Don't get any big ideas and tell him to kill Bautista. That can wait. Tell Zirco we'll wait for him . . ." He studied the map. "Here." He jabbed his forefinger far to the southwest of El Sueco. "Tell him he has my word we will not go into the mountains until he catches up with us. Take the map and show him where we'll wait."

Paco squinted at the map. "What is the name of the place?"

He had forgotten, as he had so many times before, that Paco couldn't read. Zirco couldn't either. But every *soldado* in the troop could at least make their way across a marked map—with very little help. Trini had praised him to the skies when he discovered how he had trained his men.

"Numiquipe." He pulled out his pencil and circled the town on the map. "Have Zirco make a mark as close to where he finds Fierro as he can, and have him draw a line showing where he thinks Bautista leads him."

"Why is it so important to know where Fierro is?"

"It makes a great difference in deciding exactly where we go to ground in *las sierras.* From Numiquipe we have a lot of choices. And tell Zirco to get back here fast. This town is finished. There will be no food here in a day or two. I hear even the *padre* is leaving here tomorrow."

Paco repeated the name of the town three times, folded up the map, stuck the pencil Jorge gave him in his pocket, and without another word went into the Chihuahuan night.

Maybe it would work. It wasn't foolproof, but it was the best he could do. Even if the Indian made a mistake with the map, talking to him when they met in Numiquipe might provide the answers.

"Jorge . . ." Juanita said from the bed. Something made her voice quaver. "Now that you have decided the war is over, will you be going home?"

The words pierced him to the heart. Why in God's name would such a thought occur to her again? Hadn't they been all through this before—when she agreed to have the baby? And now of all times, when he had made his mind up firmly to hide out in the Sierra Madres with her, Paco, and the child. Didn't she know that while she lived he could never leave Mexico without her—no matter how much he wanted to?

"*Querida . . .*" He had to convince her over and over again. It was probably the most important thing he would ever say to her. Well, it would never hurt to say it a thousand times. It felt good when nothing else did. Somehow he had to erase the look of disbelief she still wore.

"We will be together—always."

He meant it. She knew he meant it. She knew, too, that it wouldn't make a particle of difference. No matter how good his heart or strong his purpose, he would leave her here in Mexico. The sure feeling that this would happen had come last night, as if some spectral messenger had visited her while she slept. She couldn't doubt it. He wouldn't want to leave her, but he would leave, and when he did he would leave as well the life she carried beneath her breast.

Jorge, Jorge. I love you so.

She stood. The baby inside her felt suddenly heavy. Until now she had carried it so easily.

"I must go to that cantina down the *calle, querida.* Papá needs *cerveza.*"

"*Un momento, mi amor.* I will go with you."

Panic. But at least panic she could suppress. "No, no, Jorge! Stay and rest. You will need all your strength when you lead us out of here."

She hadn't lied. She *would* get Papá's beer. But there was

somewhere else she must go and something else she must do first.

The rumor Jorge had heard was right. The priest was leaving El Sueco. As she stepped inside the little church she found him at the altar, packing a large wooden box with the precious silver tools of his trade. There wasn't much. El Sueco was a poor parish.

She wouldn't hide what she intended doing from Jorge, but she knew she had to do it alone. She wouldn't see a church or a *padre* again until they reached Numiquipe—if they ever did—and her saint's day and her birthday had come and gone while they were all still on the run from Las Palomas. She would probably find no church at all in the wilds of the *sierras* where Jorge meant to take them. There was always the dark matter of Mamá's soul. Even Papá would understand, and he would now understand that there was more to this than Mamá.

The *padre* looked up from his chores. He was young, no older than Jorge, and the light from the few remaining candles burning under the wan terra-cotta Virgin came back from his eyes as fear.

"*¿Qué pasa, mi hija?*" the priest said.

"I have sinned, Father. I must make confession before I pray." She would have liked it better if he hadn't been so young, liked it even better if she had met him first and only in the secure gloom of the confessional itself.

"*Así . . .*" he said. "It must be done *rápidamente*. I have many *important* things to do . . ."

51

▲▲▲▲

Getting out of the camp of Black Jack Pershing had proved far more difficult than getting in. Corey hadn't figured on having any problem, but in the years since Cuba he had forgotten how hidebound Uncle Sam's army could be about some things.

Henry Richardson had come through for him. He had gotten him posted to Pershing's American forces as a State Department liaison officer—in mufti, thank God—and Pershing and his staff had given him the run of the encampment. They did, however, express mild official indignation when he told them he wanted to push on to the interior of Mexico by himself.

"You mean . . ." Berry, the lieutenant colonel adjutant from Ann Arbor, Michigan, dropped his lower jaw. "You're going to try to get to *Pancho Villa*? For God's sake, man, he's our enemy! Not only that, we don't even know where he is. I'm virtually certain the Old Man will never permit you to head south by yourself, Mr. Lane. He won't want to answer to Washington if you catch a stray bullet from one of Villa's greaser bandits. The War Department calls what we're engaged in a punitive expedition, but make no mistake about it, this is war! I'll admit it's a quiet war at the moment, but it's war all the same."

Quiet indeed. After the initial furious scrutiny by American newspapermen, the Pershing adventure seemed to have been forgotten north of the border. Carranza was still making a lot of the same noises he had made when Pershing first crossed the Rio Grande, about the United States violating the integrity of Mexican territory, but as strongly worded as his complaints were, it was easy to read between the lines how much the new President of Mexico wanted Villa found and crushed. If the U.S. Army did it—fine.

The general's headquarters, and in fact the entire cantonment, bore more resemblance to a Boy Scout summer camp than to a striking force bent on punishing the "petty international criminal," as the few dispatches back to Washington and New York described the erstwhile Tiger of the North. Sunburned young men stripped to the waist played baseball in the Chihuahuan desert or—in not very Scout-like behavior once the hot Mexican sun dropped behind the Sierras— chased off to the dusty little villages within a league of the camp in search of beer and women. From the grousing Corey heard, the enlisted men at least didn't find enough of the latter.

At a well-stocked canteen adjoining the supply depot, a portly major confided to him that Pershing or one of his aides, he wasn't sure which, had set up a bordello in one of the nearby towns, open only to commissioned officers. "Run by some Mexican madam somebody found drifting around the tail end of our column one day, peddling the services of about a dozen doxies to all comers—even enlisted men!" Corey knew a harrumph when he heard one. "Couldn't have that sort of thing, of course. The easiest thing to do was to regularize it, see that the press doesn't alarm all the mothers and the church crowd back home. Whoever called the shots apparently decided that officers and gentlemen wouldn't leak the news like common soldiers might. The girls are inspected by our medics every week. Care to indulge? I think civilians such as you qualify as officers, Mr. Lane, and I presume you're a gentleman."

Corey declined with no more than *proforma* thanks.

There was a murky air of frustration hovering over stiff John Pershing and his senior officers. As the adjutant confessed, the expedition's intelligence hadn't even the faintest idea of where Villa was, less about how to look for him, and none at all about how to tempt him into battle if they stumbled on him.

Hell, he didn't have any more knowledge of the Division's whereabouts than the military did, and he had just spent two long years in this country. He simmered in silent frustration of his own for a week before he doped out what to do.

He finally persuaded Pershing's chief signal officer, a co-operative young captain from Los Angeles, to link him up on a field phone with Mexico City. Will Hendricks proved to be of no help. "No idea. Not even a reasonable guess. Villa seems to have stepped off the face of the earth, Corey. All that's left are scattered units, all *calling* themselves the Northern Division."

The captain's eyes widened when Corey next said he wanted to talk with the British Embassy.

Fergus wasn't to be found any more than Villa was, but two days later the Scot called back. The understanding captain let Corey take the call in private.

"Corey! I miss ye, laddie."

He sounded as if he meant it. When Corey told him what he was after, the sound of sharply drawn-in breath came over the wire. "I'm not sure it's a guid idea, lad. Ye'll find a different Pancho than the one ye got on so capitally with in Celaya. He may seem to be free as the air now, but he's a caged animal. Verra dangerous, ye ken."

"Can't be helped, Fergus. How do I get to him?"

"A'richt. If ye insist. Actually, ye willna find him. He'll find *you*. Here's what ye'll have to do."

The next day Corey was on his way south again. A sixth sense, bulwarked by the warning of Pershing's adjutant, told him not to ask permission from his hosts. He simply left before dawn, leaving his clothes and gear behind him, but wearing his father's ancient Peacemaker Special under his jacket and telling a startled sentry at the break in the wire around the camp that he was merely going for a stroll. The sentry, barely out of his teens, had been leaning against a fence post, napping. He was scared stiff, but not to the point of full wakefulness.

"Have a nice walk, sir," the soldier said between yawns he did his best to hide, "if you like that sort of thing."

The stroll was seven tough miles over a stony path to a flea-bitten village called Rincón, a place too small to have an automobile for hire. Horses, yes, but not exactly prime riding stock. He found one that looked passable and bought it for three dollars American from a decent stableman who shook his head and told him a burro would be much better in the rugged country he was heading into. He almost switched to the burro, knew it would be the wiser choice, but he shuddered at the prospect of Pancho Villa ever seeing him on the back of such a mount. A saddle, bridle, and saddle blanket cost him two dollars more than did the horse.

He had Fergus's instructions pretty well in mind, but as he rode out of Rincón he thought a good deal more about Kennedy's last words to him.

"Gie me love to Luisa, laddie."

He had mumbled something he hoped Fergus would mistake for a promise. The next hour was a lonely one.

A night and half a day of hard riding brought him to the town called Galena the Scotsman had said was a hotbed for Villista agents. "Perhaps it willna be any longer, but it's where our lot used to contact Pancho's people in the early days of the Revolution. There's a cantina on the main lane called La Margarita. Just sit there and mind your manners. Take the first table to the right of the door as ye enter. Don't sit anywhere else. Take off your hat and put it on the table in front of you. Then wait. Someone will put their own tam-o'-shanter on top of yours. It may take a wee while."

"Thanks, Fergus." Whether this worked or not, Fergus Cameron Kennedy was invaluable. "By the way. What are you up to these days?"

"Same auld thing, laddie."

"You're not about to tell me, are you?"

"This time I can't. If you talk with him, Henry Richardson kens what's going on wi' Fergus. Perhaps he'll tell you. It's the big, big game at last. If all goes well, you'll hear aboot it one fine day. Wish me bonnie luck."

So—Henry ran Fergus, too, or at least figured in what the Scot was up to in Mexico. He might have guessed. Even at the last Henry hadn't played completely fair with him. It hardly mattered now. What did matter was that Richardson had come through for him in the matter of his being in Chihuahua now.

For two long, agonizingly dull days he examined every patron who entered La Margarita, not quite daring to speak with any of them. He began to wonder if he was wasting his time. No one so much as gave him more than a mildly curious glance, not even the proprietor. He drank more beer than he wanted to in order to have an excuse for monopolizing the cantina's table. Strangely, the fact that no one spoke with him was the only thing that gave him hope. If this were the run-of-the-mill watering place in semirural Mexico, someone would have demanded to know what his business was before the first day was out.

At noon on the third day, a scruffy, bearded old *paisano* with runny eyes and carrying a guitar shuffled to his table and took the seat across from him. He took his sombrero from his head, revealing a tangle of damp, gray hair, and placed it squarely on Corey's Stetson. Corey suspected the sombrero might be home to half the louse population of Chihuahua, but it couldn't be helped.

The old *paisano*'s mouth was leaking the brown stain from a monster chew of tobacco distending his wrinkled cheek. "If you will buy me a *cerveza, señor*, I will play you a song."

Corey signaled the proprietor and the old man pulled his guitar to his lap. He strummed three bars, his crooked fingers brushing delicately but uncertainly across the strings. He wasn't very good.

"You know this song, *señor*?" he said. He began to sing, his voice even more pitiful than his playing:

> *"En lo alto de la abrupta serranía*
> *acampado se encontraba un regimiento"*

"*Sí, viejo. Es 'Adelita,' no?*"

"You like people who play and sing 'Adelita'?"

"Very much."

"*¡Bueno!* Now—can this *brujo* be of help to you?"

¿Brujo? Well, if the old coot looked on himself as a sorcerer it was fine with Corey. He probably needed one.

"I wish to find the camp of—"

"Do not say it, *señor*. I know where you want to go. Tell me who you are and why you wish to go there."

"I want to find a man named Jorge Martínez. He is an officer with Regiment Bracomonte."

"*¿Por qué?*"

That was a rub with infinitely more friction than comfort. Until he reached the young man from Chupadera County he could tell no one, not even this apparently harmless oldster, that he wanted to take him north across the border. Jorge was still a soldier in Pancho Villa's army. He probably wasn't free to go, might never be. Well, if he couldn't lie to this old gray-beard, he would never be able to lie to Pancho Villa. And, face it, he was down to lies. "I have news for him. He has inherited a great deal of *dinero*, and I will be his *abogado* until he gets it."

The ancient eyes across the table from him suddenly danced with life. "I can take it to him for you."

"I do not have it with me." Yes, he had better establish that quickly or he might find his throat cut before he left this bar.

"Can you not send it to him, *amigo*?"

"No. There are papers he must sign. Those I do have. And I *solamente* can witness that Señor Capitán Martínez signs."

Fergus would be pleased with the ploy which had suddenly come to mind from God knew where. Money was in shorter supply with people like this old man than any other commodity, and the passage of it to anyone always presented the opportunity for a helper to get some of it for himself. It would be just as true for the sycophants around Pancho Villa. Someone near Villa would break his neck to get Jorge and him together. But it meant Corey might have to dummy up the papers he claimed to have.

"I will pass the word along, *señor*. If you are to move closer to this Martínez, someone will come for you by tomorrow night." Tomorrow night? Villa and whatever forces he had with him must be closer than he had dared to hope. The old guitarist smiled for the first time. "Would you like a little more of 'Adelita' now, *señor*?"

They came for him at sundown the next day, three riders in the uniform of the Dorados, trailing a much better horse than the barely adequate creature he had purchased in Rincón. Yes, they were Dorados, but not the gaudy horsemen he remembered from Xochimilco or even sad Celaya. Things must have gone hard with Villa's elite corps since Corey left Mexico. These three were on the verge of raggedness.

The timing of their arrival, of course, had been deliberate. By the time they reached Pancho Villa's camp in an abandoned-looking village of no more than a dozen structures it was pitch-dark; he wouldn't be able to find the shallow canyon they trotted into again in a thousand years. They would in all likelihood take him out in much the same semi-blinded way. He shivered a little. Maybe Fierro, if he were here, would see to it that he didn't get out at all. He doubted that he could simply stroll away, as he had from Pershing's stronghold four days ago.

The headquarters of the Northern Division were but a fraction of the size they had been at Celaya, and although he couldn't be sure in the dark, Corey got the impression that the Tiger of the North now had only the Dorados left to fight for him. Black Jack Pershing, could he find this encampment, would have things pretty much the way he wanted them.

His escort took him straight to Villa.

A pretty, plump, dark-haired woman was having dinner with him. She rose and left as guards ushered Corey through the door to the combination office/living quarters in an old building that looked as if it had been a school in happier times. Corey wondered if this was Luz Corral, the wife Villa was said to return to whenever he tired of playing in the broader fields of Eros. Villa peered at Corey and a smile of recognition broke across his round face.

"*Hola*, Señor Lane!" If El Caudillo had been buffeted by the withering cyclonic winds of the past year, his physical appearance—and his anticyclone manner—gave not the slightest hint of it. He seemed as naturally elemental as Corey remembered him. His enemies could never defeat this phenomenon while he lived. The grave danger was that Carranza and Obregón knew that, too. "What is this I hear that you wish to make *un rico* out of a junior officer of mine, one Major Jorge Martínez? You are creating rich men now, instead of *presidentes*?"

So Jorge had become a major. "It is important to Major

Martínez that I find him, General Villa." Not a lie, but not too close to the truth, either. Perhaps it was more important to Corey Lane than to the young man in question.

"You will, I fear, have to talk with General Fierro about it, Señor Lane. I do not think he knows where the major is at the moment, but he and his *tropa* are still under Rodolfo's command."

Fierro! The Butcher was truly Corey's personal *bête noir*. "May I speak with him, General?"

"*Sí*. Tomorrow." The agate-black eyes narrowed. "You have not spoken of General Ángeles, *amigo*. Have you given up on your grand plan to have Felipe become President of Mexico?"

The genie wasn't quite out of the bottle, but stuck in the neck as it was, it could pop out any moment. "It is at least in abeyance, General Villa. *Con todo respeto*, the fortunes of war have not smiled on you or your army, and without an all-powerful Francisco Villa and a conquering División del Norte this is hardly the time to advance his cause. I regret this very much."

The pop as the genie emerged was almost audible. "You don't think, then, that Pancho Villa can rally and defeat the enemies of the people, Señor Lane?"

Careful. "Certainly you can, sir. But it will not be easy, particularly with General Pershing threatening from the north."

"Spoken like a true, proud gringo. Your general and his *turistas* are *nada*! They are beginners in warfare in my country; my *soldados* and I have fought for six long years. They would be wise to return to the United States." It wasn't said with bravado or boastfulness. He meant every word. Villa's faith in his destiny hadn't been shaken yet. Yes. Carranza or someone like him would have to kill him to defeat him.

It seemed like a good time to say *adiós* for now.

"*Gracias*, General Villa."

As he left, the woman slipped in through the door again.

A silent soldier called at his tent at eight o'clock in the morning and led him through a field of dirt packed to concrete by cavalry, apparently, to a larger tent whose ridgepole was anchored at either end by broad-leafed shade trees. A group of Division men, all but one of them officers, huddled together. One raised his head. Corey knew those saturnine features. At the sight of Corey, Rodolfo Fierro's face set in an impassive mask, but the sharp eyes glittered.

"Señor Lane. Did you think I had forgotten you, gringo? You seem intent on putting yourself in the sights of my *pistola*." His gaze dropped to the Peacemaker Special on Corey's hip. "I see you are not wearing the one *mi general* had me return to you in Celaya."

"This one is only for show, General Fierro. I am not a *pistolero*."

The Butcher snorted. "Bah! Every *hombre* who *is* an *hombre* in Mexico today should be a *pistolero*. Even a *yanqui*. I think you could be one if you had to. Perhaps you would like to try with me." He laughed, pleased with himself, obviously, but pleased with something else as well. The officers around him laughed, too, but only after they had heard Fierro. Clearly this accomplished killer meant the last as some sort of grudging compliment, and they were willing to echo it. It bade a little better for the short-term future, but Corey knew he hadn't better count on it. The man in the faded khaki of a private soldier hadn't laughed.

"Has General Villa told you I am trying to find a Bracomonte major by the name of Jorge Martínez, sir—and why?"

"*Sí.*"

"He told me, General, that you didn't know where he was."

"That was yesterday, *señor*. Today I know exactly where he is. He sent one of his men to headquarters here to pick up pay for his *tropa*. In addition to being a brave *guerrero*, Major Martínez is a very conscientious commander. His men must love him." There was an ironic undertone, a cast of sarcasm, in Fierro's voice. "He is at a town called El Sueco." He turned to the private, who had now moved to his elbow. "How far is it, Bautista?"

"Thirty-two kilometers southeast of here, *mi general*," the man said.

Wonderful! "May I go to see him, General Fierro? And if so, how do I get to him?"

"*Sí*, you may see him, gringo. As for getting to him, as you put it— *no hay problema*. We here at the Division wish to get to him as well. My men will take you."

This was proving easier than he had expected. Perhaps too easy. The short hairs at the back of Corey's neck suddenly tingled as if lightning had struck very close to him, and his nostrils burned as if the bolt had released ozone into the air trapped under the canvas of the tent. But he had to play this out.

"When, General?"

"Right after *siesta*, gringo." He turned to the ordinary *soldado*, leaned over, and whispered something in the man's ear. He turned back to Corey. "Capitán Bautista here and two of his men will be your guides."

Captain Bautista? He wore no insignia that would indicate he was an officer. The man rose from his seat alongside Fierro and came toward Corey with his hand outstretched. His eyes, bedded deep in a sallow face, moved about as if he had no wish to hold them fixed in place.

He wore the blue-black patch of the Bracomontes at his shoulder and someone—some *soldadera*?—had threaded around his belt loop the tiny ribbon of yellow braid worn by the riders in Jorge's troop, well-remembered from Irapuato.

Fierro's officers had gathered round him again. None of the group watched Corey now. He knew the Butcher had dismissed him. He could kill in the same, easy, offhand way.

Two and a half scorching hours out from Pancho Villa's camp Corey and his three fellow riders found the dead horse lying in a ditch in the shade of trees like the ones which had propped up Fierro's tent.

The animal was beginning to bloat in the blazing sun, but it hadn't been dead long, hadn't yet ripened enough for the buzzards to come to dinner. An ugly dozen of them roosted in the trees, fluttered up for a second as the riders approached, and then settled in again stoically.

A look at the carcass and the ground around it told Corey what had happened. The horse, a big raw dun, must have stepped in the hole of some industrious burrower and snapped its foreleg. A thick, lumpy maroon scab had formed under its right staring eye where its rider had shot it. Bautista gave the scene a quick but thorough glance and urged his three companions on.

It was another hour before they caught up with the man who must have ridden the horse.

He was sitting on a huge rock set in the sparse grasses that lined the road, with other, larger rocks rising in a wall behind him, taking a pull at a canteen with a filthy canvas cover. Finished, he threw the canteen behind him. There was no look of surprise at the four horses bearing down on him, no look of disturbance, either. He wore the same khaki with the same markings as did Bautista, but he wasn't armed. Apparently the weight of the rifle he had shot the horse with had been more baggage than he wanted on a day like this.

He stood as Corey and the others approached, his eyes on Bautista as if the other three weren't there at all. He wasn't tall, but there was a look of great strength about him. Corey guessed he was an Indian.

"Zirco!" Bautista said as they reined up in front of him. There was no answer, just a dumb, steady gaze. "You followed me, did you not, *amigo*?" Nothing, not a flicker.

"Capitán Bautista," one of the two troopers said. "Would you like me to persuade this piece of *mierda* to answer you?"

Bautista sighed. "*No, gracias. Soldado a caballos Zirco es muy, muy hombre, verdad.* As persuasive as you are, Vico, you would get an answer from that rock before *mi amigo* Zirco would make a sound. Shoot him."

The rifle shots echoed from the nearby rocks as the man named Zirco crumpled to the withered grass, blood spraying first from his chest and then from his mouth. Corey's stomach became a rock as heavy as the one the dead man had risen from. Mexico. He shuddered. The heat was becoming unbearable.

"Search him," Bautista said. "You may share whatever *dinero* you find on him." He laughed, and the two other riders shot him identical looks of cynicism.

"*¿Dinero?*" the one named Vico said. "He won't have enough *dinero* in his pockets to buy one fucking *frijol, mi capitán.*"

The pair slid from their saddles and in a second were at the Indian's body, worrying it like mastiffs. One of them stood and held something up to Bautista. It looked like a folded map. The captain flattened it over his saddle horn and studied it. In a few moments he emitted a little cluck of satisfaction and turned to Corey.

"We will not be going to El Sueco, after all, *señor*. It seems that Major Martínez has decided to move his *tropa.*" He looked at Vico, whose hands were covered with the Indian's blood, drying fast in the furnace air blasting off the wall of rocks.

"*¿Dónde está Numiquipe?*"

The trooper pointed to the southwest. "Sixty or sixty-five *kilómetros, mi capitán.*"

"*¡Vámonos!*" Bautista turned back to Corey. "We must ride hard to make *el mayor*'s camp by nightfall, gringo. We have urgent business with him."

Urgent business? Corey knew to an absolute certainty just what that urgent business was.

Corey rode a poor fourth in the small cavalcade throughout the rest of the afternoon. From time to time Bautista looked back over his shoulder at him.

Yes, Capitán Bautista would not want to lose him. Corey Lane, the gringo, was a piece of "urgent business," too.

52

"*¡Un momento!*" Jorge said. He had enough to occupy his mind without interference from this gringo, although he would admit that he had been glad to see the man from Chupadera County when he rode in with Bautista and his two thugs. "I don't care what kind of difficulty you had finding me. No one asked you to come and rescue me, if it's rescue you have in mind."

"I made promises."

"*I* didn't!"

It had gone more or less like this for the first hour this morning, and Jorge felt battered. Only pride kept him from giving up and giving in.

Lane had touched him more deeply than he could know with the news that Andreas Martínez was dying of tuberculosis. But Lane had no clinching answer when Jorge asked what earthly, practical good his return to Chupadera County could do his father.

"He wants to see you."

"Certainly, and I want to see him, too. I am not an unnatural *hijo*. But I can't keep him alive. And I know my father would want even more that I finish what I started here."

"It is finished, Jorge. At least the part of it you can do anything about. Don't you see that?"

Sí, he saw it, if he couldn't admit it to this man. Lane's report on the condition of the Division at Villa's camp northeast of here had been sobering, but not unexpected. For half a year Jorge had known that the cause of Pancho Villa, and, consequently, the cause of Francisco Madero, was desperately lost. Until his talk with Paco three nights ago in El Sueco he had hidden the knowledge from himself. From his mind, at least. For months now he hadn't been able to conceal it from his heart.

Lane turned to Juanita again, as he had from time to time through the entire talk. "Tell him I'm right, Señorita Durán. I'm sorry—Señora Martínez." He was good. His voice was low and measured, and he had wisely kept even his revelations about Bautista when he arrived last night curiously unalarming. Even though Juanita's dark face was expressionless, it took no second sight to see that Lane was almost at the point of persuading her.

"I cannot speak for Jorge, *señor*. He must do what his *corazón* tells him he must do." Yes, she was almost persuaded, but not quite, not yet.

He wished Lane would abandon that particular line. He wouldn't be proof against a specific plea from her as well. Thank God big Paco wasn't there to add his two centavos at the moment. Lane had impressed Durán enormously in their first talks last night, when he had found them in this shed next to the Numiquipe livery stable where the rest of the troop was bedded. Jorge had sent Paco out right after breakfast to keep a close eye on Bautista while he decided what to do about Fierro's spy, but he was due back any minute. The dynamiter had begged again that Jorge give the word for Bautista's death, and he had been tempted to let him have his way.

So far Lane had made no mention of Juanita's condition. If he found a way to play on her fears for the child she was carrying, he could ally her with him immediately. Her belly was swollen now to the point of bursting. He knew in his bones that the child would scream its way into life very soon, perhaps before the week was out, no matter how she tried to reassure him it wasn't ready yet.

Lane was speaking again. "I'll wait for your decision, Jorge. The final choice is yours, of course, and once you've made it I won't press for another. We'd better talk about this man Bautista now. I think you're underestimating him. I believe Sergeant Durán agrees with me."

"Paco goes a little *loco* when he thinks he smells a spy," Jorge said. "I know he's right this time, of course. And I'm not blind to the danger. I'm just sick to death of killing."

¡Mierda! he was justifying himself. He hadn't done that since Trini died. The trouble at the moment was that on top of the respect he had always had for Corey Lane, he was beginning to like the man. Lane hadn't mentioned that he, too, was on Fierro's target list, although it was clear he knew he was. *Muy hombre, muy valiente,* he had thought of Lane in the battle of Celaya. The notion was stronger now. "Look, Corey. I think we've got time to sort things out. If Bautista rode down here just to kill me, he would have stormed in last night with his and his men's rifles blazing. I am not such a *bufón* as to expect complete loyalty from the men in the troop, but I've been their commander for a long time. They won't go over to him in an instant. Another thing: Bautista doesn't know yet that we know what his orders are. He may feel he has time."

He had barely finished when Paco appeared in the open side of the shed. He looked worried, but then Paco almost always did.

"*Qué pasa,* Paco?"

"We are losing our men, Jorge."

"How, in *el nombre de Dios?*"

"Money. Bautista is scattering *dinero* like corn in front of chickens."

"Our payroll!"

"*Sí.* He knows who the malcontents are from all the time he served with us. They are getting it all, or the promise of it. He is a clever man."

"Do you still want to kill him?"

"More than ever, Jorge. Some of the money he is giving away is mine. But I am afraid we have lost our chance. I think we must now consider leaving here before he makes his move. Have you told anyone in the *tropa* just where in *las sierras* we are headed?"

"Tonito and Aragón."

Paco's face fell even further. "Aragón was the first man Bautista bought."

"How many others do you think have sold themselves to him?"

"Eight, perhaps nine."

"That leaves seven or eight with us. Close to what is called, I believe, a Mexican standoff." He laughed. No one else did. "You've scouted this town, Paco. Where can we hole up for a fight?"

"The only place in this cesspool with walls thicker than a corn husk is the stable, *mi mayor*, and Bautista will have it. The men he hasn't bribed are moving out already."

"Then we run for it. But not before tonight." He turned to Corey. "You'll have to run with us, I'm afraid." Jorge spoke to Paco again. "We must pretend we know nothing. Let them all think we're sticking with our original plan." He looked at Juanita. "*Cariña*, are you ready for a long, long ride?"

"*Sí*, Jorge. It is not too far to the *sierras*."

"We will not be going to *las sierras, mi amor*."

"No?" Her eyes bored right through him. It hurt.

"I am sorry—no. I know how you feel about leaving Mexico, but I know now that Señor Lane is right. It is time for me to go home. But I do not wish to go home alone. I want you with me. Will you come?"

There was dead silence for a breath or two. Her look was half resolve, half fright. "*Sí*, Jorge."

"Paco?"

The giant stared at him dumbly for a moment. Then the great head began to shake from side to side.

"No, Captain Cockroach. Paco must remain in his own country." Juanita sobbed, and her father turned to her, his eyes filled with pain and sadness. "Do not change your mind, *mi hija*. It is best. Do not forget, you are Jorge's *esposa*." He turned back to Jorge. "I will go as far as the border with you, Jorge, but not one centimeter farther."

"Then I shall have to be satisfied with that, *viejo*."

"You won't get even the men who stay loyal to you to go that far, Jorge."

"I don't want them with us at all, Paco."

He outlined the plan which had been forming in his mind, even as he resisted Corey.

Paco was to order the troop to be at the edge of town at sunset, ready to ride. Lane, he, and the two Duráns would remain in the center of town. The dynamiter argued that only the loyal *soldados* of Tropa Martínez would obey his order, leaving the traitors and Bautista too close to the two men Bautista had come to kill. "We won't even have the guns of those few to help us."

"Bautista will have to send at least a few of his men to watch the troop. Now look, it's not a good plan, I will admit. If you have a better one, I will listen to it."

Paco was silent, indicating to Jorge that he wanted to hear more.

"You still have dynamite, do you not, Paco?"

"A little. Five sticks."

"Once it is dark the four of us will mount up and start west—through town. You will use a long fuse and blow up this shed behind us. Bautista will have to investigate. By the time he's finished raking through the wreckage we will have turned at the plaza and headed north out of town. When he finds we're gone, he'll ride like hell for the edge of town—*I hope*. Our men will fire as Bautista comes up on them. Tell Guil Jaramillo to take command. Tell him just one volley, and then they're to scatter into the desert. We won't have a big lead by the time Bautista finds he's been tricked, but it will be something."

Corey Lane coughed. "What if Bautista doesn't bite, Jorge?"

"We'll hole up somewhere north of the plaza and fight as long as we can."

"How about the *señorita* here? Isn't there somewhere we can keep her safe?"

"No," Paco Durán said, his voice heavy. "Jorge knows. There is no safety in all of Chihuahua for any of us now. If we have to fight, she will fight with us. She may be a wife now, but she is still a *soldadera*."

Jorge was right. She knew the child was getting ready to be born, but she would have to go on with the fiction that there was still plenty of time. She couldn't have his concern for her forcing him into a course of action decided only on the basis of what he thought was best for her. Her father had been just as right when he reminded Jorge and Corey Lane that she was a *soldadera.*

She did wish she felt better, though. Carrying the baby had been easy until the hard rides of the last week. *En el nombre de Dios,* when this baby was born, and they were all safe in the mountains, or, as it seemed more likely now, in Jorge's country, she would never get on a horse again.

But would they ever be safe again? *Sí.* She *had* to believe it. Nothing must stop her from presenting Jorge with his son. And it *would* be a boy. He had spoken of the child no other way, although once, early in her pregnancy, he had assured her a daughter would do just as well, "if she looks like you, *querida.* A boy, of course, can look any way at all."

She would have to make another prayer. It had served her well when they left El Sueco. The help for Jorge she had asked of God, the Virgin, and—may that same God forgive her—Florencia Durán, might very well be Corey Lane.

"I ask nothing for myself, *Dios.* But for Jorge and my child . . ."

53

Corey saw how exactly right Jorge had been about Bautista's reaction when the troopers he and Paco deemed still loyal to their commander rode out of the corral next door. Two years in this war had turned Jorge into a soldier with uncanny tactical instincts. In only ten minutes, nine riders, including the two who had come down from Division headquarters with the spy and Corey, set out after them. By Corey's reckoning, that left Bautista and seven or eight others still occupying the stable.

There wasn't much talk in the shed. A hot spring breeze swirled dust through the corral. Paco spent the late afternoon setting his charges against the shed's one sturdy wall. He stripped a tremendous length of fuse wire off its spool and connected it to the detonator he would carry in his saddlebag, explaining to Corey as he worked how he meant the wall to fall forward on the area where the four of them had slept. He said he hoped Bautista and his men would feel compelled to go through the debris to see if the detonation had saved them the trouble of killing their quarry. "It must take out a section of the corral fence, *también*, releasing all the horses. We must hide the fact that we will be up on four of them, and it will take even more time while they round the others up. Bautista will not try to follow us without spare *caballos*."

After he finished, he bundled up the eight or ten remaining feet of the fuse wire and stuffed it into the saddlebags with the last two sticks of the explosive he evidently felt weren't needed for his decoy blast.

Juanita fixed a supper of a sort of cornmeal mush along with a few short lengths of greasy sausage whose heavy load of spices didn't quite hide the fact that the meat was past its prime, and Paco dug four bottles of sickly warm beer from a feed box in a corner of the shed.

Corey watched the girl as they ate in utter silence. What little he had heard from her since he came to Numiquipe last night strengthened the impression he had gotten from their talk in Celaya. She seemed exceedingly bright. Her quick black eyes missed nothing.

Squatting on her heels on the straw-covered floor of the shed, she was suddenly one of those *paisana* women who seem an absolute part of their mundane surroundings, a woman who had emerged from the earth, silent, unmoving and seemingly unmoved, still as a rock, but with all the latent vitality of a stalk of corn readying itself to burst. How, he wondered, could Jorge rip such a plant away from the nutrients which had shaped it, transplant it to the bitter clay of another country, and expect it to survive?

It's not your problem, Lane. Yours is simply to get them there, if you can.

If she felt fear, the dark, pretty face that had now turned wooden—except when her gaze fell on Jorge—didn't show it, or *any* emotion for that matter. When she lowered her tin plate it did reveal that the meal had brought a slight touch of nausea. She walked around to the back of the shed, apparently to answer a call of nature. She must have moved into full view of the men still concealed in the stable.

"*Sí*, Corey," Jorge said, as if he had read his mind. "She picked the place deliberately. We want Bautista to know we are still here. When one of the three of us must piss, we will use that wall, too. Let them see us. Did Paco fit you out with a carbine?"

"Yes."

"*Perdón*. I mean no offense, but do you know how to use it? I have never seen you with anything but a pistol like the one you're wearing. A carbine is not a deer rifle."

"I used a long gun much like it in Cuba, Jorge."

"*Bueno*. And I don't suppose I have to tell you to check your canteen?"

Suddenly, it was dark. The inside of the shed had become Plato's cave.

Then, with the sound of it at first so faint he wasn't sure, he heard rifle fire in the western distance, not a fusillade, just one report separate and distinct from the three, four, six, then seven that followed it. Was this all there would be of the volley Jorge ordered?

In moments the sound of pounding boots beat against the sides of the shed and muffled the distant firing as shadows masquerading as men spilled from the stable into the deeper black of the corral. He couldn't see it, but he could smell the dust rising as Bautista's men chased down their mounts. The taste of it filled his mouth. Now and then a match flared as one of the riders lit a *cigarrillo*, the orange flames almost painful to dilated pupils. Shouts echoed against other shouts. He couldn't make out the Spanish, knew only that it was almost gutter *pelado*. Horses whinnied, neighed, stamped their hooves into the packed earth of the corral, some of them cantering alarmingly close to the open side of the shed. He knew a moment of prickly terror as it crossed his mind that Bautista might decide to finish them first before riding to the larger fight.

Then the voice of Fierro's assassin rang through the pitch-black air. *"¡Vámonos!"* The corral emptied. In moments more, after the hoofbeats faded, silence fell again like a cloak, silence for what seemed an age, broken only by Juanita's heavy, labored breathing.

"Ahora," Jorge whispered. "Paco—*los caballos.*"

The sound of the firing in the west was blending into a low, uniform crackling, the single shots now lost in a rising crescendo of reports.

"It is more than just a volley, Jorge," Paco said. "Our *compañeros* are making a real stand to give us time. They are good *muchachos.*"

It did seem that a hot, full-scale fight was raging. If it was, surely it would be good for the four of *them.* If the men still loyal to Jorge killed or at least disabled some of Bautista's first skirmishers, it might tilt the odds a tiny bit in their favor. He couldn't let himself hope, not yet. Jorge's plan would still have to fool Bautista, and the spy was anything but a fool.

When they were all in their saddles, Jorge spoke again. "How far is it to where that firing is coming from, Paco?"

"No sé, Jorge."

"Make a guess."

"A kilometer. *Sí.* Maybe a bit more."

"We'll give Bautista another minute to reach the fight. Then Corey, Juanita, and I will move out. We'll ride *toward* the firing first, to hide our tracks in theirs. In one more minute after we leave, blow the shed and join us. We won't have cleared the plaza by the time we hear your blast. We'll wait for you just north of town, in that arroyo we saw as we rode in."

"Go on without me. I'll catch up."

"I said we'd wait, *viejo.* If Bautista takes our bait, it will be morning before he digs through the rubble of the shed. We'll have all the start we need—or can expect."

"But Jorge—"

"¡Basta! Don't argue, Sargento Durán. We are already go-

ing to be forced to perform heroics I have no wish to even think about. I certainly don't want you inventing more!"

"Sí, mi mayor."

Jorge's first minute seemed like ten. At last he gave the order.

"Adelante."

It was a strange feeling to be riding *toward* the firing instead of away from it, but Corey recognized the thinking behind the move. After about an eighth of a mile, with the horses held to a walk, they turned into a narrow *calle*, emerging at the far end of it in a nondescript, refuse-littered plaza that would have been even less appealing in the full light of day. Just as they passed the dark bulk of the casing of the village well, the boom of Paco's dynamite reached them. Corey expected that in seconds lamps would glow in the windows of the stone houses on either side.

"Shouldn't we pick up the pace a little, Jorge?" Corey asked. "People will be pouring out into the street. Won't they tell Bautista which way we've gone?"

"They won't leave their beds, Corey. That firing has already sent most of them into cellars they won't leave for another week. And we want these horses with something left in their legs when Paco joins us. We won't see a soul."

He was right. Numiquipe looked like a city of the dead.

After another half mile they reached the arroyo, a deep cut in the rocky ground perhaps fifty feet above the level of the town. Behind them the sky above the stone huts near the stable and the corral seemed to have been set on fire.

A silhouetted horse and rider appeared at the mouth of the last *calle* leading from the plaza. Paco had made up a good thirty seconds of the minute that had lapsed between their two departures.

"It went *muy bién*, Jorge," he said when he reined up beside them. "There are *caballos locos* running loose all over Numiquipe."

The firing at the western edge of town had stopped.

"They will have started back to the stable now," Jorge said. "Let's get going before we lose what time we've gained."

They rode to the top of the hill and headed into the flat, dry, northern darkness of Chihuahua without a backward look at the flame-lit town.

"Will we ride all night, Jorge?" Corey said.

"*Sí, amigo.* And all day, too. The country ahead of us is as flat as a *retablo*. No place to hide. But a full day's ride will put us in some scrub-covered low hills. If we can avoid Villista patrols there we will be as safe as we will ever be."

"But the horses . . ."

"Do not worry about horses, my friend. Paco knows every farm in the part of the state we are heading into. We will have fresh mounts by ten tomorrow morning."

In the day and a half since he arrived in Numiquipe his admiration at the superb, crystal calm of Jorge Martínez and his firm grip on himself had grown by leaps and bounds. Corey had seen some of it at Zacatecas when Jorge yanked him and Fergus away from Fierro's firing party, and even more on the train, but in both those cases Jorge had been acting from a secure position. Here he was largely at the mercy of forces beyond his control. It hadn't shaken his poise at all. Clearly, though, he was worried about the girl.

Just before dawn they stopped at a water tank in the middle of what seemed open rangeland. A small herd of stringy cattle bolted away from the tank as the four settled beside it to eat and refill their canteens, their movements so abrupt and skittish it was unlikely they saw a *vaquero* too often or too close. It made him think of the stock grazing the sweeping hills of sweet grass at Hacienda del Sol, and he ruthlessly suppressed the thought of Luisa, but not before it hurt.

Funny, tied together as the four of them were in this flight, each seemed to stake out a separate place for himself. Juanita was on the other side of the tethered horses, Paco about twenty feet from Corey, and Jorge a similar distance back the way they had come. He had led during the long ride, but now he seemed to have placed himself in a position of guarding the others from the threat behind them.

Paco checked his detonator box, taking it swiftly apart and putting it back together again, his giant paws moving as surely and delicately as if he were a master jeweler cleaning a fine watch. An exercise of habit, Corey decided. The dynamiter would have little use for the tools of his violent trade on a run like this.

Juanita had turned pale on the overnight ride, but who wouldn't have? It had been a grueling six hours for Corey and the two other men; it had to be a nightmare for a woman in her condition.

The cows that had wandered away from the water tank had made a racket on the stony ground, but were now bunched together at a distance of three hundred yards or so. Perhaps it was the memory of their sharp hoofbeats, but it seemed to Corey he heard similar sounds far to the south of them. His heart skipped a beat. Bautista? No. It really was his imagination. When the first light of day broke across the plain he could see far to the south in back of them. There was no one out there now.

Juanita disappeared behind the high western embankment of the tank. Jorge gazed after her, then, to Corey's surprise, he stood and walked to him, dropping into that easy squat seen more here than north of the great river.

"A lot has happened to the two of us since we saw each other across that street in Chihuahuita more than two years ago, Corey."

"Yes."

"And not all of it good, no, *amigo*? Tell me, did you know I was no longer wanted in Chupadera County when you found me at Casa Estrellita?"

"Yes. Actually, I wasn't even looking for you any longer."

"You weren't? What were you doing there, then?"

Corey told him, hurrying the story. "Would you still have gone to Mexico if I had been able to tell you what had been decided back home?"

Jorge laughed. "Do not misread me, Corey. I really do not think this is funny. Would I still have gone to Mexico? *Sí*. I already wanted to, but perhaps you would have stopped me—or tried to."

"Why?"

"If I hadn't run from you, I would truly have become a killer. I panicked when I saw you. There was a man in that filthy *casa* I intended to kill that night. It hardly seems important now."

Juanita had returned and gone to her father, putting her arms around his huge middle. Her hands couldn't touch. The big sergeant bent his mammoth head down over her small one. *Las querencias* were breaking down.

"I have seen you watching her, Corey. You are worried for her just as Paco and I am. I read your eyes even in the dark. *Gracias, amigo.* Paco and I are grateful. You are an *hombre muy simpático.*"

"Am I forcing you to go home, Jorge?"

"No. It is time. You were right yesterday. Everything is finished for me here. My dreams drifted away from me in fragments, and it was hard for me to see that they were leaving." He laughed once more. "Again, Corey, do not think I am making a joke of this, *por favor*. It is just that if I *had* killed that man in El Paso, my revolution would not have been the total failure it has been."

At only ten minutes after ten, not far off from Jorge's prediction at Numiquipe, they found one of those farms Paco knew, and traded horses with a terrified peasant who looked at the muzzle of Jorge's pistol as if he were looking at a coral snake inches from his nose.

"I didn't mean to frighten the poor devil the way I did, Corey, but we didn't have time to stand around and haggle. *Muchas gracias* for paying him."

By early afternoon the flat stretches of the desert began to tilt upward, almost imperceptibly at first. He could only discern the rise by looking back over the immense wastes they had ridden over.

Though they were still making somewhat steady progress, it became clear to Corey that they weren't covering ground at the same swift pace of last night or this morning, in spite of being on fresh horses. Juanita, who on leaving Numiquipe appeared to ride as well as any of them, now began dropping back from time to time, and at least five times they had to rein up until she caught up with them. Corey saw her gulp air frantically just as they got under way each time.

Then a dull, hazy sawtooth against the northern sky, a barrier of broken, rocky country, showed itself ahead of them. At his first sight of it, Corey was sure it was another of the mirages that had danced around them in the heat, but as they neared to within three miles or so he saw that it was as real as the rocky anvil beneath their horses' hooves.

Juanita fell behind again, and Jorge called another halt.

"Do you know that country, Paco?" he asked as the girl moved up to join them.

"*Sí*, Jorge. When we took Juárez six years ago we came this way. If you look closely, you can pick out a break in the rocks. Beyond it the land is carved into *arroyos pequeños*. There is water and shade a kilometer or so past the opening. The trails and arroyos are all hard rock. Once we ride through that low wall you can just make out from here, we can hide in a million places. It would take a much better tracker than Bautista or his mongrel *perros* to find someone there who has no wish to be found."

In the middle of the great sigh of relief Corey permitted himself he caught sight of Jorge's eyes. He was looking back out across the scrub desert they had traversed since noon, as Corey had done a dozen times during the grueling ride. His black eyes were focused hard on something. Corey turned in the saddle.

Three or four miles in back of them—it was only a guess, it could have been two or ten—a ball of dust looking like a cloud of sepia cotton was rolling toward them. He prayed silently that it was a dust devil and nothing more, but knew immediately that it wasn't.

"It was too much to expect that we had fooled the spy forever," Jorge said. "*¡Vámonos!*"

It was a punishing ride. This time Juanita didn't lag. In about fifteen minutes they gained the breach in the rocks, a narrow opening with ten-foot-high walls capped with a crenellation of unstable-looking boulders. The horses labored up the last few feet and Jorge raised his hand and waved Paco to him.

"Where from here, *amigo*?"

Before the dynamiter could answer, a gushing sob of pain broke from Juanita. "Jorge!" She was bent forward over her horse's neck. "I am sorry, *cariño*. It is my time! My water—"

Down the long, dry stretch behind them, the cloud of dust was turning to something more defined. It was a blown plume now, like the smoke from a locomotive. Under it Corey could now make out the shapes of men and horses, six of them.

54

"Mount up again, Paco!" Jorge shouted. "We will go on together."

The first shots screamed away from the rocks on either side of them, and Corey feared it would be over even before it started. He heard a sharp cry from the girl. She must be even more terrified than she had been last night. The big sergeant was staring back down the trail. The riders behind them had turned now, deciding they had less chance of success if they rode wildly through the cut. Perhaps the four of them inside it still had a few more minutes.

"Mount up, *sargento*!" Jorge shouted again.

The immense bulk of Durán didn't move.

"Paco stays, *mi hijo*!" he said.

Corey looked at Jorge.

"We can all ride together, Paco," Martínez said. "You told me we can hide anywhere in the arroyos up ahead."

"*Sí*, but that was before this happened to Juanita. I tell you, Jorge, Paco can hold them in this little pass until you are safe. They have backed off a little. It will give me time to do my work."

"You couldn't hold them by yourself five minutes, *viejo*. She can go on without us." He turned to the girl, who was huddled at the side of the trail, her back to a boulder. "Is that not so, *cariña*?"

She nodded, her eyes wide with pain and terror.

Corey hesitated to add his voice to Paco's, but he now had no other choice. Surely Jorge, too, could see the danger she was in.

"You *can't* send her on by herself, Jorge. I don't know much about these things, but I do know that her condition is serious, perhaps critical. She could be in labor for a long time. I'll stay with Paco." Jorge's mouth opened, closed again. "Look! It's the only chance for the two of you. If we go on together, we're *all* lost. We won't be able to make any speed at all. And we couldn't fight as well, looking after her. She will need someone with her—and that someone should be you!" This was as hellish a predicament as any he remembered. Three men unable to help this frightened young woman, and with death riding toward them like the horsemen of the Apocalypse.

Bautista and his five riders had moved to the upward slope again. Dust was rising, but not as furiously as it had with the first charge they made. Two hundred yards? Less.

Jorge fixed a burning gaze on the low, rolling cloud. Corey could feel the heat from the red rage consuming him, while he shivered as if the hot wind had turned into an arctic blast.

"All right," Jorge said now. "But how will you find us, Paco?"

"Take the third arroyo and ride to the left until you find a place in the scrub that looks safe. I don't know how far that might be, but I will find you." He smiled, but he fooled no one. He wouldn't see his daughter and Jorge again and he knew it. "Señor Lane," he said, turning to Corey. "I would prefer you went with them."

"No, Paco," Corey said. "You wouldn't have a chance of stopping them by yourself, or even of delaying them for more than a few minutes, as Jorge said." He turned to Jorge. "I don't want to sound as if I'm placing myself in command here, but I think you and Juanita had better go now."

Paco helped his daughter mount. She leaned over to kiss him, and he had to put his hands up to her to get her straight in her seat again. She bit her lip fiercely as she settled into the saddle. Then Corey saw the stain of red spreading on her skirt. Blood? It hardly seemed right, but he couldn't be sure. He had no way of telling how much blood she had already lost, but it all must have come from her face. It was paler than the bleached rocks behind her. She turned her horse north and moved on up the trail. Paco didn't watch her go. He walked to the narrowest part of the opening and looked carefully at the rock walls on either side.

"Why are you doing this, Corey?" Jorge said as he turned his mount into the trail behind Juanita. "You owe us nothing."

"It's not a matter of settling a debt, Jorge." It was true, but it served no purpose to spell out that he was doing it for himself. It might give him doubts, and he could afford none now.

"*Adiós, amigo*," Jorge said. He thrust his hand down and gripped Corey's hard. *Adiós,* he had said, not *hasta la vista*. No, he wouldn't lie about it; they had gone far beyond all lies, even innocent ones.

As the sound of Jorge's and Juanita's horses died away, that of the oncoming Bautista and his men reached his ears for the first time, a low drumming finally lost in Paco's booming voice.

"We have perhaps five minutes, Señor Lane. Take another belt of ammunition from *mi caballo* and settle yourself in good cover with your carbine. While you do that, Paco has work to do." He was pulling the detonator box, the last two explosive charges, and the remaining length of fuse from his saddlebag. "They will pull up and talk for *un momento*. Bautista will not want to come through this break in the rocks until he looks us over. If you want to fire a time or two, just to remind them that it is a good idea for them to take care, that would not disappoint me. I would rather have them thinking about you than looking at me while I work, anyway.

You could move a time or two to make them think all four of us are here."

He placed the box down on the hard trail and climbed the north wall of the opening with the dull red stick in his big hand. Corey saw what he had in mind, or thought he did. At the top, a heap of rocks taller than Paco and several yards wide was balanced like a diver thinking about some fearsome plunge. Paco meant to seal the opening. It could delay their pursuers for something longer than the five minutes Jorge had talked about. Yes, it could delay them, but it couldn't stop them. The dynamiter looked down the way he had struggled up, shook his head once, and then ducked out of sight behind the loose rock.

Down on the approach to the little pass the six riders had pulled up about five hundred yards away, just as Paco had said they would. Three of them dismounted. They would come on foot. Corey lifted the carbine to his shoulder, took a breath, and squeezed off a single round. Dust and pulverized rock lifted into the air thirty or forty yards short of them and the dismounted men flattened behind growths of scrub. He moved behind another jutting rock and fired again. This time the shot landed a little closer to his target, but not much. The three men stood up, and now he could see that one of them was Bautista himself. The spy beckoned his two companions and the three mounted men to him.

"*¡Mierda!*" Paco's heavy voice crashed down on him, carrying equal loads of disappointment and disgust. He turned to him to see the reason. "The fucking fuse wire is much too short!" the sergeant said. He moved to his horse and stripped the coiled *riata* from its straps, returned to the detonator box, turned it on its side, and tied the rope to the plunger handle. He gathered four good-sized rocks and packed them tightly around the box. Done, he backed toward Corey, paying the rope out with his two mammoth hands, just as the first shots from Bautista and his men ricocheted off the walls.

Paco was hunched beside him, sagging back on his heels, before Corey realized the sergeant had been hit. It seemed to be a flesh wound in his right hip, but a lot of blood was dripping to the stony trail. Corey moved toward Paco, but the giant held him off with a wave of his free hand.

When he looked, he found the three men on foot had disappeared, probably into the low terrain below the breach in the rock wall. The men who had stayed on their horses were down from the saddle now, too, and moving through the last of the thorny bush beyond the depression.

Then the heads of the first three raised above the lip. Corey fired and they dropped from sight again.

"Do not fire the next time you see them, Señor Lane," Paco whispered. "I want them to come a little closer."

Sure enough, the heads bobbed up again, in different places this time, and now they were joined by a fourth. Then the four were up and running, right under the load of rocks where Paco had placed his charge. "*¡Fuego!*" Paco yelled. Corey fired, fired again. One sure hit. Yes. The man on the far left sagged to his knees. The others stopped in their tracks—and Paco yanked on the rope.

Nothing. The rope had pulled free.

"*¡Mierda!*" Paco thundered.

He began crawling forward on his hands and knees. Corey fired again and another of Bautista's men fell, but one more had crossed the lip at the break in the wall. Smoke from the rifles of the men under Paco's planted mine was filling the tiny canyon. Corey could almost count the bullets thudding into Paco's body. The big man inched forward until he was eight or ten feet from the box, got to his feet and lunged, soaring then like a giant dark bird across the remaining distance, his sombrero flying away behind him. His huge body hit the ground at the box just as another impacting round split his head. His hand reached up and settled on the plunger handle.

The walls shook and the sound of the explosion shivered the air. A ton of rock—more—avalanched down over Paco and Bautista and his men, and a screaming hail of stones and fragments passed over Corey's head, while the earth around him trembled.

Then—silence, broken only by the rattle of the last of the

stones and debris spilling down from the top of the wall. Sickly yellow smoke and dust billowed through and around the opening.

The blast had hammered Corey back five or more feet against the opposite wall. His carbine had been ripped from his grasp, too, and was itself half-buried, out of reach. He checked himself. Nothing broken, nothing severely damaged that he could see or feel, although something had creased his scalp. A warm trickle of blood threatened to find its way into the corner of his eye, and he brushed it away with the back of his hand.

The smoke drifted out of the canyon, and the dust settled— and Bautista, gray with ash and powdered rock, stood in the opening.

Immobile, his carbine still in his hand, the spy looked like a statue. He was dazed, certainly, but his eyes moved to Corey, and Corey knew he would gather himself in seconds.

Corey slipped his hand to his hip. The Peacemaker Special was still there. He pulled it from the holster and aimed.

The sharp report was nothing after Paco's explosion.

Bautista just sighed as the heavy round struck his chest. He sat down. The carbine fell from his grasp, and he rolled to his side and was still.

Corey got to his feet. If Bautista had survived, perhaps Paco too . . .

One of the big sergeant's boots was visible. He hurried to the pile and began pulling frantically at the rocks. No use. One monster boulder lay on top of Paco's head. If Corey could have moved it he wouldn't have. He had no wish to see what it hid.

There was one more thing to consider. Where was the sixth of Bautista's men? He moved carefully to the top of the pile. Down in the scrub he saw the last man mounting up. He watched until the rider turned south and was lost in the dust his horse kicked up.

He surveyed the pile again. A filthy hand protruded, but nothing else. Well, if any of the others had lived through it as Bautista had, they would have no stomach for following him.

Good Lord! Where were his and Paco's horses? The blast must have ripped them from their tethers.

Then a soft whinny from behind the rocks to the north kept panic at bay. He walked gingerly toward the sound. Around a bend in the wall he found Paco's big bay. He didn't have time to speculate on why the animal hadn't bolted. His own horse must have. He eased toward it, but the horse tossed its bell head just as he reached for the bridle. He barely caught it.

Once in the saddle the shakes reached him, and he leaned forward on the horse's neck and buried his face in its mane until they left. His hands were steady now, but his heart was still racing wildly.

The third arroyo, the dynamiter had said. He rode past two, a quarter of a mile apart.

Did that slender gash in the hillside he was passing now count as the third of them? Yes. *No.* He rode past. The next had to be the one.

The arroyo was choked with brush, but a hundred feet into it he found broken branches on a shoulder-high saltbush and his heart slowed.

It was heavy going, but about a mile up the arroyo the terrain opened up and he found Jorge and the girl in a broad clearing too dry to be called a meadow.

To the end of his days he would wish he hadn't found them.

Jorge was sitting beside Juanita, his head in his hands. He looked up dumbly when Corey rode up to him. Juanita was stretched out on her back beside him. Her skirt was pulled up to her waist, her underclothes and legs dark with blood. Gouts of it must have poured from her lower abdomen.

This wasn't the result of childbirth.

Then he remembered her cry when the first shots reached them. It had been the only cry. She hadn't made another sound.

"She died five minutes ago, Corey," Jorge said. "I don't know if my son ever took a breath. Will you help me dig a grave for them?"

55

They journeyed north for two days, and for two days Jorge didn't utter more then a dozen words. Something in him, perhaps the essential Jorge Martínez, had died with Juanita and the child. It was as if Corey was returning a corpse to the Ojos Negros.

The only map Corey had was the one bought when he and Fergus motored up to Zacatecas. It was a ten-year veteran, put together by some cartographer in the United States who relied as much on guesswork as on genuine information, showing only the six largest towns in Chihuahua, in the obvious belief there were no other Mexican towns in that far northern state worth mentioning. Jorge, Corey realized, wouldn't have been of much help even had he felt like talking. All his service with Villa had taken place in the center and the south; the only northern road he was familiar with at all was the one between Juárez and Torreón. Relying on him, particularly in his present condition, would have been like navigating a hidden sea with a mute, blind helmsman.

They had to avoid the northwest, of course. That was still Villa country, no matter how tenuous a hold Pancho and his Division now had on it. Were they to encounter one of their patrols, there was a good likelihood that Jorge would be recognized. Even old comrades would be reluctant to let him go, with Fierro's warrant for him probably common knowledge, and fear of the Butcher all-pervading.

Juárez, and the other Texas crossing points farther to the east of it, were out as well. All the territory along the big river was now held by the Constitutionalists. Carranza's people wouldn't be as apt to know Jorge, but if something happened, and they *did* discover that he was a Villista officer, the adobe wall and a firing party would be just as certain.

That left only a route straight north to Pershing's camp.

The only trouble with that was that Jorge had taken part in the raid on Columbus. A number of the raiders had already gone to the gallows at Las Cruces, and with the expeditionary force's frustrations in Mexico mounting as they had in the last month, tempers among the Americans under Pershing could flare as if they were phosphorus.

Corey could, perhaps, vouch for Jorge from his position as a State Department agent. Yes. It was the only chance.

He had come to fragile terms with the fact that Jorge was more than technically a traitor for taking part in Villa's depredation against the New Mexico border town across the line from Las Palomas. Not that it could be considered a *quid pro quo*, but two people had died as a result of the burning of Mex Town, one a child, both of them as innocent as anyone in Columbus. His fellow countrymen should be like Jorge—"sick to death of killing." Enough was enough.

Besides, Corey didn't actually know that Jorge had been there. The letter Ignacio Ortíz had shown him in Black Springs was a mere hint of evidence, not proof. And Corey wouldn't ask.

Still, it would be unwise to waltz into Pershing's command with Jorge in the uniform of the marauders who crossed the border a short three months ago.

Down off the low mesa where they had buried Juanita, they rode into a small village. After stocking up on food and water, Corey scouted the little town until he found the Chihuahuan version of a general store, and bought Jorge a suit of clothes. He wondered if the soldiers in the American camp would remark on its shiny newness, decided they had to take the chance. The proprietor looked a mixture of pride and wariness when they left the Division uniform bearing the Bracomonte shoulder patch with him. There was no reaction at all from the man who had worn it.

There had been no reaction from *that* man to *anything* on the two-day ride, only a resigned shrug when Corey told him they were heading for Pershing's camp.

Except for one small but frightening thing. Corey, beginning to recognize the country around them from his ride down to Rincón, rode in the lead. Twice on the first day, and twice more on the second, he turned to see Jorge with his pistol out of its holster, studying it like Hamlet holding the skull of Yorick.

Sixteen years ago Corey had watched helplessly as another friend put the muzzle of a gun in his mouth and blew the back of his head away.

"Jorge," he said finally, "I don't think it would be wise for us to ride into a U.S. Army outpost with you armed." He fought through waves of fear until Jorge pulled the carbine from the saddle boot and handed it and the pistol over to him. His own carbine was still back with the bodies of Bautista, Paco, and the others. He holstered the long gun and stuffed Jorge's sidearm in his saddlebag. The unhesitating way in which Jorge had surrendered his weapons, and a searching look at the young man's face, reassured him—to a degree; his deathlike silence could still hide the seeds of self-destruction. Corey never once mentioned Juanita, and the account he had given Jorge of Paco's death was short.

The last notes of Retreat were fading to plaintive whimpers as they reached the barbed wire at five o'clock on the second afternoon.

A young lieutenant called to the gate in the wire by a suspicious sentry rushed them to the headquarters tent of the adjutant.

"General Pershing has been most disturbed at your absence without leave this past week, Mr. Lane," the lieutenant colonel from Ann Arbor said. "Who the hell's this greaser with you?"

"This 'greaser,' as you call him, is a U.S. national, Colonel Berry. He's also a deep-cover operative who has been working for me in southern Chihuahua. He's the man I left camp to find." Risky. If the adjutant asked for Jorge's credentials they were both in deep trouble. "He might prove of value to your intelligence people," Corey hurried on. "He's watched Pancho Villa from very close for years." True enough. And, blessedly, Berry seemed not only mollified but moderately interested. Corey hadn't dared look to see if Jorge had reacted to the word "greaser." Now he did, and found him standing like a post, his face blank.

"We'll have to check him out, of course," the adjutant said. "I'll pass him through for the moment. By the by, Lane, there's a big noise here from the State Department who's been going crazy about your whereabouts since he arrived from Washington two days ago. Name's Richardson."

Henry? My God! Henry could give the whole game away. *He* would never buy the yarn about Jorge being a secret agent. Still, if the Bostonian didn't blow the whistle, perhaps Corey could turn his presence here to his and Jorge's advantage. But why was Henry here?

"He's my superior, Colonel Berry. I report directly to him, not to the army. No offense, sir. You surely know how these things work. Secretary Richardson will already have informed the general about my operations."

"Ah, yes, I understand." Berry didn't want to admit his ignorance. And the "Secretary Richardson" had conveniently cemented it. "I'll have an orderly get you billeted in a tent near his. Your . . . uh . . . man here can bunk in with the enlisted men, if—" It was plain as plain that he had nearly ended with something like *"if they'll have him."*

"I'd like him quartered with me, Colonel."

"But, Lane, he's a—"

Would the old fires blaze away in Jorge Martínez now? Corey glanced at him once more. His masklike face didn't betray so much as a feeble spark.

"I'm sure the *general* would approve." Corey was on solid ground here. Pershing had always had a reputation as an egalitarian that belied his autocratic public image.

Berry's face registered almost comic gravity—and assent. It was nearing darkness by the time he sent them on their way to the officers' mess in the canteen. Stares greeted Jorge, but no one said a word.

They hadn't really settled themselves into the assigned tent not a hundred feet from the canteen when Henry Richardson burst through the flap.

"Corey! Good heavens, man, I was worried sick about you!"

"Hello, Henry. Sit down, won't you?" Richardson took the tent's one canvas-backed chair. Jorge and Corey were each on a cot, with the younger man half in the shadows cast by the lantern hanging from the ridgepole. Henry was staring at him hard. Corey had to divert him while he worked out a strategy for explaining Jorge's presence. "What are you doing in Chihuahua, Henry? You can't have come to Mexico just to fret about me."

"No." He was still looking at Jorge, who sat like an unstrung marionette on the edge of his army cot. "Things have happened in Washington since you called me from Black Springs for my permission to carry out whatever this quixotic nonsense is that you've been engaged in." He fixed his blue eyes on Corey then. "Damn it, Corey! Who is this man, and what are you doing with him here?"

There was nothing left for it but to lay it all on the line for Henry and hope for a modicum of understanding, pray that there was still something left of the compassionate man he had known in Cuba.

"It's a long story, Henry."

"I've got time."

"And of course it's a purely personal obligation," Corey said at the end. "I can't expect you to cast all considerations of duty aside just to accommodate what I feel I owe Jorge and the people of my county, but . . ." He spread his hands, palms up.

Henry settled into one of his calm, judicious moods. Whenever in the past he had looked like this, his fundamentally decent, human instincts had taken over. He had turned once to Jorge when Corey told him how Jorge had put himself at risk in the rescue of Zacatecas.

"Since you seem to trust this young man so implicitly, Corey, I take it I can speak in front of him."

"Yes. It's gone far beyond secrets with Jorge and me."

Henry put the tips of his manicured fingers together and

lifted them to his lips. "I'll make arrangements for Mr. Martínez to get back home. But I want you to stay here in Mexico."

"What? I'm all done here, Henry. I've failed. The President's recognition of Carranza put the seal on our efforts once and for all. You and I both know that."

"I *don't* know that. You haven't failed yet. We have suffered a setback, true, but we're not defeated. Actually, that's what I came down here to talk with you about."

"It won't do you any good. I'm going home with Jorge."

"Please, Corey. Hear me out."

"I'll listen, Henry. But I'm afraid that's all I'll do."

"Did you follow the press reports of all the incursions made across our border while you were on that hiatus in Chupadera County?"

"Not really. I left Mexico late last winter pretty damned sick of everything down here."

"Then you may not know that Columbus was only the biggest of the violations—and the only one we can attribute directly to Pancho Villa. There have been sixteen separate instances of Mexican irregulars operating in U.S. territory since the first of the year. People have died, mostly the violators, but some Americans, too."

"So?"

"We can't prove it, but we know for a fact that the First Chief was behind almost every one of them. Sometimes he seems to almost be inviting us to take strong military action, something far bigger than Pershing's picayunish campaign. You might just have a word or two with your old comrade-in-arms Fergus Kennedy about it, if he didn't tell you when you spoke to him from here before you disappeared."

Another example of the way Henry Richardson did his homework. Corey had better set him straight. "I have only passed the time of day with Fergus in the past nine months. And I called him from here merely to help me find Pancho Villa—and Jorge." That Fergus was in league with Henry now seemed certain, but that was all in the realm of speculation. He could not permit it to have anything to do with him.

"No matter. It's quite beside the point, really." Why didn't he entirely believe Henry about this? "Now, we would never get a proud man like Woodrow Wilson to admit it, but there are indications he realizes at last that he made a dreadful mistake when he lent legitimacy to the presidency of Venustiano Carranza."

"I suppose that's good news, but what the devil can it conceivably have to do with me?"

"I believe it's time we begin another move to advance the fortunes of Felipe Ángeles. We need someone like you in the capital to run that end of it."

"No!" he exploded. "Don't even *think* about it for a single moment! I'm going back to Chupadera County. And for what it's worth, Ángeles now has no chance at all."

"Wait, please. There's more."

Corey glanced at Jorge. Surely this severely wounded young man would understand that his refusal was prompted not by indifference, but by the futility of the past two years.

"You said you'd listen, Corey. I'm not quite through. Something else is happening. Men from Victoriano Huerta's vicious old guard are beginning to drift back into Mexico. You, of all people, should know what that could mean. Another round of civil strife as terrible as the last six years. I know how you feel about Mexico and its people. Carranza is bad enough, but a resurgence of someone like Huerta would plunge his country right back into the Dark Ages. Strangely enough, one of Huerta's ex-lieutenants is beginning operations less than a mile from where we're sitting now."

"Can't General Pershing stop him?"

"It's not part of the general's mission."

"How did this man of Huerta's come to be in Chihuahua?" Why in hell was he asking? Henry might think he saw an opening.

"I don't know if you know this, but Pershing or someone on his staff set up a brothel for his officers in that little town just to the east. I find that utterly indefensible, but that's beside the point. They installed a madam from El Paso's *barrio* to manage the place after she'd run afoul of the authorities there some months ago. Come to think of it, you must remember her previous establishment. You kept an eye on it for Jake Cobb, remember?"

"Yes."

"One of her permanent houseguests is the man Jake set you to spying on, that slimy little general of Huerta's— Epifanio Guzmán. As you recall, he was Huerta's link to the American gunrunners his chief inherited from Porfirio Díaz, and probably the man who had Francisco Madero murdered. I can't understand how a nasty piece of work like Guzmán can rally thinking, otherwise decent men to him, but apparently he has. He has money—I regret to say a lot of it American—and connections. He's a genuine threat, Corey. Make no mistake about it."

Something, not a sound, not even a tiny, restless movement, but something, a force field of some kind perhaps, drew Corey's eyes to Jorge. He sat as motionless as before, but clearly there was something different about him. His eyes—yes, his eyes. Jorge had worked in that whorehouse in Chihuahuita. He probably knew exactly who Guzmán was. But that was in quite another time and another life.

"Again, Henry, no!"

"Before you turn me down irrevocably, Corey, let me fill you in on one more thing. Your friend Fergus has turned up something that may revive all the efforts you've made in Mexico."

"Fergus?"

"Yes. This last year His Majesty's Government has had Kennedy working exclusively on what von Rintelen and Wolf Kemper are up to. It's paid off handsomely for the British. What effect it will have on the United States remains to be seen."

"I'm not sure I care, Henry." Not quite true. If Fergus had indeed hit the big one, he did care, if only for old times' sake. He hoped it was true, and that the Scot could head for retirement from the game a winner.

"Fergus," Richardson said, "has uncovered solid evidence that Zimmermann, the Kaiser's Foreign Secretary, has been in direct cable touch with Carranza himself, not merely relying on his two principal agents here."

"To what end?" Damn it! The last thing he wanted was to have his curiosity draw him into things again.

"Fergus is now in possession of a cable in which Zimmermann proposes that Mexico take direct and massive military action against the United States. I know it sounds preposterous, but the reward Zimmermann proposes for Carranza would be Texas, New Mexico, Arizona, and California. His reasons are obvious. In spite of Mr. Wilson's desperate attempts to keep us neutral in Europe, we're drifting closer to war with Germany. We would never enter the conflict on the side of Britain and France were we to be occupied with a major war on our southern border. The news of Fergus's coup will break within the month. Carranza will be forced to deny it—and give Kemper and von Rintelen their walking papers, no matter what he eventually decides about Zimmermann's offer. Naturally, it's more important than ever that we know exactly what's going on in Mexico City in the next few months. When all this comes out, the military chiefs in Mexico might just decide to look for another leader. It could be Ángeles. But even if that fails, I want a man I can trust, and who is unconnected to the embassy, in the capital and watching Carranza."

"Look, old friend. You've tried to make something of me I can never be. I'm an insignificant man, and I've ventured too far beyond my depth already. Let me go home."

There was a long pause. "You won't reconsider, then, Corey?" Henry didn't look as if he really expected an answer. Clearly his heart wouldn't be too heavily invested in any other pleas he would make tonight. The superb confidence which had always buoyed him, and the men around him, had gone glimmering.

"No, Henry. I'm truly sorry."

"I'll have to accept your decision, reluctantly." He smiled the smile of a man making the unwanted best of things. "There's a truck convoy leaving for the border at ten o'clock tomorrow morning. If you and your young man here can be ready to travel by then, you'll be back in the United States by nightfall. I'll make the necessary arrangements."

"Thanks, Henry."

Richardson stood up. He clasped Corey's hand in both of his, and turned and nodded to Jorge. At the flap of the tent he turned back.

"Almost forgot. Major Will Hendricks called from the embassy in the capital today, with a message for you. Said to tell you a letter came for you a few days ago, and he's holding it until you can tell him where to forward it."

"A letter?" Who could be writing him there?

"Yes. I've a note on it somewhere." He rummaged in his pockets, came up with a scrap of paper. "Will says the letter is from your friend Doña Luisa López y Montenegro at a place called La Posada Melgar, and postmarked Mexico City two weeks ago."

A letter from Luisa? He didn't dare think about it. It was probably just the final disposition of what they had meant to each other.

Yes, it was time to leave Mexico—forever.

He didn't dare think about Luisa's letter. No, he couldn't let that happen. On the long trip home from Durango after she waved to him from the great door of Hacienda del Sol, and then during the dull, listless months in Black Springs, he'd come to an accommodation of sorts with his memories of her. Or had he? If he hadn't, he damned well better do so now, if he were ever to go about his life.

But he had to face things squarely. Life without her would be intolerable at times. The cause of Felipe Ángeles and all else that cause entailed wouldn't be his principal failure here.

What plagued him as he tried for sleep was the nagging suspicion that he hadn't tried hard enough in either case.

La Posada Melgar. Luisa was back in the capital again. She was in all likelihood quite comfortable with Carranza occupying the Palacio Nacional, would be more comfortable still if men such as Epifanio Guzmán succeeded in restoring a re-

gime like that of Porfirio Díaz. Her world was almost in order once again.

Not fair, Lane. For shame. None of that lady's views on
her country and its desperate needs were informed by the ve-
nality of men like Guzmán and Huerta. She was only chained
to another time, another universe, as was, unfortunately, almost everyone he had met or only glimpsed in this still-
unploughed sea of blood: Pancho Villa, Major Trinidad
Álvarez, Emiliano Zapata, General Medina Barrón, Paco
Durán and his daughter, the three Federalist soldiers he and
Fergus had slaughtered at Zacatecas, the ashen spy Bautista
and his implacable spur Rodolfo Fierro, and decent, dedicated
Narciso himself, the gentle man who had tried to tell him
what this sad land was all about.

> *The time is out of joint; O cursed spite,*
> *That ever I was born to set it right!*

But *he hadn't* been born to set it right.

He should get some sleep. The rigors of the last week
would bring him low if he didn't, and his final task remained
to be completed. Until he and Jorge mounted that truck tomorrow a small segment of that time would surely remain out
of joint.

He awoke once that night, shaken by dreams he didn't
want to face. The darkness in the tent held less terror than the
dreams.

He listened for Jorge's breathing, heard none.

Then he realized Jorge wasn't in his cot. He must have had
to go to the latrine. Well, there was little risk that anyone
would stop him in the middle of the night to ask what a
greaser was doing there.

Perhaps thinking of Fergus and his triumph could ease him
back to sleep.

It was five minutes before reveille when Jorge Martínez
settled on his cot again. Corey didn't hear his return.

▲▲▲▲▲

56

"There are not enough thanks in the world for what you have done for me, Corey. If I have seemed unappreciative at times, I am sorry," Jorge said at breakfast in the officers' mess. "You will be glad to return to Chupadera County, too?"

The Jorge Martínez across the mess table which everyone else in the open-sided tent avoided was a different man from the one Corey had seen when he snuffed the lantern the night before. Pain streaked his dark eyes, surely, but the empty look of the last few days was gone. The pain, or vestiges of it, would be there until the last days of Jorge's life. But at least he was alive again. Perhaps going home meant more than this troubled, damaged man could let himself admit.

"Yes, I'll be glad to get back, Jorge."

"But your big friend from the State Department—"

"Henry has no claim on me—not anymore."

"Has anyone here in Mexico?"

"No." Was it true? "Does anyone in Mexico have a claim on you?"

"No. As you just said about your friend, not anymore. My claimants all are dead. I am now ready to go back home."

For the first time Jorge sounded as if he meant it. Perhaps, in spite of his devastating losses of the past two years, he had reached some inner place of peace.

Corey was the real loser.

"*Perdón,* Corey," Jorge said now. "I do not mean to pry, but is the letter Señor Richardson spoke about from the lady I saw you with on the train?"

"Yes." It was like a blow. He had kept Luisa's letter pretty well out of his mind in the fourteen hours since Henry told him about it. Perhaps he could get Will Hendricks on the line before the convoy left and have Will tear it up.

"And Señor Richardson's wish that you would stay in Mexico?"

"Forget it. Henry will have to forget it, too." He studied the young man's face. It gave him nothing. "Let's get our stuff together, Jorge. What little of it there is." He pulled out his watch. "I'm going to have to find the expedition's finance officer and see if I can change my pesos for U.S. dollars. We can't buy horses at gunpoint once we're in the States again."

He watched Jorge walk back toward their tent before he turned to go to headquarters. His back was straight, and his step was firm and purposeful.

Again he wondered what swift alchemy had brought this change in him. Maybe someday, when Jorge was old and Corey Lane was ancient, they would meet in the Martínezes' Cantina Florida, with even the memory of passion spent, and maybe then he could ask Jorge how the change had come about so suddenly.

As he crossed a field where a squad was raising dust in the exertions of close-order drill under the eye of a sergeant who, despite his modern uniform, looked like all sergeants have looked since Caesar's time, he caught sight of Henry leaving the canteen. It wouldn't be pleasant, but he would have to say goodbye, not now, but when he finished changing his money and made the call to Will. Henry, with his immaculate manners, would keep any reproach from his chiseled features, but it would be there all the same.

The real look of reproach would be seen the next time he stood in front of a mirror, and on uncountable occasions after that.

He had to stop this *mea culpa* crap! It was over, ended, finished—and damn it, should be forgotten. There was nothing more for him to do.

He had just left the field table where a skinny, bespectacled captain with all the affability of an actuary had counted out his money, and was heading for the corner of the supply depot building where the signal officer kept shop, when he was bowled over, knocked to the ground, by the adjutant, Colonel

Berry. The colonel had been running right up until the moment he crashed into Corey, and was puffing like a switch engine.

"Sorry, Lane," Berry said as he dusted himself off. "I'm in an ungodly hurry. If you need me for anything I can see you right after I have a word with the Old Man."

Berry disappeared inside the partitioned section that bore the sign "Commanding Officer—J.J. Pershing, Gen., U.S.A.," leaving behind the lance corporal orderly who had been running at his side.

"You all right, sir?" the orderly said when Corey struggled to his feet.

"Quite all right, thank you, Corporal. I hope Colonel Berry is."

"He'll be fine, sir. He's a lot tougher than he looks. He ain't usually this careless, but he just got kind of a shock."

"Oh?"

"Word came out from the village that there was a couple of murders there late last night or early this morning, and I guess he feels we got to look into it on account of we're the only thing anywheres near like law in these parts."

"Murders?"

"Yeah. Seems somebody snuck into that cathouse the officers use and knifed that greasy little Mex general who's been living there."

"General Guzmán?"

"Sounds like the name the colonel used."

"You said *two* murders, Corporal."

"Yes, sir. The other guy was the greaser's bodyguard, a big American named Jimson, I think."

"Does anyone know who did it? Are there any suspects?"

The corporal laughed. "Twenty or thirty people in the village already, sir. This guy Jimson threw his weight around pretty nasty-like. And I hear that peanut greaser general wasn't too damned popular, either." He shook his head. "It took some doing. The shavetail who brought the word out said it looked like a hell of a scrap where they found Jimson. Nobody heard nothing, or says they didn't. The girls was all through for the night and out like lights. The general hisself couldn't have been much of a problem for the killer, though. From what I hear the little runt was three sheets to the wind twenty-eight hours of a day."

By the time he reached the tent, his goodbye to Henry and his call to Will both unmade, Corey had formed and discarded a hundred questions in his mind. None of them, he realized, would have brought the answers he was seeking.

Jorge had pulled the canvas chair out into the sun and their two saddlebags were at his feet.

"You're ready, Jorge?"

"*Sí,* Corey."

"No second thoughts, no misgivings?"

"None."

"The clerk at headquarters who cut our travel orders at Henry's request said we should get to the motor pool early if we want to get in one of the covered trucks."

He checked the inside of the tent, pretending to see if he had forgotten anything. He was no longer in the state of semishock that had struck him during his conversation with the lance corporal, but every move he made was like walking in his sleep. When he came out again, Jorge was on his feet with the two bags in his hands.

"Jorge . . ." he began.

"*¿Sí?*"

"Never mind. It was nothing important. Let's go."

It was a five-minute walk to the motor pool and neither of them spoke.

They passed knots of excited soldiers, all apparently caught up in the news about the killings, which clearly had come as a welcome relief from the ennui of camp life. Even the crude ball diamond next to the motor pool was a forum for gossip this morning, not a playground.

Twice on the walk, prompted by a word about the murders issuing from one of the small groups they passed, he looked at Jorge. Had he heard? If he had, his face didn't show he had, either time.

A quartermaster sergeant took the copy of the travel orders

Corey handed him, looked suspiciously at Jorge, and then shrugged. "Take the second truck in line, gents. Just throw your gear in back, and one of you can ride up front with the driver, PFC Heinke. I'll leave it to you who gets to." From the look of him, there seemed little doubt in the sergeant's mind just which of them that ought to be. "We roll in twenty minutes."

At the truck there seemed little doubt in Jorge's mind, either. He threw the saddlebags into the bed of the truck and climbed in after them. Corey didn't feel inclined to argue, although part of his half-numb mind would have welcomed the more exacting, bumpy ride in back, if only to jolt it into focus.

"We'll trade places at one of the stops, Jorge."

"That won't be necessary, Corey. I'll be fine back here."

Their driver showed up just as Corey walked to the front of the truck to be alone with his thoughts.

"Howdy, sir. Mr. Lane, isn't it? Would you take the crank for me when we get the signal?" Private First Class Heinke was a freckled redhead who looked as if he should have been at choir practice in some little town in Indiana rather than driving a brutal army truck in a foreign country.

Corey walked to the back of the truck again. Jorge had slumped against a pile of sacks in the bed. When their eyes met this time something new and electric passed between them.

"Yes, Corey, I will keep you in doubt no longer. I killed that *puerco*." Jorge paused, then went on, "If you feel you must turn me in I will understand."

"Why now, Jorge? Why? When you are almost home."

There was a long, soul-draining silence.

"I fought here in Mexico for a long time, much longer than I should have fought. I saw a lot of people die who shouldn't have, and I saw a lot of people live who should have died. Until last night, very little of what I did made a bit of difference. Perhaps what I did last night will. More important, though, is the fact that the good *Dios* gave me one more chance to keep a promise I made myself. It is not much to show for my two years here, but it is something."

Corey stepped to the side of the truck and looked to the north.

He didn't breathe, he didn't move, and if the truth were known he didn't even think, until . . .

"The crank, Mr. Lane, sir," Private Heinke called.

"Just one moment, son." He walked to the back of the truck again.

"Give me my saddlebag, Jorge, and get up front. You'll have to turn the crank for the kid behind the wheel. I won't be going with you. I may have a promise to keep just as you did."

Jorge Martínez smiled. Corey had never seen him smile before.

He found Henry in the officers' mess at noon.

"Corey! What on earth are you doing here? I thought you were on that convoy bound for the States."

"Changed my mind, Henry."

Henry's shrewd eyes wouldn't let him go.

"What are your plans, then?"

Well, what were they? First things first, and let the rest come as it may.

"I've got to get down to the capital as quickly as I can."

Richardson regarded him warily. He wasn't a man to count on things before they were signed, sealed, and delivered.

"Is an old friend and employer permitted to ask why you have to rush to Mexico City, Corey?"

"Certainly, Henry." Yes, first things first. "I have to pick up my mail."

THE BEST OF FORGE

❏ 53441-7   CAT ON A BLUE MONDAY $4.99
               Carole Nelson Douglas   Canada $5.99

❏ 53538-3   CITY OF WIDOWS $4.99
               Loren Estleman   Canada $5.99

❏ 51092-5   THE CUTTING HOURS $4.99
               Julia Grice   Canada $5.99

❏ 55043-9   FALSE PROMISES $5.99
               Ralph Arnote   Canada $6.99

❏ 52074-2   GRASS KINGDOM $5.99
               Jory Sherman   Canada $6.99

❏ 51703-2   IRENE'S LAST WALTZ $4.99
               Carole Nelson Douglas   Canada $6.99

Buy them at your local bookstore or use this handy coupon:
Clip and mail this page with your order.

Publishers Book and Audio Mailing Service
P.O. Box 120159, Staten Island, NY 10312-0004

Please send me the book(s) I have checked above. I am enclosing $ _____
(Please add $1.50 for the first book, and $.50 for each additional book to cover
postage and handling. Send check or money order only— no CODs.)

Name_____

Address_____

City _____ State / Zip _____

Please allow six weeks for delivery. Prices subject to change without notice.

THE BEST OF FORGE

❑ 55052-8	LITERARY REFLECTIONS *James Michener*	$5.99 Canada $6.99
❑ 52046-7	A MEMBER OF THE FAMILY *Nick Vasile*	$5.99 Canada $6.99
❑ 52288-5	WINNER TAKE ALL *Sean Flannery*	$5.99 Canada $6.99
❑ 58193-8	PATH OF THE SUN *Al Dempsey*	$4.99 Canada $5.99
❑ 51380-0	WHEN SHE WAS BAD *Ron Faust*	$5.99 Canada $6.99
❑ 52145-5	ZERO COUPON *Paul Erdman*	$5.99 Canada $6.99

Buy them at your local bookstore or use this handy coupon:
Clip and mail this page with your order.

Publishers Book and Audio Mailing Service
P.O. Box 120159, Staten Island, NY 10312-0004

Please send me the book(s) I have checked above. I am enclosing $ _____
(Please add $1.50 for the first book, and $.50 for each additional book to cover
postage and handling. Send check or money order only — no CODs.)

Name_____

Address_____

City_____State / Zip_____

Please allow six weeks for delivery. Prices subject to change without notice.